BLACK ON BLACK,
SOMETHING IMMENSE LOOMED
OUT OF THE MIST ...

The Elvenship juddered, timbers splintering, and the Man's right hand was jolted from the ice-clad bronze—he was going to fall. Suddenly someone gripped his wrist and he was dragged up and over the wale, a giant Man hauling him to safety amidst the sound of splitting beams and a pounding of a drum and a great splashing and churning of water.

"Iceberg!" the Man shouted, pointing at the blackness abeam. But even as he called it, he knew it was not so.

Boom!... Boom!... Boom!... Boom!... sounded the beat of the drum, and amid the splintering of hull planking, slowly the dark mass withdrew. Suddenly, the Elvenship rolled free, the darkness turning her loose and backing away to disppear in the fog. Amid the shouts of Men and Dwarves, the Elvenship began to sink, her hull holed, icy water pouring in. And out from the frigid mist, amid the beat of a drum and the splashing churn, there came the sound of cold laughter.

Voyage
Of The
Fox Rider

DENNIS L. MCKIERNAN

A ROC BOOK

ROC
Published by the Penguin Group
Penguin Books USA Inc., 375 Hudson Street,
New York, New York 10014, U.S.A.
Penguin Books Ltd, 27 Wrights Lane,
London W8 5TZ, England
Penguin Books Australia Ltd, Ringwood,
Victoria, Australia
Penguin Books Canada Ltd, 10 Alcorn Avenue,
Toronto, Ontario, Canada M4V 3B2
Penguin Books (N.Z.) Ltd, 182–190 Wairau Road,
Auckland 10, New Zealand

Penguin Books Ltd, Registered Offices:
Harmondsworth, Middlesex, England

Published by Roc, an imprint of Dutton Signet,
a division of Penguin Books USA Inc. Previously published in
Roc hardcover and trade editions.

First Mass Market Printing, September, 1994
10 9 8 7 6 5 4 3 2 1

To my sister,
Donna Lorraine,
in whom whimsy lives

Acknowledgments

Appreciation and gratitude to Daniel Kian McKiernan, without whose help the transliterated ancient Greek used as the Black Mage magical language would never have been; to Judith Tarr, without whom the Latin used as the magical language for all other Mages would have been seriously flawed; and to Martha Lee McKiernan for her enduring support, careful reading, patience, and love. Additionally, much appreciation and gratitude goes to all those who encouraged me throughout the writing of *Voyage of the Fox Rider*—if I wrote down all their names it would fill a page or two ... and I would still manage to leave several off the list.

Contents

Foreword

*B*efore the Separation. . . . Now there is a phrase that has appeared more than once in my Mithgarian sagas.

Before the Separation.

It all has to do with another phrase: *Once upon a time.*

You see, if the old tales are true, then *Once upon a time* there lived on this planet peoples of myth and creatures of fable. Alongside Mankind did these fantastic beings exist—pixies and fairies, elves and goblins, chimeras and brownies and sphinx . . . and whatever else you'd care to name.

Once upon a time . . . before the Separation.

You see, there *must* have been a *Separation* if the mythical peoples and mystical creatures are gone, for I am certain that we didn't kill them all—they are much too wily, much too magical—and so, they *must* have simply *left.*

And if gone, where gone?

Elsewhere! That's where. *In between! Into the twilight! Into the dawn!*

Why? Why are they gone?

I have a theory:

Somewhere along the way, arrogant Mankind claimed all the world as his own to do with as he willed. Man's appetites were insatiable, and he multiplied and multiplied and multiplied, seemingly without limit, and wherever he went he raped the land and poisoned the soil and air and waters of the world. Slowly, gradually, the legendary folk and fabled creatures were displaced, were pushed back, were shoved into ever smaller enclaves. Always

did they hope that Man would mend his ways, see what
he was doing, what he had wrought, and reverse the
destruction; always did they hope that Man would begin
to revere the earth which sustained him. But that was
not to be, for Man continued his wanton ways, destroying as he went.

And so, the day came when the harm reached a point
where the peoples of legend could no longer abide what
Man had done and was continuing to do. And so they
simply gathered up the creatures of fable and left, separated themselves from this destructive beast named Man.
They went *elsewhere,* away from this world, to a place
where Man was not.

This was *the Separation.*

You may ask, "Does he truly believe in *any* of this?"

My answer is, "Look around. Do you see any creatures of fable, peoples of legend? Or do you instead see
the ravage of Mankind?"

Perhaps someday if Man becomes sane and begins car-
ing for the world, begins reversing the destruction he
hath wrought, restores the soil and air and waters, restores the forests and fens and mountains and wilderness
to what they once were, and takes fair measure to re-
duce his own numbers to a tenth or a hundredth or even
a thousandth of what they are—let me see, five point
five billion divided by a thousand ... perhaps it is
enough—if he does all these things, then it just may be
that the peoples and creatures of legend and fable will
return.

I would hope so, for the world is a sadder place without them.

Before the Separation.
Words to make you cry.

—*Dennis L. McKiernan*

September 1992

Notes

1. *Voyage of the Fox Rider* is a tale which takes place before the Separation.

2. *Voyage of the Fox Rider* is also a tale which takes place *before* the Great War of the Ban, hence, the *Rûpt* are free to roam about in daylight as well as night, although it is told that they prefer to do their deeds in the dark of night rather than in the light of day

3. This tale was reconstructed from the fragments of one of the logs of the Elvenship *Eroean*. I have in several places filled in the gaps with notes from other references, but in the main the tale is true to its source.

4. As I did in *The Eye of the Hunter*, I have used transliterated archaic Greek to represent the magical language of the Black Mages. But in the case of all other Mages, I have used Latin.

5. There are many instances where in the press of the moment, the Pysks, Dwarves, Men, Mages, Elves, and others spoke in their native tongues; yet to avoid burdensome translations, where necessary I have rendered their words in Pellarion, the Common Tongue of Mithgar. However, some words and phrases do not lend themselves to translation, and these I've left unchanged or, in special cases, I have enclosed in angle brackets a substitute term which gives the "flavor" of the word (i.e., <power>, <fire>, and the like). Additionally, other words may look to be in error, but indeed are correct—e.g.,

DelfLord is but a single word, though a capital L nestles among its letters. Also note that swivelled, traveller, and several other similar words are written in the Pendwyrian form of Pellarion and are not misspelled.

6. The Elven language of Sylva is rather archaic and formal. To capture this flavor, I have properly used thee and thou, hast, doth, and the like; however, in the interest of readability, I have tried to do so in a minimal fashion, eliminating some of the more archaic terms.

7. The speech of the Children of the Sea is riddled with chirps and pops and whistles and clicks. I have used the ! and ¡ to indicate two of these sounds, the ! representing a "tick," and the ¡ representing a "tock."

8. For the curious, the *w* in Rwn takes on the sound of *uu* (w *is* after all a double-u), which in turn can be said to sound like *oo* (as in spoon). Hence, Rwn is *not* pronounced Renn, but instead *is* pronounced Roon, or Rune.

Fox Rider, Fox Rider,
Where are you bound?

After my true love,   *Deep in my dreams*
Wherever he's found.   *The whole world 'round.*

RWN

Northern Sea

N
W · E
S

Plains of Rwn

Kairn Wall

Kairn

Darda Glain

Lac Rwn

miles
0   25

Weston Ocean

Map S.S. Palmer

*Dreams are at times
nought but fanciful images
in a shifting shadowland.*

CHAPTER 1

Aurora

Winter, 1E9572-73
[Twenty-Two Months Past]

Farrix stood in the hip-deep snow on the crest of the hill under the winter sky and watched as the curtains of the aurora twisted and rippled, the colors randomly shifting among the hues of the spectrum, among the crimsons and saffrons and jades and indigos and lavenders.

Of a sudden—"Hoy, Jinnarin, did you see that?"

"See what?"

Farrix turned to the female beside him. "The aurora. It seemed to flash, and a plume, a large plume, streamed outward, southward, there"—Farrix pointed to the eastern horizon—"down low. I'm certain I saw it."

Jinnarin shook her head. "I was not looking."

"Hmm. I wonder . . ."

"You wonder what?"

"I wonder if those Mages are up to something. I mean, I've been watching the aurora all my life, and I never—"

"Oh, Farrix, you *always* think the Mages are up to something."

"Nevertheless, Jinnarin—"

"My love," interjected Jinnarin, "I say let us forget it and go back—"

"Hoy! There went another one," exclaimed Farrix. "Streaming south, just like the first."

Jinnarin turned and gazed long at the northeastern rim of the nighttime sky . . . to no avail, for no other plume streamed forth from the writhing drapery of the spectral light—at least, no plume that she could see.

Farrix, too, stared across the winter-barren branches of the hoary trees of Darda Glain, seeking but not finding.

Over the next month, Farrix watched as the aurora twisted and writhed, streamers of luminance occasionally flowing down from the north to the eastern horizon. At last he came to Jinnarin—rucksack on his back, bow in hand, arrows in his quiver—saying, "Love, I'm off to follow the flumes, to see just where they are going."

Jinnarin, noting the jut of his jaw, realizing that no amount of argument would sway his decision to chase this will-o'-the-wisp of spectral light, hugged him and kissed him, her heart somewhat heavy, though not extraordinarily so ... for she and Farrix had been mates for several millennia, and Jinnarin was resigned to his "whims."

With a whistle, Farrix mounted up on Rhu, and off through the forest of Darda Glain they headed northeasterly, Jinnarin standing before the hollow tree where they lived, waving her loved one good-bye.

CHAPTER 2

Night Visitor

Early Spring, 1E9574
[Six Months Past]

In a small cottage on the outskirts of Kairn, the city on the island of Rwn, an eld Man—that is, with his white hair and beard he *appeared* to be an eld Man—heard a soft tap on his door. He did not look away from his instrument, but instead continued to mutter to himself while peering along the arm of the astrolabe, sighting out through the open roof trap and into the springtime spangle of the nighttime heavens above.

Again came the tapping on the door.

"Go away!"

Softly, softly, another tap sounded in the darkened room.

"I said, go away! I am busy!"

Once more came the persistent tapping.

"Oh bother!" Irritated, the eld Man gestured, and a soft blue glow sprang into being before him. "All right, all right, I'm coming!" he called out peevishly, jotting a note in a journal lying open before him on the astrolabe stand.

Snapping the journal shut and sliding from the tall stool, the elder hobbled across the room, muttering all the while—"Not enough that the hearthlights and street lanterns from the city interfere, but now some *fool* has to come along and ..."

Flinging the door open and querulously snapping, "Well, what do you—?" the Man's words chopped to silence, for there afoot on the threshold was a tiny person no more than twelve inches tall. Dressed in varying shades of grey, she was, and a tiny bow and a quiver of arrows were slung across her back. Her hair was mouse brown, and her eyes were cobalt blue, and behind her stood a black-footed red fox.

She looked up at the Man, his face illuminated by the blue glow, his features ghastly in the spectral light. Nevertheless, she squared her shoulders and asked, "Are you Alamar the Mage?" Though high-pitched, her voice came softly.

"*Hmph!* I never thought to see a Pysk on *my* doorstone."

"Are you Alamar the Mage?" she repeated.

At the Man's nod a look of relief spread over her face. "Oh, I'm so glad. My name is Jinnarin"—she gestured toward the fox—"and Rux and I have come a long way to find you. You see, Farrix is missing."

CHAPTER 3

Herb Tea
and Wild Honey

Early Spring, 1E9574
[Six Months Past]

As Jinnarin uncinched a harness strap and hefted the travelling packs from Rux's back, Alamar rummaged about in a cupboard, grumbling, "Herb tea. Herb tea. *Ha!* In the back—dratted mice."

A smile flickered across Jinnarin's face. *Farrix said that Alamar was eccentric, yet surely the Mage doesn't believe that mice conspire against him, hiding the tea.* She dropped the packs to the hearthstone and then selected twigs from the fireside wood box and added them to the faint coals.

Alamar hobbled to the fireplace. "You will be wanting some tea, too, neh?"

"Oh yes, please," answered Jinnarin, placing small branches among the growing flames as Rux curled up before the hearth.

Alamar hooked the handle of a small copper pot on the kettle iron and swivelled it out above the fire. Without another word, the Mage returned to his seat at the astrolabe and once again sighted up through the open roof trap at the stars above. After a moment—*"Blast!"* He glared over his shoulder at the fire, and grumbling, jerked at a chain, the trapdoor above slamming to with a *Blam!* Rux leaped up and looked wildly about; Jinnarin, too, was startled.

With a gesture of dismissal, Alamar jotted a last note in his journal, mumbling, *"Pox!* I missed it," and slid from his stool as Jinnarin soothed Rux, the fox eyeing the Mage suspiciously.

Alamar hobbled to a large, cluttered, rolltop desk and cast the journal down among scrolls and tomes and scattered papers, pausing long enough to jerk a parchment from a pigeonhole and scowl at it a moment, then roll it up and jam it back in.

Behind, the kettle began to whistle, the unexpected sound bringing Rux again to his feet, the fox interposing himself between Jinnarin and the Mage, hackles raised, one lip slightly curled, a sharp canine showing.

Alamar simply glared at the beast and stumped to the kettle, while once again Jinnarin soothed Rux, the hair on the animal's back slowly settling down.

Spooning herbs into a porcelain pot, Alamar glowered at Jinnarin. "Have you got a cup?" The Mage filled the teapot with steaming water.

Fumbling through the packs that Rux had borne, she withdrew a carven acorn, a handle affixed to one side, a base attached to the bottom.

Alamar again returned to the cabinet, rattling about, extracting an earthenware cup and a small jar of honey. He peered into the cup and turned it upside down— "Dratted mice"—banging the rim against the tabletop and peering in, once again bringing Rux to his feet.

"Look here, Pysk, you ought to do something about that—that dog of yours. Why, he's as jumpy as a wild beast."

"Rux *is* a 'wild beast,' Alamar . . . and he's *not* a dog! And if you wouldn't make so much noise—"

"Tea's ready," interrupted Alamar, peering into the pot.

Moments later, Alamar stirred a dab of honey into the steaming amber drink, then fixed his green-eyed gaze on his visitor, Jinnarin sitting cross-legged atop the rough-hewn plank table. "All right, now, what's all this about Farrix missing?"

Jinnarin looked at the eld Man—or was he an Elf? His eyes were somewhat tilted and his ears slightly pointed, as are the Fair Folk's, but in each case, eyes

and ears both, they were more Manlike than Elf but
more Elflike than Man. Farrix had said that Mages were
like that—neither Human nor Elven but something in
between, and now Jinnarin could see it for herself. He
was dressed in a blue robe, and on his left wrist he wore
a gold bracelet set with a dull red stone.

"Are you just going to sit there and stare at me, or
are you instead going to tell me about Farrix?"

Jinnarin shook her head to clear it of these vagaries
and then began:

"The winter before last, Farrix thought that he saw
something peculiar in the aurora—great plumes streaming away to the east. Oh, not that it happened every
night, but he saw it occur several times over the month
he watched—"

"Plumes? To the east?"

"Well, down from the north to the east."

Alamar's bushy white eyebrows cocked upward. "Hm,
east of Darda Glain. How far east?"

"How far?" Jinnarin shrugged. "I don't know."

"Come, come, Pysk, was it right at hand or far away?"

Jinnarin turned up her palms. "I didn't see any—not
that I was looking—but Farrix said that it was one or
two hundred miles away."

"Ha! The other side of Rwn." With a gesture he bade
her to continue.

Jinnarin sipped from her acorn cup. "About two
Moons after he had gone on his quest, Rhu, his fox,
returned home, bearing a note from Farrix." Jinnarin
reached into her vest and pulled forth a tiny, tissue-thin
parchment, unfolding it and passing it over to Alamar.

The eld Mage peered at the wee document, squinting
his eyes. "Faugh! Too small. I can't read this." He thrust
the paper back at Jinnarin. The Pysk took the note and
smoothed it on the plank before her.

"My love," she read . . .

My love,
   *Here I am at the edge of the isle, and the plumes
continue to flow easterly. It appears, though, that they
arc down to strike in the ocean nearby. I have made
myself a coracle, and I plan on paddling a bit out to*

*sea, out to where it seems they might splash, just beyond
the horizon, I think.*

*I have told Rhu to wait awhile, a day or so. If he
returns without me, you will know that I am off on
another of my ventures.*

> *I love you,*
> *Farrix*

Jinnarin refolded the paper and slipped it back into
her inner vest pocket. "Rhu brought the note. Spring
came, then summer, and Farrix did not return. In autumn, Rux and I followed Rhu back to where he had
last seen Farrix: a headland along the southeast coast of
Rwn—"

"Hmph!" grunted Alamar. "How d' you know that he
took you to the right place? I mean, it's not as if they
are smart and all, like Wolves. Instead, what we are
talking about are *foxes!* So, how d' you know he got
anywhere *near?*"

Outrage flushed Jinnarin's face. "They are our companions! And trustworthy! Farrix's Rhu wouldn't make
a mistake in something as important as that." She
glanced down at Rux asleep before the fire, as if to assure herself that he had not overheard this—this *slur*
against Foxkind. "Set aside your doubt, Alamar—Rhu
led us to the right place all right."

Alamar, too, scowled down at Rux, then turned his
attention once more to the Pysk. "And . . . ?"

"And nothing. There was no sign of Farrix."

Again Alamar glowered at Jinnarin. "So . . . ?"

"So I came to you. Farrix always said that should trouble come calling, we could depend on Alamar the Mage
to help. After all, Farrix saved you from the boar,
and—"

"So *that's* who it was!" burst out Alamar. *"Farrix!"*
A great grin spread across his face, transforming it from
one of irascibility into one of discovered joy. Catching
up the pot, he splashed more tea into Jinnarin's acorn,
overflowing it, the Pysk scrambling back and away from
the spreading puddle. Not noticing the spill, Alamar
dropped a great dollop of honey into the tiny cup, the
sweet glob splashing out the rest of the tea and oozing
over and down the sides. "Well, Miss—Miss . . ."

"Jinnarin." She eyed her cup with some dismay.

"Ah yes, Jinnarin. Well, Miss Jinnarin, why didn't you say so in the first place? Any friend of Farrix's is a friend of mine."

"How can that be, Alamar? I mean, it appears as if you didn't even know his name."

"I didn't!" exclaimed the elder. "But as to him saving my life, well, it was a Pysk all right—brought that boar down with one of those tiny arrows, he did. But given the pain I was in ... well, I just didn't catch his name. He took care of me for a week or so, and when I was well enough to remain in camp alone, that's when he fetched help. Of course, when help came, he remained hidden, and I didn't get a chance to thank him."

"And you never knew his name?"

Alamar shook his head. "I called him Pysk. It seemed enough at the time. Then he was gone and it was too late.... I always wondered, though, just who Pysk was—"

A look of indignation filled Jinnarin's face. "He was Farrix! Best of the Fox Riders! And it's a wonder that he stopped to help anyone as rude as you. Imagine, not even knowing your benefactor's name! And you slandered his fox, too!" Jinnarin folded her arms and stiffly turned her back to the Mage.

Before Alamar could utter an astonished word—"And clean up that mess you made of my cup," demanded Jinnarin.

Alamar glared at her rigid back for a moment, seeming on the verge of a retort, but she faced him not. Finally, gritting his teeth, the Mage took up the acorn and dutifully washed and dried it, wiping down the table as well. And just as carefully, he refilled the minuscule vessel with herb tea, dropping in a tiny bit of wild honey to sweeten it. By this time, Jinnarin not only had cooled down, but had proceeded to a state of abject embarrassment at her outburst. And she sat with her head down, refusing to look at the Magus. For his part, Alamar had gotten over his glare, realizing the truth of her words.

They sat in silence for a while, neither willing to say aught.

Alamar fiddled with the bracelet on his arm, but finally—*"Ahem"*—he cleared his throat. "Has Farrix disappeared like this before?"

"Oh yes," answered Jinnarin softly. "Several times in the millennia I've known him." She looked up at the Mage, and her eyes filled with joy. "Farrix is, well, he is filled with curiosity and cannot seem to let go until he has an answer to whatever it is that he wants to know."

"Hmph. Then he'd make a good apprentice.... Be that as it may, these other times, Py—Jinnarin, these other times, was he gone long?"

"Oh yes. Seasons and seasons, in fact. Why, once he was gone for seventy-two summers."

Alamar drew down his shaggy white brows and turned up his palms. "But then, I don't understand, Jinnarin. He's only been gone this time for just over a year. Why have you come to see me?"

"I told you: Farrix always said that if ever there was trouble, to come and see you."

"And just what makes you think that there's trouble this time?"

Jinnarin took a deep breath. "Well, Alamar, this time, you see, I've been having these dreams."

CHAPTER 4

Shadowland

Early Spring, 1E9574
[Six Months Past]

Dreams?" Alamar turned his gimlet gaze upon the Pysk. "What dreams?"

Jinnarin's eyes lost their focus as her thoughts turned inward. "Dreams of a crystal castle high above a pale green sea."

"Hmm." Alamar stroked his beard for a moment, then stood and shuffled past Rux, the fox opening a suspicious eye, warily regarding the Mage's progress. Rummaging about in the wood box, Alamar cast a log on the fire, and with an iron rod he poked the coals into flame. Once more he faced the Pysk. "Dreams are at times nought but fanciful images in a shifting shadowland. What makes you think this dream is aught else?"

Jinnarin was quick to answer. "It has clarity ... but even more so, it has the feel, the aura, of Farrix."

Alamar's eyes widened. "It is not a Death Rede, is it?"

"Death Rede?"

"Something Elves do."

"Say on, Mage, for I know little of the world beyond the borders of my own Darda Glain."

Alamar set aside the poker and returned to his chair, taking up the teapot and refreshing his cup. "When one of the Fair Folk dies, somehow he can send a final message—a Death Rede—to another of his Kind."

Jinnarin shivered. "Oh me oh my, what a terrible two-edged gift! Blessing and bane both."

Alamar nodded. "That it is, Jinnarin. That it is. . . . But as to this dream of yours—"

"Oh no, Alamar, my dream is not a Death Rede. We have not that gift . . . or curse."

Spooning honey into his cup, Alamar glanced at the Pysk. "I had wondered. There is much alike 'tween the Fair Folk and the Hidden Ones. Many similarities."

Jinnarin grinned. "Height is not one of them."

"Ha!" barked Alamar, which brought Rux scrambling to his feet. "Nay, Pysk, height is not among the likenesses, though wit is."

Glaring at the Mage but sensing nothing amiss, Rux prepared to settle once again before the fire, though this time the disgruntled animal turned about and about for long moments, peering at the floor at his circling feet, as if pondering the wisdom of lying down once again in the presence of this loud old one.

Jinnarin swirled the tea in her acorn cup, staring deep within as if to see secrets held beyond the bounds of time and space. "But even if we had this—this gift, Alamar, my dream could not be a Death Rede, for I've had it many times, and it seems to me that Death Redes would come but once only, and that in a distressing time. Nay, this is no Elven rede. Instead, it is as if it were a . . . a message, a—"

"A sending?" interjected Alamar.

Jinnarin looked up at the Mage. "Yes. Exactly. As if Farrix were trying to tell me something."

Alamar fiddled with the gold bracelet on his wrist, a dull red stone set in the metal, his eyes staring into space. "Something about a crystal castle above a pale green sea?"

"And a black ship," added Jinnarin.

"Black ship?" The surprise in Alamar's voice brought Rux's head up, the fox settling back at a soft whistle from Jinnarin.

"Yes, Alamar, a black ship, or so I believe."

The elder rocked his chair back, tilting it up on two legs. "Perhaps, little one, perhaps you ought to tell the whole of this dream of yours."

The fire cracked and popped, and Rux dozed on, and Jinnarin sipped her tea, gathering her thoughts. The Mage ladled more honey into his cup and tasted the result. Satisfied, he set the spoon aside, his habitual glare fixed on the Pysk.

"It never starts the same," she murmured.

"Eh? Speak up."

"I said"—Jinnarin raised her voice—"it never starts the same. But no matter where it begins, in time it becomes the echo of nights past—rather like starting out on one path and then being tugged onto a familiar way. And that's what makes it seem like a—a sending: the bending of each new dream into the shape of the old."

Alamar squinted an eye. "Hmm. The shadowland is a wild, boundless place, with countless tangled pathways through extravagant 'scapes without number . . . and to start along fancy after fancy but to arrive always at the same destination is most remarkable, portentous, suggestive of no caprice, no vagary of the mind, but of deliberate guidance instead. . . .

"This destination—tell me of it."

Jinnarin shrugged her shoulders. "There's not that much to tell. No matter where my dream starts, there comes a point where I find myself flying among clouds. I know I am flying because far below I can see the waters of a pale green sea. The clouds begin seething and churning and they turn black. Above me, billows pile one atop another, and I know a terrible storm is building. Dark night falls, and I look for shelter. It begins to lightning and thunder, rain lashing down, great white bolts crashing across the ebony sky and into the brine below. And down upon the tossing surge is what I take to be a black ship under full sail, riding across the stormy waters, its masts struck time and again by the whelming strokes. Yet it is not damaged by the lightning but instead sails on, aiming for an island in the near distance, a crag jutting up from the hammering sea.

"Toward this island I fly, something or someone drawing me on—Farrix, I think. Of a sudden I find myself in a lofty crystal chamber overlooking the sea. I know—without knowing how I know—that I am in a crystal castle on that crag, while far below, down a sheer cliff, driven waves thunder into adamant stone, waves crashing into unyielding rock and being hurled back. And all the while I can see the black ship in the stormy distance, riding up over the churning crests and down through the roiling troughs, bolt after bolt of blinding lightning stroking its thrumming masts. . . .

"And there it ends, my dream; there it ends, the sending."

CHAPTER 5

Kairn

Early Spring, 1E9574
[Six Months Past]

Alamar threw up his hands. "That's it? Nothing more? You just wake up?"

Jinnarin took a deep breath. "Well, there is one more thing, but I don't see—"

"You let me be the judge of that, Pysk. What is this 'one more thing'?"

Again Jinnarin took a deep breath. "Just this, Alamar: as I watch the ship sailing toward me, I have this—this feeling of dread, as if something terrible is about to happen . . . or as if something horrible is drawing near. And I flee—where? I don't know—I just flee. And that's when I waken, trembling in fear, drenched in sweat, my heart racing." With shaking hands, Jinnarin took up her tea and sipped it.

Alamar shook his head. "Not a good sign, this fear of yours." He stood and added another log to the fire, then turned and faced the Pysk. "But heed: not all images within a dream are what they seem. That black ship may represent something else altogether . . as might the crystal castle, the storm, and aught else . . . even your fear. What they might truly be, or mean, I cannot say. . . . If Aylis were here instead of traipsing about the world, she would know."

Jinnarin looked up at the Mage. "Aylis?"

The elder shuffled back to his chair. "My daughter. She is a seer."

"A seer? What is a seer?"

Alamar cocked an eye at the Pysk and slowly shook his head, and Jinnarin burst out, "Well, I *told* you I didn't know much of the world beyond the borders of Darda Glain."

The eld Man shrugged. "A seer is, well, a kind of Mage . . . one who can divine much of hidden things."

"Can't you do that as well? I mean, aren't all Mages alike?"

"*Ha!*" barked Alamar, Rux opening an eye and then closing it again. "Preposterous! All Mages alike? You must be jesting. Are all Hidden Ones alike? Are all Pysks alike? Is aught of *anything* alike?"

"Raindrops," shot back Jinnarin. "Twins. Stars."

"Don't be foolish!" snapped Alamar, glaring. "Even you know the falsity of your words."

A look of ire crossed Jinnarin's face, and Mage and Pysk sat in angry silence for long heated moments, broken by Jinnarin at last: "I suppose," she said, "that raindrops are not all alike, for there are big ones and little ones, warm ones and cold ones, some are gentle and others harsh.

"And twins have differences, else even they could not tell one another apart.

"And the stars—"

"And the stars," interrupted Alamar, "sweep from bright to dim, some all but invisible while others are brilliant to the eye; some are fuzzy and others are sharp; and their hues range from red to blue to green or yellow and all colors in between; and while most seem fixed within the turning crystal vault, a very few glide about; then there are those that streak across the firmament, coming from nowhere, burning brightly, swiftly fading to nothingness; and yet others flare up in the darkness between, blazing where no star stood before, slowly ebbing, falling back into the blackness once again; and then there are those which come from that very same indigo dark and blaze for night after night, long bright tails glowing, bringing bane and bale within their wake."

Alamar fell silent and Jinnarin shivered, seemingly for no reason at all. At last she asked, "And the Mages?"

"Mages," grunted the elder, "are like raindrops and twins and stars. There are similarities, yet each is different."

"Snowflakes," murmured Jinnarin.

"Eh?"

"Snowflakes, I said," answered Jinnarin. "Each alike; each different."

"Exactly so," snapped Alamar querulously, "and don't you forget it."

Jinnarin ground her teeth and gritted, "Fear not, O One of Many Mages, ignorant I may be but swiftly do I learn."

Again an ired silence fell between them. At last Jinnarin took a deep breath and asked, "Now what, Alamar? I've told you of Farrix's quest, of his letter, of my dream. Where do we go from here?"

"To Kairn," answered the Mage.

"The city?"

"Where else will we find a library?"

"Library?"

"Is there an echo in here?"

Jinnarin sprang to her feet. "You are the most exasperating old grouch I have ever—"

"And you are the most impudent Pysk!" shouted Alamar.

Rux leapt up and, growling, trotted to the door and pawed it open. With a disgruntled glare over his shoulder, the fox skulked out into the night.

Jinnarin burst into laughter, while Alamar scowled at where the fox had been. "Enough, Mage," giggled the Pysk, "for my fox has run away since he couldn't stopper his ears from our quarrelling.

"Let us start anew. What will we find at the library in Kairn?"

Alamar stood and paced to the door, peering out, seeing nought of the fox. He swung the portal to, shutting away the night chill. "Where else," he asked as he hobbled back to his chair, "where else will we find word as to a pale green sea, a crystal castle, a black ship?"

"And exactly where is this library in the city of Kairn?"

"On the island in the Kairn River, there where the academy sits."

"And this academy, Alamar, what exactly is it?"

The Mage drank the last of his tea. "It's where Mages study, Jinnarin, where we refine our art."

Jinnarin's eyes widened. "A college of Mages?"

Alamar nodded. "And we have one of the finest libraries in all of Mithgar. You and I will go there in the morning and see what we can find."

"Oh no, Alamar," protested Jinnarin. "I cannot walk among Humankind in the daylight. At night they will not see me, but in the day . . ."

Alamar sighed. "Then we will go tomorrow night."

"Why not tonight? There are yet hours before dawn."

"Don't be foolish, Pysk," muttered Alamar. "Even Mages need rest."

Without another word, Alamar stood and stumped to his cot, leaving Jinnarin sitting upon the table. After a moment she swilled the last of her now cold tea and clambered down to sit before the fire, staring into the dying embers.

Dusk drew down upon the land, the air crystal clear, stars appearing one by one against the violet sky. Alamar plodded down the wending way, the lights of Kairn in the near distance. At his side rode Jinnarin upon Rux, the fox padding silently in the gloom.

Earlier in the day they had gathered together a few supplies, Jinnarin replenishing her packs. During this time not much had been said between her and Alamar; the Mage for the most part had sat at his rolltop desk making notes in his journal. He had, though, asked Jinnarin to make a sketch of the black ship, and she had complied, the drawing a tiny one, though it seemed to satisfy the Mage. Rux as usual had gone foraging and had slaked his appetite afield. The day had worn on, Jinnarin resting, and when from afar the many bells of Kairn had at last announced sunset—just as they had announced dawn—Alamar had arisen and had taken up his knapsack and had impatiently demanded to know just what they were waiting for, and they had set forth for the city.

And now they walked in the gathering gloom, each wrapped in his own thoughts.

"Alamar," asked Jinnarin, breaking the silence at last, "do you truly believe that we will discover aught of the black ship or the pale green sea or the crystal castle?"

"Foolish Pysk," gnarled the Mage, "of course we will. Did I not say that it was the finest library in all of Mithgar?"

"I thought you said that it was but one of the finest."

"Don't quibble! Quibbling is a sign of infancy."

Jinnarin's jaw fell open. *Quibbling is a sign of—* She began to laugh.

"What are you tittering at?" The elder's words came sharp.

"Nothing, Alamar. Nothing," she replied, trying to smother her laughter, failing, looking up at the eld infant striding along beside her.

They paced in silence for a while, and down and away from Alamar's hill, Jinnarin could see the shining lights of Kairn some two or three miles afar. And as Mage and fox and Pysk descended the gentle grade, Jinnarin asked, "Just how do we get to the college if it's on an island in the middle of the river?"

"Ferry," answered Alamar.

"Oh." And on they went.

At last they came to the base of the slope, where the meandering path they followed joined an east-west tradeway, and leftward onto this road they fared, heading west toward Kairn. Behind, the road disappeared into the easterly darkness, threading the length of the narrow cape and toward the distant War wall—a defensive stone bulwark spanning the width of the strait, sheer-sided peninsula—beyond which lay the interior of the island.

To the north, Jinnarin could hear the purl of the nearby River Kairn, the water flowing along a course which reached from the distant central tors to cross half the isle, running at last down the length of the promontory and through the city, where it tumbled across a high linn to thunder at last down into the sea.

They came to a freshet babbling alongside the road, its clear water flowing out from a small stonework structure and running down to join the river. "We stop here, Pysk," said Alamar, the elder settling down on a long length of cut log. "My legs tell me I must rest."

Jinnarin dismounted from Rux and approached the spring. As the fox lapped water, Jinnarin gazed at the arc of mortared stone cupping a large flat rock through which the rivulet burbled. "What is this place, Alamar?"

"Eh, they call it Elwydd's Spring. It's a roadside shrine."

"Oh my," exclaimed Jinnarin. "Why, it looks as if it hasn't been kept. Adon's daughter deserves better." The tiny Pysk began gathering up scattered leaves that lay upon the wide flat rock. With handfuls, she swept the springstone clean. Stepping back, Jinnarin surveyed her work. Looking about, she plucked a tiny blue springtime flower and laid it at the bow of the arch. "There now, it's set right."

"Do you do this often?" asked Alamar.

"Do what?"

"Sweep out shrines," answered the Mage.

Jinnarin shook her head. "Oh no. We have no such in Darda Glain."

"Yet you honor Elwydd."

Now the Pysk nodded. "Honor her, yes. But not in stonework shrines. Instead, I speak to her when I am in a glade or alongside a stream or other such in the forest. I especially like to talk to her when I find a circle of mushrooms."

Alamar's habitual scowl softened. "A Faery ring."

Jinnarin grinned. "Some call it that."

"Do you dance there in the ring?"

Jinnarin pirouetted and curtseyed. "At times."

Alamar fished through his rucksack, withdrawing a tin cup. "Would you fetch me a drink?"

As the Pysk filled the tin, she asked, "Tell me, Alamar: why is that Elwydd seldom answers?"

"Eh?"

Jinnarin stood, hefting the cup up into her arms, bearing it as would a Human carry a barrel. "Just this: It is said that long past both Adon and Elwydd trod the Middle World. Yet now they are absent—at least most of the time they are absent. And when we speak to them—to Adon and Elwydd and the Others—seldom do they answer. And so I ask you, Alamar ... why is this?"

The Mage took the cup from Jinnarin and drank it dry, waving her off when she reached out to take it for a refill. As he stuffed it back into his sack, he asked, "Jinnarin, have you thought what it might portend for the gods to answer?"

"What do you mean, Alamar?"

The elder spread his hands apart. "Perhaps it would lead to the ultimate evil."

"For gods to answer is an evil thing?"

Alamar shrugged. "Mayhap. Heed, long past in Adonar there was a great debate. At question was the gods' interference in the lives of the lesser folk, of mortals and immortals alike. The two mightiest gods—Adon and Gyphon—quarrelled bitterly, with Adon holding that the gods would destroy those whom they would control, and Gyphon contending that it is the right of gods to do as they will. Some of the gods sided with Gyphon, but most allied themselves with Adon, including His daughter Elwydd, for it was She who brought forth life unto the Folk of the High and Middle Worlds."

"What about the Under World, Alamar?" asked Jinnarin. "What about Neddra?"

Alamar shook his head in regret. "Ah me, tiny one, 'twas Gyphon who spawned the *Spaunen*—the Rucha, Loka, Ghûlka, Trolls, and other such *Rûpt*."

A small *Oh* escaped Jinnarin's lips, and then she added, "I have always known that Elwydd created the Hidden Ones, but I did not know about the *Rûpt*."

Jinnarin glanced up at the eld Man. "What about the Mages, Alamar? Who created your Folk? And on what world?"

"Elwydd, we believe. As to the world, we come from neither the High, Middle, nor Lower Plane ... but instead from—you might call it—the Outer Plane, from a world named Vadaria."

Jinnarin was astonished. "You mean, there're more than three Planes?"

"Of course," snapped Alamar. "Everyone knows that."

Jinnarin felt her face flush with anger, yet she held

her retort. At last she managed to say, "Well, *I* didn't know it."

The elder drew his knapsack up into his lap, looping the strap over his shoulder. "Pysk, there are more Planes than any of us realize, yet most are unknown to us, for to go between there must be a fair match from world to world. Why, look here, only on the island of Rwn is there a known crossing between Mithgar and the Mage world of Vadaria. Only on Rwn."

Alamar stood and said brusquely, "Let us be on our way."

Jinnarin whistled Rux to her side and mounted up. As they set out once again, Jinnarin returned to her original thread: "Alamar, it seems to me that if a god never answers, then He just doesn't care."

"Think, child," responded Alamar. "Perhaps a god who doesn't answer is a god who cares the most."

"How can that be? I mean, you have yet to explain why it would be evil for the gods to answer those who spoke to them."

"Child, I did not say that it would *be* evil; what I said was that perhaps it would *lead* to the ultimate evil.

"Heed me, if in every instance you were in distress or doubt you called upon your god to aid you, and if that god answered and resolved your woe, then I ask you, what would happen to your initiative? Why struggle when there is no need? Your god will see to all. Yet, would that not lead to your god controlling every aspect of your life? And if that happened, then what would be the challenge of living?

"Let me ask you this as well: if your god was not benevolent but instead were a selfish, jealous god, then would you have Him control every aspect of your life? And heed, even were He a beneficient, loving god, still, would you give up your free will for the generous life He would afford you? Would you surrender your very being in order to live in the comfort of a golden prison? And if you did surrender your very being, then what would be left of you? What would you have become?"

Jinnarin shook her head. "All this merely from speaking to a god and receiving a reply?"

"Mayhap, Jinnarin. Mayhap. For who knows where events will lead, given even an innocent start?"

"I find it difficult to believe that they will lead to the ultimate evil, Alamar."

"Then let me ask you this, Jinnarin: what is the nature of evil?"

Jinnarin's mouth dropped open. "Why, Alamar, *everyone* knows that."

"Oh? Is that so? Well then, Pysk, tell me."

"Evil is bad," responded Jinnarin.

"Don't be stupid," snapped Alamar. "To say that evil is bad is the same as saying evil is evil. Or good is good. Or tall is tall. And to define a thing in terms of itself is the sheerest of folly."

Jinnarin bristled at Alamar's remarks, yet at the same time she realized the truth of his words. She rode along in silence for a while, at last saying, "This is not an easy question, is it." Her statement was a declaration, not a query. "Even though I believe I know evil when I see it, still, to say what it is, to define it, well . . ."

Again the Pysk fell silent, contemplating. Rux padded along, easily keeping pace with the Mage, the elder plodding slowly. Once again it was Jinnarin who broke the quiet. "How can it be that something I had always thought so simple could be so complex upon reflection? Everything that I can think of has exceptions, exemptions, times when evil in one thing is virtue in another. Like, say, killing: Farrix killed a boar to save your life, but he would not kill a boar just to have done so, just for pleasure. . . . There is no easy answer, is there, Alamar?"

The elder grunted in affirmation, then added, "The nature of evil has been pondered for millennia, and you are right, Jinnarin, there is no *easy* answer . . . but there *is* an answer, though even it is hedged about with qualifications."

"Don't tell me what it is, Alamar. Let *me* ponder some more."

Alamar looked down at the Pysk in surprise, a glint of admiration in his sharp gaze.

On toward the lights of Kairn they went, the city drawing closer. At last they came in among dwellings, and Jinnarin and Rux slipped into the shadows, where darkness seemed to gather about the Pysk and fox, cloaking them, and even Mage eyes were hard pressed to spot them in the gloom. The road they followed continued westerly, paralleling the river, and alongside these stony banks they trod, passing before rows of buildings, crossing side streets now and then, some cobbled, others not. And all along the way they encountered people, hurrying to and fro or strolling in leisure or lounging. Yet, though many of these glanced at Alamar or stepped aside to let him pass, none seemed to see Jinnarin or the fox cloaked in shadow flitting through shadow—it was as if the two were invisible to ordinary eyes, though now and again, Alamar could make them out.

They passed by a bridge crossing the river, the lantern-lit span supported by pontoons floating on the water. In the near distance downstream, Jinnarin could see an island mid river, several towers rising up. And toward this place she and Rux and Alamar made their way, the Mage walking in the light of street lanterns, Pysk and fox slinking in shadow. As they came opposite the northernmost tip of the isle, they arrived at last at the dock of a ferry, three Men lounging on the torchlit quay.

Alamar stepped upon the stone pier. "Ferrymaster, I would go across."

One of the Men stood, gesturing the others to their feet. "It'll be a copper, sir."

Alamar fished a coin from his purse and paid, and stepped to the raft, the trio of Men boarding as well.

As the trio took hold of the pull rope spanning the river from this quay to that, a small cluster of shadow darted aboard to stand behind the Mage at the rear of the ferry.

Facing the opposite way, none of the Men noticed.

"With a *Huh!* and a *Huh!* and a *Huh!* and a ..." chanted the ferrymaster, all the Men hauling, pulling the rope threading through ring standards fixed fore and aft, the ferry slowly floating across, haled by muscle alone. A short while later the raft clunked against the island quay, and, *"Hoy!"* shouted a ferryman as a shadow darted past and was gone. *"Wot wos that?"*

The Men milled about, craning their necks, trying to see. Alamar hobbled slowly past and ashore, the ferrymen respectfully touching the brims of their caps as he trod by, making his way toward the towers ahead, crew voices following after:

"Oi say 'e's a Maige 'n' 'at wos 'is *familiar*."

"That as may be, but wot *wos* it?"

"Nothin' natural, 'n' you can take my word on't."

"A *shadow-cat*, Oi'd call it, six legs 'n' all, wi' drippin' fangs 'n' . . ."

Upon hearing these words Jinnarin smiled to herself and watched as Alamar approached, the Mage casting about, trying to discover her and Rux's whereabouts there beneath a bush. As he was about to pass her by, "Here we are," she softly said, urging Rux forward.

Startled, Alamar glared at her. But then his face took on a look of mystified curiosity. "Someday, Pysk, you are going to have to tell me just how you do that."

"Do what?"

"Why, gather shadows to yourself."

"Oh, that's easy, Alamar, although I don't know exactly how it's done."

"Eh? You don't?"

"Well, it's something I've always been able to do. All of my Folk can do so. We are born to it. It's rather like—oh, I don't know—like—"

"Like the flight of birds," interjected the Mage.

"Exactly so, Alamar. It is the nature of birds to fly. It is the nature of my Kind to gather shadow. Whether or not someone else can learn to do so, I cannot say, just as I cannot say whether someone not a bird can ever learn to fly."

"*Ha!*" barked Alamar. "*That* trick has been mastered by some of us."

"You can *fly*?" Jinnarin was amazed.

"Oh, I did not say that *I* could fly," responded Alamar, "but I do say that I have many tricks up these old sleeves of mine."

Onward they walked toward the towers, lantern lit against starry skies. As they approached, Jinnarin could see that there were six of them: five widely spaced apart, forming a pentagram, the sixth in the center. "Where are we headed?" she asked.

"To the middle tower. There we find the library."

"What are the other towers?"

"The various colleges," answered Alamar, pointing to each of the spires, and naming them: "Earth. Air. Fire. Water. Aethyr."

"And the sixth?"

"I already told you," snapped Alamar, "the library."

"Well there's no need to bite my head off," shot back Jinnarin, "I just thought it might have some exotic name like the others."

"Hmph!" grunted Alamar.

Now Mage, Pysk, and fox came among lesser buildings and wended their way through. "And these, Alamar. What are these?"

"Dwellings," answered the elder. "Storage. Food. Other mundanities."

Now and again the trio would stop to let a distant stranger cross their path. And twice Jinnarin and Rux took to deep shadows and hid when two groups of passersby approached, each person among them absently murmuring greetings to Alamar but not stopping their own discussions to talk with the eld Mage.

The three came to the edge of a wide flagstone plaza in the center of which stood the library tower, and there they waited until all was clear. Then Jinnarin guided Rux to pad next to Alamar, the fox brushing up against the elder's robe as across the 'spanse they went—a Mage with a shadow at his side.

At last they entered the building, Rux bearing Jinnarin darting through the archway and into the gloom within.

Inside, beyond the foyer, they came among stacks of books, the shelves arranged about a central area filled with tables and chairs, desks and benches, at which sat various people in study. Telling Jinnarin and Rux to wait among the stacks, Alamar went into the central area. Jinnarin dismounted but kept the fox close at hand. Now and again a chair would scrape, and someone would get up to find a book. At these times, if necessary, fox and Pysk would move back among the shadows, shifting from row to row to remain out of sight.

At last Alamar returned. "Up two floors," he muttered, leading the way, Jinnarin again mounted on Rux.

Along a wall a stone stair led upward, and here the

elder paused, complaining, "They *would* have to put them on the upper floors."

"Put what, Alamar?"

"The books we want," he peevishly answered.

"Oh."

Taking a deep breath, up the Mage trudged, stopping now and again to catch his wind. Rux, though, darted ahead, quickly covering the two flights, Jinnarin not wanting to dwell overlong upon the exposed staircase. Finally, Alamar came to the third floor landing and shuffled in among the stacks. Long he searched, at last finding the book he wanted, a large tome entitled *Maria Orbis Mithgarii.* "Aha! Now we shall see."

Alamar made his way to a table and settled in a chair in the sparsely occupied central area. No sooner had he sat than a slender young raven-haired Woman—or was she an Elfess?—came through the stacks and stopped at his table side. "Alamar?"

The elder looked up at her, squinting his eyes. At last he said, "Drienne?"

She smiled, nodding. "How have you been, love?"

Alamar settled back in his chair. "Getting on, Dree. Getting on."

"I can see." She sat opposite from him. "Isn't it about time you crossed over? You can't have many castings left."

Alamar sighed. "Aye, you have the right of that. It's time I took my rest."

"But, Dree, what about you? Last I saw, you were tottering, too. But now—well look at you. The same as you were on Faro."

She smiled again, her entire face lighting up. "The cottage in the woods. Alamar, I haven't thought about that for ..." Her hazel eyes fell into reflection, green flecks glinting. At last she said, "Would that we were there now. But not as you are, for I am certain that I would kill you."

"Perhaps you would, Dree, but perhaps not. Regardless, dying in your arms would be worth it."

"Why not go back to Vadaria, and when you return ... well—"

"Tempting, as always, Dree. But I can't go right now. I've something to do. Then I'll go, and when I come

back we will hike to that cottage in the woods and mayhap not come out for years."

Drienne smiled, her eyes lost in gentle memory. But
then she sighed and came to herself once more. Of a
sudden, as if searching, she looked under the table, then
toward the stacks. "I thought I saw a fox with you.
Surely you haven't taken a fox as a familiar."

"It's just an acquaintance, Dree, following me about
for the nonce."

"Good. I shouldn't think foxes would make good companions. Too feral. Not like cats—"

"Or owls," interjected Alamar.

Drienne rolled her eyes at this. "As I was saying, not
like cats and their comforting ways as well as their wild
energy. And Alamar, I've told you before, you can't cud-
dle with an owl." She glanced at the tome. "What is it
you are researching? Perhaps I can help."

"Three things, Dree: a pale green sea, a black ship, a
crystal castle."

"Sounds mysterious."

"They're elements of a dream."

"Ah well, I can't help you there. But if it were
stars—"

"If it were stars, Dree, I think I could do it myself."

Drienne nodded, then said, "Why not let Aylis—"

"She's not on Rwn."

"Oh. Well. All right. Regardless, perhaps I can help.
What other books do you need? I'll get them."

Alamar fished a paper from his pocket. He peered at
it a moment, then said, "See if you can find *De Castellis
Singularibus* and *De Navibus Notis*."

While Drienne searched, Alamar paged through the
tome before him, pausing now and again to read, then
moving on. Ere he had gone far, Drienne returned, bearing two more tomes. Alamar glanced across at her.
"Look for a crystal castle or a black ship."

"Hmm. A crystal castle shouldn't be difficult to find,
if one exists, that is. But a black ship now, I would think
there might be many. What kind of black ship is it?"

Alamar fished Jinnarin's drawing from his pocket,
handing it to Drienne. She squinted at it. "Lord, Alamar,
who drew this tiny thing? A dragonfly rider?"

"A friend."

Drienne looked at him in wonder, then back at the sketch. "A carrack or a galleon I would say. —A black one?" At a nod from Alamar, Drienne passed the small paper back to him and then opened a tome.

From the shadows Jinnarin watched as Drienne joined Alamar in skimming through the books. Long moments passed, the silence broken only by the sound of pages slowly turning. Occasionally one of the other people in the central area would get up and leave, and a person or two came up the steps to the same floor and entered the stacks, but they were on the opposite side of the room and Jinnarin and Rux remained where they were. Rux lay with his chin on his front paws, yet his eyes were open and his ears pricked, and Jinnarin knew that he was on guard against discovery. And so the Pysk made herself comfortable on a bottom shelf among musty tomes and waited . . . and dozed. "Here's one"— Drienne's voice brought Jinnarin awake—"Oh wait, it burned while in port at Arbalin. During the rebellion." Drienne resumed leafing, her eyes fixed upon the pages, and Jinnarin settled once more, leaning back against an aslant book.

How long Jinnarin drowsed, she did not know, but the scrape of chairs brought her awake. Peering out, she saw that Alamar and Drienne were getting to their feet. Several tomes lay scattered on the table before them, and it was obvious that they had sought references in each. Alamar stretched, straightening his back, groaning, and Drienne said, "Love, you simply must cross over to Vadaria."

"Not right now, Dree. Got to solve this dream first. A past obligation."

"Stubborn as always," Drienne muttered and began gathering up the books. But then she stopped and looked Alamar directly in the eye, her gaze filled with entreaty and unshed tears. "Heed me: don't overcast, Alamar. I want you alive and young; not old and dead."

Alamar took her glorious face in his hands and kissed her gently. "I'm going now, Dree. But I promise as soon as I have this dream business resolved, I'll cross over. Then I'll come back and we'll—where will I find you?"

"Try here, first, Alamar, here in the City of Bells. You see, I'm Regent of the Academy at the moment."

"The Grand Dame?"

Drienne nodded, smiling.

"What will the apprentices say when I whisk you off to—"

"What they've always said, I shouldn't wonder."

Alamar stood in thought a moment. At last he said, "I may be gone awhile. Should it take long, then where?"

"If not here," answered Drienne, "then on the Lady's island, there in my cottage of the wood."

"Faro," breathed Alamar, then he smiled and took her hands and squeezed them gently. "I must go."

Drienne kissed him on the cheek and released him, and Alamar turned and headed for the stairs, a bit of a spring in his step. And among the stacks Jinnarin swung aboard Rux, and the fox made his way through the shadows and reached the landing just as the elder started down. Urging Rux forward, Jinnarin followed the Mage. Yet ere they had gone halfway down, from behind, the Pysk heard a gasp. Jinnarin turned and glanced back, and at the head of the stairs stood Drienne, her eyes wide in wonderment. Jinnarin smiled and waved, then gathered darkness unto herself and urged Rux forward, the shadow-wrapped fox darting down in the gloom.

"Nothing? You discovered nothing?" They stood in the dimness beyond all the buildings, Jinnarin looking at the Mage in consternation.

"Right," snapped Alamar, irritated.

"But you said that this was the finest library—"

"I said that it was *one* of the finest," grated the Mage.

"Don't quibble!" flared Jinnarin.

"I'm not quibbling!" shouted Alamar.

Silence fell between them. Then in a more subdued tone Alamar said, "We may *never* discover where lies a pale green sea or a crystal castle or where sails a black ship. Did I not say that dream visions are often not what they seem? And, after all, it *is* nought but a stupid *dream*—"

"Sending!" gritted Jinnarin.

Alamar sighed.

Neither uttered aught for a while, then Jinnarin said, "Let us not argue, Alamar. Instead, what can we do now? Where can we go and who can we see to find a clue, a lead? Who knows about ships and seas and islands—?"

"Sailors!" declared Alamar. "Ships' captains. Navigators. Cartographers. Mariners all."

"All right then," said Jinnarin, "let us go see these—these mariners. But if they know not, then who shall we ask?"

Alamar stood in silence a moment, twisting the bracelet on his wrist. At last he said, "Well, my tiny Pysk, if they know not, then will we seek the Children of the Sea."

Jinnarin and Rux waited, shadow in shadow, while nearby the River Kairn thundered down into the waters of the Weston Ocean, the river at last coming to the lip of the headland to plunge a hundred feet or more to the brine below. Across a narrow street stood the Sloppy Pig, a cliff-edge tavern frequented by apprentice and mariner both, or so Alamar had said. The Mage himself was inside hoisting a tankard or two, speaking with members of ships' crews, captains and sailors alike. The Pig was the third such public house that Alamar had visited on the bluffs above the docks, having previously called upon the Dropped Anchor and the Foaming Wake.

Jinnarin was just beginning to suspect that Alamar had forgotten her when the Mage lurched out the door. *"Pysk, Pysk,"* he loudly hissed. *"Psst!* Where are you, Jinner—Jinn—Pysk?"

Reeling across the street, his eyes searching, the Mage stumbled among the bushes of the riverside grounds, one hand held high, a blue light glowing from his fingertips. *"Pysk—!"*

"Hush, Alamar!" snapped Jinnarin. "And put out that light!"

"Oh *there* you are, Jin-Jin. I was beginning to think—"

"Alamar, you are drunk!"

The Mage drew himself up in indignation and thickly protested, "Me? Drunk? Why, I'll have you know—"

"Alamar, I said put out that light."

Alamar bleared at his glowing hand, muttered a few words, and watched in amazement as it grew brighter. He muttered more words. Nothing happened. Finally he stuffed his hand into his cloak, wrapping cloth about it. "Never mind the cursed light. We've got to hurry. I've booked us passage on a ship. We're bound for Arbalin tonight."

"Ship? Arbalin? Tonight? Why?"

Alamar took his hand from the cloak and looked at it. It still glowed. He wrapped it up again. "Because, Jin-Jin, that's where we'll find Aravan, him and his Elvenship. If *anyone* knows where lies the pale green castle, the crystal ship, or the black sea, it'll be Aravan."

"Oh, Alamar, you are in no state to make such decisions. How can we—how can *I* be certain that this is the right thing to do? I mean, I've heard of Aravan of course—he's a Friend, after all . . . saved Tarquin's life—but to go traipsing off to Arbalin, well—"

"Cer-certainly it's the right thing, Jin-Jin," averred Alamar. "And we've got to hurry. The *Flying Flish,* the *Filing Frish,* the blasted ship sails on the night tide. Besides, how else are we going to find Farr—Pysk—Rix, the boar killer?"

With grave misgivings, at last Jinnarin nodded. *How else indeed?*

It was with some wonderment that the crew of the *Flying Fish* watched as the old Man lurched up the gangplank, dragging behind a most unwilling fox on a long tether fixed on its harness, the animal snarling at the elder and snapping at the rope and jerking back against it, at times lying down and being dragged on its side. " 'Smy familiar Ruxie," slurred the old Man.

When elder and fox were safely ensconced in their cabin, one crew member turned to another and asked, " 'Don's blood, did you see that?"

"Right, mate," answered the other, "take my grog but that fox were wild."

"No, no, you booby, the fox ain't what I were driving at!"

"Well then, wot?"

"It were his hand."

"His hand?"

"Yar! Bleed me but I do believe his hand were on fire!"

CHAPTER 6

Asea

Early to Mid Spring, 1E9574
[Five Months Past]

Alamar reeled into the cabin, dragging Rux behind, the fox struggling against the leash. As the door closed, the Mage dropped his rucksack to the planking—"*Ow!*" came a muffled cry from within. Paying no heed, the elder flopped down onto his bunk and lay on his back contemplating his glowing digits. "Out, damn light!" he thickly commanded. "*Exi, Lumen! Exstingue! Fiat lux!* Oops!"—once again the light grew stronger—"*Peri—perite—perde lumen ...*" Nothing seemed to work. While on the floor the knapsack began to wriggle and thump and emit muted curses dire, a tiny hand emerging to unfasten the bindings, Rux whining and licking at the wee fingers, while the Mage on the bunk mumbled. At last the sack was open and out struggled Jinnarin, the Pysk fuming, fire in her eyes.

"Alamar!" she shrieked. "You ale-fuddled old sot!—"

A snore answered her.

Alamar had passed out.

But his hand no longer glowed.

"Unh," groaned the Mage, opening his eyes, blearily peering about. "Where—oh my head."

No one answered him, yet he could hear the creak of wood and a distant plash of water. Bright daylight poured in through a roundish window, and the room seemed to be slowly rocking to and fro. He held up the fingers of his right hand and stared at them, as if trying to remember something—what, he did not know. Wincing, Alamar struggled to a sitting position.

On the floor across the room glaring at him sat Jinnarin, leaning back against sleeping Rux.

Smacking his lips and tasting his own tongue, Alamar's face screwed up into a horrid mask. *"Gahh!"*

"Serves you right," gritted Jinnarin.

"Wh-where are we?"

"On board the *Flying Fish.*"

Alamar's eyebrows shot upward. *"Flying Fish*? A ship?" He looked about, now recognizing the gentle rolling for what it was. "What in the name of Hèl are we doing aboard a ship?"

"You really don't remember, do you?"

Alamar stared blankly at her. "I seem to recall talking to a captain about"—he squeezed his eyes shut, trying to recollect—"about the Elvenship," he said at last.

"Aravan's ship, the *Eroean.*"

"Yes, that's it. The *Eroean.*" Suddenly Alamar's eyes widened, and he stood, groaning from the effort and clutching his head with one hand, his other reaching out for the rocking wall to steady himself. "Quickly, Jinnarin, we've got to get off before the ship sails."

"Oh, so now it's 'Jinnarin,' eh? Last night it was 'Jin-Jin.' "

"Whatever you are talking about, Pysk, we haven't time," snapped Alamar, wincing at the loudness of his own voice.

"Alamar, I have news for you: we sailed some twelve hours past."

As if his knees had turned to water, Alamar plopped back down upon the bunk. "Twelve . . . ?"

Jinnarin nodded, finally getting to her feet. Rux opened an eye, then closed it again.

"How could you let this happen, Pysk?" groaned Alamar.

"It seemed like a good idea at the time," she answered.

"Idea? What idea? Where are we bound?"

"For Arbalin," responded Jinnarin. "There to see—"

Alamar groaned again. "To see Aravan. I remember."

He cast a grievous eye at Jinnarin. "How could you conceive such a stupid scheme?"

"I? I?" spluttered Jinnarin. "How could *I* conceive such a stupid—"

"That's what I asked, Pysk," barked Alamar. "No need to repeat the question."

"Alamar, you ass, it was *you* who conceived the stupid plan!" she shrieked, her voice shrill and piercing, Alamar clapping his hands to his head in agony.

Grumbling, Rux stood and turned in a circle and lay back down again, eyeing the two accusingly.

Moaning, Alamar got to his feet once more, his gaze avoiding that of the seething Pysk. "Well, there's nothing for it," he muttered. "I've got to get to the captain and have him turn back."

But just as he reached the cabin door—"Wait!" called Jinnarin. And as the Mage turned and looked at her—"Sit back down, Alamar. I've something to say."

"Look, Pysk, every moment we delay just puts us that much farther from—"

"I said, *sit down!*" Jinnarin snarled through clenched teeth.

With a sigh, Alamar plodded back to the bunk and slumped. After a moment of silence, he demanded, "Speak up, speak up. The ship sails on."

"Quiet!" she ordered. "I am gathering my thoughts."

The Pysk moved to Rux and sat on the floor and used the fox as a bolster.

Alamar shook his head in exasperation . . . but he remained silent.

At last Jinnarin looked at him. "Alamar, perhaps this stupid scheme isn't so stupid after all. I mean, isn't it true that Aravan has sailed the world over? And if that's true, then who better to ask? Who else would know of a pale green sea? And, given that Aravan has indeed sailed all the seas of Mithgar, might he not know of the crystal castle? The black ship? Alamar, have you a better notion of who we might go to? Is there anyone other than Aravan who could better aid us in finding Farrix?"

Alamar looked long at Jinnarin. Finally he said, "But that in turn means we have to find Aravan."

"You said that he was at Arbalin."

"I said, Jinnarin, that he sailed out of Arbalin. That

doesn't mean he's there now. In fact, it is most likely that he is *not* there."

"If not there, Alamar, then where?"

"On his ship. On the *Eroean*," Alamar said peevishly. "He does, after all, sail the seas you know, gadding about the world in search of adventure, of treasure, of rich cargo."

Jinnarin nodded. "Yes, I do know. But list, Alamar: soon or late he brings that rich cargo to Arbalin, neh?"

"But that could take years, child," protested Alamar.

"Or merely days," she rejoined.

They sat without speaking, the silence broken only by the plash of waves against the hull and the rolling creak of ship's timber and rope. At last Alamar said, "All right, Jinnarin, we will go to Arbalin. There we will seek Aravan, and if he is not there, then we will seek word of when he might come, or where we might find him. We will wait for six months, no more—"

"A year," interjected Jinnarin.

"Six months," repeated Alamar, glaring.

"A year," said Jinnarin again. "After all, Alamar, it *is* Farrix we are after. You remember him, don't you, Farrix the boar killer?"

Alamar winced. "That was a low blow, Pysk.... All right. You win. A year."

The *Flying Fish* was a three-masted caravel, some eighty feet long from stem to stern and twenty-eight feet abeam, a swift little cargo ship plying the route between Arbalin and Rwn, a journey of seven to nine weeks, given favorable winds. Her sails abaft were lateen rigged, while those forward were square—all but the jib. Captain Dalby was her master, and she carried a crew of seventeen: two mates, a cook, a carpenter and cooper, a caulker, a cabin boy, a boatswain, and ten ordinary seamen. She had a stern castle but no fo'c'sle, and the former held three cabins—the captain's, the first mate's, and the second mate's, this last occupied by Alamar, for whenever there were passengers on board, the second mate and, if necessary, the first mate as well, slept with the remainder of the Men below decks in the forward crew's quarters.

Alamar took his meals with the captain, always bearing a small portion away from the board—"For my fox, you know"—and Dalby was struck by the wide variety of food that this carnivore ate: vegetables and soups, breads and sweets, and even dried fruits, as well as morsels of fish and fowl and other meats. And though the captain had no objection to the taking of modest bits and scraps, still he found it curious that even though he had invited Alamar to bring his animal into the cabin to eat straight from the board, the Mage had declined, saying that Rux was too untamed, too feral. Yet in spite of the fox's reputed wild ways, at night Alamar was often seen pacing the deck, the fox somewhere near. And unlike when he was first brought aboard, the animal ran free, no longer restrained by a leash.

Yet even though the crew became accustomed to seeing Alamar and Rux, still at times the sailors would gather and speculate about both the Mage and his fox, though not within the hearing of either. For ever since the two had taken passage, there seemed to be strange goings on aboard the *Fish:*

Now and again in the night a crewman would see a flicker of shadow from the corner of his eye, but whenever he looked, nothing would be there, or at times it would be the fox.

The carpenter swore that the fox was a shape changer, and the cabin boy claimed that he had heard Alamar in his cabin talking with the fox, *and that the fox had answered!*

"I was bringing tea to the cap'n when I heard it. A high-pitched voice it were, them two talkin' . . . arguing fiercelike. About wot, I don't know, and I don't want to know, and I didn't stop to see. Believe you me, quick as Jack Nimble I ran, I did. Didn't spill a drop o' th' cap'n's tea, neither."

"*Brrr!* Gives me the blank willies it does. But I take wot y' say, matey, 'cause I 'spect as all foxes wot talk have high voices, right enough."

"Wull, it don't s'prise me none, 'cause I've always known as foxes are more'n wot they seem. I mean, look at 'ow clever they are and all. And their eyes, not like those of a decent dog, but instead like th' slitted orbs o' a stealthy cat."

"Ar, y'r right at that. But 'ere naow, 'oo's to say 'e

ain't one o' them there demons wot Wizards are always foolin' about wi'?''

"Go on wi' ye. This Rux naow, a Wizard's familiar 'e is and talk 'e might, but 'e's all right wi' me, 'e is. And take my grog 'e ain't no demon. Let me ask you, though, 'ave you seen many rats since 'e's come aboard? 'E's better'n a cat, I'd say, when it comes to rattin'. Y'r meals 'r' better, too, 'cause the rats wot nibble and gnaw 'r' probably all dead by now, kilt by Master Rux, I do trow if y' want my honest opinion on it."

"That as may be, cookie, but all as I know is I'll be glad when we finally deliver Master Rux and 'is Wizard to the docks at Arbalin Isle. . . ."

As the caravel made its way across the Weston Ocean and toward the Avagon Sea, during the daylight hours Jinnarin stayed within the cabin, but at night she roamed the decks taking in the salt tang of the fresh ocean air, the shadow-wrapped Pysk for the most part invisible to the eye of Man, though now and again a member of the crew would catch a fleeting glimpse of her. Rux accompanied her on these sojourns, the fox now completely familiar with the entire ship. But during the day while Jinnarin was shut in Alamar's quarters, Rux was usually below decks hunting rats. And though Rux wasn't afraid of the Men aboard, he gave them wide berth, just as they gave him, each eyeing the other somewhat suspiciously.

When she wasn't asleep during the day, Jinnarin spent much of the time in discourse with Alamar, the eld Mage a fount of knowledge when he wasn't fuming or sulking.

One rainy day Jinnarin asked, "Tell me, Alamar, what did Drienne mean when she said you needed to cross over?"

Alamar glared at her accusingly. "Eavesdropping on a private conversation, were you?"

"Oh, never mind!" shot back Jinnarin.

A chill beyond that of the dampness filled the cabin, Jinnarin inspecting her bow and arrows for the thousandth time—or so it seemed to her—and Alamar sitting at a small desk filling a paper with arcane symbols.

"I'll trade you," he said at last.

"Trade me?"

"Pysk, there are times I suspect that your hearing has failed you."

Jinnarin gritted her teeth. "And there are times, Mage, when I know your manners have deserted you!"

Again cold silence fell between them as the ship rolled in the billowing seas, and they could hear the voice of the bo's'n calling out to the Men, setting the sails. Finally, Jinnarin asked: "What do you mean you'll 'trade me'? Trade what for what?"

"Information for information, Pysk. What else?"

"Meaning . . . ?"

"You want to know why Drienne asked me to go to Vadaria, and I want to know just exactly what is on those arrows you Pysks use. I mean, it must be powerful stuff indeed if a tiny shaft like that can bring down a rampaging boar."

Now Jinnarin glared at Alamar. "So, now it's the secrets of the Hidden Ones you'd like, eh?"

"Black kettle, black pot," retorted Alamar.

"What?" demanded Jinnarin.

"Goose and gander," replied the Mage.

"Alamar, I'd sooner you hold your tongue than to speak in riddles. I merely wished to know what was so important about going back to Vadaria, but you, on the other hand want to be made privy to special lore of the Fox Riders."

"Just as you want to know special lore of the Mages, Pysk."

"Oh. Well if it's a secret—"

"Not exactly a secret, Jinnarin. Instead, it's just not common knowledge."

"Well, uncommon knowledge or not, Alamar, I'll not trade. If the secret of Fox Rider arrows were to fall into the wrong hands . . ."

Alamar sighed, and once more a lengthy silence fell between them, and sheets of rain lashed upon the hull. But at last Alamar said, "This is the way of it, Jinnarin, the casting of spells exacts a dreadful toll: youth and energy are spent, the greater the spell, the greater the cost. For small effects, such as magelight, or magesight, or firestarting, the cost is minimal. But for large effects— stormbringing, lifegiving, and the like—the cost is great

. . . unless, of course, energy is gained by other means to satisfy the balance."

"Other means?"

"Mostly vile," answered Alamar. "Sacrifices. Death or torture. Fear. Anything that causes the crying out of a soul."

Jinnarin shuddered in revulsion and fell into thought. After a while she asked, "What about great joy, Alamar, or love? Wouldn't they also provide energy?"

Alamar smiled a rare smile. "Ah me, but you, too, would make a good apprentice, Jinnarin.

"But to answer your question: yes. Joy. Love. Grief. Hate. Any and all the great emotions can sustain a casting, furnishing the energy needed. But in their absence, youth is taken from the caster instead.

"Heed: my Folk are as yours, or as are the Elves—ordinarily, age visits us not. Even so, we can grow old . . . but only if we exert our inborn power to control and shape the energies about us, only if we mold reality and alter the world at hand, only if we do that which others call magic, only if we cast spells. . . . In the absence of castings, youth is ever ours."

"But then, Alamar, why did Drienne urge you to go to Vadaria?"

"Just this: on Vadaria, if we rest a special way we can recover from the ravages of casting—we can regain our youth."

"If rest is all you need, why not here on Mithgar?"

Alamar smiled again. "Very good, Jinnarin. You would indeed make a suitable Mage's apprentice had you the inborn power. Once more you have asked a cogent question, one that deserves an answer:

"On Mithgar, it takes many, many centuries to recover from casting spells, but on Vadaria, that time is but a tenth—nay! but one one hundredth of what it is here."

"Oh," said Jinnarin. "Now I see."

Again silence fell between the two. This time, though, it was Jinnarin who broke the quiet. "Two things, Alamar:

"First, the arrows are coated with a paste made from the bark of a certain tree mingled with the juice of a certain flower to which is added the pulverized powder of a certain rock; beyond that I will say no more.

"Second, you have implied that my Folk have not the power to become spell casters, yet this I say to you: there are many among the Hidden Ones who can and do 'cast magic,' and some Fox Riders are numbered among these."

The *Flying Fish* at last came into the Avagon Sea, Captain Dalby swinging the ship onto an east-northeasterly course, and with all canvas flying, the little caravel made the best of the light winds abaft. The weather for the most part continued fair, though now and again rain swept across the waters and down upon the craft. Dalby ran the Straits of Kistan without undue incident, although the lookout did espy the maroon sails of a Kistanian Rover, but nought came of it, and on toward Arbalin they plowed.

And in Alamar's cabin—"I have been considering the question of evil," announced Jinnarin one day, "and though I've come to no final dictum, there are a few things I can say."

Alamar looked up from the paper he scribbled on, then turned his chair to face the Pysk. "Say on, Jinnarin. I would hear you."

"Well, Alamar, it seems to me that much of what I consider to be evil falls into the realm of someone asserting control over another purely for selfish ends. This control can take many forms, but regardless, it is a control which ignores the wishes of the one being controlled. Domination is what I speak of here, domination to satisfy the whims of the dominator. In the extreme, the domination, the control, is over life itself, and the dominator may even slay the victim merely to prove that he holds the ultimate control. Power, authority, dominion, command, control, obedience—all for the pleasure of the wielder: these are the things a truly evil being seeks."

Alamar smiled. "Let us speak of these things you name, Jinnarin: power, authority, dominion, control, obedience. Are these not the rights of a King, or for that matter, anyone in authority?"

"Yes, Alamar, they are. Yet a King should exercise these with great circumspection, and only with the good of his subjects in mind. If he wields his power only for his own gratification, without regard to the needs and desires of his subjects, then I say he is evil."

"Hmm," mused the Mage. "What about, oh say, the dominant Wolf in a pack—is he not evil? He is dominant, after all, exercising his will over the other Wolves."

Jinnarin made a negating gesture with her hand. "But he does not do so merely for pleasure. Instead, he leads the pack to ensure their survival as well as his own. The fact that he dominates does not make him evil; instead, in this case, it simply means that he is the one best fit to lead."

"What about those who lie, cheat, steal."

"Alamar, I would say that there are varying degrees of evil. Some things being worse—more evil—than others. Lying, cheating, stealing, if they are done merely for gratification, if they are done merely because the liars, cheaters, stealers have no regard for the feelings of those they wrong, then they are acting in an evil manner.

"But take the case where one steals to feed his family. Or lies to protect his King. Or steals to save the lives of others. Then I think that perhaps evil is not being done, although in some cases the doer is accomplishing wrong. . . .

"Is that possible, Alamar? Is it possible to deliberately do wrong without doing evil?"

"Ah, Jinnarin, this is a question the philosophers have long pondered: the degree that motive ameliorates wrong. But I will let you search for the answer on your own, for it is a deep question deserving much thought.

"Instead, Pysk, let me ask you another: what about the control we exert over criminals? We lock them away. At times we put them to hard labor. At other times we exercise the ultimate control and take their lives from them. Is it not evil to control another being so?"

Jinnarin thought long ere answering. "We do those things because, just as the dominant Wolf cares for the pack, so too do we care for our own. To let an evildoer run loose is to allow an unfettered ravager into the midst of our own social order. Hence, because the criminal has demonstrated that he is a ravager of others, he must not be permitted to run free to the ultimate harm of any one of us, or to the harm of us all."

"Well said, Pysk. But now let me ask you this: What

about the control of children? If domination is evil, then is it not evil to dominate their lives?"

"Oh, Alamar, the young are a special case. They need to be given as much liberty as their experience allows, or perhaps even a bit more. When they are young, they have little or no knowledge, in which case they need looking after and guidance. As they grow older, they can and should be allowed more and more freedom, for after all, they are coming closer to adulthood. Here, if they've been nurtured to think responsibly for themselves, if they've received loving guidance, if they've been allowed to accumulate experiences that will stand them in good stead throughout their lives, then they will act more and more like the independent adults we would wish them to be. And, of course, there comes the time when we must let them go, to be the masters of their own fates, to control their own choices and thereby their own destinies.

"And so, the control of children is not an evil thing in and of itself unless the one doing so seeks only dominion, and that for his own pleasure, his own satisfaction, for his own sense of control of another being."

Alamar nodded, agreeing. "Tell me this then, Jinnarin. What is the nature of evil?"

Jinnarin stood and paced the floor. "This, Alamar, this I think lies at the heart of evil and defines its nature: Each of us should be free to control our own destiny. Only under very special circumstances should we yield limited control of our individual destinies to others, circumstances such as, say, defending one another against a common foe, circumstances where someone must lead and others follow. In the absence of those special circumstances, no one should be allowed to willfully interfere with the life of another, unless that other seeks in some fashion without our permission to exert control over one or more of us. Then and only then should steps be taken to stop this interference, and then in a minimal manner to do so. Evil is when a person or persons or thing for its own satisfaction seeks to wrench our destiny from our own hands, seeks to take away freedom of choice, to take away our physical, emotional, spiritual, or intellectual life, seeks to force us into a mold of his choosing and not our own.

"And that, Alamar, is the nature of evil: power, authority, dominion, command, control, obedience, removal of choice, suppression of freedom, usurpation of the destiny of others—all for the gratification of the wielder."

Alamar smiled and slowly shook his head. "Adon, but you would make a wonderful apprentice."

Jinnarin blushed. "I take it then I've well defined the essence of evil, neh?"

The smile vanished from Alamar's face, and he barked, "Don't get uppity, Pysk. It's a start. That's all. Just a start."

Jinnarin drew herself up to her full twelve inches. "What did I leave out?" she demanded.

"Why, much, child, much."

"Such as . . . ?"

"Well for starts, you spoke of giving up the right of self-determination under 'special circumstances,' yielding control of your life to someone else, someone you called a 'leader.' Yet you did not mention the fact that here you have stepped upon a very slippery slope, and that one person's view of special circumstances is another person's view of unneeded interference. One must always ask, 'Who is naming this a "special circumstance"?' and, 'Are these circumstances truly dire enough to surrender my free will to the judgement of another? And if so, then whom?'

"That is but one issue; here are others:

"Although you talked of lying, cheating, and stealing, you spoke not at all of lust, greed, avarice, gluttony, addiction, and other such; are these in and of themselves evil things? What of waste and want, and of neglect—benign, deliberate, vengeful—are they always vile, or instead are there cases where they are warranted? What of hate, fear, envy, sloth, jealousy, prejudice, and the like? And what of coldly taking of the life of another? Is it ever justified, is it evil here but good there? And what of religions or societies that attempt to control, to regulate even the finest detail of everyday living—of course, for the benefit of all, or so it is claimed—are these inherently evil? And the debate between Adon and Gyphon—was one side good and the other evil?

Were both sides good? Both evil? What does this debate say concerning the nature of Adon, of Gyphon?

"And lastly, child, we circle back to your original query: what about gods who never answer, or who always answer? Gods who ignore their creations, who let them be or who seldom interfere or who interfere continually? Gods who exert no control, or some control, or continuing control? Are we like children who need godly guidance, or are we instead adults who should be on our own, who should be allowed to make our own decisions and live with the rewards or consequences of such? And what of guidance that is not loving but instead has its origins elsewhere?

"Does your definition of the essence, the nature, of evil cover all these cases and more?"

"But, Alamar," protested Jinnarin, "you are asking me to practically define the entire body of ethics, of religion, of philosophy, of—of all!"

Alamar nodded. "I know I am, Jinnarin, but heed: any definition must be tested against all relevant cases and modified where found lacking." Alamar smiled sadly unto himself. "Perhaps, Jinnarin, you will ultimately circle back to your original definition of evil, concluding only that evil is bad."

They sailed into Arbalin in the middle of the night fifty-six days after departure from Rwn. Alamar bade his good-byes to Captain Dalby and the ship's crew, and carrying his knapsack and dragging Rux after—the fox lying on his side and thumping down the gangway while growling and snapping at the rope tied to his harness— the Mage and his familiar disembarked from the caravel.

"Lumme, didja see that?"

"Wot?"

" 'E was talkin' to 'is knapsack."

" 'E wos? Wot'd 'e say?"

"Somethin' about being glad 'e'd not 'ave to clean up no more fox poop."

Alamar rented an isolated cottage set on the marge of a wood. The Mage also intimated that Rux was his familiar ... and abruptly, almost instantly, fox hunting became a lost art throughout the whole of Arbalin Isle.

Alamar soon was a well-recognized figure down on the docks of the bay, for every day he trudged into town seeking word of Aravan and his swift Elvenship. But no one knew when the *Eroean* was due, nor even its ports of call. All they could say was that there had been times when the ship had been gone for years. And the last that it was seen in Arbalin was two years agone, and then it had laid over but a week ere it had set sail once more. But as to when it might again drop anchor in Arbalin Harbor . . . well, that was anyone's guess.

And so in the cottage on the marge of the woods, Alamar waited and worried, for Jinnarin's dream yet haunted her—a dream of a lofty crystal castle above pale green sea, and a lightning-stroked ebony ship . . . and of something *dreadful* drawing nigh.

And throughout the next months, often in the night did the old Man, the old Elf, the old Mage, pace in front of his cottage and stare down at the distant bay or up at the glittering stars remote and mutter aloud:

"Where away, O Elvenship, and your master Aravan?"

CHAPTER 7

Passage

Summer, 1E9574
[The Past Three Months]

Aravan turned his head this way and that, trying to locate the source of stealthy plashing muffled by the dense fog. Overhead the silken sails of the *Eroean* hung slackly, not a breath of air stirring in the morn, the ship slowly drifting, impelled by the remnants of the current of the distant river whose mouth lay easterly an uncertain way. Somewhere nearby stood the Dragon's Fangs, sharp rocks jutting up from the sea, and Aravan knew that soon he must either drop anchor or lower towing gigs to spare the aimless *Eroean* from foundering upon this cloaked hazard ... but not yet, not yet, for another deadly danger drew nigh.

Aravan gestured silently to Bokar, and the axe-bearing Dwarf stepped to the Elven captain's side. Bokar at four feet six inches was considerably shorter than Aravan, though the Dwarf was half again as broad in the shoulders as was the Elf.

Without a word, Aravan pointed slightly astern of starboard. Bokar nodded and trod away, moving down the line of Dwarven warriors and Human sailors, speaking not but instead pointing to where Aravan had indicated. And armed to the teeth they waited—the Dwarves wearing boiled-leather breastplates and dark steel helms fitted with cheek and nose guards and adorned with horns or studs or spikes or with metal wings flaring; the Men unarmored but bearing cutlasses.

A week past the black-haired captain and his Elvenship and crew had been in the port of Janjong, taking on a cargo of nutmeg and cinnamon, laded o'er a ship's ballast of porcelain tableware. South they had sailed, bearing slightly west, through the Jinga Sea, favorable but light winds abaft. Yet with all sails set—mains and studs, jibs and spankers, staysails, topsails, gallants and royals, skysails and moonrakers and starscrapers—the *Eroean* had churned white wake all the way to the pirate-infested Straits of Alacca, the long, narrow slot between the shores of Jūng and the rocky cliffs of Lazan ... and there the wind had utterly died. A night they had spent sitting at anchor, waiting for the return of the air. But then morning had come and with it the fog, creeping out from the jungles, a fog so thick that nought could be seen more than five strides away.

And in the mist they had heard a voice coming across the waters—a Man's sharp curse suddenly silenced. Swiftly, silently, Aravan had upped anchor just barely enough to let the ship drift free, the vessel sluggishly changing its position in the torpid flux. And all the crew had taken up arms, for they knew that pirates drew nigh.

Down from the ratlines came creeping Jatu, the huge black Man seeking Aravan. He stepped to the Elf and in soft voice said, "Captain, I cannot see aught of their ship down in the folds of the fog, but they've a Man aloft in a crow's nest, skimming the top of this lost cloud, and he's guiding them, sighting upon our rigging jutting up out of the mist."

"*Vash!*" hissed Aravan, his voice low. "Where away and how far?"

Yon, indicated Jatu, a point or two aft of starboard. "Mayhap a quarter hour at the rate they move."

"Well, there's nothing for it then except to stand and fight. Even so, wert thou sighted, Jatu? Nay? Hai, then they may yet believe to surprise us, knowing not that we know of them. Take two Men and ease the anchor back gently to the bottom."

Aravan strode down the line, coming to wing-helmed Bokar. "Armsmaster, ready the boarding ropes and a corvus or three. We shall carry the fight to them."

Through his red beard Bokar grinned fiercely, his dark eyes alight, then passed the word to his Dwarven fighters as well as to all the Men. Yardarm ropes were loosed from their belaying pins, there on the starboard side, warriors and sailors grasping the lines. And in three separate places, broad, lengthy planks ending in long curving hooks were affixed to the *Eroean*'s toprail, devised to fall as would a drawbridge—the iron hooks set to grasp the enemy vessel—each plank a corvus for invading ship to ship.

Again Aravan strode the length of the line. "Down and hide, let them draw alongside thinking we yet sleep."

Moments passed, and now all could hear the stealthy dip of oars. And through the runoffs they could see a vague shape darkly loom forth from the fog, drawing alongside the larger *Eroean*. Yet at last an obscure silhouette could be discerned: it was a two-masted junk, high sterned and low prowed, raised lugsails fore and aft with battens running across.

"Wait," breathed Aravan to the Dwarven armsmaster.

Now the junk came up amidships, and at a soft command the vessel's oars were shipped as the rowers ceased rowing and took up weaponry, and on her decks could dimly be seen moving figures readying for boarding.

With a muffled *thmp-tmp* of fenders between, softly the hull of the junk came into cushioned contact with her intended prey.

"Wait," breathed Aravan yet again.

Thnk. A cloth-wrapped grapnel was lobbed up over the *Eroean*'s rail, swiftly followed by three more, and the junk was haled snug and cinched against the hull of the Elvenship.

"Now," hissed Aravan—"Now!" roared Bokar—*NOW!* howled all the crew—and with thunderous crashes the boarding bridges slammed down on the decks of the pirate vessel, long iron corvine claws clutching and holding, trapping the coastal raider against the *Eroean*'s hull. And bellowing the ancient Dwarven battle cry—*"Châkka-shok! Châkka-cor!"*—a shout echoed by all the Dwarves—axe in hand Bokar thundered down and across a fog-shrouded bridge, giant Jatu at his back, with Aravan in his grey leathers swinging on a rope above them like a ghost in the mist, steel glimmering in the

Elf's grasp, while at one and the same time, with blood-curdling shouts and savage wordless cries, Dwarven warriors and Human sailors, weapons clenched, charged across the spans or swung through the mist-laden air on yardarm ropes to assail the beclouded Jūngarian ship.

Bokar slammed into a mass of shocked reavers, the Dwarf's double-bitted axe reaping foe, cleaving flesh, blood flying, while Jatu's warbar smashed pirates aside, skulls crushed, bones broken. Like some mist-wrapped demon, Aravan hurtled out from the fog to land square on the poop deck, the grey cloud swirling, mist tendrils clinging, his sword licking out to fell the startled steersman. The Elf turned in time to fend a whistling blow from a tulwar wielded by a cursing swarthy Man, the pirate in a leather vest, copper plates sewn thereon. *Shing, shang,* skirled steel on steel, and Aravan pressed the enemy hindward, the Man to topple howling over the taffrail and fall yowling into the sea below.

The mass of the *Eroean*'s crew poured aboard the junk and hurled the reavers back. Pirates were felled by Dwarven axes, hewn down in frightened surprise, and raiders were cut to ribbons by the cutlasses of the Elvenship's Men. The fight was over and done almost before it had begun, the brigands slain on the decks or driven overboard by the furious onslaught, some to escape in the fog, others to drown thrashing and shrieking until dragged under the brine.

And when the junk was cleared of enemy—"Take stock of our wounded," cried Aravan, his call echoed by the bull voice of Bokar. And the Men and Dwarves turned to one another, seeking to find any who were injured.

Of the Elvenship's crew, only five had taken hurt, and of those, just one required more than superficial aid. "Hegen, thou wilt be up and about and back at the wheel within a half-Moon," said Aravan, the Elf standing by as the chirurgeon put needle and gut away then poured a clear liquid over the side wound, the steersman drawing in a sharp breath through clenched teeth.

"Aye, Captain," Hegen managed to grit out, "two weeks or less, I'd say."

As Fager bound the now-sewn gash with a clean cloth wrapped 'round Hegen's waist, dark Jatu stepped to Aravan's side. The Man was huge, o'ertopping Aravan's own six-foot height by a good seven inches. Three hundred pounds if he was an ounce and none of it fat, his skin was so black it seemed tinged with blue, a color not found in his dark brown gaze. He was garbed in dusky leather, and brown goatskin buskins shod his feet. He cleared his throat, a deep rumble, and then said, "Not much in the way of booty, Captain—a bit of silk, some copper utensils, a few weapons, all inferior . . . and, oh yes, powder of the poppy, not very pure, the kind meant for smoking."

Aravan turned to the Man, the Elf's blue gaze grim. "Burn it."

"The poppy?"

"The entire ship, Jatu. Burn it all."

Jatu grinned. "Aye, aye, Captain. But shouldn't we cast off before setting it aflame?"

Aravan laughed a full-throated laugh. "Aye, Jatu. Burn it when we've a wind in our sails again."

The fog lingered for nigh half a day, burning off in late mid morn. Even so, the winds yet failed to blow, and the ship and her prize lay at anchor, a safe distance from the Dragon's Fangs. Another night the doldrums loitered, but just ere dawn the silken sails of the *Eroean* belled outward, heralding the return of the air. Easterly it blew, a light westerly, the breeze channeled down the strait.

Jatu looked up at the billowing cloth and smiled. "Bo's'n, pipe the crew on deck. And have Tink wake the Captain."

"Aye, aye, Meestan Jatu," answered the Man, a Tugalian by the name of Rico.

Moments later, Aravan emerged from the aft quarters, turning his face to the breeze. He stepped to the wheel and grinned at his first officer, the giant black grinning back. "Jatu, set the spanker to help her to come about, manage the sails for a larboard run, then up anchor." In the starlight, Aravan eyed the distant rocks jagging up from the water. "We'll take her close-hauled into the wind for we've a bit of short tacking to do."

"Aye, Captain," replied Jatu. "And the junk? Set her afire and cut her free, right?"

Aravan grimly nodded. "Aye. She'll not raid these waters again."

Jatu relayed the orders to Rico, and with a series of piping signals, the bo's'n oversaw the setting of lines, Men running this way and that, unbelaying ropes and haling on them, all to a purpose—the turning of the yardarms to bring the sails around—the spanker alone slowly swinging the ship about, tethered as she was on her anchor chain.

The junk was hauled astern, Dwarves tugging her aft. Bokar and another boarded her and splashed oil on her decks, then scrambled up a rope ladder and back to the Elvenship. Torches were lighted and cast o'er the taffrail and down onto the pirate vessel, and as the flames exploded upward the ship was cast loose, the breeze carrying her away from the *Eroean,* her battened sails afire, her decking aflame.

Aravan glanced at her but once, then looked away, for it was a ship that burned, and somehow he felt as if a wrong were being done. Even so, he would not tow her as salvage, for she would merely slow his own ship down. And he could not leave her in these waters, else she would once again be used as a raider. And so he had her burned but did not watch, feeling all the while vaguely guilty of some indeterminate unspecified crime.

And as the *Eroean* haled about and started to surge forward—"Up anchor," the Elf commanded.

Rico piped the anchor aboard, and sailors in the bow cranked the windlass deosil, the great bronze grapnel breaking free of the bottom and riding the chain upward, and the Elvenship ran unfettered at last.

Her bow quartered to the wind, a short haul they coursed and then came about and entered in among the crags jutting up from the sea, tacking along a safe channel through the sharp-toothed Dragon's Fangs. Then they swung once more onto a larboard tack, to slip past the last of the jagged rocks. And now the water was clear before them, the strait widening out. And with her face to the breeze the *Eroean* put her shoulder to the sea, cleaving the waves, running westward, sails set and billowing, dawnlight illuminating the white wake behind.

And far abaft beyond the rocks a ship burned, orange flames lighting the sky.

* * *

The Elvenship cleared the Straits of Alacca ere noon of that first day, yet westerly she continued to fare, tacking west nor'west and west sou'west, close hauled to the east-running wind. She ran this way for a night and a day before turning on a sou'western course, the wind now starboard abeam and growing in strength, the *Eroean* swift-cutting through the indigo waters of the deep, wide Sindhu Sea.

Aiming for the southern latitudes, down where the winds blow strong, sou'westerly she drove, her hull dark blue above the waterline, the color of the sea, her sails the color of the sky. And when the wind heeled her over, her silver bottom showed, a bottom no barnacle could cling to, a bottom where no weed could grow. But the wind was not strong enough to challenge her outright, and so southward she drove running upright, slicing through the waves, her colors making her all but invisible to other ships afar.

It would be a long run to the south, faring through the shifting monsoons and then the equatorial doldrums lying just ahead, beyond which they would at last come to the southern winds, first the trades and then the polars, a set of calms between. As to whither the Elvenship was bound, 'round the cape she was headed, down where the wild gales rage, that goal yet some five thousand miles distant as the albatross flies—longer as the ship tacks. Then back to the north she would ply through the waters of the Weston Ocean, aiming for the Avagon Sea. For it was to Arbalin Isle she was bound, bearing her precious cargo—nutmeg and cinnamon and porcelain ware—where it would fetch a premium.

Then it was back to adventure for this crew, seeking out legend and fable. It mattered not whether the legends were true, for the seeking was the sum of the game. Had they wanted nothing but wealth, then merchants of the seas they would have become, for with but a few trips of the Elvenship they could each make their fortune many times over.

Yet comfort and riches suited not Aravan, and neither did it satisfy his well-chosen crew. And so only occasionally did the *Eroean* bear merchandise for market, and that but to fund their quests, setting a little aside for the times after, when they would leave the sea and settle down to a more staid existence. But that was for later and not for now, and not for the times immediately ahead, for legend and fable yet called to this crew, sweet voices singing in their hearts, in their spirits, and luring them on. And so they hied across the sea, the Elvenship's holds laden to the hatches.

And when bearing cargo for sale, speed was of the essence, for the sooner sold, the sooner free, free to return to their prime mission—the pursuit of derring-do.

And it was this ship, this marvelous ship, which allowed them to follow their will, a ship conceived by Elven mind but fabricated by Red Hills Dwarves. Never before had the world seen such, and likely never again, its secrets locked in the hearts of those who made her, long ago in the mists of time. Nearly three millennia had she plied the seas, captained by the Elf who first envisioned her, the Elf named Aravan.

Three-masted she was with a cloud of sails, three-masted and swift. Her bow was narrow and as sharp as a knife to cut through the waters, the shape smoothly flaring back to a wall-sided hull running for most of her length, the hull finally tapering up to a rounded aft. Two hundred and twelve feet she measured from stem to stern, her masts raked back at an angle. No stern castle did she bear, no fo'c'sle on her bow. Instead her shape was low and slender, for her beam measured but thirty-six feet at the widest, and she drew but thirty feet of water fully laded. Her mainmast rose one hundred forty-six feet above her deck, and her main yard was seventy-eight feet from tip to tip. As to the mizzen and fore masts, they were but slightly shorter and their yards a bit less wide.

These were the things that other captains, other sailors, could readily see, and they wondered why the ship did not simply founder and sink, cleaving into the waves as she did. Why, with that cutting prow a high sea alone should sink the vessel, and that's why it was foolish to have aught but a rounded bow: everyone knew that a good ship was designed to ride up and over the waves ... "cod's head and mackerel tail" was the wisdom of the ship builders—the round cod's head smacked and battered into the waves, riding up over each crest, and the narrow stern left a clean wake with hardly any turbulence, all safe and sane. But the Elvenship was different, her design foolish, mad: prow sword sharp and stern club blunt—built absolutely backwards! And with that much sail, come a sudden gust, all her masts would splinter into flinders, or so it was surmised. Why, many claimed that it was a pure wonder then that the *Eroean* had managed to survive the sea, slicing right through each and every billow, water rolling over her decks. A wet ship, that one, and someday in heavy wind and wave she'd plow under never to return, or so some said.

But there were others who claimed that she'd never sink, her with her mad design, for there was *magic* bound into her hull and *that* was what was holding her up, saving her from a dreadful death below the rolling waves, and as long as the magic held, well, she would never founder, never be sucked adown. And that's why no one ever attempted to build another ship like her, for 'twas *magic* alone that kept her afloat, and none else knew how to cast the same spells.

But her peculiar design wasn't the only topic bandied about, for as well there was her crew, and what a strange mix they were—forty Men and forty Dwarves. Why, it was common knowledge that Dwarves *never* went to sea, though they were Hèl on foot as fighters. And then, too, it was said by some that this Captain Aravan often took on Wee Folk, too, them what call themselves Warrows; as to what these little'ns might be good for, well, that was anybody's guess.

And so the rumors persisted, for three millennia or more.

And still the Elvenship defied all the predictions of doom.

And still no one else was mad enough or wise enough to attempt another one like her.

Two more days she ran, the winds gradually shifting about, changeable in this season, now blowing southwesterly, the *Eroean* running before a following wind. But on the third day . . .

First Officer Jatu held a small sandglass. "Ready the log line," he called.

"Ready, sir," responded Artus, the sailor holding the reel.

"Cast the log."

Rico heaved the wood over the taffrail, the billet splashing into the wake. Unreeling the line to the first knot, Artus payed out a length and then stopped the spool, the log now a hundred feet astern.

"All set, sir," barked Artus.

"Ready?" called Jatu.

"Ready!" responded Artus. "Ready!" said Rico, too.

"Then loose!" cried Jatu, turning the sandglass over.

Artus released the spool, his eye on its spinning, making certain that it ran free on the greased axle. Rico watched as the cord reeled out, counting the knots as they sped past: *"Un. Dis. Tis . . ."* The Tugalian counting in his native language, though ordinarily he spoke the shipboard speech—the Common Tongue.

Moments later—"Belay!" cried Jatu, the top glass empty, the sand run through, Artus jamming shut the reel brake, halting the line.

"Ancé nutos—eleven knots—and some," said Rico.

"Pah!" spat Jatu. "As I thought: the winds are dying. Midline Irons ahead."

Over the course of the next few days, the ship slowed and slowed and slowed even more, the wind gradually becoming but a faint stir of air. And even with all sails set, still the doldrums clutched at the *Eroean* as honey traps the fly. They crossed the equator with the gigs unshipped and the crew rowing, towing the slack-sailed Elvenship southerly, Men and Dwarves alike taking turns at the oars. And the Sun beat down unmercifully in the torrid, summer days, its searing rays slashing through the stifling mute air, reflecting back from the copper-colored, molten brine.

Yet by burning day and hot still night the crew rowed onward, the Men singing chanteys, the Dwarves canting warrior chants.

Four days they rowed, Aravan sighting on the heavens, gauging the *Eroean*'s position; not only was he captain of this vessel, he was the pilot as well . . . for like all Elves he had the gift of knowing the skies, aware at all times precisely where stood the heavenly bodies—

Sun, Moon, and stars—and thus as navigator he was unsurpassed.

"The southern boundary draws nigh," he said on the fourth night to Rico. "On the morrow we should find the wind."

"Aye, Kapitan," replied the bo's'n, mopping his brow. "¡*Diantre*! I be glad when wind she come, stuck on midline as we be. I never t'ought I say this, but I going to welcome polars, blow and chill and everyt'ing. But to find wind in these lats, bah, at this time of year south equatorial she be as fickle as north. Still we be ready. Sou'easters or sou'westers or any bearing, we be ready."

The very next day, the sails of the Elvenship belled slightly as the rowers towing the craft finally came into a faint sou'westerly breeze. Swiftly the gigs were shipped back aboard as the bo's'n set the sails for a southerly run, and into the capricious monsoons the *Eroean* fared.

Due south she ran for three days, the wind shifting about, and on the eve of the third day the Elvenship came at last unto the southeasterly trades. And with the wind abeam on the larboard side, southwest she turned, running for the Cape of Storms, the wind gaining in strength the farther south she fared.

One hundred leagues a day she sailed, three hundred miles from Sun to Sun, over the course of five days, but then she came to the Doldrums of the Goat, there in the southern latitudes. Even so, gentle breezes blew, though fitfully quartering first this way then that, and the crew was hard-pressed to manage the sails in the shifting airs, yet after three days and a half the ship came into the prevailing westerlies beyond the southern calms. And south and west continued the *Eroean*, aiming now for the polar realm in which lay the Cape of Storms.

Steadily the winds increased, the farther south she fared, and the lengthening nights grew cold and colder, and chill grew the shorter days as well. The speed of the ship increased, and she ran sixteen and seventeen knots at times, logging more than three hundred fifty miles a day on three days running. And the weather became foul, rain and sleet off and on lashing against the ship, while large breaking waves raced o'er the southern Sindhu

Sea, the *Eroean* cleaving through the waters, her decks awash in the cold brine.

In the swaying light of the salon's lanterns, Aravan looked across the table at Jatu and at Frizian, third in command, the small Gelender's white face in stark contrast with that of the black Tchangan's. Spread out before them was Aravan's precious charts, marking winds and currents throughout the oceans of the world. Back in the shadows stood Tink, one of the cabin boys on this voyage, the flaxen-haired lad from far Rian. A knock sounded on the aft quarters door, and Tink sprang down the short passageway to open it, and in through wind and spray came Rico and Bokar, followed closely by Reydeau, second bo's'n of the *Eroean,* all three wearing their weather gear, boots and slickers and cowls.

·Tink took the dripping coats from them, hanging them on wall pegs in a corner. And all gathered 'round the chart table, including the cabin boy,

Aravan's finger stabbed down on the map. "In a day or three we will reach the waters of the Cape, and I would have ye all remind the crew what it is we face."

"Storms," breathed Tink, and then gasped at his own boldness, clamping a hand over his mouth to silence it.

Aravan smiled at the lad. "Aye, Tink, storms indeed. Summer storms at that."

Bokar growled. "Stupid southern seasons. Just backwards! Here winter is the warm season and summer is the cold."

Jatu laughed. "Ah, Bokar, backward or not, the polar realm is always frigid, though the Sun may ride the sky throughout the day."

Rico nodded, adding, "A bad place, this cape, by damn. Hard on crew no matter season. Snow hammer on rigging, weigh down both sail and rope wit' ice. In autumn, there be snow or sleet or freeze rain or anyt'ing, and same be true of spring. Even in heart of warm part of year it be not very different, ha! much of the time freeze rain hammer on ship. But in cold season, like now, storm always seem bear snow and ice, and wave run tall—greybeard all—¡Diantre! a hundred feet from crest to trough."

Aravan gazed down at the chart. "It is ever so in these

polar realms, that raging Father Winter seldom looses his grasp."

Tink, too, stared at the map. "And the winds, Cap'n, wot about the winds? Will they be the same as wot we came through before?"

"Aye, 'tis the very same air—westerlies, and constantly running at gale force, or nearly so. Seldom do those winds rest, and the *Eroean* will be faring into the teeth of the blow." Aravan looked up at the faces about him. "And I would have ye all recall to the crew just what it is that we likely face: thundering wind, ice, freezing rain, short days and long nights fighting our way through. Each jack will have to take utmost care to not be washed over the rails, for like as not, he will be lost. Remind them again that tether ropes are to be hooked at all times aloft ... and, Rico, Reydeau, rig the extra deck lifelines for surely they will be needed."

"The sails, Captain," said Reydeau, the Gothan's dark eyes glittering in the lantern light, "is there something spécial you would have me rendré?"

"The studs are already down," replied Aravan. "Likely we will furl the starscrapers and moonrakers as soon as we round the shoulder of the cape ... the gallants and royals as well. I deem that we'll make our run on stays, jibs, tops, and mains, though likely we'll reef them down somewhat."

"And the spanker, too, eh, Cap'n?" put in Tink.

Aravan laughed, as did Jatu and Reydeau. "Aye, Tink," answered the Elf, reaching out and tousling the towheaded cabin boy's curls, "and the spanker, too."

"Kapitan," said Rico, "I t'ink you might speak to crew about running cape. They no doubt like word straight from you."

A murmur of agreement rumbled 'round the table.

"Aye, Rico, I had intended to. Assemble the Men, and thou, Bokar, gather the Drimma as well. Shall we say at the change of the noon watch on the morrow?"

Sleet pelted down upon the ship, while in the forward quarters below, Aravan stood on a sea chest and spoke to the *Eroean*'s crew, the weather too harsh to hold an assembly above. And as the hull clove through the rolling waves and brine billowed over the decks, all the Men and Dwarves gathered 'round their Elven captain, all but three remaining up top—Boder, the wheelman, and Geff and Slane, two aides.

Aravan spoke of the cape and reminded them all of the weather at this time of year, for although each had been through this passage before, it was two years past and in a different season. Too, they had made the transit from west to east, running with the wind, and this time they fared the opposite way, into the teeth of the gale. Aravan spoke of the ice that would form on the ropes, and of the driven snow that would blind them and weigh down the sails. "Yet," he said, near the last, "we have made this run before. The *Eroean* is a sturdy ship, and ye are a fine crew. I fear not that we will see the Weston Ocean in but a week or so. Still, I would caution ye to take care, for if any be lost to the waters, we will not be able to wear around the wind in time to save ye in those chill waves, and to do so would put the entire ship at hazard. So, buckle up tightly when up top, for I would see ye all when we've passed beyond the horn.

"Be there any questions?"

Men and Dwarves stirred and peered 'round at one another. At last a seaman raised a hand—Hogar, an aid to Trench the cook, signed on just two years past. At a nod from the Elf, the Man stood, cap in hand. "Cap'n Aravan, sir, why not 'ead east across th' South Polar Sea and make for th' Silver Cape? Wot Oi mean, sir, not t' question y'r judgement or skills, Oi wos but wonderin' why run again' th' wind when we c'n run wi' it instead?"

Aravan smiled. "This time of year, Hogar, the Silver Cape is all but impassable, those rocky straits filled with mountainous waves of grinding ice and the air with churning hurricanes. The Cape of Storms is fierce, but the Silver Cape is deadly."

Hogar nodded and sat back down. Aravan looked about. "Any other questions?"

A Dwarf stood, Dask, one of Bokar's lieutenants. Gesturing with a sweep of his hand at the other Dwarves assembled, he said, "Captain Aravan, we have made this passage before, both ways, and seldom has it been easy. The weather will be fierce, cold, and the crew on short shift, rotating often to stay warm. If the weather is as it has been, then doubtless all will be needed, Men and

Châkka alike. I speak only to remind you that we Châkka stand ready."

A rumble of approval swept through the assembly, and without comment, Aravan grinned and cast a loose salute to Dask. When silence returned, Aravan looked about, seeking other questions or comments. When none was proffered, he said, "Jatu, an extra tot of rum for all, for hardy times lie ahead."

A hearty cheer rang throughout the forward quarters as the Elven captain stepped down from the sea chest and made his way among the crew, while Jatu poured rum from a cask into the eagerly outheld cups.

Two days later found the *Eroean* rounding the shoulder of the cape. And over these same two days the wind had risen in strength and had risen again, and now the Elvenship beat to the windward into a shrieking gale. Great grey waves, their crests foaming, broke over the bow and smashed down upon the decks with unnumbered tons of water, clutching and grasping at timber and wood and rope, at fittings, at sails, the huge greybeards seeking to drag off and drown whatever they could, whatever might be loose or loosened.

In the teeth of the blow Jatu ordered all sails pulled but the stays, jibs, tops, and mains. And Men had struggled 'cross decks awash—cold, drenching waves dragging them off their feet and trying to hurl them overboard and into the icy brine; yet the safety lines held fast, and the crew made their way up into the rigging, the frigid wind tearing at them, shrieking and threatening to hurl them away. But the Men fought the elements, haling in the silken sail and lashing it 'round the spars, while all about them the halyards howled in the wind like giant harp strings yowling in torment, sawn by the screaming gale.

On the very next watch the wind force increased, and once again the crew was dispatched onto the dangerous decks and up to the hazardous spars, this time at Frizian's command, and all jibs were pulled and the mains reefed to the last star. And now the ship ran mostly on the staysails and the upper lower topsails, the *Eroean* flying less than a third of full silk.

The following watch Aravan took command, and after

an hour or so, the wind picked up yet again, and the Elven captain ordered forth the crew to reef the mains and the crossjack to the full.

"*Diantre,* Kapitan," shouted Rico above the wind, "I t'ink if this keep up, soon we be sailing on bare stick alone."

Aravan grinned at the bo's'n. "Mayhap, Rico. Mayhap. But if it's to bare sticks we go, then backwards we will fare."

Tink made his way up through the trapdoor and into the tiny wheelhouse, the lad bearing a tray of steaming mugs of tea. That he managed to carry the cups in the pitching ship without spilling a drop spoke well of his agility and balance. With a grin he passed the tray about to Aravan and Boder and Rico, then disappeared below decks once more.

Aravan sipped the welcome drink, commenting, "Boder, answer me this: with the galley locked down for the heavy seas, fire extinguished, how do Trench and Hogar manage to brew hot tea?"

"Well, Cap'n," replied Boder, "I'd call it cook's magic."

As tons of icy water slammed down on the *Eroean,* the wheelhouse rang with laughter.

The moment Aravan drained the last of his drink and started to set the mug aside, as if by divination Tink reappeared, collecting the cups and away. Aravan looked at the closed trapdoor, commenting, "I suppose we've just seen cabin boy magic, too."

Again the wheelhouse rang with laughter, drowning out even the wrath of the wind shrieking over the furious waves.

Aravan wiped the frost from the window and peered at the raging sea. "Pipe the crew on deck, Rico," he called, taking a grip on the wheel on one side while Boder held the spokes across, "prepare to come about. On the starboard bow quarter this tack."

At the moment Rico opened the trap to go below and summon the crew, a blinding wall of white engulfed the *Eroean,* the Cape of Storms living up to its name as wind-driven snow slammed horizontally across the Elvenship.

*   *   *

Eleven days it took to round the cape, sometimes the valiant *Eroean* seemingly driven abaft while at other times she surged ahead. And at all times the savage wind tore at her, while the greybeards struggled to wrench her down. Snow and ice weighed heavily on her rigging, and Men and Dwarves were sent aloft to break loose the pulleys so the ropes would run free. Tacking northwest up across the wind and southwest back down, Aravan sailed by dead reckoning, for no stars nor Moon in the long nights did he see, nor Sun in the short, short days. Nor did he see the southern aurora writhing far beyond the darkness above, shifting curtains of spectral light draped high in the icy skies.

Still, battered by wind and wave, eleven full days it took before the ship could run clear on northwesterly course, free of the cape at last, Aravan's reckoning true, the crew superb in handling the ship and not a Man or Dwarf lost unto the grasping sea. Even so, all were weary, drained by this rugged pass, including her captain, a thing seldom seen by any of the crew. Yet finally the ship's routine returned to something resembling normality though the winds yet blew agale. But they were steady on the larboard, and running on a course with the wind to the port, mains and crossjack and jibs back full, up into the Weston Ocean she ran, the log line humming out at nineteen knots, the *Eroean* flying o'er the waves.

A week later across the Doldrums of the Goat she fared, this time heading north, the ship laded with all sail set yet moving slowly in the light air—"Slipping past the horns of old billy," as Frizian had said. Three days it took to cross the calms, three days ere the wind picked up again, now coming from abaft. Nor'northwest she drove, sweeping through the coastal waters of the wide Realm of Hyree.

Five days under full sail she ran on the northerly trek, the winds steady but moderate, until they came once more unto the Midline Irons, where as before they unshipped the gigs to tow the *Eroean* across the placid equatorial waters.

At last the winds returned, blowing lightly down from the northeast, and into these she fared, sailing through the gap between Hyree to the south and Tugal to the north, finally entering into the Avagon Sea along the Straits of Kistan. Easterly into this slot she swiftly made her way, and south lay the great jungle-covered Isle of Kistan, a haven for rovers of the seas.

A day she coursed as the skies turned a sullen grey, and now to the north lay Vancha, but to the south lay Kistan still.

"Sail ho, maroon!" called the foremast lookout. "Sail ho on the larboard bow!"

Frizian's gaze swept the horizon forward and left, then stopped. A heartbeat later—"Pipe the captain, Reydeau, and stand by to pipe the crew."

Reydeau sounded a signal on his bo's'n's pipe, and a cabin boy leapt up from the deck and sped toward Aravan's quarters. Moments later, the Elf came to the wheel, the cabin boy trailing behind.

"Where away, Frizian?"

"There, Cap'n," replied the Gelender, pointing.

Just on the horizon, a maroon lateen sail could be discerned, the ship heading downwind in the general direction of the *Eroean*.

"Reydeau, bring the *Eroean* to a southwest heading. Put this rover on our larboard beam."

"Aye, aye, Captain."

Aravan turned to the wheelman. "Hegen, ready to bring her to the course laid in."

"Aye, Captain."

"Tivir, fetch Bokar."

"Aye, Cap'n," responded the cabin boy and sped away.

As the *Eroean* came about, Bokar stepped to the wheel, the Dwarf accoutered for combat. "Where away?"

Aravan pointed.

Bokar looked long, then glanced up at the pale blue Elven-silk against the somber skies. The Dwarf turned to the cabin boy. "Tivir, tell the Châkka to take station. We should know within half a glass whether this rover will be foolish or wise."

Again the lad sped away, and moments later armed and armored Dwarves poured up onto the decks to take

positions next to the ballistas, readying the missile casters for battle.

Steadily the Kistanian ship ran downwind west-southwest, and just as steadily the *Eroean* haled crosswind,
southeasterly, down and away from the track of the freebooter. Time eked by, and still the rover ran on his
straight course, as did the Elvenship.

"Ready about, Reydeau. Keep her on our beam."

"Aye, Captain."

"Hegen?"

"Aye, Captain, I'm ready, too."

Gradually the *Eroean* headed up into the stiff wind,
now running on a easterly reach. Still the maroon-sailed
pirate fared southwest, running downwind, the vessel
now passing abeam, heading aft of the Elvenship.

Finally Aravan ordered the *Eroean* back on a heading
for Arbalin.

"Ha!" barked Bokar. "Cowards all. She was afraid to
take us on."

Aravan shook his head. "Nay, Armsmaster. I think
instead she didn't e'en see us."

Bokar glanced again at the cerulean sails against the
dark grey skies, and then down at the indigo hull. Finally
he looked to his Dwarven warband. "Mayhap you are
right, Captain, but then again mayhap not."

Nine days later in the heart of the night the *Eroean*
haled into the sheltered port of Arbalin, the citizens of
that town being awakened by their own criers ringing
out the good news that the Elvenship was back.

All the next day and the one after the cargo was unladed, and new ballast was taken on to replace the
weight of the porcelain ware, for it would not do to have
the *Eroean* turn turtle at the first strong wind or great
wave. When the ship was empty of cargo and laded with
the proper ballast, Aravan had her tugged away from
the docks to anchor in the bay.

He set the crew free to "do the town," and knowing
the crew as well as he did, he knew that most of them
would try.

It was on the following night that Aravan heard a
knock on his stateroom door, and when he opened it,

an eld Man, nay Elf—nay, Mage!—stood at the end of a line of wet footprints leading to the portal.

Astonished, Aravan stepped back.

"Are you Aravan the captain?" snapped the elder.

Aravan nodded. "Aye, that I am."

"Well don't just stand there gaping, Elf. Invite me in. We've got things to discuss."

"A Hidden One, a Fox Rider, thou sayest?" Aravan's mind flashed back to an earlier time, his hand touching a blue stone amulet on a leather thong about his neck, the Elf remembering Tarquin.

Alamar nodded, steepling his fingers.

Passing back Jinnarin's tiny drawing of the dark ship, Aravan took up his glass of brandy. "I know nought of crystal castles, nor of lightning-driven black galleons plying the oceans of the world. But of a pale green sea, there are several candidates, though in many places elsewhere the waters run green as well."

The Mage shook his head, then looked pointedly at the empty goblet before him.

Quickly, for the third time, Aravan poured a dram or two within.

Alamar took up the brandy-filled crystal and held it to the lantern light, peering deep within the golden swirl. "Even so, you will aid us, neh?"

"I wouldn't miss it for all the world," answered Aravan, his smile wide in delight.

"Good!" barked Alamar, tossing down the liquid. "When?"

"The crew returns eight days from now. Is that soon enough?"

"I suppose it'll have to do," grunted Alamar.

Aravan held up a finger. "One condition though ..."

The Mage cocked an eyebrow, his emerald gaze locked with Aravan's eyes of sapphire. "And that is ... ?"

Aravan did not look away. "Just this, Alamar: I do not ask my crew to do aught without their full knowledge of what it is I would have them attempt. On the *Eroean* we have this saying: Information is power. And in the sharing of information, many a good idea has come forth—some from where least expected. And so, on this mission, I would take my crew into full confidence, which means they will hear of the Hidden One, of—"

"Of Jinnarin," supplied Alamar.

"Aye, of Jinnarin. I would introduce this Fox Rider to the crew."

Alamar got to his feet. "I will ask her . . . yet unless and until she agrees . . ."

"Until she agrees," said Aravan, looking up at the Mage. "I will speak nought of thy business. But unless she agrees, I will not commit my crew, for I would not have them set forth on a mission in ignorance."

Alamar nodded, then spun on his heel, stepping to the door, flinging it open.

Aravan raised his voice, calling after the retreating Mage. "Need thou someone to row thee to the docks? I will fetch thee aid."

Without turning—"Never mind, Elf," Alamar called back, "I'll go the way I came." In that moment, the stateroom door swung to.

Aravan sat for a while after the Mage had gone, staring at the shut door. Then he tossed down the last of his brandy and stood and made his way to the deck. Of Alamar there was no sight, and Aravan's keen Elven hearing heard not the plash of oars.

"Burdun," he called, the watch hurrying to his side.

"Sir?"

"Where away the boat that ferried the eld Man from the docks?"

A puzzled look came over Burdun's face. "Eld man? Boat? Sir, there's come no boat at all tonight. Are you expecting one? I'll keep a sharp eye out."

"Nay, Burdun, yet I thank thee all the same."

As the Elf walked back to his quarters—*If he came not by boat, then how? Did he swim?*—Aravan laughed softly to himself, picturing the elder stroking through the waters of the bay. *But then again mayhap he flew, or walked on the waves*—once more Aravan laughed at the absurdity, and then his eye fell on the trace of wet footprints lingering in the aft quarters passageway, there where the Mage had stepped.

CHAPTER 8

Oaths

Late Summer, 1E9574
[The Present]

He wants what?" The Pysk leapt to her feet and stood with her fists clenched on her hips, beryl fire in her cobalt eyes.

Alamar sighed. "It is not an unreasonable request, Jinnarin. After all, it is Aravan and his crew we are speaking of, not some Kistanian Rovers."

"But to stand before Humanity is to give truth to the legends, and that will lead to harassment of the Fox Riders as Man and Woman alike hunt throughout the world to discover our whereabouts, to reveal us, to seek favor from my Folk. They think we exude magic and grant wishes and live only to do their labor and—and conform in a thousand other ways to their ridiculous beliefs. I know, for it has happened in the past, and likely will do so again should I or any Fox Rider or for that matter any Hidden One be exposed to them. Nay, Alamar, I would not have Mankind see me."

"Dwarves, too," mumbled the Mage.

"What?"

"I said," he growled, "Dwarves, too. Aravan has a warband of Dwarves on the *Eroean*."

"*Dwarves!*" Jinnarin clapped a hand to her forehead. "Gods, Alamar, I've heard they are even worse than Man. 'Hoy, little one, would you point out where I might find the richest veins of gold? Beg pardon, tiny Fey, but tell me where I might uncover silver and jewels for my treasuries.' Why, they'd drag me down into a stone hole in the ground or under a mountain and never again would I see the light of day."

"You exaggerate, Pysk." The blood had risen in the elder's cheeks, and his chin jutted out stubbornly. "Moreover, did you not tell me that Aravan was a—how did you put it? Ah yes—that he was a 'Friend'? And if so, would he expose you to such—such greed?"

Jinnarin stopped her angry pacing, though yet she fumed.

Rux trotted to the door, an irked look in his eye.

Alamar stood and stepped to the panel, letting the animal out. Then the Mage faced the Pysk. "What *would* you, Jinnarin, stay hidden in my cabin or in the hold as the Elvenship traipses all over the world searching for a pale green sea, a black ship, a crystal castle?"

"I did so on the *Flying Fish*," shot back Jinnarin.

"That was a short trip!" shouted Alamar. "Not a worldwide voyage."

Alamar shoved a teakettle under the pump and worked the handle furiously, water splashing violently over the sides. "He said that he would not ask his crew to take on a mission in ignorance, and he's right!"

The Mage slammed the teakettle onto a cook iron, swinging the arm into the cold hearth. Hurling two logs in the fireplace, *"Incende!"* he demanded, and the wood burst into furious flame.

He spun and glared at Jinnarin. "Besides, Pysk, it *is* Farrix we are after. You remember him, don't you, Farrix the boar killer?"

At these words Jinnarin burst into tears.

In the dark of the night came a tap on the door, the soft sound not rousing Aravan. Again came the tapping, and still Aravan's meditation remained unbroken, his Elvensleep deep, though his eyes glittered in the stateroom shadows. The latch clicked, the lock opening of itself, and inward swung the door. Silhouetted against the passageway lamps stood a figure holding a squirming burden. *"Lux"* came a soft word, a blue light springing up. And as the fox-bearing Mage wetly stepped into the chamber, Aravan snapped full awake.

Kicking the door to with his heel, Alamar set struggling Rux down, the fox gnarling a complaint and turning in agitated circles, glaring accusingly. Ignoring the animal—"We would have a word with you, Elf," declared the Mage, slipping his knapsack strap over his head and setting the bundle to the drop-leaf of a writing desk.

Aravan glanced from Alamar to Rux and back. "You and the fox?"

"Of course not!" querulously retorted the elder, fumbling at the knapsack buckles. "And get some light in here; I'm not a blooming lantern, you know."

Aravan turned to light a candle, and when he turned back, in its yellow glow stood a Pysk upon his writing table.

"You must be Jinnarin."

The Pysk eyed him suspiciously. "And you are Aravan."

"Indeed."

"I would see the stone."

Aravan raised an eyebrow. "Stone?"

"Tarquin's stone."

"Oh." Aravan drew the leather thong over his head, the cord running through a hole in a small, rounded blue pebble. He held it out to the Pysk.

Jinnarin merely touched the amulet and nodded, satisfied. "Friend," she said, smiling. How a mere touch could assuage her was beyond Aravan's knowing, yet he surmised that she sensed something of the power within the small rock. Aravan slipped the loop back over his head, the stone once again resting against his bare flesh.

Jinnarin sat cross-legged on the table. "I would have words with you."

Aravan nodded and then pulled a chair to the board, waving Alamar to another. The Mage sat opposite the Elf.

When all were comfortable, Jinnarin said, "I understand you would have me meet your crew."

Aravan nodded but said nought.

"Humans and Dwarves, I hear."

"And sometimes Waerlinga," added Aravan, "though none at the moment."

Jinnarin sighed and slowly shook her head, then said: "I would tell you a tale, Friend, and when I am finished

. . . well, then we shall see." She paused, gathering her thoughts.

Aravan stood and rummaged through a bureau drawer—"Hai!"—finding a new porcelain thimble. He then selected two crystal glasses. Into each of these, including the thimble, he dashed a dollop of dark Vanchan wine, Alamar eagerly reaching out for his. When Aravan was seated again, Jinnarin took a sip from the thimble, then began her tale:

"Long past, ere Men or Elves or aught others came into this world of Mithgar, the Hidden Ones were not. —Not hidden, that is. Instead, in those days we named ourselves 'the Fey,' and we lived in the open, free and unafraid. Fens, fields, forests, plains, prairies, deserts, mountains, oceans, it did not matter where, for we were the only Folk here, though Elwydd's work was not yet finished. We knew that She had already set into motion Her plans for this world, a design which was well underway long before we arrived upon Mithgar ourselves. You see, prior to coming to the Middle World, we lived . . . elsewhere . . or so legend has it—"

Jinnarin suddenly broke off and turned to the Mage. "Oh, Alamar, I don't known why I didn't think of this before, but it just occurred to me that mayhap my Folk come from a different Plane, just as do the Mages. Mayhap the legend, the fable, of our flight from Feyer is true."

Alamar held up his glass and saluted the Pysk, then downed its contents and held the crystal out to Aravan for a refill, an eager smile on his face.

As the Elf replenished the Mage's glass, Jinnarin resumed her tale:

"Millennia upon millennia we lived here on Mithgar, unmolested, content. But then Mankind came, Elwydd's latest, and never were things the same thereafter.

"They brought with them disease, and they usurped the land and ravaged it. Why, even I can remember when much of the world was woodland. But look at it now: whole forests hewn, slain, barren devastation where they once stood, ruin left in the wake of Man."

Aravan held up a hand. "In places, aye. Yet elsewhere, nay. Instead there be fertile farmland cleared. But thou art somewhat in the right, for Man is indeed a destroyer. Even so, there is hope, can he come to his senses in time." Aravan paused, then turned a palm up in apology. "Jinnarin, I am sorry. I did not mean to interrupt, to debate thee. Pray, continue."

Jinnarin inclined her head, accepting Aravan's amends. "Oh, I did not say that Mankind's intent was evil"—Jinnarin glanced at Alamar, but the Mage was staring into his glass—"now that I have some understanding of what evil is. Instead, evil or innocent, thoughtless or deliberate, Man's effect upon the Fey was brutal. As the land was usurped, the Fey were pushed back and back, and places where we had lived for millennia were taken by Humanity.

"And Man had little respect for the creatures of the world, for the land, for the waters—these were slain, scarred, polluted. And often, after the damage was done, Man would move on, leaving behind the wreckage of his deeds. And then he would come to where we had resettled and do it all over again.

"And there were those among Humankind who would capture my Folk and others like us, keeping us as pets, as slaves, as charms against evildoers—when it was they who were in truth the evildoers.

"Oh, they could not capture all, for many of the Fey were and are too powerful. As a consequence, Mankind—or more correctly, I should say, *some* Men—decided that these Fey were creatures of foulness, for they bent not to Man's will, and so, these Men and others like them set out to exterminate those Fey who defied them"—here Jinnarin's voice began to tremble with distress and her eyes lost their focus, as if she stared through the mirror of time at unwanted distant memories and heard the thunder of hooves and a savage baying and the blowing of dreadful horns—"and they slew Fey, cut them down just as though they were game to be hunted, hounded, cornered, butchered." Jinnarin paused, wiping the wetness from her cheeks, regaining her composure. "Often when these wicked Men succeeded, they were hailed as heroes when villains instead they were.

"And so, the Fey withdrew completely, went into hiding, became the Hidden Ones. And we cordoned off the refuges where we had retreated to, turning them into places of dire repute, places forbidden to Man. They became haunted forests, possessed hills, ghostly swamps, deadly deserts, hexed caverns, and the like—all filled with ominous forebodings, all promising ghastly doom to Man, promises at times we kept, depending upon the Man or Men who defied our wardings and entered our forbidden domains.

"Too, there were Fey who fled to remote lands—to the western continent, to islands such as Rwn, to locales then inaccessible or unwanted by Man, though now even these places have seen his footprints."

Jinnarin ceased speaking for a moment and, trembling, turned her thimble goblet about and about. Finally, her voice quavering with stress, she said, "And now you, Aravan, you who are named 'Friend,' you would have me stand before your ship's crew, verifying to one and all that the fables and legends are true. That Fey do indeed exist, that the tales handed down through the ages from Human sire and dam to son and daughter are valid, that here are a Folk to ward away evil, to perform domestic labor, to find gold, to yield treasure, to—to—" Jinnarin burst into bitter tears, sobs racking her tiny frame.

Anguish flooded Aravan's face and he looked to Alamar for aid, but the elder's own eyes were tear-filled and he shook his head and muttered, "Can't even hug her. Can't even hug her." Nevertheless, Aravan reached out and took her up and held her to his breast, cupping her gently in the curve of his arm, a hand lightly pressed against her, whispering *"Shhh, shhh,* little one," as she clung to the cloth of his shirt and wept.

"Set me down, Aravan," said Jinnarin at last, wiping her eyes on her sleeve, "on the floor, please. Rux needs reassurance."

Clearly upset, the fox yet paced and whined, nose in the air sniffing, seeking some clue as to Jinnarin's weeping. Aravan lowered the Pysk to the floor, Rux right there to receive her, and Jinnarin stood and stroked the agitated animal and whispered into his ear, Rux listening and casting glances at Alamar as if to lay blame.

The Mage wiped the wetness from his cheeks with the heels of his hands. "More wine, please," he requested, and Aravan refilled the crystal again.

A silence fell within the lounge for a while—all but the sounds of water lapping against the *Eroean*'s hull—but at last Jinnarin turned to Aravan and said, "Would you lift me to the desk. Rux is soothed now, and I would finish my wine."

The Elf carefully raised Jinnarin to the board, and the Pysk sat cross-legged and took up her porcelain thimble and sipped.

Finally, Aravan cleared his throat. "Jinnarin, I know thou art distressed by my request. Thou hast spent millennia hiding from Mankind as well as from others. It is not thy nature nor heritage to make thyself known unto those not of thy Kind . . . or those who are not named Friend. To do otherwise goes against the teachings of thy Folk.

"Yet heed, here is why I have asked thee to trust the crew of the *Eroean:* First, this crew is handpicked . . . I chose each and every one. Most are the sons of fathers who sailed with me in the past. And it has been such for nearly three thousand summers—the sons of sons of sons of sons stretching back through time. They are sworn to me and loyal beyond measure.

"They have been privy to Elven secrets and Drimmen secrets and the secrets of Mankind. And they have shared confidences with the Waerlinga as well. And never on a time have they betrayed one another, and some have died in the service of their shipmates.

"Look about thee at this marvelous ship. Who knows its secrets other than my crew? None else, I say—not a single soul who has not served on her. Yet many a merchant and sea captain would give all they own for a ship like her, but her like will ne'er again be seen on Mithgar, for her secrets are locked safely within my heart and in the hearts of my crew, and we will not yield them to any. And that is but one example of their loyalty, and the fact that I share the knowledge of this ship with them shows the regard I have for their honor.

"Yet heed, every Man, Drimm, or other who sails with me is chosen not only because of loyalty and honor and trust, but also for their wit and grit and skills. Many a time has my neck been saved by one or more members of this crew, and many a time have I in turn saved one or more of them.

"They are as my kindred, my family, my brothers in arms, and I would not put them in jeopardy brought about by the fostering of deliberate ignorance, for it would be deliberate if I had the knowledge but kept it unto myself. Likewise, I would not jeopardize thy mission by leaving them in such ignorance; for if we are to succeed, like as not it will take the brains and brawn and skills of all, and we cannot have that if they are kept in the dark. If they know not what we seek or *who* we seek and why, if they know not who needs aid, if they know not of you, Jinnarin, then they go into the mission fettered, lacking crucial knowledge on which to base key decisions, critical plans, and I would not have that happen—for thy sake as well as theirs.

"As I told Alamar, information is power—and the power I speak of here is the power to succeed.

"Let me turn the tables, Jinnarin: were I to come to thee and tell thee of a dire mission and ask thee for the aid of thy people, but only on the condition that thou sayest nought of who sent thee nor of who asks for aid nor of who we seek, then what wouldst thou advise? Wouldst thou counsel me to imperil my mission by such stipulations or wouldst thou instead advise me to tell all to thy honorable Kind regardless of my fears?

"And whilst thou ponder that, Jinnarin, here is my last: I will not take anyone on this mission who will not pledge it to secrecy—first to me, and then to thee."

Aravan fell silent, and Jinnarin stared deeply into her tiny thimble goblet and swirled the wine and swirled it. Long moments passed, and sleeping Rux chased fleeing field mice in his dreams, his paws lightly scrabbling on the stateroom floor. At last Jinnarin looked up at Aravan.

"What wouldst thou have it be, Jinnarin?" softly asked the Elf.

With trepidation in her voice, she replied, "It goes against ten thousand years of practice, yet what you say bears much weight. If they will pledge to you and to me, then I agree—you must share all ... for I would find Farrix."

Alamar who had been silent throughout held up his glass. "Pour me another, Friend Aravan, this calls for a celebration."

Aravan splashed a dollop of dark wine into each goblet. "Here's to the success of our mission, may we find what we seek," he said, raising his glass.

Jinnarin hoisted her thimble and added but a single word: "Farrix."

Alamar simply gulped his drink down.

Seven days later the *Eroean*'s crew returned by boat from the docks, trickling in by threes and fours, an occasional loner now and then. Many were comatose from too much celebration and were carried aboard by groaning shipmates, Bokar among the oblivious, borne over Jatu's shoulder like a half-filled sack of grain. As Aravan leaned over the railing and looked down at them, the huge black Man smiled, white teeth flashing from ear to ear as he stepped from the dinghy and clambered up the gangway ladder, Bokar limp as a rag. "Coming aboard, Captain," Jatu announced, "bearing a gift from the ladies of the Red Slipper, though it's worn to a frazzle, I ween."

Aravan laughed aloud, then called back, "Aye, Jatu, that I can see, though I'll warrant that each of thee did thy best to return the favor, neh?"

"Aye, Captain, that we did, that we did indeed ... and though we failed to wear them out, wear them thin we did."

As Jatu stepped onto the deck, Aravan said, "Well, Jatu, after thou pour him into his bunk, come see me. I have a tale to tell thee."

Jatu glanced at Aravan and then beyond to the far stern, where he could see an eld Man leaning over the taffrail and peering down at the dock dinghies ferrying the *Eroean*'s crew back to the ship. The black giant raised an eyebrow at Aravan, an unspoken question on his lips, but only enigmatic blue Elven eyes looked back at him and Jatu could fathom no answer within.

The day wore on, crew haling in from Port Arbalin, Women coming down to the docks to see their sailors or warriors off, lovers exchanging tender embraces and weeping farewells, acquaintances laughing raucously and slapping their companions on the back. By sundown the last of the crew was aboard.

As darkness fell, Jatu, Frizian, Reydeau, Rico, and

even Bokar were all assembled in the captain's salon, and a meeting was held lasting into the late hours. When Tink tried to serve tea, he was met at the door by Bokar, the Dwarf looking draggled and worse for wear. He took the tray from Tink but did not let him within. Even so, the cabin boy caught a glimpse of the old Man in the blue robes, and, *waugh!* "... I saw a fox, too!"

"Ar, go on wi' ye, Tink. Wot would a fox be doin' on th' *Eroean*?"

"I dunno, Tiv, but it was a fox all right. Mayhap it has something to do with the old Man in blue."

Tivir just shook his head in disbelief, and Tink shot him a warning glance, then said, "Well, fox or not, Tiv, keep y'r mouth trap shut. What goes on in the Cap'n's quarters is for him to say and not us."

" 'At goes wi'out sayin', Tink. Goes wi'out sayin'."

And just ere mid of night in the moonless dark the *Eroean* slipped her mooring and sailed away from Port Arbalin.

Bright dawn found the Elvenship well away from Arbalin Isle and in the open sea, a fair wind abaft. But then Jatu had her wear around the wind until her sails luffed in the air, her headway stilled, to the puzzlement of the crew. Then all were summoned to deck, and rumors and speculation flew. And amid the murmur and rumble, Captain Aravan stepped from the aft quarters and made his way to the bo's'ns' cabin, where he clambered up to the roof and called for silence. A hush quickly fell till all that was heard was the plash of wave and the creak of rigging and the loose flap of Elvensilk sail.

"Sailors and Warriors, Men and Drimm, draw close, for I have something to say to ye."

Dwarves and Men alike shuffled forward, be-ringing the cabin. When all were gathered, Aravan held up his hand and again silence fell.

"Mates, I call ye 'round to speak of the mission I would have us fare upon."

"What it be, Capitan," called a hearty voice, "a lost city, treasure, a tèmpio di òro, che?"

Aravan grinned, his eye lighting upon the Man. "Vido, none of what you say. Neither lost cities nor lost treasures nor temples of gold. Instead we look for a lost person, one who has mysteriously disappeared. One who saved the life of our guest here"—Aravan turned and gestured toward the aft quarters, and a blue-robed, white-haired elder stepped forth—"Alamar the Mage."

A gasp of indrawn air was heard, and whispers of *Mage* and *Magic* and *Wonder* murmured among the crew as Alamar came forward to stand where all could see him, sailors and warriors giving way to make a corridor for him to pass through.

Aravan's voice called to them, reclaiming their attention. "As far as any know, there are no riches waiting for us at the end of this venture, except the knowledge of a task well done. We know not even where the mission will take us, nor whether the journey will be dull or sharp along the way. All we know is that Alamar's friend is missing, but whether he is lost, captured, or wandering free, I cannot say.

"Yet if he is lost, then it's to make him found again. If he is captured, then it's a-rescuing we go. If he is wandering free, then perhaps we follow nought but a wild goose."

"Ar," shouted someone, "when did that ever stop us, Cap'n?"

A roar of laughter washed over the decks.

"Ha, Lobbie," called out another, "ye be right: ne're did the chasing of a wild goose e'er slow us adown."

Aravan let the laughter run its course, then said, "Ah, but it is in the chasing itself where the venture lies." And he was answered by a general clamor of agreement.

Now Aravan knelt on one knee. "This then is the mission: whether it be into danger, woe, or boredom we sail, our goal is to find and if necessary to rescue Alamar's friend."

Sailors and warriors alike looked at one another and shrugged. Finally, one—Lobbie it was—called out, "Hoy, Cap'n, why ask any o' us? I mean, wot's so special about this mission, other than it—no disrespect, Master Alamar—other than it bein' a friend o' a Mage? Let's just get on wi' it." A rumble of agreement rose up from Man and Dwarf alike.

Leaping to his feet, Aravan held up his hand. "There is one thing special concerning this mission, and that is

I would have ye all swear two oaths of secrecy: one to me, and the other to someone else."

Oath? Of secrecy? ¿Que? Someone else? Wot's all this then? voices murmured, whispers hissing 'round the bo's'ns' cabin.

"The oath I ask is that no matter what ye see, hear, or do on this mission, that ye will tell no one of what befalls. Tongues are to be held in spite of drink, in spite of the need to win glory in the eyes of thy lovers, mates, friends, family, or anyone else. Tongues are to be held at all cost."

"Even in the face of death, Captain?"

"E'en so, Artus."

"How about in the face o' torture?" called someone else.

Before Aravan could answer this last question, Boder called out. "Cap'n, what if someone does not wish to take the oath? Then what?"

A murmur washed over the assembly, and stilled immediately when Aravan answered. "Boder, for those who do not wish to take the oath, we will sail hence to Hovenkeep and off load them, be it one or many. And when the mission is done, we will return and take back on board those who wish to sail the *Eroean* once more, for ye are a fine crew and I would gladly have ye back."

"Pah!" exploded Bokar, turning to Aravan, the Dwarf calling out so that all could hear. "It is as I said last night: this oath is no different from that which we took when first we came aboard the *Eroean* long past—our oath to keep the secrets for her making locked away forever. And I say that we Châkka, one and all, will take on this new oath as well. And neither torture, drink, death, fever, nor aught else will pry words from our lips concerning this seeking of the missing one."

As of one voice the Dwarven warriors proclaimed, *Châkka aun!*

"Ar Bokar, 'e's right, 'e is, Cap'n," called out Trench, the cook, "this ain't no different. I'll take y'r oath! I'll take y'r two oaths, solemn and all! Who'll join me?" And the big Man dropped to his knees and clenched his right fist to his heart.

An uproar of agreement met Trench's words, and all

the Men and Dwarves dropped to their knees and clasped fists to breasts.

"This then is the first oath, the one to me," cried Aravan, on his own knees, fist to heart, "that no matter what befalls . . ."

No matter what befalls . . . intoned the crew.

"I swear by all I hold sacred . . ."

I swear by all I hold sacred . . .

"On my honor and my life . . ."

On my honor and my life . . .

"And by High Adon, Himself . . ."

And by High Adon, Himself . . .

"That no word of this mission shall ever pass my lips . . ."

That no word of this mission shall ever pass my lips . . .

"No matter what befalls."

No matter what befalls.

Aravan then stood. "Ye may speak freely aboard this ship, and under secrecy seal and guard when alone with others who took the oath here today, but none else shall ever hear of this."

Aye! shouted all, and then they stood once again, turning to the Mage and waiting.

The elder looked nonplused for a moment, then he called, "Oh, it's not to me that you will swear the second oath of secrecy. Nay, but to another instead."

Bewildered, Men and Dwarves looked to one another and then to Aravan, a rumble of puzzlement rising up among them.

Aravan smiled, as did Jatu, and the Elf nodded to the black Man. Jatu stepped to the aft cabin door, opening it. And Aravan extended his hand, welcoming forth the one within, and he called out for all to hear, "Sailors and Warriors, I give you the true one behind this mission: the Lady Jinnarin!"

Morning light glanced across the Elvenship decks, the diamond bright rays a saffron yellow. And into this golden aura stepped a fox, red with black legs. And upon the fox's back rode a tiny maiden dressed all in grey leather, a bow 'cross her shoulders, arrows in a quiver fastened to her hip. And through the early morn she came, blue-eyed and pale, her hair mouse brown and loose and falling 'round her shoulders. And only the swash of water against the hull sounded in that moment, for it is not certain that anyone even breathed.

Through the light and across the deck she came, Men and Dwarves parting before her in awe, Jatu pacing behind. And when she reached the bo's'ns' cabin, Jatu knelt and held out a hand, and she swung her leg across Rux's back and stepped into Jatu's palm. He lifted her to the roof and then raised Rux up after. And she leapt astride the fox once more.

And all the while none said aught, for they were struck dumb with wonder. Yet in that moment Aravan sprang down and turned to face her and called aloud, "Hail to the Lady Jinnarin!"

A mighty roar rang up to the sky, pent hearts and souls released at last—*Hail to the Lady Jinnarin! Hail! Hail! Hail!*—Rux standing as still as a statue during the hue and cry.

Dwarves and Men alike pressed forward to see this wonder, and Jinnarin glanced at Alamar—the Mage making a palm-down, stay-calm gesture.

Jinnarin took a deep breath and raised her chin and dismounted and walked about the brim of the bo's'ns' roof so all could see. Then she stopped on the forward edge, there above Aravan, and waited for the crew to swing 'round and stand before her. And when all had assembled in front, she said in her clear voice, "Now you see why you are sworn to secrecy, for I am a Hidden One and one of the People. I am a Fox Rider.

"I am the stuff of some of your legends, the stuff of your fables and lore. Should word of my existence become common knowledge, dire consequences will befall my Folk. We are named Hidden Ones for good reason, and Hidden Ones would we remain.

"We go to find Farrix, who is my mate. He is missing, yet I believe that somehow his fate is entwined with that of a black ship and a pale green sea and a crystal castle above. And that is why I came to you, for no finer crew of sailors and warriors exists in all the world, and no ship is better than the one on which you serve. This I know: wherever sails the black ship, wherever lies the pale green sea, wherever stands the crystal castle, you of the *Eroean* will find them. And whatever challenges we may face along the way, none shall stay this crew.

And should events dictate that we need rescue my Farrix, you are more than fit to take on any hazard and win through, for you are the very best.

"Your splendid Captain Aravan has asked you to swear a double oath: one to him and one to me, for I am a Hidden One and I need your worthy pledge."

Without a word, all Dwarves and Men sank to both knees, Aravan as well, and each one there clenched both fists over his heart. Tears brimmed Jinnarin's eyes at this display. Emotion filled her voice as she said, "Yet we go to find Farrix, another Hidden One, and so would I have you double-lock your oath and swear by his name to remain silent in all that befalls—"

—But no one there kneeling on the deck had ever known Farrix, had ever seen him, while before them stood a soul from legend, a wondrous person they could see and hear and even touch, and so they called out instead: *For the Lady Jinnarin!*—

And Alamar nodded and signalled to the Pysk and this pledge was even better.

And so Jinnarin stood as her name rang through the air . . .

. . . But at last she held up her hands, and as quiet returned she gestured for all to rise, and when the crew was on its feet again, she called out, "I do hope when all this is said and done that if you inadvertently shout out my name at a time or place where it should not be heard, that you will simply attribute it to a ship or a childhood sweetheart"—then she turned and gestured at Rux—"or even to a little"—her voice dropped to a loud whisper heard by all—"to a little dog."

A roar of laughter greeted her, and another round of cheering burst forth—*To the Lady Jinnarin!*

"Sail ho, Captain," cried Frizian, "two points off the bow!"

"Bring her about, Rico," ordered Aravan. "Jatu, retrieve the Lady Jinnarin."

As Rico piped the crew, Men scattering to the ropes to hale the crossbeams around for the sails to catch the morning wind, First Officer Jatu reached up and took Rux down from the cabin roof, the fox remaining unexpectedly calm at being handled. Jatu reached up again, this time lowering the Pysk to the deck. Jinnarin mounted the fox, and they dodged and darted among the running crewmen, agile Rux weaving his way back to the aft quarters.

"Splendid," said waiting Alamar, once she was inside the captain's salon.

"Oh, Alamar, my knees were knocking. All of those Men. Those Dwarves. And I standing before them all, in the open, for everyone to see. Me, a Hidden One. . . . *Pah!* some Hidden One, eh?"

"Nevertheless, Jinnarin, you did well."

Jinnarin set her bow aside and then turned to the Mage. "Well, I suppose, as you say, I *did* do all right."

"Don't get uppity, Pysk!" snapped Alamar.

Jinnarin's mouth flew open and then—

The aft quarters door swung inward and Aravan entered, followed by Tink, the two coming down the short passageway and into the salon. The Elven captain smiled. " 'Tis an Arbalina trader, the ship astern and falling away now that we've come about."

"Can't nothin' in all o' the seas catch the cap'n's lady," added Tink, proudly.

Alamar cleared his throat. "Speaking of all of the seas, where are we bound, Aravan? Have you decided?"

Aravan turned to the Pysk. "Jinnarin, I would ask thee this: did any other Hidden Ones in Darda Glain see these—these auroral plumes?"

Jinnarin shook her head. "No, Aravan. Farrix, you see, had the keenest of Feyan eyes."

Aravan pursed his lips. "That was not the answer I had hoped for." Momentarily he fell into thought, then asked, "Thou hast special sight?"

Jinnarin shrugged. "Perhaps you would say so, though it does not seem special to me."

"How so?"

"Well, Aravan, given even a glimmer of light, we see quite well."

Tink nodded as if he had always known. "Fairy sight," he muttered.

Alamar grunted. "Better than Elven eyes, Aravan, for even a star here and there seems enough for the Pysks, whereas you Elves need more—clear starlight or moonlight. Aye, Pysk sight is nearly as good as magesight . . . and sometimes even better."

Aravan turned to the elder. "Magesight?"

Alamar turned up a palm. "We need no light at all. Of course, it takes a casting. Too, we cannot see very far in total darkness even with magesight."

"Special sight or not," said Jinnarin, "what does it have to do with where we are bound? And where *are* we bound, Aravan, have you decided?"

Aravan leaned his hands upon the table. "Aye," he answered. "When we've cleared the Avagon, then it's west northwest across the Weston Ocean, all the way to the coastal waters of the western continent, for there I would land and seek out Tarquin."

Jinnarin's eyes widened. "Tarquin? Why Tarquin?"

"Because, Jinnarin, I believe that we should return to the place where Farrix was last known to have been. Yet, I would not do so until again the northern aurora is in the sky and mayhap plumes falling into the ocean nigh Rwn. But heed, even if plumes do fall, they will not do so until winter is upon us. In the meanwhile, I would visit Tarquin to speak with him and discover whether other Pysk eyes have seen the lights come down in places elsewhere. If not, then mayhap Farrix is chasing an illusion; but if others have seen these plumes, then mayhap Farrix chases a strange will-o'-the-wisp all about the Weston Ocean. Yet the Weston Ocean is a wide water, and I would think to narrow the search. If other Pysk eyes have seen the plumes, then mayhap they can aid us in locating precisely where Farrix may be. And Tarquin may hold the answer.

"Too, there is always the chance that Tarquin might know of a black ship or a crystal castle or of a pale green sea."

CHAPTER 9

Straits

Late Summer—Early Autumn, 1E9574
[The Present]

Flying all of her silken sails, rapidly the *Eroean* drew away from the Arbalina trader aft, the wind abaft impelling the swift Elvenship through the waters of the Avagon Sea. Southwesterly she sped, running a course parallel to but standing far out from the rugged coast of Hoven, that Realm lying some leagues beyond the distant horizon. Toward the Kistanian Straits she fared, there where the Rovers plied, pirates from the Isle of Kistan. Their maroon-sailed ships roamed through the narrows both north and south of that wild Land, for the great equatorial island itself stood in the way between the Avagon Sea and the Weston Ocean. Across the channel to the north of Kistan lay the Realms of Vancha and Tugal, while beyond the long curving seaway to the south arced the wide Land of Hyree. And toward these dangerous waters coursed the Elvenship, aiming for the northern channel, more strictured but more direct.

But these hazardous narrows yet lay some six or seven days away, and Bokar and his Dwarven warriors used the time to ready the ship for combat should it come. The ballistas were tested, casting missiles out and away, both spear-shafts and fireballs arcing far over the water, splashing or fizzing into the waves. The ballista deck mounts were cleaned and greased, the swivels rotating free.

In addition to refurbishing the great arbalests, each

corvus was refurbished as well, pivots lubricated, claws sharpened, rail-clamp screws cleansed and oiled.

Throughout it all, shy Jinnarin watched from afar, Bokar glimpsing her from the corner of his eye. Finally the armsmaster turned toward her and motioned her to come and see. Somewhat timidly she approached, Rux following. When she came near—"Would you like a tour, Lady Jinnarin?"

Her smile was his answer.

"Good!" Bokar took up his winged-helm and strapped it on, as if showing Jinnarin the ship's armament were somehow an official act.

Bokar and Jinnarin strolled along the deck, the Dwarf stopping now and again to explain some point concerning the conduct of combat aboard the Elvenship.

"There are ten ballistas aboard: two each in the bow and stern, starboard and larboard alike, whose main intent is to cover wide arcs to the fore and aft, though they can protect abeam as well. The remaining six are uniformly spaced along the flanks of the *Eroean,* three to a side. Each ballista is capable of flinging fire or stone or spear, all that need be decided is which to hurl—a javelin flung from the groove, or a ball from the cup ... some afire, others not."

Jinnarin strained her neck upward, trying to see. "How do you cock it, Bokar?"

"My Lady, if you will permit me," rumbled the Dwarf, and before she could say yea or nay, Jinnarin was lifted to Bokar's shoulder. "Hold onto my helm strap," he said. "That or my hair."

Jinnarin grasped the metal cheek guard, the dark steel cool to the touch. Then she watched as Bokar pointed out the mechanisms of the great arbalest: "Here be the crank by which it is wound, and this the slide on which rides the cup or propels the javelin. When the slide comes back to here, these teeth along the side trap the trigger catchment during the winding, the rail cogs a precaution in the event that the winder loses his grip. Here be the trigger. When she is cocked and armed and aimed, then pulling this cord looses her. Handled by two or three Châkka, a giant crossbow, you might call her, like the ones my warriors bear; the arbalests are slower winding of course, though much more deadly at range."

Jinnarin giggled. "I was just thinking, Bokar, this bow makes mine look as would a toothpick next to an immense tree."

Bokar smiled. "Ah but, my Lady Jinnarin, your bow looks as a toothpick, regardless."

"Oh but, my Armsmaster Bokar, that depends upon the size of the teeth, neh?"

A deep belly laugh and a birdlike trill rang across the decks of the *Eroean*.

At dusk the wind began to shift about, and by next morn it was blowing northeasterly, clouds piling up in the skies, great swells rolling over the waters. Driving rains came with the noon hour, cold and wind whipped. The studding sails were taken in, but all others remained flying as the *Eroean* tacked into the lash.

Below deck in an aft cabin given over to the Pysk and the Mage, the ship's carpenter, Finch, crawled back from his handiwork. "There you be, Miss Jinnarin, all done up safe and sound, and a pretty job of it, too, even if I do say so myself." Although the Man spoke to Jinnarin, his shy eyes looked everywhere but directly at her.

"The little panel under your bunk, it swings both ways, letting you and your fox in and out of the passageway beyond whenever you want. These little dogs, well twist them thisaway to latch the hatch shut should the sea want to enter, and I've seen it try, rushing down the corridor outside.

"And once I fasten this wood in place—" Finch mounted three wide, tongue-in-groove boards across the openings left behind when the under-bunk drawers had been removed, tapping in slender brass nails to hold them in place. "Right. Now you've got your own little closed-off Lady's chamber there under the bunk for the privacy you might want, with its own door opening in and out, and another door into this here cabin. And cor, who could use it but you?"

Finch got to his feet. "But as to light, well, I should think a wax taper'll have to do, and I've made these dogged ports out here and in there for ventilation, wot?

"Arlo the sailmaker is making you a bed ... out of soft blankets. One for your fox, too.

"And as to your personal needs"—Finch blushed furiously—"to wash yourself and to relieve yourself, Carly the cooper and Rolly the tinsmith is working on that very thing right even as we speak, though I be going now to help them."

Jinnarin smiled up at the large, humble Man. "Oh, thank you, Mister Finch. Rux and I will cherish what you have done for us. And"—the Pysk swiftly stepped into the tiny chamber under the bunk and then back out again—"and my private room is simply perfect for any and all my needs."

Finch shuffled his feet and touched his cap, then turned and rushed from the cabin.

Before the day was done, the sailmaker, carpenter, cooper, and tinsmith delivered to Jinnarin the things needed to furnish her "cabin," all newmade to her stature: bedding for her and Rux; a wee brass candlestick holder, with a striker and straight shavings tipped in pitch and several spare tapers; a small washstand and diminutive tin basin, with a tiny tin pitcher for water; a miniature sea chest for her clothing; and a wee commode chair with a tiny privy pot and lid.

As all four Men stood about, holding their hats and grinning, Jinnarin *ooh*ed and *ahh*ed, saying, "Why, this is better than I have at home."

Finch removed one of the boards of her chamber wall. "Now you arrange it like as you want it, Miss Jinnarin, and I'll fix it so as it won't slide about in a big blow, wot?"

Over the next few nights, Men and Dwarves alike came to look down the passageway hoping to see the glow of candlelight shining out through the wee window of the Lady Jinnarin's cabin. This was especially true of Finch and Carly and Arlo and Rolly—carpenter, sailmaker, cooper, and tinsmith—even though they knew that she had Fairy sight and probably didn't need the candles; still, she might burn them just to please the crew. And burn them she did, the soft yellow taperlight glimmering, and the four Men would look at one another and grin and nod; at other times the tiny portal would be dark, and they would sigh. But always they would go away marvelling over *their* Pysk.

*   *   *

Rux quickly adapted to *his* new door, ingress and egress to *his* den, where his mistress also happened to live. Even so, still he spent much time below decks hunting, though his take for the day was one or two at most, for the fox found the ratting and mousing on the *Eroean* to be slim pickings when compared to the *Flying Fish*. Throughout all the ship roamed Rux, becoming a familiar sight to the crew. From keelson to hold to crew's quarters, from lower deck to locker, from the tiller wheel on the stern to its mate in the sheltered wheelhouse forward of the aft quarters, from bow to bilge ranged the fox. The fact that his hunting ground pitched and rolled and yawed, and canted starboard or larboard depending on the wind, seemed of no consequence to Rux. The only thing that mattered at this juncture was rats and mice and exploring.

Of all the crew, Rux would only allow three to touch him: Jinnarin and Jatu and Aravan. Why, not even Alamar could gain the fox's trust—perhaps especially Alamar, for the elder yet snapped and fumed and fussed frequently at Rux's mistress, though now that she lived in Rux's own den, the Mage's opportunities to rail at her were severely curtailed. And so, although the crew often saw the fox, and tried to coax him and pet him, enticing him with tidbits of food, the animal was far too wary, his ways were much too wild.

On some of Rux's expeditions, Jinnarin would accompany him, or he her, for she, too, was exploring the *Eroean*, getting to know the ship from stem to stern and hatches to ribs.

On the dark rainy night of the autumnal equinox, Jinnarin and Rux on one of their forays came up to the deck, where they saw Aravan pacing a stately intricate gait in the wetness. Jinnarin stopped 'neath the shelter of a gig and watched as the Elf stepped, paused, stepped, turned, stepped, paused, stepped—Aravan moving through a complex pattern, something between a dance and a rite. And he was chanting under his breath.

"He does this four times a year." Jatu's soft voice startled the Pysk, the Man having come upon her unawares.

"What . . . ?" Jinnarin's voice trailed away, the rest of her question unsaid.

"It is an Elven thing," responded Jatu. "He celebrates the equinox."

Jinnarin watched as Aravan paced, seemingly oblivious of the rain. "You said four times a year, Jatu."

"Aye, Lady, the two equinoxes—autumn and spring— and the summer and winter solstices."

"Ah, I see. Then that is something like the celebrations of my Folk, Jatu, Year's Long Night and Year's Long Day the same as Aravan's solstices, but our other two times are at the Moon of Spring and the Moon of Autumn, when the Lady's Light is full."

"Lady's light?"

"Elwydd, Jatu. She is the Lady."

Jatu smiled. "I see. And Her light is the Moon, I take it."

"As Adon's is the Sun," answered Jinnarin.

The rain ran down Jatu's slicker and dripped on the wet deck. Beneath the stern of the gig, Jinnarin and Rux were out of the drizzle, the fox waiting patiently. And still the Man and Pysk watched Aravan.

" 'Tis the dark of the Moon," said Jatu. "When—?"

"The next full Moon," interjected Jinnarin, "that's when this autumn season will be welcomed by the Fox Riders—a fourteen-day from now."

Jatu grunted in acknowledgement and after a moment said, "I wonder if there is a Folk upon this world who do *not* celebrate the turn of the seasons?"

And as Jinnarin and Jatu both pondered this question and Rux waited stoically, out on the deck in the drizzling rain Aravan paced through his step-pause-step, turn-and-step ancient Elven ritual.

On the sixth night after leaving Port Arbalin, the rain stopped, and morning found a bright Sun rising in the sky and the wind shifting abaft. And with all sails set, the ship running braw, the *Eroean* came to the northern Straits of Kistan. Into the narrows she plunged, running at seventeen knots, her sharp prow slicing through the rolling swells, lookouts aloft.

"Straight down the middle we'll run with the wind,"

called Aravan to Boder, pointing slightly to starboard, setting the course.

"Aye, Cap'n," replied the steersman, turning the wheel a bit deosil, the Elvenship answering the helm.

"Trim her up, Rico," called Aravan, "catch every puff of this air."

"Aye, Kapitan," replied the bo's'n, and began piping the crew; and sheets were hauled and belayed, the cross-beams adjusted slightly, the staysails and jibs adjusted as well.

And blue water slid sternward past the hull, beneath the tiers of studding sails jutting out above.

"Eighteen knots and some," called out Frizian, standing aft with two of the crew.

And into the straits hurtled the *Eroean*, a white wake churning behind.

Two hours she ran thus, and of a sudden—"Sail ho, maroon!" called the mainmast lookout. "Sail ho to the fore larboard!"

"Sail ho, maroon!" called the foremast lookout. "Sail ho, starboard fore."

Motioning Rico to follow, Aravan strode to the bow. Long he looked at the blood-dark sails, first to larboard then to starboard. "They run an intercept course," he said at last. "Rico—"

"Sail ho, maroon!" cried the foremast lookout. "Sail ho, dead ahead!"

"Rico, pipe all hands, the Drimma, too."

"Sails ho, maroon," called the foremast lookout again. "Sails ho, starboard ahead! Larboard ahead! Hoy, Cap'n, 'tis a bloody fleet standing across the way."

"Rico," barked Aravan, "lookouts down. The Rovers have a gauntlet for us to run."

As Rico piped all hands, sailors and warriors alike, and piped down the lookouts as well, in the hue and cry Jinnarin and Alamar came rushing to the deck, Rux at their side. The ship seemed a madhouse, Men running hither and yon, gaudy-helmed Dwarves boiling up from the hold, bearing axes and crossbows and rushing to the ballistas, loosening tie-downs, opening javelin crates and fireball boxes. "Stand back," called Frizian to the Mage and the Pysk, "do not get in the way. In fact, 'twould be best if you'd go below to your quarters, for safety's sake if nought else."

"*Pah!*" snorted Alamar. "Here I stand and here I'll stay, like it or not."

Jinnarin found her heart hammering, and she turned and bolted back inside ... to emerge moments later, bow in hand, quiver of arrows—deadly arrows—strapped unto her hip.

Alamar glanced down at her and smiled approvingly. "Boars or pirates," he growled, "they're all pigs."

Out on the ocean ahead, lateen sails both starboard and larboard turned on downwind courses set to converge upon the Elvenship, cerulean silk running straight ahead swiftly, maroon canvass intercepting.

"Hegen," ordered Aravan, now astern, "to the wheelhouse. Should Boder get hit, thou wilt take the helm.

"Frizian, Rico, stay aft with me. Jatu, Reydeau, go with Boder, but first list:

"Running as we are with the wind, I would not have us lose speed trying to turn their end. Instead, I plan on breaking their file dead ahead. Given our rate and theirs, the Rovers far aflank will see nought but our stern. But those running on the wind in the fore quarter arc, aye, they are the threat.

"Bokar, I would have thy Drimma cast fire at any who draw nigh. Place thy best at the ballistas in the bow.

"Heed, that is my plan—the best I can conceive at short notice. Be there any suggestions? Be there any questions?"

None said aught. "Then away. And let us give these Rovers Hèl!"

As the crew carried forth with Aravan's plan, the Pysk turned to the Mage. "I had a question, Alamar, but I did not wish to interfere."

Alamar glanced down at her. "And it was ... ?"

Rico piped his pipe, and sailors made fine adjustments to the sheets. The *Eroean* slid even faster through the crystal waters. And still the bloody sails to fore and flank closed in.

"Well, Alamar, this seems to be a trap laid by the Rovers. Was it set for all ships or just for this one? If set for this one, how did they know that we were coming? Why spend so many ships to set a trap for one?

And last, why oh why do the Rovers fly maroon sails? I mean, if they would hope to surprise unwary ships, to sneak up on unsuspecting prey, then their sails would seem to be contrary."

Alamar shook his head. "I thought you had but one question, Pysk, and here you've asked four." The Mage glanced at the foe hurtling toward them, distances and courses rapidly closing. "Perhaps I can answer all before it's time to fight.

"As to maroon sails, they are to strike terror in the hearts of those they would plunder. And of those merchants and captains who pay tribute, the maroon sail signals 'stand and deliver.'

"As to a trap laid, I think you are correct, Pysk—it is an ocean-going ambush, set specifically, I believe, to ensnare this very ship, the *Eroean,* for she represents a mighty prize. Look, if the Elvenship were to become a freebooter, it would be the terror of the seas, and so these pirates would dearly love to have it be theirs.

"As to how they knew we were coming, I can think of many ways . . . the most likely of which is that some pirate ship must have seen the *Eroean* on her way toward Port Arbalin. And given that Aravan stays but a short while at that city . . . well, they knew he was due back through within a Moon. And what better place to set a trap than right down the center of the narrows, where he is likely to go?"

Jinnarin looked at the dark sails closing in and the racing ships they drove—sleek two-masted dhows, each vessel bearing a pair of lateen-rigged sails. On the decks could be seen dusky Men rushing about, trimming sails, readying ballistas of their own.

"Alama—" Jinnarin turned to speak to the Mage, but he was gone. *There he is! Striding toward the bow! What in the world does he think he is—?*

"Hoy, Master Alamar!" shouted Frizian.

"Let him be," commanded Aravan.

Not turning, not deigning to notice, Alamar continued forward.

Thnn! In the bow a ballista let fly at a closing Rover. The flaming ball arced upward and then down, falling ten yards short, splashing, *sizz*ing, in the sea.

Alamar clambered onto the foredeck.

"Stand back, old Man, out of the way," called a Dwarf loader, placing a ball in the cup. "You are like to get hurt."

"Listen to me, you young squat," snarled Alamar, "if anyone around here is like to get hurt—"

"Inbound fire!" shouted the crank winder.

Alamar looked up to see a flaming ball arcing down at them. The eld Mage threw a hand up and shouted *"Crepa!"* and the fireball detonated, flaming chunks and sparks showered down upon them, and immediately two Dwarves scooped up the largest burning fragments in flat shovels and pitched them overboard, while others cast sand on the smaller bits.

"All right," shouted Alamar, shaking a fist at the Rover ship. "Now you've asked for it!"

He turned to the ballista crew. "Lob another at the skuts. We'll show them what's what."

The crew turned to Bokar.

"Do as he says," growled the armsmaster.

Aiming the ballista and lighting the missile—*Thnn!*—another fireball was loosed. Alamar watched its arc. *"Longius,"* he whispered, and the trajectory appeared to flatten out and carry farther, to burst upon the mainmast, the sail and spar igniting.

Hai! cried the ballista crew, jeering at the foe afire.

"I told you we'd show you," shouted Alamar. "Jump us, would you, ha!"

"Sir."

Alamar felt a tug on his sleeve and turned. An armed Dwarf stood at his elbow.

"Sir," said the Dwarf respectfully, then pointing, "a pair on the larboard bow."

Alamar looked. Two maroon-sailed Rovers drew nigh.

"How fast can you load?" the Mage snapped at the Dwarf.

"Ten heartbeats, sir."

"Good! We'll get them both."

"But sir, one is but barely in range, the other farther still."

"Don't be a fool, Dwarf. Trust me, we'll get them both. Now fire at the first."

Bokar grunted in agreement, and the crew aimed and loosed.

Thnn!—the fireball arced up and over the waters, Alamar watching it fly. He whispered nought as the missile arced down to crash into the poop deck of the foe, setting the tiller aflame, the ship falling away on the wind. "Good shooting," he said querulously, as if somewhat disappointed. It is doubtful that the cheering ballista crew heard him or the annoyance in his voice.

Ten heartbeats later—*Thnn!*—another fireball was loosed. *"Longius,"* whispered Alamar, then, *"Ad laevam."*

The missile arced far out over the waters, veering left as it flew, and it burst upon the aft sail of the enemy ship, fire whooshing up. Again a mighty cheer shouted out from the decks of the Elvenship, while aboard the foe bedlam reigned.

Sailing far aflank of the *Eroean,* Rovers strove to overtake the ship, but fell behind instead. Even so, they cast their fires, the missiles falling short, though one or two came close.

Alamar merely watched, gauging the trajectories, saying nought.

"Ahead starboard," called a Dwarf.

Alamar turned about. "Stand by," he said.

But ere the *Eroean* fired, the Rover cast first, and once again the missile flew true. *"Crepa!"* called the Mage, the fireball exploding in the sky, flaming chunks arcing down to *pssst* in the sea.

"Ready, sir," said the starboard ballista crew leader, the Dwarf aiming the missile caster.

"Whenever," murmured Alamar.

Thnn!—the fireball arced upward through the zenith and then over. *"Brevius,"* whispered the Mage, the arc steepening, angling downward, the ball slamming into the enemy ballista crew and blasting apart, fire exploding outward.

Horrid screams sounded from afar, Men aflame leaping overboard, others running amok.

On the *Eroean* the cheering fell subdued.

"Dead ahead," called Bokar.

Alamar turned his gaze toward this Rover. "Ready the ballistas." He sounded weary.

But the sailors on the Elvenship foredeck began cheering lustily, shouting. "She's turning tail! Turning tail! Running!" and in the distance the Rover ship sails were haled about and her tiller pressed hard over as she heeled on the wind to flee.

And as the dhow sailed off abeam, the *Eroean* sliced swiftly onward through the waters and past the shattered gauntlet, past the broken line of Kistanian Rovers, her cerulean sails embracing the wind and holding it, the Elvenship driving away from the collapsed ambush and toward the horizon afar, leaving the freebooters nought to grasp but her churning ephemeral wake.

The forward ballista crews gathered 'round Alamar, shouting in acclamation, and they would have hoisted him onto their shoulders but he stopped them short, the Mage pale and trembling. And as a flame quenched by an onslaught of water, the cheering voices chopped shut. "Help me back to my quarters," he said hoarsely. Dwarves leapt forward to aid him, and as one took hold of each arm, his knees gave way completely, and he collapsed, the Dwarves lowering him gently to the deck.

"Fager!" shouted Bokar. "Fager, to me, to me!"

The ship's chirurgeon made his way to the foredeck and bent over the Mage. "He's fainted," said Fager after a bit. "Bear him up and to his quarters."

Rux came scrabbling up the steps, Jinnarin on his back. The Pysk hurled herself from the fox and darted to Alamar's side, crying anxiously, "Is he wounded? Is he bleeding? Will he be all right?"

Fager stood and scratched his head. "No wound or blood, Lady Jinnarin. But as to whether he'll be all right . . . if he were Human, then I'd say yes. But he's a Wizard, and so I just don't know."

Men bearing a litter arrived, and they gently lifted the Mage to the canvas. Two sturdy Dwarves took grip on the handles and hoisted the elder.

In that moment, Alamar opened his eyes. "Brandy," he croaked.

"What happened, Alamar?"

Mage and Pysk were in the captain's salon along with Fager, Bokar, and Aravan.

"Another, please," requested Alamar, holding out his glass. Aravan glanced at Fager, and at a nod refilled the elder's crystal.

Jinnarin repeated her question: "What happened, Alamar?"

Alamar sipped the drink—*"Ahhh"*—and smacked his lips, then leaned back in his chair. He glanced at Jinnarin kneeling on the table before him. "Too much too fast," he said.

"Too much brandy?" Jinnarin looked at his glass.

Alamar clutched his glass protectively. "No, no. Too much . . . casting."

"Oh."

Aravan sat down opposite the Mage. "Regardless, Alamar, thou didst much to protect this ship and crew, as well as break the blockade."

"Hai, warrior Mage!" cried Bokar, slamming a clenched fist to the table. "I will war at your side against your enemies whenever you call, Friend."

A look of shock flashed upon Alamar's face. "No, no," he protested. "Mages are forbidden to fight except in the defense of themselves or others."

A scowl fell upon Bokar. "Forbidden? Who would do such?"

Alamar paused, sipping his brandy. "Why, we do. The Mages I mean. Heed, for us to war against others would lead to"—he glanced at Jinnarin—"to evil. Our power is to be used wisely—not to gain advantage for our own satisfaction."

Bokar tugged on his beard. "Tell me, Alamar, if not to gain advantage, what do you call what you just did against the Kistanee?"

Alamar's jaw jutted out. "I call it protecting this ship, Dwarf. That's what!" He tossed the last of the brandy down his throat and slammed the glass to the table.

Aravan leaned back in his chair and smiled, his tilted Elven eyes glittering, watching these two fiery-tempered allies go at one another.

Bokar ground his teeth. "Guiding our fireballs is protecting this ship?"

"In the long run," shot back Alamar.

Fager held up his hands. "Hear, hear, gentleme—gentle beings. No need to argue 'mongst ourselves. Besides, Alamar needs rest, not debate."

After glaring a moment, Bokar stalked out from the lounge, heading back to the deck, grumbling to himself.

"I suggest you lie down and rest, Master Alamar," said Fager. "Take your ease. Recover from your ordeal."

Aravan stood and placed the brandy decanter back in the cabinet, Alamar watching with some disappointment.

"Let's go, Alamar," said Jinnarin, turning, leaping down from table to chair to floor. "Heed the chirurgeon."

The Mage shuffled down the corridor and to his cabin, Jinnarin at his side. When they entered, the Pysk stepped into her under-bunk quarters and set aside her bow and quiver. Returning, she found Alamar reclining on his own bunk, sighing wearily.

"Are you all right?"

Alamar rolled on his side and looked at her. "Just remembering, Pysk. Just remembering."

"Remembering what?"

"Why, when I was not old and frail, as I now find myself, I could have tossed those fireballs right back at them. Better yet, I could have made them spin and circle in the air as would a jongleur tossing colorful balls while singing humorous ditties."

Jinnarin laughed at the mental picture. Of a sudden she sobered. "How do you do it, Alamar?"

Alamar yawned. "Do what?"

"Do your—your, uh, castings."

Alamar blinked slowly at Jinnarin. "More secrets, eh, Pysk?"

Jinnarin sighed. "Well, if it's a secret ..."

Alamar pursed his lips. "Look, Pysk, everything has a—an astral fire within, be it alive or dead, animal, mineral, vegetable, or aught else. This astral fire has five pure forms—fire, water, earth, air, aethyr—or can be an amalgam or admixture or alloy of such. My Folk can *see* this astral fire, with a vision which goes beyond that of the eyes. And, with much training, we can cause the flame to flow this way or that, changing it, controlling what it does, and that in turn controls whatever is housing that fire, whatever it may be—all things alive or dead or never alive—"

"Even people?" interjected Jinnarin.

Alamar grunted. "Even people."

Jinnarin sat cross-legged on the floor, her chin resting on one fist. Long did she sit this way, lost in deep thought. At last she glanced up at Alamar, a question on her lips. But she did not ask it, for the Mage was fast asleep.

Two more days did the *Eroean* fare through the long Kistanian Straits, but no more pirates did she come across, the waters free of maroon sails. At last the Elvenship cleared the narrows, though she was yet in the waters of the Avagon Sea, the Weston Ocean lying some hundred leagues ahead.

Westerly she ran another day, in the wide gap between Tugal to the north and Hyree to the south, the wind yet abaft though more gentle.

And at noon on the following day, with a bright Sun overhead, just as the *Eroean* came upon the marge between the two oceans—"Castaway!" called the foremast lookout. "Castaway, on the starboard bow!"

Alamar and Jinnarin on the foredeck shaded their eyes and peered ahead, the Pysk standing on the stem block, up where she could see. In the distance bobbed a small gig, a single mast rising but no sail mounted. A figure stood in the boat, one hand braced against the bare spar, bare that is but for the square of cloth flying at half-mast, a signal of distress.

Aravan stepped to the foredeck as well, looking long as the *Eroean* sliced toward the small boat. "Reydeau, pipe her to wear around the wind. Luff her nigh that gig. We will take him aboard."

Bokar, too, stood on the foredeck. "Beware, Captain, it could be another Rover trap."

"Reydeau, any maroon sails?"

The bo's'n piped a signal, and from the forward crow's nest came the response, "No ships nigh but the castaway, Captain. None starboard, larboard, fore, or aft."

Aravan nodded. "Wear her around, bo's'n."

"Aye, Captain."

As the bo's'n piped the signals, Alamar turned to Aravan. "You could give him a sail, Aravan, and enough provisions to reach the mainland. For if you take this castaway aboard, he may see Jinnarin, and he is not sworn to secrecy."

Aravan nodded then turned to the Pysk. "Lady Jinnarin, I suggest that thou and thy fox take to a hiding place—below deck."

"But, Aravan, I want to see."

"Now, Pysk—" growled Alamar.

"Look, Rux and I will hide under one of the deck gigs."

"Pysk—"

Jinnarin stamped her foot. "No, Alamar. You can go below if you want someone out of the way, but Rux and I are staying above. Hiding, but staying above."

Alamar looked at Aravan and shrugged as if to say, *I did my best.*

Climbing the rope ladder came the boat's occupant, swinging up and over the rail.

Clutched in shadow beneath a deck gig, Jinnarin gasped for it was a female, reed slender and dressed in brown leathers. Her light brown hair was cropped at the shoulders and seemed shot through with auburn glints in the bright sunlight. Her complexion was fair and clear, but for a meager sprinkle of freckles high on her cheeks, and her eyes were green and flecked with gold. And she was tall, the top of her head level with Aravan's startled eyes.

As to her Race, that soon came clear, for upon stepping aboard she turned to the Wizard Alamar.

"Father," she said, her voice soft.

"Aylis," he responded, embracing her.

CHAPTER 10

Portents

Early Autumn, 1E9574
[The Present]

As Aylis returned her father's embrace, her eyes flew wide in astonishment, for over the elder's shoulder she saw stepping toward her a tiny female, twelve inches tall, and at her side came a fox.

"A Pysk!" she gasped and pulled back to look at her sire in wonderment. "Father, I knew that you travelled in strange company, but a Pysk!"

Alamar turned. "Daughter, this is Jinnarin, mate of Farrix who saved me from the boar."

Aylis kneeled and held out a hand, her smile wide. "Jinnarin."

The Pysk lightly touched Aylis's palm. "I've heard somewhat of you, Aylis."

Aylis glanced up at her sire then back to the Pysk. "Filling your head with tales of my waywardness, I shouldn't wonder."

"Oh no," responded Jinnarin in all seriousness. "He's quite fond of you, you know."

Aylis nodded. "I know," she said softly.

"Harrumph." Alamar cleared his throat. "Daughter . . ."

Aylis grinned and stood. "Yes, Father."

"Daughter, this is Captain Aravan."

Aylis turned to Aravan, her green gaze falling into his of blue, and of a sudden her face flushed, blood rising hot to her cheeks, and she seemed neither able to speak nor breathe.

"Art thou well, Lady?" asked Aravan, stepping forward, reaching out to take her hand and steady her, and when fingers met fingers, a spark leapt between, startling Aravan and Aylis both. Even so, he held her hand in his, and Aylis, her color returning, grinned up at him, saying, "Quite well, Captain. It's just that, I did not expect to see . . . you."

Aravan's eyebrows rose and again Aylis blushed. "I mean . . ." she began, and then her voice seemed to fail her, and flustered, she pulled her gaze from his, though she made no attempt to retrieve her hand.

A dawning look came over Alamar's features and he began to laugh, his cackle rising upward in merriment.

Jinnarin looked up at the eld Mage in puzzlement. "What is it, Alamar. What can be so humorous?"

Holding his fingers to his lips and chortling, the Mage glanced down at Jinnarin. "Nothing, Pysk. Nothing. Or maybe something—a silver mirror—"

Dropping Aravan's hand as if it were a hot coal, Aylis spun about and sharply said, "Father!"

Alamar's voice dropped to a loud whisper. "We'll speak of it later, Pysk."

In that moment Jatu stepped to Aravan's side. "Captain, I've ordered the Lady's gig brought aboard. Men are unstepping the mast now. We can be underway in a trice."

Aravan nodded. "Lady Aylis, this is my first officer, Jatu."

Aylis smiled, acknowledging Jatu, receiving a wide grin in return.

As Jinnarin peered through a runoff port and down at the Men working below, Tivir came scrambling up over the railing, sea bag in hand, the lad beaming at Aylis. "Y'r belongin's, Laidy. Oi've brought them, Oi 'ave."

As she reached for the bag, the cabin boy drew back and blurted, "Hoy, Laidy, Oi'll carry it f'r y', that is, if y' don't mind."

Aylis smiled. "Why, thank you, Mister . . ."

"Tivir, Laidy. Tivir's m'name. And no mister at that."

Aylis laughed a deep throaty laugh. "All right then, Tivir it shall be, with no mister in front."

Tivir bobbed his head and stepped aside and smirked at Tink in victory, the other cabin boy standing by.

Jatu gestured toward the railing. "Is there aught else in the gig you would have special care of?"

Aylis shook her head. "No, Jatu. All I had with me was my sea bag and a bit of food and water."

Aravan turned to Tivir. "Lad, bear Lady Aylis's belongings aft. We will quarter her opposite Mage Alamar."

"Aye, Cap'n." Tivir sped away.

Jatu peered over the wale at the gig now being hoisted on davits. "My Lady, the ship you were on—gone down I take it."

"I came on no ship, Jatu."

"But then, your distress flag—"

"I was in no distress. I merely needed you to stop and take me aboard."

Jatu's eyes widened. "But how did you get here? Surely not by that bit of a gig below."

Aylis smiled and nodded. "I sailed south from Tugal yestereve."

Jatu shook his head. "Most foolish, Lady. Foul weather alone could have foundered you, to say nothing of what the Rovers might have done had they come across you ere we did."

Alamar grunted impatiently. "Jatu, my daughter would not have come in that gig if storms or pirates were in the offing." The elder turned to Aylis. "Tell me, Daughter, just what *were* you doing out here bobbing about in the ocean like a cork adrift?"

"Waiting for this ship, Father, waiting for you."

"Waiting?" burst out Jinnarin. "Waiting for this ship? The *Eroean?* For Alamar? But how did you know—?"

"Argh!" growled Alamar. "Pysk, I think you never listen to me. That, or your memory is a sieve. Did I not tell you that she is a seer? And seers *know.*"

Jinnarin stamped her foot angrily. "Unlike you, Alamar, *I* have not lived among Magekind all *my* life. How *could* I know?"

"Because I told you! And what I say I expect you to remember."

"Oh? Every last phrase you utter, I suppose?"

Aylis moved between the two, effectively shutting off the brewing argument, though Alamar tried to step around her to continue, but failed.

Aylis turned to Aravan, as if to appeal to him to reason with these two, but she gave up when she saw the Elf futilely attempting to suppress a grin.

Managing a sober look, Aravan asked, "My Lady, just why *wert* thou waiting for my ship? Surely 'tis a most uncommon way to visit with thy sire, neh?"

Aylis took a deep breath, her gaze sweeping from Aravan to Jinnarin to Jatu and across the decks of the *Eroean,* stopping at last on the visage of Alamar. "Father, I have done a casting. You, this ship, the crew, everyone aboard, we are all in dreadful danger, though what it is I cannot say."

"Shielded?" Alamar's eyes flew wide. "But that would mean . . ."

Aylis, Aravan, and Alamar were seated 'round the map table in the captain's lounge. Jinnarin sat cross-legged upon the board, and Rux was curled up below. At Alamar's outburst, Rux snorted and stood and trotted out from under the table and to his door in the passageway, disappearing into the privacy and quiet of his den, there where he and Jinnarin slept.

"Yes, Father, I know," replied Aylis, her voice soft.

"Well, *I* don't," snapped Jinnarin. "I don't know what it means at all."

"It means, Pysk," muttered Alamar, "that some Mage somewhere is blocking Aylis's castings, concealing from her scrying whatever it is that's going on."

Jinnarin threw up her hands. "Why would someone block her?"

Aylis leaned forward in her chair. "I do not think that it is just my attempts being thwarted, but rather all attempts."

Jinnarin turned to Aylis. "Even so, why?"

Aylis shrugged. "There are any number of reasons to shield against scrying, but they all come down to a person or two ensuring their privacy."

"Lovers?" Aravan's sapphirine gaze again caught at Aylis's emerald eyes, and somewhat discomposed she nodded as her cheeks reddened.

Jinnarin's voice cut through Aylis's diverted silence. "Besides lovers, who?"

Aylis counted off several. "Merchants, war commanders, misers, alchemists, cooks"—she turned up her palms—"anyone wishing to keep a secret. Oh, do not assume that I and my kind spend our waking hours snooping upon the private acts of others, nay. 'Twould be most unethical to do such. Moreover, it takes considerable power to see through time or space or both in detail, hence the need must be great enough to justify the cost ere such castings are made ... just as must the need for privacy outweigh the cost of shielding. I hasten to add, though, that the price paid to hide something is much less than that of its finding."

Alamar stroked his beard. "And the cost to break through this particular shield—?"

"Father, this shielding is strong beyond measure. I deem I cannot break it."

"Then, Lady Aylis," asked Aravan, "how dost thou know that danger lurks?"

"Because, Captain"—from a pouch at her waist Aylis extracted a small wooden box—"I have cast several simple readings." The box was made of sandalwood. A small golden hasp latched it. Aylis opened the clasp and raised the lid. Inside was a black silk cloth wrapped about ... a deck of cards.

"You use cards?" blurted Jinnarin.

"At times, tiny one," Aylis answered, "particularly when I wish to demonstrate to others what I have seen." Taking the pack in hand, she began shuffling the deck, blending the cards time and again, and on the final shuffle she murmured, *"Simplicia, propinqua futura: Aylis."* Setting the pack before her, she fanned the deck wide and selected a card at random and turned it faceup. It showed a lightning-struck tower bursting apart, stone blocks flying wide, a person falling from the castellated top. Aylis glanced up at those watching.

"What does it mean?" asked Jinnarin.

Alamar answered. "Disaster."

Aravan reached over and took up the card, commenting, "A single pick does not a future make."

Aylis reassembled the pack and handed it to Aravan. "Captain Aravan, you mix and select."

Aravan cocked an Elven eye her way and slipped the single card into the whole. Then he shuffled the deck, while this time Aylis murmured, *"Simplicia, propinqua futura: Aravan."* At last Aravan spread the cards and selected—

Jinnarin gasped. "The tower!"

Aravan slowly canted up and over one of the end cards of the lapping spread such that the remainder of the cards turned faceup. Revealed was a variety of illustrations—people and places and animals, the Sun, Moon, and stars . . . more—each card different from the others, some representations ordinary, others arcane.

Aylis gazed at Aravan, her green eyes atwinkle. "Did you think they were all towers?"

Aravan smiled at her. "My Lady, wouldst not thou, thyself, scrutinize all ere deciding what may lie within a riddle?"

Aylis's own smile answered his. "Perhaps, Captain, some things should be taken on faith."

"Perhaps," responded Aravan, his grin widening, his eyes lost in hers.

Alamar looked at Jinnarin. "While those two are canoodling, Pysk, would you care to try?"

Jinnarin drew in her breath sharply. "Oh no, Alamar. I don't want to know. Besides, I am too small to handle those cards."

The Mage took up the pack and began shuffling. "Then I'll see what they have to tell me. —Daughter. —Aylis!"

Aylis started, then turned away from Aravan's smile and toward the frown of her father. She gathered her scattered thoughts and whispered, *"Simplicia, propinqua futura: Alamar."*

The Mage spread the deck, his right hand wandering back and forth above the cards, index finger pointing, touching first this one and then that. Finally he teased one facedown card free and pushed it out and away from the deck, the elder glancing up and at Aylis. And then his hand darted back to the spread to select another card altogether. This one he turned over.

It was the tower.

"Blast!" snarled the elder. "I hoped to fool it." Casually he reached out and turned up the card he had pushed to the fore. Jinnarin suppressed a shriek and Aylis turned pale, for portrayed thereon was the skeleton of a Man.

CHAPTER 11

Reflections

Autumn, 1E9574
[The Present]

Northwesterly fared the *Eroean* out into the deep blue waters of the Weston Ocean wide, all of her sails unfurled and driving her full, the wind abeam and brisk. She was bound for a distant Land, her goal some seventeen hundred leagues hence, some five thousand miles away, though tacking as she did, the Elvenship would sail half-again that far. But the *Eroean* was swift, and given fair winds she would be but four to six weeks in the crossing.

Jinnarin sighed. "Four to six weeks. Ai, but I would that we could go faster."

She and Jatu with Rux between sat atop the steps leading up to the low poop behind the aft quarters. Dusk had fallen, swiftly followed by night racing across the waters. And in the gathering darkness Jatu looked down at the tiny Pysk. "Lady Jinnarin, could we catch a constant polar blow abaft, then we would cross in two weeks or less, mayhap in but ten days. Yet such is not the case, for the wind does not come at our beck ... that is, it does not answer *my* summons, though perhaps Mage Alamar could whistle it up."

Jinnarin shook her head. "I don't think so, Jatu. Alamar once told me it took great power to call the wind, to make storms."

Jatu cleared his throat, a deep rumble, then said, "Even the Jujubas of Tchanga, as powerful as they claim they are, make no weather magic of their own . . . though when it is dry for long seasons—so dry that the lakes have dwindled to nothing but pools of stirring dust and the land is pitted and cracked and the trees and vines and brush and grasses are reduced to arid tinder merely waiting for a spark—the Jujubas sometimes call upon the gods and ask for rain."

"And are they answered, Jatu?"

The black Man laughed. "Sometimes, my tiny one. Sometimes. And sometimes the gods bring more rain than is wanted."

"Then, Jatu, those gods must be different from mine, for seldom if ever do Adon and Elwydd answer, no matter how dire the need."

A silence fell between them, and Jatu reached over and petted Rux, scratching him behind the ears, the fox closing his eyes in pleasure. At last Jatu said, "Perhaps, Jinnarin, the Tchangan gods do not answer either. Perhaps instead it is merely the rain come again and the Jujubas simply take the credit . . . or, if the rain is overmuch, blame the gods."

Again a silence fell between the two. Overhead the crescent Moon rode the sky. Jinnarin looked up at the spangle of stars above. After a while she said, "Do you think that much of worship is that way, Jatu? I mean, priests claiming credit for the good things, saying that their prayers were answered, or disclaiming the bad, blaming each dire event as an act of some maleficent, vengeful god."

Jatu grunted. "In my village, Lady Jinnarin, during hard times our Jujuba alleged that the gods were meting out punishment to the tribe, claiming that we deserved whatever woe the gods now descended upon us—be it drought, pestilence, plague, famine, war, or aught else— for we had strayed from the one true way."

Jinnarin looked up at the huge Man. "The one true way? What . . . ?"

"I think the one true way was whatever the Jujuba had decided it should be on a given day." Jatu slammed a fist into an open palm, his look sullen, angry.

Rux peered up at Jatu and then stood and cast about, as if enemies or danger drew nigh, the fox glancing to Jinnarin for any command she might issue.

Yet the Pysk looked not at the fox but instead eyed the Man. "You are ... disturbed, Jatu. Is there anything I can ... ?"

Slowly Jatu relaxed. "I did not mean to give you concern, Lady Jinnarin. I was merely ... remembering."

Once more silence descended between them. After a moment Rux again lay down. The *Eroean* continued slicing through the dark water, the wind yet abeam as it had been for the past two days upon the Weston Ocean.

Without preamble Jatu said, "When I was fourteen, my father was ill and wasting away. No matter what the Jujuba did, my father seemed to slip further into his misery. It was the will of the gods, said the Jujuba.

"One night I followed the Jujuba into the jungle, and there I saw him foraging. He found what he was searching for, a yellow flower, and he dug up its root, pounding it to a pulp, draining the juice into a small clay vessel. The flower is named the viper's eye, and its root sap is poison. The Jujuba mixed this juice into the medicine he was giving my father. When I told my mother, she confronted the Jujuba, and that was when he told her that he wanted her. He tried to force her and that's when I killed him.

"I ran away to escape the punishment of the elders. Then it was that I took to the sea with Captain Aravan. He taught me much—including reading and writing and ciphering ... and language and manners and knowledge of the sea and its ways, and of the sailing of this ship. I was nought but an ignorant lad fleeing from a dark deed when I came aboard, yet thanks to Captain Aravan I am now an officer on the *Eroean*, the best ship in all of the oceans and all of the seas in all of the world. And on this ship I have seen more than any Tchangan child could ever have imagined—marvelous wonders and dangers dire, things precious and deadly and of unsurpassed beauty and charm.

"Years later, I had a chance to go home. There I discovered that my mother was yet alive as was my father, for he had miraculously recovered after the Jujuba was found dead of a broken neck, though a new Jujuba had later come to take the other's place.

"I could have gone back into the tribe then, but by this time it was no longer my way of living.

"And so you see, Lady, given my experience with the Jujubas and their claims concerning the wills of the gods, I hold little faith in religion ... though of late I am beginning to believe in the teachings of Adon."

Jinnarin glanced again at the black Man. "Teachings of Adon? What do you mean, Jatu?"

Jatu shrugged. "Oh, that He created the Planes and the worlds, that He brought forth life unto the waters and the earth and the air. That His daughter, Elwydd, created the peoples of the worlds and gave them free will. That Adon leaves us alone to become whatever we can without His aid or interference."

"Oh," said Jinnarin.

Jatu again ruffled Rux's ears. "I am not at all certain, though, that I believe the rest of it."

"The rest of what?"

Jatu took a deep breath. "The rest of the teachings: that each Folk has a hidden purpose, and that it is our destiny to try to discover what that hidden purpose is. Too, Bokar tells me that each person is reborn time and again and that—"

"Bokar is your mentor?" interjected Jinnarin.

Jatu nodded. "In these teachings, yes."

Jinnarin began to laugh, her tiny voice trilling as would a bird song.

Jatu looked at her in puzzlement.

Finally she managed to gasp out, "Jatu, when you've been converted by Bokar, you will be the tallest Dwarf of all."

Jatu's great belly laughs joined her giggling twitters to ring out over the sea.

A week fled into the past, and now they came to the Doldrums of the Crab, the wind falling to fitful zephyrs first blowing this way and then that, finally dying out altogether, the Elvenship's silk hanging slack—"Caught on the claws of the old pincher, himself," claimed Frizian. Aravan called for the gigs to be unshipped and crews to row them across the unruffled sea, this time heading straight north, the shortest way through the calms.

Aylis and Jinnarin stood in the bow watching as the Men canted their chanteys, oars dipping into the glassy waters, ringlets and riffles spreading outward, the hulls drawing widening wedges behind, vees and circles merging in mingling patterns.

Jinnarin on the stem block stood bewitched by the rhythmic sights and sounds, Aylis just as entranced, Men rowing, voices chanting, sunlight glancing from the ever shifting, never changing ripples spreading 'cross the sea.

At last Jinnarin looked down into the pellucid waters, seeing her own reflection far below. "It was in a mirror such as this that I first saw my true love," she said, breaking the silence between Aylis and her.

Aylis turned, her eyes widening. "You, too?"

"What?" Jinnarin twisted about and stared at Aylis to find the seeress blushing.

"Please say on," said Aylis. "I interrupted."

After a moment, Jinnarin continued. "It was in Darda Glain nearly five thousand years past. Rux and I were—"

Aylis held up a hand. "Wait. How can that be? Rux is a fox, and they are short-lived."

"Oh, it was not this Rux, but another. An ancestor long past. You see, we keep a fox for some seven seasons, and in the last two we raise one of the kits from a litter, training him—in some cases a vixen—to take the place of the sire or dam, calling the kit by the same name."

Aylis tilted her head. "Ah, I see. Then you have always had a Rux, neh?"

The Pysk nodded. "For as long as I can remember."

"Pray, continue."

"Where was I? Oh yes. Rux and I were travelling through the north of Darda Glain. The day was hot, and I asked Rux to find water. Foxes are especially good at that, you know. In any case, he raised his muzzle and scented the air all 'round and then, straight as a bee flies to the comb, Rux ran through the forest, coming at last to a wide mere, the pool shaded by overhanging trees, reeds standing along the banks. It was fed by a small stream, watercress growing in the run, its clusters of white flowers matching the white floating blossoms of the lilies in the mere. Beneath the trees the ground was carpeted by cool moss, and violet blooms nestled down among the brye.

"The water was cool and clear and marvelous, and Rux and I drank our fill. I told Rux that here we would rest, and sent him to find a meal for himself, the watercress would provide ample fare for me. Rux slipped into the woods, and as I watched him go I plucked a blossom from the moss. Thinking to put the bloom in my hair, I knelt on a poolside rock and leaned out over the still water to see my reflection. To my great surprise the face I saw was not my own, and I leapt up and whirled about, looking behind . . . but no one was there. Thinking perhaps it was a water sprite, carefully I peered again into the mere. And there once more was the face. Surrounded by leaves. Then I looked overhead, and there was another Pysk, laughing in the tree above, lying along a branch where he had been watching me.

" 'Ho, my lovely,' he stood and called down, 'I, Farrix, who have never been known to lie, declare that no flower, no matter how fair, can do aught but pale in comparison to your own shining tresses.'

"Well, with such a bold overture, how could I do other than fall in love with him—immediately and completely. But then he did the most foolish thing: without hesitation he dived into the pool—gracefully and cleanly and with hardly a splash. And I screamed in horror—"

Aylis held up a hand. "But why, Jinnarin, why scream? 'Tis clear that he was merely trying to impress you. There is nothing of horror in that."

"Oh, Aylis, it is plain to see that you are not a Pysk. Think you what would have happened had there been a great trout or pike living in that pool. For me or anyone of my size, 'twould have been swish, gulp, and good-bye. And that's why I screamed in horror, for had there been such a monster lurking below, Farrix would not have survived. Fortunately, there was not, and my newfound love was not eaten."

Aylis mouthed a silent *O* of understanding.

"I could see him swimming underwater to my rock, but he didn't emerge and didn't emerge and didn't emerge. I became frightened for him and when I knelt down and leaned over to see if he was caught on a root or trapped in some manner, he popped up and kissed me and laughed. Now I ask you, how could I not love him?

"And when he climbed out he bowed deeply to me,

his grin lighting up the whole world, and he said, 'In case you have forgotten, my name is Farrix and I never lie, and my fox there behind you is Rhu.' "

Once again Jinnarin leaned over the wale and peered down at the placid sea rising and falling below. And as gentle swells from the towing rowers passed across the undulant surface she said, "And that's where I first saw the face of my true love—reflected in a mirrored pool."

Six days and nights it took to escape the claws of the Crab, for upon the dawn of the seventh morn they haled into a light wind, Reydeau piping the tow-crew aboard, Rico piping up the hoisting of sail, and ere the break of fast the *Eroean* was once again cutting the waves, her white wake churning behind.

It was on this same morn, though, that Jinnarin woke refreshed after a peaceful night of sleep. And the moment she realized such, she burst into tears. Rux whined in anxiety, licking at his mistress's face, and he cast about for sign of threat, finding nought.

"What's all this ruckus?" called Alamar, knocking on the wooden wall of Jinnarin's under-bunk quarters.

"Oh, Alamar," sobbed Jinnarin, "I slept the night through."

"Eh?" Alamar rattled the tiny door.

Jinnarin opened the panel and stepped into Alamar's room. "I said, I slept the night through."

A frown came over the Mage's face. "Oh my, not good. Not good at all."

Jinnarin, sobbing, plopped down on the floor, burying her face in her hands, whining Rux alternately nudging her and glaring at Alamar, as if to place blame.

"No dream at all?" asked the Mage.

Without looking up, Jinnarin shook her head.

"Not of any kind?"

Again Jinnarin shook her head, *No*.

"Well, Pysk, we will just have to wait and see."

Snubbing, at last Jinnarin looked up. "Wh-what might it m-mean, Alamar?"

Alamar stroked his white beard. "Any number of things, not all of them bad."

"Such as . . . ?"

"Look, just because you didn't have your usual nightmare, it doesn't mean—"

"Don't try to cozen me, Alamar! Tell me straight out."

Alamar sighed. "Well ... it could be that whoever is sending this vision was troubled last night and too busy to cast you your nightmare. Likewise, it could be that he or she no longer needs to send the dream—why? I know not. Perhaps his problem is resolved. On the other hand, the sender could be injured or ..." The Mage fell silent, his words sputtering to a halt.

"Go ahead, Alamar, you can say it: the sender could be injured or dead!"

Chapfallen, Alamar nodded, and at this confirmation again Jinnarin burst into tears. Now Rux growled a warning at Alamar but made no move toward the Mage.

At last Alamar spoke, saying, "Let us ask Aylis. Mayhap she will know ... or can find out."

Aylis stared into the small silver basin of jet black water, her face reflected from the ebon surface. Her emerald eyes were lost in intense concentration, and sweat beaded on her brow. To one side stood Aravan, his own features filled with concern. Alamar sat across the table, and Jinnarin kneeled in front of the dark liquid, peering deep within. The portholes were blackened out, and a single taper burned in a silver candlestick on the table beside the Pysk.

"*Patefac!*" demanded Aylis for the fifth or sixth time, a strain in her voice, but the raven-dark water did not change.

"*Patefac!*" she gritted again.

Yet nought altered in the silver bowl, and with a groan Aylis slumped back, her eyes closed.

Jinnarin gasped, and Aravan leapt forward, catching up the seeress's hand. "My Lady Aylis," he called, chafing her wrist.

"I am all right," she murmured. "Just exhausted. The shield ... it is too strong. Beyond my power to discern aught past."

Aravan touched her hand to his cheek, and she looked up at him, startlement in her gaze. He smiled and sat beside her and clasped her cold fingers between his two warm hands.

Tears welled in Jinnarin's eyes. "I am so afraid," she said, her voice quavering.

Alamar sighed. "I don't think that there's anything to be afraid of—"

"Oh, Alamar," burst out Jinnarin, "I am not afraid *of* something. Instead I am afraid *for* Farrix."

"Look, Pysk, we don't even know who is sending this dream, much less whether it has anything to do with Farrix."

"Father"—Aylis's voice came quietly—"I deem that Jinnarin has cause to worry, for who else would send such a vision to her?"

"But, Daughter, 'tis a nightmare, this dream. Would Farrix send such to his love?"

Jinnarin leapt to her feet and paced back and forth upon the table, and in the flicker of candlelight, shadows seemed to gather about her and disperse and gather and disperse and—"Alamar, you said yourself that dreams are oft not what they seem. Farrix would not deliberately send me a nightmare."

Aylis glanced at the Pysk and then to her sire. "She is right, Father. Besides, the vision she sees—the storm, the black ship, the pale green sea, the crystal castle— these things in and of themselves are not frightening. Instead, there is something else in her dream that brings fear with it, something that remains unseen."

Alamar grunted in acknowledgement. "And, Daughter, you have no idea as to what it might be, or of the meaning of the dream itself?"

Aylis made a negating gesture with her free hand. "None. As I said when Jinnarin first told me of her vision, it seems indeed to be a sending, yet what it means, I cannot say, for I could not then nor can I yet see unto the source."

Alamar stood and shuffled to one of the three curtained portholes on the starboard side. "Let's get some light in here," he growled, sliding back the velvet drape.

As the bright morning Sun streamed into the captain's lounge, Aylis reluctantly freed her hand from Aravan's and snuffed out the candle. The Elf stood and stepped to the larboard ports and slid back the covering cloths.

Jinnarin plopped back down to the tabletop and sat with her legs drawn up and her arms wrapped about her knees. "What can I do, Aylis?" she asked, a tormented look on her face.

"Oh, Jinnarin, there is little you *can* do. Merely wait, that's all. It may be that Farrix, if indeed he is the sender, is tiring, for it takes energy to give a dream unto another."

A tear rolled down Jinnarin's cheek. "Tiring? You mean weakening, don't you?"

Aylis turned up her hands. "I don't know, Jinnarin. I simply do not know."

Over the next several days, Jinnarin went about the decks of the *Eroean* in poor spirits and weary. Her days were cheerless and her nights filled with fitful sleep, the Pysk tossing and turning and unable to rest, for no nightmare plagued her dreams. All the crew noted her downtrodden stance and a glumness fell upon them as well. Even Rux seemed dispirited, his tail hanging lank, and his hunting of rats and mice fell to nought.

"We must do something about this," said Finch to Arlo and Rolly and Carly, the carpenter and sailmaker and tinsmith and cooper concerned over Jinnarin's despondent state. "Our Pysk is disheartened and needs cheering up, she does."

"How about music?" asked Rolly. "I could play me pipe."

"Sea stories," suggested Arlo, "we have some tales that'd set your hair on fire, we do. Mayhap that'll take her mind off her bother, wotever it might be."

"How about a spree of sorts, wot d'y' say?" chimed in Carly. "We c'd get Trench 'r Hogar t' make a cake, wot?"

"Celebrating wot?" asked Rolly. "I mean, sprees is for something or other—a victory, a remembrance, an anniversary, wotever."

"How 'bout twelve years since I come aboard?" asked Lobbie, the sailor lying on his bunk and listening to the four.

Rolly and Finch and Arlo and Carly looked at one another then shrugged. "Seeing as there is no objections," declared Finch. . . .

And so it was that a celebration was engendered—Lobbie's Dozen, it was called.

And two days later as evening drew down upon the *Eroean*, lanterns were lit and all hands gathered on deck and a shipboard spree was held. Songs were sung and tales were told and arm-in-arm jigs were danced.

Some of Bokar's warband demonstrated their skills with axes, whirling the double-bitted blades about, casting them spinning into the air, catching them by their oaken helves, clanging steel on steel with one another while stepping through an intricate drill, all cheered on by their fellow crew mates.

Alamar the Mage juggled balls of light and pulled vanishing doves and disappearing fish from the hair and beards of various members of the crew, to the *Oooo*s and *Ahhh*s of the others. Why, he even pulled a huge red jewel right out from Bokar's left ear, he did, the giant ruby to turn into sparkles and twinkle away even as the armsmaster reached for it, the onlookers howling in glee.

And then, while Lobbie played the squeeze box and Rolly his pipe and Burdun banged on his drum and all the Men and the Dwarves stomped in time and clapped their hands, Captain Aravan and Lady Aylis danced a wild, wild fling, stepping and prancing and whirling about and laughing into each other's eyes. And when they were done a mighty shout rang up into the sky, and the Captain picked up the Lady by her waist and spun her around and planted a kiss on her lips, and wild pandemonium reigned, sailors and warriors alike cheering in reckless abandon.

When this madness died down, Trench and Hogar, with Tink and Tivir helping, brought out the cakes and a vat of green brew, this latter made from limes. And upon one cake were written the words, *Lobbies Duzzen,* and this one they set before Lobbie for him to cut and serve.

And as the Men and Dwarves and Mages and Elf partook of the cake and sipped on their cups of green squall—for so the lime drink was named—a Pysk and her fox took center deck, Jinnarin mounted upon Rux.

Jinnarin whispered something to her fox and commenced a measured clapping of her hands.

Slowly, slowly, did Rux begin, following Jinnarin's stately beat, the fox pacing an arcane pattern.

Step, step, turn and pause. Step, step, and turn.

The crew looked on, their eyes following Pysk and fox, wonder in their gaze.

Step, step, turn and pause. Step, step, and turn.

Gradually, gradually, the beat increased, Rux keeping pace.

Step, step, turn and pause. Step, step, and turn.

And all the onlookers stood entranced, cake and brew forgotten.

Step, step, turn and pause. Step, step, turn.

Faster came the beat, faster paced the fox. And a member of the crew took up the rhythm, clapping in time with Jinnarin.

Step, step, turn and pause. Step, step, turn.

More joined in, and more. And still the pace increased, Rux no longer stepping stately but now prancing through the gait.

Step, step, turn and pause, step, step, turn.

Pysk on fox, Jinnarin's hands free and clapping, still the beat increased.

Step step turn and break, step step turn.

Now someone began to stomp in time, others joining in.

Step touch turn break step touch turn.

"Hai, hai, hai, hai . . . !" called out Jinnarin, clapping even faster, her voice sharp and piercing, Rux's feet now but a blur, the clapping hands and stomping feet of the crew climbing in deafening crescendo, Men and Dwarves crying out a raw wordless shout.

Touch touch turn hitch touch touch turn, Rux whirling and gyring yet keeping pace with the frenetic beat and dancing a tattoo.

And of a sudden—*"Ya hoi!"*—cried Jinnarin, Rux leaping high, landing, spinning, leaping high again, Jinnarin dismounting even as they were in the air and coming down beside the fox to alight simultaneously with him.

And as the crew went mad, Jinnarin and Rux both bowed 'round to all, and Jatu, roaring in delight, swooped out and scooped Jinnarin up and set her on his shoulder and with Rux following marched among the howling crew, shouting, "The Lady Jinnarin and Rux! The Lady Jinnarin and Rux!" all joining in, Jinnarin smiling and bowing her head to each and every one.

And among the clamor, four sailors—Finch and Arlo and Rolly and Carly—looked at one another and grinned great grins even though tears brimmed their eyes. For with her dolor broken, they deemed the party they had given to cheer up a single soul to be an unqualified smashing success.

Their Pysk was well again.

CHAPTER 12

Shadows

Autumn, 1E9574
[The Present]

Through the prevailing westerlies fared the *Eroean*, running long reaches across the wind, tacking only as necessary, trimming now and again as the air shifted. North and west she sailed aiming for the western continent, where only uncivilized forest folk were said to dwell.

Jinnarin's sprightly mood had generally returned, though still there were days when she seemed glum. At these times any number of persons would try to cheer her—Jatu, Aravan, Bokar, Tink, Tivir, and others of the ship's crew, as well as Aylis. On occasion even crotchety Alamar tried, though he typically broke her doleful moods by getting into arguments with her, inadvertently most of the time.

But time and again it was to Jatu that Jinnarin turned for comfort, the big black Man listening with a sympathetic ear, offering little by way of advice, now and then restoring her spirits by telling her tales of his childhood in his Tchangan village as well as stories of the sea. Too, Rux found Jatu to his liking—and to Jinnarin's way of thinking anyone who gained Rux's trust would gain hers as well. And so it was that a giant of a Man became the confidant of a tiny Pysk.

Three nights after the spree, Jatu stood at the wheel of the *Eroean*, guiding on the fixed northern star, steering the Elvenship across the wind in the crystal night.

From the corner of his eye, Jatu saw movement, and he watched in amazement as a scanty cluster of shadow glided silently up the steps and across the poop deck.

"Hullo, Jatu," said the shadow, speaking in a tiny clear voice.

"Lady Jinnarin? Is that you?" Jatu rubbed his eyes.

A sigh was his only answer.

"My, my, in a dark mood, are we?" Then Jatu barked a sharp laugh.

"What's so funny, Jatu?"

"I made a jest without knowing," he answered.

"Jest?"

"Aye. There you stand wrapped all in shadow, and I ask if you are in a dark mood."

"Wrapped in—? Oh." Suddenly the shadow dispersed, revealing the Pysk.

"Ah, much better, Lady Jinnarin. I like to see you when we talk." Jatu made a small correction of the wheel. "Besides, I did not know that you had such a power."

Jinnarin sat glumly on the deck, cross-legged, her elbows on her splayed knees, her chin on her fists. "I don't think of it as a power."

"Oh my, but it is, Jinnarin. Shadows have great power."

"They do?"

Jatu nodded. "Why, some say that the shadow is the very soul of a person, and that if you cut it away with an enchanted silver knife at high noon on Year's Long Day, it will be lost forever—just as you yourself will be lost, too, a priceless essence gone away from you."

"Surely, Jatu, you don't believe that."

"Mayhap I do, mayhap not. But if I ever see a Man or aught else without a shadow, I will know him to be without a soul."

"Would you run?"

"It depends, tiny one. It depends."

"On what?"

"On whether or not there was a need to flee."

"Oh."

Jatu made another small correction of the wheel, trimming against the westerly. After a moment he said,

"Still, that is but one tale of shadows and their powers. There are other tales as well."

Jinnarin peered up at the Tchangan. "Other tales?"

"Aye. Would you like to hear one?"

"All right."

Jatu stood silent for a moment, then began:

"Long past and far to the north of Tchanga, where the jungle gives way to grasses and they in turn give way to a vast desert lying beyond the mountains where the great eagles fly, in the heart of the burning wasteland there dwelled a demon beside a crystal pool in a heavy-laden grove of pomegranate trees. Now you must realize that this was a marvelous place, being in the core of sandy furnace as it was, for water is priceless in such a fiery realm, and to have the precious gift of pomegranates as well ... ai, it was as if a part of paradise itself had fallen unto the earth.

"Now it so happens that one day while the demon was in the golden city on the other side of the world tending to several of his many affairs, a young Man whose caravan had been attacked by robbers and he himself left for dead, a young Man who came stumbling and reeling over the burning dunes and falling and crawling and lurching to his feet only to stumble and reel and fall and crawl again, a young Man who was delirious and within a hairsbreadth of death, that young Man came slithering on his belly down a last long dune and into the oasis of the demon.

"And the young Man plunged his face into the crystal pool and drank deeply.

"And at that very moment across the world in the golden city the demon screamed, 'Someone is stealing my water!' And in fury he flew up into the sky and raced across the world.

"But ere the demon could get to the oasis, the young Man plucked a pomegranate from one of the trees and bit into the flesh, red juices staining his lips and running down to drip from his chin.

"And the demon, who by this time was halfway there, shrieked, 'Someone is stealing my pomegranates!'

"Onward flew the demon, maddened with rage, and when he came to his oasis he found the exhausted young Man asleep, his thirst quenched, his hunger sated.

"Reaching out with his long claws, the wrathful demon was on the verge of rending the youth asunder. But of a sudden the demon bethought to himself, 'Ai, I could tear him to shreds with my mighty talons, but would he truly suffer as he should? Nay! He would be dead ere he even awakened. And I would not have him get off so easily; instead I want to make him agonize for the remainder of his life for his heinous crimes against me.'

"And so the demon drew back his swordlike talons and did not rend the young Man to ribbons. Instead he went to his nearby forge, and—bellows whooshing, fire roaring, hammer clanging—he began crafting a magic nail, muttering all the while.

"Now the clamor and clash of this noise served to awaken the young Man, and he crept near to discover the source of the thunderous din. And when he saw the demon at work he was sore afraid, yet he crouched down behind a rock and watched and listened.

"And in between mighty hammer strokes he heard the demon cursing: 'Steal *my* water, would he?'—*clang!*—'And eat my pomegranates, *too?*'—*clang!*—'This will fix him forever'—*clang!*—'A punishment to fit the crime'—*clang!*

"The young Man immediately knew that the demon was crafting some magical item to punish him for nothing more than saving his own life. Oh, how he did fret, wondering what to do. He knew that appealing to the demon for mercy was futile, for demons have no mercy. He knew, too, that he could not flee, for the demon would find him no matter where he ran. He could not fight the demon, for demons have enormous strength and terrible claws and tusks and fangs. The young Man was in despair, for how could he, an ordinary mortal, hope to escape the hideous fate of the demon, whatever that might be?

"At that very moment the demon cried, 'Ha! It is done!' and he turned away from the anvil and began rummaging about in a great tool chest.

"In stillness the young Man crept forward and saw what appeared to be an ordinary nail lying on the anvil. Quickly, he substituted a nail from a nearby barrel of nails for the demon-forged one, slipping the demon-forged nail into his waistband. And, although he did not know what the nail was for, he took up a nearby hammer and slipped that into his waistband as well. And then swiftly and silently he ran back to the poolside and lay down and feigned deep sleep.

"Shortly came the demon who shook the young Man by the shoulder and roared, 'Wake up, robber, miscreant, thief! Accept your just punishment!'

"The young Man sat up and rubbed his eyes and yawned. 'Punishment? How so? What for?'

" 'For drinking my water!' roared the demon, and with a wave of his hand the pool disappeared. 'And now it lies where you'll never reach it, ninety-nine leagues to the east!'

" 'You punish me for drinking water!' cried the young Man. 'Oh how terribly unjust and cruel.'

" 'And for eating my pomegranates!' roared the demon, and with a wave of his hand the grove disappeared. 'And now they lie where you'll never reach them, ninety-nine leagues to the west!'

" 'You punish me for eating fruit?' cried the young Man as the hot Sun shone down from above, now that the shade was gone. 'Oh how unjust and cruel.'

" 'Unjust and cruel? You know not the half of it!' roared the demon, and he waved his hand again and now the sand underfoot became a vast adamant rock. 'I'll show you how unjust and cruel I can be.'

"The demon knelt down and with a hammer he nailed the young Man's shadow to the rock. And at the youth's puzzled look, the demon laughed a wicked laugh and said, 'Now you are trapped here forever, and any magic you might have had is gone. You may travel only as far as your shadow permits, nailed as it is to this forever rock by my unremovable spike. You may run anywhere you wish, as long as your shadow falls across the nail. Now what do you think of that?'

"The young Man knelt at the demon's feet and said, 'Oh, demon, it is a cruel, cruel punishment, a punishment fit only for one who is just as cruel.' And with that he hammered the true magic nail into the demon's own shadow.

"The demon roared in pain and made a grab at the Man, but the youth was too agile and swift and leapt away, beyond the reach of the demon. And the demon waved his hands in arcane patterns, but all of his magic was gone. And he bent down and tugged at the unremovable nail, but it did not budge from the forever rock. And weeping and gnashing his teeth, the demon cursed the young Man, dreadful words rolling off the demon's forked tongue, calling for crows to pluck out the youth's eyes, for foul disease to rot his bowels, for virulent sand wyrms to poison him—all to no avail for the demon's power had vanished.

"The young Man struck out across the desert and nearly died ere he was rescued by a passing caravan.

"The demon, though, was trapped by the nail hammered through his shadow. In the dark of the night, when there was no Moon, he could travel wherever he wished, for in the blackness his shadow was everywhere, and so he was free to roam. But at sunrise every day he was compelled to be east in order for his shadow to fall across the nail—oh, he could be leagues and leagues to the east, just as long as his shadow was pinned. But as the day grew toward noon and his shadow shortened, he had to move westerly, and as the Sun came to the zenith, he had to stand on the nail, for the Sun was directly overhead and his shadow directly underfoot. And as the Sun sank in the west, to the west the demon could fare, his shadow cast easterly behind him and lying over the nail.

"But the greatest irony of all was that at ninety-nine leagues to the east and west the pool of crystal water and the grove of pomegranate trees were just barely beyond the demon's reach, where he could see them but never sip the refreshing water nor taste of the sweet fruit, the tantalizing prizes right where he had placed them to torment an innocent young Man.

"The demon roared in rage and wept in frustration and slaughtered any wayfarer unfortunate enough to come within his reach, and soon the region became a place to shun for there a demon dwelled. They say that even unto this day the desert in that compass is unsafe at night, for the demon yet roams the waste, and he is terribly angry and terribly strong.

"They also say that at high noon you can see the demon, standing still in the sunlight like a great tall rock, faintly stained red as if from pomegranates eaten long past.

"They also say that other demons heard of this one's plight and they came to see for themselves, and they shuddered in terror at his dire fate, and although they tried to free him they did not succeed, for the spells he had cast were entirely too strong for any of them to break.

"And they say that the demons took an enchanted silver knife and tried to cut away the trapped one's shadow at high noon on Year's Long Day, but the magic in the charmed nail was beyond the power of the silver blade and so they abandoned that plan.

"And lastly they say that the terrified demons cut away their own shadows that day, so that they themselves could never suffer such a dread fate . . .

". . . And now, Lady Jinnarin, you know the whole of the tale and why demons are without souls, all but one that is, and that demon's soul is nailed firmly to a rock, surrounded by hot, burning sands."

Jatu broke out in deep laughter, and Jinnarin beside him was wreathed in smiles.

After a moment she said, "Thank you, Jatu, that was just what I needed."

Jatu grinned and adjusted the wheel a bit.

Water slid past the hull, the ocean churning into phosphorescent wake swiftly left behind, while overhead the stars sparkled and twinkled and slowly wheeled through the vault above. Somewhere on the deck a voice rose in song, a plaintive descant in a language which neither Jinnarin nor Jatu knew. And down on the main deck strolling into view came Aylis and Aravan, and these two stopped and leaned over the rail and watched the starlit water glide past.

"Hmm," murmured Jatu.

"What?" asked Jinnarin.

"I was just thinking . . . speculating."

Jinnarin waited. At last Jatu said, "I deem that Captain Aravan is like to lose his shadow to the Lady Aylis."

Jinnarin frowned, puzzled. "Lose his shad—? Oh, I see. And yes, I think you are right, but she will give him hers in return."

*   *   *

That night Jinnarin awakened covered with sweat and trembling, her heart pounding in fear, and she was ecstatic. "Alamar!" she shouted, slamming out through the tiny under-bunk door and into his quarters, Rux scrambling up and following after, "It's back! My nightmare is back! Oh, I feel so good!"

Nought but a snore greeted her joyous announcement.

Northwesterly fared the *Eroean,* each day covering leagues upon leagues, drawing nearer to the distant goal. Southwest of Gelen they sailed, though that island Realm was far too distant for any to see, lying some one hundred miles north of their course, beyond the vision of even the lookouts atop the tall masts above. The weather stayed fair for the most part, though now and again it did rain. And the ocean remained a deep blue expanse, ceaseless in its movement, like some great creature breathing in and out, waves rolling across its heaving surface. At times fish could be seen, schooling, racing, veering. Occasionally, too, there were flocks of seabirds, wheeling, diving, plunging after fry. And one day were seen whales—"Lords of the sea," said Aravan. Occasionally a distant sail would be glimpsed, or a lone soaring bird, but for the most part from horizon to horizon the vista was empty of visible life. But then one day—

"Smudge ho!" called the foremast lookout. "Smudge ho on the starboard bow!"

Standing on the stemblock, Jinnarin looked. There to the north and low against the distant horizon hung a dark stream in the air.

"What is it?" she asked, turning to Aylis and Aravan. "Cloud or smoke?—Oh, Aravan, is a ship on fire and sinking?"

The Elf shook his head. "I think not, Lady Jinnarin," answered the Elf. "Instead I would say that it is Karak."

"Karak?"

Without taking her eyes from the smear in the sky, Aylis said, "The firemountain on Atala. Now and again it stirs, Jinnarin, sending ash and smoke into the air."

"How about molten rock? I hear that firemountains sometimes issue such."

Aylis nodded. "At times, though not within my memory. What say you, Aravan?"

Aravan reflected back. "I recall that the last time Karak sent molten stone flowing was some three or four thousand summers past. Exactly when, I cannot say. I had been on Mithgar for perhaps one or two thousand summers."

Nearby, a sailor coiling a rope gasped in astonishment and stared at Aravan, dumbfounded by the age of his captain, though neither Aylis nor Jinnarin found aught remarkable in the Elf's words.

"Is that where you crossed over?" asked the seeress.

Aravan shook his head. "Nay, Aylis. I could have though, for on that island is an In-Between place connecting Atala with Adonar. I came instead into Hoven, near the shores of the Avagon Sea. There is where I saw my first ocean, and it sang to my soul."

Jinnarin sighed. "I don't know where my parents crossed over into Mithgar from Feyer. All I know is that many of my people fled to Rwn when the Humans began hunting us down. I was just a youngster at the time." The Pysk shuddered, and in her mind she could hear the blaring of horns and the baying of hounds and the thunder of horses' hooves, that and the headlong splashing of foxes running through water, desperately evading the hunt. "I never got a chance to ask them."

Silence fell among the three, and they watched as the smudge on the horizon fell to the aft and away. Finally Aylis said, "Well, it is no mystery where we of the Mage world cross over. On the island of Rwn is the only known passage twixt Vadaria and Mithgar. Even so, it is but a pallid match, and it takes long in the ritual to go between."

"Couldst thou not step first unto Adonar and thence unto Mithgar?" asked Aravan. "Or even unto Neddra first?"

Aylis shook her head. "Mithgar seems to be a nexus for us, the only way for Magekind to gain access unto other worlds, other Planes."

Aravan grunted. "Curious, I think neither Adonar nor Neddra nor any other world has a crossing into Rwn—only your Vadaria, and if Vadaria in turn has but a single In-Between unto Rwn and nowhere else ... I find that passing strange."

Aylis shrugged. "I repeat, Aravan, Rwn has the only *known* crossing. There may be others as of yet undiscovered."

Aravan turned up his palms. "Even so, for the Mage world to have but a single crossover ..."

Jinnarin giggled, and when Aravan and Aylis gave her questioning looks, the Pysk said, "Perhaps Adon made it that way so that Mithgar would not be overrun by Alamars."

Aravan broke out in laughter, and Aylis smiled. Aravan then reached out and took Aylis by the hand, his bold blue eyes catching at her green. "How could an irascible elder as is your father have such a wondrous daughter as thee?"

Aylis smiled at the Elf, not looking away, her gaze just as bold. "He gets like this when he is aged—crotchety, querulous, argumentative, secretive, overfond of ale, wine, brandy, and other spirits. Yet he will change considerably when he returns to Vadaria and regains his youth, for he will also regain his resilience and his winning ways."

Jinnarin looked surprised. "He will change?"

Aylis turned to the Pysk. "Oh yes. Then his querulous manner will be completely gone, though I must admit he will still have his argumentative moments."

"Oh my," fretted Jinnarin, "I am not at all certain I will welcome that. You see, I like him just as he is."

Freeing her hand from Aravan's grasp, Aylis knelt by the stemblock, her eyes level with those of the Pysk. "So do I, Jinnarin. Yet I love him as a youth, too. And so, I believe, will you."

Jinnarin smiled tentatively. "Well, it's just that, as he is, he makes me think ... really think. Why, he asked me a question months ago which I am still puzzling out."

Aylis laughed and stood again. "Believe me, Jinnarin, *that* will not change."

Again a silence fell among them, and they watched as the smudge slowly disappeared over the horizon aft.

When it was gone, Aravan glanced down at Jinnarin. "Tell me, Lady Jinnarin, how didst thou and thy Kind get to Rwn?"

Jinnarin smiled. "There are Friends other than yourself, Aravan, people who can be trusted—Magekind for the most—and they bore us there on ships."

Aravan sighed. "I was hoping that thou and thy Kind had gone by some fabled means—on the backs of Great Eagles, or by Gryphon, or borne on the fins of the Children of the Sea. Instead I find nought but ordinary means transported ye all there."

"Oh, Aravan, I did not say that 'ordinary' means were used . . . only that we went by ship. The merchant men who sailed us across thought that we were livestock—sheep, cattle, horses, dogs, poultry, and the like—as mazed as were their minds. The Friends who made the trip possible, well, let us simply say that they had considerable influence on the captain and his crew."

Aravan grinned. "Powerful Friends, indeed."

Aylis looked over at the Elf. "Tell me, Aravan, how did you become a Friend of the Hidden Ones?"

" 'Tis a simple tale," answered Aravan. "When I rove the seas on the Dragonships of the Fjordlanders—"

"Dragonships?" Jinnarin exclaimed. "What are Dragonships?"

"Long, open-hulled ships. Square-sailed, oar-driven boats. Narrow of beam and swift. A hundred or so feet in length, but only twenty wide. And they measured but seven feet from keel to top wale. Shallow draft and lightweight, they are. Klinker built and flexible— But wait, I burden thee with detail. Let me just say that it was while plying the oceans in the Fjordsmen's longboats that I began to understand the relationships between hull length and width and draft and speed, for no other ships in the world sailed as fast . . . that is until the *Eroean*, and her slim design owes much unto the Dragonboats."

Jinnarin glanced about at the Elvenship, with her three tall masts and cloud of sails and the watertight deck atop her hull. The Dragonship Aravan had just described didn't seem related at all to the *Eroean*. "Someday I would like to see one of these longships," she said. "In the meanwhile, please continue. You were roving the sea in a Dragonship, and . . ."

"And we sailed across the Weston Ocean beyond the blue known sea unto the land afar, where the Fjordsmen traded for furs with strange-speaking Men, clannish in their ways, peaceful unless provoked.

"While on one of these trading voyages we put to shore for water. I had taken a cask and began a hike inland. It was a blustery day, but above the gusts I heard the distant barking of foxes, and having no better way to go, I journeyed toward that sound.

"And then I smelled smoke, and as I topped the next ridge, on a facing slope I saw the woods afire. And from that conflagration came the barking cry of foxes.

"I ran down and through a stream and up to the burn. Beyond the blazes I could see two foxes, trapped by encircling flames. But lo! there, too, were a pair of tiny people, Hidden Ones, Fox Riders they were.

"Back to the brook I dashed, plunging into the water, wetting myself down, soaking my cloak. And then sopping wet and streaming water, drenched cloak in hand, back I ran, plunging through the encircling flames to come into the fire itself, blinding smoke all about.

" 'To me! To me!' I shouted, dropping to the earth, covering my head with the cloak, the fire roaring up among the treetops so loud that I could but barely hear mine own voice.

"Yet others heard me as well, and the two mounted Fox Riders came to my side. 'Hold on to my clothes,' I called, scooping a fox up under each arm, the twain riders grabbing on as best they could. And beneath my drenched cloak, now steaming in the heat, back through the flames I dashed and down the hill, plunging again into the stream.

" 'Twas Tarquin and his mate, Falain, I saved that day. And thereafter I was declared a Friend of the Hidden Ones."

Aylis reached out and took Aravan's hand in her own, saying nought.

But Jinnarin said, "And that's when he—when Tarquin gave you the wardstone, neh?"

Aravan touched the small blue stone at his throat. "Yes."

Aylis looked, her eyes widening slightly. "It has power, yet I am not familiar with its manner."

Aravan slipped it over his head and handed it to Aylis. "It grows cold when things of utter vileness are about."

Jinnarin's own eyes now widened. "I just realized, Aravan, that it detects evil."

Aravan shook his head. "Nay, tiny one, not evil. Instead only some of the foul creatures capable of causing harm."

Aylis passed the stone back to Aravan. "Such as . . . ?"

"Such as creatures from Neddra—Rucha, Loka, Trolls, Gargoni, and the like." Aravan slipped the thong back around his neck. "Too, it grows cold in the presence of Hèlarms—Krakens—as well as some Dragons, though not all—"

"You have seen Dragons?" blurted Jinnarin.

Aravan smiled and nodded. "But not up close, Lady Jinnarin. Not up close."

Aylis reached out and touched the blue stone again. "Tell me what creatures of evil intent it does not detect."

"Humans who are vile," answered Aravan. "Pirates, thieves, brigands, and the like: these it does not warn of. Nor of other Mithgarian Races whose intentions are vile."

"Dwarves?" asked Jinnarin.

Aravan smiled and shook his head. "I deem thou shouldst not let Bokar or any of the warband hear that comment, Lady Jinnarin, for Dwarves hold honor above all else."

Aylis loosed the amulet. "From its astral fire, with few exceptions, I ween that it will detect nothing of Adon's or Elwydd's creations."

"But that's practically everything," protested Jinnarin.

Aylis shook her head. "Nay, it is not."

Jinnarin thought a moment. "But that only leaves . . ."

In that instant Alamar came shuffling onto the foredeck. "That's right, Pysk," he called. "It only leaves the creatures of Gyphon."

That night Jinnarin's dreams were filled with scenes of forests and fields, of streams and pools, of flowers and of everyday tasks. She had no sending, no dream of dread, and she awoke filled with misery, for once more her nightmare had fled.

But the following night, again it was back, and she awoke atremble in sweat.

Yet afterward it was gone for four nights running, ere returning on the fifth.

"Sporadic," declared Alamar.

"He is weakening," wept Jinnarin. "Oh, my Farrix dwindles."

"I can see nought," said Aylis wearily, "though Adon knows I have tried."

Under a full Moon of the third night of November of the year 1E9574, the *Eroean* dropped anchor in the shelter of a headland along the rocky shores of the western continent, six weeks and six days after setting sail from Port Arbalin. Her crossing of the Avagon Sea and of the Weston Ocean had been swift but by no means spectacularly so, for the Elvenship in the past had made the same journey in as few as four weeks and two days. Even so, Aravan was satisfied that the ship had done as well as could be expected, given the state of the winds, though Rico was certain that they had lost a day overall, while others disputed his claim.

We took a solemn oath to Lady Jinnarin ... fought pirates ... rescued the Lady Aylis ... rowed for days to get out o' the grasp of the claws of the Crab ... why, we even had a shipboard spree. Now given all of that, don't you think, Rico, as we done as well as could be expected?

By damn, no! I t'ink we be one day faster do we row better. Next time, eh?

Regardless as to whether the trip could have been swifter, the fact was that the *Eroean* now lay at anchor along a shore where Fox Riders were said to dwell. And on the morrow, Aravan and the Lady Jinnarin and Rux, along with Alamar and the Lady Aylis, would go inland and seek out Tarquin, though just what aid he might give them, none aboard the Elvenship knew.

CHAPTER 13

Ashore

Autumn, 1E9574
[The Present]

Just after dawn two gigs were lowered, one with Alamar and Jinnarin and Rux aboard, while Aravan and Aylis climbed down a ladder after, a rowing crew boarding as well. The other gig took on a mixed band of sailors and Dwarven warriors, Jatu and Bokar among these. With sailors manning the oars, toward the rocky shore they rowed, the gigs riding in on the high tide. A thin shingle of sand rimmed a tiny cove, rough crags rising above, and toward this landing they made their way.

"Look smart, anow!" called Boder to the rowers, the helmsman manning the tiller. "A bit more on the larboard oars, lads. Now steady. Steady.... Now hard!"

The gig rode in on the crest of a wave to scrape against rocky sand. Forward, two sailors jumped over the wales and haled the boat up, riding the next wave onto the landing. Five yards away the second boat settled into the shore as well.

Clambering over the side, Alamar looked up at the craggy rise. "Why is it that adventures always seem to involve difficult obstacles. Just once, mind you, once, I would like to go on an undertaking where level grassy lawns are all that is ventured, and the goal nearby at that."

Jatu laughed. "Ah, but Mage Alamar, what then would the bards sing of? How Alamar the Great walked upon grass a few hundred feet and then rested for a while?" Again the big black Man laughed, while Alamar cast him a scowl.

"Eh, I don't care what the bards sing of, you big idiot. I'd rather walk on level grass than climb up rocks."

"Father, you don't *have* to go."

"Oh no? Well let me ask you, young lady, just who do you think saved the ship from the Rovers, eh?"

Jinnarin shook her head. "No Rovers here, Alamar."

"Of course not, Pysk. I'm not a complete fool, you know. Savages though, well, that's a different matter."

"Leave any savages to me," growled Bokar, the Dwarf thumbing the edge of his axe.

"Nay, Bokar," spoke up Aravan. "Any so-called savages are my province, for I have been here many times before and they know of me."

Aylis looked at Aravan. "How long past?"

"Most recently?—mayhap a hundred summers, no more."

"Then are they like to remember?"

Aravan nodded. "My ship and I are now woven into their lore."

"Well, I'm going up now," said Jinnarin. "The last thing I want is for the Humans of this Land to see me."

"Hold!" called Bokar, but he was too late, for Jinnarin on Rux disappeared among the crags, the fox scrambling upward. "Dask, Brekka, up after, swift!" Two Dwarven scouts began a hasty ascent. "Fool Pysk," he hissed, "running off like that, mayhap into the very jaws of danger."

Jatu leaned down to the Dwarf. "Nay, Bokar, no fool she. She has the magic of shadow and stealth to protect her and Rux. Besides, as soon as we gain the top, these five go on without us, for they would find Tarquin, an unlikely end if we are with them."

Bokar scowled at Jatu, plainly disliking the plan to let these searchers go forth without Dwarven escort. "Five? I count but four: Captain Aravan, Mage Alamar, Seer Aylis, and Lady Jinnarin. Who else do you have in mind?"

Jatu smiled. "I include Rux among their number."

Now Bokar grinned. "Aye."

A low whistle came from above, and on the verge stood Dask, signalling the all clear.

Leaving a boatwatch behind, up through the crags the others wended, choosing the easiest path for Alamar, at times merely steadying the elder, at other times lifting him bodily up the jagged way. At last they reached the crest, and Alamar sat and rested while others scouted about, ranging out across the grass-topped headland and toward the nearby pine tree forest ... yet no sign did they find of Jinnarin or Rux.

As they gathered together once more near the place where Alamar rested, Bokar growled, "Captain, I like this not. Lady Jinnarin is missing. Mayhap the forest dwellers have captured her. I would set search parties out ... and bring more from the ship to aid, if needed."

Aravan shook his head. "Nay, Bokar. Although we found no sign of Lady Jinnarin, we also found no evidence of the forest dwellers—nor of the Hidden Ones, for that matter. I ween that she and Rux are off on their own to find Tarquin."

Unconvinced, Bokar took a deep breath but said nothing, though Jatu nodded in agreement with Aravan's words.

Turning to Alamar, Aravan asked, "Deem thee ready for travel?"

The eld Mage stood, a look of irritation on his face. "Hmph! Of course I am ready, Captain. Couldn't be more ready if I was a thousand years younger. It's not me who's holding up the march. It's that dratted Pysk gone missing, that's who."

Shouldering a small knapsack of supplies, Aravan looked at Aylis, a smile playing at the corners of his mouth, as if to ask her how could she possibly be the get of this blame-laying old grouch.

"Come, Father," said Aylis, offering Alamar her arm. "Let us find this Tarquin."

Sneering at her proffered aid, Alamar barked, "Ha! More like he will find us than the other way about." And the eld Mage tramped off in the direction of the woods, while in his wake stepped Aylis and Aravan, seeress and Elf casting grins at one another as if sharing a secret.

Toward the pine tree forest went the three, while Bokar stood behind and clenched his teeth, for only Aravan bore weaponry, and that nought but bow and quiver of arrows ... and a long-knife in a scabbard strapped to his thigh, and Bokar's opinion was that they were virtually defenseless without the Châkka at their sides. The Dwarf watched until they disappeared into the woodland and he could see them no more. And then he turned and began aiding Jatu and the remaining sailors and warriors as they set about establishing a campsite along the top of the cliff.

When they came in among the trees, Alamar stopped and faced Aravan. "What now, Elf? Where do we go from here?"

Aravan gestured forward. "Ahead, a short way, a league or less, we will find the clearing where we will wait. Tarquin will come to us there if he is of a mind to meet ye twain. If not, then on the morrow I will go to him alone."

"Well, if you know where he lives," grumped Alamar, as they started forward again, "then I say we march straight to him. No need for this shilly-shallying about in the woods."

"Father"—Aylis's words came sharply—"these are Hidden Ones. We need to respect their rights."

"Pah!" snorted Alamar "Foolishness! All foolishness!"

Stopping now and again for Alamar to rest, at last they came through the thick pines to the grassy clearing sought by Aravan. Here the Elf dropped his knapsack and they sat and waited, while a soft breeze soughed in the crowns overhead and a stream could be heard burbling nearby.

Aylis stood. "There is a rill somewhere close. I am going to taste of its water." Hearing no objection, she walked through the tall yellow grass and across the glade toward the murmuring of the run. Aravan watched her go.

As she strode away, Alamar shifted about and then shifted again, fingers probing the earth. "The ground is chill. Winter is near. I feel it in my bones."

Aravan nodded, his gaze yet following Aylis. "Aye, Alamar. At these latitudes, winter comes early."

"Drat that Pysk!" complained the elder. "Where is she? She should have found Tarquin by now."

Aravan stood, taking up his bow and shading his eyes, peering across the clearing. "That she will find him I do not dispute, for little passes in Fox Riders' domains that goes unnoticed by them, and the *Eroean* has been at anchor now a goodly while. That we have been seen by them, I ween there is no doubt. All that is at question is whether they wish to be seen by us."

"Foolish Pysks, I say again," grumped Alamar. "Why, there is every reason to trust us, and little reason to—"

Aravan set an arrow to bowstring, his gaze intent.

Alamar fell silent, and huffing, he stood and peered across the clearing, too. Aylis was not in sight. "Now where—?"

At that moment Aylis reappeared, standing, wiping her mouth with the heel of her hand, the tall grass all about her.

Aravan relaxed, replacing the arrow in its quiver.

Alamar sat back down with a grunt.

Mid morn, Aylis and Aravan heard a fox bark, and Aravan placed two fingers in his mouth and gave a sharp whistle, startling Alamar awake. "Eh, wha—?"

"A fox, Father," murmured Aylis.

"Foxes don't interrupt perfectly good meditation with shrieks that'd wake the dead," grumbled Alamar.

Aylis raised an eyebrow. "Meditation, Father? It sounded more like snoring to me."

Alamar bristled, readying a retort, but Aravan whistled again, then pointed, and a furrow came rippling through the tall grass. In moments, Rux and Jinnarin appeared, the Pysk grinning.

"Tarquin said I would find you here," she announced, leaping down from the fox, "and so I have."

Alamar glared at her. "Pysk, how many times do I have to tell you not to run off like that?"

Jinnarin looked surprised. "Why, Alamar, you never told me to 'not run off.'"

"Don't evade the issue," Alamar snapped. "We were worried sick." The elder looked to Aylis and Aravan for confirmation, but Aravan simply cocked an eyebrow, while Aylis said, "Father, you were asleep."

Jinnarin giggled. At a glower from the Mage she tried to look solemn but failed, breaking out in titters again. "Oh, Alamar, don't be angry. You see, I found Tarquin, and he has a plan."

CHAPTER 14

Dreamwalk

Autumn, 1E9574
[The Present]

A plan?" The eld Mage raised an eyebrow. "And just what might this plan of his be?"

"I don't know, Alamar," answered Jinnarin. "He just told me to fetch you three to him and then he would explain."

Aravan squatted down. "I take it then that thou recounted all to Tarquin."

Jinnarin nodded. "Yes. I told him about the plumes and Farrix missing and about my dream and about you and Alamar and Aylis and the *Eroean* and everything. And before you ask, Aravan, Tarquin told me that no one he knows has seen any plumes. Even so, he is sending word to other Hidden Ones to discover if any of them has. But whether or not the plumes have been seen, still Tarquin thinks he can aid."

Alamar fixed Aravan with a gimlet eye. "Well, I suppose there's nothing for it but that we have to go see this Tarquin."

Shouldering his bow and picking up his knapsack, Aravan held out a hand to the Mage, helping him to his feet, the elder grunting and straightening slowly, complaining about his back. At a gesture from Jinnarin, Rux scrambled to his own feet and she leapt astride. Alamar glanced down at her. "And just how far is it to this Tarquin?"

"No more than a league or so."

Alamar groaned.

*   *   *

Shadows flitted among the trees as Jinnarin led the trio through the pine-scented forest, shades flickering at the corners of the eyes, but when Aravan and Aylis and Alamar looked, nothing was there ... that is, nothing that they could see straight on.

"Eh," grumbled Alamar, "I'm of a mind to—"

Aylis shook her head, *No.* "Father, that we are being escorted, I have no doubt. To confirm it with a casting is a waste of power."

"But I would see, Daughter, just who and what accompanies us."

"Father, they would rather remain hidden from prying eyes such as ours."

"Pah!" snorted Alamar. "Again I say it is foolishness."

Aravan glanced at the elder. "Nay, Alamar, not foolishness. Thou knowest the Hidden Ones were sorely pressed in times past, especially the Fox Riders, particularly by the hand of Man, though at times others joined in as well."

Aylis sighed. "I wonder why."

Aravan shrugged. "As is oft the case, what Man cannot control, he deems evil. And in the past, among the things Mankind named evil were the Fox Riders, for they resisted unto death the controlling hand of Man. And so, Men hunted them, ahorse with hound, riding over the open wolds and through the forests, horns ablare, hounds baying, thinking it great sport to run the fox to earth. Now and again would they capture a Fox Rider and cage him or her, though more likely they killed those they caught, for after all, were they not evil? Even unto this day, in some lands fox hunting remains a grand sport, a blood sport, though Mankind has long forgotten how it got its start—the destruction of evil where no evil lay."

"Grand sport!" Jinnarin exploded. "Hunting for 'sport' is wicked, cruel, one of Mankind's worst evils, for they do not even eat that which they kill. The killing alone is what drives them—the lust for death and proof of their prowess in trophy—and not the protection of their flocks nor hunger nor need for fur to clothe them. Cruelty alone is the sought-after end."

Aravan held up a hand as if to deflect blame. "Jinnarin, I did not say that I thought hunting was a great sport. I merely spoke to Aylis of the nature of Man and the need for the Feyani to hide."

Alamar glared at Aravan. "You tell us nothing new, Elf. We know what drove them to cover. And still I say that it is foolish for them to conceal themselves from me, from Aylis, for we are no threat to them."

"Ah, but Father, they know not that we are allies," demurred Aylis.

Alamar sighed and trudged on.

Down into a forest vale they fared, a tumbling brook at the bottom, and alongside this watercourse they made their passage upstream, resting along the way. At last they came in among a jumble of moss-laden boulders cupped in an arc of a rocky bluff. Through a slot cut deep in the wall cascaded a fall of water. A pathway angled up beside the cataract, at the top of which stood a silver fox, a rider astride. Aravan raised a hand, palm outward, the rider doing likewise. " 'Tis Tarquin," said the Elf.

"King of the Fox Riders?" asked Aylis.

"In as much as they have Kings," responded Aravan.

Jinnarin said, "If I understand the role of a King, Tarquin is not one of those. Instead, I would call him a trusted leader or a chieftain, for they more accurately describe his standing among the Hidden Ones. He led us when we took flight from Feyer."

As they made their way up the path, Alamar groused, "Climbing, always climbing. Why must we always go upward? Doesn't anyone live on level ground?"

"Look who's talking," called Jinnarin above the *shssh* of the cascade.

"Eh? What do you mean, Pysk?"

"You live on a hill, Alamar."

"That's different!" shot back the Mage. "I need it to see the stars."

"Still in all, what's sauce for the goose is sauce for the gander, or so you once told me."

"Bah!" exclaimed the elder, then trudged uphill in silence.

When they came to the top, Tarquin dismounted. "Welcome," he called out above the waterfall, "I am

Tarquin"—he made a sweeping bow, then gestured toward his fox—"and this is Ris."

"Well-met again," answered Aravan. "May I present Lady Aylis and Mage Alamar."

As Tarquin bowed to daughter and sire, they saw before them a Pysk perhaps a half inch taller than Jinnarin. His hair was black and long, reaching down nearly to his hips and held back from his face by a headband of leather. His eyes were a brown so dark that they, too, seemed black. He was dressed in moleskin leathers, and his feet were shod in soft buskins. The leather belt at his waist carried his only ornamentation, incised as it was with tiny red runes.

"This way," he called out, leaping on the back of Ris and riding away, not looking hindward to see if they came after.

Into the high-walled canyon they went, proceeding upstream 'round twists and turns, the sound of the cascade behind fading in the distance. The walls of the chasm steadily drew away until they widened into a broad gorge. Here grew grass and trees—pine and larch and birch—the vale bottom rich with loam. Now they came to broad pools of water, lakelets and meres and such, and rushes grew in the shallows, the reeds now brown in the autumn and rattling in the breeze.

Tarquin led them away from the stream and into a hollow carved in the vale side. And there they came unto his home—an undermound dwelling in a grove of silver birch, the burrow much too small for any to enter but Jinnarin. And there they met Tarquin's consort, Falain, a ginger-haired, hazel-eyed, leather-clad Pysk, and her black fox, Nix.

Aravan knelt and rummaged through his pack. "I will make us some tea, and then shall we speak upon the events that brought us here."

Alamar cleared his throat and scowled at Tarquin. "And I would hear of this plan of yours, Pysk."

"Dreamwalking?" Aylis's eyes flew wide. "I have never heard of such. What is it? How is it done?"

Tarquin shrugged and sipped his tea, then set the tiny cup aside. "Falain learned of it from Ontah."

"Ontah?"

"One of the Humans," said Falain, gesturing westerly. "A Healer."

Aylis looked at the Pysk. "A Human. One who lives nearby?"

Falain nodded.

"A savage?" Alamar's voice came sharply.

Tarquin looked mildly surprised. "I would not call him a savage, Mage Alamar. He is a forest dweller."

"And a Friend," added Falain.

Aravan turned to Alamar. "Rumors notwithstanding, those who dwell in the forest are a gentle people."

Jinnarin looked to Tarquin, and he laughed and nodded in agreement, saying, "It is perhaps but rumor that keeps others away from this land, for who would dare walk in the domain of bloodthirsty savages."

"Aye," added Aravan, "it is as Tarquin says. Oh, the forest dwellers paint themselves with fierce colors when trading with outsiders, but that is to maintain the savage facade. Unless riled, unless defending themselves or their domain, they are a most gentle folk, though that is a secret they would have us keep."

"Humph!" grunted Alamar, but he said no more.

Aylis turned to Falain. "This dreamwalking, just what is it and how is it done?"

Falain glanced at Tarquin, then said, "As to how it is done, we do not know. But as to what it is, it allows someone to enter another's dream, to walk within it, to see things that the dreamer cannot see."

Aylis nodded, looking to Jinnarin then back at Falain. "And you think that Ontah can walk in Jinnarin's dream and discover ... whatever there is to discover?"

Falain held up her hand in a gesture of demurral. "That I cannot say. All I can say is that Ontah knows the secret of dreamwalking."

Alamar growled. "I wouldn't want someone prowling about in my dreams. Why does he do it, this dreamwalking? I mean, what is it good for?"

Falain turned her palms up. "All that I do know is that he uses it at times to heal someone who suffers from nightmares, waking or sleeping."

"Oh," said Alamar, enlightenment dawning, "someone who isn't right in the head, eh?"

Jinnarin bristled. "Alamar, I'll have you know that my

head is perfectly all right. If anyone around here has a noggin that needs fixing up then I'd say it's—"

"Look, Pysk," began Alamar.

"Stop it, you two!" flared Aylis. "You're worse than a pair of bickering brats. Incessantly quibbling. Seeing insult where none is intended.

"Remember, both of you, just why we are here. Farrix is missing. Jinnarin is having nightmares, a sending we believe. And someone is shielding knowledge from us."

Both Alamar and Jinnarin stared at the ground, refusing to meet anyone's eye.

"Where can we find this Ontah?" Aravan's words came quietly.

Tarquin stood. "We will lead you to him. It's not far. Two leagues or so."

Alamar groaned. "Uphill, I'll wager."

It was nearing sunset when they walked into the clearing where sat the lodge of Ontah, a one-room square house of logs, white clay filling the chinks, a smoke hole in the sod roof. On a bench out before the house sat a Man dressed in buckskins, and at his side perched Falain, with Nix on the ground below, for Falain had ridden ahead to tell the Healer of the impending visitors.

Ontah's hair was long and grey, his eyes brown, his skin a bronze hue. His silvery mane was bound in a ponytail, hanging down his straight back. He was thin and aged, his coppery skin raddled with delicate wrinkles, like antiquated parchment.

Speaking in an unfamiliar tongue to the eld Man, Falain gestured at the four visitors. Jinnarin glanced at Aravan. "She introduces us to him," murmured the Elf.

"Oh," said Jinnarin.

"As I thought," added Aylis.

Ontah stood and gestured into his dwelling, speaking. Aravan replied in the same tongue, then turned aside to his companions, saying, "Now he invites us in."

They entered the dimly lit shelter. Mats of woven reeds lay on an earthen floor. In the center of the single room was a ring of firestones, from which rose a small, virtually smokeless blaze, wisps of vapor rising up through the hole in the roof. Ranged along the walls were shelves on which lay clutches of herbs and plants, piles of nuts and seeds, stone and fired-clay bowls, earthenware cups, wooden tools. Several woven baskets sat about, containing grain and tubers. In one corner was piled firewood, and in another lay blankets. From the rafters bracing the sod roof, there hung more clutches of herbs and plants as well as dried roots and other such. Too, there was smoked fish and a haunch of venison. An axe sat beside the door and a coil of rope hung from a dowel. A large clay vessel contained water, and a gourd dipper dangled by cord from a nearby peg.

Ontah gestured at the mats about the tiny blaze, saying, *"Takla."* Aravan murmured, "Sit."

As they seated themselves, Aylis muttered, "I like not this waiting for translation." She raised a hand and made a gesture, speaking a word under her breath: *"Converte."*

Ontah gazed at Jinnarin, saying in his native tongue, ["You would have me walk a dream?"]

Not understanding, Jinnarin looked blankly at the old Man.

As Aravan translated Ontah's words to Jinnarin and Alamar, Aylis responded directly to the Healer, ["Yes, White Owl, she would."]

Both Aravan and Ontah looked at Aylis in surprise, the old Man saying, ["I did not know you spoke the tongue of the People."]

["I know the tongue but temporarily, White Owl. Nigh mid of night, I will know it no more."]

["How can this be?"]

["I have spoken a word of <power>, White Owl."]

The old Man's eyes widened, then he tilted his head in understanding, saying, ["If I were younger, I would ask you to teach me this word."]

Jinnarin turned to Alamar, whispering, "Aylis is speaking to Ontah."

The Mage nodded. "She must have done a seer's casting."

"Why don't you do a casting, too, Alamar?"

"Pysk, again you didn't listen to what I said," he hissed.

"I did, too. You said she must have done a seer's casting."

"Well, there's your answer."

A look of confusion spread over Jinnarin's face. "My answer?" Her bewilderment turned to ire, her voice rising. "Answer? I don't even know the question."

"Then why did you ask?" snapped Alamar.

"Ask what?" Jinnarin was near to exploding.

"You asked why didn't I do a casting, too."

"And . . . ?"

"Pysk, it's a seer's casting."

"So?"

Now Alamar gritted his teeth. "I am not a seer."

"Oh," said Jinnarin. "You mean you can't do it, right?"

"Of course I could do it if I trained at it." Alamar fumed.

Aylis reached out a hand. "Father, we're not here to argue."

Both Alamar and Jinnarin fell silent, each glaring at the other.

Aylis turned back to Ontah. ["White Owl, will you walk Jinnarin's dream and tell us what you see?"]

Ontah looked into Aylis's eyes. ["Yes, I will walk her dream. Would you care to walk it with me?"]

["I know not how."]

["You are young. You know the way of <power>. I will teach you."]

["Then I will gladly walk the dream with you, White Owl."]

Aravan, who had remained silent until now, asked, ["White Owl, is there danger in walking a dream?"]

Ontah sat in contemplation for a long while, and Aravan thought that the old Man would remain silent, yet at last he said, ["There are times when dreamwalking is filled with danger, especially if the dream is laden with evil spirits. Then the dreamwalker's own spirit can be wounded, even slain, by the bad ones."]

Aravan glanced at Aylis and then back to Ontah, and although he spoke to the Healer, Aylis knew that his words were intended for her. ["White Owl, Jinnarin's dream is filled with fear."]

The old Man peered into the fire. ["That does not prove there are evil spirits within her dream, though it does not disprove it either."]

Aylis looked into the flames as well. ["Is there any

way that we can know if evil is present before we dreamwalk?"]

Ontah shook his head, *No*. ["Only by walking the dream can we know what lies within."]

Silence fell on the group, and only the crackling of the fire disturbed the quiet. At last Aravan asked, ["White Owl, are there other dangers in dreamwalking?"]

The old Man looked up, his gaze shifting from Aravan to Aylis and back. ["If the dreamer wakes before the walker steps free, then his spirit will be trapped until the dreamer enters the same dream again."]

When this last was translated for Jinnarin, she gasped, "Oh, Aylis, I *always* startle awake. I cannot help myself. You may be trapped. And I would not want to snare you or Ontah or *anyone* in that horrid, fear-filled nightmare."

Aylis reached out to Jinnarin. "Ah but, my Jinnarin, we won't be trapped forever, for at least you return to the same dream night after night."

"No, no, Aylis, not night after night," protested Jinnarin. "You know the dream comes much less frequently these days, these nights."

Aravan turned to Aylis, his face carefully composed, neutral, his voice controlled, but shadowed in his eyes was grave concern. He spoke softly, softly, his words for her ears alone. "This is thy decision to make, Aylis, and none can stand in thy way. Yet heed, thou must think long and carefully ere taking this step, for the way is fraught with danger. I cherish thee, and if thou wert to suffer harm . . ."

Aylis reached out and took Aravan's hand, but she said nought.

In the dark of night at the cliffside camp Jatu startled awake. What had roused him, he could not say. By the light of the low-burning fire he peered about the encampment, seeing his sleeping comrades and a Dwarven sentry standing guard. Jatu shook his head, deeming his waking nought but a vagary of the night. Yet as he settled back, he felt a crackling at his breast, and in his jerkin at the laces he found a fold of parchment, a missive from Aravan. Again Jatu looked about, yet no evidence of the messenger did he see. By the light of the fire he read the note:

Jatu:

We are well and with Tarquin. He has guided us to a forest dweller named Ontah, a Healer. Ontah is a "dreamwalker," and he proposes to walk in Lady Jinnarin's dream accompanied by Lady Aylis. We may be here for some days waiting to accomplish that goal, for Lady Jinnarin must dream her dream and Ontah must walk his walk.

Until we return, I will send thee a message every three days or so. If in the meanwhile thou and Bokar decide to return to the Eroean, *a small signal fire on the cliffs where thou now encamp will let thee know that I have sent another message.*

             Aravan

Even as Tarquin on Ris set out to deliver the note to Jatu, in Ontah's lodge Aylis and the old Man sat in deep counsel, all others outside. The fire burned low, wavering shadows looming upon log walls. Ontah sat crosslegged at the edge of the fire ring, Aylis opposite, and the old Man gazed intently through the thin rising tendrils of smoke, his brown eyes peering into Aylis's eyes of green. His voice came softly:

["There is a word in my tongue which is similar to your name: *aylia*. It means, brightwing."]

Aylis tilted her head. ["When you said it, I knew."]

Ontah grinned, his face wrinkling. ["I will need to call you by a name when we dreamwalk."]

Aylis's own face broke into a smile. ["White Owl, I would be honored if you would call me Brightwing."]

["Good. I was hoping you would see reason."]

["Oh?"]

Ontah nodded. ["This old head of mine has seen four score and some years, and old habits are hard to break. I was afraid I would forget and call you Brightwing regardless, and I wanted you to know."]

Aylis looked at the old Man, a peculiar tightness in her chest. *Oh my, he is but eighty and some odd years of age, yet how ancient he looks, as if he were a Mage* *who had spent all his <power>. Ah, but then again, he is Human . . .*

Ontah cast another bit of kindling on the fire, his words bringing Aylis back from her musing. ["Brightwing, have you ever had a dream where you knew you were dreaming?"]

["Yes, White Owl, though not often."]

["When you knew that you were dreaming, did you try to change the dream, make it into something . . . wonderful?"]

["No, White Owl. I merely knew that I was dreaming at the time. I did not try to control it. I did not know that it could be changed."]

["That is the second step to dreamwalking, Brightwing—to walk into your own dream and know that it is a dream."]

["If that is the second step, then what is the first?"]

["Your own dream must begin at the same time as the dream you wish to walk begins."]

["Oh my. How will I even know that the dreamer's dream has begun? How will I know that Jinnarin is dreaming?"]

["Her sleeping eyes will move back and forth."]

["And then I must immediately begin to dream . . . and shape the dream?"]

Ontah nodded.

["But how . . . ?"]

["I will teach you."]

["All right, let us say that I begin my dream and enter it and know that it is a dream—then what?"]

Ontah smiled. ["Then you must shape the dream, bend it to your will, make it into what you would have it be."]

["Which is . . . ?"]

["Which is to dream that you are stepping into another's dream, stepping into the dream you wish to walk."]

["But how—?"]

["I will teach you."]

["And then . . . ?"]

["And then, Brightwing, you walk the dream of the other, observing, seeing, and remembering."]

Aylis took a deep breath and then nodded.

Ontah held up a cautionary hand. ["Here is where an

evil spirit might be encountered, and you must be ready to banish it or to escape."]

["Banish it? How?"]

["Sometimes you can merely tell it to begone, and it will leave. Sometimes you must threaten it. Sometimes you must fight it, and here your own spirit may be killed. Sometimes you must flee."]

Aylis felt her heart thudding at Ontah's words.

["Do not let me frighten you, Brightwing, for evil spirits are not often encountered."]

Aylis grinned with a bravado she did not feel, saying, ["My heart tells me otherwise, White Owl, but I will try to remain calm."]

Ontah reached across the fire ring and squeezed her hand. ["That is good, for you must remain calm in order to leave."]

["Leave? Leave the dream?"]

Ontah nodded. ["Yes. When you have seen enough you must leave. At times you must leave before you are ready."]

Aylis turned up a palm. ["And the reason?"]

["You must stop walking in the dream before the dreamer wakes, else you will be trapped."]

["How will I know when to leave, White Owl?"]

["I will teach you."]

["There is much for me to learn."]

Ontah canted his head in agreement. ["Do you remember the steps?"]

["When the one whose dream I wish to walk begins dreaming, I must enter my own dream and know that I am dreaming. I must shape the dream and dream that I am entering the dream I wish to walk. I must observe well and remember. I must be wary of evil spirits, which, if encountered I must banish or flee from. Regardless, I must leave the dream I am walking before the dreamer wakens."]

Ontah smiled. ["Then you must waken, leaving your own dream behind before you forget what you have seen in the dream you walked."]

["Oh? Am I likely to forget?"]

["Most dreams are forgotten, Brightwing, even those we would wish to remember. Let me ask you, have you ever wakened from a dream in the night and said to yourself that you must remember this dream in the morning, but when morning comes all you recall is that you wanted to remember a dream, but it is gone from your mind?"]

Aylis smiled a rueful smile. ["Yes, White Owl, I have forgotten dreams I wanted to remember ... exactly as you say."]

["Then, Brightwing, it is necessary that you waken quickly after a dreamwalk so that you can recall most of what you have seen."]

Aylis sighed. ["There is much for you to teach me, White Owl. I hope I am up to it."]

Ontah made a negating gesture with his hand. ["Of that, I have no fear, Brightwing, for you know the ways of <power>."]

["Then let us begin."]

Ontah cast another stick of kindling on the fire. ["Tell me this: do you know how to sleep without sleeping?"]

Sleep without sleeping? Momentarily Aylis was nonplused, but then she asked, ["Do you mean—?"] suddenly Aylis realized that there was no word in Ontah's tongue which meant meditation ... in particular, deep meditation ...

... And so began Aylis's instruction in dreamwalking.

In the early afternoon of the next day, a Dwarven warder called out, "Someone comes!"

Bokar and Jatu stood and peered toward the pine tree forest. In the near distance toward them came Alamar, tottering and disheveled and panting. "Something is wrong," gritted Bokar, hefting his double-bitted axe and setting out at a trot toward the eld Mage, Jatu jogging at his side. Even before they reached Alamar he waved them back, wheezing out in an irritated voice, "No need to come and get me. I can make it on my own. I'll not have anyone carrying me, even though it has been an ordeal."

By this time, Bokar and Jatu had reached his side. "Is there danger?" demanded Bokar, axe at the ready, his gaze sweeping the wood for sign of threat.

"Danger?" gasped Alamar, whirling about, facing the forest. "Where?"

"I don't know where," snarled Bokar, "you are the one running."

"Running? Me?"

"You mean you are not fleeing?"

"Of course not, you bloody fool."

"Then what are you doing here?"

"Well there was nothing for me to do!" Alamar peevishly snapped, yet puffing and blowing. "Aylis and Aravan have everything well in hand. The Pysks are all right. Ontah knows what he is doing. The savages are no threat. And besides, it was bloody uncomfortable out there in the woods."

Bokar seemed unwilling to concede that nothing was amiss. "Are you certain?"

Alamar threw up his hands and stomped off toward the encampment, muttering, "It's not enough that I have to walk miles and miles out to that lodge and back, and it was uphill both ways, but now my very judgement is being questioned, and . . ."

Bokar and Jatu turned and followed the Mage, the Dwarf scowling, the black Man laughing.

That night, Ontah and Aylis sat at the lodge fire, aromatic wood shavings filling the air with fragrance. They faced Jinnarin, who lay nearby on a soft blanket, the Pysk trying to sleep, failing. Neither Aylis nor Ontah spoke, the silence broken only by the slight crackling of the fire. At the doorway, Aravan sat with his back against the outer wall, the Elf resting his mind in gentle memories. Neither Tarquin nor Falain were present, having escorted Alamar back to the cliffs where he would return to the *Eroean*.

An hour passed and then another, and the wind in the pines strengthened, the soughing *shssh* drowning out all other sounds. Aylis regarded Jinnarin, watching as her breathing slowed and her hands fell lax—she was asleep at last.

Aylis slipped into a state of light meditation, noting that Ontah did likewise.

A time passed. And there came a soft word from Ontah. Beneath their lids, Jinnarin's eyes began to whip from side to side.

Now Aylis slipped into deep meditation, and using

the now-ingrained <word> of <suggestion> taught her by White Owl, Aylis began to dream. She stood in her father's cottage in Vadaria, looking about in wonderment, for here she had not been since childhood. And as she stared at her dwelling of yore, a young Man with black hair and brown eyes and coppery skin stepped through the wall toward her. "Brightwing," he said, reaching out his hand, tugging her into the cave.

They walked toward the light at the distant end. When they emerged, they were alongside a still mere.

"See and remember," whispered White Owl.

Aylis peered about. They were in a forest. Oak trees. Willows. It was summer. Reeds stood in the lakelet near the shore. The water was faintly undulant. She could hear a stream purling softly. Across the way a fox and rider stopped.

"Remember," whispered White Owl again.

The fox bounded away. The rider—Jinnarin? yes, Jinnarin—knelt and plucked a flower. She stepped to the edge of the mere and knelt on a broad stone, fixing the flower in her hair and using the water as a mirror. From above came laughter, and out from a tree a Pysk dived into the pool. Jinnarin screamed.

"Remember."

That must be Farrix. Aylis watched as the black-haired Pysk popped up from underwater and climbed out. He wore no clothes. Suddenly, Jinnarin's clothing disappeared. Farrix kissed her. They lay down in the moss.

Aylis turned to the Man, her heart thudding. "White Owl, we must not—"

"Brightwing, see the trees."

Aylis looked. They were beginning to lose form.

"Brightwing, we must leave now."

They stepped into the tunnel, White Owl striding swiftly. Aylis looked behind. The opening disappeared, the tunnel walls began to collapse, rushing toward her from the far end.

"Do not look back!" White Owl commanded, his voice sharp.

Aylis's head snapped 'round, but she knew that at the speed of the approaching cave-in, only moments remained until they would be buried.

"Do not believe it!" commanded White Owl. "Control the dream and it will not fall."

Her heart hammering, Aylis envisioned the walls solid, adamant, unable to give way. The crashing behind her stopped.

They stepped forth from the tunnel and into a smoke-filled lodge. A tiny fire burned in a ring of stones. An old Man and a young seeress knelt in meditation, a Pysk asleep before them.

"Remember," said White Owl. "And awaken."

Aylis said the other deep-rooted <word> of <suggestion> White Owl had drummed into her ...

... and she opened her eyes.

Aylis was ecstatic. She had dreamwalked. She turned to Ontah, and he smiled at her, saying, *"N'klat sh'manu, Aylia."*

"What?"

"N'klat sh'manu. Chu doto a bala."

"Converte," evoked Aylis. Then she turned to Ontah. ["You must forgive me, White Owl, it seems that I lost my ability to speak your tongue when I dreamwalked."]

Ontah made a gesture of understanding. ["I said, it was well-done, Brightwing, this first dreamwalk of yours. Not everyone of <power> can do as well even after many Moons of training."]

Aylis bobbed her head, proud and slightly embarrassed at one and the same time.

["As to losing your gift of speaking the tongue, perhaps that is because when dreamwalking all tongues are the same."]

["The same?"]

Ontah nodded. ["Do you remember the language we spoke in the dream?"]

Aylis's eyes were lost in reflection. ["Yes. It was ... we spoke in ..."] She looked at Ontah in puzzlement, then fell silent.

["All tongues. All the same."]

Aylis and Ontah sat without speaking a moment. Without awakening, Jinnarin turned on her side. Finally Ontah asked, ["Do you remember, Brightwing, all that happened?"]

["Yes."]

["Then tell me."]

["In my dream, I was in my father's cottage. You came—or rather a younger version of you came—and you made a tunnel into Jinnarin's dream. She was dreaming about how she and Farrix met, and then it became a dream of intimacy. We left then, because her dream was dissolving. The tunnel began to cave in, but you had me stop the collapse by taking control of the dream. Then we came here and wakened."]

Ontah smiled. ["Good. Now tell me the details."]

Thrice more that night they entered Jinnarin's dreams, each time Ontah allowing Aylis more and more control of the feat. Now that she knew what to look for, in each of the dreams Aylis was first to notice the signs of dissolution, warning White Owl that it was time to disengage.

In none of the dreams did Jinnarin experience her nightmare.

For much of the next day, Aylis and Ontah slept, resting from their essays of the night. Aravan and Rux went hunting, the Elf bringing down three rabbits with his bow. In mid afternoon, the smell of rabbit stew was redolent on the air. As Jinnarin and Aravan took a meal, Tarquin and Falain came riding in, the Pysks reporting that Alamar had been safely delivered, although it appeared that the Mage had immediately started an argument with a Dwarf and the black Man, Jatu.

After Tarquin and Falain had gone, Aylis and Ontah awakened, and as they ate they spoke to Jinnarin and Aravan of what they had seen in their dreamwalks, the Pysk remembering nought but a fragment of her visions, and that of the last dream only.

["Tonight, Brightwing, you shall speak with Sparrow's dream spirit."]

["Sparrow?"]

Ontah pointed to Jinnarin. ["Sparrow."]

Aylis smiled. "He names you Sparrow, Jinnarin, and tonight in your dreams I am to speak with you."

"Sparrow?" Jinnarin giggled. "Somehow it seems fitting. Do you have a name, Aylis?"

"He calls me Brightwing. In the Common Tongue, his

name, Ontah, means White Owl. You need not commit
the names to memory, Jinnarin, for now that you have
been told, in your dream you will simply know . . . it is
the way of dreams."

"Well, I may not need to memorize each of our names
beforehand, Aylis, but oh, I do hope I remember the
dreams after I waken."

They stood on a high bluff overlooking a deep vale,
Aylis's arm about Jinnarin, the seeress surprised to find
that she and the Pysk were of a like size. At their side
knelt Ontah, the Man gazing out over the forest far
below.

The seeress turned to the Pysk. "Sparrow, tell me
where we are."

"In Darda Glain, Brightwing."

"On Rwn? I have never seen this place."

"It is closed to outsiders."

Aylis nodded in understanding.

Ontah stood, pointing to the wavering of the clouds
in the distance. "We must go now, Brightwing."

"Oh, please stay." Jinnarin yawned. "I don't want you
to go." Her eyes were heavy-lidded and losing their
focus.

Aylis squeezed the Pysk's shoulders. "We have no
choice."

As Aylis turned to Ontah, he said, "You make the
way, Brightwing."

A tunnel mouth appeared in the air next to Aylis.
"Good," grunted Ontah, and they stepped inward.

"How many dreams?"

"Five," answered Aylis.

"But I don't remember any, and I did so wish that
I would."

It was the afternoon of the next day, Aylis and Ontah
having awakened but a short while ago.

Jinnarin sighed. "Again, no nightmare."

Ontah smiled and said something to Aylis. "He says
that you are remarkably healthy, Jinnarin."

"In my dreams, you mean, neh?"

Aylis translated this to Ontah. Again the old Man
smiled at the Pysk, and then tapped his head and

pointed at her, speaking to Aylis. "Healthy of mind, of spirit, of soul, he says."

Bearing his knapsack, Aravan came striding into the lodge site. He squatted by the outside fire, withdrawing oatcakes from the pack, saying, ["I have been to see your people. They send food."]

Ontah smiled. ["I am glad. It takes much food to walk among dreams."]

Without comment, Aylis agreed, for she felt drained of energy.

They flew above the roiling dark clouds, the storm gathering about them. Now Jinnarin swooped downward, Aylis and Ontah following. Below, a pale green sea churned with high-tossed waves, and a black galleon under full sail hurtled across the face of the heaving waters, lightning stroking the masts in the howling wind.

Aylis peered through the ebony night, and in the distance she could see a craggy isle, but other shapes, too, could dimly be seen scattered across the surface of the thundering sea . . . yet what they were, she could not tell.

Of a sudden the three stood in a crystal castle and looked out over the rage. How they could see through the solid walls, Aylis did not know, but see they could, and the black ship hove across the hammering waves and toward the isle, toward them.

And a thrum of fear whelmed at Aylis, taking her breath from her.

Even so, she stood with her arms about Jinnarin, the tiny Pysk trembling in terror. What caused this mauling dread, she did not know.

"Beware, Brightwing, there is an evil spirit nearby," White Owl called out above the crack of lightning and roar of thunder and rolling boom of wave.

Aylis turned and looked at Ontah, the coppery young Man stepping to her side. "Remain with Sparrow and ward her. Flee at need. I will search."

As White Owl moved away, Aylis felt herself drawn, as if into another dream, yet she did not move from where she stood. All about her the walls of the castle shifted, changed. "Hold on, Jinnarin!" she cried. "A moment more."

The glittering chamber lost its smoothness, became irregular and sharp-edged and jagged, as if—

A wave of terror whelmed at her, and in the distance, the black ship altered.

Jinnarin moaned, sweat beading on her brow.

"No, Jinnarin!" cried Aylis, her own heart running away in her breast. "Do not flee, not yet."

And suddenly the dark ship became a giant black spider running toward them across an undulant grass-green sea. And hideous dread hammered into Aylis, terror exploding throughout her entire being, shattering fear erupting up and out. And howls burst forth from her throat, horror-driven endless screams.

Jinnarin shrieked and shrieked—

And from somewhere, nowhere, White Owl cried, "Get out, Brightwing!"

—and the walls began to judder and fade, racing toward oblivion.

A tunnel flashed into existence. "Run!"

Aylis scrambled inward, panic driving her, hoarse screams tearing from a throat raw with dread. And a wall of blackness engulfed her, sucking at her, dragging her down—

—and her wild shrieks filled the lodge as Aravan held her tightly, Aylis thrashing about, her eyes wide in unseeing madness, Jinnarin's shrills lost in the din.

Of a sudden Aylis collapsed.

But Jinnarin was awake and crying—"Oh. Oh. Oh . . ."—sobbing in remembered dread.

Reaching over, Aravan gently drew the Pysk to him, and she clambered up into the crook of his arm and pressed against him and clung tightly, seeking comfort, her gaze wide but unfocused, terror crowding vision aside. And Aravan held both Aylis and Jinnarin and rocked gently, for he knew nought else to do. Of a sudden, Aylis's eyes snapped open and she drew in a great breath as if to scream. *"Shh, shh,"* shushed Aravan. "You are safe, *chieran*. You are safe."

She looked at him, her gaze no longer insane. "Ontah," she gasped, struggling to free herself, "is he all right?"

Aravan loosed Aylis, Jinnarin climbing down, and together they turned to the old Man.

He lay on his back, not moving, not breathing, arms and legs akimbo, as if he were a broken doll. Aylis flung herself to his breast, placing an ear to his chest, listening, listening, and then moaning, "Oh no, no, no . . ."

Tears in her eyes, she raised up, and kneeling, rocked back on her heels. "He is dead. White Owl is dead."

Ontah lay sprawled before her, his eyes wide in terror, his mouth stretched in a silent shriek of dread, the old Man slain by a dream.

CHAPTER 15

Tides

Autumn, 1E9574
[The Present]

A chill wind swirled as Aylis and Aravan walked among the silent cortege of forest dwellers passing through the sacred ground in the high grove of silver birch. All about them stood lofty platforms on tall corner poles. On the scaffolds lay the enwrapped remains of those who had died, their bindings tattered and bleached by wind and rain and Sun; in places the cerements were completely gone and yellowed bones jutted through. At last the procession came to a new-built flet, and, swathed from head to toe in ceremonial wrappings, Ontah's body was lifted high onto the stand atop the uprights. From Ontah's funeral jar the chieftain took four tufts of owl feather-down, placed there long ago by Ontah himself against this very day. And while the clan softly chanted, the chieftain and three others lay the downy strands loosely upon the top of each corner pole, for the forest dwellers knew that each person's soul is borne into the afterworld by totem spirits—in Ontah's case, owls would take him to the Land Above—and when they came, the wind of their passage would blow the feathery down away, and Ontah's spirit would be carried into the sky.

And even as they placed the tufts onto the poles and freed them, the chill swirling breeze spun the strands up and away, the forest dwellers releasing a glad muted sigh, though here and there among them tears flowed from dark brown eyes, wetting coppery faces—Aylis's own quiet tears shed as well.

Once more in utter silence, away from the funeral ground they trod, taking care not to disturb the dead, for who knows what havoc might result should a corpse rise up whose spirit is gone. And so they walked in stillness away from Ontah's bier, none looking back, their eyes deliberately downcast so that none of the dead would follow them home ... hence none saw the shadow-wrapped foxes slipping inward among the trees.

From a somber sky a light snow fell as Aylis, Aravan, Jinnarin and Rux, Tarquin and Ris, and Falain and Nix stood at the edge of the pine tree forest, a pall of sadness dragging upon them, weighing down their spirits. Too, remnants of dread lingered deep in the eyes of Aylis and Jinnarin, though neither as yet had had the courage to relive aloud those dire moments of Jinnarin's dream, and so they had not yet spoken of what had befallen within. In the distance at the edge of the cliff they could see the campsite of Bokar and Jatu and the Dwarven warriors, a small fire burning as evening drew over the land.

"None we spoke to has seen the plumes," said Tarquin, breaking the dismal silence. "Of course, we did not speak to all, for you have been here but six days. Even so, in that time, all those we could reach said nay."

Falain glanced over at Jinnarin. "Nevertheless, it does not prove that your Farrix was chasing a will-o'-the-wisp, for no one was especially looking for streamers in the sky."

Aravan squatted down. "I did not deem that we were certain to find answers or even confirmation ... though I was hoping we might."

"What will you do now?" asked Tarquin.

"Sail to the seas nigh Rwn," replied the Elf, looking up at the snow falling through the gathering darkness. "Take up station and wait. Mayhap more plumes will flow, given that now is the season for the return of the aurora to that realm."

Tarquin dismounted and stepped to Aravan. Touching a tiny hand to Aravan's palm, the Pysk said, "Though I believe that you step toward evil, go in safety, Friend."

"I thank thee for thy aid, Friend," answered Aravan. "Would that we could stay yet awhile, but we cannot. Fare thee well, Tarquin. Fare thee well, Falain. May Adon cup ye two in the palm of His hand."

Now Jinnarin and Falain dismounted, the Pysks hugging one another, Falain whispering, "I wish you well, Jinnarin, and pray that you find your Farrix, for I know how I would feel were it my Tarquin instead."

Jinnarin said nought as she embraced Falain and then Tarquin.

Aylis knelt, Tarquin and Falain each touching her hand in farewell. "As Aravan says, may Adon watch over you both," said the seeress.

And then the twain leapt upon Ris and Nix and with a final wave turned and sped away, silver fox and black disappearing among the dark pines.

Wearily, Aravan and Aylis stood, and with Jinnarin and Rux stepped forth from the woods, setting out through the falling snow and toward the distant camp.

"Dead?" Alamar's eyes flew wide. "Ontah dead? What happened, Daughter?"

Aylis, Aravan, Jinnarin and Rux, and Alamar stood in the captain's lounge.

Aylis took a deep breath and let it out. "I don't know, Father. All I know is that he was slain while walking Jinnarin's dream."

"Slain? By a dream? Oh no, a dream alone cannot be the sole cause. Surely there is more to it than that, Aylis. I mean, if Jinnarin's dream can slay someone, then why isn't she herself dead?"

Jinnarin burst into tears.

"What?" barked Alamar. "Why are you crying, Pysk?"

Jinnarin's sobbing grew worse.

Aravan crouched down, cupping a hand about Jinnarin's shoulders.

Aylis turned to her sire. "Father, Jinnarin believes that she killed Ontah. That it was her dream which slew him. But it is not so. Instead it was something . . . evil."

"Come, let us sit and speak of it, Daughter. You can tell me all."

Aravan glanced up at the Mage. "Nay, Alamar, not now, not tonight. Instead, she needs rest."

The eld Mage drew himself up, glaring down at Aravan, preparing to challenge the Elf's words. But Aylis laid a hand on his arm. "He is right, Father. I need sleep, for I am spent."

Alamar looked at Aylis, her face drawn, her eyes sunken, her shoulders sagging, her entire stance speaking of a weariness beyond measure. He glanced down at Jinnarin, the weeping Pysk no better off. With a sigh, Alamar relented. "Yes, I see it now. To bed with you, Daughter. You, too, Pysk. Tomorrow will be soon enough."

On the predawn tide in a blinding snow they sailed away from the cove, the blizzard spinning black in the night, as of ravens' feathers driven before a howl. Aloft in the thrumming rigging Men bore storm lanterns, haloed glimmers in the blow, members of the crew setting the crossjack and main and foremain sails; and even as this was done, down on the decks other crewmen winched the jibs and staysails and the spanker up into place. These sails and no more would be used to drive the ship easterly, or so Frizian declared. Oh, the masts and spars of the *Eroean* could easily bear more silk in this wind, harsh as it was, and fly well before it. Nay, 'twas not the Elvenship that limited the amount of sail. Instead it was the crew, for in this frigid squall they could not safely remain aloft to set the other sails, else they risked frostbite and worse. Only at dire need would the crew scramble up to rig the higher silks, and the need this day was not dire. And so it was that the *Eroean* haled away from the western continent in the dark of night, driven easterly under partial sail enmeshed in a whirling storm.

It was late mid morn when Aylis groaned awake. By the slant of her cabin she knew the ship was heeled over sharply, and the sound of wind in the rigging confirmed that they were in a heavy blow. Dim light seeped inward through the porthole, and a damp chill pervaded the cabin. Struggling up, she clambered out from her bunk and washed her face and dressed warmly. Then she stepped forth in the canted passageway, and bracing a hand against the bulkhead, she made her way toward the captain's lounge, where she found her father and Jinnarin waiting. A single lantern swinging from a head-beam cast swaying light over the two as the ship cut through the rolling swells. "Hmph," grunted Alamar, looking up, "thought you were going to sleep all day."

"Mayhap I could have, Father, but then what would I do tonight?"

"Exactly!" growled Alamar, disarmed by her reply.

As Aylis sat down, Jinnarin leapt from the table to a chair to the floor. "Are you hungry? I'll fetch Tink. He'll get you something to eat."

"Oh no you don't, Pysk," barked Alamar. "You'll be blown off the decks if you go out there."

Jinnarin laughed over her shoulder. "Even I know that, Alamar. Instead, I'm going through the passage to the wheelhouse and down through the trap." She disappeared into the gloomy corridor.

Alamar grunted his approval, then swung about and studied Aylis's face, at last softly saying, "Daughter, you still look pale, drawn. Fare you well?"

Aylis drew in a shuddering breath, and her heart thudded in her breast. And she realized that somewhere deep within, her soul was clutched in dread. "No, Father, I am not well. Instead, I am frightened."

Alamar reached out, his hand covering hers. "Can you yet speak of it . . . your dreamwalk?"

"I must, Father, for something"—now Aylis's heart began hammering, and she took another deep breath and let it out—"something hideous dwells within Jinnarin's nightmare. Something that slew Ontah. And we must discover what it is and what is behind this—this terror."

Alamar took up her trembling hand and held it. "After you get something to eat, Daughter, then will we speak of the dreamwalk and of what occurred therein."

Aylis nodded, squeezing Alamar's hand. "Aravan, too, Father. I would have him here when—"

A swift smile flashed over the elder's face. "Ha! That goes without saying, Daughter, without saying. In fact, I am surprised that he's not here now. He's been popping in and out like a blooming jack-in-the-box to see if you are yet awake."

The howl of the wind blasted down the corridor as

the door to the deck opened then closed. The eld Mage cackled. "If I am not mistaken, Daughter, that would be him now." Aravan stepped into the lounge, and Alamar crowed, "No sooner said than done."

Doffing his foul-weather gear, the Elf turned to Aylis. "Hast thou yet eaten?"

"Jinnarin has gone through the wheelhouse to fetch Tink."

Aravan added charcoal to the small iron stove, turning the damper a bit in the vent pipe leading up and out. He then took the chair next to Aylis. "Should this wind hold, we are now but five or so days from Rwn."

Alamar snorted. "Do you truly believe that we will discover anything there?"

Aravan shrugged. "Who can say?"

Aylis sighed. "I could . . . were not someone blocking all visions concerning—concerning whatever it is we pursue."

"The recovery of Farrix" came Jinnarin's voice, the Pysk just now stepping from the passageway, Tink in tow behind, the lad bearing a tray. "We are trying to find Farrix. That is what we pursue."

Aylis smiled. "Aye, Jinnarin. That we are. But there is more to this than a missing loved one, though just what it is, I cannot say. We will speak of it after breakfast . . . including the dreamwalk, Jinnarin. Including the dreamwalk."

Jinnarin took a deep breath and then exhaled and nodded sharply but once. "Yes, Aylis, after breakfast."

Alamar leaned forward as Tink uncovered the tray. "Cap'n, sir, I brought enough for all," said the cabin boy, smiling. "I reck'd that more than one would be hungry, given when they ate this morn."

"Thou didst well, Tink," said Aravan, "we could all use a bite."

"Thank you, Cap'n," said Tink. "Be there aught else?" At Aravan's negative shake of his head, Tink headed across the rolling floor and into the passageway beyond.

Alamar, needing no urging, took up a bowl and spooned in a ration of oatmeal, adding a dollop of honey to it, stirring it about then digging in. Aylis on the other hand ate tentatively—honey and bread for the most part—and in this she was joined by Jinnarin, the Pysk picking at her food. Aravan took nothing but tea and watched the others instead, noting that both Aylis and Jinnarin seemed to be bracing themselves for a distressing ordeal. None said aught for a while, wind and wave and the sounds of the *Eroean* were all that broke the silence. At last Aylis pushed her plate aside, a half-eaten crust of bread remaining, and she looked at Jinnarin, the Pysk cross-legged upon the table. "Let us begin."

Jinnarin glanced up and asked, "Where shall I start?"

Alamar growled, "At the beginning, Pysk."

As if anchored by his remark, Jinnarin nodded and took a deep breath. "I don't remember what I was dreaming before I found myself once again flying above the pale green sea, though however the dream started, whatever it was about, I don't think it matters. All I know is that there I was in the dark storm clouds, the black ship below me, lightning striking the masts."

Alamar looked at Aylis and asked, "Did her beginning dream have any bearing on the sending?"

Aylis shook her head. "No, Father. At least I think not. When Ontah and I stepped into her dream, she was standing upon a fallen oak."

"On a bank above a pool?" asked Jinnarin.

"Yes."

"It is near my home in Darda Glain."

"You walked out on a limb above the water and made ready to dive."

"Farrix and I swim there."

Aylis smiled. "When you dove, instead you flew. Up and away. Ontah and I flew up after. Soon we were among the storm clouds, the nightmare ship below, lightning crashing down upon it."

Alamar leaned forward. "Did you see anything strange?"

"Everything was strange, Father."

"No, I mean, did you see anything that Jinnarin had not before described to us?"

Aylis's eyes were lost in reflection. "No . . . or wait, perhaps. I saw other shapes on the sea, but it was too dark . . . they were too dim and distant to make out."

Jinnarin tilted her head. "Other shapes? Do you mean the island?"

"No, Jinnarin. The island I could see. These were perhaps other islands. Smaller."

"Hmm," mused Aravan. "Mayhap an archipelago or . . . I will scan my charts for a scattering of islands in a green sea."

Alamar held up a cautionary hand. "Remember: not all visions seen in dreams are what they seem. The storm, the ship, the sea, the islands, the crystal castle: they are perhaps but symbols representing something else entirely."

Aylis agreed. "Yes, Father, indeed as you will see, at least one or two were something else altogether."

"Oh?"

"Yes."

Jinnarin shivered in remembered horror, but she spoke on: "It was as before: suddenly I found myself in a crystal castle watching the black ship afar sailing toward me across the storm-tossed sea, and I was afraid.

"Then Aylis and Ontah came, and the dream *changed* into something different from before . . . and the fear got much, much worse."

Jinnarin looked up at the other three. "Even now my heart is pounding."

Aylis reached out and gently took Jinnarin's tiny hand in her own. "Mine, too, Jinnarin."

Alamar stroked his beard. "Changed? How so? Just how did the dream change."

Jinnarin took a deep breath. "Well, when Brightwing and White Owl—"

"Brightwing and White Owl? What's all this, Pysk? Who are they?"

"That's their dream names, Alamar. Aylis is Brightwing and Ontah is—was, White Owl. I was named Sparrow."

"Hmph," grunted Alamar, then signified that she should continue.

"When they came, the fear got worse. I would have fled but Brightwing called for me to stay. The crystal walls wavered, changed, and the ship, too. I wanted to run, but Brightwing— I thought my heart would burst, and even though I tried, I couldn't stay any longer. I had to flee."

Jinnarin stopped speaking, her gaze lost.

Alamar looked at Aylis. "The dream changed? How, Daughter?"

"When the fear came, White Owl called out that there was an evil spirit nearby. He then told me to stay with Sparrow and to flee at need, while he searched. That's when the dream began to change. The walls shifted, and it was as if I were seeing double: the finished crystal castle walls seemed overlaid with a roughness, as of unworked crystal. I felt as if I were being drawn into another dream, one different from Jinnarin's. And the fear, the dread, became almost more than I could bear. Even so, I called to Sparrow to wait, and the ship became a black spider running toward us. I began shrieking; I could not help myself. The walls wavered and began to fade as the dream, Jinnarin's dream, started collapsing. White Owl shouted for us to flee. A tunnel appeared, and I bolted in terror."

Fright once again welling within, Aylis began sobbing, and Aravan drew her to him, embracing her. Jinnarin, too, wept.

After a moment Aylis disengaged from Aravan and wiped her cheeks with the heels of her hands. "White Owl—Ontah—didn't escape. Instead he died there in that nightmare, in that sending, slain by something. . . ."

"The evil spirit?" asked Jinnarin, her face stark with remembered dread.

Aylis turned up her hands. "I know not, Jinnarin. Perhaps it was a spirit. Perhaps instead it was the fear."

Alamar took up the teapot and replenished his cup, spilling a bit as the ship rolled with the sea. "Would a spider cause such fear?"

Jinnarin nodded, her eyes wide. "It was a giant spider, Alamar."

"Even so . . ."

Aylis shrugged. "I don't know, Father. It seems to me that White Owl searched for the fear . . . elsewhere . . . as if he were not in Jinnarin's dream at all. I did not seek him, for he had charged me with Sparrow's safety. Regardless, I could not seem to take my eyes away from the ship, the spider."

Alamar glanced up at his daughter. "Perhaps then, Daughter, the spider wasn't—isn't the evil spirit at all, but is a diversion instead ... something to keep you from seeing past the symbols and into the true nature of the dream."

"Perhaps so, Father. But then again perhaps they are exactly what they seem."

Driven before the storm, late on the fifth day they sighted the island of Rwn, and southerly turned the *Eroean*, the ship cutting through the austral waters to come to the cove on the southeast coast mid of the sixth day, where she hove to and dropped anchor.

"Now shall we wait," said Aravan as the crew clambered down from the rigging, Elven silk furled 'round yardarms, jibs and staysails stowed.

It was the fifteenth of November, winter now gripping this northern clime.

Aylis peered at the sky. "I am afraid that we will see nothing through this overcast."

"Clear or cast," replied Aravan, "we may see nought regardless."

Aylis turned and faced the island. In the near distance, dark waves lapped the rocky shore. Above, on the rising, snow-covered land, tall pines stood, and where they shone through the white mantle the laden boughs were dressed in a green so dark as to seem a shade of blue. Here and there stretched tangles of deciduous trees, stark and barren in their winter dress, gnarled, frosted limbs clawing upward at the desolate sky.

Cloak-wrapped Alamar came stumping toward the aft deck, Jinnarin at his side, Rux following after. "We are going to bed now," called the Mage. "Got to be rested in order to stay awake throughout the night."

Jinnarin looked up at the elder. "I don't think I'll be able to sleep."

"Nonsense, Pysk. Besides, you've got to sleep. Only you have the eyes to see the plumes. Of course, with my magesight I'll be able to see them, too."

"Wait, Father," called Aylis, "let me do a weather casting. Unless the sky clears, no one will see anything this night regardless, plumes or no."

"It doesn't matter, Daughter," growled the Mage.

"We've got to become accustomed to staying awake. After all, we will be the ones on watch."

Aylis trod down the steps to the main deck. "Do not forget, Father, I have magesight as well. Even so, it is not certain that either you or I will see anything."

"Pah!" snorted Alamar. "If a Pysk can see them, then—"

"Then that's no guarantee that either of us will, magesight notwithstanding," interjected Aylis. "That aside, I will forecast the weather; it will take but a moment."

Tugging her cloak about her, Aylis walked forward to face the chill wind, the Elvenship having swung at anchor until her bow pointed into the draught. The seeress stood on the foredeck and gazed westerly over the bowsprit and intoned, *"Caelum in futura."* She watched as ship, water, and land disappeared and only the sky remained and hours passed in mere moments—day raced past, dusk but a flicker as starless night splashed across the skies, and then dawn burst into cloudy day but a lucid blue swiftly rived the grey and swept it away—and then her vision expired.

"It will clear by this time tomorrow," she said upon returning. "Tonight, though, the overcast remains."

Alamar growled under his breath. "Doesn't matter," he snapped. "I'm off to bed. From now until we see the plumes and discover where they are going, it's down in the day and up in the night. A schedule no different from the one I use when charting the stars, see."

He turned and trudged toward the aft-quarters door. "You coming, Pysk?" he called back over his shoulder. "Can't have you falling asleep on watch, you know."

"In a moment, Alamar," answered Jinnarin, watching until he disappeared through the door. She turned to Aravan standing on the afterdeck atop the steps. "I really am not at all sleepy."

Aravan stepped down to the main deck and squatted beside the Pysk. "Jinnarin, there is no need for thee to be on watch unless and until the boreal lights are in the skies. As to when that may be, I cannot say, for none I know commands them and they come at their own will. Thou need be awake and alert then and only then. Hence, were I thou, I would sleep as usual and waken only at need—only when the lights are in the sky. And my crew will rouse thee when such events occur. And should the lights come several nights running, well, thou wilt adapt quickly unto a backward day."

Jinnarin glanced at the door where Alamar had gone, then she grinned at the Elf. "We will tell Alamar in a bit, eh?"

The Pysk and fox wandered off to find Jatu, and when they were gone, Aylis turned to Aravan. "You said that none you know commands the boreal lights, and that is true. Yet if we are to believe the words of Jinnarin's Farrix, then perhaps someone does indeed hold dominion over the aurora ... or parts of it. But why, I cannot say."

In the late afternoon, Alamar came stumping up onto the deck. Aylis stood in the starboard bow, leaning against the forward mainrail. The elder took a place at her side. "Couldn't sleep," he grumbled when she turned her head to look at him.

Aylis faced the island again, and the two stood and looked at the waves crashing against the shore. At last the elder bade, "A copper for your thoughts."

Aylis sighed, then said, "Father, here we stand off the shore of Rwn, less than a day's sail from Kairn, less than a day from your cottage. But even more importantly, less than a day from Vadaria."

"Eh?" Alamar looked at Aylis. "What's Vadaria got to do with anything?"

Now Aylis turned to her father, tears in her eyes. "Father, I look at you and see that your <fire> has burned low. Not many castings are left within you, and should you attempt something major, it could cost you your very life. You are nigh spent, and you well know that it is time for you to go home and regain your youth, your <power>."

Alamar bristled. "Pah! I am as good as—"

"No, Father, you are not!" burst out Aylis in anger, thrusting out her hand, palm forward, to stop his words. "Father, you look upon this quest as a lark, as one last fling. Yet it is anything but!"

"Bah!" snorted Alamar, his jaw jutted stubbornly.

Confronting Alamar, Aylis saw an eld Mage before

her, but saw as well the aged face of Ontah. "Father, you know the truth of what I am saying, and you must not pretend otherwise. One has already died on this mission, and I would not have the next be you."

Huffing and grinding his teeth, Alamar turned his back to Aylis.

"Please, Father, listen to me. Were you filled with the energy of restored youth, none better could be enlisted to see the mission through. Yet you are not and we are opposed by someone of great power, and I fear for your life. For at this moment you are old and nearly spent, no match for another Mage."

Alamar spun, his palm raised as if to strike her. She stood unflinching, weeping, her hands at her side. Of a sudden he looked at his upheld hand in wonder, and the rage left him. He pulled her to him, hugging her fiercely, or as fiercely as his frail form would permit. And she clutched his thin frame to herself and wept. At last he held her at arm's length and growled, "Aylis. What you say is true. I am old. There, I said it: I am old. No one likes to admit that he is old. No one. But I am. Old.

"I should—I must journey to Vadaria, and soon, for I have not much <fire> left within me. Even so, I'll not leave this expedition until we've settled what's happened to Farrix"—Alamar held up a hand to stop the protest springing to Aylis's lips—"I gave my sworn word, and I will not go back on it . . . after all, he saved my life. But heed, I will be careful, spending as little as possible, for as you can see, I know my limits. Once we've found Farrix, once this mission is done, then will I go, I promise—first to Kairn, the City of Bells, for I would say good-bye to someone there, and then to Vadaria to regain my youth."

Alamar cocked an eyebrow. "And that, Daughter, is the best I can do. Does it suffice?"

Aylis studied his elderly face. At last she sighed and pulled him to her and gave him a hug. "Yes, Father, it will have to do." Then it was she who held him at arm's length. "But you must remember your promise—to husband your <fire> and spend it only at great need. This is not a lark, not a last grand adventure. I will have no more of this showing off in battle, exploding enemy fireballs, or anything else of the like."

Alamar looked long at her, but at last nodded. "You drive a hard bargain, Daughter."

Again she embraced him, a timorous smile on her face, for deep inside she doubted that he would keep his promise.

Jinnarin sat with Aylis in the seeress's quarters, the Pysk cross-legged on the drop-leaf of the writing desk, Aylis sitting on her bunk and leaning back against the wall, each sipping tea. Night had fallen and the cabin was lit by the soft yellow glow of lantern light. The two were alone and had been since the evening meal—Aravan and his officers were in the ship's lounge setting the order of the watch for the days to come, and Alamar had retired to his own cabin. And so the two sat and spoke of things that had been and things that were and things that might never be.

"I learned something today, Jinnarin."

"Oh?"

"From my father. Something he said."

Jinnarin said nought, waiting for Aylis to continue.

"Yes, and I think that it applies to Mages and mortals alike."

Jinnarin set her tiny cup aside. "You Mages are passing strange, I think. But then so are mortals." Jinnarin laughed. "Perhaps so are we all.

"Regardless, what did Alamar say?"

"He told me that no one likes to admit that they are old."

Jinnarin shrugged. "I wouldn't know. I'm not mortal."

"Neither am I, Jinnarin. Nevertheless, my father's remark has raised questions within me, bringing issues to light."

"Such as . . . ?"

Aylis gazed at the Pysk. "Do you remember what White Owl looked like in the dreamwalks?"

Jinnarin nodded. "Yes. He was dark-haired. Slender. Strong."

Aylis leaned forward. "Yes. Not at all like the Ontah we first met, for in his waking life he was white-haired and frail."

"Rather like your father, Aylis."

"Yes. But I remember when my father was filled with

the vigor of youth, his hair dark brown, his limbs strong, his body lean and firm."

Jinnarin glanced up. "Like Ontah in the dream."

"Yes. Still, my father will regain his youth, whereas Ontah's was gone forever . . . except in his dreams."

Jinnarin sighed. "Do you suppose that aged mortals think of themselves as being old? I mean, in their thoughts, do they think that they are the same as they were when they were young?"

"I don't know, Jinnarin, but that is one of the things I wonder about. Mortals cannot but help knowing that they are getting frail, weakening, their health failing, their bodies losing the power to swiftly recover from injuries, even perhaps suffering from injuries that never heal. Still, taking account of their infirmities, in their thoughts as well as in their dreams, they must consider themselves yet vital."

"Does anyone ever dream of themselves as being truly old?"

"Again, I don't know, but if they do, then perhaps they have given up on living."

"Is that what it means to be old? To give up on living?"

"Perhaps, Jinnarin, perhaps." Aylis smiled, for the Pysk's thoughts were tracking her own. "But if so, then how long one has lived—the number of seasons, of years they have seen—has little to do with being old. Age alone does not determine elderliness. Instead it is attitude, outlook, an interest in life, neh?"

Jinnarin shrugged. "Perhaps." She glanced down at her hands. "I have lived . . . hmm . . . oh, several thousand years, yet it seems to me as if I've always thought as I do now, that my embracing of life is the same. I wonder if it is different for mortals?"

Aylis shook her head. "I don't know, Jinnarin. But what you say of yourself is true for me as well: it seems as if I have always considered life as I do now. It may be the same for mortals, too . . . at least for some of them—all mortals are not alike. Perhaps many think of themselves as they did when they were younger. On the other hand, perhaps infirmities change one's outlook, leading to bitterness, leading to agedness. Certainly my father is infirm ... and crotchety ... not at all what he will become when he regains his vitality."

Jinnarin steepled her fingers. "Is it the inevitability of death that ages mortals, or is it instead the ageing process that makes death inevitable?"

Aylis shrugged. "I cannot say, for although I age—by that I mean I gradually become more elderly as I loose energy in castings—I can regain my spent youth. Hence, I cannot say what determines mortality, for I am not mortal."

Jinnarin scratched an eyebrow. "Neither of us are.... Perhaps we will never know."

A soft knock sounded on the cabin door. Aylis opened it and found Aravan standing there. The Elf saw the Pysk. "Oh, I did not mean to interrupt—"

Jinnarin stood, stretching, yawning. "No interruption at all, Aravan. I was just saying that it was off to bed for me."

As Jinnarin jumped down to the chair and then to the floor, Aravan said, "In that case, Aylis, wouldst thou care to take some fresh air with me?"

Aylis turned to fetch her cloak, and Jinnarin smiled to herself, noting that where Aravan stood, his shadow was lost in the darkness of the corridor. *Indeed, I do believe that Jatu was right about the captain losing his shadow to the Lady Aylis.*

Riding at anchor, the ship slowly rose and fell as long swells passed under the hull. Aylis and Aravan strolled the length of the main deck, their way dimly lit by a single lantern astern. Overhead the sky was yet clouded and neither stars nor Moon shown down. A chill drift of air flowed over the ship, but neither Aylis nor Aravan seemed to note its passage, comforted as they were by each other's presence. They stopped and leaned on the forward rail and peered at the dim silhouette of Rwn in the near distance looming against the dark sky. From somewhere below there drifted the sound of a concertina and Men singing, as well as the rhythmic clack of Dwarven batons striking against bucklers, measuring out the music's gleeful beat. Laughter washed up as the song ended, but then another began.

"You have a good crew, Aravan."

"Aye. Worthy in all respects."

Elf and seeress listened as the chorus rose up and fell back, the piping and clacking momentarily drowned out.

Aylis turned to Aravan. "I have something to ask you." Of a sudden her heart began thudding in her breast.

Aravan straightened up from the railing and turned toward her, waiting.

"When Ontah, when I—" She took a breath and began again. "When I awakened from my last dreamwalk, you called me by an Elven word—"

"Chieran," said Aravan, his eyes lost in shadow.

"What does it mean?"

Aravan took her by the hand. "It means, my love."

Aylis's heart raced. *"Chieran?"*

Aravan raised her hand to his mouth and kissed her palm. "My love." He pressed her hand against his cheek. "All my life I knew that something was missing. I did not know what it was until I saw thee."

With her free hand Aylis reached up and took his face in her hands, pulling him to her. *"Chieran,"* she whispered, then kissed him full on the mouth, gently at first but then with exploding passion. His arms went 'round her, and he crushed her against his breast, fire flowing between them, lips burning, hearts hammering, souls soaring, her arms clasping him, their bodies pressing together.

Slowly, gently, he pulled back, shadowed eyes gazing into shadowed eyes. Then with a shout of elation he lifted her up and spun 'round and 'round proclaiming *"Chieran!"* to the sky, Aylis laughing in unfettered joy.

On the stern, Jatu leaned against the taffrail and peered down into the waters, a smile creasing his face.

CHAPTER 16

Flux

Winter, 1E9574–75
[The Present]

Aylis wakened to the sound of rustling paper. The surroundings were unfamiliar, but she knew precisely where she was and she smiled. Unclothed, Aravan stood at a table, his frame lean and firm and showing no scars. Maps were scattered before him, and he intently studied a chart then cast it aside, selecting another. In silence Aylis watched entranced, as if she were observing some beautiful, enchanted creature, a creature that might fly from her were she to speak. She lay and reveled at how the light played across his body, at how his black, black hair framed his face and fell 'round his shoulders, black hair in one other place as well. Memories flooded her, and she languorously stretched. Aravan turned at the whisper of her movement, smiling to see her awake.

"Chieran," he said, dropping the parchment and stepping toward her.

"My love," she responded, her heart quickening. And as he came to the edge of the bed, Aylis lifted her arms and pulled him to her, kissing first his hands and then his lips. His arms went 'round her, and passion again flared. They made slow, gentle love.

Spent, they lay side by side, Aravan on his back, his arm around Aylis, she with her cheek upon his chest, Aylis taking in the clean scent of him, of salt and leather

199

and something elusive but undeniably masculine. After a while she raised up and gestured at the littered room. "Quite a mess you've made, love. Why so?"

Aravan turned his head and looked at the scatter of maps. "I was searching for an archipelago in a green sea. I found many chains, but there is no note as to the color of the waters. Yet Jinnarin speaks of it in no other terms but that of a pale green sea."

Aylis shivered, and drew down against Aravan, clasping him tightly, her thoughts returning to the nightmare sending. "Adon, but I wish that there were no hideous dream."

Aravan kissed the top of her head and stroked her light brown hair, wild-tossed and fine. "Ah, but were there no dream, *chieran*, then I would not have met thee, at least not this soon."

Aylis clutched him tighter.

They lay without speaking for long moments, Aravan finally breaking the silence. "I would have thee move thy things herein, for I would not live away from thee now that we are discovered of one another."

Aylis raised up and looked down at him, saying nought, as if she were searching for some truth.

"*Vi chier ir,* Aylis," he said. "I love thee."

At last she smiled and nodded and then kissed him. "I will move in this very moment, *chieran*." And growling, she slid astraddle him, but as he reached up for her, she laughed and slipped away.

As Aylis stepped from the stateroom, Jinnarin and Alamar looked up from the game of tokko they played, the Pysk sitting at the edge of the six-sided board scribed with black and white hexagons, red and green coin-shaped pieces scattered thereon, other, taller, carven shapes ranged 'round the edges ready to assault the center.

Jinnarin smiled as Aylis nodded then walked toward the corridor.

Alamar called after her. "Not that you need it, Daughter, but you have my blessing."

Then the eld Mage peevishly shouted, "No, no, Pysk! You can't move an eagle that way! Here, let me show you—it's up and over two hexes and down front left or right on the third ... unless, of course, there's a storm in between, in which case the eagle is deflected rightward or leftward two, unless there's a storm there as well."

"You didn't tell me about the storms, Alamar" came Jinnarin's tart reply.

Minutes later, when Aylis came back through the captain's lounge, Jinnarin was standing in the middle of the tokko board, pieces scattered about as if she had kicked them aside; her fists were on her hips, and she glared up at the Mage. "What do you mean locusts? Where did *they* come from? You're making this up as you go along, Alamar."

"Argh," growled Alamar, huffily crossing his arms and turning his back to her. "You never listen, Pysk."

Laughing, Aylis kissed her father in passing, and bore her bundle into the stateroom. Aravan was by this time dressed, and again he stood at the table and pored over the maps, yet looking for an archipelago in a pale green sea.

As Aylis returned on her second and final trip, Alamar and Jinnarin were intently studying the tokko board, the pieces in disarray, Jinnarin grinning wickedly, Alamar muttering, "You blew up my eagle."

Rux came trotting down the passageway, his tail held high, a dead rat in his mouth. He proudly looked up at Jinnarin, then dropped the rat on Alamar's foot.

Aylis surveyed the scene and burst out in ringing laughter, her heart free and soaring in joy. She was, after all, utterly in love.

In late morning the overcast began to clear, faint patches of blue gradually showing through, as if the sky were carving down through the clouds from above, shaving away the vapor. Soon, long streaks of azure rived the overcast, splitting it, gaps growing. A westerly wind drove the remnants before it, and the Sun appeared, winter-low in the southern sky. When evening fell, the vault above was crystal clear.

Jinnarin stood on the foredeck and marvelled, "It was just as Aylis said, Alamar. Her seer's casting held true."

"Of course," snapped Alamar, the Mage yet smarting from his loss at tokko. And to a rank beginner, no less!

No doubt it was the rat dropped on his foot that had caused him to lose his concentration. No doubt.

"And you can't cast seer's spells, you say?"

Alamar glared at the Pysk. "I could, had I the inclination . . . and, of course, the training."

"How many different kinds of Mages are there, Alamar?"

"Why, we're all different."

"No, no. I mean, how many different *types*? Aylis is a seer. And you are . . . *hmm* . . . just what *are* you, Alamar?"

Alamar glowered down at Jinnarin. "Still fishing for secrets, eh, Pysk?"

"Well, if you don't wish to tell me . . ."

"Oh, all right. It's no secret. I shape the elements: earth, air, fire, water, aethyr. Bend 'em to my will."

"How does it work, Alamar? How do strange words in a special language cause things to—to *happen?*"

"Pah, Pysk. Things just don't 'happen.' Instead, a Mage has to spend energy, astral fire, to bring about an effect. Look, it's like finding a special leverage point and using a small bit of force to cause a big thing to occur. Rather like tipping over a huge balanced rock with nothing more than a slender prying pole, or causing a massive rockslide with but a small pebble.

"The astral fire within each thing can be manipulated with an expenditure of the Mage's own astral fire. Usually it takes but a small amount—such as for magesight. At other times it requires a great deal of astral fire to bring about the effect—for example, causing the collapse of a well-built castle would claim much <power>."

"But Alamar, how do mere words bring this about?"

"Oh, Jinnarin, the words themselves are nothing but keys to unlock the ingrained casting rituals. Depending on their nature, the castings themselves well from the heart, or the mind, or spirit, or soul. In our training we begin with very small castings, quickly discovering that different castings require different applications of <fire> for different effects. In order to master a given effect, we ritualize the specific application of the leverage fire, so that each new time is identical to the previous. Part of that ritual is to give it a key word, something that will recreate the proper conditions in the Mage's heart, mind, spirit, or soul to reproduce the effect without undue time being spent to rediscover how it is done—rather like learning to do something without having to actually think about it. Take for example, walking, running, throwing, catching, swimming, and the like ... when we first begin, these things are difficult, but with practice they become second nature. The same is true of learning how to apply <fire> in such a way as to produce a desired effect, and the resulting method is ritualized and triggered by a word—different words for different rituals, which produce different states of being, which shapes the astral fire differently, which leads to different effects. And as it is with any training, Mages start small and work their way up.

"And that, my curious Pysk, is why I do not cast seer's spells. I have not the training. But likewise, most seers do not cast elemental spells, for their training has taken them down a different path from mine."

Jinnarin slowly nodded. "I think I understand, Alamar. But tell me: how many different kinds of Mages are there?"

Alamar pondered a bit, finally saying, "As I said, we are all different, but I suppose you could say that there are perhaps a dozen different kinds of—"

"A *dozen?*" blurted out Jinnarin, her eyes wide.

Alamar nodded. "Elementalists, seers, sorcerers, mystics, illusionists, mentalists, healers, alchemists, artifactors, and—and— Look, Pysk, just take my word for it. There are many different kinds of Mages—those who shape the elements or thoughts or emotions or vitality or growth, or those who peer into the past or future, or those who do any other number of things—all of whom manipulate the <fire>, all of whom are trained in their own, special rituals."

Jinnarin gestured toward the island of Rwn. "At the college in Kairn?"

"Mostly."

"Why Kairn, Alamar? Why do Mages train there and not on Vadaria?"

"Because, Pysk, the <fire> burns brighter in Mithgar than it does in Vadaria. Hence, castings come easier here, and so training is conducted here rather than on the home world."

"Oh. So all the Mages get their training in Kairn, eh?"

"All but the Black Ones."

Jinnarin looked up in surprise. "Black Ones? You mean black like Jatu?"

Alamar snorted. "Bah. No, Miss Nosy Pysk, I mean the Black Mages—those who practice the forbidden ways." Alamar held up a hand, stopping Jinnarin's question. "Before you ask, I'll tell you. Mages have certain powers and talents that others do not. It would be rather easy for a Mage to dominate, to subjugate, those who are without the ability to control the <fire>. Hence we have adopted a code of conduct, an ethic to prevent such domination. But some Mages do not adhere to this ethic. Do you recall our discussion about the great debate between Gyphon and Adon?"

Jinnarin nodded. "Yes. Adon was for free will; Gyphon for domination and control."

Alamar smiled. "You have the pith of it, Pysk. And that is what separates most of Magekind from the Black Mages: we follow the precepts of Adon, while they follow the teachings of Gyphon. They seek dominion, control, power over others; we do not."

Jinnarin looked down at her hands. "Well then, Alamar, it seems that they fit my definition of evil."

Alamar sighed. "Yes, Jinnarin, they do. They fit my definition of evil, as well."

"In that case, Alamar, I hope there aren't too many of them about."

Alamar canted his head in agreement then looked up at the darkening sky, stars now appearing in the firmament. "I'm off to get my rest, Pysk. There might be an aurora tonight."

"Yes, there might," replied Jinnarin. "How about a game of tokko before you go?"

Alamar glared down at the Pysk. "A challenge, eh? Well, Miss Lucky Beginner, I pick up your flung gauntlet. But no rats, you hear, no rats allowed!"

There was no aurora that night.

And the game ended with Jinnarin kicking the pieces off the board.

Aravan lay in bed with his arm about Aylis. "This eve

I heard thy father and Jinnarin speaking of Kairn and of Mage training. Is that where thou learned thy craft, *chieran*?"

By the starlight shining in through the porthole, Aylis raised up on an elbow and peered at her Elven lover. "Yes. Kairn, the City of Bells."

"Is it difficult to learn to be a seer?"

Aylis shrugged. "Not for me. Of course, each person has a natural bent. Mine was to be a seer. Perhaps just as yours was to be the captain of a fleet ship and ply the waters of the world."

"I had never seen an ocean until I came to Mithgar."

"Tell me of it, love."

Aravan's thoughts returned to a day long past. "When I rode out of the dawn and into Mithgar, I came into the youth and wildness of this new world, leaving behind the stately grace and beauty of ancient Adonar. I found myself in a misty swale, the grassy crowns of mounded hills all about. I was not surprised by the cast of the terrain, for as thou knowest, crossings between are fair matched to one another. Unexpectedly, though, there came unto mine ears the distant sound of *shssh*ing booms. Curious, I turned my horse toward the rolling roar, riding southerly among the diminishing downs. Upward my path took me, up a long, shallow slope, the sounds increasing, the wind in my face, a salt tang on the air. I found myself on a high, chalk cliff, the white bluff falling sheer. Out before me, as far as mine eye could see, stretched deep blue waters, reaching to the horizon and beyond. It was an ocean, the Avagon Sea, its azure waves booming below, high-tossed spray glittering like diamonds cast upward in the morning Sun. My heart sang at such a sight and mine eyes brimmed with tears, and in that moment something slipped comfortably into my soul. And although I had not before come unto this world, I felt as if I were home at last."

Aravan fell silent, and after a moment Aylis bent down and kissed him.

Aravan looked up at her. "It was the same when I first saw, thee, *chieran*. When thou clambered up out of thy gig and over the side of the *Eroean,* my heart sang with the wonder of thee. It does each time I see thy face and form, it does each time I drown in thy gold-flecked green gaze. I am drunk with thee, Aylis, and always will I be so.''

Aravan pulled Aylis to him, their kiss long and lingering, passion kindling. ''No, wait,'' whispered Aylis, ''I have something to show you.''

She scrambled over the top of him, and padded across the floor, her flesh glowing ivory in the shining starlight. Rummaging through a drawer where she had stowed some of her things—''Aha''—she came back to the bed, once again climbing over Aravan and settling at his side.

''I was just a girl among many when I first entered the college at Kairn. Almost as soon as they are able, many who are seers do a casting upon a silver mirror, a casting to see their true love. In public I scoffed at those who had done so, thereby demonstrating my superiority over those who practiced such childish rituals. But in private, when I had the ability, I did my own casting upon my own silver mirror.''

''And what didst thou see?''

Aylis held up a small disk of polished silver. ''Look deep within and tell me what you see.''

Aravan steadied the mirror in the starlight and peered within. ''I see nought but mine own face,'' he said at last.

Aylis looked down into his deep blue eyes and said, ''Exactly so.''

Two more days and nights passed, and still the northern lights did not shine. But against the stars of the third clear night the spectral flare of the aurora shimmered, the eerie display writhing high in the winter sky, pastel hues shifting among the colors of the spectrum.

Jinnarin and Alamar, Aravan and Aylis, Jatu and Frizian and Bokar, and nearly all the crew—Men and Dwarves alike—stood watch upon the decks . . . but no plumes did they see.

''Storm takes eagle,'' crowed Alamar, snapping up the piece.

Jinnarin looked up. ''Oh,'' she said, her attention once again on the board. ''I didn't see it coming.''

Alamar glowered at her. ''I don't even know why we are playing, Pysk. You haven't been here all evening.''

Jinnarin reached out and turned her throne on its side,

signifying resignation. "You're right, Alamar. My mind isn't on the game."

"What then?"

"Oh, I've been thinking about Gyphon and Black Mages and the nature of evil."

"Back on that, eh? Well, have you come to any conclusions?"

Jinnarin leaned against the book she used as a backrest. "Not much more than before. Just a few observations, that's all."

"Such as . . . ?"

Jinnarin took a deep breath. "Such as, well, I started with the premise of someone trying to control, to dominate another. That led me to thinking about acts of evil." Jinnarin looked up at the Mage. "You know, I don't even like to think about this, Alamar. It does nothing but drag my spirit down."

"Then why do it?"

"Because I can't get it out of my mind!" snapped Jinnarin, leaping to her feet. "You started it, Alamar, and I can't seem to stop it."

"Oh no, Pysk. It was your curiosity that—"

"Oh, stop it," demanded Jinnarin. "It really doesn't matter who started it. It's just that I can't seem to turn loose of it. And it makes me feel bad."

Alamar stroked his white beard. "What that usually means, Pysk, is that you're still working on a problem. In this case, you are still trying to understand the nature of evil. Look, sometimes talking to others helps clarify the thoughts and clear the mind. So I suggest that you sit down and tell me what you've come up with."

With a sigh, Jinnarin resumed her seat. Alamar got the teakettle from the stove and replenished their cups. As the Mage settled down again, Jinnarin began:

"I have thought that one cannot be directly controlled by another without deliberate submission. This can come about in several ways, among which are: the person wants to be controlled, has no will of their own, or is driven by fear of the consequences.

"This led me to believe that purveyors of evil use coercion, intimidation, and force to control others.

"And that, Alamar, is as far as my thinking got."

The eld Mage nodded. "Perhaps that is enough, Jinnarin, though I would add to your list manipulation—be it overt, covert, subtle, or blatant. Given our previous discussions as well as this one, perhaps you now have enough of a foundation to see acts for what they are: good or evil, fair or foul. Can you name me some evil acts?"

Again Jinnarin took in a deep breath and let it out slowly. "Murder for gain. Murder of innocents. Thralldom. Whippings and beatings to force people to do as you will. Threats. Rape. Pillage. Wanton destruction. . . . Oh, Alamar, I don't wish to think of it any longer."

Alamar gazed down at her. "You will turn loose of it when you are ready, Jinnarin," he said, gently. "Until then I would have you consider the following: you have named several of the great evils; but can you name some of the small ones? Those which seem on the surface to be nothing more than, say, callous or even thoughtless acts, but which are evil at their core? I speak here not of the big things, like, say, torture, but instead of the smaller things."

"You mean like the hunting of foxes for sport?"

Alamar smiled. "Perhaps."

"Well, that's a rather big thing with me, Alamar."

"Yes, Jinnarin, I know."

More days passed and winter deepened, the lines and masts and spars of the *Eroean* lading up with ice, crews clambering in the shrouds to break the pulleys free and to shake the ice from the silken ropes and loosen it from the outer layer of the fully reefed sails, keeping the ship at the ready, for who knew when they would be called to raise sail and get underway to chase a streamer, to chase a will-o'-the-wisp? But night after night came the boreal lights, night after night . . . yet no plumes did they see.

"Argh," spat Alamar after a week of such, "nothing at all. Oh well, at least we are anchored for the moment where I will see the occultation."

"Occultation?" asked Jinnarin.

"Didn't I just say that, Pysk?"

Jinnarin bridled, but said nothing.

Aravan looked down at Jinnarin. "Mage Alamar is

right. Here in these latitudes the Moon will eat the Sun late next month, two days before Year's Long Night."

Alamar nodded in confirmation, then sighed. "Would that I had the Elves' gift, Aravan. The Sun, Moon, and stars are my passion, yet I must cipher what will be their patterns, whereas you and your Kind simply *know*."

"Do all Folk have a gift?" asked Jinnarin. "I mean, Mages can control the astral fire; Elves know where stands the heavens; my Kind can gather shadow. What gift have the Dwarves?"

"They cannot lose their footsteps," replied Aravan. "No matter where they travel on land, they can always unerringly retrace their paths."

"How about at sea?"

"Nay. Neither, I deem, through the air. Only on land, and then only when they are in good health—not, say, when they are delirious with fever ... or so Drimma have told me. Time and again have I seen Drimma make use of this gift of theirs."

Alamar cleared his throat. "I understand that they can retrace their steps blindfolded."

"So, too, do I understand, though I have never seen it," replied Aravan.

"Tell me," asked Jinnarin, "what is the gift of Man?"

Alamar looked at Aravan and then replied, "Fecundity."

Aylis removed the blindfold and examined the cards laid out before her, some of them faceup, others facedown. She sat at the table in the lounge. To the left sat Aravan, Jinnarin to the right. Across the table opposite sat Alamar. None said aught while she studied the layout of the arcanely scribed flats, and yellow lantern light cast slowly shifting shadows as the Elvenship rode at anchor upon the gentle swells.

"Arr," growled Aylis, frustrated, slapping her hand down upon the cards, "this makes no sense at all!"

"What?" asked Jinnarin, leaning forward as if to better see. "What doesn't make sense?"

"None of it. None of it at all," replied Aylis. She reached out and turned over one of the cards and sharply drew in her breath. "No wonder," she muttered, her finger stabbing down. "See this?"—she pointed at

the newly revealed picture, someone in a dark robe—
"It is the Mage, and he sits in the strait, blocking all."

"The strait?"

"Yes." Aylis gestured at the layout—four cards in a row across the top, three cards in the next row, then two, then one, followed by two, then three, then four. "See, we have a pyramid tapering down, then flaring back out. The strait is the narrowest part. It represents the key, the critical juncture. And the Hidden Mage Reversed blocks all." The picture of the person in the dark robe sat alone at the key.

Jinnarin stood and walked over to the spread. "Reversed?"

"Aye," answered Aylis. "With respect to the Delver, a card takes on six positions: Open, Obverse, Upright, Reversed, Leftward, Rightward. Open means faceup, the picture showing, a factor not hidden. Obverse means just the opposite, the card facedown, a hidden factor. Upright means that the picture is rightside up to me, the Delver, whereas Reversed means it is upside down to me. Upright aids; Reversed opposes."

Jinnarin cocked her head. "What about Left and Right?"

"Leftward is sinister; Rightward is beneficent."

Alamar glared at the card in the strait, the cloaked figure upside down to Aylis. "So this confirms we are opposed by a hidden Mage, eh?"

"Didn't we already know this?" asked Jinnarin. "I mean, Aylis's other attempts—with the black water, and the card showing the shattered tower, and all—revealed that we were being blocked."

Aylis inclined her head in agreement. "Blocked, yes. But *if* the cards show true, they now tell us that it is indeed a Mage and not a god or demon."

Aravan's voice came softly. "Then the spread is not entirely without use. What else say the cards?"

Aylis again peered at the dual pyramid. At last she said, "It seems to be entirely at random, as if the cards were selected haphazardly with no purpose at all. Except for the Obverse, Reversed Mage, I would say that chance alone governed the layout."

Jinnarin looked up at Aylis. "Well isn't it true? Doesn't chance alone determine what befalls the cards?"

Alamar snorted. "In hands less skilled than those of my daughter, Pysk, you are right. But in Aylis's hands, or those of other seers, random chance plays little or no part."

"Unless blocked, Father," murmured Aylis, placing a finger on the card in the strait. "Unless blocked by a higher power."

Aravan reached out and laid a hand on Aylis's. "If thou canst see nought of the mission, then mayhap individual readings will reveal what a general reading will not."

Aylis sighed. "I tried to do so when I was in Tugal, but I found only danger in the cards."

"You didn't know us then," suggested Jinnarin.

"I knew my father," replied Aylis, "and still I discovered but a meager bit: only that he was in jeopardy and on the *Eroean*, which would soon pass through the Straits of Kistan."

Alamar stood and went to the porthole and peered out.

Aravan leaned back. "But now that we are known to thee, *chieran*, mayhap a reading on one of us will reveal something new."

Aylis turned up her hands. "Perhaps. Perhaps not. I can but try." She turned to the Pysk and gestured opposite. "Be seated, Jinnarin. I will start with you."

Somewhat timorously, Jinnarin sat atop the table across from Aylis.

Aylis replaced the black blindfold about her own eyes, and reached out and began spreading and swirling and mingling the cards, blindly turning some over and then others while whispering under her breath. At last she drew them all together into a single pack. "Jinnarin, close your eyes and then divide the cards into three separate stacks, first one to my left, then one to my right, but leave the final one in the center. Try to keep your mind clear as you do so, for we strive to find how outside events impinge upon your life."

"Do you mean blank? Keep my mind a blank?"

"Yes."

"I don't know if I can think of absolutely nothing whatsoever."

In the shadows Alamar growled but said nought.

Jinnarin stood and stepped to the cards. She drew in a sharp breath, for staring up at her was a picture of a skeleton. Kneeling down and closing her eyes, she divided the deck as Aylis had said. "It is done," she said. "Can I open my eyes now?"

"Yes."

Jinnarin opened her eyes, and backed away as Aylis reached out and blindly reassembled the three stacks into one—left on the right, with the center turned completely over and placed on top—and then she cut the cards once and then once more. The seeress then began dealing out the cards. In the first row, she placed four straight-up cards side by side. In the second row, she placed three cards: the left one sideways, the center one straight up, and the right one sideways. In the third row she placed two sideways cards. In the fourth row went a single card, straight up. Then she arranged four straight-up cards in a column to the right of all. She laid the remainder aside and then reached up to remove the silken blindfold as Jinnarin studied the layout: some of the cards were faceup, Open, their pictures showing; others were facedown, hidden, Obverse. Jinnarin could also see that some were Reversed and others Upright as well as both Left and Right.

"Tell me what the arrangement means, Aylis."

Aylis frowned at the cards, then said, "This inverted pyramid of ten cards is called the Spread. The top row of four represents significant events you will face, for good if Upright, for ill if Reversed. The second row of three depicts other factors involved, opposing or aiding if Left or Right, the middle card for good or ill. The third row of two shows Fortune's hand, aiding or opposing or both. And the single card on the final row represents the critical factor, the strait. The four cards to the right represent the Cycle of Time, and from top to bottom they demarcate the past, the present, the future, and a key moment. If a card is faceup, it represents something that was, or is, or will be in the open, whereas a facedown card is something that is hidden."

"All right. Then how do you read them, Aylis?"

"Initially I will read the Spread in general. Then we will examine it through the Cycle of Time: first, as it is affected by the past; then in light of the present; then

with an eye to the future; and finally we will see where
the key moment fits in.''

Aylis studied the layout. "Exactly half the cards are
Open, half Obverse. Not a rarity, yet a bit unusual.''

She began turning up the Obverse cards, setting them
somewhat lower in their rows so that they could easily
be identified later. As she turned them, a frown came
over her features. "This makes little or no sense," she
muttered. When all the cards were faceup, she shook
her head. "Random, all but one.''

From his position by the porthole, Alamar said, "Let
me guess: the Mage is in the strait, neh?''

Aylis turned and looked at her sire. "Yes, Father. And
he is Reversed.''

Alamar stalked to the table and leaned forward on his
hands. "Then, Daughter, I suggest that it is not random
at all.''

Aylis nodded. "Blocked again.''

Aravan asked, "Is there nothing thou canst see within
the Spread—past, present, future, or e'en the key
moment?''

Aylis turned up the facedown cards in the Cycle of
Time and studied the whole for long moments. After a
while she looked up at Aravan and shook her head.

Aravan moved to the chair across the table from
Aylis. "Then try me, *chieran*.''

Again Aylis tied the black silk across her eyes then
blindly stirred and mingled the cards, turning them over
and over at random, all the while chanting under her
breath. At last Aravan divided them in three stacks, and
Aylis reassembled the deck and cut it twice. Then she
dealt out the Spread—again five were Open, five Obverse. And she dealt out the Cycle of Time—two were
facedown, two faceup.

Aylis removed the blindfold. As she turned up the
Obverse cards in the Spread, Jinnarin, Alamar, and Aravan looked on intently. Jinnarin drew in a sharp breath
as the straight was revealed—the Mage Reversed. After
a long moment of study, Aylis looked up at Aravan and
shook her head.

She then reached out and turned up the two Obverse
cards in the Cycle of Time. As she revealed the final
one, she gasped uncontrollably and looked straight at

Aravan—*through* Aravan—her eyes wild and unfocused, and she hoarsely cried, *"Introrsum trahe supernum ignem—pyrà—in obscuram gemmam!"*

And then her eyes rolled up and she fell forward unconscious, Jinnarin shrieking her name.

CHAPTER 17

Streams

Winter, 1E9574–75
[The Present]

Aylis!" cried Jinnarin, leaping to her feet as the seeress swooned and fell forward, scattering cards across the table.

Cat quick, Aravan was at her side, scooping her up in his arms. "Brandy, Alamar," he barked, and he bore her toward the captain's stateroom.

Inside, as Aravan gently lowered Aylis to the bed, Alamar stepped to a cabinet and took from it a decanter of brandy, pouring a bit into a small glass and holding it out to the Elf. Cradling Aylis, Aravan gauged her pulse —"It's steady"—and waited until he saw her eyelids flutter, then he took the jigger from Alamar. Aylis opened her eyes and looked into Aravan's.

"Chieran," murmured the Elf, lifting her to a sitting position. "Here, drink." He held the shot to her lips.

With shaking hands, she reached up and took the glass from him.

"Steady, Daughter," said Alamar.

Aylis took a sip and grimaced, shivering.

"All of it, *chieran,"* whispered Aravan. "Drink it all."

Again Aylis sipped, once twice, then downing the last, squinting her eyes and shuddering, her lips pursed in a moue.

Aravan handed the glass back to Alamar. "Another?" asked the Mage, pouring.

"N-no," said Aylis. "Please, no more."

Alamar looked about, as if seeking another who needed a drink, then downed the dram himself.

"What happened?" asked Jinnarin, standing on the bed beside Aylis.

Aylis looked nonplused. "Why, I don't know. One minute I was turning over cards, and the next I was in here. I think instead it is you who must tell me what happened."

"Thou swooned, *chieran*," said Aravan.

"Swooned?"

"Aye, swooned."

Alamar poured himself another dram and set the decanter aside. "Fainted dead away, Daughter. Took one look at the cards and fainted dead away." The Mage sat in a chair and took a sip of brandy.

"But first you said something," added Jinnarin.

"Blurted it out, in fact," declared Alamar.

Aylis looked at Aravan. "What was it? What did I say?"

Aravan shook his head. "It was in a tongue I know not, *chieran*."

"You said," proclaimed Alamar, downing the last of his brandy, *"Introrsum trahe supernum ignem—pyrà—in obscuram gemmam!"*

Aylis's eyes widened, as Jinnarin looked at Alamar and nodded vigorously. "Yes," said the Pysk. "It sounded like that. But, tell me, what does it mean?"

"It means," said Aylis, "Draw the heavenly fire ... um, something ... into the dark gem." Aylis turned to Alamar. "Father, do you know what *pyrà* means?"

Alamar sighed and seemed weary. "Yes, Daughter, though it is only by happenstance that I do. It is a word the Black Mages use, and it means fire."

"Pyrà is fire?"

Alamar nodded. *"Ignem, pyrà:* I am certain they are the same." He poured himself another dram of brandy. "Comes from the word *pŷr,* I suspect."

Jinnarin looked at the eld Mage. "Speaking of samenesses, Alamar, is 'heavenly fire' the same as the astral fire you told me about?"

Alamar shrugged then cocked an eyebrow. "Seems likely."

Aylis glanced at Aravan. "I'm all right now, love."

He kissed her on the forehead then released her, and she swung her feet to the floor. As she stood, she fixed Alamar with a puzzled look. "Tell me this, Father: why would I use a word of the Black Mages?"

Again Alamar shrugged, a frown on his features. "Daughter, you are the seer, not I."

Jinnarin hopped down from the bed. "Perhaps, Aylis, it is something you saw in the cards."

"Yes," said Aylis, standing. "The cards. I must see them."

"They are scattered," said Aravan.

"Nevertheless, I must see them."

She stepped to the door and out, Jinnarin at her side, Aravan and Alamar following. In the captain's lounge they found Tink, the cabin boy, with the deck in his hand—reassembled. "Hullo, Cap'n. Just straightening up, I was."

"Do you remember any of the cards?"

Aylis's question hung on the air as Jinnarin, Aravan, and Alamar looked at one another.

"More importantly, Daughter, do *you* remember any of them?"

Aylis shook her head. "No, Father, I don't. All I remember is that I was turning up the Obverse cards—the hidden factors."

"They were all faceup when you fainted, Aylis," said Jinnarin.

Aravan nodded and gestured at the table. "Thou hadst just turned up the very last when thou swooned."

Aylis looked from one to another. "Surely you remember some of the cards ... don't you?" Silence answered her. "Not even one?"

"The Hidden Mage was in his usual spot," said Alamar at last.

"There was a—no, wait, that was in my Spread," murmured Jinnarin. "Oh, Aylis, when you fell across the table, whatever cards were laid down, well, it was knocked right out of my head."

They sat in despondent silence for a while, Aylis finally asking, "What was the last card I turned up?"

Aravan glanced at the others. "It was the key moment in the Cycle of Time."

Both Jinnarin and Alamar nodded their agreement, the Mage saying, "It was then you seemed to be gripped in a trance."

"And you called out those words," added Jinnarin.

Aylis took Aravan's hand in her own. "Try to remember: what was the card?"

Aravan closed his eyes. "A dagger, a sword, I think. A blade of some sort."

"No," said Jinnarin. "Not a sword. Instead, it was two swords crossed. I remember now. Two swords crossed. Definitely."

Aylis riffled through the deck, withdrawing a card. "This one?" She laid down a card depicting crossed blades, but they were daggers, not swords.

Aravan looked at Jinnarin, and they both turned to Alamar. The eld Mage shook his head and turned up his hands in a gesture of I-don't-know. At last Aravan said, "Mayhap, Aylis. All I remember was that it was a blade or blades."

Aylis held up the card. "This is the only one with crossed blades. If this was the card, then it signifies combat, personal combat, such as a duel, a match, one opponent against another." Aylis took a deep breath. "Tell me, was it Upright or Inverted?"

"Upright.—No, wait. Upright to me but Inverted to thee."

Aylis grew pale and her voice was grim. "Inverted to me means the outcome is unfavorable to you, Aravan. Unfavorable to you."

"Bah!" barked Alamar. "First of all, we don't even know if that was the card or not. Second, the Hidden Mage, whoever he is, is blocking all critical readings. Who's to say that he isn't also sending false information?"

Aylis leaned forward on her elbows, her head in her hands. At last she looked up. "Father is right. The cards are unknown. In fact, they may have had nothing at all to do with my rede. Seers under stress have at times spontaneously foretold the future, and Adon knows, we are—I am—under stress."

As they pondered Aylis's words, Jatu entered the salon. "My Lady Jinnarin, you are needed on deck; the northern lights have begun to flicker."

*   *   *

"Aylis," asked Jinnarin, not taking her eyes from the sky, "are the cards always right?"

Aylis looked down at the Pysk. They stood on the deck of the *Eroean,* the aurora flaming overhead. "Jinnarin, the cards only tell what might be, not what must be."

"But I thought your seer castings were—were—" Jinnarin searched for the right word.

"Infallible?" asked Aylis.

"Yes, infallible."

"No, Jinnarin, seer castings are not infallible. Oh, a divination by a skilled seer is indeed a powerful thing, and most likely to have been, to be, or to become true, depending upon where within the Cycle of Time the seer looks. Regardless, the futures presaged by the cards are not immutable ... especially not in this case, for I am thwarted by an unseen power, and the cards make no more sense than were they dealt by random chance."

"But, Aylis, surely you saw something in the Spread you dealt Aravan."

Aylis shrugged. "Perhaps, Jinnarin, yet we will never know."

"Unless it comes true," said Jinnarin, scanning the skies.

Aylis inhaled deeply, then exhaled, her breath white in the winter air. "A losing duel?"

Jinnarin nodded. "Or something about heavenly fire and a gemstone. —Wait! Do you think the heavenly fire could mean the aurora?"

Aylis's eyes flew wide, and she gazed at the burning display above.

Though the boreal lights shuddered and shifted throughout the long winter night, no plumes did they see, and in the hour ere dawn, the aurora faded until it was gone. Weary, the watchers made their way unto their beds.

It was nigh noon when Aylis awakened, and after she had completed her toilet and dressed, she found Aravan and her father on deck with Jatu and Bokar, Jinnarin nowhere to be seen. As Aylis joined them, Jatu repeated his question: "And just how does one go about 'drawing heavenly fire into a gemstone,' eh? Answer me that, Mage Alamar.''

The elder ran his finger 'round the dull red stone in his gold bracelet. "For me, it would be a matter of discovering the proper casting. But for you, the gemstone would need to be special, a token of power, one you could invoke by Truenaming it."

Jatu raised an eyebrow. "Truenaming?"

Bokar looked up at the black Man. "Like Durek's Axe. It has a Truename. Speak it and the axe will cleave through stone or metal . . . or so they say."

"Ah," said Jatu, his face lighting up with understanding. "Like Nombi's Spear: it never missed, did you call it by its secret word."

"A Truename, no doubt," said Alamar.

Jatu turned to the Mage. "How do these 'special' things acquire a Truename?"

Alamar glanced at Aylis, and she nodded, as if giving permission, or as if agreeing that the knowledge should be shared. Alamar cleared his throat. "A very simple token of power is sometimes simply found in nature and requires no crafting at all. Other simple tokens can be made by a single crafter, an artificer, usually a Mage, but sometimes not. Some of these are continuously active and do not need to be Truenamed—such as your blue stone, Aravan—whereas others do. Examples of a single artificer's work which are invoked by a Truename are the swords made by Dwynfor, the Elven smith, as is perhaps Durek's Axe, Bokar . . . or Nombi's Spear, Jatu. More complex tokens of power usually take two or three Mages to complete the crafting—an alchemist, an artificer, and someone to embed it with its special power. A very potent token, however, requires the crafting of many Mages, or even the crafting of a god."

"A god?" Jatu's eyes widened.

"Adon, Elwydd, Gyphon, the Others."

Bokar took off his winged helmet and looked within, as if seeking something inside. "Tell me, Mage Alamar, what kind of a gemstone could draw fire into itself?"

Alamar shrugged. "I don't know, Bokar. There are many kinds of gems, any one of which might be made into a token: *adamas, crystallus, smaragdus, carbunculus, sappirhus, corallum*—"

"Argh," growled Bokar. "You name gemstones I am unfamiliar with."

"My father gives them their Magenames, Bokar," said Aylis. "You know them as diamond, crystal, emerald, ruby, sapphire, and coral."

"Hah!" exclaimed the Dwarf. "It sounds as if *any* gemstone will do."

"That's what I was telling you, Dwarf," retorted Alamar peevishly.

Bokar bristled, then settled. "Well, Mage Alamar, what *I* was wondering is whether or not the dark gemstone of Seeress Aylis's rede could be the stone Aravan wears about his neck?"

Alamar's eyes flew wide, and he turned to Aravan. "Let me see it," he demanded.

Aravan fished out the stone from beneath his jerkin and slipped the leather thong over his head, handing it to Alamar. The Mage studied the blue rock for long moments. "Wrong fire," he muttered. "Entirely the wrong fire within. Aylis was right when she examined it before: this is a warding device, pure and simple, one that will detect creatures of Neddra, and a few of this world as well." He handed it back to Aravan, who threaded it over his head and slipped it back beneath his jerkin. "Nevertheless, Bokar," added the Mage, "it was a clever thought."

"Those gemstones, Alamar," asked Aravan, "know thee the gemstone names in the speech of the Black Mages?"

Alamar shook his head, *No,* then asked, "Why would that matter?"

Aravan glanced at Aylis, then said to Alamar, "Thy daughter spoke a word in the tongue of the Black Mages, and I thought the name of the dark gemstone might be called in that tongue as well."

Alamar slowly nodded, saying, "Perhaps. Were we in Kairn, Aylis and I would visit the library at the college of Mages. There we might find reference to those names. Still, though, it would be at Fortune's whim for us to find anything worthwhile, for we do not even know what kind of gem or jewel the dark gemstone of her rede is. And there are tens, even hundreds of types of gems, and to discover the Black Mage words naming all of them is most unlikely. And even should we find a name of a gem or two, and even should the name we find be the correct one, to infer from that a Truename, well, I would say it is a virtual impossibility, especially since we are being blocked."

Days fled by, winter deepened, and often the spectral lights of the aurora burned above in the long cold nights. Yet no plumes did they see. Jinnarin's moods swung between glumness and cheer, depending upon whether she dreamt of a black ship or not, the nightmare coming sporadically. December arrived, the first week passed and then another, and the tempers of all began to fray, crew and officers alike snapping at one another. Alamar's complaints and criticisms grew by leaps and bounds, and Jinnarin thought that she would scream whenever he opened his mouth. Finally Aravan held a shipwide meeting, and even as he climbed upon a table to speak, someone called out, " 'Ow much longer we goin' to ride at bloody anchor, Cap'n?" A concurring murmur of discontent rumbled through the crew.

Aravan spotted the complainant. "That's what I am here to talk about, Geff."

Aravan slowly turned, his gaze seeking the eye of every Man and Dwarf. Some returned his scrutiny straight on; others glanced down at their feet, as if ashamed or guilty of some unspecified infraction. When he had turned full circle, he spoke:

"I know we are all impatient to get on with the mission, and that sitting at anchor off the coast is wearying to the spirit of each and every one. Yet, heed, we may be here all winter—another full hundred days." A groan rose up at this pronouncement, then quickly died as Aravan held up his hands for silence. "We seek to see the same as Lady Jinnarin's mate saw—plumes from the aurora. Mayhap in but a night or so they will come; mayhap in a week or two; mayhap not at all. Yet, sitting here may be the swiftest way for us to find Farrix, can we find his plumes.

"Do we not succeed in seeing what he saw, then will we hale anchor and go aroving, seeking instead the pale green sea.

"I know ye chafe to be off and running, for I do so

myself. There is little to occupy us while riding at anchor, and loitering about is not a thing we do gracefully. For we are folk of action, folk who are used to roving the waters of the world and seeking the truth behind legends, we who if we are not sailing the seas are instead striking inland on the trail of wonder.

"Yet now we find ourselves sitting idle, waiting for an event that might never come.

"But we are sworn to serve the Lady Jinnarin, and at this moment we serve her best by waiting. But we serve her not at all with our bickering, and I would that we set these petty things aside.

"And so, I charge us all with the following: to find again our good spirits; to find again that fellowship which draws us together; to find again our good cheer; and to find again our sense of mission, of purpose, of direction—of our service to Lady Jinnarin."

Aravan paused, and in the silence someone—Geff, it was—called out, "Hoy, the cap'n's roight, 'e is. 'Tis only a 'undred days we've to wait—that or less. Hi can do that standin' on me 'ead—"

Jatu called out, "Now that's something I'd like to see: Geff standing on his head for a hundred days."

A roar of laughter burst out, and Aravan let it run its course. When it died down, he said, "I ween Geff's words ring true: on our heads or not, we can easily put up with a hundred-day wait. What say ye all?"

Geff called out, "Hi say let's give the cap'n three cheers—roight?"

Hip-hip, hooray! Hip-hip, hooray! Hip-hip, hooray!
Geff himself led the cheering.

Smiling, Aravan stepped down, but as the crew began to disband, Jatu sprang to the table and called for quiet. When it fell, the big black Man said, "I say we get up a lottery as to when the first plume will be seen."

"A hundred days," roared Bokar, agreeing, surging forward to participate, his warband crowding in after. "A hundred-day lottery for all!"

"With two hundred numbers," shouted someone else, "two numbers for each night, one before the midnight hour and one after."

"Pick 'em out of a hat!"

A general shout of agreement rose up, and Aravan

smiled as he left the meeting. It seemed as if morale had been restored—perhaps for one hundred days.

The next day Jinnarin sat with Jatu at the stern of the ship and watched as the crew clambered up the rigging to clear the ice that had accumulated overnight, and one of the Men was canting a chantey, and the others responded in chorus.

"They seem happy, Jatu," said the Pysk.

"Yes, Lady Jinnarin," responded Jatu. "They *are* happy. You see, Captain Aravan spoke to them last night. He cheered them up and reminded them of the mission we are on."

"Oh, I wish he had spoken to Alamar, cheered him up, too."

Jatu looked down at the Pysk and raised his eyebrows.

"He's become nearly impossible, Jatu, picking fights at every turn."

"Fights?"

"Arguments. Niggling arguments over picayune things."

"Perhaps, Lady Jinnarin, it is his only 'entertainment.'"

"No, Jatu. Instead he is frustrated. He has nothing else to occupy him, nothing but arguments, debates."

Thoughtfully, Jatu scratched his jaw. "Perhaps we should set him a riddle to solve. It would occupy his mind."

"Oh, he has already set me a riddle."

"And it is . . . ?"

"First it was to define the nature of evil. This I finally did to my satisfaction as well as his—at least as concerns the greater evils. Then he set me a task to think of some smaller evils. Well, Jatu, I do not know if there can be such a thing as a small evil."

"What did he consider to be the greater evils?"

"The quenching of free will for gratification. Using force, dominance, intimidation, or other means to slake one's own need to control others. Torture, pillage, slavery, and the like. Those are examples of the greater evils."

"What of things such as lying, cheating, stealing, breaking promises, and—"

"Oh, Jatu, lying, cheating, stealing, and the like, perhaps at times are small. Here, I am on shaky ground, for is a lie, even a small one, ever anything but evil? Can a lie be virtuous? And if so, where is the line between a virtuous lie and an evil one? Perhaps it is in the intent. If they are done only to gratify the doer, well then, I think they are evil, large or small. If there are so-called small evils, I do believe that they can become greater evils, too, depending upon the purpose behind them. But I do not believe that the greater evils can ever become small."

Jatu sat in silence for a moment, then said, "So this is the problem Mage Alamar set before you, eh? No little task, I say. Even so, if you would surprise him, would shake him from his querulous ways, why not try to anticipate the next problem he will ask you to consider and skip ahead—answer his question before it is asked?"

Jinnarin smiled. "Oh my, but that would surprise him, indeed."

Jatu grinned down at the Pysk and nodded. "And perhaps delight him as well, breaking the foul mood he is in."

"Well," said Jinnarin, "since he's asked me to define the nature of evil, perhaps he will next ask me to define the nature of good."

Jatu shook his head. "I think not, Lady Jinnarin. Defining the nature of good would seem to be the opposite of evil . . . or perhaps a bit more. I think instead he will ask you how a person should live in order to avoid doing evil to others."

"That's too easy, Jatu."

"It is? Then tell me, tiny one, what is the answer?"

"Do no harm to others, and let them do no harm to you."

Jatu laughed and, seeing the puzzled look Jinnarin gave him, said, "I've never heard it put quite that way before."

"What?"

"Well, among the wise Men of the far lands to the east, they say, 'Do not do to someone what you would not have done to you,' or, 'Do no harm to others.' "

"Isn't that what I just said?"

"Oh no, Lady Jinnarin, what you said is altogether

different. Your rule is quite a bit more—shall we say—active?"

"How so, Jatu?"

"Well, your rule begins the same as theirs—'Do no harm to others'—but then you part company—wildly, I might add—for your rule says, '. . . and let them do no harm to you.' To me, that implies should someone try to harm you, then it is all right for you to prevent them from doing so."

"So . . . ?"

Jatu laughed again. "I *like* your rule, Lady Jinnarin. The wise Men in the east could learn from you. You see, *their* rule implies that *if* you do no harm to others, *then* they will do no harm to you . . . and we all know that is not so at times. By their rule, should someone attempt to harm them, they either accept it or they run away. But *your* rule seems to say, 'I won't harm you *unless* you try to harm me first, in which case I will stop you.'"

A look of enlightenment came over Jinnarin's face. "Oh. Now I see what you mean. —But wait, Jatu. Their rule doesn't prohibit someone from taking steps to prevent harm."

"No, it doesn't. Yet it implies that it would be evil for you to harm someone to stop him from doing harm, no matter how evil he is. Hence, you may not cause harm to prevent harm. —I do not happen to agree, by the way, for at times the only way to stop evil is to destroy the evildoer."

They sat quietly for long moments watching the chanting crew clamber along the icy rigging, hammering on pulleys and lines, breaking loose the ice, glittering shards twinkling down to shatter upon the deck.

Jinnarin stood. With a sigh she said, "I'm going to go talk to Alamar about this. He'll want to argue, I shouldn't wonder."

Jatu held up a hand to keep her from going just yet. "Why don't you disarm him before he gets a chance?"

"Disarm him? How?"

"Change your rule slightly. Instead of focusing on harm, try to focus on doing good. Ask him if he believes that people should treat others as they themselves would wish to be treated. When he says yes, then you have him: he cannot then treat you shabbily unless he himself wishes to be treated the same."

Jinnarin smiled and clapped her hands. "Good, Jatu. Very good." The Pysk turned on her heel and began hopping down the steps. When she reached the bottom, she stopped, as if in deep thought. Facing Jatu once more, she called up, "But what if he doesn't agree that each person should treat others as he himself wishes to be treated?"

Jatu laughed deeply. "Then, my Lady, you are on your own."

Sighing, Jinnarin turned and trudged onward.

Alamar blearily gazed at Jinnarin. "Ha, Pysk, sought to trap me, eh?" The Mage reclined on his bunk, his back against the wall, a glass of brandy in his grasp, a nearly empty bottle at hand. "Well, this wily old fox is up to your tricks, Pish . . . tish, Prix . . . tricks, Pysk."

"Alamar, you're drun—"

"But you know, you have hit on three of the great thoughts of civiliza-civiliz-civilization. One, do no harm; two, do only good; three, treat me like I treat you. Not the same things, you know. Different. And do you know why?"

"Well—" began Jinnarin.

"I'll tell you why," interrupted Alamar, speaking now to the air instead of Jinnarin. "As far as good is concerned, one is more active than the other. And as far as evil is concerned, one is more active than the other. . . . Did I just say that? Well I meant it. Anyway, as far as getting along is concerned, one is more active than the other. You see, one is for good, one is against evil, and one is some of each." Alamar paused to swill from his glass of brandy.

Jinnarin took the opportunity to get in a word edgewise. "Isn't being for good the same as being against evil, Alamar?"

The Mage peered back down at the Pysk. "Oh, are you still here, Pish?"

"Answer my question, Alamar. Aren't they the same?"

Alamar looked around, his eyes searching. "What?"

"Being for good is the same as being against evil, isn't it?"

"Who told you that?"

"No one. I just—"

"There. You see?" said Alamar triumphantly. "I told you so."

"You told me what?" Jinnarin was ready to scream in frustration.

"Doing good, preventing harm: of course they're not the same. One tells you *what* to do; the other tells you what *not* to do: one would have you aid the victim, do only good; the other would have you forgo badness, do no harm. Of course, there's an extension to doing no harm—and that's to prevent others from doing harm to others."

"But wait, Alamar, preventing harm is not the same as doing no harm."

"Right again, Picks. Doing no harm applies to yourself; preventing harm applies to others. In the one case, you leave others be; in the other case, you can kill whatever evil bastards you run across."

"They don't have to be evil, Alamar. I mean, Farrix prevented harm to you by killing the boar, though it was not an evil creature."

"The Hèl it wasn't!" cried Alamar. "Tried to kill me."

Jinnarin threw up her hands in exasperation. "Never mind. But say, what about the third way?"

"What third way?"

Jinnarin ground her teeth. "The some-of-each, as-you-would-be-treated way."

Alamar peered through his empty glass at the distorted image of Jinnarin. "It's the best of all. Pick and choose, I say. If you only do good, you'll do a lot of volunteering to help, such as aiding someone to harvest his grain. If you do no harm, you do nothing to hinder his harvest—leave him alone ... let him get his grain by himself. If you prevent harm, you'll spend a lot of time in dreadful danger, working in causes that you might not even understand, except that they prevent harm. But if you live and let live, if you treat others as you would be treated, well then, you can pick and choose when to help, when to leave 'em alone, and when to fight. —Best of all, I tell you; best of all."

"Hmm." Jinnarin fell into thought. After a while a snore interrupted her musings. Alamar had passed out.

Mid December came, the aurora flaming above, but no plumes were seen in the moonless dark. But on the night of the seventeenth—"There it is! There it is!" cried Jinnarin, pointing northwesterly, the Pysk dancing in excitement. "A plume! A streamer! Look! Look! Oh, don't you see it?"

Alamar whirled about, peering intently, muttering, *"Visus."*

Then the Mage called out, "Frizian! Frizian! To me!"

The second officer came running forward, bo's'n Reydeau at his side. "Mage Alamar?"

Alamar pointed, his arm at a low, upward angle, west and north. "There is the plume. Get Aravan, get the crew, and get this ship moving."

Both Men stared where Alamar pointed, and Frizian said, "But I don't see a thing."

"You don't have the vision, lad. We do! Now hop to! We've spotted the quarry at last!"

"But sir, it looks to me as if you are pointing inland. And if it's landed on Rwn, well, sir, we cannot sail through rocks and soil."

"Damnation, Frizian, I've studied the stars all my life, and I know, y' hear me, I *know,* where that plume came from and where it is like to land, and it's well beyond the island. Now delay no longer. Either give the orders or get out of the way!"

Frizian turned to Reydeau. "Pipe the captain and crew, bo's'n. Ring the bell. 'Tis time for the *Eroean* to cut the waves."

Moments later, as some of the Men scrambled up the ratlines and others haled on the halyards lifting the spars, Aravan and Jatu strode to the foredeck. "Where away?" asked the Elven captain.

"There, Aravan, there!" said Jinnarin, pointing, her voice effervescent. "It's gone now. But it was there. Oh, Aravan, a plume at last!"

Aravan glanced at Alamar, the eld Mage saying, "My guess, Aravan, is that it came down a hundred miles or so beyond the far coast. Look. See the Serpent's Tail, just now setting? Third star up? That's the direction."

Aravan peered at the constellation. "I'll mark the chart, Jatu, then thou wilt know where we sail."

Jatu nodded. "Aye, Captain, but that comes later. At the moment, Rwn stands in the way. We can't sail across the land, but we can go around the isle. Widdershins or deosil, which do you choose?"

Aravan glanced up at the pennons flying in the wind. "Deosil, Jatu, given the air."

As Jatu strode away, Aylis arrived. "Where?" she asked Jinnarin, gazing in the direction the Pysk pointed. "Did you see it, Father?"

"Not without magesight."

Aylis glanced at the elder. "Well, Father, at least that's something."

"Come," said Aravan. "I will strike a line on the charts and show ye all where we are bound."

They followed the Elf to the captain's lounge and gathered about the table, Jinnarin standing atop. Aravan selected a chart and rolled it out flat, holding down the corners with paper weights. "Here is Rwn, and here we are, in this cove on the southeastern quarter. Given Alamar's estimate"—Aravan laid a straight edge from the cove across the center of Rwn and beyond, marking a point some hundred miles northwest of the isle—"and given that we can run twelve to thirteen knots in this wind"—with a pair of dividers, Aravan gauged the distance along the southern route they would sail—"we are some twenty-five to thirty hours away."

Jinnarin, now standing on the map, looked up fretfully. "A full day?"

Aravan nodded. "Or a bit more."

Alamar growled. "Nothing we can do about it, Pysk. It would take too much <fire> to call up the wind."

Aylis studied the chart. "We sail past Darda Glain, neh?"

A glance at Aravan confirmed her words. "Seven or so hours from now."

Aylis looked back at the map. "Kairn, too, I see."

"You can put that right out of your mind, Daughter," growled Alamar. "I won't do it."

"Do what?" asked Jinnarin.

"Be put off at Kairn, that's what!" snapped Alamar.

"But, Father—"

"I said no, Daughter! Just when the quarry has been sighted, you want me to run away. Well, I said it before and I say it again: I won't do it! I'm in this to the end, and that's that!"

Jinnarin stood in map center, her arms crossed, her jaw jutted out. "And I won't be put off in Darda Glain! And that's that, too!"

"Oh, Jinnarin, I wasn't thinking of putting *you* off," protested Aylis.

"Just me, eh?" barked Alamar.

Jinnarin turned to Aylis. "Well, if you weren't going to put me off, why did you ask about Darda Glain?" The Pysk pointed at the woodland marked on the southern marge of Rwn.

"Just this, Jinnarin: it occurred to me that Farrix might be back home by now. And if so, then this mission takes on new meaning."

"Oh, if he were back home, then that would be wonderful," exclaimed Jinnarin. "But he isn't there, I'm certain, not as long as I'm having the dream."

Aylis held her hands palm up. "You assume, Jinnarin, that Farrix is the sender, and I agree most likely he is. Yet if we are wrong and Farrix is indeed in Darda Glain, then we would have to ask, if not Farrix, then who is sending you the nightmare . . . and why?"

Leaning on his hands, Aravan looked across the table at Aylis. "What dost thou propose, *chieran?* If we would find the secret behind the plumes, we cannot delay at Darda Glain."

Aylis gestured negatively. "I was not thinking of stopping there, Aravan. Instead, when we are closest, I will use ebon water in a silver basin to search for him."

Jinnarin mouthed a silent *O,* then a frown came over her features. "But, Aylis, how will you know when you've found him? I mean, you don't even know what he looks like."

Aylis smiled. "Oh, but I do, Jinnarin. After all, I saw him swimming naked in the pool of your dreams."

In the spectral auroral glow and by the light of the stars, in less than an hour they weighed anchor, bringing the Elvenship about, running southerly and then southwesterly and then swinging to the west as they sailed along the southern marge of Rwn. Yet the isle was roughly circular and one hundred and fifty miles across, or there-abouts, depending on where one measured, and so the trip to the waters beyond would cover in all some three hundred miles by sea. And so it would be a day or more before the *Eroean* would come into the region where Alamar gauged had fallen the plume from the distant high heavens above.

In the hours before dawn, Aravan awakened Aylis. "We sail nigh Darda Glain, *chieran*."

Aylis rummaged about, finding her small silver basin along with its bottle of jet ink and the candle in the silver holder. Lighting the candle, she stepped into the salon, where she discovered Jinnarin and Alamar awaiting her, the two of them yet awake having watched for additional plumes—none had been seen. Aylis set the silver bowl on the table and filled it with water, dropping four droplets of jet within, the water turning ebony. Aylis sat at the table and concentrated, peering deep in the surface, murmuring, *"Patefac Farricem."*

Jinnarin stood on the table next to the candle, her eyes wide and watching. Alamar stood across from Aylis, the eld Mage staring at the black water. Aravan stood behind Aylis, ready to support her should she faint again.

"Patefac Farricem," she repeated, gazing into the ebon mirror of the darkling water.

Though she did not expect to, Jinnarin could see no change in the surface; even so, a sense of disappointment crept into her heart.

A third time did Aylis call, *"Patefac Farricem."* At last she looked up and shook her head, *No.*

Jinnarin's shoulders slumped, but before she could say aught, "Come, Pysk," muttered Alamar. "Back on watch. There's yet some aurora left, and we would not miss a plume ... though we may have missed one already."

Dawn came and onward they sailed, beyond the town of Kairn, the City of Bells, eastward over the horizon from the course where they fared. Onward they went, the low chill Sun arcing its track across the cold winter sky, the Elvenship moving at a good clip through the grey waves, driven by a stiff winter wind. Darkness fell, yet on they ran, and just ere the mid of the moonless night they came at last into the waters one hundred miles northwest of Rwn.

With a winter wind blowing, the crew stood upon the decks, sailors and warriors alike dressed in quilted, down-filled parkas and pants, the clothing proof against the brumal blow, the warriors armed and armored as well, for none knew what they might find. At the stern stood Jinnarin and Aylis and Alamar, father and daughter dressed like the crew in parkas and pants. To a lesser extent was Aravan affected by the chill and so the clothing he wore, though warm, was lighter. But Jinnarin was dressed in her usual garb, the Pysk seemingly untouched by the winter blast, as if being Feyan was somehow proof against the cold.

All eyes scanned the dark, night sea ... finding nothing.

"Wot'r we looking for, Cap'n?" asked Tink, the lad jittering about in the wintry wind.

"I don't know, Tink—something untoward ... large or small I cannot say."

Tink's eyes scanned the horizon. "Lor, no matter if it's as big as a house, in all this vastness it'll be like searching for a needle in a haycock."

Bokar growled, "Or a cork bobbing about on the sea."

"I see nothing here," said Jatu. "Where now, Captain?"

Aravan glanced overhead at the stars. "We will sail the line drawn on the map. Guide on the third star up in the Serpent's Tail."

"Aye, Captain. —Reydeau, pipe the sails. Boder, follow that star."

Sailing this course they ran tor an hour and then another, faring along the uncertain boundary between the icy waters of the Northern Sea and the milder Weston Ocean.

Still nothing did they find.

In the third hour on this track, overhead the glimmerings of the northern lights began. And Jinnarin and Aylis and Alamar remained on deck to watch for plumes.

"Captain," said Jatu, "by my reckoning we are now

over forty leagues from Rwn, one hundred twenty miles."

Aravan glanced at the stars again. "Aye, Jatu, thou art fair exact. Bring her about. We will run the line opposite, but tack larboard and starboard a league or so each way." Aravan turned and pointed to a constellation southeasterly. "Guide on the Shepherd's Crook."

Alamar harrumphed. "I say, Aravan, what if we are zigging when we should have zagged?"

"Then, Alamar, we shall have missed whatever there is to miss. E'en so, we saw nought when we ran a straight course, and so if something lies a league left or rightward, then if Fortune smiles upon us, we will come across it; otherwise we will not."

Reydeau piped the sails about, reversing the *Eroean*'s course, the ship now tacking back along the southeasterly line.

Another hour passed, the night deepening, and of a sudden Jinnarin shrieked, "There's another one! Another plume!"

Both Alamar and Aylis muttered *Visus,* and looked to where Jinnarin pointed. A great long stream detached itself from the aurora and flowed down toward the eastern horizon, disappearing beyond.

"Line it up," barked Alamar. "Pick out a star where the plume disappeared."

"The red one on the horizon," said Aylis.

"I agree," responded Alamar. "Axtaris, it's called."

By this time Aravan had reached their side. "In line with Axtaris, Aravan," said Alamar, "that's where it went down."

"Due east, Jatu," called Aravan. "Due east we sail, Reydeau."

As the ship was heeled over to sail easterly, Aravan turned to Alamar. "Hast thou any estimate as to how far?"

"Less than two hundred miles, I would say. Perhaps no more than a hundred fifty."

Alamar turned to Aylis. She shrugged. "Beyond the horizon, Father, that is all I can say."

Jinnarin nodded in agreement.

And with a stiff winter wind off the starboard stern quarter, eastward ran the *Eroean*.

*   *   *

The Sun had not set late in the day when they came to the waters off the northern coast of Rwn. The lookouts aloft had seen nothing unusual as the Elvenship cruised easterly, the Men relieving one another often because of the cold, cold air out upon the open sea. Another shift was just changing when Aravan came to the wheelhouse, where the officer of the deck and the steersman now stood out of the blow.

"Anything at all, Frizian?"

"Nay, Captain."

Boder at the wheel spoke up. "Where to next, Cap'n? I mean, what be the course?"

"East, Boder, east. We'll run at least until dark."

"Then what, Cap'n?"

"Then we'll see, Boder. More I cannot say."

Aravan held an officers' meeting just after sunset, the *Eroean* yet running east.

Gathered 'round the map table were Jatu, Bokar, Frizian, Reydeau, Rico, and Fager. There as well were Jinnarin, Aylis, and Alamar. Aravan spread a chart upon the board. Two places were marked thereon: one where Alamar had judged the first plume had fallen, the other at his less-certain placement of the second.

Aravan looked up from the map. "Though we have seen two plumes and have followed them to their landings, we have found nought but waves in the water."

Bokar growled, "Aye, Captain Aravan, nothing but waves. But that is not all, for we pursue something that I cannot even see—another 'nothing' to my way of thinking. Kruk! I feel as if we are chasing an invisible will-o'-the-wisp!"

Alamar bristled. "Well *I* can see it, Dwarf. And I tell you that it is a *something* and not a *nothing* we pursue."

"Father," said Aylis, "Bokar is not doubting our word. It's just that it is difficult for a warrior to grapple with something he cannot see."

Bokar nodded vigorously. "You have the right of it, Lady Aylis. Give me a foe I can see and I will soon put him down. But invisible will-o'-the-wisps are not at all to my taste."

Jinnarin sat down on the map, pondering. "What we

need is a way of being at the place where a plume comes down at the time it comes down."

Jatu slammed a fist into palm. "Exactly so, Lady Jinnarin. In pursuit, perhaps we will never find out what is happening. But let one come to us, and, well, mayhap things will change."

Aravan smiled. "My thoughts exactly."

Frizian looked back at the map. "What do you propose, Captain."

Aravan drew a line between the two marks, then extended it on eastward another hundred and fifty miles, and there he put a third X. "I say we sail on another fifty leagues to this point and wait. Should a plume come down after we arrive, then surely it will strike nearby."

Jatu grunted. "That assumes, Captain Aravan, that the next one—the third plume—will be eastward by the same distance that the second one was from the first."

"Aye," replied Aravan. "Same distance, same direction."

Alamar cleared his throat. *"Hem!* But, Aravan, I am not at all certain that the second one was fifty leagues away from the first."

Frizian looked at the Mage. "But, Mage Alamar, you were dead certain about the location of the first, e'en though that was more than two hundred miles away."

"Right!" exclaimed Alamar. "But I was sighting out across Rwn. And gauging the likely size of the plume, and given the scale of the island, I could better judge where it landed. This time, though, we were on open water, and"—Alamar's jaw jutted out defiantly—"I'd like to see you try to size something up when you've got no reference. Fifty leagues, sixty, seventy—I doubt you'd come even that close!"

Aravan turned up his palms. "Nevertheless, Alamar, thine is the best estimate we have. Hence, I suggest we sail easterly to this mark." Aravan's finger stabbed down on the third X.

Jinnarin looked up at the others 'round the table. "Seems as good a chance as any."

"By damn, third time, she be charm, Miss Jinnarin," said Rico with a grin.

Aravan also looked about at the others. "Any additions, amendments, alternatives?" Silence answered him.

"Then set sail, Rico, all she will bear. Run east another fifty leagues and hope that we are in position before the next plume falls."

"Aye, Kapitan," replied the bo's'n, and he turned on his heel and left.

Aravan turned to the second officer. "Frizian, run her hard and true, for I would catch this will-o'-the-wisp."

Frizian saluted. "Aye, Captain. Be there more?"

Aravan shook his head negatively, and the officers returned to their duties or to rest, each frowning, as if secretly fearing that the chase would be long and hard.

When they were gone, Jinnarin sat alone in the center of the table, her head down in reflection. Aravan reached for the map, clearing his throat, for the Pysk sat in its center. When Jinnarin looked up, Aravan said, "Thou art troubled, Lady?"

"Oh, Aravan, I was just thinking of something that Rico said."

"And that was ... ?"

"Well, he said, third time's the charm."

Aravan raised an eyebrow.

Jinnarin added, "I am reminded that the fourth time's the harm."

They had sailed some thirty-five leagues—mid of night drawing nigh, the boreal lights writhing above—when in the remote distance ahead another plume streamed down from above and toward the ocean beyond the horizon afar.

"Where away, Alamar?"

"Close, Aravan. No more than fifty or sixty miles ahead."

"Twenty leagues." Aravan turned and called aft, "Rico, what be our speed?"

"Fourteen knots, Kapitan" came the reply.

"Four hours," gritted Aravan. "Again we are late."

"But on the right course," said Jinnarin, pointing easterly. "It was nearly straight ahead."

Aravan sank into thought. Finally he turned to Jatu and Frizian. "Cut through the position where fell the plume, but maintain our course and sail on past if nought is seen. I deem that we can reach the expanse *wher... ...ne* next one will fall ere the Sun sets on the morrow."

Aye, Captain, they each replied.

But a coldness clutched at Jinnarin's heart, for throughout her mind echoed the bodeful thought, *Fourth time is harm ... is harm ... harm ...*

At four in the morning on the twenty-first of December the *Eroean* sliced through empty chill waters where Alamar had judged the third plume had fallen, and neither lookouts nor deck watch saw aught. And not slowing at all the Elvenship sailed on easterly, running before the steady winter wind. Thirteen knots and fourteen was her speed, and leagues of cold ocean slid under her keel as the day drew on, dawn arriving at last, the low winter Sun rising later and later as Year's Long Night approached.

Jinnarin and Aylis and Alamar took to their quarters, for in a bare nine hours the Sun would set, and they needed sleep.

Jinnarin found Rux curled up in her under-bunk cabin, and she spent some time grooming him and speaking softly, for she felt as if she had neglected him of late, though it was not so. Nevertheless she used a small comb to groom his cheeks and chest and the tip of his tail— in those places where his fur was white. And then she curled up at his side and promptly went to sleep.

Alamar came into his cabin and fell into his bunk, and shortly his snores filled the chamber. A partially full bottle of brandy sat untouched on the writing desk, the elder completely uninterested in drinking, now that he was engaged in the chasing of plumes.

Aylis and Aravan lay side by side, the Elf clasping the Lady Mage. And when she slipped into slumber, carefully he disengaged his arm from around her and softly slid from bed. He sat on the floor with his back against a bulkhead, resting his mind in gentle memories, meditating deeply ... as Elves are wont to do.

Yet Aravan had been resting but an hour or so when a loud knocking came on his stateroom door. After a moment and another knock, Aravan roused. He stood and glanced at Aylis, the seeress sound asleep. Stepping to the door, he found Frizian standing outside.

"Captain, the Sun. 'Tis being eaten by the Moon."

"Ah me, Frizian, I had forgotten. An occultation will come this day. I will speak to the crew."

All day the gloom grew as the Moon slowly crept across the Sun, steadily blocking out the light, while in the darkening skies above glimmered faint traces of the aurora. Protecting their eyes, sailors and warriors only occasionally glanced at the spectacle, and then but briefly. And they muttered to one another in low voices and timorous whispers, for no matter the fact that Captain Aravan had spoken to them, and no matter the fact that they knew the cause, still, old tales and superstitions hang on grimly to the hearts of Men and Dwarves alike. And every Man and Châk among them looked upon this occultation as an ill-starred omen.

Alamar arose just after the noon hour and railed at the sky that no one had thought to awaken him, for his passion was the study of the heavens, and now a full half of the Sun was obscured and he'd missed all to this point. It was Aylis, however, who reminded him that he, too, had forgotten the significance of this date.

Steadily the eclipse deepened, and was at its fullest less than an hour ere sunset, though still a sliver of the Sun showed. "Were we at my cottage on Rwn, we'd have seen the whole of it for there the Moon has eaten all."

But Jinnarin looked at the darkness with disquiet in her heart, for her thoughts kept repeating, *Fourth time is harm . . . Fourth time is harm.*

"Keep her under constant sail, Frizian," ordered Aravan. "Run her about a tight, closed course. I would have us lose no time and already be in motion when the next plume comes down."

Frizian glanced back at the slender limb of the setting Sun, yet obscured by the Moon. "Aye, Captain. We'll be under all silk when the next plume falls. We may be going the wrong way at that moment, but if we are, we'll bring her about straightaway and leave wake aft."

"We'll run it down, whatever it be, Captain," added Hegen. "It'll not get away from us this time, will-o'-the-wisp or no."

The ecliptic penumbra slid into night as the Moon-obscured Sun finally set, and the ship began running a triangular course, cutting through the same waters again and again.

Hours passed, and still the ship continued orbiting about, the crew haling on the sheets to bring her onto the same repeated headings over and over.

"Lor," said Artus, "I thought it was bad running all day beneath a disappearing Sun, but it's even worse sailing the same course over and over. Why, I say it's just like being on a ghost ship sailing to nowhere."

"*Ooo,*" shuddered Lobbie, "don't say that. It's bad enough that we're runnin' under these ghostly lights in the sky above wi'out you pronouncing a ghostly doom on us all down here as well."

Reydeau's piping broke up their conversation, and they moved to hale on the lines and bring the ship about once more.

"Argh!" growled Bokar among his armed and armored warriors. "I feel as if we are chasing our own tails."

Beside him Dokan nodded and inspected the blunt face of his warhammer. "Just give me something to fight, Armsmaster. Pirates, Grg, even a Madûk—it doesn't matter which."

"Aye," added Dask. "We've been too long without action, chasing will-o'-the-wisps."

Bokar nodded and thumbed the edge of his axe. "Mayhap tonight, Châkka. Mayhap tonight."

Still the ship ran its tight course, another hour or so, and then Jinnarin called out, "Overhead, Aravan! Overhead! A plume! A great plume! —Oh, Adon, it's going to hit us!"

Aravan looked up, the plume plunging down, and even his Elven eyes could see it, it was so close, the luminous streamer flowing toward the *Eroean*. Huge it was, and palely lucent, pouring down from above, yet roaring as would a vast fire, it hurtled on past them and aft. Even the Men and Dwarves, though they did not see it, knew that something immense raced by, for hair stood on end and the rigging glowed, and witchfire raced along the yardarms and masts, and there was a great bellowing in the sky. Above the ship the streamer arced past, racing aft to strike the ocean just over the near horizon.

"Bring her about starboard, Reydeau," called Aravan, but the bo's'n seemed frozen in awe.

"Reydeau!" barked Aravan. "I said bring her about."

Reydeau shook his head as if regaining awareness. "Aye, Captain," he said at last, and he raised his pipe to his lips, a series of piercing whistles relaying the commands.

Even so, still the Men moved cautiously, as if afraid to touch the sheets, for they yet glimmered here and there with the glow of spectral fire. But Bokar raged across the deck, shouting, "Be you a bunch of superstitious poltroons? Take hold those lines and bring her about!"

Spurred into action by the warrior, at last the Men sprang to the sheets and haled the yardarms 'round, bringing the ship to a southerly course, Hegen spinning the wheel hard over. Slowly the *Eroean* turned deosil, the wind aiding in swinging her from the northerly course through the east and toward the south.

"Alamar!" called Aravan. "To me!"

The eld Mage came aft to where Aravan stood. "How far?" asked the Elf.

"No more than ten miles. Mayhap less."

"Even mine eyes saw it this time, Alamar, and I would say thou art right."

Aravan turned to Frizian. "Our speed on this course, give me a mark as soon as able."

As the Elvenship steadied up on the southerly course, Frizian and Artus let out the knot line, the sand running through the glass. "Eleven knots, just under, Captain," called Frizian.

"Damn!" cursed Aravan. "Nearly an hour away."

On ran the *Eroean,* gaining no speed, aiming for where the plume landed. And in the bow stood Jinnarin and Aylis, peering forward through the starlight.

Southerly they raced, and as they drew nigh—"Look sharp," called Aravan.

Jatu rumbled, "Would that there were a full Moon above, then mayhap we could see something."

"Fear not," said Aravan. "Lady Jinnarin stands in the bow. Lady Aylis as well, with her magesight. Mine own eyes are sufficient to see by starlight. And the Drimma see well in the night. Between the lot of us, we should espy whatever there might be."

"Aye, Captain, but the Men aboard would like to see as well."

"Hola, Captain," came Bokar's shout from the bow, "Lady Jinnarin sees something bobbing about in the waters ahead."

"Where away, Bokar?"

"A point or two off the starboard."

"Run for it, Hegen."

"Aye, Captain," responded the steersman, turning the wheel a bit.

A minute or so later Bokar shouted, "Someone is in the water. Dead ahead."

Aravan's gaze swept to the horizon all about. "I see nought in the way of threat. Wear her around the wind and luff her up, Reydeau. Jatu, ready a gig. We'll take him aboard, whoever it is."

"Stand ready at the ballistas," called Bokar when the Dwarf heard the piped signals. It is questionable whether the Dwarven warriors needed the command for they already crewed the missile casters.

"He's not swimming, Captain," called Bokar. "Just bobbing about."

"Take him up regardless, Jatu," ordered Aravan.

Swiftly the gig was lowered, and Jatu and five others clambered aboard, two Dwarven warriors among them to act as eyes and to provide arms should combat be called for.

Aravan watched as the gig rowed out, and then came Jatu's voice calling across the water. "He's dead, Captain."

They fished the naked body from the icy brine, the gig returning to the ship. Jinnarin and Aylis and Alamar joined Aravan as a litter was davit-lowered and the corpse laded and brought aboard.

"Oh, Adon," gasped Aylis when she saw the cadaver, for it was the horribly mutilated remains of a Man: he had been eviscerated, his eyes were gouged out, some fingers were missing, his privates were torn loose, and his arms and legs flopped unnaturally, as if the bones within were broken, and he was slashed with hideous burns.

Horrified, Jinnarin turned her head aside. "What did this?"

Tink looked. "Shark?"

"Nay, lad," growled Bokar, "neither shark nor other fish. The evil that did this does not swim in the sea, but walks about on two legs instead."

"I am the seer," said Aylis, kneeling at the dead Man's side. She laid her hands on the mangled corpse and closed her eyes and murmured, *"Percipe praeteritum."* Suddenly her face blanched, and she gasped, "The pain. Oh, the pain." Her breath came in great gulps, and she wrenched back and forth, as if she were trying to break loose but could not, and she wept in agony.

Aravan leapt forward and pulled her away, Aylis swooning in his grasp.

Now Alamar bent down and laid hands on the corpse. *"Quis?"* he demanded. His face went white and filled with rage, and with venom in his voice he hissed, "Durlok!"

CHAPTER 18

Marge

Winter, 1E9574–75
[The Present]

"Durlok?" asked Bokar. "What is a Durlok?"

"Durlok is not a 'what,'" gritted Alamar, rising from the corpse, "but a 'who.'"

"Well then, Mage, *who* is this Durlok?"

Jinnarin looked up at Aravan, the Elf kneeling on the deck, holding Aylis. "Brandy, Aravan? Do we need brandy?"

"I'll get it, Cap'n," said Tink, and he bolted aft.

"No brandy," murmured Aylis, opening her eyes. "I am all right. Breaking the connection was ... difficult."

"Not surprising, Daughter," said Alamar bitterly. "Durlok is behind this all."

Aylis's eyes widened, but she said nothing.

Bokar growled. "Again I ask, just who is this Durlok?"

Jatu came clambering over the rail. He glanced at the corpse and then at Aylis, the seeress now sitting. The black Man leaned back over the wale and called down, "Run the gig to the aft davits, the deck is crowded here."

Tink came rushing back with a full decanter of brandy but no glass. The lad wheeled about and ran off again.

As Aravan helped Aylis to her feet, Bokar roared, "Kruk! Will you not answer my question? Who is Durlok?"

Shocked from his asperity, Alamar stared at Bokar.

244

Then the bitterness filled the elder's face again, and he harshly replied, "A Black Mage, that's who, Dwarf."

Jinnarin gasped, but did not speak.

Bokar's eyes narrowed. "I take it that Black Mages are vile."

Alamar nodded once, jerkily.

Jinnarin turned to Aylis. "Is he the hidden Mage of your cards, Aylis?"

Aylis turned up her hands, but Alamar answered, his voice grating out, "It is the way of his kind."

Jinnarin gestured at the mutilated corpse. "And is Durlok the one who did this to the Human?"

Fury filled Alamar's eyes. "Yes! Of that there is no doubt."

Bokar looked at the Mage. "How know you this?"

"Because I see the traces of his <fire>, that's how!" exploded Alamar.

"Father, calm down," appealed Aylis "Bokar is not the enemy."

Again Tink arrived, this time bearing both decanter and glass.

Glaring about, Alamar snatched the brandy and crystal from Tink and then stalked away muttering to himself.

"There is more here than meets the eye," said Aravan.

Aylis nodded. "You are right, Aravan. My father and Durlok—they are ancient foes."

Aravan raised an eyebrow.

Aylis elaborated. "Long past, my father and Durlok dueled."

"Dueled?" blurted Jinnarin, gazing at Alamar's retreating back. "I cannot imagine Alamar with a sword in his hand."

"Oh, it was not a sword fight they fought," demurred Aylis. "Instead it was a duel of Magekind: casting against casting."

Tink's eyes flew wide. "A *magic* fight," he breathed. "Spell against spell."

Aylis sighed, then said, "I suppose you could call it that, Tink."

"Cor, Lady Aylis, wot happened?"

Aylis glanced about at the others. "Durlok followed

the teachings of Gyphon and was practicing the forbidden arts, using the sufferings of others to power his castings. Father discovered this and confronted him, and there was a terrible battle. In the end, Durlok was defeated, and the Council imprisoned him and banned him from all castings. Both Durlok and my father were ravaged by the duel, and it took long years for them to recover. When he was well, Durlok escaped and disappeared. Whence he had gone, none knew, yet Father always suspected that he had flown from Vadaria, had fled to Mithgar; my father was right, it seems."

Jatu glanced from Aylis toward the rear quarters where Alamar had gone. "When did this take place, Lady Aylis?"

Aylis shrugged. "Millennia past, before I was born."

Behind them a chanting began, the Men hoisting the gig back aboard.

Jatu now looked at the corpse. "Captain, what would you have us do with this . . . Man."

Aravan turned to Aylis. "Is there aught else thou or thy father can learn from the slain one?"

Aylis shook her head. "No. I know how he was murdered and why. And my father knows who did the deed. We need nothing more."

Aravan looked at Tink. "Fetch Arlo, Tink. Have him sew the body in canvas with ballast. We will see that he gets a decent burial at sea."

"Aye, Cap'n." The boy sped away.

"What be our course now, Captain," asked Frizian. "Where do we sail next?"

Aravan looked at Jatu and Bokar, and then down at Jinnarin. "East, Frizian, due east. A hundred and fifty miles, for there I deem the next plume will fall, and we must stop Durlok from committing another of these foul deeds."

Jinnarin glanced once again at the mutilated remains. "Why would this Durlok do such a thing, Aylis?"

"To power his castings, Jinnarin. It is the way of the Black Mages to use the rage and fear and suffering of others to gain <fire> for their castings."

They found Alamar in the captain's lounge, the Mage in deep thought, the full brandy decanter on the table before him yet stoppered, the glass unused. As they came into the salon, Alamar glanced up and about, fixing at last on Aravan. "Captain, you've got to sail east, go to the next place where Durlok is likely to be. We cannot let him do this again."

"Thou art right, Mage Alamar," replied Aravan.

Even as Aravan spoke, the silks of the *Eroean* were piped about to catch the wind once more, and the ship fell away before the frigid southwesterly breeze.

Bokar took off his helm and laid it on the table. "We are making a great assumption here," he growled.

"Assumption?" asked Jatu.

"Aye, assumption," responded the Dwarf. "We are presuming that the Black Mage will be where the next plume falls, yet who is to say that he follows these will-o'-the-wisps at all?"

"Oh my," ventured Jinnarin. "Do you believe that it was merely happenstance that the plume came down where Durlok's victim was found?"

Bokar shrugged. "Mayhap."

Jatu cleared his throat and said, "On the other hand, perhaps he doesn't merely follow the plumes. Perhaps instead he causes them."

"To what end?" asked Bokar. "Why would he do such?"

All eyes turned to Alamar.

The eld Mage made a chopping motion with his hand. "It doesn't matter why. The only thing that matters is that we stop him."

Aylis sat down beside her sire. "And how do you propose we go about stopping him, Father?"

"I did him in the eye once before, Aylis, and I can do it again."

Jinnarin frowned in puzzlement. "Did him in the eye?"

Alamar nodded sharply. "Defeated him, Pysk. Did him in."

Aylis took his hand in hers. "Father, you were in your prime then."

Alamar's jaw jutted out and he glared at her, but Aylis's gaze was unwavering, green eyes staring into eyes of green, neither looking away. At last Alamar said, "But he's got to be stopped."

"We can go to Kairn," said Aylis. "Surely at the college will be someone who can defeat him."

"Daughter, if we go to Kairn now, we will lose Durlok's trail."

As if appealing for aid, Aylis glanced at Aravan, but the Elf said, "I deem thy Father has the right of it, *chieran*. If our assumption is correct, then Durlok will go to the next place of the plumes." Aravan pulled a map from the chart box, spreading it out before them in the lantern light. "Given that the plumes move fifty leagues a day, by the time we can sail to Kairn and back, and then onward to where the plumes will have gotten to, *aro*! they will have marched another two hundred leagues easterly—six hundred miles in all. And that puts them at"—Aravan stabbed a finger down to a landmass on the plot—"this point: the Realm of Thol. In fact, if they continue along the same course, they will be well inland. Nay, Aylis, if Durlok fares east and we would catch him and put an end to his vile deeds, now is the time."

Jatu nodded in agreement, adding, "And remember, we depend upon the wind, and should it die as we fare to or from Kairn, then we must await its return before we can take up the chase again. I would rather follow a trail that is hot on the wind than one grown cold, the scent lost."

Aylis looked 'round at each of them. "And what will we do if and when we overtake him, eh? Has anyone here the power to oppose him?"

Bokar hefted his axe. "Just let me stroke his neck with this. Then no matter his power, it will be of little concern."

Alamar snorted. "I doubt you will get the chance, Dwarf . . . if Durlok sees you coming, that is."

Jatu gazed at the Mage, then said, "Then we will need to take him unawares."

Aylis turned her palms upward. "Again I ask, who among us has the power to do so?"

"Perhaps I do," said Jinnarin. Her voice came from a cluster of shadow gathered in table center.

None said anything for a moment, and then Jinnarin spoke: "I could slip upon him unawares. And remember, my arrows are deadly."

Bokar growled. "Assassinations have no honor to them."

Jatu raised an eyebrow but remained silent.

"No, Pysk," said Alamar. "It is too dangerous. We must find another way."

The cluster of shadow disappeared, and Jinnarin stood revealed in the lantern light.

Jatu looked at Aravan. "He must be in a ship, Captain. Sink the ship and he will drown."

Again Alamar snorted. "Nay, not drown. Sink his ship and he will merely walk away."

Aravan's thoughts flashed back to the wet footprints Alamar had left behind when he first had visited the *Eroean* riding at anchor in Port Arbalin.

Bokar slammed a fist to the table. "Burn him then. Cast fireballs at the ship and set it aflame."

Again Alamar snorted. "Do you not remember what I did to the Kistanian Rover's fireballs? He will do the same . . . or worse."

"Not if we take him unawares," said Jatu, "slip up on him in the dark. Perhaps we can fire the ship when he is below decks."

"Fat chance," sneered Alamar.

"Well, Mage," gritted Bokar, "have you a better scheme?"

"Not at the moment, Dwarf. But before we get there, I will think of something."

A silence fell upon the group, none saying aught. After a moment, Aylis looked at those gathered 'round the table. "That's it? That's the best we can come up with? Somehow sneak this great tall ship up alongside Durlok's and shoot fireballs at it in the hopes that the Mage is below decks? That's our plan? Ha! Some plan!"

"Daughter!" barked Alamar, "I said I'd think of something."

"Well, I hope so, Father. I hope that at least *one* of us comes up with a better strategy, and soon, for we've less than a day to do so."

In his cabin, Alamar paced back and forth, the eld Mage muttering to himself. Finally he turned and said to Jinnarin, "The only way to fight fire is with fire."

Jinnarin's eyes flew wide. "But *I* thought it was the better to quench flames with wat—"

"Argh, Pysk! Where is your head? I don't mean ordinary flames. I mean <fire>. Castings."

"My head is right here, Alamar!" shot back Jinnarin, pointing to her temple. "If you want me to know what you are talking about, then I suggest you say what you mean!"

"Well what I mean, Pysk, is that it will take a spell to overcome a spell."

"But Aylis said—"

"Never mind what Aylis said."

"But, Alamar, isn't she right?"

Alamar growled, then said, "In some things she's right, Pysk. —But look here, what I plan to do is to get the jump on Durlok, surprise him, as Jatu says catch him unawares." The elder rubbed his hands together in anticipation.

"And just how do you propose to do that, Alamar?"

"Well, Pysk, think on this: what if Durlok cannot see the fireballs, eh? Then what?"

"Um ... I suppose they would strike his ship unimpeded."

"Exactly so," cackled Alamar. "Exactly so. And I can conceal them with a casting, make them, *hmm*, unnoticed."

"But, Alamar," protested Jinnarin, "won't he simply use his magesight to see them coming?"

"He could, Pysk, and that's why we have to surprise him, so that he doesn't get a chance. Then we'll burn his ship, and if he escapes, skewer him with a bolt from a ballista. That will put an end to his plans, whatever they may be."

"But, Alamar, you assume that he is indeed on a ship. What if he is not? Then what?"

Alamar stared at Jinnarin. "How else would he travel about in the middle of the ocean, Pysk? Tell me that."

"I don't know, Alamar. You're the Mage. You tell me."

"Pah! It's not even worth considering."

Jinnarin reluctantly acquiesced, then gazed up at the Mage. "That's your plan? The whole of it?"

Alamar nodded. "What do you think?"

"Well, Alamar, I think that it's full of holes. See here, if Durlok is the Mage you think he is, then won't he counter your spells with castings of his own? Won't he quench any fire we burst upon his ship? Won't he turn any ballista bolt hindward in its arc and send it back at us? I mean, look at it this way: if you, Alamar, were on a ship being attacked thusly, what would you do? And whatever you decide, isn't that exactly what Durlok will do?"

Bokar, Jatu, and Frizian sat drinking hot tea at a table in the ship's mess. "I say we do it just as we did the pirate ship in the Straits of Alacca," declared Bokar. "Only this time it is we who will hale alongside. Then we drop the corvuses and charge across, while some swing over on yardarm ropes, and take the ship. It is as simple as that."

"Oh?" murmured Jatu, a skeptical look on his face. "As simple as that, eh? You forget, Bokar, there's a Mage aboard that other ship, and where Mages are concerned, nothing is simple."

"Bah!" exclaimed Bokar. "There are forty Châkka warriors upon the *Eroean*, all armed and armored. I doubt that any Mage can withstand such an assault, especially if it comes as a surprise."

Jatu nodded, but Frizian said, "Perhaps so, Armsmaster, yet surely this Durlok does not sail alone. He must have a crew of his own. And if so, they will not simply be standing about while we board their ship and go after the Mage. I mean, we'll be fighting for our very lives."

Bokar canted his head in agreement. "True, Frizian, yet heed: I will have ten of my Châkka bear crossbows, and assign them the task of finding the Mage and bringing him down. Surely one or more bolts will find their mark. He cannot turn them all aside."

Before the ship's second officer could reply, a seaman came to the table. "Mister Frizian, sir, the wind is beginning to shift. It's running a bit warmer and up from the south."

As Frizian stood and made ready to leave, Jatu shook his head and said. "Perhaps this plan of yours will indeed succeed, Bokar, yet it does have a weakness, one which Lady Aylis pointed out: just how will we slip this tall ship alongside Durlok's without being noticed?"

"Fainting is not my wont," said Aylis, standing in the center of the stateroom she and Aravan shared.

Aravan canted an eyebrow. *"Chieran?"*

Aylis shook her head. "Twice now it has happened to me: the first time when I was trying to read your cards, love; the second time when I laid hands on the ... on Durlok's victim. Never before have I fainted, but now it seems to be on the verge of becoming a habit."

Aravan pulled her to him, his strong arms going about her. Of a sudden he pulled back and looked at her. "Thou art trembling, Aylis."

She drew him back to her, resting her head on his shoulder. "I am afraid, Aravan, afraid for my father."

Aravan stroked her hair. "Dost thou wish to speak of it?"

Aylis sighed and then pulled away and moved to the bed and sat. Aravan swung a chair about and threw a leg astraddle and sat facing her.

"Durlok is a Black Mage," began Aylis, "and they get their <power> not from within but rather from without. They use the pain and agony and sufferings of others, their hatred, their fear, their terror, whatever, to power their vile castings. Hence, given that they have enough victims, their energy is without bounds.

"My father, by contrast, uses his own internal energy for his castings. And he is at the end of his ebb, or nearly so. Hence, he has only a limited number of castings ere he will be past redemption, and should he use all of his <fire>, he will perish.

"And the terrible thing is, I cannot aid him, for my strength lies in the gathering of information, though at the moment I am blocked. I cannot even lend him some of my <fire>, for I know not how. Oh, there are spells which would transfer <power> from me to him, but I am not privy to such ... nor do I believe is my father. Yet even did we know them, it is questionable whether he would employ castings of that kind for they are much too similar to the lamia-like drainings the Black Mages use to empower themselves.

"And that is why I am afraid, Aravan, for should we

meet Durlok face-to-face, I know my father will not hold back. He will pit his limited <fire> 'gainst the inferno of a Black Mage. And he will die does he do so."

The wind continued to shift from southwesterly to south, and as it did so, its force began to abate. The air itself was somewhat warmer, though only slightly so, for it was yet deep winter there on the marge between the wide Weston Ocean and the great Northern Sea. And onward sailed the *Eroean,* easterly ever easterly, Rico now piping the sails about to catch the failing wind abeam.

Early mid morn Captain Aravan came on deck and the entire crew gathered for a simple ceremony, a burial at sea for Durlok's victim. As all stood assembled beneath silken sails, the captain uttered a prayer, asking that High Adon gather the soul of the slain Man unto Himself. And with Rico piping farewell, they tipped the funeral plank and let the canvas-wrapped body slide down into the waters, the ballast dragging it under the cold grey waves.

Hours passed, the low winter Sun crawling across the sky, the wind continued to diminish, the *Eroean* making the most of the breeze, yet creeping across the water.

"What be our speed, Boder?"

"Six knots and falling, sir."

Aylis came on deck, seeking Aravan. And when she found him she said, "I have been thinking, love, about the rede I uttered while trying to divine your cards. It seems to me that I should begin teaching you some of the tongue of Magekind, for if you are to draw fire into a dark crystal, you will need the words to do so."

Aravan gazed at the seeress. "*Chieran,* it is not at all certain that the rede was meant for me. After all, thou wert not looking *at* me but *through* me instead."

"Nevertheless, love, I would teach you words which you might need in speaking an object's Truename."

Aravan acquiesced, and together they strolled toward the bow, Aylis speaking softly, Aravan repeating her words.

And still the wind diminished.

Jinnarin and Alamar sat in the ship's mess, breaking their fast, Rux lying under the table, gnawing on a slab of dried jerky. As they ate, from the galley came Trench the cook. "Oi've got somethin' special 'ere for y', Laidy Jinnarin. A bit o' a sweet, if Oi do say so m'sel'. 'Ere y' be, Laidy—a dab o' a 'oney comb. It ought t' go roight nice on th' bit o' y'r biscuit, naow."

As Alamar eyed the honeycomb, his mouth watering, Jinnarin looked up at Trench. "Why, I thank you, Trench, but tell me, what did I ever do to deserve such a treat?"

Trench shuffled his feet then said, "Well, miss, y'see, y' won th' plume lottery f'r me, y' did. Two 'underd coppers, 'twas, one f'r each slip pulled out o' th' 'at. And when y' spotted that first plume, wellanow, it were Oi 'oo wos th' winner. Two 'underd coppers, it ain't much naow, but it were th' prestige o' winnin' wot counted. Oi c'n crow it over m' shipmates, Oi can, 'n' f'r naow Oi'm known as 'Lucky Trench,' 'n' f'r that Oi thank'ee. Y'see, th' crew, wellanow, they think m' cookin' is even better, naow that Oi'm a proven lucky charm 'n' all. 'N' that's why Oi'm givin' y' th' bit o' th' comb Oi've been savin' j'st f'r a special occasion, 'n' this wos it."

"Why, I thank you, Mister Lucky Trench. I will savor every scrap of it."

Trench bobbed his head and strode back to the galley, a spring in his step.

"Are you going to eat all of that?" Alamar's voice was plaintive.

"As much as I can, Alamar," answered Jinnarin, stuffing her mouth. "Yb cn mrv htvr ss lft."

"What? What did you say, Pysk?"

Jinnarin's jaw worked up and down as she chewed and chewed and finally swallowed. "I said, you can have whatever is left." She smiled wickedly and took another big bite.

When Jinnarin and Rux and Alamar came up on deck, Aylis and Aravan were amidships, the seeress yet teaching the Elf the words of Magekind. Alamar, licking his lips yet sweet from honey, stood and listened for a while. At last he said, "I wish we knew the Black Mage words for the various gems. You could learn those, too."

"How did you learn their word for fire, Father?"

"*Pŷr?* It was in the duel with Durlok. He yelled *pŷr*

several times, trying to set me aflame. Succeeded once. I quenched it the other times."

Jinnarin's eyes flew wide. "You were on fire?"

Alamar nodded, then made a negating gesture. "Oh, it was not *me* that was on fire, but my clothing instead."

"Oh," said Jinnarin. Then her eyes flew wide again, and she gasped, "What did you do? Didn't you get burned?"

"What a question!" exclaimed Alamar. "Of course I got burned, Pysk. You can't have your clothes on fire without getting burned."

"But what did you do?"

"What do you think I did? I set *his* clothes on fire, too."

Jinnarin stamped her foot. "No, Alamar. I mean, what did you do about your own clothes being on fire?"

"Well why didn't you ask that in the first place? I sent them away, that's what I did."

"Sent—?"

"Yes. Made 'em go elsewhere. Finished that fight stark naked, I did."

"Oh."

Aravan was laughing and holding onto giggling Aylis, and when Alamar glared at them, Aravan said, "Forgive me, Mage Alamar, but I cannot help myself. Thy plight was dire, that I do not doubt, but the sight of thee with thy clothes afire and then standing naked, well, it must have been a wonder to behold."

Alamar's chin jutted forth—"Being on fire is nothing to jest about"—and he spun on his heel and stalked away.

Aravan turned to Aylis. "I will apologize to him later, *chieran*, when he has had time to cool somewhat."

Aylis glanced down at the Pysk and Rux. "Jinnarin, would you go to him and try to soothe his ruffled feathers? In spite of his manner, he cherishes you."

Jinnarin sighed and turned to go. A step or two later she turned and grinned. "You know, I cherish him, too, despite his ways. —And, oh, by the way, I had the nightmare again yestermorn. It's coming now every three or four days." Turning once more, Jinnarin strode in the direction Alamar had gone, Rux at her heels.

Behind, Aylis turned to Aravan. "I asked her to tell

me when it came. With her awake at night and sleeping during the day, well, I wondered if it changed anything."

"Mayhap we could call it a daymare, now," said Aravan, smiling grimly.

Aylis winced mockingly. "Ah, Aravan, *iocatio* in the midst of all."

"Iocatio?"

Aylis nodded. "Another mageword, and it means, sirrah"—her smile answered his own—"that you lack appropriate seriousness in these matters grave."

"Ah but, *chieran,* I would rather smile in the face of adversity than to become glum and dour, no matter the stakes."

Aylis reached out and took his hand. "I know, love, and so would I."

Aravan raised her fingers to his lips, his sapphire gaze holding fast her emerald eyes. Her own gaze softened, and she said, "First, love, more lessons, and then will we take reward."

Aravan's grin widened. "Then on with it, Lady. Delay not."

Aylis retrieved her hand then said, "When you combine two magewords, usually you change the ending of the first, sometimes adding an 'o,' at the other times adding . . ."

The south wind died just after sunset, and the sails on the *Eroean* hung slack. Frizian turned to Aravan. "Caught on the horns of a winter calm, Captain. Shall I unship the gigs?"

Aravan glanced at the stars. "We are some leagues short, Frizian. Too far to row and hale the ship. *Ahn!* too far to row, regardless, towing the ship or not. Nay, leave the gigs aboard."

"Kruk!" spat Bokar. "That means Durlok is likely to work his evil again."

Boder strode to Aravan's side. "Cap'n, there's a mist forming on the sea."

Aravan and Bokar and Frizian stepped to the taffrail and peered over, the second officer holding high a lantern for his Human eyes to see the waters below, though neither Aravan nor Bokar needed such. "Garn!" exclaimed Frizian. "Warm air over cold water. I knew that a south wind boded ill. There'll be fog tonight, Captain."

"Kala!" crowed Bokar. "If the fog is thick enough and reaches far enough, the Black Mage will see no aurora tonight."

Aravan turned to Bokar. "Armsmaster, if Durlok is indeed behind the plumes, then mayhap thou art correct and a fog will set his plans awry. Yet heed: it is winter and we are on the marge of the Northern Sea, and a fog will clad the *Eroean* with ice."

Frizian glanced up at the silken sails. "Captain, shall I reef her tight? Keep ice from the 'spanse?"

Bokar growled. "But if the wind returns, then we'll be just that much longer getting underway."

Aravan nodded, then said, "Frizian, if the fog starts climbing up the masts, then pipe the crew and reef. I'd rather take time raising sail than to try to shake loose ice."

"What about the sheets and pulley blocks, Captain?" asked Boder. "They'll ice up, too."

"That can't be helped, Boder," replied Aravan. "We'll have to work them often to keep them running free."

Bokar glanced back at the mist rising. "Bane and blessing," he grumbled. "Bane and blessing alike."

Slowly, steadily, the fog rose up from the surface of the sea, gradually enveloping the *Eroean*. Frizian had Reydeau pipe the crew, and up the ratlines they clambered, taking care, for even now a thin coating of ice covered the rope-ladder mesh. They reefed the yardarm sails to the full and haled in the jibs and stays, and now the Elvenship drifted free, no silks flying on her masts. Up and up rose the icefog, obscuring the stars above, until nothing of the heavens could be seen. Lanterns were lit, ghostly yellow halos in the stirring grey. The mist breathed a clear crystal sheath to lie over all, and the decks became hazardous, nearly too slippery to walk upon, and deck lines were strung to aid the crew, though all but the lookouts now quartered below. All sound became muffled in the cloak, and only the lapping of water against the hull broke the silence . . . that and the stamping of the deck watch, tromping in place to stay warm.

Mid of night came and then passed on, and still the fog thickened, layering the drifting ship with its icy grasp. And the Men on watch could but barely see a foot or two beyond their reach. Even so, the Elvenship lookouts remained alert, listening, depending upon their ears more than their eyes to detect if anything was amiss.

Below decks, suddenly Aravan wakened from a sound sleep, jolting upright, his hand clasping the frigid blue stone amulet about his neck. Beside him, Aylis looked up, her eyes muzzy with sleep. "Wha—?"

"Get dressed!" hissed Aravan, throwing on his pants and boots. "Danger!"

Lobbie amidships cocked his head for it seemed he heard a plashing above that of the waves lightly slapping against the hull. *Starboard,* he thought, and using a deck line, across to that side he went. He leaned over the railing and listened with care, trying to hear through the muffling fog. *There!* a splash, another, many, and of a sudden in the darkness, black on black, something immense loomed forth, swirling mist driven before it.

"Iceber—!" shouted Lobbie, but his bellow was lost in the crash of timbers as the great, dark mass plowed into side, and the hull of the *Eroean* was breached. Lobbie was hurled over the rail but managed to grab a frozen stanchion. Grimly he hung on, yelling for help, his gloved hands clutching ice, slipping. The ship juddered, timbers splintering, and Lobbie's right hand was jolted loose from the ice-clad bronze—he was going to fall. Suddenly someone gripped his wrist and he was dragged up and over the wale, giant Jatu hauling him to safety midst the sound of splitting beams and a pounding of a drum and a great splashing and churning of water.

As the ship juddered and jolted, Lobbie grabbed the railing and dragged himself to his feet. "Iceberg!" he shouted again, pointing at the blackness abeam. But even as he called it, he knew that it was not so.

Boom! ... Boom! ... Boom! ... Boom! ... sounded the beat of the drum, and amid the splintering of hull planking, slowly the dark mass withdrew, the *Eroean* jolting and jarring like a ravaged hare in a savage hound's mouth.

Of a sudden the Elvenship rolled free, the darkness abeam turning her loose and backing away to disappear in the fog. And amid the shouts of Men and Dwarves the *Eroean* began to sink, her hull holed, icy water pouring in.

And out from the frigid mist, mid the beat of a drum and the splashing churn, there came the sound of cold laughter.

CHAPTER 19

Gelen

Winter, 1E9574–75
[The Present]

"Man the bilge pumps!" roared Jatu. "We are holed!" In the icefog, crewmen slid and slithered across the glassy decks. Someone somewhere began ringing a bell, while someone else winded a brass bugle, both bell and trump sounding a needless alarm, for the ship had been struck a murderous blow, shivering timbers, slamming Man and Dwarf and Mage and Pysk and Elf and fox into whatever stood in the way. Below decks, water thundered in through the gaping cleft where something massive had rammed through and then had withdrawn. Men and Dwarves alike regained their footing and led by Frizian they charged down the ladderways, hurtling past the lower deck and into the main hold, where icy brine of the cruel Northern Sea relentlessly poured inward, inundating all, the water so cold that it *burned*. Men cried out from the deadly chill, and even hardy Dwarves gasped as they fought their way toward the breech through the frigid rush. Taking up planks and hammers and long, heavy nails, and saws and axes and mauls and wedges, toward the break they struggled, the bitter sea washing them back, knocking Men down and dragging them under, Dwarves as well, trying to freeze them or drown them in their very own hold. Dwarves reached out and grasped struggling Men, pulling them up from beneath the flow, the Men benumbed and in shock from the merciless cold. And the frigid Northern Sea continued to roar inward.

Aravan now among them gathered together a crew and up the ladderways they raced.

"Cap'n!" panted Hogar, "we've got t' ready th' boats! If we go down in this sea, we won't last ten heartbeats in th' icy water!"

"We are not going down, Hogar," gritted Aravan, in the lead.

Pausing only long enough to light lanterns, onto the slick decks they scrambled and through the fog to the main hatch. "Get it open, Arlo!" commanded Aravan. "You three help. And, Arlo, bring up a crossjack! Lay it out flat on the starboard side, lengthwise to the ship, above the breech! The rest of you, come with me!" And toward the bow he skittered, hanging onto the deck lines to keep from falling, and Men and Dwarves struggled after their captain, all of them drenched to the bone and freezing in the harsh winter air, the lanterns they bore casting luminous halos in the clinging ice-crystal mist.

Opening the forward deck lockers, Aravan heaved free a heavy hank of rope, shouting, "To me, Dokan! Hogar and Hegen, fetch a second halyard! Artus and Dask, fetch a third!" And as the crew sprang forward to follow the commands, Aravan unknotted the hank and handed one end to Dokan. "To the bowsprit!" he barked. "Ye others, follow after! Do as Dokan and I do!"

"Captain," rasped Dokan, as up the foredeck ladder they scrambled, "what be the plan?"

"We are going to keelhaul the leak," gritted Aravan. They came to the bowsprit and Aravan slithered onto the ice-laden outjutting mast and called, "Hang on tight to thy end, Dokan," and he hurled the bulk of the halyard into the sea while clutching the other end. As the line uncoiled and struck the water, Aravan dangled his end down two yards or so and whipped it under the bowsprit and caught it on the opposite side. He then slid back onto the foredeck, the Elf clinging tightly to the cordage, the halyard now a great loop under the bow. "Now we must drag the line back amidships, Dokan, thou on the larboard, I on the starboard. Keep a firm grip. —Hogar, Hegen, Artus, Dask, take care, the sprit is slick. Cast thy lines over as did we, and follow."

Dragging the halyard under the keel, they struggled

back amidships, each clinging tightly to his end of the rope, passing it out and around ratlines and deadeyes and other such, Dokan on the larboard, Aravan on the starboard. When they came to the main hatch, Arlo and his helpers were back up from below, the unfurled crossjack lying out before them.

"Arlo, to me. Ye others, get three more lines," Aravan ordered, the crewmen shuffle-sliding across the ice to lockers to fetch them. "Hold tight, Dokan!" Aravan called to the Dwarf 'cross ship. Swiftly Aravan and Arlo clipped the halyard to the lower left-corner eyelet in the crossjack border.

"Cap'n!" shouted one of the Men frantically cranking the wheel of the mid deck bilge pump. "She's goin' down!"

The drifting *Eroean* was beginning to list in the frigid, icefog sea.

In that moment Hogar and Hegen came dragging the second line aft, one Man on the starboard, the other Man opposite, unseen in the fog. "Arlo, clip that line to the lower middle eyelet!"

No sooner had they done so than Artus and Dask came amidships dragging the third halyard. As Arlo fastened this line to the lower right-hand corner, Aravan and the other three crewmen—Geff, Jon, and Jamie—fastened three ropes to the middle and corner eyelets of the upper border of the crossjack.

"We're going to use the jack to cover the hole," shouted Aravan. "Geff, Jon, Jamie, take two turns of each halyard about a stanchion"—he pointed—"there and there and there.

"Ye Men on the bilge pump, get ye over to the larboard. Lend a hand."

"But, Cap'n," called one of the pumpers, "she'll sink if we don't crank!"

"She'll sink faster if ye don't do as I say!"

"Do as the captain orders!" roared Jatu through the fog, the huge black Man just then coming back onto the icy decks.

Aravan skittered across to the larboard, accompanied by Jatu. "Take two turns about stanchions, there and there and there, then hale in the slack."

Dokan, Jatu, and Dask each took a line, Hogar and

the two bilge pumpers dividing themselves among the three. Quickly, all slack was gone, the great silk crossjack now spread wide and flat against the hull, the sail pulled down over the starboard side, the top edge at the railing, bottom edge just at the surface of the sea, just above the hole. "Now," called Aravan, "slowly pay out the starboard lines as we take up the larboard. Arlo, sing out when the jack covers the breech."

"But, Cap'n," came Arlo's voice, "I can't see down through the fog!"

"Jatu," hissed Aravan, "stay here and follow mine orders. I'm going starboard."

"Aye, Captain," grunted Jatu, as Aravan disappeared into the mist.

Aravan leaned over the starboard wale, and dangled a lantern down on a cord, his Elven sight able to discern what mortal eyes could not. "Pay out and take up!" he called. Down into the water slid the crossjack sail, the silk hugging the side of the *Eroean*. "Pay out and take up again!"

Down went the crossjack.

"Pay out and take up more on the bow lines, less on the stern line!"

When the jack was squared up—"Pay out even and take up again!"

Now it became a struggle as the sail edged farther down over the breech, the rushing sea trying to shove the silken cloth into the hole. Struggling, the Men and Dwarves haled on the lines, and down slid the crossjack, now firmly plastered against the hull by the press of inrushing water. Were it not for Jatu and the two Dwarves—Dask and Dokan—the venture would have failed, the sail would have been sucked into the hold . . . yet the strength of these three proved critical in resisting the brutal flow, and paying out and taking up, at last the silk covered the gape and the halyards were haled tight and belayed. And in the hold below, as the crossjack sail was pulled down over the breech, the thunder of water slowed to a roar and then to a gush and finally to a heavy runnelling. But the hold was awash, and Men and Dwarves alike were suffering from the cold, the heat drawn from them, and they could but scarcely function, barely able to clamber up and out from the flood, for if they did not get warm they would die.

The midship bilge pump crew returned to their task, and together with the forward and aft pumpers were now able to keep ahead of the inflow.

Aravan turned to the others, exhausted, chilled, their wet clothes rimed with ice. "Get ye below and into dry garments and warmed. Jatu, this fix is but temporary. As soon as thou canst, find able crew to lash more lines about the vessel to trap the sail e'en tighter against the hull. Too, find Bokar and send him to me in the aft quarters. And when thou canst find suitable replacements, relieve the pumping crews."

As Aravan entered the aft-quarters passageway, he heard Rux whining in Alamar's cabin. Entering, he found Jinnarin looking on starkly as a grim-faced Aylis wetted a cloth. On the bed lay Alamar, the eld Mage motionless, his hair matted with blood. Rux whined, the fox smelling gore in the air and sensing his mistress's distress. Tokko pieces were scattered across the floor.

"Oh, Aravan," cried Jinnarin, "Alamar was hurled against the wall."

"Is he . . . ?"

Aylis glanced up. "He is breathing, his pulse strong, yet he has suffered a blow to the skull." Aylis began washing the back of her father's head, clearing the blood away.

Aravan stepped to Alamar's side. "Jinnarin, fetch Fager. I know not where he is; he may be attending others. As soon as he is able, have him come here."

Jinnarin leapt to Rux's back, and the fox sprang out the door.

Aylis washed away the last of the blood, though a gash yet seeped in the center of a large knot standing forth on the anterior of the elder's head.

"I will get bandages, *chieran*," said Aravan, stepping from the cabin. Moments later he returned, cloth and a healing salve in hand. Aylis took both from him and gently applied the salve. Then she folded a pressure bandage and bound it to the back of Alamar's head with a strip of cloth, tying it in place.

Bokar stepped into the cabin. He glanced at Alamar, then said, "Captain?"

Aravan turned to the Dwarf. "Bokar, thy Drimma will recover more swiftly than the Men. I would have thee gather a crew to cut away the burst timber and rig a fix until we can sail to a shipyard for repairs."

"Shipyard?"

"Aye. The port of Arbor in Gelen, I deem; it is nearest."

"But, Captain," growled Bokar, slamming a fist into his palm, "we will lose Durlok if we do so. And I wager all I own that he is behind this calamity."

Aravan shook his head. "Bokar, we have already lost Durlok, whether or no he is responsible. As it now stands, the *Eroean* cannot fare after him; we cannot pursue him with our hull holed. And, if he runs to dangerous waters, a jury-rigged repair is like to fail."

"Kruk!" spat Bokar. After a moment he said, "My Châkka will be ready in mayhap a half a candlemark. I will assemble a crew; we will repair the ship well enough to reach Gelen."

Aravan nodded. "Find Finch. He will tell thee what needs doing, though keep him from wading in the frigid water; I would not have him dead, the heat sucked away from his body. Divide thy Drimma into several crews and have them work in short shifts, for even thy hardy Folk cannot withstand the chill of this ocean overlong. I will join thee when I can."

As Bokar left, Jinnarin and Rux returned. "Fager will be here soon, Aravan. He is treating those who were in the water below." The Pysk looked to Alamar. "Any change?"

Aylis shook her head.

"*Chieran,* there is nought I can do here, yet much I can do below. I will return when I can."

Aylis looked at Aravan and nodded.

Working in short shifts, and guided by Finch, the carpenter, Dwarves waded through the icy brine in the flooded hold to saw and chop away the shattered hull planking. And as the bilge pump crews steadily lowered the water inside, boards were sawn and fitted across the breech and nailed in place, and caulking was forced into the seams. By mid morn the *Eroean* had been repaired to the point where she was marginally seaworthy again, though there was some question whether the jury rigging would hold in a battering storm.

Exhausted, Finch and the Dwarves took to their beds, while Aravan and the ship's officers surveyed the damage below, Quartermaster Roku accompanying them, the little Jingarian muttering over the loss of goods and marking it down in a ledger. And as the bilge pumps glugged away, down through the hold they all clambered.

Much of the stores of food had been ruined by the seawater, especially that which was stowed in bags or packed in crates, though anything stored in kegs had remained undamaged for the most part. All cloth goods were sodden through and through, and would be rimed in salt were they ever to dry. Other supplies fared well or poorly, depending on their makeup and their method of storing. Some goods had been stowed on racks above the reach of the brine, and these were completely undamaged. Other goods were wholly submerged, and yet they fared well, such as the ballista fireball Bokar fished up from below the water; after a cursory examination, he declared it fit for battle, tossing it back into the brine. The lances, though, would need be recovered and dried soon, else the shafts would warp.

The inspection tour ended back at the boarded-over hole, water seeping in, and Aravan said, " 'Tis well enough done for us to sail to Gelen when the wind returns, though I deem we need leave the crossjack lashed to the outside in the event that something goes amiss."

"Like to have dashed my brains out," declared Alamar, feeling the back of his head. The elder pointed at his sternum. "My chest hurts, too."

Jinnarin sighed. "I'm afraid I did that, Alamar."

"Hurt my chest?"

"Yes," she replied. "You see, when we were thrown across the room, you hit the wall, and I hit you."

"You hit me?"

"Well, I couldn't help it, Alamar. You were in the way."

Alamar glanced at the tiny Pysk. "You hit me!"

"I'm sorry, Alamar. There was nothing I could do. Besides, would you rather it had been you who slammed into me? If so, then I would be just a flat spot on the wall."

Alamar grinned in spite of himself. Jinnarin giggled.

Of a sudden, Alamar sobered. "This has got to be Durlok's doings. I've got to get to the hold and see for myself."

"It's still awash, Alamar."

"As soon as the water is out, then."

"Rux and I will go down shortly. When it is safe, I'll let you know."

Alamar stood and made his way to a porthole. Peering out, he said, "Go ask Aylis when this fog will lift, when the wind will return. The sooner we get to Gelen, the sooner we get the ship repaired. And the sooner repaired, the sooner we can be back on Durlok's track."

"But, Alamar, he's lost to us, don't you think? I mean, who knows where he'll be by the time the *Eroean* is repaired?"

Alamar turned away from the porthole, bitterness in his eyes. "Regardless of where he's gotten to, Pysk, he *must* be stopped." The elder trudged to his bed and sat down wearily. Finally he said, "Go ask Aylis when we will be underway."

Jinnarin found Aylis standing on the deck, Aravan at her side. The seeress gazed at the unseen sky and summoned her energy. *"Caelum in futura,"* she murmured, and watched as all disappeared but the icefog, and hours passed in mere moments—grey day raced past, dusk but a flicker as dark night fell sharply, but then the grey mist swirled away and stars splashed across the skies, and then dawn burst into clear day, and here and there a cloud raced across the blue—and then her vision expired.

"It will clear sometime tonight," she said upon returning from the depths of the vision. "This day, though, the fog remains."

Aravan looked down at Jinnarin. "Today is Third Yule, and tonight is Year's Long Night, the winter solstice. And tonight we shall turn for Gelen, riding a crippled ship, breaking away from our pursuit of Durlok, the Black Mage. Not a good portent for the coming year, eh, Jinnarin?"

Unexpectedly, Jinnarin shivered, though not from the cold. "Oh, Aravan, I do hope that it bodes no ill for Farrix ... or anyone else, for that matter."

Aravan glanced over at Aylis, then back to Jinnarin. "Aye, tiny one, so do I hope as well. Regardless, tonight is Year's Long Night, and I will step the ritual. Wouldst thou care to join me?" He looked at Aylis. "Thou, too, *chieran?*"

"Oh no, Aravan," answered Jinnarin. "Rux and I will celebrate as my Folk have done throughout the years."

"I don't know the steps," said Aylis, smiling, "but I would gladly learn."

The Elf's gaze grew gentle. "Thou need not know them, *chieran,* for I will pace thee through."

Thus it was that in the night of the twenty-third of December the wind returned and blew the icy mist away and the stars shone down. And as the Men clambered up the ice-laden lines and unfurled the sails, and as the *Eroean* hove about and headed southward for Gelen, on the deck of the Elvenship were conducted three rituals celebrating the winter solstice:

Aravan and Aylis paced through the Elven rite: Step ... pause ... shift ... pause ... turn ... pause ... step. Slowly, slowly, move and pause. His voice rising, her voice falling, notes like silver as they sang. Aylis in harmony, euphony ... step ... pause ... step. Aravan turning. Aylis turning. Step ... pause ... step. Aylis passing. Aravan pausing. Step ... pause ... step. Counterpoint. Descant. Step ... pause ... step ...

On the aft deck, Fox Rider and fox, bowed to the six cardinal points—north, east, south, west, above, and below. Rux arched his neck down and Jinnarin mounted and faced the stars and spread her arms wide, as if to grasp the whole of the heavens above, and Rux slowly turned so that his rider could see the entire glory of the sky. And as Rux continued to slowly turn and turn, Jinnarin sang to Adon, though her song had no words. Even so, that it was a paean unto Him, there was no doubt, for what else could have such liquid beauty? It was as if a soul had been set free to soar among the stars.

While on the foredeck, Bokar and the Châkka warriors chanted to Elwydd, renewing their ancient pledges

of honor and industry and bonding and faith—the armsmaster lifting his face and hands to the star-studded
heavens and raising his voice to the sky, calling out the
great Châkka litany, the unified response of the gathered
Châkka warriors alternating with his, cantor and chorale
speaking in Châkur, the hidden tongue:

> *[Elwydd—*
> > *—Lol an Adon . . .]*

> Elwydd—
> > *—Daughter of Adon*
> We thank Thee—
> > *—For Thy gentle hand*
> That gave to us—
> > *—The breath of life*
> May this be—
> > *—The golden year*
> That Châkka—
> > *—Touch the stars.*

And as Elf and Mage, and Pysk and fox, and a Dwarven warband each in their own ways reverently hallowed
the longest night, southward turned the wounded *Eroean*, sailing away from the waters where she had nearly
gone down, away from the waters where mayhap a Black
Mage lurked.

Finch came into the captain's salon, the carpenter bearing a fragment of wood. He stepped in among the ship's
officers and handed Alamar the scrap of mahogany, a
splinter from the breech. "As you requested, sir, this
came from the very point of impact, or as near as I
can determine."

His head bandaged, Alamar fingered the wood, murmuring, *"Quis?"* After a moment he said, "As we
thought, it's Durlok's doing, all right." He handed the
scrap over to Aylis. "What do you get from it?"

The seeress held the wood and canted, *"Patefac!"* She
gasped and dropped the chip. Catching her breath, she
said, "A great dark beak rushing at me."

"Ha!" barked Bokar. "Just as we expected—a ram!"

Fager shook his head. "Lady Aylis called it a beak. It could be a monster instead."

All eyes swung back to Aylis, and Jinnarin asked, "Was it a monster, Aylis?"

"I"—Aylis turned up her hands—"I don't know. A dark beak is all I saw, pointed, rushing forward . . . underwater, I think."

Fager turned to Aravan. "Captain, what did your stone detect, if anything?"

Aravan fingered the blue amulet. "Danger is all, Fager. It could be a creature. It could be other evil."

"Most likely from Neddra," said Alamar. "Someone or something sent by Durlok . . . or travelling with him, I think."

Jatu glanced over at Bokar. "I side with Bokar. It was a ram. Forget not that both Lobbie and I heard drums, and a great splashing. What could it be but a ship?"

"Aye," averred Bokar, clenching a fist in affirmation. "The ship of the Black Mage. And something on that ship caused Captain Aravan's stone to chill."

Jinnarin turned to Aravan. "What kind of a ship could crash into us and not be damaged just as we were?"

Frizian answered, "One that's built to do so, Lady Jinnarin."

"Don't forget," said Jatu, "it backed away. That would make it some kind of galley."

"Galley?" asked Jinnarin. "But I thought that a galley is where the cook works. Is there another kind?"

Aravan leaned forward on his hands. "Aye, Jinnarin. There is a type of ship having the same name. It is sail powered and bears oars as well. Some have great underwater rams jutting out from the bow. In battle, her crew rows her at speed at another ship, the ram to crash into the enemy vessel below the waterline, holing her hull, as was ours. The galley crew then backs water, withdrawing the ram from the foe, and the sea does the rest, sinking the enemy ship."

"Aye," added Jatu. "And a drum is used to keep the beat of the oars together, and we heard a drum. And the splashing we heard—what would it be but the oars stroking her away as she backed water and left us to sink, eh?"

Fager shook his head. "I yet have my doubts. Heed,

what kind of crew could row a hundred and fifty miles a day, day after day, eh? I mean, that's how far apart the plumes were, right?"

"Perhaps they had ... magical help," said Frizian, looking at Alamar. "Is such a thing possible?"

Alamar shrugged. "It would take a lot of <fire> to do so." At his side, Aylis nodded in confirmation.

A silence fell, then Aravan said, "Mayhap it was a galley, yet those kinds of ships are of ancient vintage and are not now used. The last I saw was in the waters off the coast of Chabba, and she was sinking, burned by a ship from Sarain during one of their frequent Wars. Since then, I know of no galley left in all of the world."

"Well, Captain," growled Bokar, "that may be as you say. But I believe that at least one galley yet roams the seas with one or more Grg aboard."

Two days later on the morning tide of the sixth day of Yule, the *Eroean* sailed into the port of Arbor in Gelen. Word spread like wildfire, and citizenry from miles about came to see the wonder of her. That the Elvenship was damaged was plain to see, yet her master did not put her in dry-dock there in the shipyards, for none was of a size to take her length; yet even had one been suitable, still it is unlikely that her captain would have used it, for it seemed he was on an urgent mission, and had other plans. Instead she was haled up to dockside and unladed of her spoiled cargo as well as much of her ballast. Thus lightened, and with bales of rope and cloth acting as fenders between the ship and the dock, lines were affixed well up on her masts and used to winch her over onto her larboard side, her starboard rolling up until her injured hull was well exposed. And then Aravan and Finch and the crew began her repair, Dwarves and Men alike swarming over her starboard side, helping her Elven captain and the ship's carpenter.

That this was a remarkable event, of that there was no doubt, for the Arborites flocked down to the docks in droves. Even had she not been injured, the *Eroean* would have drawn crowds just as large, for this was a seaport and the Elvenship was legendary.

Cor, this'll be a Yuletide long remembered, eh? Oi mean, th' Elvenship roight 'ere in our very own docks!

None else like 'er in th' whole wide world.
'N' damaged, too, naow what d'y' make o' that, eh?
Probably fightin' sea monsters, wouldn't y' know.
That, 'r' pirates, eh?
They'd put 'em all t' death, if hit wos pirates, roight?
They'd put 'em all t' death if they wos monsters, too.
Coo, naow look't that, would y': she's got a pure silver bottom, she does!
Clean as a whistle 'n' nary a barnacle.
Ar, but did y' see them what took rooms at th' Storm Lantern? Dwarves, they wos, 'n' filled hit roight up, they did. Naow what 'r' th' loikes o' Dwarves doin' sailin' ships, eh?
Sailin' ships? Ar, y' big gob, they don't sail no ships. This be th' way o' hit: j'st 'oo d'y' think kills them pirates, Oi hasks? Them Dwarves, 'at's 'oo! They be th' Elvenship's army, don't y' know.
Yar. But did y' see ... th' cap'n, 'e's got a Wizard aboard, too. They say 'im 'n' 'is fox familiar took rooms hat th' Blue Mermaid, they did, along wi' th' cap'n's laidy 'n' more o' th' crew.
Coo, th' laidy, she were a looker, wot?
Ar, but th' fox naow, 'e didn't loike bein' dragged on that leash, did 'e?
Oi'm o' a moind t' go t' th' Mermaid 'n' th' Lantern both, 'n' see wot's wot, Oi am.

Thus nattered the onlookers as the *Eroean* was heeled over and the work to repair her was begun. While in a room in the Blue Mermaid . . .

"Ha! Some familiar, this fox," snarled Alamar, dragging Rux into the room. "I'd sooner have a large stone for such; at least a rock wouldn't pull backwards."

Slamming the door behind, the Mage set his knapsack down on the table and dropped the leash. Discovering that he was free, Rux sat up and glared at the Mage, then began backing about the room, trying to slip out of the rope tied 'round his neck. Alamar opened the pack and Jinnarin climbed out, the Pysk leaping down from table to chair to floor and calling Rux to her. As she untied the rope, Jinnarin said, "Rux would make an excellent familiar, whatever they are and whatever it is that they do."

"Ha!" barked Alamar, sitting down and crossing his arms defiantly.

Jinnarin unknotted the rope at last and pulled it free. Rux sat down and began scratching furiously, as if the line about his neck had been full of fleas.

Clambering back up to the tabletop, Jinnarin began rooting about in Alamar's knapsack, the Pysk looking for the comb. "Tell me, Alamar," she said, her voice muffled, "just what is a familiar ... and what do they do?"

"Nothing you would understand, Pysk. But I'll tell you this: they don't drop rats on your feet."

Now Jinnarin disappeared completely into the knapsack. "What did you do with my comb?"

Alamar glared. "I didn't steal it, if that's what you are implying."

"Oh, here it is." Jinnarin said, then popped back out. "Did you ever have a familiar, Alamar?"

"Once," he muttered. "An owl."

Now Jinnarin glared at the Mage. "I might have known! You had an owl! A murdering owl!"

"What are you talking about, Pysk?"

"Owls, that's what, Alamar. Owls! Don't you know that at times they've tried to kill us?"

"Tried to kill Pysks, Pysk?"

"Exactly so."

"Well it wasn't *my* owl," declared Alamar.

"How do you know that?"

"I *know,* Pysk. That's how."

"Hmph," snorted Jinnarin, leaping down to the floor. She began combing Rux's fur all 'round where the rope had been. After a while she said, "Really, Alamar, I'd like to know about familiars."

Alamar glared.

"Truly, Alamar, I would."

After a moment, he uncrossed his arms and hitched his chair about, facing her. "Given the amount of study we do, the life of a Mage is a rather solitary one. The last thing we need is someone chattering about all day and night. Even so, a companion of sorts breaks the loneliness, the solitude, especially a companion that is useful. An apprentice is one kind of companion— someone to talk to, someone to teach, someone to run and fetch, and as his experience grows, someone to share ideas with. But taking on an apprentice is a weighty responsibility, and if there is no time to teach, then it is of no benefit to the apprentice: might as well merely have a servant.

"A familiar, though, is a different kind of companion. Still, a familiar is someone to talk to, even though most cannot answer back, or if they do, their answers are limited and long conversations are rare. Even so, they are useful, for they run and fetch if you know how to ask them . . . and if it is within their means. Mostly, though, they are a second pair of eyes and ears, and occasionally another nose, warding us in times of danger. And for those of us who know how, we can send the familiar out scouting or spying, and see through their eyes, hear through their ears, smell through their noses, feel through their touch, taste with their tongues. This is, however, not without its dangers, for if the familiar is harmed while merged with the mind of the Mage, then we suffer the harm as well . . . and vice versa.

"If throughout the long years the Mage merges often with the familiar, then they become part of one another, and if or when one or the other dies, it has profound effects. In both cases, Mage and familiar, they sink into deep melancholia. If the familiar dies, it is as if a part of the Mage has been ripped from his existence, and frequently it takes long years to recover. On the other hand, if the Mage dies, then often the familiar goes away into isolation and refuses food and water and dies from what can only be termed a broken heart.

"And that, my dear, is what a familiar is."

Jinnarin looked at Alamar with tears in her eyes, and she softly asked, "What happened to your owl, Alamar?"

"She died." Alamar's gaze glittered. "I did not take on another."

Jinnarin's eyes brimmed over, tears running down her cheeks. She turned and leaned her head against Rux and threw her arms about his neck and did not move for some time. At last she straightened and resumed her combing. After a while she said, "I'm sorry that I called your owl a murderer."

*   *   *

Alamar looked up from the tokko board. "Eh, what did you say?"

"That I had my nightmare again last night," answered Jinnarin.

"Same dream? Nothing changed?"

Jinnarin nodded, then smiled as Aylis moved her Bridge across Alamar's Chasm. "Guard your Throne, Father."

Alamar lowered his brow and squinted at Jinnarin and then Aylis. "Oh-ho! So that's the way it is, eh? You two in cahoots to distract me, right?"

Both Aylis and Jinnarin looked at the elder, innocence in their faces. Then they both burst out laughing.

"Aha! I thought so!"

Still laughing, Aylis stood and stretched.

After a moment, Alamar turned his Throne on its side. "Ask your Aravan to come and see me, Daughter. I will tell him of your devious, scheming ways."

"I will, Father, that is if he ever comes to our room." Aylis sighed. "He hasn't left the *Eroean* since we got here two days past."

"Now, Daughter, he has much to do, and—"

"I know that, Father. Even so, he and the others need rest and hot food and warm drink and even entertainment."

"But, Daughter, they've got to be finished before the storm strikes in, what did you say, six days?"

"Seven days when we docked: four days now. Twelfth Yule—New Year's Day—that's when it's due, late in the night."

"All right. Four days, then. But we can't have the *Eroean* lying over on her side when the storm hits, now can we? Besides, they are getting hot meals and warm drink and rest."

"Yes, for most of the crew, Father, working in shifts as they are. But not Aravan, Father, not Aravan. Only he knows the secrets of the oil they rub into the wood. Only he knows the secrets of the black caulking. And only he knows the secrets of the starsilver paint . . . or the dark blue, for that matter. Only Aravan. And so, he needs to be there at all times, hence is getting little rest and certainly no entertainment."

Alamar grinned. "And just how would you propose that he be entertained, Daughter?"

Alamar did not quite duck in time to evade the thrown pillow.

And down at the docks where the Elvenship lay, holes were being drilled with a silver auger and wooden pegs fitted, for no iron nails graced the hull of the Elvenship.

Two days later the repair of the vessel was complete, and the winches holding the ropes heeling her over on her larboard side were loosened and allowed to slowly slip opposite, the windlasses acting as brakes as the *Eroean* gradually uprighted. Ballast was reloaded onto the ship, and the hold was restocked with fresh supplies, Quartermaster Roku overseeing the lading of the goods he had purchased throughout the previous days from many a happy merchant. Finally, the ship was towed away from the dock and anchored in safe harborage, for it would not do to have the ship pounded against the quay in the forecasted storm.

And Aravan came to the Blue Mermaid and collapsed into bed and slept for two more days.

On the evening of the twelfth day of Yule—New Year's Day—a gentle snow began falling. That same evening, a grand celebration was held in the common room of the Blue Mermaid. It was attended by all of the Elvenship crew and a Mage and Lady Mage and a red fox, as well as by a shadow lurking in the darkness at the top of the stairs. There was singing and dancing, and Lobbie played his squeeze box and Rolly his pipe and Burden banged on his drum, and as they had during the spree, all the Men and the Dwarves stomped in time and clapped their hands while Captain Aravan and Lady Aylis danced their wild, wild fling, stepping and prancing and whirling about and laughing into each other's eyes. The Châkka chanted marching songs, the words in a brusque language strong. Then Mage Alamar made the air sparkle with untouchable glitter of all different colors, and caused a strange musical piping amid the sounds of wind chimes. And then Captain Aravan played a harp and voiced stirring sagas, odes to make your heart pound and your blood run hot. And Aylis sang in a high, sweet voice and not an eye was dry when she finished. And while Dwarves or Men stood guard at the bottom of the steps, allowing no townsman to go up, many a member of the crew went and sat in the darkness at the top of the stairs, where it seemed they talked to themselves, laughing and joking with the empty air and sharing sweetmeats with the shadows.

And when the celebration came to an end, it was in the wee hours of the morning. Outside the gentle snow had become a storm. It was the second of January, and the twelve days of Yule were ended.

The howling wind hammered throughout the night and was yet squalling about the eaves of the Blue Mermaid when the morning came. Aravan and Aylis snuggled down in the warmth of their bed, the Elf clasping the Lady Mage unto him. Wan light seeped inward through the window and snow pelted 'gainst the rippled panes, and sometime after mid morn Aravan raised up on one elbow, his sapphirine gaze searching Aylis's features.

"What?" she asked, wondering at his intense scrutiny.

He grinned. "I am counting the faint freckles sprinkled across thy nose and onto thy cheeks."

"Eleven," said Aylis.

"Eleven?"

"Exactly."

"Well, my lovely *chier*, I seem to see fifteen."

Aylis's eyes flew wide. "You do? Where?" She scrambled from the bed and found her silver mirror, nipping back under the covers in the cold. Aylis held up the polished silver and peered within, searching.

Aravan's grin widened. "And now I have proven that thou art not the only one of us who can cast a mirror spell, *chieran*, for now it is in this silver speculum I see mine own true love."

Aylis burst out laughing. "You are a trickster, sirrah, a trickster."

Aravan's laughter joined hers, and she grabbed him and rolled atop, pinning him down. "Confess, miscreant, or I will have your ... your ...!" But then she kissed him and kissed him again and laughter turned to love.

Chapter 20

Seekers

Winter, 1E9574–75
[The Present]

"Of course," proposed Alamar, "I could make each fireball look as if it were ten. It's a simple matter of bending the aethyr, splitting the light. Durlok would not be able to explode them all before the true one hit his ship." But then the elder shook his head and growled. "Though as you say, Pysk, he could simply call upon his magesight and see through the trick."

As the wind howled 'round the Blue Mermaid and snow pelted against the window panes, Jinnarin sat in quiet contemplation for some moments. "It seems, Alamar, rather difficult to fool a Mage, eh?"

Alamar puffed out his chest and thumped on it. "Certainly it's difficult to fool *this* Mage," he declared.

Jinnarin raised her eyebrows. "Oh?"

Alamar nodded sharply. "It's not like fooling mortals and foolish Pysks and the like. We Mages are extraordinarily alert to tricks and traps and other such. After all, we have the great advantage of being able to see the astral fire, and that gives us an edge over all other beings."

Jinnarin looked at the Mage in wide-eyed innocence. "Oh, Alamar, I'm so glad that you told me." She reached forward and took up a tokko piece. "Stone crushes Throne," she said, dropping the agate on Alamar's Throne. "Game's over."

A look of surprise and then petulant rage flashed

across Alamar's face. "You distracted me again, Pysk! That's cheating!"

Jinnarin jumped to her feet and stood before the Mage, her hands on her hips. "Oh? Cheating, eh? Well if that's cheating, Alamar, I suggest that you find a similar way to 'cheat' Durlok!"

Alamar shook his fist at Jinnarin. "If you weren't a female Pysk, Pysk, I'd invite you outside!"

"And if you weren't so decrepit, Alamar, I'd take you up on it!" shot back Jinnarin.

They stood fuming and blustering at one another, and suddenly Jinnarin burst out laughing. "You look like a fish out of water, Alamar," she giggled.

In spite of himself, Alamar grinned. "Well, Pysk, if I'm a fish out of water, then you're a beached minnow."

Jinnarin's giggles were joined by Alamar's cackling glee.

After a while, still smiling, the elder gazed back at the tokko board. Then a thoughtful look came over his features. "Perhaps you are right, Pysk. Perhaps we've been looking at this at the wrong angle."

Jinnarin raised an eyebrow. "Meaning . . . ?"

Alamar steepled his fingers. "Meaning that instead of taking on Durlok dead straight, perhaps we should find a way to distract him. And while he is looking the wrong way, we sneak up behind him and drop a rock on his head."

"Well, Captain," rumbled Jatu, "where do we go from here?"

Bokar stood at the window of the Blue Mermaid and peered out at the storm, now diminishing in its second day. He turned and growled, "I say we sail the northern waters and look for more plumes. That is the only chance we have of catching up with the Black Mage, wherever he and his galley may have gotten to."

The others in Alamar's room—Jinnarin, Aylis, Alamar, Aravan, Frizian, and Jatu—looked at Bokar, Frizian musing, "Do you think that he's still up there lurking about in the Northern Sea?"

"That is where the aurora is," answered Bokar. "Find the aurora, and we are like to find the Mage."

Jinnarin sighed. "But who's to say that if we find the Mage, we'll find Farrix?"

Aylis shook her head. "It's the only lead we have, Jinnarin: Farrix went looking for plumes; Durlok's ship was where a plume fell. They are all we have linking the two."

Aravan's gaze swept across the others. "If Durlok is indeed behind the plumes, then in the eleven days since we were rammed, he could be nigh six hundred leagues from his last position."

Alamar did a swift reckoning. "That assumes he travels fifty leagues a day, a hundred and fifty miles."

Aylis nodded. "That's how far apart the plumes were, Father."

Frizian took a sip of his tea. "If he is eighteen hundred miles straight away, and if we knew where he was, then given favorable winds we could be there in a week to ten days ... but I think he will not stay in one spot for us to catch him, even if we knew where to go. Nay, he will have gone onward to somewhere else."

"I agree," said Jatu. "But on the other hand, if Durlok instead sails back and forth under the aurora in the Northern Sea, then Bokar's plan is sound. We should take station along the course where last we were."

Bokar gnarled. "It does not suit my nature to take up station and wait. I say we run back and forth along his route until we spot a plume. I would rather come upon him than for him to come upon us: the last time he did so, we were holed."

Aravan unrolled a map. "Ye both then assume that Durlok runs a course east and west along a track just north of Rwn, shuttling back and forth between the western continent and Thol to the east." With his finger Aravan traced the route across the map, following the marge between the Weston Ocean and the Northern Sea.

Jinnarin looked closely. "But wait, Aravan. Farrix saw the plumes streaking down to the south and east of Rwn. Couldn't Durlok have more than one course he sails?"

Aravan rubbed his jaw. "Aye, Lady Jinnarin, he could at that. Mayhap it depends upon where the aurora shines. What say thee, Mage Alamar?"

All eyes swung to the elder. Alamar turned up his

hands. "He could have a *thousand* routes for all I know," he answered peevishly, frustrated. "I don't even know what he's up to! —But whatever it is, it's not to anyone's benefit, and that's a fact!"

At that moment the door opened and inward bustled the innkeeper, bearing a tray of pastries and another pot of tea. " 'Ere naow, Oi've brought y'—" His words chopped off as first he glimpsed Jinnarin and then a cluster of darkness standing in the center of the table. "Lor! Is that—?"

Jatu stepped smoothly between the table and the innkeeper, blocking off his view. "I'll take that, Mister Orgle." The innkeeper tried to step around Jatu, but the black Man intervened, taking the tray and standing in the way. "Thank you, Mister Orgle."

"Arfoozle arapp!" loudly said Alamar, as shadow-wrapped Jinnarin scrambled down and away. "Harrum!" he cleared his throat. "There now, that illusion is gone. Let me show you another. *Flores rosae pendete!*" Of a sudden the room was filled with floating rose blossoms.

Mister Orgle's eyes flew wide with pleasure as he backed out of the room, Jatu shepherding him aft, the innkeeper craning his neck, unsuccessfully trying to see over the big black Man. "Maige Aliamar, y' be a wonder, and that's hall there is to that! Coo naow, what wi' y'r sparkly lights 'n' tinkly sounds 'n' wee dark bogles 'n' floatin' flowers, if y' e're need t' pay f'r y'r room 'n' board, Oi'd taik these hillusions o' y'rs in hexchainge." As he passed through the door he called out, "O' course, Oi'd hask y' t' do hit whin m' paying customers wos habout. They'd no doubt come f'r supper, 'n' hafterward they'd drink plenty, they would, wos y' t' be 'ere t' put on y'r show, naow." Jatu smiled and closed the door in his face and pegged the latchlock, then turned and bore the tray to the waiting group.

Shadows now dissipated, Jinnarin climbed back onto the tabletop and asked in exasperation, "How soon will we be leaving?"

The *Eroean* made ready to set sail the very next day, and nearly all citizenry of Arbor tramped through the snow and down to the quay, following the Dwarves from the Storm Lantern and the ship's Men from the Blue

Mermaid. The air was festive, almost paradelike, as townsfolk chatted and laughed with the crew and with one another, and snickered as Alamar struggled with Rux. And down to the docks they went, where the crew boarded launches and were rowed out to the Elvenship. And when they all were aboard, still the crowd hung about, waiting to see her raise silk and up anchor and glide majestically out of the harbor on the morning tide. And as she did so, Men and Women alike *ooh*ed and *ahh*ed with the wonder of her. Long they stood and watched, some even running up to the headland to catch a final glimpse of her before she sailed from view. And at last she was gone, northerly, on her mysterious mission, and the citizens of Arbor returned to their businesses and dwellings and other such, and for years after they talked of the time the Elvenship herself came unto their very own town, and rightly so, for she had been damaged in battle with a thousand terrible monsters, and what better place to put in for repairs?

Covered with sweat and gasping for air, Jinnarin jolted upright in her bed, the dread of her nightmare coursing through her veins. Gazing wildly about, she saw that she was in her under-bunk cabin, Rux now awake beside her. "It's all right, Rux. It's all right," she said, more to reassure herself than the fox. "He's still sending me the dream, and for that we can be thankful." She smiled at Rux and rolled over . . . and finally returned to sleep.

"Adon misereatur," said Aylis.

"May Adon have mercy," translated Aravan.

"Cui bono?" she asked.

"Who stands to gain?" responded Aravan.

"Alis volat propriis."

"She flies on her own wings."

"Virtutis fortuna comes."

"Good fortune is the companion of courage."

"Ah, love, you learn swiftly," said Aylis. "But now I would have you speak to me in the tongue of the Mages."

Aravan nodded, then said, *"Amor vincit omnia, et nos cedamus amori. . . ."*

. . . and so they did.

*   *   *

Frizian stepped into the wheelhouse, and by the lantern light he peered at the gradations scribed on the astrolabe, then glanced at a chart. Setting the instrument aside and removing his gloves, he pulled down a heavy tome and opened it, thumbing through the pages, revealing table after table filled with numbers. Stopping at one, his finger ran down a column, pausing at one of the entries. Muttering to himself, again he looked at the chart, and nodded in confirmation. Pulling on his gloves, once more he stepped out to the deck, where the winter wind blew icy cold. "By my reckoning, Captain, we are back at the latitude where we were holed."

Aravan glanced at the stars above. "Close enough, Frizian. Close enough."

Frizian shook his head in envy. *No charts, no tables, he just knows!* "Which way then, Captain?" asked the Man.

Aravan took a breath then said, "West. If the Black Mage shuttles back and forth, then west along this track is most likely where we will find him."

"How so, Captain?"

Aravan gestured to starboard. "Landfall lies some hundred twenty-five leagues to the east, Frizian, but some seven hundred leagues to the west. Thus, westerly there is nigh six times as much of an ocean track than to the east. Hence, if the Black Mage sails this course, then unbiased Fortune would put him to the west some six times out of seven."

"Ah but, Captain, is Dame Fortune ever unbiased?"

Aravan sighed. "Sometimes I think not, Frizian. Sometimes I deem she is the most fickle creature of all."

"More fickle than the ocean, Captain?"

"Mayhap, Frizian, mayhap. *Akka!* At times I think they are one and the same."

Frizian nodded, then turned toward the poop deck and pulled down the scarf from his face. "Reydeau!" he called. "Pipe her due west!"

"Aye, sir" came Reydeau's response from aft.

The yards were pulled 'round and the tiller turned, the Elvenship answering the helm. And close hauled to the wind, westerly she fared, racing into the night.

*   *   *

Below decks in the Dwarven quarters, Jinnarin sat with the warriors and listened to them speaking in Châkur, the hidden tongue. With its abrupt starts and stops, their language was harsh to her ear, and it seemed to her that everything started with a *b* and ended with a *k*, though it was not so. As to Châkur, it is an ancient tongue, tracing its roots back to the time when Dwarves first walked upon the world . . . or rather, within it, for it is a tongue eminently suitable for use in underground caverns, where echoes and reverberations tend to distort other languages beyond all recognition. And so Jinnarin sat and listened to the Dwarves talking among themselves—sibilance absent, murmurs, mumblings, and undertones missing, contractions nowhere to be found—each word separate and sharp and crystal clear, though she understood none of it at all.

"Tell me, Kelek," she asked, "just how did it come about that Dwarves sail upon the *Eroean?*"

The black-haired Dwarf stroked his beard and looked at her, his dark eyes glittering in the lantern light. It seemed as if he were judging whether or not to answer her question, though it may have been that he was considering the answer itself. "You think it odd, eh?"

Jinnarin nodded. "Frankly, I do. I had always thought of Dwarves as being dwellers in the earth."

"In the earth, nay; in the Mountains, yea."

"But inside the very mountains themselves, right?"

Kelek canted his head, *Yes,* adding, "It has always been so that the Châkka have dwelled within the living stone."

"Then how did Dwarves, that is, how did some Dwarves become seafarers?"

Kelek nodded, then stood and stepped to a small iron stove and poured himself a cup of tea, offering to refresh Jinnarin's wee cup, but she shook her head, *No.* Returning to the table, Kelek sat and took a sip, then set the cup down. "In the time of my ancestors—and perhaps myself, before I died in that bygone cycle—some three thousand years past, Aravan the Elf came to the Red Hills, seeking Tolak, who was at that time DelfLord of the caverns. And when he found him . . ."

*　　　*　　　*

The Châk before the gate eyed the tall Elf suspiciously. "I am to escort you to Lord Tolak. And your name is . . . ?"

"Aravan. Alor Aravan of the sea. And thou art . . . ?"

"I am Barad, gate captain."

"Well then, Captain Barad, lead on."

Instructing Aravan to leave his weapons with his horse, Barad led Aravan across the broad forecourt of polished granite and up a low set of wide steps to another stretch of stone. As they passed in through the great iron gates, Châkka sentries on duty nodded to their captain and hefted their axes, as if to say they stood ready should this Elf give trouble.

Out of the bright sunlit courtyard they stepped and into the shadowed halls of the Châkkaholt, entering into a long wide hallway fetching at its far extent up against another iron gate. Barad noted that Aravan glanced overhead, the Elf eyeing the machicolations in the ceiling, murder holes from which would rain death should an invader breech the outer gates. And then Aravan's gaze swung alongside where in the walls were slots in the stone through which crossbow quarrels would fly. "Formidable defenses, Captain," he murmured as their footsteps echoed about.

Captain Barad did not reply.

Beyond the second gate the halls were lit with phosphorescent Châkka lanterns, the blue-green light casting a ghastly aspect over all, and down through this spectral glow they trod, twisting through passages, ascending and descending stairs, walking along crevasses left and right. Halls and corridors crossed and recrossed and joined and forked away from the passage they followed; millennia had gone into their delving, and had Aravan not been escorted, the Elf would soon have been lost within the maze. But at last they came to a doorway leading into the throne room, where Captain Barad bade Aravan to stop. Through the opening, Barad could see Lord Tolak sitting upon the chair of state. Down before him and to one side on the steps of the dais sat a slender figure swathed from head to foot in layers of diaphanous veils; it was a Châkian, Erien, Tolak's trothmate. And when Barad announced the presence of Aravan, Erien gracefully arose and glided from the room, and Barad saw Aravan's eyes widen slightly as he looked upon the form of the retreating female, for Châkia were rarely glimpsed by outsiders.

When she was gone out through a portal behind the throne, Barad led Aravan into the chamber, then took station at Tolak's side—the captain standing ready should Tolak need him, standing ready as well to escort Aravan back to the gate when his audience was done. That Tolak would need protection is questionable, for he was a Châk in his prime, and at hand leaning against the throne stood his double-bitted axe, oaken-helved and iron-beaked. Tolak himself, as all Châkka, stood between four and five feet tall, and his shoulders were broad—half again as wide as the Elf's. He had chestnut-colored hair, and he was dressed in brown leathers beneath his black-iron shirt of mail— much the same as was Barad's dress, though the gate captain also wore a metal helm with a molded dragon for a crest. Tolak's mien was one of gruff curiosity, wondering what errand had brought an Elf unto his domain.

"Lord Tolak," said Aravan, bowing.

Tolak arose. "Alor Aravan," he said, and returned the bow. "It is not often that Elves come to the Châkkaholt of the Red Hills. And when they do, it is usually to trade for iron or steel. Yet I understand that you come neither to trade nor to buy or sell."

Aravan smiled broadly. "Nay, Lord Tolak. Instead I come to ask for help."

Tolak's eyes widened. "Elves needing help? From the Châkka? Are your people in trouble?"

Aravan laughed. "Nay, Lord Tolak. The help is for me alone, and not for the Lian."

"Ah," said Tolak, gesturing to a side table and chairs, "this I must hear."

As they took seats, Tolak rang a gong, and a tray-bearing Châk served tea. Leaning back, they took their leisure, and Tolak said, "Now about this aid . . ."

Aravan set down his cup. "Lord Tolak, I have sailed the seas now for some two millennia, and I have spent most of that time on all manner of ships, learning their nature—from the dhows of Gjeen to the Dragonships of Fjordland, from the carracks of Arbalin to the junks of Jinga, from the leather-bound coracles of Rwn to the oaken ships of Gelen to the reed vessels of Khem. I have sailed knorrs and coastal traders, raiders and whalers and more ... I have sailed them all. And everywhere I went I worked in shipyards, learning all I could about the construction of every type of vessel in every Land. I have learned much, and though I know that there is yet more to learn, still I believe that the time has come."

Tolak looked across his cup at Aravan. "The time for what?"

"The time to build mine own ship."

"And why have you come to our Châkkaholt? Do you need fittings or other such that we can forge for you?"

Aravan smiled at Tolak. "Nay, Lord Tolak. I need more, much more."

The DelfLord set down his cup. "Just what is it you want from the Châkka?"

"Lord Tolak, I want a warband of Drimma to fare with me across the world to find that which I need to make a ship such as the world has never before seen nor will ever see again. Further, when all material is in hand, I want the Drimma to build my ship."

Tolak looked at Aravan as if the Elf had lost his mind. "Alor Aravan, we are not a seafaring Race! We are the Châkka! We dwell within the living stone! What do we know of building ships? Are you a fool to ask for such?"

Aravan laughed. "If I am a fool, then I am the wisest of them, for no other are more suited to accompany me on my quest than the Drimma—warriors beyond compare. What I seek—woods and oils and silks most rare—are scattered across the world and will not be easily found nor won. And once all are found, none are better fitted to build my ship than the best crafters in the world: again, the Drimma. In this task, I ask thee for thy aid, Lord Tolak, for thee and thy Kind are without peer."

"And you want us to build the entire ship?"

"All but the sails and ropes, Lord Tolak; they will be Elven made."

"And what do you offer the Châkka of the Red Hills for our aid?"

"Four things, DelfLord: First, I will pay ye gold and gems, though that is the least of all rewards. Second, ye will learn much in the crafting of my ship, though ye will be sworn to secrecy in the manner of its building, and may not construct another without my leave; even so, the knowledge gained will be suited for the crafting of other things, things both precious and rare. Third, the quest itself will yield ye great knowledge concerning much of the unknown world, knowledge from which trade and commerce will spring if ye but seize the opportunity of it. And fourth, there is the adventure itself, the seeking, the exploration, and though at times it will be perilous, this alone I deem to be the greatest prize of all, especially for those of stout heart and strong hand who come with me across the whole of the world."

Tolak nodded, then asked, "What is needed to build this ship?"

"Special woods for the hull and decks and tall straight trees for the masts, oils to treat the woods, special caulking to keep the sea at bay, silks for the sails and ropes, starsilver for a special paint for her bottom, cobalt for a special blue paint coating her above, and a special alloy that will not corrode for the anchor and fittings, and more, much more."

"Did I hear you say starsilver to be used in a *paint*?"

"Aye. For her bottom."

"Starsilver is too precious to be used in paint!" averred Tolak.

"Not for this ship, DelfLord."

Tolak pondered for a moment. "How much will you need?"

"A pound, no more."

"*A pound!* A whole pound?"

"Aye. I have a formula from Dwynfor the swordmaker."

"And where do you expect to get this starsilver?"

Aravan gestured northerly. "From DelfLord Durek in Drimmen-deeve."

Tolak nodded, then asked, "And just where do you

propose that we build this ship of yours? We cannot put it at our gates, for it would be long in its launching were we to do so."

Aravan's laughter rang throughout the Châkkaholt. "Aye, a long way indeed, the sea being some seventy leagues hence, the River Argon some fifty. Nay, Delf-Lord, not here at thy gates. Instead I know of a secret grot in Thell Cove. One that if thou knew not it was there, thou wouldst never find it, and even wert thou told of its existence, still it is nearly impossible to find unaided." Aravan touched a small blue stone on a leather thong at his throat. "I was aided."

Tolak glanced over at Captain Barad who had remained silent throughout. "Well, Barad, what say you?"

Barad glanced over at Aravan, then back to Tolak. "I have but one thing to ask, DelfLord, and it is this: when do we leave?"

Jinnarin looked up at Kelek. "And that's it? That's the way that Dwarves became involved with the *Eroean* and the sea?"

Kelek nodded. "Aye. And a grand adventure it was. It took more than two hundred years to gather together those things needed for her making. And then we were another twelve years fashioning her."

"And Dwarves did it all?"

"Nay. The Elves made her silks and her rigging. Some Men aided in her final construction. But Captain Aravan and the Châkka did all of the rest."

"Men? Men helped, too?"

Kelek nodded, then smiled. "When she was finished, one of the Men looked at her in awe. 'She will last for a thousand years,' he said. We laughed, did the Châkka. And when he asked why, we said, 'A thousand years? Nay, Man, not a mere ten centuries, but more, much more.' "

"Tell me, Kelek," appealed Jinnarin, "just how do you know this?"

"Because, Lady Jinnarin," answered Kelek, "Gate Captain Barad of the Red Hills was my ancestor."

Jinnarin mouthed an *O*, but then asked, "Even so, that was long past ... for a Dwarf, that is. What I mean is, it seems to me that the tale would be lost in three millennia . . . or at least distorted."

Kelek shook his head. "No, Lady Jinnarin, it remains true. It is a fact that has been passed from sire to son as each of us in turn sailed with Captain Aravan. Rarely does he take on someone whose ancestor he did not sail with long past. And as we grow old and he does not, we at last take to land while he sails on, our sons and the sons of other old hands taking our places aboard the Elvenship."

Jinnarin's face fell. "Only sons? No daughters? He takes on no daughters?"

Kelek bristled. "It would be unthinkable, unforgivable for him to take on a Châkian!"

"Well then, if not a female of your Race, what about females of other Folk?"

Kelek pondered a moment, then his face lit up. "I seem to recall that he has taken on at least one female. A Waeran, I believe. Yes, a Waeran. They name themselves Warrows, in the Common Tongue. A small Folk"—Kelek held his hand a yard or so above the floor—"though not as tiny as you, Lady Jinnarin."

Jinnarin sighed. "One daughter . . . and all the others sons."

"Sons, and sons of sons, and sons of sons of sons, and so it goes, down through the descendants of those who served him before. He follows a proven line."

Jinnarin shook her head, then nodded, then turned up a hand, and said, "Loyalty."

"To the death," Kelek responded.

West sailed the *Eroean* throughout the short days and long nights, beating into the prevailing westerlies, hauling and tacking along the straight course, zigzagging across the wind. At times the blast was brutal, hurtling snow and ice before it and driving huge waves ahead. At other times, though, it was less harsh, though always blustery and frigid. Ice formed on the rigging and coated the sails, and the crew was hardpressed to keep the *Eroean* smoothly underway, weighted down as she was and glazed over, her blocks and pulleys jammed, her lines made stiff as iron rods. Even so, on a typical day she covered some hundred and forty miles along the straight course, though veering back and forth in the teeth of the blow she sailed half again as far.

In the gelid nights whenever the aurora shone, Jinnarin and Aylis and Alamar stood ward on the ice-rimed decks and watched as the ghostly lights writhed in the sky above. But as of yet they had seen no plumes flaring down to the sea below.

Some fifteen days after heading westerly they sighted land to the fore starboard, a headland coming into view. They had arrived at the marge of the western continent, and as yet had seen no sign of either plume or ship nor any sign of a Black Mage.

"Lookouts aloft," ordered Aravan, and Rico knelled the bell a coded ring and parka-clad Men scrambled up from below, clambering up the ratlines and to the crow's nests above.

Onward they sailed, the headland rolling up over the rim of the world. Aravan stepped to the starboard rail, where he was joined by Aylis and Jinnarin, Alamar coming after, and then Jatu. Aylis bent down and lifted Jinnarin up to see and held her in the crook of an arm. Steadily the land drew nearer.

"Keep a sharp eye!" called Jatu to the lookouts aloft. "Ship, sails, movement on land or water—sing out!"

Now the shoreline could be seen in the distance.

"Ready to fall off and run downwind, Jatu," said Aravan.

"Aye, Captain," replied the Man, turning and calling to Rico and repeating the command.

Bokar came to stand beside them.

Aravan's gaze swept across the bleak headland, seeing nought but a barren stone shore lashed by waves, with winter dressed trees above. "Lookouts report, Jatu," he said.

Nought! all three called down.

"Kruk!" growled Bokar.

Jinnarin sighed. "What now, Aravan?"

Aravan looked at the Pysk. "Now we turn and run the track opposite."

"To where, Aravan? I mean, we've run most of the

track and have seen nothing of plumes or Durlok. So I ask, where now?"

Aravan gestured easterly. "Back along the track, Jinnarin. All the way to Thol if necessary."

Bokar gripped the railing, his gloves taut. "And if we do not find this Black Mage, Captain, then what?"

Aravan took a breath and let it out. "Then Bokar, we need take another tack, but what it might be ... I cannot say."

The Elf turned to Jatu. "Fall off, Jatu. Run her due east before the wind."

"Aye, Captain," responded Jatu. He cupped his hands and called up, "Lookouts down!" then turned toward the wheelhouse. "Wear her eastward, Rico!"

As Rico piped the crew, Jatu and Aravan stepped to the wheelhouse and Bokar headed below decks.

Aylis set Jinnarin down, and the Pysk and Alamar began walking aft. "You coming, Daughter?" asked the Mage.

"In a moment, Father."

"Loosen the mizzen stays! Ready to fall away!" called Jatu, Rico piping the orders, and the triangular sails were set to flapping, while all the crossjack and mizzen- and mainsails were clewed up and the braces were coiled down for running. "Up helm, furl the spanker, and square the mizzen- and mainyards!" called Jatu, the Men swiftly obeying. With the rudder over and no silk aft, the jibs and foresails began bringing the Elvenship 'round as she fell off before the starboard draught. Larboard turned the vessel to come directly downwind. "Center the wheel, Boder," said Jatu, then called out, "Square the fores and reset the stays and jibs!" And as Rico piped, some of the Men hauled the yards about and clewed them down, while others reeled in the sheets and set the staysails and spanker. And with her silks belling to the full in the following wind, easterly ran the *Eroean,* picking up speed.

Jatu turned to Rico. "All right, Rico, trim her out to make the most."

"Aye, Meestar Jatu," answered Rico, and again he signalled with his pipe, but this time he stepped forward to personally oversee the final adjustments of the sails.

And all the while the ship fell off before the wind, Aylis stood in deep thought, saying nothing, paying no heed to the bustling activity all 'round, and as the ship came about and squared away and put her shoulder to the sea, Aylis at last looked up and squared her own shoulders and strode purposefully aft, the glint in her eyes resolute.

CHAPTER 21

Dark Choices

Winter, 1E9574–75
[The Present]

Day and night the *Eroean* ran before the cruel winter wind, ice and rime lading her flanks and decks, and her masts, rigging, and sails as easterly she clove through the frigid waves of the Northern Sea. Toward the Realm of Thol she fared, that chill realm of bleak castles and high moors and windswept, craggy tors, of sod-roofed longhouses and scattered fishing villages along the shingled shores, and of immense reaches of deep woods dark, stretching far inland. Thol was peopled by hunters and crofters and fishers and traders and raiders, as was Jute to the south and Fjordland to the east, and her longships were much the same. But the folk of Thol and their manner of living were not on the minds of the crew of the Elvenship. Instead they sought someone else, someone perhaps at sea in a galley ship, someone vastly more dangerous. And so the *Eroean* sailed easterly through the Northern Sea—or rather along the uncertain marge between it and the waters of the Weston Ocean—on the track of a Black Mage . . . or so they deemed.

One hundred and fifty miles a day she fared, more or less, sailing from station to station—fifty leagues or so, depending upon the wind, the cold winter blow strong at times and falling off at others. In the frigid days lookout after lookout scrambled aloft, relieving each other often, for none could withstand the terrible cold overlong. And they watched the seas for signs of ships, though none came into their view.

Dusk to dawn was spent on station awaiting the boreal lights. And some nights the aurora twisted and coiled above, while some nights it did not; and on yet other nights it was hidden, for thick snow filled the air. When the boreal lights could not be seen, the *Eroean* remained at that station all the following day, not wanting to run too far along the route and inadvertently pass beyond Durlok in the night and fare such a distance as to miss a subsequent plume aft. Yet when the boreal lights could be seen, easterly they ran the next day to take up station fifty leagues away.

In this time of eastward sailing, of running before the wind, Jinnarin's nightmare came but thrice, her dream yet sporadic.

They sighted land some twenty-four hundred miles and twenty-two days after setting out from the verge of the western continent, and in all that time it was as if they had sailed the seas alone. No sign of Durlok did they see: no ship, no plume, no ghastly sacrifice, nor any other mark of the Black Mage.

And as they came into the coastal waters of Thol in the early afternoon—"Smoke ashore!" cried the foremast lookout. "Smoke ashore larboard fore!"

Bokar stared long and hard. High on a headland a stone turret could be made out. From the turret smoke coiled up and over, driven inland by the wind. "This may be the work of Durlok," he growled, then called out, "Rico, pipe the warband!"

The bo's'n rang the bell and piped the pipe, and Aravan stepped to Bokar's side. As the ship drew nearer, he said, "It is the tower of Gudwyn the Fair, or so it was called long past. Below is Havnstad, a town of commerce—of fisherfolk, traders, merchants, artisans."

'Midst the scramble of Dwarves pouring onto the deck, Jinnarin and Aylis came forward, Alamar shuffling after. Jinnarin clambered up onto the stem block and gazed at the smoking tower and at the harbor town below. After a moment she asked, "If this is Durlok's work, then where is his ship?"

"Good question, Jinnarin," murmured Aylis. "All I see are fishing vessels and a few traders riding at anchor, none at the jetties. Certainly there is no galley at the quay."

"Perhaps it is disguised by a casting of Durlok's," suggested Jinnarin.

"Visus," whispered Aylis, then after a moment she shook her head. "Nay, Jinnarin, none is other than what it seems."

Aravan nodded. "The ships ride at anchor because they are laid up for the winter. This is not the whole of their fleet, for many have been haled ashore for refurbishing ... such as their Dragonships being refitted for the spring raids." Even as he spoke, Aravan's gaze swept from turret to town to ship to shoreline, gauging, warding, wary.

Alamar peered long at the smoldering tower. Finally he said, "This is not Durlok's work, for the turret is not destroyed, it merely burns."

Bokar's eyes widened. "The Black Mage has the power to destroy a stone tower?"

Alamar nodded, adding, "He did when last I knew him. He may be even more powerful now."

"Hmph," grunted Bokar. "He would have to be if it were Châkka built."

"Rico!" called Aravan. "Sail nigh the harbor and luff her up, but be ready to get underway at an instant."

Aravan then turned to Bokar. "Armsmaster, I would have thee go ashore and find out what passes. Select those Drimma whom thou wouldst have accompany thee."

Bokar nodded, then said, "By your leave, Captain, I will take Jatu as well."

Aravan smiled. "I see. Thou wouldst have a friendly, trustworthy face to gull the citizens, someone to protect them from the ravages of savage Drimma, neh? And then after saving them he will ask what passes. Have I the right of it, Bokar?"

Bokar grinned. "Recall, Captain, it worked in Alkabar. The natives fell over their own tongues to tell him all, while we Châkka merely stood in view and thumbed our razor-keen axes. And those who had temporarily stolen our cargo ... perhaps they are yet running."

Aravan laughed and called for Jatu.

In addition to Jatu, Bokar selected nineteen Châkka to accompany him, and three gigs were readied. The *Eroean* sailed into the mouth of the harbor and luffed into the wind, and the landing party was lowered, the boats abristle with Dwarves bearing crossbows and war-hammers and axes, and Jatu bearing his warbar. As soon as the gigs were away, the Elvenship fell off on the wind and took up a triangular course, a mile to a leg.

It was late in the day when the gigs put back out to sea, and as the Sun set they rendezvoused with the *Eroean*. Among members of the warband, Bokar and Jatu clambered up over the rail, where Aravan, Alamar, Aylis, and Jinnarin waited. Jatu shook his head. " 'Tis a feud, Captain, nothing more. The Jarl of Klettstad came overland with his warband last week and set siege; and yester, when the Jarl of Havnstad surrendered, the winning Jarl put the place to torch. It yet smolders."

"It has nought to do with Durlok?" asked Aravan.

Jatu shook his head, *No,* and Alamar nodded unto himself, his own suspicion confirmed.

To make certain, though, Aylis asked, "Do they know anything of him or of his ship ... or anything of the plumes?"

"Nay, Lady Aylis, they do not," replied Jatu, then, as Jinnarin's face fell, added, "I am sorry, my tiny one, but life goes on heedless of our own quest. Though we would perhaps like the whole world to revolve about our concerns, it does not."

"I know," said Jinnarin, disappointment in her voice. "Still, I am so frustrated by our lack of knowledge. I was hoping against hope that here we would at last discover something to guide us, something leading to Farrix, yet all we found was a feud."

"Is the town on War footing?" asked Aravan.

"Nay, Captain," answered Jatu. "They paid tribute to be left alone. The Jarl of Klettstad is gone home."

As the gigs were brought aboard, Aravan said, to Rico, "Sail us into the harbor and drop anchor, Rico, well out from the town but sheltered by the shoulder of the headland. Set double ward, and should any approach, sound the alarm." Then he turned to the others. "Come, let us fetch Frizian and Fager and then take counsel and examine the choices before us."

As they strode toward the captain's lounge, Bokar growled, "Disgusting!"

"What?" asked Jinnarin.

"That he surrendered," replied the Dwarf.

Jinnarin looked over her shoulder at the smoldering turret, smoke rising against the emerging stars. "The Jarl of the tower? But he has his life, doesn't he? He was spared, neh?"

Bokar nodded, then said. "But he is now without honor."

"Isn't it better to surrender—?"

"Surrender is not a Châkka word!" snapped Bokar.

"But I would think, Bokar, that it is better to live to fight another day than—"

"I said," growled Bokar, "surrender is not a Châkka word!"

Jinnarin fell silent and on they walked toward the salon.

In the swaying yellow lantern light, Aravan rolled out a large map before the others and placed paperweights at the corners to hold it down. Displayed on the chart was a broad reach of the northern part of the world, extending from the Latitude of the Crab in the south to the polar realm in the north, and from the coastal waters of the western continent to just beyond the eastern bound of the Boreal Sea. Leaning on his hands, Aravan glanced up at the others gathered 'round, shadows swinging slowly to and fro in the room beyond.

"Let us discuss his options, this Durlok, and see can we lay out a likely course to follow." Aravan stepped to a cabinet and took from a drawer a modest pouch. Returning to the table, he said, "First, let us try to list all of his choices, and I will mark them." He opened the pouch and poured out a complete set of tokko game pieces, these carven from jade and ivory, flint and obsidian, crystal and tourmaline and malachite and amber and garnet and other such. Jinnarin's eyes flew wide and she glanced up at Alamar, for here was a set far more precious than those they had been using. "Once marked," Aravan continued, "then we will discuss the merits of each."

The Elf reached out and took up a piece—an ivory ship—and placed it in the Northern Sea. "He could yet be following his former track."

Aravan looked at Bokar. "He could have gone inland," said the Dwarf, stabbing his finger to the map, and Aravan placed a jade castle in the Realm of Thol.

Saying nought, Jatu reached across the table and took up an obsidian ship and placed it in the Boreal Sea.

Alamar pointed to the Weston Ocean southeast of Rwn, and there Aravan set a spheroidal stone of flint.

Frizian chose the Polar Sea, marked by a malachite eagle.

Fager said, "The western continent," and it was distinguished by a carnelian miter.

Aylis seemed distracted, as if lost in deep thought, and though she peered long at the map it is questionable whether she even saw it. Of a sudden she became conscious that all eyes were on her, and she quickly placed an onyx throne in the ocean west of Atala.

Jinnarin was last, and she took up a crystal castle and walked completely off the map and to the edge of the table, setting it down on bare wood, saying, "Perhaps he's gone to his crystal castle on the island in the pale green sea, wherever it may be."

Aravan again looked at the others through the swaying amber light. "Let us now go back 'round the table and discuss the merits of each." He pointed at the ivory ship he had placed in the Northern Sea. "Consider whether Durlok yet plies his former route, shuttling to and fro between Thol and the western continent." Aravan glanced from one to another, awaiting comment.

Frizian cleared his throat, then said, "I think not, Captain. We searched this track long and carefully. If he had been there, pulling down plumes, we would have seen some sign of him—either his ship or a plume." Frizian looked at Jinnarin, and she nodded in agreement.

"On the other hand," put in Fager, "there were some nights we did not see the lights—when it stormed or when they did not shine above."

"Even so," responded Frizian, "no two nights running did that occur, yet when it did we held station, sailing a triangular course, waiting until the boreal lights did shine down on that position. And given the range that the plumes are seen ..." All eyes swung to Alamar.

The elder nodded. "If Durlok were on the track and had called down a plume, I do not think that Jinnarin would have missed it. Recall, the first one she saw came down some two hundred miles away. Ha! She would have seen any others, and that's a fact!"

Jatu slowly shook his head. "Be that as it may, the ocean is a wide place, and the Black Mage could easily sail past us during the day—and certainly at night—without us ever seeing him. And if he did not draw down a plume while we were in range, well then . . ."

All fell silent and after a moment Aravan asked, "Has any aught else to add concerning whether or no he sails the same track?" He glanced about the table at the mute company, none saying a word. Aravan then pointed to the jade castle in Thol. "Did Durlok fare inland when he reached the Realm of Thol?"

Alamar glanced up at Bokar and then back to the map. "It is possible that Durlok is compelled to continue along a given track to gather plumes. Stranger constraints have been known to bind the workings of certain castings."

"If so," mused Aravan, "then he would need a place to harbor his ship, and this coast is riddled with fjords and coves. It will take long to search them all out."

"But, Captain," put in Frizian, "perhaps he sent the ship elsewhere, while he alone, or with a small following, landed and trekked inland."

Jatu jerked a thumb in the direction of the nearby harbor town. "Forget not, however, that the people of Havnstad saw no galley nor any other ship of late. And had Durlok landed, surely someone would have seen it. This town *is* closest to where we think his track would bring him."

Alamar shook his head. "He is a Mage, a Black One, but a Mage still. And if he had wished to land unseen, he could have managed it."

Frizian sighed. "Given our position and the date when he rammed us, if he did go straight from here to the coast of Thol and land—and go on—then he is deep within that Realm by now."

Again a silence fell on the group. Once more Aravan asked for additional comments, and when none was forthcoming, he said, "Very well, let us now consider whether or no Durlok is in the Boreal Sea. What say ye?"

Bokar looked at the map. "Even though it is not on the track, the Black Mage could have turned north and east, sailing along the coast and past the island of Leut and into the Boreal. It would give him another"—Bokar gauged the distance—"thirty-six hundred miles of ocean. And the aurora shines above it as well."

Aravan pursed his lips. "The Boreal at this time of year is even more fickle than the Northern Sea, and savage storms and great greybeards rage across its 'spanse, trying to drag all to their doom." He turned to Alamar. "Would Durlok risk such?"

Alamar shrugged, a nettled look on his face.

Frizian said, "Too, there is the suck of the Great Maelstrom there by the Seabanes, yet any captain worth his salt can easily avoid that Kraken-infested maw."

Scanning the faces at the table, none had anything to add, and so Aravan pointed to the flint spheroid southeast of Rwn. "What say ye of this?"

"It's where Farrix saw the plumes," said Jinnarin.

Fager spoke: "There is an old saying: thieves oft return to the place of the stealing. And who can deny that this Durlok comes like a thief in the night. Regardless, as Lady Jinnarin said, it's where Farrix saw more than one plume come down."

Jatu leaned forward on his hands. "Even so, we were anchored along the southeast coast of Rwn for nearly a month and in all that time no plume fell nearby. And when finally Lady Jinnarin saw the others, they were on a track that fared north of Rwn."

Alamar nodded but added, "Again I say, castings are nearly always hemmed in by constraints. It could be that in the year when Farrix saw the plumes, well, perhaps southeast of Rwn was one of the few places—or even the *only* place—where conditions were right for drawing them down."

"Damn!" exclaimed Bokar, slamming his fist to the table, jolting the tokko pieces. "No matter where we look, it is the same tale, full of could be's and might be's and do not know's!"

Frizian nodded sharply, agreeing wholeheartedly with the Dwarf, and he pointed at the malachite eagle marking the Polar Sea. "Captain, the Polar Sea, where it is not locked in ice, is even worse this time of year than the Boreal. And in spite of the fact that the northern lights shine strongly there, the Armsmaster is right, and I say that the might be's and could be's of the Polar Sea are no better nor worse than the others—probably worse, now that I think of it."

"Aye," chimed in Fager. He pointed at the carnelian miter. "And what was said about Thol could as well be said about the western continent."

Aravan looked about the table, then at Aylis, the seeress yet distracted, pondering. *"Chieran,"* he said, then, *"Chieran,"* louder.

"Wha-what?" She looked up and about. "Oh, my onyx throne." She reached down and touched the piece. "I put it here because the lights reach farther south at this time of year. I think that perhaps Farrix saw Durlok on a different track, one which runs below Rwn. It occurred to me that Durlok may have moved to a new path, and that's why we didn't see him or any plumes when we ran along the northerly reach."

A murmur of agreement muttered 'round the table, but Jatu added, "Still, Lady Aylis, it is but speculation, as has been all said here this night, just as full of could be's and might be's and don't know's. Even so, your offering seems a shade more apt than other conjectures this night."

Aylis held up a palm in demurral. "Oh no, I disagree—the most **likely** course is that suggested by Jinnarin." Aylis pointed, and all eyes followed her outstretched finger to find the crystal castle sitting off the map at the edge of the table.

"So, Daughter, you think that Durlok has turned tail and run home, eh?"

"I don't believe that we can claim that he has 'turned tail,' Father, but this I do know: we could sail the wide seas forever and *never* discover Durlok. Yet can we find his home . . ."

"She is right, Captain!" growled Bokar. "The best place to snare a vulture is in its nest."

"And that's where we will find Farrix," added Jinnarin, "or so I think."

Alamar turned to Aravan. "Tell me, my lad, just what

have you discovered concerning the location of pale green seas?"

Aravan smiled at being called "lad" by Alamar, though no one else seemed to note it, for had he been a mortal, Aravan appeared to be no more than twenty-five or thirty years old, whereas Alamar seemed ancient by like comparison. But as to which of the two was eldest in reality ...

Aravan stepped to the chart cabinet and hauled out several of the drawings. "None seems promising," he said, unrolling a map and laying it atop the one on the table, weighting the corners down. He pointed. "Here, we have a green sea in this long cusp at the northwest marge of the Great Gulf, yet there are no islands within."

Aravan unrolled a second map and laid it atop the other two. "Here in the Avagon are the Islands of Stone, frequented by pirates. The waters thereabouts are aqua-marine. Yet I know of no crystal castle therein. Too, the islands are quite close together, separated by a maze of channels running among them rather than by wide 'spanses as Jinnarin's dream would have."

A third map was laid out. "This is the Sindhu Sea. Here and here are pale green waters surrounding islands, yet these are well peopled, and traders ply this route. Again, no crystal castle sits therein."

On the fourth map, Aravan pointed out island group after island group. "These are the wide waters of the Bright Sea, where rings of coral islands abound. They have white beaches and lucid waters, yet all are set low in the sea and are covered with palm trees; none corresponds to the craggy isle described by Jinnarin and Aylis."

Aravan unrolled a fifth map. "Here we have the Ramanian Archipelago on the rim of the Jinga Sea, green waters about. Yet once again all these islands are well-known and no crystal castle stands above any of the shores.

"There are many other archipelagos, but none with pale green waters.

"Hence, of all the places I have examined, none seems to be an acceptable candidate for none matches the dream."

Alamar cleared his throat. "Again I say, dreams are misleading. It could be that the waters are not truly pale green. It could be that the crystal castle represents something else entirely. It could be that the island is not an island at all, but a place that lies upon a continental shore, or even far inland."

Bokar ground his teeth in frustration. "More could be's and might be's and do not know's."

Alamar shook his head. "Indeed, Dwarf. What we need is less speculation and more information."

Aylis took a deep breath. "I agree, Father, and that's why I must walk Jinnarin's dream again."

"What?" exploded Jinnarin, aghast.

Alamar looked at her wide-eyed, and Aravan's face fell grim.

"I said," responded Aylis, "that I must walk your—"

"Oh no you don't," interrupted Jinnarin.

"Daughter—"

"Chieran—"

Aylis raised her voice above the clamor. "It is the only way!"

Jinnarin strode back and forth across the table. "Oh no, Aylis, I have already killed one person. I'll not have the blood of another on my hands."

Aylis reached out and blocked her path, the Pysk stopping and looking up at the seeress. "Jinnarin, you are not responsible for Ontah's death. Instead it is Durlok who—"

"It's my dream!" shouted Jinnarin.

"No it isn't," gritted Aylis. "It is a *sending!* Whose? Farrix's, we think. But Durlok has done something to make it into a thing of dread. How? I cannot say, yet he is behind this just as certain as he is behind the plumes and the hideous sacrifice we found. So, Jinnarin, take not this guilt upon yourself; instead, place the blame where it rightfully belongs—at the feet of a Black Mage."

Jinnarin turned to Alamar, appeal in her eyes. But Alamar slowly shook his head, though his face was drained of blood. "I cannot stop her, Pysk. I will not even try. She is her own person, and I would not have it be otherwise. What she proposes to do is fraught with danger, yet she has the right of it: the only way for us to gather more information is for her to walk your dream again. Unless she does so, we may never discover Durlok's schemes."

"I don't care about Durlok!" Jinnarin cried and spun away, turning to Jatu.

The big black Man turned up his hands. "Unless she walks your dream, tiny one, we may never find your Farrix."

Tears welled in Jinnarin's eyes, and she turned to Aravan.

For what seemed to be endless moments he did nought but look at her, his face bleak. At last he spoke, his voice but a whisper: "The choice is thine and hers alone, Lady Jinnarin. None else here can make it for either of ye. It is thine alone to choose, and if thou choose to do so, it is hers and thine to do. She will not walk in thy dream without thy permission; she will not enter without thy leave."

In the swaying lantern light, Jinnarin turned to Aylis. As shadows shifted to and fro, long did Jinnarin look into the face of the seeress. At last the Pysk nodded, and that but once.

Aylis let out the breath she discovered she was holding. "Good. I will go."

At these words, Jinnarin fell to her knees and buried her face in her hands and wept as if her world had come to an end.

CHAPTER 22

Phantasms

Winter, 1E9574–75
[The Present]

The next morning, Quartermaster Roku, along with a crew of sailors and an escort of armed Dwarves, made ready to row across the harbor to the town of Havnstad, there to arrange for the replenishment of the ship's store of fresh water and to restock their reserve of supplies. " 'Ware," called Bokar down to Kelek, his second in command in one of the gigs, "this town has just paid tribute to raiders. Some will be touchy, and belike to act before they think."

As Kelek acknowledged the warning, Jatu standing at Bokar's side murmured, "On the other hand, they are chary of warriors armed and armored; I think the towns-folk will act as they did yester—overpolite and eager to please, so as not to upset a fierce foe. Unless there be a hothead or two, Roku and Kelek and the others will see no belligerence this day, just as we did not. Too, since they've just paid tribute, their coffers run low, and they will be eager for our business."

As the gigs rowed away, Aravan and Frizian came to join Bokar and Jatu. Without preamble Aravan said, "When Roku and the others return, I am of a mind to set sail on a westerly course running south of Rwn."

Jatu smiled. "Following the route suggested by Lady Aylis, eh?'

"Aye, Jatu, it is as thou said: her offering seems more apt than all our other conjectures."

Frizian blew out his breath, white in the chill air. "What about her dreamwalk, Captain?"

Aravan glanced at the morning Sun and took a deep breath. "Lady Aylis believes that she may begin walking dreams with Lady Jinnarin within a sevenday."

"Why wait, Captain?"

"There is more to dreamwalking than we know, Frizian, yet can the Lady Aylis teach Lady Jinnarin the lore of it, mayhap it will increase their chances of evading the peril within the sending, for in that dream deadly dangers lie."

"Argh!" growled Bokar. "Give me something I can see, something I can bury cold steel in. That is the foe I would fight. Not some dream phantom!"

Aravan held up a hand. "Bokar, thou name a dream phantom, yet we know not *what* foe lies within."

Bokar's eyes narrowed. "A giant phantom spider, Captain, was it not?"

"Lady Aylis does not deem the spider slew Ontah. 'Twas something else altogether."

"Durlok!" exclaimed Frizian.

Bokar's eyes widened. "The Black Mage? Think you he is somehow within the dream itself?"

Frizian turned up his hands, but Aravan said, "If one can walk a dream, then so might another."

A pall of silence fell upon the group. At last Frizian said, "Captain, I'll tell the Men to make ready to get underway when Roku returns."

As Aravan nodded and Frizian turned to go, Bokar gritted, "And I'll keep the warband ready, in case these craven Havnstaders decide to pull some underhanded trick."

Now Bokar stepped away, and Jatu said quietly, "Captain, he is spoiling for a fight. If we don't find action soon . . ."

"Nay, Jatu, worry not about Bokar. He is well disciplined, as is all his band. Yet thou hast the right of it: he *is* spoiling for a fight, and I pity those he finally faces if it comes to combat."

Below decks, Aylis and Jinnarin sat in darkened quarters, a single candle illuminating the room, daylight blocked from showing through the cloth-covered porthole. Aylis sat on the floor, her back against a wall, Jinnarin on the bunk, her back against the opposite wall. "Breathe deeply and relax," murmured Aylis. "Look at the candle flame; concentrate on it until all else fades from view. Then close your eyes and let the image of the flame remain. Slowly it will begin to wane, and as it does so, picture a peaceful scene—a stream, a glade, a quiet dell, a field of nodding flowers. Let your mind float free from your body and enter what you envision. Once you have entered ..." And as the *Eroean* slowly and gently rocked to and fro, Jinnarin began a journey into peaceful meditation, Aylis her learned guide.

Roku returned from the port town in mid afternoon, a small flotilla following. Bokar and his warband stood wary guard as goods were passed up from the merchants' boats, the townsfolk aboard them marvelling over the cut of the Elvenship. Dried vegetables and fruits, grain, flour, slabs of cured meat, dried fish, kegs of pickled cabbage, jerky, barrels of water, keglets of rum and wine, wheels of cheese, more: all were passed up and over the rail, some winched aboard in nets. And when all had been laded and the boats were away, Frizian had Reydeau pipe the silks, and the *Eroean* weighed anchor and majestically sailed out from the harbor, running easily against the incoming tide.

South fared the *Eroean* for a full day, running with the wind abeam. Then westerly she turned into the blow and began tacking a zigzag path. Another day followed and then another one after until altogether a week had fled, and still westerly she drove, beating windward, sailing the waters above Gelen and below Rwn and on beyond Atala. And all that time though the boreal lights shone, no plumes in the night did they spy. Nor during that time in the daylight hours was any galley seen. And day after day in a darkened cabin Aylis quietly led Jinnarin into the secrets of drifting free, of meditation, of consciously walking a dream.

Aylis lay with Aravan, her head on his breast, he stroking her hair, she listening to the beat of his heart. "I think we are ready," she said after a while.

"When, *chieran?*"

"Tomorrow we begin."

"So soon?"

"Yes."

"And Jinnarin?"

"She is as ready as I was at the same stage of learning, love. She has mastered both light and deep meditation. Too, Ontah's <words> of <suggestion> are well ingrained, and though they are not true words of <power>, they will serve her well. Now all she needs is to be schooled in the ways of controlling a dream, to shape it to her will, and for that we must walk within the dreams of another."

Aravan lay quietly for a while, then said, "She learned quickly, neh?"

"Yes. Ontah marvelled over how swiftly I learned, but he would have been just as pleased with Jinnarin."

"Is it difficult?"

Aylis pondered Aravan's question. "I did not think so . . . nor for that matter did Jinnarin. But I had been schooled as a seeress, and so it came easily to me. Jinnarin, on the other hand, has had no such schooling, but she learned swiftly regardless."

"Hmm," mused Aravan thoughtfully, then added, "Mayhap what comes easily to Pysks or Magekind or others of similar ilk is difficult for Humans. Someday thou must try to teach me, then we perhaps shall see."

Aylis raised up and peered into Aravan's eyes. "Oh, love, how wonderful, for then we would walk our dreams together and shape them as we will."

Aravan smiled. "I am already walking my dream with thee, *chieran.*"

Aylis leaned down and kissed him gently, then returned to listening to the beat of his heart.

After a long silence, Aravan whispered, "Tomorrow?"

"Yes."

His embrace tightened but he said nought.

Soon she raised up and kissed him again, and they made gentle love.

"It is not easy to sleep while someone else is watching," rumbled Jatu.

Neither Jinnarin nor Aylis answered.

"I mean, here I lie like a stiff log while you two sit as would a dark, silent *Uhra* with her little *Jeju* familiar at her side ... or in this case, the Jeju perches to my left while the Uhra sits to the right."

Still Aylis and Jinnarin said nothing, each maintaining her state of light meditation.

The three were in Aylis's old quarters, having commandeered it for dreamwalking purposes. Jatu lay on a pallet in the floor, the bunk being entirely too short for his giant frame. Aylis sat cross-legged with her back to a wall, her hands, palms up, resting lightly on her thighs, her eyes mere glittering slits. Jinnarin sat in a like manner but up on the bunk on the opposite side of Jatu. Rux lay beneath the bunk asleep. The room was dimly illuminated by a single shielded candle.

"Even though I can see you two, I feel as if I were prey to some unseen jungle predator."

Both Jinnarin and Aylis remained silent.

Jatu sighed and shifted about, attempting to quell his uneasiness by means of physical comfort.

It did not help.

After a while of tossing and turning, Jatu leapt up and slammed out of the cabin. Though Rux lifted his head and looked, neither Jinnarin nor Aylis made a move. The fox went back to sleep.

Shortly thereafter, Jatu came back in and lay down once more, and moments later, somewhere nearby a sailor began to sing, his words distant and sometimes lost in the blustery wind, sails slapping in the blow, rope and tackle creaking, waves *shsh*ing against the sides, the *Eroean* rising and falling across the long ocean swells.

"*<Añu>*," said Aylis softly, using one of Ontah's <words> of <suggestion>.

Although Jinnarin could not see Jatu's sleeping face, she knew that his eyes must be whipping back and forth beneath his lids. She slipped into a state of deep meditation and used another of the ingrained <words> of <suggestion> taught to her by Aylis, and Jinnarin began to dream. She sat on a branch high in a tree. Below, on the bank of a creek, a pair of otters tumbled and slid on their stomachs down a mud slide. As she laughed in pleasure, a brown-haired Lady Mage came striding through the sky. "Sparrow," said the Lady, holding out her hand. "Brightwing," replied the Pysk, taking the hand in hers. And together they stepped through the tree-trunk passage to a distant dream, emerging in a withy hut.

An ill black Man dressed in a loincloth lay on a woven mat, a young, bare-breasted black Woman in attendance, plying wet cloths to the Man's brow. Peering in 'round the edge of the doorway was a tall black youth, his face twisted in torment. In the distance beyond the youth could be seen an approaching Man dressed all in rushes, his black face painted a ghastly white, and in his hand he bore a cup, a viper, a flower, a cup, a snake, a root, a cup.

"I don't want to see this," said Sparrow, turning away.

"We must watch and remember, Sparrow," responded Brightwing.

Sparrow shivered and shook her head, *No*. "Bright wing, it is where Jatu killed the Jujuba. That is Jatu's father and mother. The youth is Jatu. The black Man coming with the poisoned cup is the Jujuba. I do not want to see this. Let us go. Let us go now!"

Brightwing sighed and turned, and in the wall appeared a hole leading elsewhere. But even as they approached it, the withes of the wall began to shudder and shift, melting and running down.

"Quick!" shouted Brightwing. "Flee!"

They leapt out through the hole in the hut and into the ship's cabin where three people were—a Pysk, a Lady Mage, and a thrashing black Man—along with a fox pacing nervously back and forth alongside the bunk on which Jinnarin sat.

"No!" shouted Jatu, bolting upright, sweat runnelling down his face and neck and chest.

Rux flinched down and back but then recovered, and he stood stock-still between his mistress and Jatu, his wary gaze focused on the face of the black Man.

Sparrow flew over and alighted by the Pysk—her corporeal self—and then she said a <word> of <suggestion> . . .

. . . and opened her eyes.

*   *   *

"All right, Sparrow, now you form the bridge to Jatu's dream."

They stepped through the burrow tunnel toward the light, to emerge on the seat of a gig. Men rowed mightily, and in the fore Jatu held onto the haft of a great harpoon, his laughter ringing through the air.

Sparrow stepped among the sweating Men, making her way to the bow. "Jatu! Jatu!" she called, "What is it you hunt?"

Jatu swung his head about, his face lighted with joy. "Aha, little Jeju, we hunt that!" Jatu turned and pointed at a swift-running white cloud.

"A cloud, Jatu?"

"Aye, Jeju, a great cloud whale."

Of a sudden Sparrow realized that the gig was high in the sky above the world, and behind sailed a great sky galleon up among the clouds, following the hurtling gig, Men and Dwarves aboard her cheering Jatu and his rowers onward.

Now Sparrow turned, peering forward, and the cloud they chased wafted a great tail up and down, propelling it ahead. "But why, Jatu? Why chase the clouds?"

Jatu doubled over with laughter, but he managed to gasp out, "'For the fog blubber, little Jeju. For the precious fog blubber." His great guffaws shattered the air, the rowers giggling and snickering even as they pulled hard on the oars.

"Sparrow," said Brightwing, her face wreathed in smiles, "we must go. See the distant sky?"

Sparrow looked. As would a curtain blow in the wind, the sky at the horizon shifted and shimmered. The sky galleon began fading, and the clouds started vanishing one after another, like candles being snuffed out. "Oh my, this glorious dream is coming to an end," she said.

"Bridge out," said Brightwing.

Sparrow formed an opening into which she and Aylis stepped, and behind they heard Jatu laughing. "She blows! The cloud whale blows! She blows in the wind!" Again his laughter belled up.

As Brightwing and Sparrow murmured the <words> of <suggestion> . . .

. . . Aylis and Jinnarin opened their eyes to the sound of soft laughter, Jatu chortling in his sleep.

* * *

"Fear not, Jinnarin, we will not dreamwalk the sending until you are ready."

"When will that be?"

"I would say ... one more night walking in Jatu's dreams."

Jinnarin smiled. "He has such wonderful dreams, doesn't he? Quite unpredictable, neh?" Jinnarin's smile vanished. "All but the one about the Jujuba, that is."

Aylis nodded. Then a pondering look came over her face. "I wonder ..."

Jinnarin glanced up at the seeress. "What?"

Aylis's eyes were lost in reflection.

"What?" said Jinnarin again.

Aylis shook her head, as if rousing from the depths of her thoughts. She took a deep breath.

"You wonder what?" asked Jinnarin, hoping that this time she would be heard.

Aylis turned up her hands. "Oh, several things: I wonder if appalling events are forever repeated in one's dreams. I wonder if those of great joy are oft relived in the shadowland as well. And I wonder if a grim event, such as Jatu's, can be set aside so that it never troubles a dream or a dreamer again. If so, how? —Oh, if I had only asked Ontah ... perhaps there is something we could do to ease Jatu's dreams of this horrid event from his past."

Jinnarin nodded. "Or anyone else's, for that matter."

Aylis smiled. "Perhaps we can find another teacher— one wise in the ways of dreamwalking and dream shaping."

"On the other hand," mused Jinnarin, "if we can't, then perhaps we can discover on our own just how to cleanse one's dreams of these awful events ... eliminate them entirely."

"Oh, Jinnarin, in that we must be most wary, for dreams in some fashion provide a way to purge fear and rage and other strong emotions, else they will feed upon themselves, to the harm of the person involved. To totally eliminate a dream, I think would do great damage. Instead a dreamhealer must find a way to bring harmony within a person's mind and spirit and soul, and yet not dispose of the dream."

"Aylis, are you saying that nightmares and other dreams of dread are good for the spirit, the mind, the soul?"

Aylis shook her head. "No, Jinnarin. What I am saying is that I simply do not know. Hence, we must not interfere such that we take the dream away."

"But I thought that Ontah reshaped dreams in the minds of those he aided."

Aylis nodded. "He did. But, Jinnarin, Ontah was remolding the dream, making it into something else, something safe, not eliminating it. How he did it, I do not know . . . and until I know, until we know, meddling with another's dream represents a risk we should avoid."

Jinnarin pondered a moment, then said, "The sum and substance of it, Aylis, is that Ontah knew what he was doing, whereas we do not."

Aylis smiled. "'Yes, my tiny Pysk . . . although we are not entirely ignorant in the art of dreamwalking, we know nothing yet of the art of dreamhealing, of reshaping another's dream from something harmful into something benign."

"Well, I certainly do not want to tamper with the sending."

"Oh, I do not plan on attempting to remold it. Instead, I think that we must merely find out more of what lies within."

Jinnarin shivered. "Something dreadful is what we are likely to find—something dire and dangerous . . . something that killed Ontah."

Aylis reached out toward the Pysk. "Yes, Jinnarin, yet remember, it is a sending and not a dream of your own. But you are right—something dangerous lies within—and I would avoid the danger."

"Just how will we do that? Have you a plan?"

Aylis spread her hands. "Not exactly a plan. A strategy instead. This I think is the truth of it: I believe that you must sleep a natural sleep to be guided into the sending. However, since it *is* a sending, it represents *someone else's dream*. Hence, once you have begun the dream, if I intercept and alert you, you *might* be able to disengage from the sending *just as if you were dreamwalking*. Then, should aught go awry, we can both escape across a bridging—out from the sending and home."

"Oh, Aylis, do you think it will work, this strategy of yours? Am I ready? Do I know enough?"

"As to the strategy, I can only hope it will work, Jinnarin. But as to your readiness, we need only to walk in but a handful more of Jatu's dreams for you to gain experience in seeing when it is time to leave as well as shaping the bridges out.

"Then I want to walk some dreams of yours to practice making you aware within the dream itself.

"Then and only then will we walk within the sending." Aylis pursed her lips. "I know of nothing else we can do to prepare us for the journey. Can you suggest anything?"

Jinnarin sat cross-legged and reflected deeply. At last she said, "I will take my bow and a quiver of arrows."

Aylis's mouth dropped open. "Bu-but, Jinnarin, this is a— How can—?"

"Easily," interjected Jinnarin. "Since we can shape our dreams when we are aware, I will merely call my bow and arrows to me."

Aylis laughed and clapped her hands.

The floor was transparent, and below a brawl raged to and fro within the barroom. Jatu rolled over in bed and said to the naked Woman, "Sorry, my fancy, but I—"

—he found himself hurling Arbalinian dockworkers out the doors of the Red Slipper, Bokar roaring at his side, the Dwarf without clothes yet covered with a thick matting of hair, and his arms were elongated and his knuckles dragged the ground. A dockworker charged and Bokar ape hurled the laughing Man through the window and out into the waters of the bay. Suddenly the bordello was entirely empty, except for Bokar—who was now restored to his normal state, chainmail, helm, and axe, but no clothes. And down the stairwell came the many ladies of the Red Slipper, nude and inviting. Jatu quickened, responding to the lure. . . .

Jinnarin laughed, looking at Aylis standing beside her. "Perhaps we ought to go now."

The walls began to waver.

"Now I *know* we ought to go," said Jinnarin, forming

a hollow log leading out from the dream. The two stepped into the cavity, leaving Jatu's dissolving fantasy behind, and passed through the length of the log and into the cabin.

Jinnarin spoke the <word> of <suggestion> and opened her eyes in the candlelight. Jatu moaned and rolled over, somewhat awake, his body and mind yet mazed by the dream. Jinnarin grinned shyly and said, "Go back to sleep, Jatu." At the sound of her voice, Jatu wakened wholly. Groaning, he wrapped the blanket about himself and stood and stumbled out from the cabin.

Aylis watched him go. After a moment she said, "Men—males—are not the only ones who have such dreams."

Jinnarin smiled to herself. "I know."

Jinnarin crouched down, trembling in the grass. She could see the huge owl perched on the branch of the tree, its great unblinking yellow eyes fixedly locked upon her. Fumbling about, she didn't have her bow, and Rux was nowhere to be seen.

"Jinnarin, look at me!"

It was Aylis.

"This is but a dream, Jinnarin—your dream."

"My dream?"

"Yes. And as such, you can control it, do with it as you will."

"Control . . . ?" Of a sudden, her bow appeared in her hands—"Hai!"—and Rux was at her side.

The owl launched itself toward her. As the great slayer swooped down, its talons extended for the kill, "'Rux!" cried the Pysk, and the fox ran up through the air and, snapping, leapt upon the raptor, and the two tumbled down toward the ground to fall beyond seeing in the deep grass. There sounded a din of skrawking and snarling, and then silence, and Rux came trotting through the meadow, an owl feather clinging to his mouth.

Sparrow turned to Brightwing standing beside her. "What now, Brightwing?"

"Ah, so now you are aware."

"Yes," responded Sparrow. "This is my dream, or

rather Jinnarin's, and I am in control." Suddenly they stood on a high mountain overlooking a waterfall pouring out from the sky, a flutter of rainbows all about. "See?"

Brightwing laughed.

Now they stood upon a drifting cloud, peering down at a great forest with leaves of scarlet and gold. "Tell me something, Brightwing, if I were to make a bridge back to the cabin at this moment and say the <word> of <suggestion>, would I then be able to waken myself?"

Brightwing's eyes flew wide. "Oh, Sparrow, what a novel idea. But I know not the answer—perhaps it would be so, but then again perhaps not. If White Owl were here, he could advise us; yet he is not, and I do not know if there are risks involved, and without knowing, I think we had better not try."

"If we take no risks, Brightwing, then we gain no knowledge," said Sparrow. "Yet I will wait to try it another time ... after we have found Farrix. Even so, I wish I knew the answer, for it may be a trick we will need when we venture the sending."

Brightwing nodded as they floated on a burgundy oak leaf down a burbling rill mid a swarm of iridescent dragonflies. "If we are somehow left without choice, then will be the time to attempt such."

When Brightwing stepped into the dream, she found herself among churning dark clouds above a pale green sea, Jinnarin flying ahead. *We are not yet ready for this.* Forming a bridge out, Brightwing returned to the cabin where Jinnarin lay, the Pysk covered with a sheen of sweat.

Moments later, Jinnarin bolted upright, panting, her heart hammering with dread. Temporarily she was disoriented, but then she focused on Aylis. "It was the sending," she gasped.

"I know."

"Why didn't—?" Jinnarin paused, catching her breath. "Why didn't we go?" she said at last.

"We will, Jinnarin, but just not yet. We both need a bit more practice: I, in awakening you within the dream; you in controlling a dream and in making bridges."

Jinnarin sighed glumly. "I think I am ready now."

Aylis spread her hands. "Next time, Jinnarin, next time we go. I promise."

They lay in bed side by side, the Lady Mage and the Elf. She clasped his hand and brought his fingers to her lips, kissing each one separately. He looked at her and smiled a gentle smile. Of a sudden she shook her head, and looked hard at him.

"'What is it, Aylis?" asked Aravan, concern in his eyes.

She took a deep breath and then exhaled. "Oh, love, it's just that I've walked so many dreams of late that I sometimes find it hard to tell which is reality and which are but phantasms of the mind."

Aravan nodded slowly, then said, "Once while serving as navigator on the Dragonship *Wavestrider,* the captain, Rald was his name, woke up with a start, his eyes wide and staring and full of puzzlement. When I asked him if aught was amiss, he told me of the dream he had had. He said, 'I dreamed that I was a bee gathering honey. The dream was so real, so very real. I had six legs and two wings, but I had no trouble in knowing how to use them. When I had gathered all the nectar and pollen that I could carry, I flew straightly and swift, back to the hollow tree where the hive took all my gatherings from me to make honey. Darkness fell, and each of the bees went to sleep, including me. That's when I awoke here on the *Wavestrider,* and then it was that I wondered if I was a Man who had dreamed he was a bee, or instead a sleeping bee dreaming of being a Man on a Dragonship.' Rald then moved his limbs and felt along his chest as if seeking to discover another set of legs. Finding none, he looked over his shoulder, trying to see his wings. Detecting neither extra legs nor wings, he looked long at me and then broke out in laughter. It was thereafter, though, that he developed a special fondness for flowers, seeking them out at every opportunity."

Aylis laughed, but then grew sober, thoughtful. Finally she said, "Perhaps that is what we are—nought but dreaming dreamers, fast asleep in some far Realm, dreaming our lives away as we live here in this existence."

Aravan smiled. "'Mayhap, *chieran,* but if so I would

not wish ever to awaken unless thou wert there as well." He raised up on one elbow and leaned down and kissed her on the lips. Then he reached down and took her hand and kissed her fingers as well. Finally he looked into her eyes, sapphires gazing into emeralds. "Although I have no way of proving it, this I deem is the reality, *chieran*, though for me it is a dream come true."

Aylis pulled him to her and kissed him long. Then holding hands they lay once again side by side. After a while she murmured, "She is ready, love; Jinnarin is as ready as I can make her, and so am I. When next she enters the sending, then will I follow her, and together we will venture to discover whatever we can."

Aravan said nothing, though he gripped her hand tightly. They lay and listened to wind and wave and creaking rope as the *Eroean* fared westward along the briny track. Time passed, and there came a faint cry from above decks. Aravan swung his feet over the flank of the bed and sat listening, his head cocked to one side. Again came the cry. Moments later a knock sounded on the door. "Land, Cap'n" came Tivir's voice, "land ho off th' starboard bow."

CHAPTER 23

Web

Winter, 1E9574–75
[The Present]

"Jatu's dreams—all but one—well, they were strange and wonderful and wild and often rather bawdy," said Jinnarin. "It was quite an experience. I laughed and was amazed and at times embarrassed."

"Hmph," snorted Alamar, "I'll wager."

"Sometime, Alamar, I'd like to walk your dreams. Why, there's no telling what I might find in there."

"Oh no you don't, Pysk," snapped Alamar. "I won't have anyone walking about in my head, stepping all over my brains, poking about in my dreams. No thank you. Especially not a Pysk."

"Why not, Alamar? I mean, it's not as if it would do damage."

"Ha!" barked the elder. "No damage? Why, you—particularly you—would be looking for all my secrets, stealing every bit of privy lore hidden in my mind, to say nothing of prying into my private affairs to see what you could find to hold over me."

Jinnarin leapt to her feet infuriated, her hands clenched into fists on her hips, her cheeks puffing and blowing with outraged dignity. "Steal your secrets?" she shrieked. "Pry into your affairs? Alamar, you old fossil, now even if you invited me, I wouldn't go into that creaky shut-up mind of yours. Why, why, I'd get squashed to death in those narrow confines. Besides—"

A knock sounded on the door and, snarling, Alamar jerked it open, shouting, "What?"

Startled, Tivir quailed backwards. "It's land, sir, that's all, land." His message delivered, the lad fled down the passageway.

Grumpily, Alamar and Jinnarin made their way to the deck, where they found Jatu and Bokar standing along the starboard rail. Five miles or so in the fore distance they could see the high cliffs of a long, curving shoreline creeping up over the horizon. Atop the bluffs they could make out greenery—a pineland running along the edge of the precipice.

"Where are we?" asked Jinnarin. "What Land?"

" 'Tis the western continent again, Lady Jinnarin," answered Jatu, "though farther south and west than where we were before. East and a bit north lies Tarquin's Realm, and north beyond that is where last we saw this continent ere turning east for Thol."

"Oh." Jinnarin sighed.

"Well what'd you expect, Pysk?" growled Alamar. "I mean, given the direction we were sailing, where else could we have gone?"

"I—I don't know, Alamar. I was just expecting ... expecting ..." Dejectedly, Jinnarin slumped to the deck.

In that moment, Aylis and Aravan arrived, and the seeress shot a look of reproach at her father and knelt by the Pysk.

Alamar threw his hands up to the sky and stormed off, muttering to himself.

"Yaaaahhh!" shouted Bokar, slamming the butts of his fists down on the wale, startling Jinnarin and Aylis, Alamar at a distance whirling about, Aravan and Jatu looking on in consternation. "Kruk! I know just how you feel, Lady Jinnarin. Nothing! No one! Empty sea! Dark land!" The Dwarf turned and bellowed out over the ocean, "Where are you, Durlok, you skut?"

Now Jinnarin leapt to her feet, and turned and kicked the starboard railboard and shrieked out through a run-off hole, her tiny voice piping, "Where are you, Durlok, you skut?"

Of a sudden, Jatu began laughing, immediately joined by Aravan and then Aylis. Bokar doubled over roaring, and finally Jinnarin, her birdlike trills ringing. Alamar, glaring, came stomping back and demanded, "All right, you bunch of jackfools, just what's so funny?" which started them on a roar again.

"Where now, Captain?"

Aravan looked at Jatu. "Bring her in close and drop anchor. We'll lay up in this bight for a while. Send a landing party ashore to fetch water to replenish what we have used. In fact, rotate the crew through this water duty—give them a stretch ashore. In the meanwhile we will wait for Lady Aylis and Lady Jinnarin to walk the sending and see what they can see. Then shall we determine our course."

As Jatu and Bokar turned to carry out the orders— Jatu to bring the ship to safe anchorage, Bokar to form up mixed teams to go ashore afterward—Aravan turned to Aylis and Jinnarin. "Now it is up to ye twain," he said quietly, his eyes full of desperate concern.

Four nights later, on the tenth of March, during the third dream of the darktide, Brightwing found herself once again flying through dark roiling clouds above a pale green sea. Rain lashed down, while far below a black ship sailed, her masts stroked by lightning. In the remote distance stood the dark shape of a storm-lashed island, and other dim shapes were scattered widely across the raging sea.

Just ahead, she saw Jinnarin. Flying swiftly, she caught the Pysk and took her by the hand, Jinnarin and the seeress of a matching size. "Sparrow! Sparrow!" she called above the sound of thunder and rain and wind and lightning. "Sparrow! Wake up! It is the sending!"

Jinnarin looked over at her, the Pysk's eyes mazed. But then her gaze filled with awareness, and Sparrow called out, "Brightwing!"

Brightwing laughed. "Come, my Sparrow, let us fly down to see the sea. I would inspect these pale green waters." But even as she said it, a thin tendril of fear snaked up her spine.

"Do you feel it, Brightwing?" called out Sparrow. "The evil, I mean."

"Yes. Be wary. Be ready to flee. Watch close for the dissolution of this dream, for I would not be trapped within."

Sparrow shuddered. "Oh my no. Neither would I."

Even as they sped down toward the heaving waters below, the fear grew.

"My bow and arrows!" cried Sparrow, and suddenly they appeared, the bow in her hand, the quiver strapped to her hip.

Now they came down nigh the ocean, and in the distance the black ship thundered toward them, capturing their eyes. Down they settled to the surface of the sea, yet *lo!* they landed not on water, but instead on a great green web!

"Oh, Brightwing, I'm stuck! I'm stuck!" cried Sparrow, the Pysk trapped, her foot caught by the monstrous snare.

Yet even as Aylis turned to help her, the great dark ship shimmered and changed, becoming an immense black spider, fangs adrip and long legs scuttling as it rushed toward them, the web shuddering as onward it came.

Fear hammered upon them as Brightwing tried to haul Sparrow upward, the spider hurtling at them.

"I can't—!" gritted Brightwing through clenched teeth, her straining arms about Sparrow. "It's too—I need a—

"*—Sword!*"

Suddenly a sword appeared in Brightwing's grip.

Now the web bounced and bounded, the horrendous spider rushing down on them, dread whelming through their veins.

Brightwing slashed the sword down on the great strand holding Sparrow, but the blade rebounded and did not cut.

And the hideous monster now was but steps away, its many eyes glittering as onward it came.

"*Incende!*" shouted Brightwing, and the blade burst into flame. Again she slashed at the web, the green strand giving way before the fire!

Once more she slashed, and Sparrow was free!

And the huge dark spider now loomed above, rearing upward and lunging down.

"Up and away," shrieked Brightwing.

But even as they tried to fly, great green ropy tentacles lashed up from the sea, clutching at them.

"Bridge out!" cried Sparrow, a black hole forming before her, and she dived through, a virescent tentacle whipping through the breach after, lashing about and groping for her even though she was back in the cabin.

Ducking and dodging, "Brightwing! Brightwing!" she called, for the Lady Mage had not come through with her.

Of a sudden, another gap appeared, and Brightwing dove through, rolling, grass-green tentacles grasping after. She leapt to her feet, shouting, "Close the bridge, Sparrow! Close the bridge!"

With a <word> Sparrow slammed the hole shut, hacking off the tentacle to flop and writhe and vanish in a sickly green vapor. Brightwing, too, chopped shut her portal, severing off a length of the clutching tentacle to lash and coil and dissolve in yellow-green smoke.

Hearts hammering, they looked at one another, Sparrow trembling, Brightwing gasping. Still quaking, they sat beside their physical selves and uttered the <words> of <suggestion> . . .

. . . and opened their eyes in the candlelit room.

And in that very moment, Aravan came crashing into the cabin, his sword in hand, his eyes sweeping the chamber, the Elf ready to slay whatever it was that had caused his blue stone amulet to run icy chill.

"The thing that puzzles me," inserted Frizian, "are the giant tentacles. Only the Krakens are known to have such hideous arms, and although they live in the deeps, the only place where the Krakens are known to congregate—"

"Is the Great Maelstrom!" blurted out Tink, serving tea, the lad clapping a hand over his own mouth for butting in.

Aravan looked at the cabin boy and smiled. "Quite right, Tink." Then Aravan turned to the others. "Yet heed: though the Seabane Isles lie nearby, the Great Maelstrom is not a pale green sea"—he glanced at Alamar—"yet as thou sayest, Mage Alamar, things in dreams are not always what they seem."

Alamar jerked his head up and down. "Quite right, Elf: nothing may be as it seems, and that includes the ship, the spider, the pale green sea, the storm, the island, the crystal castle, or whatever else this blasted sending shows us!''

Jatu turned to Aylis and Jinnarin. "The fear, did it come from the spider?"

Aylis glanced at Jinnarin, and the Pysk said, "Oh, Jatu I was terrified of the spider, yet I don't think that the fear we first felt came from it. Instead I would say . . . well, I just don't know." She looked at the seeress.

Aylis turned up her palms. "Jinnarin is right. Though terrifying, the spider is not the source of the dread. I believe instead that it comes from the island."

A silence fell on the group, broken only by the clink of pottery as Tink stepped 'round the gathering and served tea. At last Aravan said, "Let us list all. Mayhap by seeing it written down in one place we will be inspired."

He pulled open a drawer in the table and took pen and parchment from it. "In order now, there was—?" He looked at Aylis.

"Clouds. Jinnarin flying. A storm. The black ship below, lightning stroking the masts. The pale green sea. The island. Other shapes—"

Aravan paused, holding up a hand. "These other shapes, what deem thee they were?"

Aylis shrugged. "They are too vague, distant."

"Make a guess, Daughter," directed Alamar.

Aylis looked at Jinnarin. "Perhaps islands. Small islands. I simply don't know, Father. They are too distant, too vague in the storm to see well."

Alamar turned to Jinnarin. The Pysk shook her head. "I don't know either."

Aravan took up his pen. "Let us continue."

Aylis glanced at the list. "Um, let me see, oh yes—I wakened Sparrow. We flew down to look at the pale green sea. It was a vast green web. Jinnarin trapped. The ship became a great black spider. I cut Jinnarin free with a conjured, flaming sword—"

"But, Daughter," interrupted Alamar, "you don't know how to conjure flames."

"I do in my dreams, Father. I merely said the word that I've heard you use a thousand times: *Incende*."

"It cast?"

"Yes, Father. —How? I do not know. Yet had it not, then we would not have survived."

"Hmph!" grunted Alamar, turning his bracelet 'round his wrist.

Aravan took up his pen once again, signifying for Aylis to continue.

"There's not that much more. The great black spider was upon us. Green tentacles clutching. Bridging out, the tentacles following. We slammed the holes to, which cut off the tentacles, which vanished in yellow-green smoke."

"*Ooo*," breathed Frizian, peering around at the shadows in the salon. "They followed you right into the cabin?"

Jinnarin nodded.

Aravan fingered the amulet at his throat. "I deem the tentacles in the cabin is what caused this stone to run chill."

Bokar cocked an eyebrow. "A dream creature?"

Aylis slowly nodded. "A dream creature it was, Bokar, yet forget not, it was no ordinary phantasm, but instead was one we brought from the dream shadowland and into the ship's cabin ... into the reality of the world."

Frizian shuddered. "Rather frightening."

"That's spooky, all right," said Tink, "but, Lor! even worse is thinking of a great big green web in the sea, trapping all wot sails into her."

At Tink's remark, Aravan's eyes flew wide, and he glanced at Jatu, and by the look on the black Man's face he saw that Jatu's thoughts followed the same track as his own. He leapt up and pulled a map from the chart cabinet and spread it out, his finger stabbing to a shaded area in the south Sindhu Sea. "Here, my friends, here may lie the pale green sea."

All looked, and Frizian said, "But, Captain, that's the Great Swirl."

"Aye Frizian, but Tink I ween is right; here is a great green web trapping all within."

Jinnarin looked at Aravan. "What *is* this Great Swirl?"

It was Jatu who answered. "Ah, tiny one, it is a vast area of clinging weed, more than a thousand miles across, slowly turning 'round about with the surrounding currents. Many a ship has been storm driven into that monstrous clutching whirl to be caught forever, never to be seen nor heard from again."

Jatu fell silent but Frizian added, "Ships trapped within are drawn to the center, or so they say, ever changing position in the slow churn."

Bokar growled, "Is it true that salvage and treasure expeditions have been lost as well?"

Frizian nodded. "So it is said. It is told that something evil lies within."

Bokar slammed his fist to the table. "If it is evil, then it might be the Black Mage! It could be a place where he gets his victims, eh? Sailors trapped by the weed?"

A ripple of conversation muttered around the table.

Aylis held up a hand for silence. When it came, she asked, "Can this be where we should search for Durlok? For the crystal castle? For the pale green sea? For Farrix? Have we facts to support this thesis—that the Great Swirl is the seat of the mystery—or is it but mere speculation?"

Alamar shrugged. "All we have to go on is the sending, Daughter, and dreams are deceiving and not what they seem."

"Yet Tink may be right, Mage Alamar," said Aravan. "The green web could symbolize the clutching weed of the Swirl."

"Wot about its color, Cap'n?" asked Tink. "Is it pale green?"

Aravan nodded. "Aye, Tink, I have seen it up close, and pale green, grass green, they both apply."

"And the tentacles of the dream," asked Jinnarin, "what are they?"

Now Jatu spoke up. "Green tentacles? Perhaps they, too, are the clutching weed, Lady Jinnarin."

Aylis slowly nodded. "Perhaps. But the spider, it is no weed in the water. What might it represent?"

Silence fell 'round the table, each looking at one another in puzzlement. Suddenly Tink blurted out, "The galley! The Black Mage's galley! The legs are—"

"—The oars!" exclaimed Jatu. "Ah, Tink, m'lad, you have the right of it!"

"Ha!" exclaimed Bokar. "It all fits. The green is the weed. The spider is the galley of the Black Mage!"

"Pah, Dwarf," declared Alamar, "how many times do I have to repeat myself? Things in dreams are not necessarily what they seem. These things may be something else altogether. Take Tink's conjecture—the spider doesn't have to be a galley."

Bokar glared at the Mage. "What else can it be?"

Before Alamar could reply, Aravan said, "Bokar has a point, Mage Alamar. Thou sayest thyself that dreams are not what they seem. A giant spider, especially one as large as a ship, seems unlikely. Instead, I think Tink's posit is apt: the spider is but a symbol for the galley, legs representing oars." Aravan glanced across the table at Aylis. "It began as one kind of ship and ended as perhaps another, the spider but a dream token—"

Jatu nodded vigorously and interjected, "Farrix—or whoever it is sending the dream—could have all along been trying to tell Lady Jinnarin that it is a galley, yet the dream became garbled somewhere along the way."

Alamar threw up his hands. "I'm not saying it is and I'm not saying it isn't . . . what I am saying is that we just don't know."

Frizian blew out his breath. "What about the lightning stroking the masts? And the island? I know of no island in the Swirl."

All eyes turned to Aravan. The Elf shrugged. "Neither do I, Frizian, yet heed, the weed is more than a thousand miles across. It could hide many things within, and they would remain unknown. An island is the least of them."

"Ships!" exclaimed Aylis.

"Eh?" grunted Alamar. "What are you going on about, Daughter?"

"Ships, Father. The other shapes in the sea. Small. Indistinct in the storm. They're not islands, but ships instead. Trapped ships. Oh, Father, now even I am beginning to believe."

Jatu looked at the shaded area. "Ah but, Captain, it is a circle a thousand miles across. How we will find a single island within . . . well, all I can say is that I think it will be a nearly impossible task."

Jinnarin, sitting cross-legged on the table, asked, "Can

we sail through those waters? I mean, if other ships are trapped, won't the *Eroean* get caught as well?"

Aravan nodded. "Even the starsilver bottom of the *Eroean* will not keep her free of the clutches of the weed should we sail therein. Oh, at the edges the weed is sparse, and the *Eroean* can easily fare through. But deeper within, the weed becomes thick, and there I would not take the ship. Nay, we will have to use flat-bottom boats of single sail to explore the central part, mayhap rowing as well."

Alamar glared up at all those standing around the table. "You are bound and determined to go there?"

Each person looked at all the others, and one by one, each nodded, though Frizian added, "Jatu is right. A thousand-mile circle contains some seven hundred fifty *thousand* square miles to search. I think it will be by the good graces of Dame Fortune alone that we find an island in such."

"Faugh!" snorted Alamar. "*Finding* the island is the trivial part. What will be difficult is *reaching* the island through mile after mile of that grasp."

Bokar cocked an eye at the elder. "And just how do you expect to find the island, Mage? Have you some magic spell of location which will do so?"

"Magic spell?" sneered Alamar. "Oh no, Dwarf, no *magic* spell."

Jinnarin leapt to her feet and stalked across the table and stood in front of Alamar, her fists on her hips. "You make me just want to scream, Alamar, clutching secrets to your bosom and sneering at others. Stop shilly-shallying about! Tell us, just *how* do you expect to find this tiny needle in its vast haycock?"

Disgruntled, Alamar's jaw shot out stubbornly, as if he were about to refuse to answer, but Jinnarin stomped her foot. Alamar sighed, and said, "Oh all right, Pysk, it's no great secret. You see, I plan to ask the Children of the Sea."

CHAPTER 24

Voyage Afar

Late Winter–Early Spring, 1E9575
[The Present]

The Children of the Sea!" blurted out Tink. "Bu-but they're just shipboard fables, aren't they?"

"Ha!" barked Alamar, "Fables? Oh no, boy, the Children of the Sea are anything but."

Tink turned to Aravan, and the Elf smiled. "Mage Alamar is right, Tink. The Children of the Sea are as real as thou or I."

"Exactly," declared Alamar. "And this Great Swirl . . . if there is an island within, the Children of the Sea will know."

"Hast thou had dealings with the Children before, Mage Alamar?"

"If I hadn't, Elf, well I wouldn't know how to call 'em to me, now would I?"

Aylis sighed. "Father once saved a Child of the Sea who had been blown ashore by a great cyclone. 'Twas on the Isle of Faro, I believe . . . right, Father?"

Alamar nodded, his gaze lost in reflection. "Um, yes. Water and waves nearly carried us away, running as they did way up into the very forest itself. Never saw such a blow. Anyhow, I found the Child unconscious at the foot of a great oak—stumbled across her, really. At first I thought she was dead, but faint breath stirred her breast. I took her to Lady Katlaw's tower—she's a healer, you know. Fixed her up, did Lady Katlaw, though the Child was a long time in recovering. I learned her language—

strange as it was, filled with clicks and chirps and other such—works well underwater, she said. Sinthe was her name. When she went back to the sea, she gave me this." Alamar slid back a sleeve revealing his golden bracelet set with a stone of red coral.

Aravan's hand strayed to the blue stone amulet about his own neck. "Has it any . . . power, Alamar?"

Alamar glared at Aravan but then glanced at Jinnarin, the Pysk yet standing before him, her fists still on her hips. "It lets me call them," he growled, adding, "though they won't come if just any jackfool is standing about. Too, they need to be somewhere nearby, else they don't, um, hear it."

"Hear it?" asked Jinnarin. "Does it make a noise?"

"Of course not, Pysk."

"Well, if it doesn't make a noise then how—?"

"Feel it, then," snapped Alamar. "Sense it. Whatever." He peered closely at the red coral, as if trying to see something.

"What Father is saying," murmured Aylis, "is that we don't know how it calls them or how they know. It is a thing beyond our ken . . . somewhat like your stone, Aravan."

Alamar looked up. "One of these days I'll know how it does what it does . . . when I've had a chance to study it."

"Father, you've been at it for two or three millennia and—"

"Not all the time, Daughter. Not steadily. When it becomes important to know, then I'll delve out its secret."

"Aha!" crowed Jinnarin. "So you would know another's secrets, eh? Black pot, black kettle, or so someone said once apast."

As Alamar puffed up to retort, Aravan intervened, stabbing his finger to the shaded area of the map. "It is settled then. Here is our goal. When we arrive, Mage Alamar will call upon the Children of the Sea. If there is an island in the weed, we will need flat-bottom boats to reach it, not the gigs we have"—Aravan glanced at Bokar—"and enough to take all of Bokar's warband. Jatu, tell Finch to make . . . eight flat-bottomed, single-sail, six-oared, eight-person dinghies. Have him put a sculling oarlock on the rear thwart." Aravan looked up and around at the others. "Unless there are objections . . ." None said aught. Aravan turned to the second officer. "Frizian, ready the crew to unfurl the silks—we sail at dawn's light."

"Aye, Captain," replied the Gelender. "And our course . . . ?"

"Make for the Cape of Storms."

"Aye, sir."

As Frizian strode from the salon, "Coo," breathed Tink, staring at the map, "that weed's halfway 'round the world, right?"

"Aye, Tink," said Jatu. "Very nearly the opposite side from where we now lie at anchor."

"How far is it 'tween here and there?"

"Some fourteen thousand miles 'round Old Stormy."

Tink's eyes narrowed. "Say, wouldn't it be closer to go the other way—past the Silver Cape instead?"

Jatu smiled. "Closer in miles, Tink, but longer in time." Jatu unrolled another map and his finger traced a route as he spoke. "You see, we could fare down alongside the western and southern continents and then angle for the Swirl. But we'd have to sail into the teeth of the polar winds, not only through the straits of the Silver Cape, but nearly all the way to the weed as well. Whereas, running 'round the Cape of Storms the winds favor us on the journey from here to the Swirl—that is, if the winds blow normal; if they do, the air will be mainly on our beam or at our backs most of the way. And should Dame Fortune favor us, we'll be there in eight to ten weeks."

Tink gazed at the map and let out a low whistle. "Oy, all that way and in such quick time. She's a wonder, she is, is the captain's lady, um, er"—Tink spluttered and, red-faced, looked up at Aylis in embarrassment—"I mean the *Eroean*, Lady Aylis. —Oh, not that you're not a wonder yourself"—he hastened to assure her—"I mean, you're the captain's lady too and all, and I, um, that is, I—"

Aylis tried to hold back her laughter, but Jatu's guffaws broke her resistance and carried her along as well, Jinnarin's trills providing counterpoint. Aravan threw a hand over his own mouth and tried to look stern, failing miserably.

"Stuff and nonsense, boy," cackled Alamar, "I think you put it very well, myself."

Amid the laughter, Tink grinned and said, "It's not every day someone like me gets to talk through his toes."

Alamar frowned. "What are you nattering about, boy? What's all this blather about 'talking through toes'?"

"Well, sir," replied Tink, "how else could a person like me speak but through my toes when my foot's in my mouth, eh?" At this the lad broke out in braying laughter, with Jatu, Aylis, Jinnarin, Alamar, and Aravan gleefully joining in.

When a modicum of quiet returned, Aravan clapped the cabin boy on the shoulder and said, "Tink, thou didst well here tonight, for it was thy cleverness which pointed the way—first to the Great Swirl and then to the link 'tween spider and galley. Well-done, Tink, well-done."

Tink ducked his head in acknowledgement, then swiftly gathered up the tea service and cups and fled. When he had gone, Aravan turned to Alamar and said, "When first we met I told thee that clever ideas oft come from the least expected quarters. Tink's contribution tonight is an example of such."

Alamar glared at Aravan. "Do you think I am so ignorant that I did not already know that?"

Before Aravan could reply, Jatu said, "I am not so certain that it was an unexpected quarter, Captain. Tink, well he is a bright lad. I think he'll go far."

Aravan smiled. "Aye, Jatu, he reminds me of thee at the same age."

"Oh no, Captain," rumbled Jatu, "I was much taller."

Again the salon rang with laughter.

The *Eroean* sailed out on the morning tide, a waning half Moon overhead, a following wind quartered off her aft starboard. Jinnarin watched as the land slid over the horizon abaft. She looked at the fox beside her and sighed. "Oh, Rux, it seems as if we've been on this ship forever."

Boder at the wheel peered down at the Pysk. "Well,

Lady Jinnarin, you came on board back in mid September and here it be nigh mid March. Now if my ciphering be right, that'd make it some six months gone—a half a year, or just days short of."

Jinnarin's eyes widened. *Two full seasons on the* Eroean, *and still no sign of Farrix!* Again she sighed. "Oh, Boder, six months? And according to Jatu, we are perhaps two Moons or so away from our destination. It seems I *will* sail the seas forever."

Boder sucked in his breath. "*Ooo,* Lady Jinnarin, don't go saying things like that. You'll curse the ship with those kind of words. Why, then we'd be like the *Grey Lady* herself, we would, and that's a fact."

"The *Grey Lady?*"

"Aye. A cursed ship sailing the night, her masts and rigging glowing with green witchfire, her ghostly crew forever trapped aboard."

"Oh, Boder, how ghastly. How came this to be?"

"Well, you see, they say that the ship wasn't always called the *Grey Lady*. But no one knows what her original name was, it was so long ago. Regardless, she set sail to round the Silver Cape, and on board there was but a single passenger, the son, it seems, of a sorceress—"

"A sorceress?"

"Yes."

"No, Boder, what I meant to ask is, what is a sorceress?"

"Oh. A sorceress, well, she's a Lady Mage, she is."

"Ah. Like Aylis."

Boder's eyes flew wide. "Oh no, Lady Jinnarin. I mean, Lady Aylis, she's a real Lady, whereas sorceresses, they're not Ladies at all. Instead, they be what you might call wicked."

"Oh. More like a Black Mage, then?"

"Yes. I suppose that'd describe them right enough."

Jinnarin turned up a palm. "I interrupted, Boder. Please go on with your story."

Boder made a small adjustment to the wheel. "Well, it was like I was saying, with a single passenger aboard, the ship set sail to round the Silver Cape.

"Now that passage is difficult in any season, and sudden storms are like to blow even in the calmest. But the ship was sailing in the autumntime, when unexpected storms are most likely down there. The cap'n, he warned the passenger of this and told him that should it come to a blow, to get to his cabin and stay there and not come on deck, else he'd likely be washed over.

"They sailed from their home port of Alkabar in Hyree, heading south and west, till one day they came to the waters of the Silver Cape. And lo! all was calm for an entire week, the ship beating her course into the polar wind, circling 'round the bottom of the world as it does.

"But just as they got to the clinch of the straits, came a monstrous blow—great greybeards rolling over the ship, slamming her and rolling her and pitching her this way and that, and driving her sideways and forwards and backwards and every which way.

"The passenger, he was screaming and shrieking for help and calling for someone to save him. But when he saw a bit of the brine sloshing under his door and jerked it open to see waves washing back and forth in the passageway outside his cabin, well he thought they were sinking, the fool. And ignoring the cap'n's orders, he bolted for the deck where the gigs were kept—ha! as if a tiny gig could weather such.

"No sooner did he run topside than a great greybeard rolled over the ship and when it was gone, well then, so was he.

"The cap'n, he couldn't do anything for it, and when the storm died down two days later, all he could do was sail back to Alkabar.

"Now the sorceress was shrieking mad when she heard her only son was lost, and she cursed that ship and all her crew to find her son or to sail the seas forever. And so, you see, Lady Jinnarin, that's why the *Grey Lady* is a ghost ship, sailing endlessly through the nights, her masts and rigging burning with witchfire.

"But now here is the worst of all. They say the *Grey Lady* sails about, trying to find the lost passenger, the ghost cap'n calling the lost one's name out over the waters. They also say if you hear what that name be, then you will suddenly find yourself trapped aboard the *Grey Lady* herself, sailing the seas to the end of time."

Boder fell silent and turned the wheel a bit.

"Do you believe this tale, Boder?" asked Jinnarin. "Has anyone ever seen this *Grey Lady?*"

Boder glanced down at the Pysk. "Those who told me, Lady Jinnarin, they swear it is true, though they themselves were told long ago."

"You mean it's been passed down from sailor to sailor?"

Boder nodded.

"And none you know has ever seen her?"

"No. Though none I know doubts the facts either, Lady Jinnarin."

"Hm," murmured Jinnarin, then whispered to Rux, "sounds like a sea story to me, Rux. What do you think?"

Rux swung his head toward his mistress and gave her a little lick, but he kept whatever opinion he might have had concerning the tale entirely to himself.

Southeasterly sailed the *Eroean,* the wind starboard aft, until she came to the Doldrums of the Crab some seven days later. The wind fell and shifted about till it ran off the port beam, but at no time did it die entirely and so the Elvenship fared steadily across the belt of the calms, and a day later she was sailing briskly again.

Steadily, too, the climate had warmed, for they had sailed south away from winter's grasp and toward spring, the vernal equinox drawing nigh.

Springday found them in tropical waters south of the doldrums, and that night, as a warm wind blew, Jatu and Jinnarin watched as Aravan and Aylis paced the slow Elven rite celebrating the coming of spring.

Still south and east sailed the *Eroean,* and early in the morning of the twenty-ninth day of March they came to the edge of the Midline Irons, the wind dying completely, the silks of the Elvenship falling lank. Gigs were unshipped and manned, the crews rowing, towing the *Eroean,* the Men canting their chanteys in the hot, still air. All that day they pulled southward, the fierce Sun a burning furnace shining down on a molten copper sea. Crews were changed often in the torrid heat, Dwarves taking turns and stroking to War chants. The Sun set and sultry night fell, yet the rowing continued without letup, sweat pouring down, and steadily the ship was drawn southward across the hot, glassy sea.

The following day, late in the sweltering afternoon a darkness gathered low on the eastern horizon, roiling clouds mounting up and up. Slowly the dark grew, moving toward them, and high on the masts the starscraper sails belled slightly as a faint breeze drifted 'cross the deeps, the air beginning to move at last. "Ship the crews and gigs," ordered Aravan, and all boats were recalled and taken up. Moonrakers, gallants, topsails, stays, jibs, and mains, all silks clutched at the frail zephyrs now stirring as the storm crept toward them. Lightning could be seen stroking in the core of the darkness, and grey rain fell down into the sea, sweeping across the waters as would a giant broom. Now the wind sprang into fullness, blowing toward the storm, the air rushing inward and up. "Trim her, Reydeau," called Aravan, "run south." The bo's'n piped the sails about, the crew haling on the halyards and sheets, the wheelman setting the rudder. Now the wind shifted full 'round as the storm rushed over them, plunging the ship into darkness, and rain sheeted down, cold and drenching. Lines were haled and belayed, the silks catching the blow, the *Eroean* running due south, wind on the larboard beam, lightning shattering the skies, thunderclaps hammering the air.

Alamar, wet and dripping, came muttering across the deck, heading toward his cabin. "Isn't it wonderful," cried Jinnarin, her face to the chill rain.

"What a damnfool notion!" snapped Alamar, a glare of lightning illumining the deck. Suddenly, his finger shot out as he pointed at Rux, the fox dashing past, running for the rear quarters door. "Of the two of you, Pysk, only he seems to have any sense." Alamar stomped onward, Jinnarin's trilling laugh following, though she herself stayed put.

And southward drove the *Eroean,* escaping the Midline Irons, flying through a darkness rived by thundering glare, rain hammering down, Fortune favoring the Elvenship running on the wings of the storm.

As bolt after bolt stroked down through the night, of a sudden Alamar jolted upright in his bunk, exclaiming, "Aha! So *that's* what it is!"

Again a flash of lightning shattered the blackness, the glare flaring through the porthole, momentarily etching all with dazzling light, brilliant afterimages dancing in the eyes when darkness returned.

As another flare lit the cabin, Alamar stumbled out from his bed. Crossing the rolling floor, he leaned over and pounded on the boards nailed across the lower side of the other bunk. "Pysk! Pysk! Wake up!"

He then made his way to the lantern in its wall sconce and fumbled about with its striker, lighting the lamp at last, its yellow glow filling the quarters. "Pysk! I said wake up!" he called, crossing back to the bunk. He kicked at the tiny door—"Ow!"—stubbing his toes, and hobbled to a chair and plopped down. As he clutched his foot and massaged it, the wee door opened and Jinnarin stepped out from her under-bunk quarters, rubbing her eyes, Rux following after.

"What is it, Alamar?" Jinnarin yawned.

Another glare of lightning flared outside.

"There, see!" called Alamar, pointing at the porthole.

Again Jinnarin yawned. "See what? The window? You called me to look at a window?"

Thunder hammered above the wind and wave and pelting rain.

"No, no!" barked Alamar. "Outside!"

"Oh, rain." Slowly, she smacked her lips, tasting her tongue, still trying to shake the dregs of sleep from her.

"What's in that head of yours, Pysk? Solid rock?"

Jinnarin glared at him, now awake. "If you're going to insult me, I'm heading back to bed." Jinnarin turned to leave, Rux ahead of her disappearing under the bunk.

Once again a bolt flashed down, this one nearby. "The lightning," called Alamar as a thunderclap boomed.

Jinnarin turned back, her head cocked to one side. "The lightning? Are you afraid of the lightning, Alamar?"

Alamar gritted his teeth in frustration, but said through clenched jaws, "The lightning, the plumes— they're one and the same."

"What are you trying to tell me, Alamar? Make it plain."

Alamar threw up his hands in exasperation and said,

"Make it plain? Make it plain? Why, it's as plain as the nose on your face."

"What?" shrieked Jinnarin. "What's as plain as my nose?" She looked cross-eyed down at her nose, then back at Alamar as the Mage began to cackle, his frustration turning to wild laughter.

"Oh, if you could only see how you just looked, Pysk," crowed Alamar. Then the Mage crossed his own eyes down at his nose. "Like this."

Jinnarin stomped her foot, but her giggles betrayed her.

Another lightning bolt flared outside.

Alamar uncrossed his eyes and, smiling, turned to the porthole. Suddenly he sobered. "In your dream, in the sending, the black ship's masts are stroked by lightning, neh?"

Jinnarin nodded. So . . . ?"

"So just this, Pysk, I told you that things are not what they seem in dreams, right?"

Again Jinnarin nodded, but said nothing.

"Well then, Pysk, I think that whoever is sending this dream—"

"Farrix," murmured Jinnarin.

"All right, have it your way," conceded Alamar, then continued, "Farrix is trying to tell you that someone on a ship is drawing down plumes from the aurora; but in the dream, the plumes become lightning bolts instead."

"Yes!" cried Jinnarin, enlightenment illuminating her face. "You have it, Alamar! That's exactly what it must be! The plumes and the lightning: they *are* one and the same. And that means—"

"What it means, Pysk, is that Durlok is behind it all. The plumes, Farrix's disappearance, the sending, all. And in the sending, the ship is supposed to be Durlok's ship, his galley, drawing down plumes—that is what you are meant to see in the dream."

Jinnarin nodded. "But instead it's a lightning-stroked galleon, which then becomes a spider, but never a plume-gathering galley."

"Because," interjected Alamar, "dream images are not always what they seem to be."

"And the green web?"

Alamar shook his head. "I am beginning to believe that it is indeed the trapping weed in the Sindhu Sea."

"If it is, Alamar, then we've solved it all."

"Oh no, Pysk, we will have solved only the least of it."

"Least of it? What do you mean."

"Just this: although we might discover where Durlok lurks, we still don't know why."

"Why what?"

"Why he draws down plumes from the boreal lights, Pysk. What are they for?"

"Oh," said Jinnarin. Then she added, "Or for that matter, Alamar, just what does all this have to do with Farrix? I mean, that Farrix is involved, I do not question. But the hows and whys ... well, therein lies another mystery."

Alamar nodded, stroking his white beard. "One thing for certain ..."

As lightning flared outside nearby, thunder whelming close after, Jinnarin looked up. "And that is ... ?"

"That is, Pysk, with Durlok involved ... it can't be good."

On the following day, the first of April, the storm abated, the clouds running westerly as the *Eroean* escaped the Midline Irons and slowly came back to its intended course, now tacking a zigzag route back and forth across the southeasterly wind. And when evening drew down, the skies were clear, and the Sun set and the full Spring Moon rose. And late that night under Elwydd's Light and beneath the bright spangle of stars, Jinnarin and Rux paced out the Fox Rider rite of spring, Aravan, Aylis, Alamar, Jatu, and Bokar watching as the tiny Pysk and her fox made obeisance to Adon and His Daughter for renewing the life of the world.

When the rite came to an end, they retired to the captain's salon to drink a toast to spring, Aylis with a crystal of sherry and Jinnarin with a porcelain thimble of Vanchan dark, the others sipping brandy from crystal cups.

"To the renewal of life, eh," proposed Bokar, to which they all raised their cups and said, *Aye!* then downed a sip.

"Peculiar," declared Jatu, when the toast was done.

"In Tchanga, or for that matter, in all the Lands south of the midline, especially those below the Latitude of the Goat, the coming of spring heralds the end of the growing season in those southern Realms. Then is when we harvest. Just the opposite of the northern lats. Were I to have made the toast, then I would have given thanks not for the coming of new life, new growth, but instead for the reaping of crops, for the yield of nature's bounty."

"Hmm," mused Jinnarin. "I never thought of that, Jatu. Spring in the north is autumn in the south—"

"Aye, and summer and winter are reversed as well."

"Oh my," declared Jinnarin, "do you think I got it all garbled—my prayers to Elwydd and Adon, that is?"

Jatu laughed, as did the others, the black Man shaking his head and saying, "Fear not, Lady Jinnarin, I think They will sort all out."

Alamar's shaggy brows drew down, a dark look on his face.

"What is it, Father?" asked Aylis.

"Ahh, I was just thinking that we're sailing into winter down 'round the Cape of Storms and wondering what the weather will be like when we reach there."

Aravan shrugged. "Depending on the winds, we should be at the cape some four weeks hence. It will be cold, stormy, blizzards sweeping the waters."

"Damnation!" spat Alamar, scowling. "We've sailed all the way from the end of one winter to the beginning of another. These old bones can't take too much of such . . . not without fortification, that is." He emptied his glass then held it out for more brandy, smiling as it was refilled.

Jinnarin grinned at the elder, then sobered. "I was talking to Boder. He told me of the storms 'round the Silver Cape. Is the cape where we're going the same?"

Aravan shook his head. "Nay, Lady Jinnarin. The Silver Cape is much worse, especially in the winter."

"Oh, good," said Jinnarin, taking a sip from her thimble of dark wine, then adding, "I mean it's good that we're going to the gentler place."

"Ha!" barked Bokar. "Gentle? I should say not! It is not called the Cape of Storms for idle reason."

"Oh, bad," said the Pysk, to the agreement of all.

*   *   *

In but ten days they came to the Calms of the Goat, and once again Fortune favored them, for they were not trapped in doldrums, a light, shifty wind bearing them across, the towing gigs remaining on board. And during this time, as on all the voyage, shipboard life maintained its routine: Aylis continued to instruct Aravan in the tongue of the Mages; Jinnarin and Alamar played tokko and squabbled; Rux ranged the holds, hunting elusive rodents; Bokar and the warband drilled at arms; and Jatu, Frizian, and the sailing crew kept the ship steadfastly bearing southeastward, while below decks, Carpenter Finch and his apprentice, Quill, along with the Dwarves, when they were not drilling, constructed flat-bottomed dinghies.

Too, during this time, Jinnarin's fearful nightmare continued to come sporadically, but she and Aylis did not venture another dreamwalk within.

As they passed beyond the Calms of the Goat the wind shifted about, until it blew steadily from the west, across their starboard aft quarter, and they set their sails to make the most of it, tacking and hauling no longer required. Gradually, toward the polar latitudes they sailed, the air now chill at night, the wind strengthening the farther south they fared.

Now they began to swing more and more easterly, as into icy rains and frigid clear days and snow squalls they ran, and in the skies above, the southern lights flickered. In but another month or so this austral aurora would burn brightly and writhe in great luminous folds, just as had the borealis in the north.

"Lor, Alamar, do you think that Durlok calls plumes down in the south as well?" asked Jinnarin, her eyes peering at the night sky, a faint corona occasionally glimmering above.

Alamar squinted at the gleam, then growled, "Maybe yes, maybe no. If I knew why he did it, I could say for certain."

Fifteen days beyond the Calms of the Goat they rounded the southernmost point of the Cape of Storms, the *Eroean* driving hard through a blizzard, the wild wind directly aft.

As the ship cut through the heavy waves, Aravan stepped from the wheelhouse and into the passageway leading to the captain's lounge, the Elf heading for his and Aylis's quarters beyond. Passing Alamar's room, he heard Jinnarin crowing in victory while the Mage cried foul, and Aravan chuckled to himself and strode on.

Entering the cabin, he found Aylis sitting at the table, a spread of cards lying open before her, a stricken look on her face. "*Chieran,* what is it?"

Aylis looked up at Aravan, then gestured at the cards. "Deadly danger, my love. Though I am blocked from discovering specifically what it is, still there is no doubt that we sail toward peril dire."

"At the Great Swirl?"

Aylis gazed again at the layout. "So it would seem."

Aravan glanced at the cards—a random spread to his eyes. He took her hand in his. "If so, *chieran,* then we should know its nature within a twenty-one day or less, for even now we pass the horn of the cape. From here it is a straight run to the weed. And given that the winds do not desert us . . ."

"Three weeks?"

Aravan nodded, then lifted her hand and pressed his lips to her fingers.

Steadily, a point or so north of east sailed the *Eroean,* leaving the frigid polar waters behind, faring into the more temperate clime of the variable zone. And in the noon hour on the fourteenth of May, seventeen days after rounding the cape, the foremast lookout called down to the watch below, "Weed ho! Weed ho, dead ahead!"

Jinnarin and Aylis stood on the foredeck—the Pysk on the stemblock, the seeress at the rail—and peered into the distance ahead. And with hammering hearts they glanced at one another and nodded, their visages grim, for in the noontime Sun, slowly, inexorably, the Elvenship fared into the waters of a pale green sea.

CHAPTER 25

Children of the Sea

Spring, 1E9575
[The Present]

Aravan stepped onto the foredeck and peered over the side at the *Eroean*'s bow cleaving the pale green water. Within the brine running aft could be seen long branching tendrils of grass-green weed. "Jatu!" he called. "A weighted line forward! And furl all silks but the forestay and spanker and mains and cro'jack!"

As Rico piped the crew, Jatu himself brought a sounding line, a heavy lead bob at its end. "Captain?"

"Cast it over and let it run deep, Jatu. We will use it to gauge the grasp of the weed."

At Jinnarin's puzzled look, Aravan explained. "To keep the *Eroean* from being trapped, we will take the measure of the weed and stop while we are yet in safe waters, for the closer we come to the center, the thicker it becomes until it is nought but a clutching snare. I would not have us suffer the doom of others . . . ships unwittingly caught—storm blown, ill-captained, or ill-fated, it matters not—all have been lost."

"Oh, Adon," breathed Jinnarin, scanning the horizon, "a sea of lost ships."

"Aye," said Jatu, giving the plumb a vertical length of slack, "some call it that." He whirled the bob 'round a time or two and cast it hard, the cord uncoiling smoothly, the lead weight flying far to the fore and landing with a small splash.

Aylis turned to Aravan. "How far inward can we sail?"

Aravan glanced up at the Men furling the silks and turned up his palms. "I know not, *chieran*. Running only on the stay and spanker and mains and jack, mayhap a day or two; mayhap but an hour. It all depends on the weed."

Alamar came shuffling forward. Looking up at the crew in the rigging, he said, "I see you take down silk. Slowing the ship, eh?"

Aravan nodded. "Aye. It would not do to run full tilt through these dire waters."

Jatu drew up the sounding line. "A small amount of weed, Captain. No threat at all. We could run through such forever."

Aravan shook his head. "Fear not, Jatu, it will change."

"For the worse, too," called out Bokar, the Dwarf just then coming up the steps, the rest of his warband—armed and armored—pouring onto the decks, axes and warhammers and crossbows at hand, all Dwarves moving to the ballistas to make them ready as well. Bokar eyed his warband, then turned to Aylis and Jinnarin. "But if there be some green-tentacled monster in this weed, we will be prepared."

Another twenty-eight hours they sailed, moving steadily toward the center of the Swirl, the ship covering another one hundred sixty miles. And all the while the weed gradually thickened until the amount gathered by the plumb line at last became substantial. Aravan once again stood on the foredeck, and he finally called out, "Heave to and maintain!" and Jatu headed her up into the wind, the silks flapping lank, the bosom of the sea slowly rising and falling as of a sleeping creature softly breathing, the weed acting to smooth the waves into long, gentle swells.

Aravan turned to the Dwarves at the foredeck ballistas. "Stand ready, for we are dead in the water."

Slowly the ship drifted, the current forming the Great Swirl carrying her deosil. "Were we north of the midline," mused Aravan, "I deem we would run widdershins."

"There's a difference?" asked Jinnarin.

"Aye, Lady Jinnarin. In the north the air, storms, water . . . all tend to turn widdershins—against the Sun.

To the south it is just the opposite . . . deosil—with the Sun. —Why? I know not. Part of Adon's plan, mayhap."

"Oh," said Jinnarin, peering down over the side, puzzled, seeing nought but drifting weed and pale green water, the Pysk, no closer to understanding why things north of the midline should be any different from those south. At last she said, "I suppose it's for the same reason that the seasons are opposite, too."

Aravan glanced at the angle of the Sun and looked at the Pysk as if to say something, but before he could comment Jinnarin turned, peering aft. "Well, it's up to Alamar now. Where is he?"

"When last I saw, he was in the salon arguing with Bokar as to whether warriors are wanted on this task."

"And . . . ?"

"See for thyself, Lady Jinnarin," answered Aravan, pointing sternward.

Bokar and Alamar came up out of the aft quarters, the armsmaster scowling, the Mage with a triumphant sneer on his face. Aylis and Jatu came after, the seeress looking exasperated, the black Man laughing. Jatu called Rico to him and gave instructions, and swiftly the bo's'n assembled a boat crew, two Dwarves included. Leaving the others behind, Bokar came stomping toward the foredeck, muttering in his beard, only part of which Jinnarin overheard—the words "obstinate old fool" among his grumbles.

Aylis embraced her father and kissed him on the cheek, and the elder clambered into one of the newly built dinghies, which was then swung out on davits, the rowing crew entering the boat after. The dinghy was lowered, Aylis watching until it floated free, then she came forward with Jatu.

As they came onto the foredeck, "Lady Aylis," growled Bokar, "does your sire never listen to reason?"

Before Aylis could answer, Jatu said, "Oh come, Bokar, he was right, you know."

Bokar bristled. "Jatu, we don't know *what* kind of creatures lurk beneath this weed."

"Agreed," responded Jatu. "But this we *do* know: no Child of the Sea will come to Alamar as long as one of us is about—be we Man, Dwarf, Lady Mage, Pysk, Elf, or aught else."

"And just *how* do we *know* this?"

Aylis turned to Bokar. "We know this because my father said so."

"Is he always correct?"

"No, Armsmaster, but he is always truthful."

Bokar turned his face to the sea and watched as the dinghy drew farther away. "Then let us hope that he is correct as well as sincere."

Tivir came to the foredeck bearing a tray of tea, offering it all 'round. Aravan and Jatu each took a cup, the others declining, their eyes fixed on the now distant boat.

"Oy," said Tivir, peering at the dinghy as well, "they tell me Maige Aliamar needs t' be alone t' meet th' Children o' the Sea. Naw, if 'at's so, then just 'ow is 'e going t' do it, eh?"

Jatu turned to the cabin boy. "Tivir, your meaning . . . ?"

"Just this, Mister Jatu: Oi mean, if 'e's got t' be alone, then is th' crew going t' leap from th' dinghy 'n' swim back? Or is 'e instead going t' tread water? Wot'll it be, eh?"

Jinnarin grinned. "Just watch, Tivir."

Bokar growled, "I told him that he should tow a dinghy after, but did he listen? Oh no. No sitting about in a boat for him. Instead—"

"There he goes," interjected Jatu.

While the Men and Dwarves aboard the dinghy gesticulated wildly, as if arguing with Alamar, the elder clambered over the starboard wale and walked out on the surface of the sea, as if the long, low swells were nought but dry land gradually rising and falling.

"Oh, lor!" breathed Tivir. "Naow Oi've seen it all, Oi 'ave."

With a disdainful wave of a hand, Alamar dismissed the crew of the dinghy, and they turned about and pulled oars for the *Eroean,* coming back considerably faster than they had gone.

When they had nearly reached the ship, Alamar drew up his sleeve and squatted down, immersing the wrist with the bracelet into the brine. He remained motionless for some lengthy time, then with effort stood upright again, holding his hands to the small of his back and slowly twisting and stretching.

"Oh my," murmured Aylis, "he does so need to return to Vadaria."

Time passed, an hour or so, the ship continuing its deosil drift as the Sun crept down the sky, and all the crew stood transfixed at the larboard rail and marvelled over the old Mage standing as he did on nought but water, the dinghy crew below marvelling as well. And on the foredeck, Aylis, Aravan, Jinnarin, Jatu, and Bokar stood watch . . . and slow swells passed below in the pale green sea.

At times Alamar paced in a small circle; at other times he squatted and plunged his bracelet into the brine, each time getting up more slowly.

"How long can he keep this up, *chieran?*" asked Aravan.

Aylis shook her head. "Father says that it is a simple casting. Even so, given his lack of youth, it must be draining. —Oh where are the Children of the Sea?"

Tivir brought more tea, along with slabs of bread and a new jar of Tholander honey, and this time all partook of his bounty. And still the Sun crept down toward the horizon and still the ship drifted. Until . . .

"Cap'n," called down the mainmast lookout, "something moving under the weed!"

"Where away?" called Jatu.

"It's making a run at the Mage!" the lookout cried.

"Kruk!" spat Bokar. "I *knew* that he should have warriors with him! —Stand by ballistas!" he called to the crews. "Ready to cast!"

Jinnarin's heart hammered in her breast, and Aylis's lips drew into a grim line.

"Hold, Bokar!" barked Aravan, the amulet at his throat emitting no chill. He called to the mainmast lookout, "Man-size or bigger?"

"There's more than one—"

"Look! Look!" cried Jinnarin.

In a wide ring about Alamar five dolphin came leaping out of the water, gracefully arching up and over and down, splashing into the weedy brine, ripples marking the surface where they had been. Again the pod leapt, still in a ring, this time closer to the Mage.

"Oh my," breathed Jinnarin, "how elegant."

Aravan glanced down at her. "I deem, Lady Jinnarin, that they herald the coming of the Children of the Sea."

Once more the dolphin arched up and over, even closer to Alamar, the splash of their entry showering the Mage. Jinnarin burst out laughing as Alamar raised a clenched fist and shook it at where the dolphin had been, though she could not hear what he was yelling.

Now in a wide ring about Alamar, the dolphin came to the surface and took up station, their sleek muzzles out of water, their curious eyes fixed upon the Mage, their high-pitched voices chattering, calling.

And then another sleek head broke through the water, and another and one more—three altogether, with flowing silver locks . . .

. . . The Children of the Sea had arrived.

Slowly the Morfolk swam to and fro, seldom pausing, maintaining a margin of four yards or so between themselves and the stranger.

Alamar gazed down at the three, with their translucent, pale jade flesh and delicate elfin features, their large, catlike light green eyes and their silvery hair spreading in the water. A bit smaller than Magekind, they were, and a long, wide, webbed fin ran down each side of their supple bodies, from shoulder to ankle, merging with their finlike feet, and a similar fin ran along the outside of each arm. All three returned the Mage's gaze, and one—the one slightly to the fore—glanced at the drifting ship and then back at Alamar and raised a hand, his long, webbed fingers spread wide. *"¡Tklat!"*

As the pod of dolphin slowly swam a circular path, stopping every now and again to turn a dark eye to the proceedings, Alamar searched his mind for the tongue he had learned long past, for unlike his daughter, he could not simply say a <word> and *know* a language.

["Yes, it was I,"] he said. Alamar drew back his sleeve and turned his wrist so that the bracelet glittered in the angling sunlight.

The Child to the fore cocked his head to the side, his slitted pupils expanding slightly. Then he smiled, his wide mouth showing a row of pointed white teeth. ["You are a Friend?"]

["Yes. I was given this by Sinthe, she whom I saved at the Isle of Faro."]

["Faro?"]

["Yes. It is in the ... hm ... it is a small island in what are called the Twilight Waters, there on the edge of the Bright Sea. It has a tower on it: Lady Katlaw's tower."]

Now the swimmers looked at one another and smiled, and the one to the fore turned back to Alamar and said, ["Ah, Lady Katlaw. Another Friend."]

One of the Merfolk swam 'round the leader and said, ["I would see this bracelet of yours."]

Alamar grunted down to one knee on the water and held out his wrist. Timidly, the one came forward and reached up a slender finger to the circlet, gently touching the red coral inset. Now through the pellucid water Alamar could see that she was female, somewhat like Sinthe, with her small breasts and sleek form, the cartilaginous gill slits along her rib cage now closed since she was breathing air. She turned her exotic face to his and smiled, and Alamar felt his heart clench, she was so strangely beautiful.

["I am Rania"]—liquid as silk, she turned and gestured toward the others—["this is Nalin, and that is Imro beyond."] Rania faced Alamar once again. ["And you are ... ?"]

["Alamar. I am a Mage."]

Rania wafted backwards and looked at him kneeling on the water and laughed. ["That, Mage Alamar, we deduced, given where you now stand. What we didn't know was whether you were the Friend who called. Your bracelet, though, answers that question."]

Imro surged forward. ["That ship"]—he raised a hand and pointed a finger toward the *Eroean,* a talon unsheathing, indicating his displeasure—["you came aboard it?"]

["Yes,"] responded Alamar, grunting back to his feet.

["You are accounted a Friend, yet you bring others with you? Those who are not Friends? Destroyers?"] Now a full set of talons sprang forth from the tips of Imro's fingers, and the web down the length of his arm spread stiffly wide, with evenly spaced, wickedly sharp spines jutting out the full of its length.

Alamar glared at Imro, but before he could reply, Nalin spoke: ["We know that ship, Imro. Long has it plied the Mother Waters, never to the harm of the"]— Nalin thumped himself on the chest—["¡Nat!io ... nor to the"]—he swept his arm toward the encircling ring of dolphin—["A!miî. Imro, I think this vessel no threat, even though it bears those we ordinarily name destroyers."]

Rania added, ["Imro, you know that there has ever been a Friend aboard that ship. I can feel the token he bears even now."]

Alamar smiled at the female. ["His name is Aravan. He has always been master of the *Eroean*."]

Nalin drifted back and grinned. ["Ah, so that is his name: Aravan. —And her name, too. We ¡Nat!io call her *Silver Bottom*. Long has she plied the Mother Waters. She is swift, through not as swift as we."] His voice took on a tinge of pride. ["When she comes through our demesne at night, at times we race before her bow ... along with the A!miî."]

As Imro's claws slowly retracted and his arm fins relaxed, he faced Alamar again. ["Why are you here and why have you called us? Especially, why have you called us to this foul place?"]

["Ha!"] barked Alamar. ["So you name it a foul place, too."]

Rania took up a tendril of green weed, holding it out of the water. ["Long ago it was a place of great bounty, and we hunted and frolicked within. But now we like it not, and we were far from here when you summoned, else we would have come sooner."]

["You have not answered my questions,"] said Imro impatiently.

Alamar glanced over from Rania to Imro, and his eyes narrowed as he readied a retort, but Rania interrupted, ["Why have you called us, Friend?"]

Alamar looked back down at her. ["We pursue an evildoer, one who caused great harm long past and is like to cause even more. We think he sometimes comes to the Great Swirl, here to the clutches of the weed. His ship ... although we are not certain, we deem to be a *galley*."]

["G-¡g!alley?"] Nalin had trouble pronouncing the

Common word and he added tick-tock clicks to it. He cocked his head. ["What is a *¡g!alley?*"]

["A ship of many oars, long and sweeping, propelled by rowers. Sails, too."]

Rania sucked air through her sharp teeth and backed water and said, ["It is black, with evil aboard. Vile destroyers. We give it wide berth."]

Alamar demanded, ["You have seen it?"]

All three nodded, ringlets spreading outward, Imro adding, ["And this one you hunt, you say he is aboard?"]

["Yes,"] gritted Alamar. ["Do you know where it is, the black *galley?*"]

The three looked at one another and shook their heads.

"Damnation!" spat Alamar in Common. Puffing his cheeks, he blew out his breath, then said, ["We think there might be an island somewhere in the weed. Do you know of any?"]

Rania's cat-eyes widened. ["Yes. But it is an evil place now. We do not go there."]

["Will you lead us there?"]

Startled, Imro sounded a harsh clattering clack, and the ring of dolphin disappeared, diving under. ["You do not hear well, Mage,"] snapped Imro. ["Rania said that we never go there."]

["Listen to me, you stupid minnow,"] shouted Alamar, ["I've had about enough of your suspicions, your gall. We came to rid the world of an evil, and you keep—"]

A piercing shrill note came from the throat of Rania. She spun toward Imro. ["Imro, he is a Friend!"] she declared. Then she rounded on Alamar. ["And you, Alamar, you must remember that we are Friends, too!"] A subdued quiet fell upon the sea.

Imro submerged and emitted a clicking clatter of chirps. Of a sudden the dolphin reappeared, once again forming a ring.

Nalin's exotic features were sunk in thought as he drifted. At last he said, ["If those on the *Silver Bottom* rid the island of the evil, and rid the Mother Waters of the black *¡g!alley* as well, then perhaps the weed will become ours again."]

["Exactly!"] proclaimed Alamar. ["If that *Child*"]—he

pointed a finger at Imro—["had only listened long enough before getting uppity—"]

Rania's warning voice cut sharply through Alamar's tirade: ["Friend, remember my words."]

Alamar spluttered to silence.

Nalin looked at the others. ["I say we go."]

Imro asked sourly, ["Go where?"]

["Show them the way."]

Rania again sharply sucked air in through her pointed teeth. ["Go to the island? Shouldn't we put this to the *Grex?*"]

Nalin shook his head. ["Those elders? It would take them a spawning season to make up their minds."]

Rania nodded grudgingly, sunlight sparkling off the ripples of her movement. ["What about the weed? On the surface it becomes impassable, or nearly so."]

Imro scowled. ["It's a stupid plan. They will never be able to get *Silver Bottom* through."]

["Ha!"] barked Alamar. ["We don't plan on taking the *Eroean* any farther. We have flat-hulled boats for that task. All we need to know is where to go."]

Imro yet scowled. ["*We* can pass the weed by swimming far under, down where it does not reach. But then how will the *A!miî* go? They need to breathe air, and they cannot swim up through the thick weed from below. They are faithful protectors, and I would not wish to leave them behind while we go alone into the dangerous weed. And these destroyers, they breathe air as well. They, too, cannot go under ... which means if we are to guide them, then we must do it by swimming on the surface, through the weed, which will only grow thicker the farther inward we go. And so, Nalin, just how do you propose that we and the *A!miî* pass the weed?"]

["Simple,"] replied Nalin, ["we will call a *¡th!rix.* We will let *it* clear the way."]

Rania shook her head. ["We cannot ask a gentle *¡th!rix* to go to the island. That would be wicked."]

Now it was Alamar who scowled. ["What is this—this *¡th!rix?*"]

["Besides,"] added Rania, ["*I* will not go all the way to the island. It is an evil place."]

Nalin drifted over to Rania. ["We will only ask the *¡th!rix* to take us to where the island can be seen, guiding

Friend Alamar and his companions through the weed. Then we will turn back, riding the *¡th!rix* out."]

Alamar threw up his hands. ["Would one of you young *jackfools* tell me what a *¡th!rix* is?"]

Nalin looked at Rania and Imro. ["Well, shall we do it?"]

Rania glanced back and forth between the two. ["And none of us goes to the island—neither you, Nalin, nor Imro nor I . . . nor the *¡th!rix,* right?"] At Nalin's nod she inclined her head, *Yes.*

Imro stared long at the *Eroean,* then at Alamar, and finally he nodded, too.

Nalin spun to Alamar. ["We will take you to within sight of the isle."]

Alamar stood glaring at the sky, his arms folded tightly, his chin jutting out stubbornly, his foot tapping the water, ringlets rippling outward. ["I am not going anywhere until someone tells me just what this blasted *¡th!rix* is!"]

Rania laughed up at him, her voice liquid silver. ["You will see, Friend Alamar. Oh yes indeed, you will see."]

At the sound of her voice, Alamar looked down at her incredible elfin face and could do nought but smile.

"Oh, oh, look, there they go," cried Jinnarin. "Oh my!"

In the distance the Children of the Sea rolled a surface dive, the silver-haired Merfolk speeding down and away, and some of the crew at the rail cried out that the Children had the tails of fish, claiming that they had glimpsed them, though it was not so. As the Merfolk dived, the ring of dolphin broke, and leaping and plunging alongside one another they swiftly sped away.

Alamar turned toward the *Eroean,* gesturing wearily, and the crew in the dinghy below pushed off and began rowing out toward him. When they reached him, aided by two sailors Alamar clambered over the side and in. The crew then turned about and rowed back to the *Eroean.* Davit ropes were lowered and affixed, and the dinghy was winched upward. As the boat was swung aboard, Aylis looked at the drawn face of her father—he was weary yet strangely flushed. Aravan helped him to climb out, and Jinnarin, bouncing and jiggling on the balls of her feet in excitement, asked, "Well, Alamar, what happened out there?"

Alamar looked down at her, a beatific smile on his face. "What happened? Out there? I'll tell you what happened, Pysk: I fell in love again, that's what."

"Oh, lordy, he's been charmed by a Mermaid," declared Artus, standing nearby.

"Pish tush!" poo pooed Jamie. "There ain't no such thing as Mermaids."

Artus turned and pointed out to the sea where Alamar had stood. "Then tell me, Mister Smarty, what do you call those we just saw dive under if not Mermaids?"

"Is it true?" asked Jinnarin. "Were you charmed by a Mermaid, Alamar?"

"Of course not, Pysk," snapped Alamar, but Aylis looked at her father and wondered if his denial hadn't come a bit too swiftly.

Bokar cut through the chitchat. "Is there an island, Mage Alamar? If so, where?"

"Island? Yes." Alamar nodded. "Where? They did not say. Inwards, is all."

"If you did not discover where lies the island," growled Bokar, "then how are we to find it?"

Alamar drew himself up, peering down his nose at the armsmaster. "They will guide us, that's how. Dawn tomorrow they return to do so, bringing with them a ¡th!rix to clear the way."

"A th-th," stuttered Jinnarin, unable to cope with the clicks. "Hmm, whatever you said, Alamar—what is it?"

Alamar threw up his hands in delayed frustration and snapped, "They wouldn't tell me!"

"Bah!" burst out Bokar, his own frustration mounting. "Tell me, Mage, just what *did* you find out?"

Alamar glared at the armsmaster. "What I found out, *Dwarf,* is that Durlok plies a black galley in these waters."

"Aha!" crowed Jinnarin. "The black ship! So then we were right!"

Aylis looked down at the Pysk. "Oh, Jinnarin, then this must truly be the pale green sea."

Jinnarin nodded vigorously, then turned to Alamar. "What about the crystal castle? Is it on this island?"

A stricken look came over the elder's face, but then his jaw jutted out and he said, "I didn't ask."

"What?"

Alamar raised his voice. "I said, Pysk, I didn't ask."

Jinnarin was stunned. "You . . . didn't . . . ask?"

"Have you lost your hearing, Pysk?"—Alamar's voice was a near shout—"I say once more: I didn't ask!"

Her eyes narrowed, and she gritted out through clenched teeth, "Alamar, how could you not ask?"

"Ha!" exclaimed Bokar. "Just as he did not ask about the location of the isle! Ten thousand things could happen between now and dawn tomorrow, yet this Mage—"

Aravan's voice cracked out, "Armsmaster, 'tis enough!"

Alamar puffed up to reply, but Aylis stepped before him. "Aravan is right, Father: 'tis enough. Bickering among ourselves serves no end."

Jatu squatted down beside the Pysk. "Regardless as to whether or no the crystal castle stands thereon, Lady Jinnarin, we are bound for the isle on the morrow. We will know soon enough."

Throughout the evening the *Eroean* maintained station—first, drifting in the current, and then setting the jibs, stays, and spanker to return to the starting point, where they began drifting again. And as the Elvenship sailed and drifted and sailed and drifted, all those who would go to the island made ready for the journey. Not knowing where the goal lay, Bokar insisted that they take along three weeks of rations—mainly crue and kegs of water. Too, not knowing the threat they faced, he ordered the warband to take axes and warhammers and shields, as well as crossbows with enough quarrels to conduct a small war. To this they added climbing gear and several healer's kits along with other miscellaneous field equipment.

That evening as well, Alamar called Jinnarin out from her under-bunk quarters and nearly apologized.

Jinnarin plopped down in the center of the floor and sighed. "I suppose Jatu is right. I mean, crystal castle or no, we are going there regardless."

Alamar said nothing.

Jinnarin continued, "At least, you verified much of the sending."

"Hmph," grunted Alamar. "Don't forget, I also arranged for us to be taken there."

Rux came out from under the bunk and lay down beside his mistress. Jinnarin scratched him behind the ears. After a while she asked, "Did you see what Bokar is doing? If I knew no better, I would say we are setting out to conquer the world."

"As much as he grates on my nerves, Pysk, what that Dwarf is doing is right," said Alamar. "The island is an evil place, or so say the Children of the Sea, and I believe them. We don't know just what Bokar and his warband may be called upon to do, or for that matter, any of us. We know not what foe may be on the isle. But whatever or whoever it is, we need to be ready."

Jinnarin stepped to her quarters and then back out, the Pysk carrying her tiny bow and quiver of arrows. "This is the best I can do, Alamar. Though if the foe on the island is the same one that slew Ontah, well then, I'm not certain that even *my* arrows will be enough."

CHAPTER 26

The Great Swirl

Spring, 1E9575
[The Present]

In the hour before dawn, in the captain's salon, Aravan held an officers' meeting, Jinnarin, Aylis, and Alamar included. They reviewed the preparations and the order of the dinghies, seven in all to go on the expedition: In the first six boats, each would have six Dwarven warriors, one Human sailor, and a passenger—Bokar, Aravan, Alamar, Aylis, Jinnarin and Rux, and Jatu. The seventh and final dinghy would bear three Dwarves and three sailors. All dinghies would carry a proportionate share of the supplies. The Elvenship would be left with a crew of thirty-one, Human sailors all, Frizian in command. Aravan turned to Frizian. "Keep a sharp eye on the weed, Frizian. Let not the *Eroean* become entangled. Maintain this station and set sail only at need. Should a storm blow, hie thee a safe distance hence, and come back to the weed when all is done, taking this position once more."

"Aye, Captain," replied Frizian. "And should the black galley appear, what then?"

"Should it appear, let it be," answered Aravan. "I deem it is likely well armed, and it will take all of us— sailors and warband alike—to put it down."

"Ha!" exclaimed Alamar. "Mages too, Elf. If Durlok is aboard, magery will be needed, like as not."

Aylis turned to the elder. "Father, should it come to a duel—"

"Should it come to a duel, Daughter, have we any choice at all?"

"Yes, Father, we do have a choice—we can run."

Alamar's cheeks puffed up, but before he could say aught, Bokar exploded: "Run? Run! Pah! There is no honor in running away like a cowardly cur with its tail between its legs."

"Finally, Dwarf," exclaimed Alamar, "finally something we agree on!"

Jinnarin leapt to her feet. "Well I agree with Aylis!" The Pysk's cobalt gaze flicked back and forth between the Mage and the armsmaster. "I mean, you two would have us stand toe-to-toe with any foe and whale away until one or the other falls dead. Did you hear me? Until one or the other falls dead! And that could just as well be us as them.

"But my Kind has a saying: 'When choosing how to fight, look not to the Bear but to the Fox instead, for cunning and guile will out.' Many a time have we outwitted stronger enemies, defeating them by using our brains instead of our brawn."

"Pah!" snorted Bokar, slapping the table. "That is because you are but a mite and have no brawn. All you *have* is cunning and guile—and a tiny bow with pin-prick arrows—whereas we Châkka have the strength of arms."

A frown came over Alamar's features, and he looked at Bokar and said, "Take care, Dwarf, for should you go against this 'mite' or one of her Kind, you will see just what those pin-prick arrows can do."

The Mage turned to Jinnarin. "Nevertheless, Pysk, Bokar is right. Only the weak run."

Aylis peered at the low-burning astral fire in her father and said, "Exactly, Father, and that is why we must follow Jinnarin's advice and outwit the foe. Seldom if ever does strength alone defeat true cunning and guile."

Jatu laughed. "Aye, always should one use cunning and guile. Even so, at times strength need be added to the mix, while at other times pure trickery."

Aravan leaned forward on his hands. "Enough. The manner in which a hazard is fared depends upon the hazard. Let us not sail those waters until we come to them."

As the meeting had progressed, the *Eroean*'s gangway

was brought up from the hold and affixed to the larboard of the ship. Seven dinghies were lowered to the sea and tethered to the foot of the ramped catwalk. Sailors and Dwarves stood by, waiting. Finally, onto the deck came Jinnarin and Rux and Alamar, Aylis and Aravan, Jatu, and Bokar. All were armed but Alamar and Aylis . . . and Rux, if fang and claw counted not. Frizian came out with them, the second officer unarmed as he was remaining aboard the Elvenship.

As the Sun lipped the horizon, the mizzenmast lookout called, "Dolphin, Cap'n! Dolphin off the port stern!"

Leaping through the water coursed a pod of five dolphin, racing in a file toward the *Eroean*. Swiftly they came onward and then abeam—their line carrying them a distance out from the Elvenship—and then they sped beyond. They took up station some two hundred yards past the bow of the ship, once again in a ring, though spread wider than before, their dolphin voices chattering and clicking and calling to one another over the slow-rolling swells.

Aravan turned to Alamar. "Mayhap thou shouldst have a crew row thee out to where the dolphin—"

"Cap'n!—oh, Adon!—Cap'n!" called the foremast lookout. "Off the bow! Som'thin' monstrous large comin' up from the bottom!"

"Kruk!" snarled Bokar. "Warriors to the ballistas!"

As Dwarves sprang toward the missile casters, Aravan dashed toward the foredeck, Jatu on his heels, Bokar coming after. Aylis, too, ran forward. But swiftest of all was Rux, the fox racing ahead, Jinnarin on his back.

As the Pysk leapt to the stemblock, Aravan sprang up the steps behind, the Elf having outdistanced all but the fox. Jinnarin peered to the fore, and out midst the dolphin ring she could see a great stirring and churning, water roiling in agitation, a vast upwelling, as if something immense rose from below, pushing weed and water upward as it came, waves rolling out over the sea. Aravan joined the Pysk, and then Jatu and Bokar and Aylis arrived. In that moment a gigantic rounded form emerged—smooth and heart-shaped and dark green, water runnelling down—and standing atop was a jade-hued figure with fins along his sides and flowing silver hair.

Once again had come a Child of the Sea, but this time he brought with him a creature of the deep. A head emerged—wedgelike and huge and ending in a beak, and bearing two ebon-dark eyes. A flipper as well swashed through the water.

"Captain," breathed Jatu, "we look upon the father of all—"

"Or the mother—" interjected Aylis.

"Cap'n," called down the foremast lookout, "I see it plain. 'Tis a sea turtle, big as an island no less!"

Bokar stared at the figure riding the immense tortoise. "Is that—?"

"Call off your dogs, Bokar," barked Alamar, the Mage just now reaching the foredeck. "I think we look upon a *¡th!rix*, for that is Nalin on its back. And see"—two more figures clambered into view—"Imro and Rania join him."

Alamar turned to Aravan and Jinnarin. "Come with me, you two, and meet our escort. It will set their minds at ease to see who fares on this mission. They know you, Elf, as a Friend—they can sense your token. And Pysk, with you along—a Hidden One—it should assuage them, for they, too, remain hidden for the most part from those they term 'destroyers.' "

"Destroyers?" asked Jinnarin.

"Mostly Humans, I think," replied Alamar.

"Oh, I see," said Jinnarin, "and agree." She looked out to where the Merfolk waited. "I think you are right, Alamar; I should go meet them now. Rux, too."

Alamar sighed. "All right, Rux, too."

"Who will row?" asked Jatu. Before any could respond, he answered his own question: "I say it shall be me and Bokar—"

"Then I will come as well," interjected Aylis.

Alamar threw up his hands and said, "Why not? Why not the whole bloody crew?"

Dwarves and Men surged forward, but Aravan put out a hand and said, "Nay. We would not have them disappear under the waves. I deem that we seven shall go first and accustom them to our presence."

Bokar turned to Kelek. "At my signal, bring all other boats and crew."

The seven entered the first dinghy and headed toward the gigantic turtle: Jinnarin and Rux in the bow, Alamar at their side; Bokar and Jatu next and rowing; Aylis and Aravan in the stern, Aravan plying the steering oar.

Steadily they drew across the weedy water, and as they neared, curious dolphin swam alongside and regarded those in the boat, especially Rux, and chattered and called. For his part, Rux excitedly eyed the dolphin, his head bobbing up and down and side to side, his nose taking in their scent, the fox turning to Jinnarin and whining, as if to ask for guidance. Jinnarin laughed and stroked his head, the fox turning his attention back to these denizens of the sea.

Now they passed through the ring of dolphin and drew near the turtle, the hard-shelled reptile floating at the surface and drifting with the slow current. It was an immense creature, spanning some forty feet from side to side and fifty or sixty in length. Dark green was its carapace and splotched here and there with mosslike growth. Great paddle flippers could be seen, occasionally stirring the water. And it turned its head as the dinghy drew near, a great ebony eye fixed upon those within.

Atop the tortoise, the three Merfolk stood, clothed in nought but their silver hair and their pale jade skin. Their stance was guarded, though somewhat haughty: Nalin in the fore, facing them, his fists on his slender hips; to the right stood Imro sideways, his back to Nalin, his arms crossed defiantly, peering over his left shoulder at those in the boat; Rania stood on Nalin's left, her hands on her hips as well. Three pair of large, catlike green eyes peered at the seven with chary curiosity— lighting with a hint of surprise upon seeing Jinnarin and Rux—though when their gazes fell upon Jatu and Bokar, they became wary, distrustful.

["So this is a *¡th!rix*,"] called out Alamar.

Rania smiled at the Mage. ["Yes, Friend Alamar. Are you surprised?"]

Before Alamar could answer, Imro butted in. ["You said that forty or more destroyers would be going to the isle. Why have you brought just these?"]

Nalin turned to Imro, but Alamar's voice cut past what Nalin might have said. ["Listen to me, sprat, I came out here in good fellowship and what do I find but a crotchety, querulous, self-centered, ill-mannered—"]

Rania's shrill cry split the air. ["Stop this assailing one another! You are like two coral fish battling over possession of a tiny patch of sand."]

Jinnarin looked up at Alamar's blustering red face. "What's the matter, Alamar?"

Aylis whispered, *"Converte."* Then she turned to the Children of the Sea. ["I am Aylis, daughter of Alamar. Is something wrong?"]

Alamar called out, ["I need no help in taking care of this fry, Daughter."]

["Oh, I see,"] replied Aylis, sighing in resignation. ["Father, there are more important things to do than to argue with Friends."]

Rania smiled at Aylis. ["Exactly so."]

["You have still not answered my question,"] declared Imro, arrogantly. ["These are not enough to challenge the evil on the isle. Why have you brought only them."]

"Bah!" said Alamar, the elder turning aside and pouting, refusing to look at or even to speak to Imro.

But Aylis said, ["The plans have not changed; all promised are going. Yet we came first so that you would know that more than just one Kind have banded together to confront this evil in your Realm. You already know my father, a Mage. I, too, am a Mage. Here at my side is the Elf known as Aravan, master of the *Eroean*."]

["The Friend,"] said Nalin, smiling.

["We feel the power of his token,"] added Rania.

"I am introducing all," murmured Aylis. "I have told them your name, Aravan."

Aravan smiled a greeting and raised an open hand, palm outward.

["The black one is a Human known as Jatu"]— hearing his name, Jatu grinned and inclined his head toward the trio of Merfolk—["and the one at his side is Bokar, our Dwarven Master of Arms."] Now Bokar nodded his head, the Dwarf trying to look friendly but he only managed to project a stern image of unbending will.

["In the fore is my father, and beside him are Jinnarin, a Pysk, a Hidden One, and her bright fox, Rux."]

Jinnarin whispered something to Rux, and she and the

fox bowed to the Children of the sea, much to Rania's delight.

["I am Nalin. This is Rania. And Imro.]"

The three sea Folk bowed. Then Nalin glanced at the rising Sun. ["The island is far from here—two Suns and some at the rate of the *ıth!rix* through the weed, and if we would reach it . . ."]

"Bokar, call the others," said Aylis. "The island is two and a half days hence, and the Merfolk would go now."

Upon hearing this, Jinnarin's face fell, but before she could speak—"Two and a half days!" exclaimed the armsmaster. "My warband will be exhausted rowing that far. If there be trouble on the isle, we will not be able to lift an axe."

Aylis repeated Bokar's concern to the Children of the Sea, and Rania laughed, saying, ["Fear not, Lady Aylis, if you have ropes, the *ıth!rix* will tow you all the way."]

["Not to the island itself,"] amended Nalin, ["but to within sight of it."]

The Dwarven warband rowed the remaining dinghies out, and Jinnarin and Rux, Aylis, Aravan, Jatu, and Bokar transferred to their own boats, Alamar staying put, a crew coming aboard, joining him. Quickly the boats took their assigned positions in a file, the stem of each dinghy tied by a length of rope to the stern of the one ahead; the first in line—Bokar's boat—was harnessed to the *ıth!rix*. "Slipknots," had ordered Bokar, "in case this monster takes it in his head to sound."

When all was ready, Bokar signalled the Merfolk, and they dived forward from the shell of the immense turtle, and in a moment, ponderously, the *ıth!rix* began to move, slowly gaining speed, its huge flippers stroking the brine as would great bird wings stroke air. Inward it went, deeper into the weed, cutting a wide swath, leaving a broad channel behind, dinghies towed after like beads on a necklace. And running alongside or aft of the boats swam the pod, dolphin chattering to one another, rolling up to curiously eye the ones they escorted—especially Rux. Occasionally swimming alongside as well came one or two of the Merfolk, their arms extended out before them, fins erect down each side running from wrist to ankle, their supple bodies undulating in smooth, dolphinlike motions, their gill plates open along their rib cages now that they were swimming completely underwater.

Northwesterly into the weed of the pale green sea they fared, the great turtle now moving at a steady rate, gauged by Aravan to be some nine knots, and he called back to the others, "Can he keep up this pace, we will reach center in less than two days."

"Two days," sighed Jinnarin, disappointment filling her face. "That's what the Children of the Sea told Aylis."

"Aye, Lady Jinnarin," said Jamie, the sailor aboard her boat. "The Swirl, well it be nearly a thousand miles across in all—five hundred from edge to center, though the *Eroean*, well it came some third of the way in, or so they told me."

Jinnarin sighed. "Oh, Jamie, I am just anxious to get there. Farrix is in the crystal castle, or so I believe, and if it's on the island . . ."

Lork, one of the Dwarven warriors, asked, "Do we know where lies this island?"

Jinnarin shook her head then glanced down at the water. "The Children of the Sea know."

Relk, another of the Dwarves, barked a laugh. "How about the turtle, does he know?"

Jinnarin giggled. "Even if he does, who can ask him?"

Jamie smiled but cocked an eyebrow. "The Mermaid can talk to him, I'll wager. The Mermen, too. Here, if you look real close, you can see that one or the other of them is always up there telling him where to go . . . that, or urging him on."

Jinnarin moved over to the wale and leaned out and watched for a while, verifying what Jamie had said, seeing that always one or another of the Merfolk stayed near the creature's head.

And deeper into the Swirl they went.

Hours passed, the Sun riding up from the horizon and overhead then sliding down the western sky. There was little to do but sit and talk, or to carefully stand and stretch, and only Jinnarin did not feel cramped by the close quarters. They took meals and water, and modesty notwithstanding, they relieved themselves over the side, even Rux.

Gradually the weed thickened, and when clumps of it floated past, Jinnarin could see small fish wriggling among the leafy tendrils and tiny crabs scuttling over the strands. She fished up a branch and wee shrimp scurried away, fleeing to other strands. Jinnarin and Rux examined the tendril, the fox sniffing and nosing this treasure from the sea. The frond was long and lank, thin stemmed and branched, with narrow pale green leaves curled at the very tips to form tiny snags to ordinarily hook onto other strands to form an entangled mass floating just under the surface. Diminutive berries grew on tender stems along the branches, and as she watched, a tiny snail slowly enveloped one.

As she and Rux examined the plant, Jamie said, " 'Tis only green hereabout, Lady Jinnarin, here in the Great Swirl. In the other waters of the world, 'tis reddish brown, this weed, and not thick."

"Reddish brown?"

"Aye."

Jinnarin looked at the pale green sea to left and right. "Must be something about the water, eh?"

Jamie peered over his shoulder, as if seeking something aft. "That or the curse of this place." At his words, all the Dwarven warriors—Lork, Tolar, Relk, Engar, Koban, and Regat—peered warily about, their hands straying to their weapons.

Shuddering, Jinnarin cast the weed back into the ocean and onward they fared.

As the Sun sank in the west, the giant tortoise progressively slowed, and now its stroke began to change, its front flippers sweeping forward to spread the weed and clear the way. Even so it maintained a goodly pace, judged by Aravan to be some seven knots.

Now one or two or sometimes all three of the Merfolk rode on the creature's back, one always near its head, as if whispering instructions to guide the *¡th!rix* across the slow-turning churn. When not riding, the other two sometimes swam back among the dolphin, the pod yet following in the wake of the turtle, there in the long curving channel behind. At times, the Children would swim alongside the wall of weed, now and again their quick hands darting out to snag a fish on their sharp talons, which they would laughingly cast to a nearby dolphin or eat with great relish, sharp teeth tearing. Too, the Children would gather sea bounty and bear it forward, presumably to feed the tortoise. Occasionally a Child of the Sea would swim alongside a dinghy and would look upon the destroyers within, the eyes of the Child filled with unspoken accusations, especially Imro's eyes.

And still they fared inward, ever inward, while the Great Swirl slowly turned.

It was just after dusk in the dark of the Moon when they saw the first ship to the fore, a half-sunken hulk floating in the weed, dismasted, its timbers shattered, much of it clutched by a sickly green growth. A Jingarian junk it was, its battened sails long rotted and dragging alongside. The *¡th!rix* gave it wide berth, refusing to swim near, though Aravan's blue stone amulet remained warm as they passed it by.

"Why doesn't it sink?" asked Jinnarin. "I mean, it looks half drowned already."

"The weed, Lady, the weed. It'll hold her up forever."

"Oh."

And on they went, deeper and deeper, a chill wind springing up at their backs.

Mid of night came, and with it an overlay of dark clouds driven before the wind, and lightning sheeted low across the western horizon. Two more hulks they passed, one to the starboard, the other larboard, yet they were too distant to see what manner of ships they had been. None of the Human sailors could see them, for not even the stars shone down, but Dwarf and Elf and Mage and Pysk could yet just make out the silhouettes, though details were beyond even their extraordinary <sight>.

On fared the *¡th!rix* through the thickening weed, its rate continuing to diminish, while behind the storm drew ever closer, driven on a hard wind, large swells running under the weed. And Jinnarin looked at the boiling clouds above and shivered, for it was as if the nightmare itself had entered her waking life.

" 'Ware!" came a cry from the fore, and Jinnarin

leaned over the wale and peered ahead and gasped in
fear, for in the distance she could see another hulk, one
directly in their path, its rigging burning with green
witchfire.

And in that moment, a great flaring bolt of lightning
shattered into the sea, blanching all with a blinding glare,
a deafening thunderclap whelming after.

And drenching rain hard-driven by the wind lashed
down from the ebony sky.

And Jinnarin looked about in terror, expecting now
to see a black ship, its masts stroked by lightning, plunging toward them across the pale green sea.

It rained without letup through the rest of the night,
the occupants of the boats in chill misery. And in each
dinghy they wrapped themselves in their all-weather
cloaks and draped the sail over as much as they could
and huddled beneath for comfort and warmth and to
escape the rain. Even so, water steadily ran into the
boats and sloshed about their feet, and all but Jinnarin
and Rux took turns at bailing.

Drawn and weary and lacking sleep, dismal daylight
found them yet faring inward, a thin drizzle coming
down through a fog on the sea. And Jinnarin fretted
about the state of Alamar's health, for the elder lacked
the resilience of youth, and surely he would suffer more
than any of the others. Yet there was nothing she could
do about it, and so she turned to Rux and did what she
could to make the fox more at ease, Rux grumbling in
cold discomfort, while the Pysk worried about her friend.

Throughout the day the fog lingered, the cloud cover
preventing the Sun from dispersing the mist. And every
now and again they would pass another trapped hulk,
the ship looming dimly on the edge of vision there in
the swirling fog. Some of these wrecks caused the stone
amulet at Aravan's throat to turn chill, warning him of
danger. Always it seemed the turtle knew of the peril as
well, for the beast swung wide to pass beyond the hazard. And they did not pause to investigate the source of
a given jeopardy, for they were on a different mission
altogether.

Rania, Nalin, and Imro became more subdued the farther inward they progressed, and even the trailing pod

of dolphin now seemed restrained. But there was no change in the manner of the *¡th!rix,* the great creature ponderously moving forward through the weed.

In mid afternoon the day brightened, and Jinnarin guessed that the skies above the fog had cleared, and by sunset the mist had burned away and weary spirits took heart. When night fell, they set the watch, and all others bedded down, Jinnarin curling up against Rux and immediately falling asleep.

And the *¡th!rix* swam on.

Jinnarin awoke to another grey sky, and once more a chill wind blew. It was the beginning of the third day of travel, and still the great turtle fared through the weed, towing behind seven dinghies. Bokar, Aravan, Alamar, Aylis, Jinnarin with Rux, and Jatu rode in separate boats, roped together in that order. As before, each dinghy also carried an experienced small-craft sailor, and each of the first six boats bore six Dwarven warriors as well. The seventh dinghy carried three Dwarves and three sailors. All supplies were evenly distributed again, so that if a boat sank, it would not carry all of a given stock down with it.

Behind the boats came the pod of five dolphin. And on the turtle rode the three Children of the Sea. How the dolphin or tortoise or Merfolk had slept, or whether they even needed sleep, Jinnarin did not know.

And as Jinnarin awoke, she looked up to find Jamie peering white-faced and grim-lipped at the sea about. The Dwarven warriors, too, glanced around with flinty eyes, and they hefted their warhammers or thumbed the edges of their axes. Jinnarin climbed up to see what was amiss, and as she looked over the wale she gasped, for no matter in which direction she turned, it seemed that her eye fell upon the trapped hulk of a ship, its rigging draped with long ropy strands of greyish-green growth dangling down, like snares set to strangle the unwary, while weed and slime reached up to clutch at the hull as if to drag it under.

"It is like a great web, Lady Jinnarin," muttered Jamie, "just as I heard Tivir say, a lair of a monstrous spider, trapping all that sails in to her, this Sea of Lost

Ships. I had always known about it but never thought I'd see it. But now here I am, I am."

These ships were weatherworn beyond endurance, devoid of color where the slime grew not, bereft of original paint, assuming that they had been painted to begin with.

Grey and lifeless they were, or so Jinnarin assumed, though Aravan passed word back that his blue stone ran chill, and the Dwarves cocked their crossbows and loaded them with quarrels.

Decayed were these vessels and strange their designs, the like of which Jinnarin had never seen before, though her experience was limited. But Jamie, too, commented upon their shapes and the manner of their construction, for he had not seen such either.

One relic seemed made entirely of reeds, its stern and prow high and bundled, a roofed-over canopy amidships, now fallen into ruin, sharp-pointed oars hanging awry.

Another ship was made of heavy timbers, its hull round-bellied and blunt on both ends. Perhaps it once had a deck cabin, yet none stood there now. Instead, it seemed scarred by fire, as if long past it had been aflame.

One trapped hulk looked like nothing more than a huge hollowed-out log—though it was so weed-covered that it was difficult to tell—and no mast could be seen. What appeared to be two large poles jutted out to the side, but as to their purpose, Jinnarin could not guess, though Jamie told her that another, smaller log had once been affixed across the outer ends, lending the craft stability.

"Look!" gritted one of the Dwarves, Tolar by name.

Jinnarin's gaze followed his outstretched arm and her heart leapt into her throat, for though she had never before seen such a ship, she knew without question exactly what it was—there where he pointed was the rotted, weed-covered hulk of a three-tiered galley, splintered oars hanging out through openings in the hull. "Durlok!" she hissed, a mutter of confirmation rising up about her.

"Aye, Lady," agreed Jamie. "His ship'll most likely be somewhat the same, though more seaworthy, I ween."

Word filtered back from Aravan that they must be

close to the heart of the Swirl, for these relics were from
elder days, their designs long since abandoned.

And through this ancient graveyard passed the turtle,
towing seven dinghies behind.

The chill wind blew and the day grew darker, even
though it was not yet noon. Of a sudden there came a
shrill cry from the fore. The *¡th!rix* stopped swimming.
The boats drifted aimlessly on the ends of their tethers.
Jinnarin stood and looked, and in the distance ahead she
could see the crests of rocky crags.

It was an island.

They had come to the center of the web.

Now the dinghies were untied from the turtle and
from one another as well. Alamar's boat, third in file,
was rowed to the fore. Coiling Bokar's line, Rania and
Nalin and Imro strode across the back of the great turtle
and cast it to the Dwarf, then turned and spoke with the
Mage. What they said, Jinnarin did not hear, nor would
she have understood it regardless. Even so, she knew
that the Merfolk had fulfilled their part of the bargain,
for the island stood at hand. Now it was up to those in
the boats to fulfill their promise and clear the island of
evil, though just what that evil might be, none knew.

Rania dived into the water and came swimming back
alongside the dinghies, and she stopped at Jinnarin's
boat. There she was joined by the pod of dolphin, and
lo! she raised her pale jade elfin face from the water
and spoke to *Rux!*—her words filled with clicks and tiks
and pops and chirps—completely unintelligible to anyone at hand, though Aylis in the next boat laughed. The
dolphin chattered, and Rux barked, and then like liquid
silver Rania turned and swam to the *¡th!rix,* her long-
finned feet appearing to be nothing more than the
sweeping tail of a fish.

With the Children of the Sea atop, ponderously the
tortoise swam in an arc, turning back toward the channel
it had left behind. When it reached the open slot, the
silver-haired Merfolk turned and called a singing farewell, Aylis answering in kind, her own voice soaring.
And in the clear water of the channel, the pod of dol-

phin leapt with abandon, speeding away in the distance toward the far-removed open sea.

Jinnarin watched for a long while, as the Dwarves stroked easterly, the flat-bottomed rowboats gliding over the weed. At last she turned toward Aylis's boat and called out, "What did she say, this Rania? What did she speak to my Rux?"

Aylis smiled. "She told your little fox, Jinnarin, that if he was ever of a mind to leave the land behind and join them, the dolphin would like nothing better."

Jinnarin laughed and turned to Rux and ruffled his ears, and glanced back toward the receding *¡th!rix*. But the Children of the Sea had long since dived into the water and could no longer be seen. The destroyers had been left behind at the lair of the spider to confront the peril on their own.

CHAPTER 27

Island of Stone

Spring, 1E9575
[The Present]

"Ship oars and raise sail!" called out Aravan, and the Men aboard the dinghies affixed the sheets to the silks and ran the cloth up the masts, trimming sail to make the most of the chill southern wind.

The flat-bottomed dinghies skimmed over the surface, the rounded bows riding the weed down and under. With the steering oars being used as rudders, toward the rocky isle all boats fared, running in a ragged file beneath the cold grey skies, wending past waterlogged hulks half-drowned in the clutching weed.

Jinnarin and Rux had moved to the bow where she could better view the course ahead. And in the distance perhaps seven miles away rocky crags reared up from the sea. This was their goal, the Lair of the Spider—Jinnarin thought of it as such. Bleak and windswept it appeared from here, grey stone tors jutting up, barren of greenery, perhaps devoid of life altogether. In grim premonition Jinnarin shuddered and clutched her cloak tighter about. And she threw an arm over Rux's neck and whispered, "Don't worry, old fox, we will be all right." Yet whether she said so to assure herself or her companion, she did not know. Sensing her uneasiness, Rux freed himself and turned and cocked his head this way and that and peered at her, his cat-eyes seeking assurance that she was fit. She smiled at him and ruffled his ears, and heartened, he took a lick at her cheek then faced front once more.

373

Past relics they sailed, hulls drawn down into the weed and awash, algae and sea moss enshrouding all that remained above. In one place only a mast jutted out from the brine, and to Jinnarin's eye it seemed thickly covered by pallid mushrooms growing up the length of the shaft. On they fared and Jinnarin looked down into the water, trying to see past the weed. Of a sudden she gasped and drew back in apprehension, for below she saw the curve of a hull on its side, the ship dragged completely under and drowned, and her mind conjured up visions of dead sailors trapped within and clawing at the hull to get out.

"Oh, what a horrid place," she murmured, glancing about at the drifting graveyard, Rux the only one to hear.

They sailed onward for perhaps an hour, the island looming larger, the dinghies running slower as the weed thickened, until they were but moving at a crawl. "Fend weed," bade Jamie, and as Dwarves took up oars to do so, Jinnarin and Rux moved back to the stern. But even with the Dwarves kneeling in the bow and along the sides and sweeping the sea plant aside and back, still the craft slowed, the wind no longer able to overcome the drag, the weed was so heavily grown. Not even the Children of the Sea could have swum through such without the aid of a *¡th!rix*.

"We'll try to row from here," said Jamie. "I'll leave the sail up for whatever push it can give."

Oars were settled in oarlocks, and with Jamie canting a chant, the Dwarves began to row. Steadily they haled across the clutching waters, molasses thick, or so it seemed, the rowers grunting with the effort, sweat pouring down. And Jinnarin was glad that it was not she who had to row, though in looking down at the brine she thought she might almost be able to run upon the weed-thick surface, as if she were Alamar himself.

The other boats, too, rowed through the weed, the last one struggling the most, for it was crewed by three Dwarves and three Men, hence could not bring the same force to bear. But then Bokar hit upon a scheme, and he ordered all boats in close file behind his, the thought being that his craft would break a channel, just as the giant turtle had done when bringing them here. And so all the dinghies lined up behind Bokar's, and thereafter the rowing became easier for all but the lead craft, the other boats switching off at intervals to break the trail, sharing the burden.

They fared this way for another mile, and *lo!* of a sudden the weed came to an end, the dinghies breaking into clear water, the growth behind like a great green wall falling sheer into the abyssal depths.

And some two miles ahead lay the island, be-ringed by this clear water, or so it seemed.

"Ship oars," called Aravan, "and form up on me— geese on the wing."

Swiftly the boats were maneuvered into a vee formation, Aravan at the point of the wedge, with three craft trailing to the right and three to the left. And across the open water and toward the isle they sailed.

Stern and forbidding towered the land, jutting up from the sea, and to left and right for as far as the eye could range steep-sided rocky bluffs rose sheer two hundred feet or so, and the long ocean swells crashed upon the adamant stone, hammering against the base. Atop the cliffs Jinnarin could see wind-twisted trees desperately clutching at the rocky land, but of shrubs or grass or other growth, there was no sign. Jinnarin judged the island itself to be roughly three miles wide, but as to its length, she could not tell from where they now fared.

"Cor, that's strange," muttered Jamie.

"What?" asked Jinnarin.

"No birds, Lady Jinnarin. No birds at all. In fact, there ain't been no birds ever since we came to the waters of the Great Swirl."

Jamie's words caused Jinnarin's heart to pound, and she reached out and stroked Rux, her gaze vainly searching the grey cliffs and leaden sky above for sign of bird life. As she eyed the barren steeps, word came from Aravan's boat that they would sail deosil about the island until they came to a place to land. And swinging to larboard, all craft followed Aravan's lead.

Faring along the towering bluffs, they had covered some four miles when they came upon a place where a portion of the cliffs had crumbled, a long, scree-filled, vee-shaped notch clove down from high stone to the water, a rubble-strewn shingle of beach at the base.

Toward this strand they made their way, Aravan calling out, " 'Ware the landing, the water is deep!"

As they neared the crumble of stone, Jinnarin looked down through the clear water into the blackness below, and she could see no bottom. But suddenly they passed over an underwater precipice rising up sheer from the abyss to a flat underwater shelf, the ledge some twenty feet down, or so she judged, and strewn with a scattering of talus from the collapsed cliff above, pebbles and rocks and boulders—now becoming more and more densely packed as they sailed inward, finally ramping up toward the wide notch cleaving down through the grey bluff.

As their boat neared, Jinnarin strapped on her quiver of arrows and slung her bow across her back. Then she fastened the travelling packs on Rux, the fox in the prow and yipping in joy, his head bobbing up and down, Rux eager to take to land, as were they all. One after another the sailors grounded the dinghies on the rocks of the gravelly shore, flat-bottomed hulls grinding onto stone. And with Jinnarin mounted, Rux leapt out onto the slope of rubble, the warriors and Jamie coming after and dragging the boat well up the rock-laden shore.

Scrambling across the talus, Rux came to where Bokar and Aravan stood eyeing the cliffs above, while Dask and Brekka, the Dwarven scouts—crossbows in hand—started up the gloom-laden notch toward the top of the bluff, pebbles and stones sliding down from their footsteps. The Pysk dismounted and whispered a command in Rux's ear, letting the fox roam free nearby, the animal darting about here and there and marking the beach as his own. Jatu joined the trio, as did Kelek, then Aylis, and finally Alamar, the eld Mage picking his way across the scree and muttering something about it being a trap to turn unwary ankles. As he arrived, he looked up at the steep slope of loose stone and groaned, "Uphill. I might have known."

"Captain," asked Jatu, "it is near high tide; shall we secure the boats?"

Bokar glanced toward the scouts, now a third of the way up, and said, "When we are given the all clear by the scouts, then will be the time to make the boats fast; not before."

"Scouts?" blurted Jinnarin. "Why, there aren't any

better than Rux and I." With that she put her fingers to her lips and her cheeks puffed out. Neither the Dwarves nor the Men nor Alamar heard anything, though Rux's head snapped up alertly and he came running.

"What are you doing, Lady Jinnarin?" barked Bokar.

"She whistles," said Aravan, Aylis nodding in agreement, for both the Elf and the Lady Mage could hear the sound beyond earshot of the others.

As Jinnarin leapt on Rux's back, Bokar stepped out as if to block her way, saying, "My Lady, it may not be safe for you to—" but the red fox dodged past the armsmaster and darted up the ramp of scree.

"Kruk!" spat Bokar.

Alamar nodded in agreement, muttering, "Might as well talk to one of these pebbles, for all the good it does."

As Rux scrambled up the talus and passed beyond Dask and Brekka, Bokar growled, "I like this not. There may be foe atop."

Aylis turned to Aravan. "What says your stone, Aravan?"

Aravan touched the amulet at his throat. " 'Tis slightly chill, as if danger lies far off."

Jatu peered out past the clear water at half-sunken relics trapped in the weed beyond. "Could it be something aboard the hulks?"

"Mayhap, Jatu. Many of those wrecks held something to cause the stone to chill. In any event, the danger the amulet now detects is not nigh."

Bokar growled and shook his head. "Take no comfort, Jatu, for the blue stone does not scent all foe."

Kelek turned to Bokar. "Armsmaster, shall I assemble a squad to go up after? I would not have Lady Jinnarin face a foe alone."

Bokar nodded, and Kelek barked out orders in Châkur, the hidden tongue. As members of the squad stepped forward, Pysk and fox, now shadow-wrapped, skittered out through the top of the slot and were gone.

A chill wind blew 'neath cold dark skies, and Jinnarin's eager gaze swept across the stony mesa, seeing craggy tors jutting up here and there, snaglike peaks clutching at the blustering air. Gnarled trees and clumps of scrub grass were scattered among the grey rock, the plants clinging tenuously to the adamant land. Jinnarin's face fell, and tears blurred her vision. "Oh, Rux, we've come all this way and there is no castle—no castle at all. Perhaps this is not even the place."

A scrape of stone sounded hindward, and up through the slot came Dask and Brekka, just now topping the slope. "Now where has she got to, her and her fox?" asked Brekka.

Dask shrugged, peering about.

"I'm right here," said Jinnarin, dropping the cloaking shade.

The scouts started in surprise, for it seemed to them that she and Rux had sprung from thin air. Dask laughed and squatted down, peering at the Pysk. But then, swift as quicksilver his expression changed. "Why so chapfallen, tiny one?"

"Oh, Dask, there is no castle."

The Dwarf looked up and about. "Be not certain of that, Lady Jinnarin. Although we cannot see one from here, a castle could stand among the tors . . . or beyond."

"Too," added Brekka, "a castle might be set down at the water's edge over the cliffs afar."

Dask nodded in agreement. "Take heart, my Lady, for as of yet there is no cause for gloom." He turned and gestured at the stone bluff behind, saying, "The castle of your dreams could just as well be a bartizan clinging to the face of the island."

Jinnarin brightened, then frowned. "Bartizan?"

"Aye," answered Dask, "a turret, a chamber, clutched against a wall."

Jinnarin looked out at the mesa and nodded and sighed. "I suppose. —It was just that I was expecting a crystal palace in plain view."

Brekka smiled ruefully and shook his head. "Nothing about this venture would be that easy, Lady Jinnarin."

Dask took one last sweeping look across the isle. "I will signal the others."

As Dask stepped to the precipice, there sounded the clack of sliding scree as Kelek and the squad came up through the slot. Dask signalled the all clear to those yet waiting down at the water's edge.

While the boats were beached well above the mark of the high tide and anchored to large boulders, Kelek set a perimeter of sentries out around the head of the slot. The remainder he sent back down to aid in the hauling of the supplies to the mesa, some goods to be left cached in the boats for the return journey—stored there in case of a hasty retreat, for who knew if there would be time to reload all? And so, some supplies were left stowed while others were set out on the rocky slant, and Dwarves and Men alike shouldered loads and began the climb.

The first one up was Bokar, bearing a keg of water. He set the cask down and peered about, announcing, "We will found our base camp here at the top of the fissure. Then we will send out scouting parties to see what we can see." With that pronouncement Bokar turned and started back down for another load, passing by Aylis and Aravan and a train of sailors and warriors, each bearing cargo and climbing up the sliding scree.

Aided by two sturdy Dwarves, last of all came Alamar struggling up the slope, cursing at those ahead for deliberately kicking rocks at him.

Within an hour they had established their camp at the top of the notch. Bokar then laid out the scouting assignments, and patrols fared forth to discover the width and breadth of the isle and to seek sign of a castle or bartizan or the like, as well as anything else of interest. The Dwarves were particularly suited for this mission, for with their uncanny ability to unerringly retrace their steps, they would soon know the measure of this bit of land. "Location sense," Alamar called it, but at one and the same time it was both much more and much less.

After forceful argument by Jinnarin, Bokar at last acceded, and she and Rux were sent with a Dwarven squad in among the island tors, the Pysk especially equipped to scout the lay of the land, with Rux and shadow and stealth at her beck. On the fox she would go well before them, she and Rux cloaked in shade to slip in secret among the twisting ways.

All squads were cautioned merely to measure and observe, to avoid confrontation and combat should they sight foe—for who knew what this dreadful place might conceal? And so, under gloom-cast skies, across the isle spread the explorers, leftward and rightward and inward. And within the vanguard spreading wide, a clot of shadow slipped among the weed and scrub and stone and headed into the craggy tors.

Using the face of a shield as a drawing table, Dett sat on the ground and added a section to the parchment map as Aravan and Bokar peered over his shoulder. When the scout set the pen aside, the armsmaster growled, "That completes the perimeter."

Aravan glanced at the scale. "Hm ... some three miles across and four miles long."

Alamar scowled at the seated Dwarf. "No castle, eh? Nothing of the sort?"

Dett looked at the elder. "No, Mage Alamar. Not where we walked."

"You looked down the sides, did you?"

The ginger-haired Dwarf nodded.

"Bah! It is the same with all reports," Alamar said sourly, then spun on his heel and stooped under the brim of the sail-made tent, where Aylis paced back and forth in the chill wind, peering out through the gathering darkness.

"You'll wear out your legs with all your worry," muttered Alamar.

"Where is she, Father?"

Alamar waved a hand toward the silhouettes of crags. "Out there."

"But she should be back by now. All the other squads have returned."

"She is with warriors, Daughter. Besides, she can take care of herself."

Surprise in her eyes at this admission, Aylis looked at the elder. "Even so ..."

It began to rain.

Jinnarin and Rux, along with Brekka, Dask, and Dokan, came through the cold downpour an hour after full darkness fell, though under the pall of the rain, just when that had occurred was nought but a guess. Drenched to the bone, they came in under the tent, and by the slump of her shoulders Aylis knew that the Pysk and Dwarves had found nought—"Nothing but stone crags," confirmed Jinnarin.

When they had dried off, by the phosphorescent glow of a Dwarven lamp and the flicker of the small scrub fire, Dask added their knowledge to the map. As had all other patrols, he noted the elevations as well as the general features observed, while he sketched with precision their exact route.

When he was finished, Jinnarin stood beside the shield and peered at the drawing. Soaking cold rain drummed down on the silk above. "Where is it, this castle?"

Bokar turned up his hands, saying nothing.

"No one found anything?"

"Nothing," growled Bokar.

Near tears, Jinnarin looked at Aravan, seeking answers. None were forthcoming.

Alamar cleared his throat. "Perhaps Durlok has enwrapped it in a spell so that it is not seen."

Jinnarin's eyes flew wide. "Invisibility?"

"I did not say that, Pysk," snapped the Mage, nettled at her response. "Bah, you are like all the others—expecting miracles."

A spark of fire glinted in Jinnarin's eyes. "Well you said—"

"What I said, Pysk," interrupted Alamar, "was that he might have used a spell so that the castle is not seen."

Jinnarin ground her teeth. "If that isn't invisibility, then what is it?"

"Oh, any number of things—but they all boil down to disguise or misdirection."

Bokar cocked an eyebrow. "Disguise I understand, Mage, but misdirection? How can that be? Hiding a castle is no sleight of hand trick."

"Ha! Do you presume to instruct me in magery, Dwarf?"

Aylis sighed in resignation. "What Father means is that there are castings which cause an onlooker to simply not see what is before his very eyes. In some, the beholder cannot even look at the object, but instead he is forced to peer around the edges, so to speak. Some of these castings cause the observer to mistake an object for something completely familiar, something to dismiss entirely from attention. Others cause the witness to forget the object even as he is looking straight at it. Still other castings camouflage the object to meld in with the surroundings, or to become obscure, such as does your mastery of shadow, Jinnarin. Illusion, misdirection, obfuscation—these are three ways to hide a castle."

"See? I told you!" sneered Alamar. "Invisibility, pah!"

Ignoring the affront of Alamar's manner, Jinnarin asked, "And you believe that Durlok may have done such a thing?"

Aylis turned up her hands. "It is a possibility."

"Then how will we overcome it?"

"Aha!" crowed Alamar above the sound of rain. "I will counter it with a casting of my own, using my mage-sight to see through Durlok's cheap trick."

During the night it stopped raining, and bright Sun came with the dawn. Two heavily armed parties were sent out, fifteen Dwarves in each: one accompanying Alamar; the other with Aylis. Mage and Lady Mage would use their gift of <sight> to see through whatever ruse Durlok may have cast . . . if any.

Using the map, they divided the isle into sections, Alamar and his party to start out westerly, Aylis and hers to the east. First they would merely walk the perimeter along the top of the cliff, their <sight> sweeping across all they could see. If anything was spotted, they would hold their position and send runners to fetch the other party. If nothing was seen, they would meet at some point along the opposite side, then Aylis and her team would walk among the crags, the Lady Mage seeing whatever she could see. As proposed, should Aylis and her party enter the tors, Alamar and his team would return to the campsite, the crags deemed too rugged for the elder to pass among. Alamar had argued strenuously that he was as good as any of them, but finally acceded to the plan when Aylis reminded him that the tors were mostly uphill.

Jatu and Bokar accompanied Alamar's team; Jinnarin and Aravan and Kelek went with Aylis. The remainder of the force remained at the campsite, warding the boats and supplies.

Jinnarin on Rux took point as Aylis's party marched

east, the Lady Mage whispering *"Visus,"* her gaze sweeping across the isle.

Along the top of the bluff they marched, cliffs falling sheer to the water. The ocean below boomed against the grey stone bulwark, attempting to wear it away. The morning Sun burned brightly as it rode up into the sky. It would pass overhead far to the north, for it was the middle of May and they were far south of the midline—in fact some five hundred miles south of the Lat of the Goat.

An hour passed, no more, and they had reached the eastern extent of the island, when Jinnarin called, "Look! In the crags—a glittering!"

A quarter mile away, among the upjutting grey stone, a sparkle shone. "It is no illusion," murmured Aylis, "but a real glint—source or reflection, I cannot say."

"Let's go," cried Jinnarin, Rux bounding away.

"Wait," called Aravan, too late, for the Pysk was by then gone.

"After!" ordered Kelek, Aravan gainsaying him not. "At a jogtrot!" and the Dwarves and Elf and Lady Mage set out on the heels of the fox.

Within sixty heartbeats Rux had covered the distance to the gleam, and Jinnarin's face fell, for it was merely sunlight reflected off glittery stone. Moments later, the Dwarven squad arrived. "It's just shiny rock," said Jinnarin bitterly. "And I was so hoping . . ."

Kelek stepped forward and ran his hand over the stone. *"Kwarc,"* he said, other Dwarves muttering in agreement. Turning and sweeping his arm wide, Kelek added, "All rock here among the crags and elsewhere on the island is *kwarc* bearing. It is the nature of such stone."

Jinnarin sighed. "Well, it's not enough to make a crystal castle from."

"Not here," agreed Kelek, turning, gesturing. "But elsewhere—who knows?"

They marched back to the periphery and continued about the isle, now heading 'round the southern marge. They had gone some miles or so, when Aravan held up a hand. "Mine amulet, it gathers chill the farther we go. Take care, for we approach something of harm."

All crossbows were cocked and weapons were eased

in their harnesses, and those who bore shields on their backs unslung them and kept them loosely at hand—not such as to interfere with the crossbows, but available nevertheless. Jinnarin was recalled and apprised of the forewarning, and she readied her tiny bow and gathered shadow to herself and Rux. And in spite of arguments to the contrary, she took point again, for none else was as well suited to the task. Even so, Aravan cautioned her to keep an eye on him, for he would signal should the stone betoken imminence of the threat.

With Jinnarin and Rux thirty yards in the lead, south and west they fared, still on the rim of the bluff. And the farther they went, the colder became Aravan's stone. Aylis's magesight revealed nothing untoward—no illusion, misdirection, obfuscation—and no threat. Past the southernmost reach of the isle they trod, eyes alert, weapons ready, yet nothing of menace did they see. Yet when they moved on westerly, Aravan murmured, "The threat slowly fades; the stone is less chill."

Aylis swept the isle with her <vision> then said, "Does it move away from us, or instead do we move away from it?"

Aravan's eyes widened slightly at her canny question. "When we join up with Bokar and Jatu and the others, then we shall see, *chieran.*"

On they marched another mile or so, the stone warming with every stride. And then in the distance they saw Alamar's group resting, the elder sitting on a rock.

"Here it is coldest," murmured Aravan, his hand clutching the blue stone amulet, the Elf surrounded by a ring of Dwarven warriors, Aylis and Alamar inside as well.

"If your stone is chill," muttered Alamar, "then most likely it responds to creatures from Neddra—Foul Folk and the like."

They had returned to the place where the stone grew chill and, arms ready, had followed its influence to where it grew coldest, moving inward toward the tors. And now they stood at the edge of the crags perhaps a quarter mile in from the bluffs.

On the perimeter of the ring, Jinnarin looked about in puzzlement. "But there is nothing here."

"Do not be certain of that," gritted Bokar, tapping lightly on an upright face of stone. "Perhaps there is a secret door leading underground."

"A secret door?" asked Jinnarin. "Where would it lead?"

"Into the living stone," answered Kelek.

Aravan turned to Aylis. "Dost thou see aught with thy magesight?"

Aylis shook her head, *No,* as did Alamar.

Bokar barked a sharp laugh. "If a hidden door lies nearby, even one as poorly crafted as are those of the Ukhs, it is not likely we will find it."

"Ha, Dwarf!" snapped Alamar. "That's what you think. You forget, Aylis is a seer." He turned to her. "Daughter."

Aylis held out a hand to Aravan. "May I hold the stone?"

The Elf slipped the thong from his throat and over his head and handed the amulet to her. She gripped the chill stone in her hand and closed her eyes and murmured, *"Unde?"*

After a moment she whispered, "It comes from below."

"Uah!" grunted Kelek. "It is as I said—from the living stone."

Aravan softly asked, "Is there aught else thou canst divine, Lady Aylis?"

Aylis opened her eyes and looked at Aravan, then slowly shook her head and handed the stone back to him. "Below is all, nothing more."

"Kruk!" spat Bokar. "If there is someone or something down within the living stone, the entrance could be anywhere on the entire isle!" He flung his arms out in a wide gesture. "In the crags. On the flats. Anywhere!"

Aylis nodded, then said, "Yes, Bokar, but heed: If Durlok is involved, then perhaps the entrance is hidden by magery. We have searched the perimeter. The tors we have not. I say that we continue with our original plan. I would add that perhaps the creature below has nothing at all to do with Durlok, but is merely a thing which causes the stone to chill. —All the more reason to continue the search."

Aravan slipped the thong back over his head. "Let us go on, then."

Once more Alamar protested. "No need to prevent me from coming along. There's places in here I can walk. You need my <sight>."

"Father, that we could use your <sight> I do not doubt. Yet we agreed this morning, the sooner done, the sooner we can take advantage of whatever we find. I can search these tors swiftly, and quickly return to camp with word of our discoveries, if any. In fact, we may arrive at camp before you get there."

"Oh, you think so, eh? Well we'll just see about that, Daughter." Alamar spun on his heel and stomped off, followed by Bokar and Jatu and the Dwarven squad.

"Nicely done, *chieran,*" whispered Aravan. And trailing Jinnarin on Rux, into the tors went Kelek's Dwarven squad, Aylis and Aravan in their midst.

"Nothing!" exclaimed Alamar. "You found nothing?"

Aylis nodded. "No sign of magery at all, Father."

Alamar turned to Kelek. "What about hidden doors, Dwarf?"

Kelek shook his head, *No,* but Bokar exclaimed, "Mage, did I not say that secret doors are all but impossible to find. Even with a map they are difficult to locate."

Alamar growled but did not retort.

Aravan glanced at the mid afternoon Sun then turned to the others. "We searched yester and today, finding nought—"

"Nothing but bare rock and scrubby plants, Aravan," interjected Jinnarin glumly.

Aravan nodded in agreement. "Aye. But no sign of crystal castle or Black Mage."

"There was the chill on your amulet," Aylis reminded all.

"It's got to have something to do with Durlok!" declared Alamar.

"Mayhap, Mage Alamar, yet what?" asked Aravan.

Alamar turned up his hands, peering about at the others.

"I seek suggestions," said Aravan.

"About the chill on your stone?" asked Jinnarin.

"About aught," replied the Elf, "be it the chill, places we might look, or things we have overlooked."

Jatu cleared his throat. "Captain, I have been thinking. If Durlok indeed comes in a black galley to this place for who knows what reasons, then he needs safe anchorage for his craft. And can we find that anchorage, then maybe we will find whatever else there is to discover on or in this isle."

Aravan cocked his head to the side and slowly smiled. "Ever the sailor, eh, Jatu. I like thy reasoning. Thy thought, it has much merit. Hast thou additional words?"

Jatu shrugged, then added, "Just this: the brine is deep where we landed. No anchorage at all. But we have not looked at the water completely 'round. I suggest we once again circle the isle and look down within the sea, seeking a place for the Black Mage to heave to and lay up along the shores."

Alamar held up a hand, and when Aravan turned to him he said, "I agree, but let me add this: the first place we should look is along the shore where your stone amulet grew chill."

"Wait!" exclaimed Aylis, peering over the rim and down the face of the bluff. "That ledge of stone, I cannot see under it."

The others looked down at the overhang. "Even so," said Jatu, "the water is black, deep. No anchorage at all ... that is, unless Durlok ties the black galley to moorings in the stone."

"I will climb down and see," said Bokar.

Aylis dotted her cloak. "I'm going with you, Armsmaster."

Bokar looked at her in surprise, and Aylis added, "Moorings may be disguised by magery. You will need my <sight>."

Bokar shrugged, then asked, "You climb?"

Alamar barked a laugh. "Like a doe goat, Dwarf."

Ignoring Alamar, Bokar asked, "Can you rappel?"

Aylis smiled. "I have been known to walk down a wall or two."

Now Alamar hooted. "Why, once at the college in Kairn, Aylis—"

"Father, hush!" commanded Aylis, reddening, glancing at Aravan but not meeting his eyes. For his part, Aravan raised a curious eyebrow but said nought.

Ropes were lashed together and passed through snap rings anchored by pitons driven into stone crevices, the free ends cast over the side. Looping the doubled line under her left thigh and over the right shoulder and down, the right hand back gripping the rope low, the left to the fore and high, Aylis looked at Bokar, the Dwarf handling his rope likewise. Nodding to one another, over the rim they backed, slipping the line as they went walking down the vertical wall.

A hundred or so feet below they reached the ledge, Bokar first, Aylis following. They each cast loose from their ropes, and Bokar lay belly down and peered over the edge. "Kruk!" he grunted. "Nothing but rock down to the water's edge."

Now Aylis lay beside him. *"Visus,"* she murmured, then gasped. "Look! False rock!"

"False? It seems sound enough to me."

"Believe me, Bokar, it is false. See the waves—they roll straight through the so-called stone."

Now Bokar's eyes widened. "By Elwydd," he breathed. "You are right!"

Chapter 28

The Lair of the Spider

Spring, 1E9575
[The Present]

There is a sea-level cavern down there," said Aylis, the moment she climbed up over the rim, "hidden behind an illusion of stone."

Illusion! exclaimed several voices at once.

"Durlok!" spat Alamar.

"This cavern, how large?" asked Aravan.

"The entrance is some seventy or eighty feet wide at the sea, and tapers up to a central point nearly reaching the ledge, say ninety feet high."

Jinnarin, her eyes wide, asked, "What did the illusion look like?"

Bokar stooped down and took up a stone. "Like this rock," he grunted. "I could see nothing of the cavern. To me the wall fell sheer to the ocean below. But as Lady Aylis pointed out, the waves rolled on through. —*That*, I could see."

"How deep is this cavern?" asked Aravan.

"From the ledge I could not tell," answered Aylis, "though Bokar says it is very large."

Kelek raised an eyebrow, then asked, "How so, Armsmaster?"

"It has the sound of a large cavern, Kelek. The waves surge in and softly boom with a low, rolling echo."

"Ah," said Kelek, satisfied.

"I could see some distance in," added Aylis, "and for forty or fifty feet it runs straight on back. Beyond that, I cannot say."

Jatu looked at Aravan. "Safe harbor for Durlok's boat?"

Aravan nodded. "Aye, Jatu, or so it seems."

"Ha!" barked Alamar. "As to how far it reaches, this cavern must run inward at least two furlongs."

Jinnarin looked up at the elder. "Why do you say that, Alamar?"

"The stone amulet, Pysk." The Mage pointed toward the tors. "It was a quarter mile back from the rim where Aravan's amulet grew coldest." Alamar glanced at the Elf. "Foul Folk from Neddra are likely holed up in this cave, eh?"

Aravan turned up a hand. "Most likely, Mage Alamar, though it could as well be something else—even a creature of the sea."

"Creature of the sea?" blurted Jinnarin.

"Aye," responded Aravan. "Some are known to cause the stone to grow chill—Hèlarms, for one."

Jinnarin swallowed. *Hèlarms—Krakens.*

"Eh, Hèlarms or no," declared Alamar, "still we've got to investigate. The illusion alone says that this is Durlok's lair."

Jinnarin's heart pounded, her thoughts running wild—*The Lair of the Spider, he means*—but she said nought.

Bokar turned to Aylis. "Is there a place to land if we rappel down and in?"

Aylis shook her head. "I think not. There are no ledges within that I could see—nowhere to stand."

"Then we'll have to enter by boat," rumbled Jatu.

Aravan glanced at the low-hanging Sun. "The daylight is nigh gone. I deem 'twould be better to make this essay in morning light."

Two hours after dawn the boats drew near the bluff below the ledge. Sheer stone rose up to the shelf—or so it seemed to Jinnarin.

[Drop sail,] ordered Aravan, using silent hand signals. Swiftly all silks were lowered, and while some Dwarves took up already cocked and loaded crossbows, others set muffled oars in locks and began rowing toward the opening that only Aylis and Alamar could see, Aylis in the lead boat with Bokar, Alamar in the next with Aravan. Jinnarin, Rux, and Jatu in the third boat.

Following Aylis's lead, all seven boats rowed in file toward what seemed to be a solid stone wall, the dinghies bearing the entire complement of Dwarves, Men, Mages, Elf, Pysk, and fox, for they knew not what they would encounter behind the illusion and so they came in full force.

Of a sudden Jinnarin gasped, for Aylis and Bokar's boat disappeared, passing through the stone. Then Aravan and Alamar's craft slid through the wall. In spite of what she had just seen, when Jinnarin's boat came to the bluff—*We're going to crash!*—she squeezed her eyes shut as the wall intangibly rushed over her. And then cautiously opened them when they were within. Turning, she looked over her shoulder—from this side there was no illusion of stone, only the large jagged opening, wide at the base and narrowing to a point high above.

Jinnarin leaned over the side and peered down into the water; it was deep and made luminous by the daylight shining in under the surface; she could see no bottom. Facing front, she saw that they had entered a long, jagged strait, stone walls rising sheer, the channel leading inward. Glints shone in the stone, fragments of *kwarc,* or so it was named by the Dwarves.

On inward the boats fared, the channel some eighty feet wide down at the water's edge. The angled ceiling of the cavern rose and dipped, coming down as low as fifty feet in places. And Jatu whispered, "If Durlok's ship has a tall mast, he must step it to bring the craft in."

"Step it?"

"Aye, Lady Jinnarin. Step it up and out from its footing and take it down."

"Oh."

On inward they went, their shadows preceding them down the strait, daylight receding behind, the hollow sound of surge echoing from the gloom ahead, rhythmic, like some great creature breathing. Of a sudden the channel came to a broad lagoon, some hundred and fifty feet across to the opposite shore, with perhaps twice the breadth, the ends left and right cloaked in dimness.

And *lo!* the walls all about sparkled like diamonds.

"*Kwarc,*" breathed Brekka, pointing with his crossbow.

"Crystal!" hissed Jinnarin. "Oh, Jatu, could this be

the crystal castle? Alamar says that images in dreams are at times nought but misleading shadows of truth."

"Perhaps so, Lady Jinnarin," responded Jatu, his voice low. "Perhaps this glittering cavern is indeed the gleaming manse of your dream."

While crystalline walls danced in the light reflected from the undulant waves, across the understone lagoon they fared, the cavern sighing and breathing with the surge. Aylis angled the file of boats left and toward a landing clutched in the shadows on the far side of the grotto, there where stood a long stone quay.

As they passed above the dark, heaving waters, again Jinnarin looked over the side. All below was clutched in a blackness so impenetrable that a thousand hideous creatures of the deeps could dwell therein unseen; and remembering Aravan's words about Hèlarms, Jinnarin envisioned great ropy tentacles rushing up from the abyss to lash out and clutch the boats and drag them all to their doom, and she gasped and drew back from the wale.

The first boat came to the quay and drew alongside, warriors quietly clambering up and out, the sound of their landing lost under the echoing swash in the cavern. As one warrior paused to secure the boat, the others spread wide, crouching down along a defensive perimeter, crossbows at the ready, flinty eyes scanning the shadows as the other boats came to the stone dock. As each crew landed, more Dwarves joined the ringing guard.

Jinnarin's craft came to the quay, and at a whispered command from her, Rux leapt up and out, the Pysk on his back—but it was a cluster of shadow that landed on the stone and darted to the perimeter ring.

Alamar's boat docked at the very end of the quay, where stone steps led up from the water. Dwarves helped the eld Mage out and up the treads.

Soon all had gathered on the pier. " 'Ware, my amulet is chill," murmured Aravan above the rolling echo of waves washing against stone. Quickly the warning was passed throughout the warband.

A single corridor led away from the landing, a rough-hewn tunnel some thirty feet wide and half again as high. In the distance down the curving hall glowed a faint light, its unknown source beyond a far turn. Gesturing silently, Bokar formed up his warriors into two columns and down this broad way they went, shields ready, weapons in hand, twenty Dwarves loosely spread along each wall, those in the fore with crossbows cocked. Brekka and Dokan stepped out in the lead, though a tiny cluster of shadow went with them. Bokar and Aravan fared near the head of the column, Bokar bearing a double-bitted axe, Aravan with an unsheathed sword in his right, a long-knife in his left. With Dwarves before and after, near the midpoints of the columns walked Alamar on the left and Aylis on the right, Mage and Lady Mage unarmed. Bringing up the rear came the Men, cutlasses and cudgels in hand, two bearing hooded Dwarven lanterns, each metal cover slightly raised to show but a tiny thread of light, the sight of the Humans not as keen as those of the others. Jatu came last, the giant black Man bearing his great warbar.

Walking softly, down the corridor they fared, the walls about them layered with crystal, Aravan's stone amulet growing more chill with every step. And a faint stench seemed to overhang the air. Steadily they advanced, the passageway gradually curving leftward as they moved toward the dim light ahead. Now some distance in the lead, cloaked in shadow trotted Rux, his mistress on his back, the fox chary for he did not like the smell of the place. Nevertheless, ahead they went, Jinnarin pressing Rux forward. They came to a junction and stopped, waiting for Brekka and Dokan to arrive. A small tunnel split off to the left, while the main channel ran on, curving gently to the right. Faint light seeped from the narrow, left-hand way, its floor a gradual slope upward, the tunnel no more than three feet wide and just tall enough to admit passage of a Man.

The two Dwarven scouts stepped to where the shadow waited, though she had to move to let them know she was at hand. Brekka cautiously peered down the passage to the left, while Dokan took a few steps ahead and looked down the main corridor. Nought but gloom and silence greeted them both.

Bokar and Aravan and the main column came to the junction, Bokar hand-signalling a halt, swiftly passed back down chain. His wary eyes glancing at the choices before them, at last Bokar signalled Brekka and Dokan to scout the left-hand passage, while the main body waited at the junction.

Before they could move, the shadow dropped away from Jinnarin and Rux, and she vigorously signalled that Brekka and Dokan should remain here while she and Rux explored the dimly lit passage. Without awaiting an answer, again darkness clotted about her, and the tiny cluster of shadow slunk off up the narrow way.

Bokar reached out as if to stop her, but Aravan grasped the armsmaster by the shoulder and held him back, murmuring, "She is right, Bokar. None are better suited to the task."

Grinding his teeth, Bokar turned to Brekka and Dokan and signalled them to go down the main passage ahead. The remainder of the force stood fast, flinty eyes searching the darkness, seeking foe, while a Pysk and a fox slipped down a dimly lit fissure toward the source of light.

The floor of the cleft gradually rose as Jinnarin and Rux went onward, the light ahead slowly brightening as they neared the source. Quietly Rux moved, and Jinnarin held her bow in readiness, a tiny arrow nocked. The walls crookedly shifted this way and that, but mainly they hewed to a south-bearing course, back toward the rim of the isle, or so Jinnarin judged. The passage itself remained narrow, shrinking to a width of two feet in places, expanding out to no more than five feet at others. A faint sprinkling of dust covered the floor, and she looked for tracks, finding none, although from the scuff marks here and there it was clear that the route was used.

They had travelled some four hundred feet, when Jinnarin murmured, "I smell the sea, Rux," and on they went, coming at last to the end of the passage, where a narrow vertical slit a foot or so wide and some three feet high opened to the outside and daylight shone in. A scattering of debris lay on the floor. Jinnarin dismounted and glanced at it—fish scales and bones, a moldered fragment of bread, dried fruit peelings, the cracked bone of something not a fish, and other such— remains of meals eaten weeks past, or so she thought. Jinnarin stepped to the slit and clambered upon the sill and peered out. She could see the ocean to the horizon, entrapped hulks jutting up through the drifting weed here and there. Some ninety feet straight down the rough face of the sheer bluff the ocean boomed against the rock wall of the isle. But two hundred feet to the left at the base of the wall the waves rolled through the stone. *That has to be the illusion covering the entrance to the cavern.* She looked up, and just overhead a ledge jutted out. *Yes, I am back on the outer perimeter of the isle. This must be a lookout post.* She turned to remount Rux, and daylight sparkled off the crystalline walls of the passage, and she gasped. *Is this where I stand during the dream?* Her heart thudding, Jinnarin whirled and looked once more across the waters, but no black ship or giant spider came hurtling over the waves. Quelling her fears, Jinnarin leapt upon Rux and back down the narrow crevice they ran.

When Pysk and fox returned to the junction, Jinnarin discovered that the column had moved somewhat forward, for now Aylis and Alamar stood nearby. As the shadow came flitting from the crevice, the seeress whispered something to a Dwarf and then squatted down, intercepting fox and Pysk.

"Where are Bokar and Aravan?" Jinnarin asked.

"I have sent for them."

"Oh, Aylis, perhaps I have discovered the place where we stand in the dream and look out over the sea."

"It is there?" asked Aylis, gesturing at the slot.

"Not as it is in the dream—"

In that moment, Aravan and Bokar stepped to the pair.

"Bokar, Aravan," said Jinnarin softly, "the cleft leads to a sentry post, a narrow slot just under the ledge, above and to the left—to the west—of the entrance."

"Do any other passages split off?" asked Bokar.

"No."

"Jinnarin," whispered Aylis, "next time, before darting off, wait until I have done a casting."

"A casting?"

"Yes. When I focus, I can detect the presence of <sentient> life."

"But Aravan's blue stone—"

Alamar hissed, "It detects Foul Folk for the most part, Pysk. Some foe it does not sense at all."

"Neither does it tell direction," added Aravan, "only near or far."

Bokar tugged on his red beard. "Even so, Lady Aylis, I do not want you to be in the vanguard, nor Mage Alamar—"

"Bah, Dwarf," growled Alamar. "We can take care of ourselves."

Aylis laid a hand on her father's arm to quell him. "Father, Bokar is right—the vanguard is a place for warriors." She turned to the armsmaster. "Even so, Bokar, when we come to passages, let me do a casting before you send scouts in."

Bokar gave a short sharp nod, then said, "Just ahead, Lady Aylis, Brekka and Dokan have discovered another passage splitting off to the right."

"I'll be right back, Father," murmured Aylis, stepping swiftly away before he could volunteer to go with her. Jinnarin on Rux followed on her heels, with Aravan and Bokar coming after.

They trod along the curve, and some fifty feet down the passageway they came to the juncture, a wide corridor sheering off at a right angle to the main artery. Here Rux snorted, trying in vain to clear his nostrils of the stench emanating from this cavern way.

" 'Ware," hissed Jinnarin, "Rux likes this not."

Bokar signalled Dwarves with crossbows to stand ready. Then he turned to Aylis and whispered, "My Lady, from the echoes, to the Châkka it resounds as would a single chamber a distance within." Aylis nodded and prepared to step before the dark opening.

With crossbows warding her, Aylis murmured, *"Patefac vitam patibilem,"* and peered down the hallway, her brow furrowed in concentration. After a moment she relaxed and stepped back. "Nothing," she whispered.

"Ha!" hissed Alamar. Jinnarin whirled about. The eld Mage had come up behind them. "No <sentient> life, but other kinds of creatures could be in there—some deadly."

"I know that, Mage," sissed Bokar. "Brekka, Dokan . . ." the armsmaster paused, looking down at the cluster of shadow that was Jinnarin and Rux. Finally he added, ". . . and Lady Jinnarin. You three make a quick trip in and back. Be wary, for it is as Mage Alamar says, there yet may be life within."

Into the passage the scouts went, Jinnarin in the lead, Rux reluctantly forging into the stench. The passage curved slightly to the left and then back to the right, and at this second curve, Brekka and Dokan each un-shuttered a Dwarven lantern, the phosphorescent glow pressing back a darkness too deep for even their Châkka eyes, though Jinnarin and Rux could yet see.

They came into a large chamber filled with a stench that Pysk and Dwarf alike nearly gagged upon. And scattered across the floor were huge pallets. "Trolls!" hissed Brekka, his face grim in the gleam of the lantern. "This is a Troll sleeping chamber."

Jinnarin shuddered. She had never seen a Troll, but she had heard of them. Farrix said that they were huge—twelve to fourteen feet tall—with enormous strength and endless endurance. Like monstrous goblins they were, but dull-witted. They had pointed teeth and bat-wing ears and glaring red eyes, and stonelike hides, greenish and scaled. And some people called them Ogrus while others called them—

"Count the beds," sissed Dokan, breaking into Jinnar-in's thoughts. "We need know the threat."

Rapidly they circled the room. "I add up twenty-eight," gritted Dokan, Brekka and Jinnarin agreeing.

Brekka's gaze swept the chamber. "I see no other en-trances and exits."

"Just the passage we came down," concurred Dokan.

"Let's go," urged Jinnarin. "Rux would leave now."

Swiftly, they made their way back to the main corridor.

"It is a vacant Troll chamber," growled Dokan. "It sleeps twenty-eight."

"Elwydd!" exclaimed Bokar. "Twenty-eight?" The armsmaster looked in alarm at Aravan. "We cannot hope to take on such foe, Captain. We would be hard-pressed to defeat just one."

Aravan's hand strayed to the chill amulet at his throat. "Let us hope that we do not meet even one, Bokar. Yet Troll or no, we must press on, for now I am certain that we stride through Durlok's very own strongholt, and somewhere herein lies the heart of an evil that we must seek out and destroy."

A small cluster of shadow added, "The key to finding Farrix must lie within as well."

A grim look came into Bokar's eye. Turning to Brekka and Dokan ... and Jinnarin, "Let us go forward then," he gritted, signing for the scouts to take the point.

Another hundred feet they went, the passage sloping upward and continuing to curve gently to the right, and they came to a passageway angling sharply leftward. Again Aylis cast a spell, and once more found no <sentient> life within. And down this way Jinnarin and Brekka and Dokan discovered two more sleeping chambers, one apparently housing sixteen Rucha, and the other, four Loka. Once again, Jinnarin reviewed what Farrix had told her of such goblinlike creatures: Rucha—bandy-legged, bat-wing eared, pointed teeth, four to five feet tall, with swart skins and yellow eyes. Loka—like Rucha but taller, Man-sized, with straight limbs. And just as Trolls, these creatures, too, came from Neddra—the unskilled Rucha and the skilled Loka, all creatures of Gyphon.

Still the main corridor continued to slope up and curve to the right, the echoes of the ocean fading as they went. And still Aravan's amulet continued to gather cold unto itself as they pressed onward, denoting that they drew nearer to peril.

Some four hundred fifty feet onward, again they came to a junction, one corridor bearing left and the other straight ahead. Both passages were level, but as to which was the main route, they could not say. A faint bluish light, however, shone down the corridor to the left.

"Let me hold your amulet, Aravan," whispered Aylis.

Aravan slipped the thong over his head and handed the stone to Aylis. *"Unde?"* she murmured, closing her eyes. Slowly she turned, until she was facing down the left passage. Opening her eyes, she handed the amulet back to Aravan. "It comes from that passage," she said, pointing.

"How about the right hand way?" muttered Bokar. "I would rather not go into peril without knowing what lies behind us."

Now Aylis faced the dark passage. *"Patefac vitam pati-*

bilem," she murmured, then shook her head. "No <sentient> life, Armsmaster."

Bokar jerked his head at Brekka and Dokan, gesturing at Jinnarin's clump of shadow as well, and down the right-hand corridor sped the scouts.

As they approached they could hear the sound of running water, and they came into a large gathering hall, where there were tables and benches sized to fit Trolls as well as Rucha and Loka. Rotten bits of food were scattered about, and along one wall stood a trough and water trickled out from the stone wall to fill it, the overflow spilling down through a crack in the floor. "A mess hall," growled Brekka.

Two passageways split out from the back of this huge chamber, a small one to the right and down, a larger one level and left. While Dokan explored the left-hand way, Brekka and Jinnarin and Rux sped down the small corridor to the right. As they went down, Jinnarin could hear the sound of waves lapping against stone. They came to another split, a barred door standing ajar to the left, an open passage to the right. Glancing at Brekka, down the right-hand way they sped, coming into a chamber, and a stench was mingled with the smell of the sea. A filth-laden crevice jagged across the floor, feces lining the lip, and they could hear the ocean swashing far below. "Ugh," muttered Brekka, "this is a Grg privy."

Back to the barred doorway they went, and inside they found another chamber, this one with rotted straw pallets scattered about. A thin, feces-lined crevice jagged through this floor, too, the sound of waves splashing in its depths. Jinnarin looked at Brekka. "Prisoners, captives, most likely were kept here," he growled, jerking his head back toward the barred door.

Back to the gathering hall they went, telling Dokan what they had found. For his part, Dokan jerked a thumb toward the way he had explored. "A cookery," he growled. "Vent cracks up into the stone above."

Brekka threw the shutter on his lantern wide and looked upward. The *kwarc*-laden ceiling also showed vent cracks overhead. "Ha. I suspect it is the same throughout, the swash of the lagoon acting as a great pump to exchange the air."

Back to the waiting party they fared, reporting all to

Bokar. The armsmaster nodded and then turned to Aravan and gestured at the left-hand corridor, faint blue light shining down the glittering way. "Well, Captain, let us go see what evil it is your stone detects."

Into the passage they went, each treading silently, Brekka and Dokan and a moving cluster of shadow in the lead, the sound of the ocean all but lost in the darkness behind. A hundred feet they fared, passing a large area on the left filled with crates and bales and barrels. "Supplies," hissed Brekka, as they went past. Another hundred fifty feet they fared, the light ahead growing brighter, and once again they passed a cache of goods stowed in a hollow on the left. Now they came toward an opening into a chamber from which the bluish light glowed. Brekka stopped them a few paces away and quietly breathed, "Take care, for this is not daylight we see, nor do I think it is lantern light, but something else altogether."

Jinnarin whispered, "It looks like a casting of magelight, like Alamar makes."

A soft voice whispered right behind. It was Aravan crept upon them unnoticed in his Elven stealth. " 'Ware. My stone is icy chill. I ween the peril lies within."

Behind came the force of Châkka, and with them, Aylis.

Aravan looked at her then jerked his head toward the lighted chamber. *"Patefac vitam patibilem,"* she muttered, then nodded, whispering, "Take care, there is <sentient> life within. Just who or what, I cannot say."

"I will see," hissed Jinnarin, and the scant cluster of shadow crept toward the opening.

With her heart pounding, Jinnarin and Rux eased forward, and slowly a side of the chamber came into view. Jinnarin gasped in astonishment, for the ceiling and walls were made up completely of foot-wide, yard-long shafts of crystal—six-sided, blunt-pointed steles closely packed and jutting out at random angles into the room. The uneven floor was transparent crystal as well, as if there once had been huge crystals jutting up here, too, but ones that had been broken away and the surface crudely adzed. And all was permeated with a blue light that seemed to emanate from the very air. And as Rux crept closer, a rune slowly came into Jinnarin's view, its form hacked in the floor, the shape somehow jarring to the senses, almost as if it were writhing obscenely even though it was fixed in rough crystal.

Rux took an additional step or two, and more corrupt runes slid into view and caught at her eyes, the scribings malignant in their very shapes. Now she could see that to the left the floor jagged down toward the unseen center of the room.

Jinnarin glanced back over her shoulder. Behind crept Dokan and Brekka, while all the others waited.

With her heart hammering in her breast, Jinnarin turned back toward the crystalline room and urged Rux forward, the fox stepping to the doorway. Again Jinnarin caught her breath, for the chamber was huge, circular, fully two hundred feet across and lined with great sparkling crystals. The rough-cut floor formed a large, shallow hollow, and Jinnarin could now see down to the center where on a raised dais, or perhaps an altar, lay

"Farrix!" she shrieked, the shadow dropping away from her and Rux, fox and Pysk now standing revealed. "Farrix!" she cried again, and into the room she plunged.

CHAPTER 29

The Crystal Chamber

Spring, 1E9575
[The Present]

Kruk!" spat Brekka, leaping toward the doorway after Jinnarin, Dokan on his heels, crossbows up and ready, while through the shadow behind came Aravan running, with Bokar and the warband flying after.

Into the crystal chamber they poured, spreading wide, eyes darting this way and that, seeking foe. Following Jinnarin, Brekka and Dokan dashed down across the rough-cut crystal floor and toward the central dais, where Pysk and fox had gotten to, Rux just then leaping upon the altar, a great crystal block.

Jinnarin flung herself from Rux's back and down to her knees at Farrix's side, crying out his name. But Farrix moved not, the black-haired, leather-clad Pysk lying motionless on his back, and his chest did not stir with the breath of life. Dread filling her soul, Jinnarin pressed her ear to Farrix's breast, listening for a heartbeat, finding none. And she rocked back on her knees and raised her face to the ceiling and keened a silent wail, her face twisted into grief beyond measure. And Rux whined and turned about in indecision, and bared his teeth and growled as others drew near.

Brekka and Dokan had come to the central dais, as well as Aravan, and they took a defensive stance about the altar. And still Dwarves poured inward through the doorway.

Bokar reached Aravan's flank. "Another opening," he

barked, pointing up to the side of the chamber, where, a third of the way around the room, a slit of a doorway yawned pitch-dark along the crystal wall. The armsmaster turned to Aravan. "What says your amulet, Captain?"

"It is deadly chill—peril is nigh," answered Aravan, his eyes seeking foe, finding none.

"Kelek!" Bokar called his second in command.

As Kelek made his way down to Bokar, Aylis and Alamar entered the crystalline room, the elder pausing at the runes scribed in the transparent stone floor. "Gyphon!" he hissed, then looked up and about. "This is a temple to Gyphon."

Now all the Dwarves had come into the chamber, followed by the Men, weapons clutched in white-knuckled hands . . . all but Jatu's. And they spread across the crystalline stone glittering in the blue light.

Aravan motioned Jatu unto him, the black Man striding down into the shallow hollow, Aylis at his side. When they came to the crystal block, both looked upon Jinnarin and sorrow flooded their eyes. Jatu reached out to Jinnarin in her agony, but then withdrew his hand, for now was not the time to comfort the grieving—that would come later. Tears ran freely down Aylis's face, the seeress weeping, yet she too knew that solace would have to wait.

Leaving the runes at the doorway behind, Alamar hobbled down to the center. He gazed at Jinnarin beside the still form of Farrix, and a grave look of deep sadness crossed his face. But he shook his head, and ignoring Rux's growlings, he began examining the altar, muttering unto himself.

"Blood channels. Sacrificial. Damn Durlok! This is his slaughter house, or one of them. . . ." Still muttering, he backed away, peering at the writhing runes scribed here and there in the floor. ". . . Damn Gyphon! . . ."

Jerking his head toward the second opening, Aravan said, "Jatu, there are yet passages to follow to their ends, seeking the peril my stone warns of. Even so, I would have thee and the Men remain here at Lady Jinnarin's side, warding her, while the rest of us press on."

"Aye, Captain," said Jatu, looking about, motioning the Men to his side.

Aravan turned to Aylis. "My Lady, I need thee to search for life where we fare."

Aylis nodded, then followed Aravan as he and Bokar and Kelek and the rest of the warband moved toward the narrow opening in the wall, ebon-dark—not even the blue light seemed to shine through. All paused while Aylis stood before the doorway and cast her spell. Of a sudden, she jerked. "Blocked!" she hissed.

Upon hearing these words, Alamar looked up from one of the runes he was examining. *"Visus!"* muttered the elder, peering at the darkness just as Bokar stepped to the black opening, axe raised. "Wait, Bokar! It is trapped!" Alamar cried. At Alamar's words, all stepped back a pace or two.

While everyone waited, the eld Mage hobbled up to the doorway, and hissing and mumbling, he ran his hands around the verge of the opening. Nodding sharply unto himself, he stepped back and raised a hand and called out, *"Resera!"* and the darkness vanished. Cackling aloud, "Try to stop *me,* would he?" Alamar stepped aside and made a sweeping gesture to Aylis. "It's all yours, Daughter. But should you encounter another such, come for me. I must examine these runes." Alamar stumped to the nearest of them and bent over it, muttering and stroking his beard.

Once again Aylis stood before the doorway and murmured, *"Patefac vitam patibilem,"* then turned to Aravan and Bokar and said, "No <sentient> life." And with Brekka and Dokan in the lead, into the opening fared the Dwarven columns, Aravan and Aylis among them. While behind at a writhing rune an eld Mage mumbled and hissed to himself—"Damn Durlok! And damn Gyphon, too!"

The narrow corridor they entered slowly widened as they went, and some fifty feet down the hallway, Brekka and Dokan entered a room. By the blue light shining from the crystal chamber behind, they could see that the room was large, with tables scattered here and there, alembics and astrolabes and burners and vials and other such strewn upon them. Jars of powders and flasks of liquid sat here and there, as well as stone urns filled with colored minerals. Too, there were clear glass vessels containing things which had once been alive—small furry animals and birds and reptiles and amphibians, some dissected, others not ... and additional containers held hearts and livers and cold staring eyes and other such vital organs—all were stored in liquid. In the center of the chamber hanging down from the roof was a large, crystalline stalactite, and glistening water seeped down its sides to fill a small darkling pool cupped in a modest hollow in the floor. Along the crystalline walls stood shelves, with tomes and scrolls and piles of parchment stored thereupon. And sitting about on the floor were mechanisms made of gears and wire and metal frameworks. Yet Brekka and Dokan did not stop to examine any of these wares, noting instead that another opening loomed along the right-hand wall. Toward this way they went, as others of the warband came into the room behind, Aylis among them.

"This is a Mage's laboratory," she muttered, glancing about, then she made her way to the opening where waited the scouts.

"Visus," she murmured first, and then, *"Patefac vitam patibilem,"* and she concentrated on the dark way ahead. "Nothing."

With their Dwarven lanterns now illuminating the way, into the passage stepped Brekka and Dokan, and ten strides later they entered a chamber where stood a large canopied bed, black velvet drapes closed about. A crimson rug covered the floor, with a black-leather couch and chair sitting thereon. Too, a writing desk stood against a wall, lacquered black with a scarlet Dragon twining up and across the closed cover.

As others of the warband quietly entered the room, Brekka pressed a finger to his lips and jerked his head toward the bed. Dokan nodded, and handed his bow to another Châk, taking his axe in hand instead, and quietly the scouts stepped to the bedside. Brekka raised his crossbow to his shoulder, while Dokan reached toward the curtain.

At a nod, Dokan lifted his axe high and with a free hand threw the drapery wide.

The bed was empty.

Brekka looked at Dokan and grinned. Dokan shrugged, then stared about the room. On the far wall hung another black velvet drape, with no decoration. Stalking to the wall, the scout cautiously looked behind, then motioned others to him, Aylis among them. Jerking a thumb toward the drape, he signified to Aylis that there was a chamber on the other side of the cloth. Aylis stood before the drape and whispered her castings, then turned to Dokan and shook her head, *No.*

Carefully, Dokan drew the drape aside, revealing a narrow doorway. Peering within, the Dwarf gasped, for the room was piled high with treasure—chests, ingots, bags, silks, incenses, perfumes, and other such. Dokan turned to Aravan, a question in his eyes. " 'Tis the plunder from the weed-entrapped ships, I ween," murmured the Elf.

Dokan nodded, then stepped into the room, with Brekka following as well as others. Ignoring the treasure, they scanned the walls for another opening, an exit to elsewhere, but they found none.

Finally, Bokar turned to Aravan. "Unless there are secret doorways hidden along the routes we travelled, we have come to the end, Captain. The place is empty— no Durlok, no Ûkhs, no Hrōks, and best of all, no Trolls."

"Yet my stone is chill," said Aravan, his hand to his throat.

Aylis stepped to Aravan's side. "Give me the amulet, Aravan; I will find whence the peril emanates."

Once again Aravan handed the blue stone to Aylis. Holding it she said, "I will need aid, for my eyes will be closed as we follow the trace."

Saying nothing, Aravan smiled and offered her his arm.

"Unde?" she whispered.

Slowly Aylis turned, yet she faced toward a blank wall of the treasury. Bokar and Kelek examined it, tapping on the crystalline stone. After a moment Bokar growled, "Bah, I find nothing."

"Yet the peril lies in that direction," declared Aylis.

Brekka stroked his dark brown beard. "Beyond that wall lies the crystal chamber." His Châkka talent of knowing where he had walked made his statement a certainty. "Mayhap that is where you would have us go."

Aylis nodded, and they all moved back out from the treasure room and through the bedroom and the laboratory to come once again to the temple. Aylis stood in the doorway, her gaze sweeping the chamber. Down at the central dais, Jinnarin yet wept at Farrix's side, the Pysk now holding the lax hand of her mate. Behind her, Rux lay upon one end of the crystal block, his head down on his paws. Jatu and the Men stood with their backs to the altar, their chary eyes scanning. One Man stood in the other doorway, warding at that entrance. Alamar was on the far side of the chamber, yet examining the runes carved in the crystal floor.

At last Aylis closed her eyes. *"Unde?"*

With Aravan at her side, the seeress slowly paced down into the shallow hollow, her right hand outstretched before her, index finger extended, the amulet clutched in her left, her eyes closed, a frown of concentration on her brow. Down she trod and down, toward the great crystal block. At last she came unto the altar, and with her eyes yet closed she reached out with her finger to touch the source of peril. "Here," she murmured, "here lies the evil."

Aylis opened her eyes.

Her finger rested on Farrix.

CHAPTER 30

In the Garden
of Dreams

Spring, 1E9575
[The Present]

Slowly Jinnarin raised her face to Aylis, tears flooding her eyes and streaking unchecked down a visage twisted in torment. In a voice but a whisper, she rasped, "What? Evil? My Farrix? It is not so, Aylis! How can you— He's dead, Aylis, dead! He can't be evil; Farrix is dead. . . ." She broke into desolate sobs, choking on her grief, her heart broken.

Her own eyes flooding, Aylis wrenched about and buried her face against Aravan's chest.

Aravan embraced her and whispered, "Not evil, *chieran,* the stone does not augur evil . . . it signals peril."

Clenching the cold amulet tightly, Aylis drew back. "Peril, evil—regardless, I do not understand." Blinking away her tears, she thrust the chill stone into Aravan's hand then turned toward Farrix's still form. "How can someone who is dead be a danger to—" Aylis gasped and started, staring intently, then cried, "His eyes! Jinnarin, his eyes! Look at Farrix's eyes!"

Jinnarin looked. And even through her tears she could see that Farrix's eyes were rapidly moving back and forth beneath their closed lids.

"Farrix!" she shrieked, flinging herself forward, clasping him, weeping now in joy. "Oh, Adon, he's alive!"

Aylis turned to Aravan, tears streaming down her face. He held her close.

Jatu grinned and opened his mouth to say something, yet Jinnarin's next words drew him up short. "But wait," moaned the Pysk, her head on Farrix's chest, "he has no heartbeat. He does not breathe."

Aylis spun 'round and stared at Farrix. *"Visus!"* she hissed, her gaze locked on the Pysk. Moment later, "Father!" she called, not taking her gaze from Farrix. "Come to me!"

Alamar looked up from the rune he now studied. "Father!" Aylis cried once again. Grumbling at this interruption, Alamar demanded querulously, "What is it, Daughter? I'm busy! Grief and mourning must wait for I need to look at the rest of these runes."

"No, Father, not the runes, at least not now. Instead you need to look at Farrix. He has a casting upon him. Is he alive or dead?"

"How would I know? You are the seer."

"But you have had experience with—with Durlok's necromancy. And I fear that he has done something—"

"Necromancy!" Hastily, Alamar hobbled down across the rough crystal floor toward the altar.

"If it is necromancy," hissed Aravan, "then the stone did indeed detect evil."

Now the elder arrived at the dais and stared intently at Farrix. In a moment, "Aha!" he crowed, leaning down closely, noting the twitching of Farrix's eyes, the eld Mage grinning. "Corpses don't dream, and neither do the undead."

"But he has no heartbeat," wailed Jinnarin.

"Don't be foolish, Pysk," snapped Alamar, "of course he has one."

"But I've listened and—"

"Well listen again!"

Jinnarin laid an ear to Farrix's breast. After a moment she raised up and shook her head. "No, there's—"

"I said listen!" barked the Mage.

Once again Jinnarin laid an ear to Farrix's breast, remaining there a long while. Of a sudden her eyes widened in surprise. "A beat!" she hissed. Still she remained listening. Long moments passed, yet finally, "Another!" And a lengthy while after, "Another!"

Jinnarin raised up. "But he is not breathing."

Alamar turned to Aravan. "Your long-knife," he demanded. The Elf unsheathed the blade, handing it over to the Mage. Holding the steel between his hands, *"Refrigera,"* murmured Alamar. A moment later he turned to the altar. "Now watch, Pysk, but do not breathe on this cold blade." Alamar held the blade next to Farrix's mouth and nose. Finally a trace of mist condensed, then evaporated, and after a long while, another trace condensed. "See, I told you. He breathes." Still holding the blade, he called out to Aylis, "Farrix is not dead, Daughter, nor is he one of the undead. There is no necromancy at work here, though Farrix *is* enwrapped in a spell, but one I cannot fathom for I have never seen its like."

"Enchanted sleep?" asked Jinnarin.

"Bah! Foolish Pysk, looking for more miraculous 'magic'?"

Jinnarin jumped to her feet. "Well if it isn't magic, if it isn't enchanted sleep, then just what *is* it?"

Aylis, examining Farrix, looked up. "It is a dangerous casting, Jinnarin."

"Dangerous!"

"That's what she said, Pysk, dangerous." Alamar handed the long-knife back to Aravan.

Jinnarin wrung her hands, her gaze repeatedly darting from Farrix to Alamar to Aylis. "What'll we do? What'll we do?"

"I've no time for this twaddle," querulously snapped the elder, "I've got to get back to the runes. You tell her, Daughter." Alamar hobbled away.

Aylis sighed, then turned to Jinnarin. "Farrix is in no immediate danger, Jinnarin. This sleep of his, it's more like the winter sleep of a Bear."

"Then how do we waken him?"

"Only if the spell is removed can we waken him."

Jinnarin glanced down at Farrix. "How do we do that—remove the spell, I mean."

Aylis shook her head. "If I had cast it in the first place, it would easily be done, for I would know the exact intricacies of the spell. Yet, to try to remove the casting of another . . . well, it is very dangerous, both for the one enspelled and the one attempting to lift the spell."

"This danger you speak of, what is it?"

Aylis looked down at Farrix. "Should I try to remove the casting and fail, I could send him into a permanent sleep . . . or into death. As for the danger to me, failure might mean that I would fall under the same spell—then there would be two victims entrapped. Too, I could as well be slain. —I am not an expert in this particular form of casting, though I do know a meager bit."

"Oh," murmured Jinnarin.

"Why not take him back to Rwn?" suggested Jatu, glancing at the enspelled Pysk. "Surely someone there has the experience needed."

Aylis sighed. "That is part of the problem. The casting binds him to this place. To remove him from the isle, perhaps from the altar itself, would mean his death."

"Oh," said Jinnarin. "Then we shall not move him."

"Hmm," mused Jatu. "That means either we must leave him behind while we go and get someone who can lift the spell—"

"No!" barked Jinnarin. "Now that I have found my Farrix, I will not leave his side."

Slowly Jatu nodded, then said, "Then it seems that we must capture Durlok and force him to remove the casting . . . or Lady Aylis or Mage Alamar must attempt to remove it."

Aylis shook her head. "Not my father. Although I have little skill in this art, he has none at all."

Jinnarin's face fell. "Oh, Aylis, I would not have you endanger yourself. Is there no other way of bringing Farrix back to me—other than lifting the spell, I mean?"

"One other, but the chances of it happening are remote."

"What is it?"

Aylis looked at Farrix. "If he wakens himself, then perforce the spell will be broken."

Jinnarin sighed and sat down beside her mate, her shoulders slumped in dejection.

Aravan glanced from Farrix to Aylis. "Now is not the time to decide. Let us think on it awhile. Mayhap another course will suggest itself."

"Ha!" came Alamar's call. "None of these runes are now empowered, though they have been in the past." The elder began stepping down toward the central dais.

"What do they do, Father?"

"Well, my best guess is that they let Durlok talk to Gyphon, but that is merely a guess—a damn fine guess I might add. In fact, I am most likely right."

"Talk to Gyphon?" Aylis was dismayed. "But Adon forbade—"

"I know, I know, Daughter." Alamar arrived at the altar. "Nevertheless, that is what I think."

Now Bokar came down to the dais, to Aravan. "I am sending out a squad to seek hidden doorways along the route we travelled, though it is unlikely we will find any whether or not they are there."

"Nonsense," snorted Alamar. "Finding secret portals is a trivial task." The Mage glanced at the sleeping Pysk, then turned back to Bokar. "I can do nothing here. Instead I will go with your squad and use my <sight> to reveal any doors that may be hidden."

"Father, <sight> will likely only reveal doors hidden by castings and not those cunningly carved."

"Daughter, this cavern was hidden behind an illusion. Durlok may have disguised other openings in a like manner."

Aylis sighed and glanced at Farrix, then said to Aravan. "We will cover twice the ground in half the measure if I go with another squad and look as well. It will give me time to consider our dilemma with Farrix."

Bokar turned to Aravan and asked, "Just what *do* you plan on doing, Captain? I mean, shall we stay in Durlok's lair until he returns? Take him prisoner? Force him to remove the casting from Farrix? Haul him to Rwn for a trial by his peers? Or do we, instead, take our leave before he comes back? What?"

"He's already had his trial," barked Alamar. "Sentenced to exile on Vadaria, he was, before he escaped to Mithgar. And now, dead or alive he's to be returned to Vadaria before he can do any more harm. Myself, I'd prefer to see him dead."

"Father, now that we know of this place, can we return to Rwn, then shall we muster the aid needed to capture Durlok in his lair."

"Daughter, if we waken Farrix and remove him, Durlok will know that his strongholt has been discovered, and he will flee elsewhere."

"Father, we cannot let Farrix remain in the grasp of that monster."

"But, Daughter, we also cannot let Durlok escape."

At these words, Jinnarin burst into tears.

Jatu growled and turned to Alamar. "Durlok will know we have been here regardless, Mage, for you tampered with his door, disarmed his trap."

"Bah!" snorted Alamar. "That is easily set back to the way it was. Nothing that I have done will alert Durlok that he is found."

In dismay, Aravan looked upon the weeping Pysk. After a moment he said, "We will counsel after the search. Bokar, form up another squad for Lady Aylis. Too, set a sentry at the lookout post Lady Jinnarin found. I would not have Durlok surprise us."

"Neither would I, Captain," gritted the armsmaster. "That is why I sent Arka and Dett to the lookout post—they should be there by now." As Aravan shrugged and faintly smiled, Bokar turned to Kelek. "Lead Lady Aylis's squad. I will go with Mage Alamar." In a trice a second squad was formed, and the search for hidden doors begun, Aylis and Aravan going with one squad toward the distant quay, Alamar with the other beginning at this end of the long hallway. Soon a quietness fell upon the crystal chamber, and with tears running down her face, Jinnarin sat beside her Farrix and held the sleeper's hand.

After a while Brekka came to the dais and stood for a moment with Jatu. The black Man looked up and around at the chamber, then asked the Dwarf, "Tell me Brekka, have you ever seen a place as this?"

Slowly Brekka shook his head. "The Loremasters tell of crystal caverns, but I had never seen such until now. In our delving, we Châkka at times discover the miniature of this—hollow stones with crystals clinging to the interior walls . . . *kalite, lamethyk, kwarc,* and other such. But compared to this, those hollow stones are small—I have found several myself—whereas this cavern is enormous."

Of a sudden Brekka's jaw clenched in anger. "But this cavern has been defiled. Look at the floor—mutilated. We Châkka would have made this into a place of wonder, yet the despoiling Grg have ravaged it nearly beyond redemption. And Durlok has carven foul runes within the living stone itself. For this alone I would slay him."

Jatu stroked his chin. "Among your Kind, such is a crime?"

Brekka nodded. "Elwydd gave us the under-Mountain realms to husband. We honor Her and strive to make them into domains even She would find worthy. To despoil the living stone is to slur Her name, and we would exact retribution for such."

"But Brekka, sometimes my People, Mankind, sometimes we destroy the stone—mines and the like."

Brekka turned to Jatu. "Mining is an honorable calling. To extract precious metals and rare gemstones from raw earth, ores, rock, or to delve for tin and iron and copper and such, or to quarry stone—common or semiprecious—there is nothing wrong with such. It is the wanton destruction of irreplaceable beauty which constitutes the crime ... that or unjustified destruction of life."

"Oh, I see."

The two fell silent, but after a moment a soft voice came from behind them, Jinnarin saying, "Evil. It is evil which must be destroyed." She looked down at Farrix. "For this, Durlok must die."

"Aye," gritted Brekka, striking a fist into palm.

Jatu growled, "But only after we force him to waken the sleeper."

Jinnarin sighed, then nodded.

They looked down upon Farrix, the Pysk lying motionless, not seeming to breathe, apparently dead. In that moment beneath their lids his eyes began switching rapidly back and forth. "He dreams," said Jinnarin.

"The sending, do you think?" asked Jatu.

Jinnarin shrugged. "Perhaps. I just wish—" Suddenly Jinnarin's eyes flew wide, and she leapt to her feet. "Jatu! That's it! I know how—where's Aylis? Brekka, where is Aylis?"

Brekka gestured at the doorway leading toward the quay, but before he could say aught, "Rux!" Jinnarin shrieked, waking the fox from his doze, the animal leaping to his feet. Springing to Rux's back, "Away!" she cried. "Find Aylis!"

Down from the altar sprang the fox, hitting the crystal floor running, flying toward the exit. "Jinnarin, wait!" called Jatu, starting after, but she paid him no heed, as out the doorway and into the crystal-laden passage she sped.

As the ocean swells hollowly boomed against the walls of the understone lagoon, *"Visus,"* murmured Aylis, her gaze sweeping all about the great grotto. After a moment she turned to Aravan and Kelek and shook her head and muttered, "Nothing." Lightly concentrating to maintain her magesight, she stepped into the passage leading inward from the landing, and down this way she trod among the squad of Dwarves, Aravan at her side, the seeress intently scanning the walls as she went. Soon they came to the narrow fissure on the left, the one leading to the sentry post, and into this strait they went, Kelek and a handful going before her, Aravan and the others following after, the Dwarves now and again having to turn sideways in the crevice, their shoulders wider than some places along the slot.

And even as they pressed forward, Aylis's mind gnawed at the problem of Farrix and Durlok, as a dog would worry a bone. Still, she maintained her <vision> and searched the fissure for the telltale signs of magery, for concealment of whatever might be hidden along this way.

At last they came to the end of the cleft, where Arka and Dett stood ward, daylight yet shining through the narrow slot in the wall of the tiny sentry chamber, now crowded with Dwarves shuffling about to get out of Aylis's way.

"The slot, too, is covered by illusion," she muttered. "I would think that from the outside it appears to be stone." Looking out and glancing up, she said, "Ah, it is up against the overhang of the ledge where I could not see it, and that's why I did not find it with my <vision> when Bokar and I lay atop."

Pulling back, her gaze darted about the small chamber, crystal glittering in the daylight. *Ah, now I do see.*

This is where Jinnarin said might be the place she stands in the sending. Aylis turned and looked back out over the sea. Of a sudden, her eyes widened as an unexpected thought burst upon her consciousness, the power of it such that she lost her concentration. Whirling toward the passage, she slapped a palm against her forehead and cried, "Adon, how stupid! I know a way to try!"

"Try what?"

Even though she stood next to Aravan she did not hear his words, lost as she was in her sudden illumination. Urgency filled her voice. "I must get to Jinnarin." And she plunged through the press of Dwarves and back into the cleft crying, "Out of my way," to the warriors inadvertently barring her path, the seeress struggling to get past.

"Go before her!" shouted Kelek, and the Dwarves blocking the slot turned and started back toward the main passage, Aylis calling out and spurring them to swiftness.

Down the cleft they pressed, moving now in haste, feet clattering, armor jingling, Aravan and Kelek and a handful of Dwarves trailing after. They had rushed nearly back to the entrance to the fissure, when above the chinging of mail and slap of feet and the sound of their own breathing, from ahead they heard the barking of a fox and Jinnarin crying out, "Aylis, Aylis, I know, I know, I know how." And running toward them came Rux and the Pysk, the fox with his nose to the floor following the scent of the seeress.

The Dwarven warriors in the lead skidded to a halt, those coming after jostling into one another at the sudden stop, Aylis among these. Rux, too, slid to a halt, and Jinnarin leapt from his back and ran weaving through the press until she came to Aylis. And her whole face lit up at the sight of the seeress, as did Aylis's own face. And the moment they sighted one another, *Dreamwalk!* they simultaneously cried.

Jinnarin stood on the altar and looked down at Farrix, while Aylis argued with her father.

"Daughter, are you forgetting that Aravan's amulet runs chill? The stone detects the antipathy between

Aravan's *essence* and that of a born foe ... which is why it runs cold at the vile creatures from Neddra, but gives no hint of a Human enemy. Heed me, Daughter, there is something evil in this casting which entraps Farrix."

"The stone detects peril, Father, not necessarily evil. And we already know that peril lies within the sending. Yet can we find Farrix in his dream, we can talk to him, cause him to become aware that he is dreaming, and let him take control and awaken himself, breaking the spell. For such a gain we will risk the peril."

Alamar nodded then scowled. "Last time, you brought a green monster back with you."

"Tentacles, Father, tentacles only. And they were chopped off when we closed the bridge."

"But what if something horrible follows you again? Something worse. Something which doesn't get chopped off."

Aylis sighed. "There are hazards all about, Father. Yet I think that walking Farrix's dream is the least risky chance of all. I do not think I have the knowledge or the skill to dispel the casting laid upon him by Durlok. But should I try, then both Farrix and I are at peril—and death or disaster lies along that route. And our chances of capturing Durlok and forcing him to lift the spell—well, who can assess such? Not I. Besides, Durlok may do something even more evil should we give him an opportunity to cast a spell—whether or no it be on Farrix, or on us all instead. And we cannot move Farrix to let the Masters at Rwn lift the spell. And I think that Farrix will not spontaneously awaken himself, removing the casting. No, Father, I think that this is our best chance to lift this foul curse that lies on Jinnarin's mate."

Alamar growled, "Knowing Durlok, Daughter, this is like to be a trap of his. There was a trap on the doorway, you know. But just what kind of trap he may have laid on Farrix, well, I don't know. Yet this I do know: the spell is linked to someone or something, but who or what I cannot say. And to disturb that link ... well, it just might bring on even more trouble."

Aylis kissed her sire on the cheek and grinned. "We will be most wary, Father. If there is a trap and we are successful, then you and I will both have defeated him, father and daughter alike. "

A faint smile flickered over Alamar's face, but then he sighed and said, "Of course waking Farrix will mean that Durlok is likely to slip through our fingers again."

Jinnarin rounded on Alamar. "I don't *care* what happens to Durlok! We set out to find Farrix and rescue him if need be, and we have done so—found him that is. But his rescue yet lies before us. And you are sworn, Alamar. You are sworn. Now leave us be! Your battle with Durlok can wait! You can do him in the eye some other time."

Alamar ground his teeth in ire, then spun on his heel. "Bokar, get the squad together. There's walls and halls and rooms yet to examine for secret doors."

Aylis watched her father leave, the Mage to use his <sight> on the laboratory, bedroom, and treasury, and the passages between. When he was gone from the crystal chamber, she turned to the Pysk. "Jinnarin, I do not think that my father would try to stop us from awakening Farrix just so that he could face Durlok once more and 'do him in the eye.' Instead he is frightened for us both, for he knows that walking a dream is a most dangerous undertaking—especially this dreamer's dream."

Jinnarin sighed. "You're probably right, Aylis. It's just that we've come such a long way to find Farrix, and now that we've done so . . . well, I just want him back."

"I know, Jinnarin. I know. And given that Fortune turns her smiling face our way, we will have him with us shortly."

Jinnarin looked up and about at the room. "This light, Aylis, is there some way we can at least dampen it?"

"My father can, of that I am certain."

"Well and good then, for I have some candles." Jinnarin fished through one of the packs Rux had borne and drew out three tapers, each one nearly as tall as she.

Aylis gestured at the floor beside the altar. "When my father gets back and we begin, I will sit down here. You sit beside Farrix and when he starts to dream, signal me."

As Aylis looked for a smooth place, of a sudden she cocked her head this way and that and stared at the roughly adzed crystal. Then she glanced up at the walls. "Hmm. Jinnarin, when I walked the sending with Ontah, we found ourselves flanking you in a fine crystal castle. But then the dream changed, the walls of the chamber becoming less finished, the floor rougher, as if we were being drawn into another dream. I note that here the floor is rough, the walls unfinished."

Jinnarin's face fell as she thought of Ontah—of White Owl—who had been killed by the very same dream they would perhaps walk once again, the Pysk remembering the look of terror frozen upon the slain elder's face. She shook her head to dispel the horrid vision, and then looked about the room and finally at Aylis. "Yes, the walls and floor are rough, unfinished." Then Jinnarin blenched. "It changed as the dreadful fear came upon us. What does it mean, Aylis?"

Aylis took a deep breath and then let it out. "I think it's just one more indication that the sending comes from here."

"From Farrix," said Jinnarin.

Aylis looked at the enspelled sleeper. "Aye, from Farrix."

The Pysk set her bow and quiver of arrows at Farrix's side. Taking a deep breath she said, "Well, come what may, I'm ready."

"So am I," said Aylis.

A time passed, and Alamar at last came back into the temple, Aravan and Bokar with him.

"Nothing," said the eld Mage. "No doors, panels, or anything else hidden by a casting."

"Your warriors yet tap the walls," said Aravan to Bokar, gesturing, "both back there and toward the quay. Mayhap they will find a hidden door."

"Unlikely, Captain," responded Bokar. "If their crafting is at all worthy, we will find nought. Even so, we are looking for seams and splits, cracked crystals, hollow soundings—anything that would reveal a door, a hidden hall."

Alamar strode 'round the crystal chamber, a look of concentration on his face. At last he called out, "Nothing here as well, Bokar. You can stop worrying about a secret Troll hole."

Bokar shook his head and gritted, "You jape me, Mage Alamar. Yet Trolls are nothing to gibe about. They are a terrible foe, their skins like stone, turning blades aside. Not even a crossbow bolt will penetrate, except in the eye or ear, and perhaps the throat, and that a shot guided by Fortune's hand. And twenty-eight of such"—Bokar stabbed a finger in the direction of the Troll quarters—"would squash us like beetles under a heel."

"Faugh!" Alamar dismissed the threat with a wave of his hand as he hobbled down toward the central dais. "Any Trolls come along, well, you just leave them to me."

"Father," Aylis said sharply, "Bokar is right. That many Trolls would be nearly unstoppable. I have not the training to thwart them, and although you do, you must remember your promise to me and not squander the <fire> you have left."

"All it would take is a bolt or two—"

"Father!"

Hissing in exasperation, Alamar clenched his jaw but remained silent otherwise. Aylis turned to Bokar. "Armsmaster, I would have you remove your warriors from this room, for Lady Jinnarin and I will need the chamber to be quiet to walk Farrix's dream."

"I would not leave you unwarded," protested Bokar.

"Then leave one or two behind."

Bokar shook his head. "One or two is not sufficient."

"Fiddle-faddle!" exclaimed Alamar. "These caverns are deserted, Bokar. Where Durlok has gotten to, who can say? Regardless, if Aylis and Jinnarin need peace and quiet, then I say let be."

"We will also need darkness, Father. Can you extinguish this blue light?"

"Ha!" barked the Mage, raising a hand, muttering,

"Exstingue omnino," and the chamber was plunged into total darkness.

"Father!" exclaimed Aylis.

The soft phosphorescent glow of a Dwarven lantern filled the chamber as Jatu raised the hood on the one he wore at his belt.

Jinnarin glanced at the lamp but still lighted one of her candles, and Jatu closed the lantern shield, the blue-green glow extinguished.

As the soft yellow light of the candle on the altar glittered and glimmered among the crystals, Aravan said, "Jatu, Bokar, Mage Alamar, and I will remain within the chamber while ye dreamwalk, Lady Aylis, Lady Jinnarin. All others will aid in the search for hidden doors."

Bokar cocked an eyebrow but said nothing, as Aylis murmured her agreement, adding, "Caution them to quietness should they have need to enter the chamber, Bokar."

In the flickering flame of the candle on the crystal altar, Jinnarin sat cross-legged at Farrix's side, her thoughts drifting, her mind in a state of light meditation. Down beside the carven block, Aylis sat on the rough-cut floor, her back against the mass, her mind too in meditation. Spaced at wide intervals in the deep shadows 'round the chamber sat Bokar and Jatu and Aravan and Alamar—Bokar at the entrance to the hallway, Alamar at the opening leading to Durlok's laboratory, with Jatu against the crystal wall across from Bokar and Aravan opposite Alamar. And there drifted on the air distant echoes of faint murmurings and soft tappings as Men and Dwarves searched afar for hidden doors.

A time passed, and after a long while Alamar quietly stood and stretched, his elderly muscles stiffly protesting. He motioned to Jatu and when the black Man came to him he whispered in his ear. Jatu nodded, and Alamar turned and left the chamber, heading into the laboratory. Jatu softly stepped to Bokar, murmuring something, then came on to where Aravan sat. Squatting, Jatu whispered, "Mage Alamar has gone to search through Durlok's papers to see if he can deduce what the Black Mage is up to."

Aravan nodded, then murmured, "Take station at his

doorway then, where thou canst get to him quickly in case he needs help."

"I had planned on that, Captain, for should aught happen then we in here may need Alamar's aid as well." Jatu rose and crept back to where Alamar had been sitting and positioned himself there.

And more time passed.

The candle had burned some halfway down when Farrix's eyes began to twitch back and forth.

"<*Añu*>," murmured Jinnarin to Aylis, the <word> of <suggestion> alerting the seeress. Jinnarin then slipped into a state of deep meditation and used another of the ingrained <words> of <suggestion> and began dreaming. And she found herself . . .

. . . before the hollow tree in Darda Glain that served as a home for her and Farrix. Sighing with memories of past days, Jinnarin called her bow and arrows to her. Then she formed a bridge to Aylis's dream, and stepped onto . . .

. . . the afterdeck of the *Eroean*, where Aylis stood with Aravan, the Elf laughing freely while the seeress spun the wheel to heel the ship over in the wind. Aylis looked down at the Pysk and sighed, then turned and kissed Aravan. "I must go, love," she said.

The air divided and Pysk and seeress together walked into the fissure, and out into . . .

. . . the shadowed marge of a sunlit garden.

The air was gentle, cool, a breeze softly blowing. A crystalline stream burbled nearby, running among the verdant growth, and grassy pathways wended through a riot of colors, blossoms of all hues nodding in the zephyr as humming bees coursed among clusters of flowers and over rill mosses and around stands of delicate grasses. Ornamental trees were scattered here and there, the garden itself set within the expanse of a broad forest glen, and the songs of unseen birds occasionally echoed from afar. A noontime Sun stood directly overhead in a clear blue sky and shown down into the glade, and in garden center grew a tall hedge, a green rectangular wall, some hundred feet from corner to corner, four hundred feet 'round all.

"Oh my," murmured Aylis, "how lovely."

"Yes," agreed Jinnarin, looking about, "but where's Farrix?"

They stood in the shade of a great oak tree on the edge of an ancient forest. Aylis slowly turned in a complete circle, her gaze sweeping across the garden and then in among the huge-girthed boles down within green dappled shadows stirring in the gentle breeze. But when she had turned full 'round, once again her eye rested upon the central hedge within the glade. "There," she said and pointed. "There within the square bounded by the hedge, there I would think to find him."

They followed one of the grassy pathways wending toward the hedgerow, the rill burbling alongside. They passed among the nodding flowers and sighing grasses and softly rustling trees as the breeze gently urged them onward, ruffling their unbound hair. Up across a tiny arched bridge they trod, and Aylis leaned over the railing to see golden fish swimming above a white sandy bottom and among fronds of green watercress wafting in the purling current, the auric fish darting under the water plants, fleeing from her shadow cast straight down.

At last Pysk and seeress came to the hedge, but when they walked all way 'round, no entry did they find. Aylis smiled and took Jinnarin's hand, and up and over they flew . . . to find . . . a garden within the garden, this one much the same . . . except in the very center, on a crystal block lay—

"Farrix!" Jinnarin shrieked, and flew down to land at his side.

He was asleep.

"Wake up, my love! Wake up!" she called, shaking him by the shoulder—to no avail.

Jinnarin laid her ear on his breast, and after a long while, "A heartbeat," she said, and waited, and finally called out, "Another."

Her eyes brimming with tears, Jinnarin glanced up at the Lady Mage. "Oh, Brightwing, it is the same. He is in an enchanted sleep here as well."

Sadness filled Aylis's eyes and she looked at Farrix, then startled, looked again, her eyes widening. "Sparrow, he dreams!"

Jinnarin jerked her head up from Farrix's breast and

stared at Farrix's eyes as they whipped back and forth beneath their closed lids.

Confusion filled Jinnarin's face. "A dream within a dream?"

"Yes, Sparrow, that's what it must be. We must hurry and enter this dream as well."

"Can we do that?"

"I don't know, but we must try. And quickly, for if he wakes, we'll be trapped."

"Even if he doesn't wake, but merely stops dreaming, we'll be trapped. Perhaps this is the snare that Durlok set, and no matter how many dreams we enter, we'll always find him asleep. Oh, let's hurry."

Jinnarin formed another bridge, the air rippling apart. They stepped into the fissure and found . . .

. . . themselves in a crystal castle overlooking a pale green sea where a black ship with lightning-stroked masts plunged across the storm-tossed waves.

And dread filled their very beings, hammering at their hearts, rending their guts, riving their very souls. The room began to shift, to change, to become rough, unworked crystal. And with terror mauling them, Jinnarin and Aylis whipped about to see a writhing mass of blackness boiling toward them, great claws forming on massive arms and lunging out to rend and tear as hideous yellow eyes gloated in insane triumph.

"Bridge out!" shrieked Aylis.

Through a hole dove Jinnarin, landing and rolling in the sunlit garden, her bow lost to her grasp. Aylis, too, leapt into the sunshine, both Pysk and seeress slamming the bridges shut. But the air before them rippled, and roiling blackness came through—not a single writhing mass, but five, ten, twelve, more!

"Again!" shrilled Jinnarin. "Bridge ou—!" But before she could complete her thought, terror whelmed into her mind, filling it entirely. She could not think. She could not see. She could not hear. She could only scream.

But Aylis's mind had not been seized, and she managed to reach out an arm toward one of the writhing masses and hiss past lips taut with dread, *"Fulmen!"* and a bolt of lightning flashed from her outstretched hand and through the boiling black.

Of a sudden, Jinnarin could see and hear and think.

But Aylis was frozen in place and screaming, unable to do aught else.

And blackness boiled toward her, ebony talons raised. Nearly paralyzed with terror, Jinnarin managed to reach out a hand and clutch her bow. Panic hammering at her, her breath nought but hoarse gasps, with fear-frozen fingers still she succeeded in nocking an arrow. She raised the bow in her trembling dread, the shaft rattling against the wood of the grip. "Adon," she groaned through fear-clenched jaws, and aimed and loosed, the bolt shrinking to a tiny Pysk-arrow that flew straight through one of the writhing blots of darkness and beyond, to no effect.

Even though she despaired, again she strung an arrow. "Demon spawn!" she shrilled, dread whelming at her. "Die!" and she loosed at another of the roiling shadows. But again the wee shaft flew into the seething blackness and out the other side, and still the writhing mass moved with the others through the sunlit flowers and toward Aylis.

Of a sudden Jinnarin shrieked, "Demons!" And she strung another arrow, this time choosing her target carefully. But once again the diminutive shaft flew without effect through the churning darkness. And now the writhing, boiling black had reached Aylis, clustering about the dread-whelmed seeress, who could neither think nor see nor hear nor do aught but scream in unremitting terror.

Massive black claws were raised to rend her, insane gaze flashing in mad triumph, a gaping red maw leering—

—but in that moment a tiny arrow flashed into a particular yellow eye—

—and all the creatures vanished but one!

—and that one—"*RRRAAAAWWWW!*—bellowed in agony and clawed at its amorphous face, its fang-filled crimson maw stretched wide in anguish—

—and another tiny arrow flashed into the shapeless creature's mouth, slamming into tissue—

—and deadly poison burst into the demon's brain—

—flaring, flashing throughout—

—and the creature fell dead, slain by an etheric poison on a spectral arrow from the phantom bow of a Pysk.

CHAPTER 31

The Dreamer

Spring, 1E9575
[The Present]

The hideous dread vanished, and Aylis slumped to the ground. Jinnarin sprang to her side and called out, "Brightwing!" The seeress had not fainted, though, and she looked at Jinnarin. "I—wha—? The fiend! — Where?"

"Dead."

"Dead?"

"I killed it. It was a demon, and I killed it."

"How?"

Jinnarin raised her bow. Aylis nodded. "I tried lightning, one of my father's spells, to no effect."

"You missed the real one."

"Real one?"

"Yes. All but one were illusions."

"How did you—?"

Jinnarin smiled. "Jatu told me about demons. I shot at the one with no shadow."

Aylis turned to stare at the demon, and *lo!* even as she and Jinnarin looked on, an oily darkness rose up from the ebony form, the wind swirling it up and away and shredding it. In moments the demon had vanished.

"This was Durlok's trap," gritted Aylis. "This was the evil spirit that slew White Owl. Sparrow, by your bow, he is avenged."

Jinnarin looked at where the demon had lain and nodded. And suddenly she began to laugh wildly, from relief, from the snapping of tension.

Aylis looked at her in amazement, and then she, too, began laughing.

Soon both were howling, and pointing at one another. Covering her mouth, trying to get control of herself, Jinnarin turned away from Aylis and looked in garden center where lay Farrix's sleeping form.

Abruptly she was sober. "Farrix! Brightwing, we've got to waken Farrix! And swiftly, for he will soon stop dreaming."

Aylis, too, sobered. "Yes! You are right. We must find him quickly."

"Back into the dream within the dream?"

Aylis nodded, even then forming the bridge between.

Once again they stepped through the rippling air and into the crystal castle. Now there was no fear, no dread, within. In haste they searched the chamber, and in an alcove they discovered Farrix asleep upon a crystal altar.

"Oh no, not again!" cried Jinnarin, kneeling beside him. "He's under a casting here, too!" But at the sound of her voice, Farrix stirred.

"He moved, Sparrow! He is not enspelled in this dream!"

Jinnarin gently shook him by the shoulder. "Farrix. Farrix. Wake up, my love."

Slowly Farrix stretched, yawning, and opened his eyes—

—And in that moment the crystal castle shifted, the floor became rough-adzed crystal, and whole crystals jutted out from the walls. It was Durlok's temple to Gyphon—

"Hullo, love," said Farrix, starting to raise up, but unable to move because Jinnarin flung herself atop him, weeping in joy.

"Here, here, what's the matter? Why this crying?"

Jinnarin tried to tell him, but her words were incoherent, a sobbing babble.

"It's a strange tale, Farrix," said Aylis, as he looked up at the sound of her voice and saw her for the first time. "But know this: you are somehow involved with Durlok—"

"Durlok!" spat Farrix, sitting upright even though Jinnarin yet embraced him. "I had forgotten!" He looked about the crystal chamber then grasped her by the shoulders and held her at arm's length. "How did you get here? —Oh never mind, the only thing of importance now is that we've got to get out of here, love! You are not safe!"

Taking her by the hand, Farrix struggled against Jinnarin's resistance, trying to leap with her from the crystal block, but Jinnarin held him back, crying, "No, no, Farrix!" He turned to her, and with her eyes red and running, her nose adrip, Jinnarin shook her head. "You need not fear Durlok, at least not at the moment. You see, this is a dream you are having, and you've just got to wake up! Break the spell."

Farrix gaped. "Dream? Dream! What are you talking about, and who is this?" He jabbed a finger at Aylis.

Jinnarin clenched her fists in frustration. "Oh, Farrix, it doesn't matter. You see, you've got to wake up before you stop dreaming."

Again Farrix's jaw dropped open. "Wake up before I stop dreaming? But—but if this *is* a dream, if I wake up I *will* stop dreaming. This makes no sense." He looked at Aylis, turning his hands up in an unspoken appeal to sanity, adding, "And I still want to know who you are."

"She's a Lady Mage, Farrix. Alamar's daughter."

Aylis nodded. "We are in your dream to break an"— Aylis sighed—"an 'enchantment' placed upon you by Durlok. It is important that you waken before this dream ends."

Farrix took a deep breath and then explosively blew it out through puffed cheeks and shook his head. "I can't believe I'm dreaming." He looked about and pinched himself—"Ow!"—wincing. "It is so *real!*"

Jinnarin stomped her foot. "Is *this* real?" she barked, then floated up off the crystal block.

"Adon!" hissed Farrix, leaping to his feet. "It *is* a dream!"

"See? I told you!" proclaimed Jinnarin, settling back to the altar.

"What do I have to do?" asked Farrix.

Suddenly Jinnarin realized that she didn't know *what* Farrix had to do to awaken himself. She looked at Aylis.

"Tell me," the seeress asked him, "have you ever wished to awaken at a certain time, say at dawn, or when

the Moon rises, or at mid of night, and been able to
do so?"

Slowly Farrix nodded.

"Then here is what you must do. Convince yourself
that at the moment we leave, that is the very moment
you must awaken."

"When you leave?"

"Yes. That is the signal to yourself."

Farrix looked about the crystal chamber. "Where are
you going? Into the tunnels? Into the Troll hole? Back
to the grotto? Where?"

Aylis shook her head. "None of those places, Farrix.
Instead we go to a garden. To the garden of dreams."

"That's where you are," added Jinnarin. "Asleep."

Farrix's eyes widened in confusion. "Asleep?"

"Yes, love. Dreaming this dream."

"Oh," he said in a small, still voice. "I sleep in a
garden dreaming this dream, and when I awake, all will
be set to rights."

"Not quite—" began Jinnarin, but Aylis interrupted.

"We will explain what comes next when you awaken
from this dream."

Again Farrix took a deep breath and blew it out. "I'm
getting confused, but I'll do my best to waken when you
go from here." He looked at them, then frowned. "But
I say, look here: I don't know how I go about setting
my mind to wake at a certain time or event. I just do it."

Aylis grimly smiled. "Wish or want is what drives it—
strong enough desire or need."

"Oh."

Jinnarin stepped to his side. "Farrix, I really need you.
You *must* do this thing, else I fear we are all in dire
straits, and Durlok will do something utterly evil, something we need to stop before he kills any more."

Farrix gritted his teeth. "Damn Durlok! He is a monster and needs stopping."

Aylis caught his gaze with hers. "Then, Farrix, you
must awaken."

He nodded sharply. "Let us do it, then."

"Though I am not certain, I believe that it would be
easier if you would lie back down," advised Aylis.

Farrix reclined on the crystal block.

Jinnarin leaned over and kissed him and then stepped back. "Brightwing . . ."

Farrix turned his head toward them and watched as the air rippled, a cleft forming, a portion of a sunlit garden could be seen through the fissure. His eyes widened as they stepped through, the breach closing behind them.

Jinnarin climbed upon the crystal slab where Farrix lay sleeping in the heart of the verdant glen, Aylis at hand. The Sun yet stood at the zenith, having moved not at all. And the two of them peered at the dreamer's eyes, twitching back and forth. Of a sudden the movement stopped. "Oh," wailed Jinnarin. "We were too late. He has stopped drea—"

—Farrix opened his eyes.

"Ha!" exulted Jinnarin. "You did it!" And she kissed him soundly.

Farrix sat up and looked about. "So, what I was dreaming wasn't a dream after all. Or, no, wait—it *was* a dream, but not an ordinary one. Instead, it was a—a true dream? Does that make sense?"

"Oh yes, love!" said Jinnarin, kissing him again.

Farrix started to get up, saying, "Well, let's get out of here and stop Dur—"

"No, no, Farrix. Wait," called Jinnarin, pushing him back down. "This is but another dream."

"Another dream?" He looked about, once again pinching himself—"Ow!"

Jinnarin floated upward. "See?"

Farrix groaned. Then sighed. Then muttered, "Damn Durlok! Is this like one of those puzzles—links and rings and boxes within boxes?"

Jinnarin grinned. "No, love, this is the last one. When you awaken from this one, you will really and truly be awake."

Aylis leaned over. "Are you ready to try again?"

Farrix rolled his eyes, but nodded.

"It may be a bit harder this time, Farrix, for as Sparrow—Jinnarin—has said, this is the last one."

"I am ready," he said, lying back down on the crystal slab. "Let us get on with it."

Again, Jinnarin kissed him. "I will be waiting, my love."

And once more Farrix watched as the air rippled and a fissure formed and Jinnarin and Aylis passed through, the cleft closing behind.

Jinnarin and Aylis stepped into the crystal chamber, where bedlam reigned, with shouting Dwarven warriors hacking and chopping at some huge creature lying on the rough-adzed floor halfway up to the wall. Between the creature and the crystal altar stood Aravan and Jatu, weapons in hand, warding a motionless seeress and unmoving female and male Pysks—Aylis and Jinnarin and Farrix. And striding down from the door to the laboratory came Alamar, a strange, dark fire playing about the eld Mage's hands, while up on the crystal block stood Rux, his teeth bared, the fox between his mistress and the mêlée above. Swiftly the dreamwalkers rushed to their forms and plunged within and spoke the <word> of <suggestion>, opening their eyes to the riot in the room.

Aylis sprang to her feet, Jinnarin as well. The Pysk nocked one of her tiny arrows and leapt to Rux's back as Aylis stepped to Alamar's side, the elder taking a stance by the altar. "Father, what is it?"

"A Gargon, Daughter, a Gargon!"

Aylis's heart jumped into her throat. A Gargon! Dreaded fearcaster. A huge, hideous creature, grey and stonelike, but walking upright on two legs, a malevolent monster of the nether world, a demon, said some, able to paralyze its victims with fear.

Aravan stepped before Aylis, sword in hand, standing between her and the downed creature, the Elf's face to the threat. Jatu took up station at her side.

"It just fell out of mid air and crashed to the floor," rumbled the black Man. "Kelek and a squad were passing through," he added.

"Châkka-shok! Châkka-cor!" Bokar's war cry crested above the rage, the Dwarf slamming his axe—*Chnk!*—down into the unmoving creature's flank.

"Hold!" shouted Kelek, his voice lost in the uproar, the Dwarven warrior among those hewing and smashing upon the felled monster. "Hold, by Elwydd, hold! It is dead!"

At last he was heard in the tumult, and the shouts and cries and fury diminished, dwindled, stopped altogether. And as quiet returned, slowly, suspiciously, the warriors backed away, and by the light of the Dwarven lanterns scattered across the floor, they peered at the creature, an evil parody of a huge, reptilian Man eight feet tall, ponderous, with taloned hands and feet and glittering rows of fangs in a lizard-snouted face, the Dwarves ready to leap forward again should the monster give even the slightest twitch.

And in the ensuing stillness—"I say, what's all the ruckus about" came a piping voice from behind.

Jinnarin, Aylis, Alamar, Aravan, and Jatu all whirled about, to see Farrix standing, the black-haired Pysk yawning and rubbing his eyes.

CHAPTER 32

Links

Spring, 1E9575
[The Present]

With a cry of joy, Jinnarin leapt from Rux's back and hurled herself at Farrix, staggering him hindwards with her fierce onslaught. She clasped him to herself and wept with gladness, showering him with kisses.

He held her in a tight embrace and kissed her in return. And just as he opened his mouth to speak, boiling inward through the doorway came charging a warband of Dwarves, weapons hefted, shields at the ready, flinty gazes sweeping the chamber, Châkka seeking the battle they had heard, responding to Bokar's war cry.

Startled, Farrix shoved Jinnarin behind him, leaping between her and potential danger, his empty hands reaching for his bow, finding naught, and all the while his glance darted about, seeing Humans and Dwarves, Elves and Mages, Rux the fox ... and one very dead Gargon.

Farrix whirled to Jinnarin. "We've got to hide before they see us," he hissed, gathering shadow.

She shook her head. "No, love, these are Friends."

"Friends? Friends! So many?"

At her nod and grin, he dispensed the darkness and turned back to the confusion in the chamber.

Holding up his hands, Bokar was shouting in Châkur above the milling chaos, calling for quiet, saying that the fight was over, the *Ghath* slain. And when a semblance of order returned, once again Alamar, Aravan, Aylis, and Jatu faced the dais and the Pysks thereon, and wide smiles wreathed their faces.

Over his shoulder Farrix asked, "Hoy now, love, this is not another dream is it?" Before she could answer, he pinched himself—"Ow!"—then muttered, "Oh wait, that didn't work before."

Jinnarin laughed and stepped before him, placing her hands on his shoulders. "Oh no, Farrix, this is not a dream. You've broken the spell and are truly awake at last."

He tore his gaze from the stir above and looked into her eyes. "Then you can't fly?"

"No, love. I can't fly."

"Oh," said Farrix. "Too bad. I would imagine it's rather a nice talent to have." He was smiling as he said it. He pulled her to him and kissed her soundly, then gestured outward. "I say, Humans, Dwarves, Mages, and an Elf—just who are all these strangers?"

"Strangers to you; Friends to me." Jinnarin disengaged, adding, "That is, all but two are strangers to you. Regardless, these are Friends who helped me to find you and aided in breaking the spell." Turning, she motioned the others to her, saying, "Farrix, you've met Lady Aylis—"

"Wha—?" Farrix looked up at the seeress. "I thought you were a Pysk!"

Aylis smiled. "We met in a dream, Farrix, where you and Jinnarin and I were all of a size—strange as that may seem."

"Oh," said Farrix, then bowed to Aylis. "In any event, Lady Aylis, I am most glad to meet you in the real flesh, and I thank you for helping Jinnarin break the spell."

As Aylis smiled, Jinnarin said, "And this is Jatu."

The black Man stepped forward and rumbled, "Ah, Master Farrix, she described you well, did your Lady Jinnarin."

As he looked up at the huge Man, Farrix's eyes widened. "From the southern lands, I take it. I always wished to go there."

"Someday, perhaps, we will go together," replied Jatu, a grin splitting his face.

"And this is Aravan." Jinnarin gestured at the Elf.

"A Friend!" Farrix smiled, then explained, "I sense a token you bear."

Aravan's hand strayed to his throat. "It came from Tarquin."

Alamar jerked his head toward Aravan. "The amulet, Elf, what does it sense?"

" 'Tis warm ... no longer chill, the peril gone."

"Ha! As I thought!" The elder jerked a thumb toward the slain Gargon. "There, Daughter, there was Durlok's trap! Linked to Farrix! Whoever tried to break the spell, ha, they would have a Gargon to deal with."

Slowly Jatu shook his head. "Gargon, yes, and we would have all been slain. Yet, Mage Alamar, I could swear it was dead when it fell from the air...."

Farrix's eyes flew wide in surprise. "Mage Alamar?"

Alamar looked down at him. "Eh? Oh, Pysk. Hmph, glad to see you awake."

Again Farrix asked, "Mage Alamar? Is it really you?"

"Of course it's really me, you young jackanapes!"

Farrix shook his head as if to clear it from confusion. "Well, I just seem to remember that you were a lot, uh, hmm, darker haired."

"I was," snorted the Mage. "If you'd've cast as many spells as I, you'd be a bit grey on the top, too."

"Oh," said Farrix, cocking an eye at Jinnarin as she whispered, "Casting spells drains youth. I'll tell you all about it later."

"And oh by the way, Pysk," added Alamar. "Good shot, and thanks."

Puzzlement washed across Farrix's face, and Alamar barked, "The bloody pig, Pysk—the boar!"

Enlightened, Farrix simply nodded, but Jinnarin spoke up: "A thousand years late, Alamar, but thanks accepted."

Alamar grunted sourly then muttered, *"Visus,"* and looked sharply at Farrix. "Aha, Daughter, he's no longer enspelled. And the link is gone, too. Tell me, just what did you do?"

"Well, Father, in the first dream we—"

"First dream?"

"Yes, Father. There were two: a dream within a dream."

Jinnarin shook her head. "No, Aylis. I think there

must have been at least three. Remember, Farrix was asleep and dreaming in the second dream, too."

Aylis nodded. "As Farrix told us within one of the dreams, Father, it was like one of those puzzles—boxes within boxes, rings within rings, or the like."

"Aha," murmured the elder, raising his chin, then gesturing impatiently. "Well, go on, go on."

"In the first dream we found Farrix asleep in a garden—lying on a crystal altar like this one." Aylis tapped the crystal block. "He was dreaming in that dream, and so we walked within that dreamed dream as well."

Alamar raised an eyebrow. "That might have been dangerous, you know."

"It was!" blurted Jinnarin. "That's where we found the demon!"

"Demon?"

Jinnarin's head bobbed up and down. "Yes. Demon. And it was dreadful. But Jatu saved us, and you as well."

Alamar threw up his hands, snapping, "Hold on, hold on! You aren't making any sense, Pysk."

Aylis looked at Jinnarin. "Oh but she is, Father, or at least I think she is"—Jinnarin nodded vigorously—"but let me tell it as it happened, at least as much as I know, and then Jinnarin will tell the parts I know not."

"In the first dream—in the garden—we discovered Farrix asleep on a crystal altar. In the second dream, we stepped into the crystal castle of the sending. But a hideous creature of some sort lunged toward us, a writhing blackness with great talons and evil eyes and a fang-filled mouth. This I think is what your amulet detected, Aravan. I think as well it was the creature that slew White Owl—Ontah. An evil spirit, he named it; a demon by Jinnarin's words; yet by any name it was terrible, and nearly proved our end."

Aylis's eyes were wide in remembered dread, and Aravan put an arm about her. Fleetingly she smiled at him and then continued. "We escaped the crystal castle, fled, bridged out to the garden, but the monster pursued—not just one, but many, a dozen or so. Before we could bridge out of that dream, the monster froze Jinnarin simply by looking at her."

Jinnarin gasped and reached out to take Farrix's hand.

"I couldn't move. I couldn't flee. I thought my heart would burst with dread."

Aylis nodded, "Me, too, Jinnarin. I thought my heart would burst as well." She gave the Pysk a tiny smile and then continued:

"I cast a lightning bolt at it—"

"A lightning bolt? A lightning bolt, Daughter? But you don't know how."

"You are right, Father—I do not know how. Yet recall, it was a dream, and as I discovered in the dream where we escaped the spider, in the dream where I made the flaming sword, all I needed to do was say the right word to cast a spell. And in spite of my dread I managed to utter one of your words, '*Fulmen,*' and out leapt the bolt from my hand. But it had no effect, passing right through one of the creatures. Yet loosing the bolt did accomplish one thing: the monster now mistakenly thought I was the greater threat, for in that moment the dread creature abandoned Jinnarin and turned all of its vile power on me, and my mind was seized and I only knew terror from then on . . . until Jinnarin set me free."

Alamar turned to Jinnarin, the Mage waving his hands in small, impatient circles. "Well, Pysk, what then?" he demanded.

"Then you saved us, Alamar, you and Jatu."

Jatu cocked his head in puzzlement, but Alamar snapped in agitation, "Get on with it, Pysk! Just how did Jatu and I come galloping to the rescue."

"Well, after a couple of my arrows"—Jinnarin gestured at one of the wee shafts—"did nothing to stop two of the creatures, I recalled that you said you could make one fireball seem to be ten. And I thought that there were ten or so demons there, and decided that all but one had to be illusions, false images like the illusory stone over the entrance to these caverns. Then I remembered Jatu's story about all demons but one having no shadows, and that's the one I shot next—the demon with no shadow. My arrow flew through it though, having no effect. And it was now about to kill Aylis. . . ."

"Cor, love," breathed Farrix, "what did you do?"

"Stop interrupting, Pysk," snapped Alamar, glaring at Farrix. Then he looked to Jinnarin. "What did you do?"

"I killed it, that's what," replied Jinnarin.

"How?" barked Alamar, nearly shrieking with frustration.

"Well, you might say I did him in the eye."

"Did him in the eye?"

Jinnarin raised her bow. "Yes. I did him in the eye . . . and then the mouth."

"And that killed it? Killed the demon, the evil spirit?"

Here, Aylis spoke up. "Yes, Father, that killed it and set me free. And after a moment the slain monster turned into a vile, black vapor that vanished in the wind."

"Hmm," mused Alamar, then sharply said, "but the spell was not yet broken, right?"

"It was not yet broken," replied Aylis, nodding. "We went back into the dream within the dream, back to the crystal castle, and there we discovered Farrix on another crystal altar."

Alamar's eyes widened. "Another crystal altar? Well, well. That must be the icon which links the dreams together, links them to here as well."

"Exactly my thought, too, Father."

At that moment Bokar strode down from the slain Gargon, joining the circle. Jinnarin turned to Farrix. "This is Armsmaster Bokar, Farrix. He, too, is a Friend, as are all you will meet in the coming days."

Bokar bowed stiffly to Farrix, the Pysk grinning but bowing likewise. The Dwarf glanced over his shoulder at the doorway to the caverns and then said, "I would ask you a question, Master Farrix—"

"Ask him later," snapped Alamar, "we're in the middle of something here"—Bokar's beard quivered in fury, but he held his tongue—"Go on, Daughter. You discovered Farrix on a crystal altar in the crystal castle of the sending—what happened next?"

"He was dreaming, Father, but when Jinnarin called out, he moved. We wakened him, and suddenly the castle disappeared and the chamber became the duplicate of this one. I believe that it was at that moment the linkage to something evil was broken."

"Aha!" barked Alamar. "That's when the Gargon appeared here! So it *was* dead when it crashed into the chamber! Damn good thing, too, else as Jatu said, we'd have all been killed by such a monster."

"But, Alamar," protested Jinnarin, "I do not understand."

"Look, Pysk, the Gargon was, hmm, somewhere on the island, I would imagine, but linked to Farrix, and whoever tried to break the spell would summon it."

"But wait," rumbled Jatu. "If there was a Gargon somewhere on the island, Captain Aravan's amulet would have detected it, would have run chill."

"It did detect it, you big lummox," snapped Alamar. "Right here in this chamber. Y'see, the Gargon's essence was trapped in Farrix's dream ... hence, wherever its body was hidden, it did not trigger Aravan's stone. The stone *did* detect, however, that the Gargon's essence was linked to Farrix, shackled to his dream. —Oh what a clever trap Durlok set, damn his eyes!"

Jatu nodded, then turned to look at the slain Gargon. "And the moment the link was broken—"

"Was the moment the Gargon came from ‹elsewhere› and crashed to the floor dead."

"Already slain by my Jinnarin!" crowed Farrix, picking her up and whirling around.

When he set her down, he kissed her and released her and she turned to Alamar, her eyes wide. "You mean the demon of the dream was really the spirit, the essence of the Gargon?" At Alamar's nod, she gasped, "Oh my, then the fact that I chose a particular image to shoot was even a greater gamble than I thought."

"Why so, Pysk?"

"Well, Alamar, I did not think that Gargons were demons, and had I known ..."

Aravan shook his head. "Nay, Jinnarin, it was a wise choice thou made to slay the one with no shadow, for long have my Folk believed that the Gargoni are of Demonkind."

"Most likely, Elf. Most likely," said Alamar. Then the Mage turned again to Aylis. "Then what, Daughter."

"Well, Father, after that it was rather simple. We merely had to convince Farrix that it was a dream and to wake up—after we left, of course, for we did not want to be trapped."

"It was so real," added Farrix. "I mean, if Jinnarin hadn't flown, I believe that I would have thought that she had lost her mind, and had convinced another

Pysk—Aylis—to go mad with her. And when I awoke from the dream within the dream, well, I had to be convinced all over again. And, of course, when I awoke from the last dream, well, here I was in a madhouse itself, what with yelling warriors beating upon a giant dead lizard, or the like. Then I wasn't at all certain that I hadn't gone 'round the bend myself.''

Jinnarin began giggling and Jatu roaring and Aylis laughing as well. Aravan joined in the mirth along with Farrix. Even Alamar cackled. All laughed but Bokar, his visage grim. When the laughter died, the armsmaster stepped forward. "Master Farrix, I need ask a vital question." He jerked a thumb over his shoulder and toward the passageway leading toward the quay, saying, "Where be the Trolls?"

Farrix looked up at him and replied, "Why, with Durlok, Armsmaster Bokar, rowing his black ship."

CHAPTER 33

Façade

Spring, 1E9575
[The Present]

Bokar turned to Aravan. "Captain, now that we have Farrix, I suggest we leave, and quickly. Before Durlok and his twenty-eight Trolls return."

"Still afraid of the Trolls, eh, Dwarf?" snorted Alamar. "As I said before, *I* can deal with them."

"Father!" Aylis rounded on her sire. "We have already had this argument. Twenty-eight Trolls are too many for us to face."

"Bah!" replied Alamar.

Farrix looked up at Aylis. "How did you know there were twenty-eight?"

Bokar answered the question. "We counted the beds, Master Farrix."

"Oh my"—Farrix turned his hands palms up—"of course. How thick of me."

"There *are* twenty-eight, aren't there?" asked Jatu.

The Pysk nodded. "Yes. And fifteen Rucha and four Loka, too."

"Fifteen Rucha!" exclaimed Jinnarin. "But we counted sixteen beds."

"One is dead," replied Farrix. "Killed by—"

"Argh!" snarled Bokar. "Ūkhs and Hrōks are of little threat, but the Trolls are a different matter."

"Captain," rumbled Jatu, "Bokar is right. We should go, and now."

"No!" barked Alamar. "If we go now, Durlok will

441

know that we've been here, what with the Pysk gone and a dead Gargon hacked and splattered all over his floor. He'll run and find a new place to hide, and we'll be millennia tracking him down again. And all the while, he'll be performing hideous rituals—slaughtering the innocent, gaining in power—all to some evil end."

Farrix's face had gone flat, the blood drained from it. "Alamar is right, you know—about the rituals, I mean. Durlok is a monster."

The elder nodded vigorously, then turned and gestured at a trail of scattered papers leading from the crystal chamber back into the laboratory. "I have been in his sanctum, examining his tomes, his scrolls—I was there when the Gargon fell and Jatu called, and I came running." Alamar stalked to one of the papers and scooped it up and held it on high before him. "These are the horrors of a Black Mage; they are vile, terrible things, filled with dreadful rites and depraved sacraments—wicked, malevolent abominations. And all are dedicated to the gathering of power over others, to utter dominion and the destruction of free will, and to the glorification and ascendancy of Gyphon."

Alamar crumpled the parchment and flung it down. "No, say I. I will not allow such a fiend loose upon the world. If I must remain here alone to face him, then let it be so."

"But, Father," protested Aylis, "you cannot hope to defeat both a Mage *and* an army of Trolls. Instead, let us return to Rwn, gather the aid we need. Durlok's trail will be warm, and we will have the master seers to track him. They will have the power to break his wards, to find his essence."

"Is it so, *chieran?*" asked Aravan. "We will not lose the opportunity to rid the world of such a monster?"

Aylis nodded. "Yes, my love. He cannot escape, now that we have something of his and know where to start."

"But wait!" exclaimed Jinnarin. "If that's all it takes, couldn't you have tracked him down long past, when he crossed over from Vadaria? That was a known place to start."

Aylis shook her head. "Although we knew where

to start, we had nothing of his, nothing embedded with his essence. What he did not take with him, he destroyed before he escaped." Aylis gestured toward the sanctum. "But now we have much to choose from, all imbued with his very <fire>."

Aravan turned to Alamar. "Is it so, Mage Alamar?"

Alamar looked about as if seeking allies, but all faces were grim, waiting. At last he sighed, his shoulders slumping. "I had forgotten about the seers. —Yes, it is true."

Aravan's gaze swept over each one there. "We will leave, and swiftly, for I will not jeopardize the lives of all just so that one elder can wreak his revenge. Yet we shall return, fit for the fight, on that ye have my word."

Alamar ground his teeth. "You realize, Elf, that by running away with your tail between your legs, you are condemning more innocents to die."

Aravan's gaze was steely. "Mayhap, Mage Alamar. Yet by garnering the help we need, we make certain that the monster is slain. To do otherwise is to virtually ensure our failure and give Durlok a free hand."

Farrix pounded tiny fist into tiny palm. "Yes! And Durlok must be stopped, and to that end I'd rather be certain than sorry."

Alamar's jaw jutted out stubbornly, but Aylis stepped to him and embraced him, whispering, "Father, Farrix is right: Aravan's way is best. I know it and so do you. But even if you think otherwise, still there is your pledge to me—to return to Rwn now that Farrix is found—and I now ask you to honor it."

For long moments he stood rigid in her clasp, his arms at his sides, not returning her press. But at last he nodded jerkily and patted her on the back, saying, "All right, Daughter. You've made your point. Aravan, too." Tentatively Aylis drew back and looked at his face, and he smiled at her . . . but his smile did not reach his eyes. And once again his jaw shot out, and he looked at Aravan and waved in the direction of the laboratory and declared, "But we won't go till I've burned those unholy incantations to ashes—epistles of torture, primers of agony, scriptures of pain and suffering." Alamar turned on his heel and marched back toward the sanctum.

Aylis stepped to Aravan. "I will go with him and make certain that we salvage something of Durlok's essence."

Aravan canted his head. "I will go with thee, *chieran.*"

"We're coming, too," said Jinnarin, as she and Farrix leapt down from the crystal block, Rux jumping down after. Jatu glanced at Bokar and shrugged, and scooping up the scatter of papers as they went, together they all followed Alamar into Durlok's lair.

As they came into the laboratory, Jatu waved a hand toward the hall leading farther inward. "What about the treasure, Captain?"

"Leave it behind, Jatu," replied Aravan. "We have no need of such, and I would not weigh down our small craft on the return journey."

"Leave it behind for Durlok?" asked Farrix. "He will use it for evil ends."

Jinnarin looked at Aravan. "We could hurl it into the sea."

Bokar shook his head. "There is a great amount, Lady Jinnarin, a veritable Dragon's hoard. To cast away all will take much time. Yet if we do not, it will be as Master Farrix has said, Durlok will use it for his own ends."

Alamar, throwing scrolls and tomes into a pile, called out, "Pah! If Durlok has Foul Folk at his beck, treasure is of no matter. He can always have them ravage and pillage for more, or even dig for it."

"Finding gems or precious metals in the ground is not such an easy task," growled Bokar.

Alamar turned and glared at the Dwarf. "Hah! For a Mage it is a trivial matter."

Bokar's eyebrows shot up, but he said nothing, and instead began throwing papers and scrolls and such onto the growing pile.

Farrix turned to Aylis. "I say, if Mages can easily find things, well, could you find my bow? Durlok took it and put it somewhere, and, burn me, I'd like to get it back."

Aylis smiled. "Perhaps I can at that, Farrix. Jinnarin, will you let me have yours?"

Jinnarin handed over the tiny bow to Aylis. *"Iveni simile,"* the seeress murmured. Deliberately Aylis turned and cast about as if seeking and finally began slowly pacing down the hallway toward Durlok's sleeping chambers, with Aravan at her side and the Pysks at her heels. Bearing a Dwarven lantern, Jatu followed. Through the bedchamber Aylis trod, each step more sure than the last. Into the treasure room she strode and swiftly to the pile where she took up the mate to Jinnarin's bow. She turned and stooped down to Farrix. "Thy bow, tiny one," she said, grinning, casting Aravan a sideways glance.

A great smile split Farrix's face, but then he craned his neck, looking into the gleaming mound. "Uh, d'you see my arrows anywhere?"

Without a word, Aylis held out a hand to Jinnarin. "Be careful," said the Pysk as she took back her bow but handed the seeress one of her tiny arrows.

"Iveni simile," muttered Aylis. At first the seeress turned to Jinnarin, for the tiny Pysk had additional arrows in the quiver at her hip. But Aylis murmured, *"Aliter,"* and turned again. Soon she paced into Durlok's laboratory, where Bokar and Alamar yet cast papers onto the heap. In a drawer she discovered Farrix's arrows. As she handed the tiny quiver to him, Aylis frowned and shook her head. "I suspect that Durlok was saving these to analyze. It would be a sad day were a Black Mage ever to discover the secret of your poison."

"Indeed," replied Farrix. "That's why we tell no one ever."

At these words, Jinnarin glanced at Alamar, but the elder was muttering to himself and did not hear.

Aylis looked at the mound of tomes and scrolls, of journals and books and papers. "Oh my, do we need burn this all, Father?" asked Aylis. "I mean, I have always revered all scribings for the knowledge they contain, be it precious or mundane. Are you certain we are not about to destroy something that will prove useful in the future?"

Alamar paused and looked at the pile. "I am not

certain, Daughter. But this I do know: Many of these things are written in Common. Others are scribed in the Black Mage tongue. Some are in Slûk. Those languages I recognize even though I do not speak or read or write some of them. There are other tongues, too, ones I do not recognize. Many of the papers are illustrated; others are not. But of those that are, all show monstrous rituals—eviscerations, castrations, flensing, torture, ritual rapes, and the like, all to leech power, of that I am certain. But there are also writings here without any illustrations, and so, indeed we may be throwing away irreplaceable knowledge ... but I think it is knowledge of devastation and ruin, and I would keep it out of Durlok's grasp. With the castings you have at your beck, you or other seers could easily read what is written, but we don't have the time needed for you to examine all. Could we bundle it up and bear it back to Rwn to be used to combat the Black Mages, then I would do so, and gladly. Yet, just as is the case with the treasure, there is too much here as well; it would merely weigh us down. And so, I would destroy it all to prevent its use by Durlok ... destroy it all but this"—Alamar held up a black journal—"a Black Mage lexicon, I think. Durlok's very own; see, it has his <fire>. *This* we will use to track him when we are ready to do so."

"Then, Father, if that is what we are keeping, I suggest that we each take a page from it so that if one is lost, we still have the means to trace his whereabouts."

"Ah," said Alamar, "a splendid plan," and he ripped six pages from the journal and stuffed one of them into his robes. Then he handed a page to everyone but Aylis, giving her the remainder of the book instead. "Here, Daughter. When you get a chance, use your seer ability to decipher what is within." Satisfied, he glared at everyone but Bokar and gestured at the mound of paper and said, "Now, if you've all finished your traipsing about, shirking the task at hand, then I suggest you pitch in so that we can finish this off."

Swiftly the chamber was stripped of writings, Durlok's bedchamber, too, all of it thrown onto the pile.

At last Alamar said, "All right, let's set it afire and then get out of here."

As Jatu bent down and made ready to set the whole of it ablaze, a hubbub sounded from the crystal chamber, and a Dwarven warrior came bursting into the sanctum. It was Dett, one of the sentries from the lookout post.

"Armsmaster! Captain!" he urgently said. "A ship! There is a black ship on the southern horizon and it is heading this way."

"Durlok!" spat Alamar. But then a gleam came into his eyes, and he rubbed his palms together. "Well, well. So it's come to a fight after all."

Jinnarin stood on the sill of the slot at the lookout post and watched the black galley coming onward in the eventide; its oars beating, its dark sails canted at an angle to catch the westerly wind, hull and canvas casting long shadows in the setting Sun. And as it raced across the pale green sea, her heart hammered in her breast and fear coursed through her, and she half expected at any moment to see the ship disappear and a great spider come charging across the weed and waves. She gripped Farrix's hand and glanced at him—his face was white and grim—then she looked back out on the undulant waters, pale green turning to malachite as the Sun sank in the west. *Is it only late afternoon? It seems we've been here forever.*

"Five miles," gauged Jatu.

As the black Man stepped aside, again Bokar looked through the slot and growled, "How is it getting through the weed? It seems not slowed at all. —Shallow draft? Special hull? Magic? What?"

"Here, let me see," snapped Alamar.

The eld Mage stepped around Rux and toward the window slit, crowding past Aravan, Jatu, and Bokar. *"Visus,"* he muttered, then peered out. And as he looked upon the distant galley, his face drained of blood. "Adon!" he breathed, his shoulders slumping. "Oh, Adon."

Now Aylis moved to Alamar's side and invoked magesight as well, and she, too, peered at the far ship.

And she blenched and sucked air in through clenched teeth. "So much <fire>, Father. So very much <fire>."

Below, Jinnarin gripped Farrix's hand tightly in her fright, his return grip just as firm, and she asked, "I don't see— What are you talking about, Aylis?"

Aylis did not look away from the galley as she answered the Pysk's question. "The ship, it is bright with astral fire. If it is Durlok that we see burning so, then we cannot hope to defeat him. Perhaps all the Mages in Mithgar combined could not do so." She turned to Aravan. "We cannot take on such <power>; instead we must flee."

But it was Alamar who replied, and his voice was filled with weariness. "No, Daughter, we cannot hope to flee without his detecting us."

"Captain," said Jatu, "we can return to our boats and row to the far dark end of the understone lagoon and hide. Then slip out after the galley is docked and unladed."

Again Alamar spoke: "There is no place we can hide from Durlok. He will know that his sanctuary has been invaded the moment he enters, for he will cast a revelation to see that all is as he left it. And we have broken his grasp upon Farrix, and this he will detect."

Bokar grunted, "Mayhap we can find an escape through the vent fissures overhead."

Aravan shook his head. "A temporary evasion at most."

"Whatever we do, we must hurry," rumbled Jatu, "for the galley draws nearer with every stroke."

"Can we not use cunning and guile?" asked Farrix. "Trick them somehow?"

"Trick twenty-eight Trolls? Perhaps," muttered Bokar. "But how do you trick a Mage?"

Silence fell upon them all and they peered at one another as waves broke against the rock below, while in the distance the galley came on.

Alamar took a deep breath, then slowly blew it out through puffed cheeks. "How do you trick a Mage? That Mage? That Black Mage? Perhaps there is a way. Though I am not certain that I have the <fire>."

Fright leapt to Aylis's eyes. "What, Father? What do you—?"

"I defeated him once, Daughter; he cannot have forgotten that ... he cannot have forgotten it was me who"—Alamar glanced at Jinnarin and smiled at her—"who did him in the eye."

The Mage turned to Bokar. "If I fail, Dwarf, ignore the Trolls. Instead have all your warriors concentrate on killing Durlok. Perhaps a crossbow bolt or axe will get through."

"Father, you can't—"

"Daughter, I must ... and to trick him I need your aid. Stand close behind me—close as you can get. The rest of you back away and let be. I need all my attention on what I do."

As Alamar turned to the slot and gathered his energies, and as Aylis stepped close to her father to stand right behind, Bokar whispered to Aravan and at the Elf's nod, the armsmaster went into the narrow passage, taking Arka and Dett with him. "He goes to set ambush," murmured Aravan to Jatu.

The black Man grunted, then whispered in return, "I'll go get the Men and join him." Without awaiting permission, Jatu slipped into the crevice where Bokar had gone.

Jinnarin and Farrix started to climb down from the sill, but Alamar hissed, "No, stand there together, one behind the other. At this range, Durlok will see you as one."

Farrix started to step in front of Jinnarin, as if to shield her. "No, Farrix," she exclaimed. "You are taller, and I would see." Sighing, he gave back, and Jinnarin stood before him instead.

Alamar raised a hand and pointed out the slit and down to the ocean some hundred yards away. *"Imago mei igens in eo loco."*

Jinnarin gasped, for of a sudden, on the ocean where Alamar had pointed towered a giant figure facing south, facing away from the isle, facing the direction whence came the black galley. Even though she couldn't see its features, Jinnarin knew that it was an image of a Mage, for it was dressed like Alamar. Upward it loomed, a hundred feet or so, and she guessed that it bore the features of a younger Alamar, for its hair was brown instead of white, and its form looked sturdy, strong, with no hint of the elder's frailty.

"Cande," hissed Alamar with effort, and in the twilight a spectral glow first limned the figure and then flared into brightness—a burning giant on the malachite sea.

Jinnarin glanced back and up at Alamar, and sweat beaded his brow. *"Imita me,"* he sissed, his voice shaking with effort. Behind him, Aylis grew pale, fear in her eyes.

"Vox valida," he uttered, his words but a groan, his lips drawn thin with trial, sweat runnelling down his face, and he seemed to be ageing even as Jinnarin looked on. She wanted to reach out, to aid him in some fashion, but she didn't know how, and she knew that anything she might attempt would perhaps do more harm than good.

Agonized, she watched as with great effort Alamar straightened and raised his hand and pointed into the distance. His mouth moved, as if he were speaking, but no sound came from him. Yet from behind, from the outside, a great voice boomed out across the darkling sea: "DURLOK!"

Jinnarin whirled and looked outward. The huge glowing figure stood with an outstretched arm, a finger pointing at the far black galley. For long moments nothing changed the oars yet beating through the twilight, the sails bearing the wind. Again the fiery image called out—"DURLOK!"—then motioned the black craft onward, as if inviting it to near. "COME, MY OLD ADVERSARY, IT IS TIME WE BATTLED AGAIN."

Now the oars ceased beating and the black craft slowed, borne forward only by the wind.

Again, long moments passed. Yet of a sudden a gigantic figure loomed on the distant ocean, this one dressed in dark robes and illuminated by a black fire, and Farrix hissed, "He has slain a victim."

Jinnarin glanced back at her mate. His face was filled with rage, and his hand strayed to his arrows, as if he would shoot someone. Behind him, Alamar stood trembling on the verge of collapse, his features even more aged. And Aylis wrapped her arms about him and held him up, tears running down her face.

"I SEE YOU ARE FILLED WITH THE <FIRE> OF RE-
NEWED YOUTH" came a voice booming across the
tides.

Jinnarin spun and faced outward again. At this distance she could not be certain, but the long angular
features of the image of the Black Mage seemed
twisted in a rictus grin, a skull-like grin.

Alamar's image called out, "I HAVE DESTROYED
YOUR GARGON, DURLOK, AND SET THE PYSK FREE. YOU
ARE NEXT."

Surprise flashed across the face of Durlok's likeness,
and it turned its head slightly, as if looking elsewhere
within the caverns. Then once again it faced Alamar's
icon and anger filled its features, making it seem even
more skull-like for the image had no hair—not even
brows stood above its eyes.

Alamar's semblance boomed out, "DID YOU TRULY
EXPECT A GARGON TO BE A CHALLENGE TO ME? PAH!"

Now Durlok's simulacrum raised a hand, and a
great bolt of lightning flashed out, not at Alamar's
image, but at the lookout slot instead.

"Averte!" hissed Aylis, and the great jagged bolt
crashed into stone, barely missing the slot, shattering
white light stabbing inward through the opening, deafening thunder whelming in on the heels of the glare,
hammering into Jinnarin and Farrix and slamming
them sideways against the rock wall of the slit, stunning them.

Ears ringing, Aravan stepped toward Aylis but she
shook her head and waved him back. He reached out
to aid the Pysks, who even then were beginning to
stir, but once again Aylis waved him back, not daring
to risk anything which might distract her father in the
slightest. And so Aravan stepped hindwards, back to
where Rux whined and cowered, and the Elf squatted
down and soothed the fox.

Her own ears ringing, Jinnarin shook her head trying to recover, while behind her Farrix stirred.
Through swimming eyes she looked up at Alamar, the
eld Mage shuddering in the agony of maintaining such
a potent spell, given the meager limits of his astral
fire, which even now was draining swiftly, the <fire>
of his life nearly spent.

Yet his glowing icon stood straight, and laughed at Durlok, the likeness afar enraged. "Is THAT THE BEST YOU CAN DO?" boomed out Alamar's figure.

"BAH!" sneered Durlok's image. "I COULD SQUASH YOU AS EASILY AS I COULD AN INSECT, ALAMAR. YET I HAVE NO TIME FOR THIS NONSENSE. I MUST CONSERVE MY ENERGIES FOR THEY ARE NEEDED TO DELIVER MY GRAND WEDDING GIFT TO ALL OF YOUR ILK, ALAMAR, BUT AFTERWARDS, IF YOU YET LIVE . . ."

Of a sudden, Durlok's simulacrum vanished. In the twilight Jinnarin could see that the black galley oars again took up a beat, but this time one side backed water as the other side pulled forward, and the sails were shifted about as the galley turned away. And something white was cast over the side as Durlok surrendered the field.

"His victim," gritted Farrix.

And in the chamber behind, Alamar hoarsely whispered, *"Dele,"* his image vanishing even as the aged Mage collapsed in Aylis's arms, and weeping, she lowered his frail form to the stone.

CHAPTER 34

Plumes

Spring, 1E9575
[The Present]

Alamar!" cried Jinnarin, leaping down from the lookout slot. "Alamar!"

The Mage lay on the stone floor, reedy air rattling in and out of his thin chest, and he looked as if he had aged decades, his hair now sparse, the flesh on his face like translucent parchment mottled with brown spots. On her knees, Aylis wept at his side, and Aravan knelt down and put his ear to Alamar's breast and after a moment said, "Thready."

"We've got to get him to Rwn," gritted Aylis, "to Vadaria. His <fire> is almost gone. It was too much, this spell of his. It was too much. . . ."

Opposite Aylis and Aravan, Farrix stood next to Jinnarin, his arm about her, the distressed Pysks powerless to aid. Rux stopped his agitated pacing and came and nosed his way between the two, seeking comfort.

Aravan raised up from the elder. "Jinnarin, find Jatu, Bokar. Tell them what has passed. Tell the armsmaster we need a healer for Alamar and a litter to bear him to the quay. Have Jatu and the Men ready the boats. We are leaving as soon as it is safe."

Jinnarin nodded, glad of something to do, and she shook the tears from her eyes and leapt upon Rux and sped away.

Aravan turned to Farrix. "Keep watch on the black galley. I would not have Durlok turn back and catch us unaware."

* * *

As Koban and Relk set the litter down on the quay, Alamar's eyes fluttered then opened, and he tried to raise up but failed. Jamie leaned down. "Here now, Mage Alamar, you shouldn't be wanting to get—"

Alamar reached up and grasped him by the shirt, and with surprising strength pulled Jamie to him and murmured something, his quavering voice nearly lost in the echoing surge *shssh*ing in the cavern. Alamar lapsed back into unconsciousness.

Bokar squatted beside the litter. "What did he say?"

"Burn the papers, Armsmaster. He said to burn the papers."

Bokar knelt and even though he did not know whether Alamar could hear him, he spoke to the elder: "Even now, Mage Alamar, Jatu is setting the fire. The documents will be burned."

A dinghy was maneuvered to the steps of the quay, and the litter was borne down to it. Alamar was lifted into the boat and made comfortable on the bedding that had been laid for him. Burak, one of the Dwarven warriors, clambered into the boat with Alamar. Burak would watch over the eld Mage and administer whatever herbal medicines might help from those they had brought along. Though not a chirurgeon, Burak—along with three others in the warband—was nevertheless trained in the arts of treating warrior's wounds and sicknesses in the field, and as the most experienced, he was the one who accompanied Alamar into the boat.

As the Dwarven rowers followed and arranged themselves in the craft, a piercing whistle from the passage behind sounded above the waves, and after long moments, Jatu and Farrix and Jinnarin came out from the darkness of the corridor, both Pysks mounted upon Rux.

Aravan looked at Jatu. "They burn, Captain," said the black Man. "Durlok's writings burn."

Farrix and Jinnarin had been standing watch at the lookout post, and as Farrix dismounted he turned to the Elf. "The black galley is now gone over the horizon. It is safe to leave."

Swiftly they entered their boats, Farrix going with Jinnarin and Rux, and soon the dinghies came out through the channel from the understone lagoon and into the nighttime air, a spangle of southern stars glittering in the skies above, a thin crescent of a quarter Moon hanging low in the west.

Silks were raised in the southwesterly breeze, and the flat-bottomed craft sailed across deep, black waters, heading due west along the southern ramparts of the high stone island looming off to the starboard side. A mile they went and then a league, the black waters clear of hindrance, but at last they came to the wall of weed dropping into the depths below. Oars were then set in their locks and used to press forward, and out into the hulk-laden waters of the clutching swirl they went.

"I wish we had our turtle," murmured Jinnarin as the Dwarves stroked over the undulant swells.

"Turtle?" Farrix turned his questioning gaze upon her.

"It towed us here."

"A *turtle?*"

"It was a big one, a giant, you might say. It pulled all the boats."

"Ha!" barked Farrix. "It would have to be. But tell me, my love, just how did you come about this—this monstrous turtle?"

"The Children of the Sea brought it with them, though they called it a—a, oh, I can't say it, but something like tok'th'tick'rix. Regardless, it was a giant turtle."

Now Farrix's eyes flew wide. "Children of the Sea! You met some Children of the Sea? Oh, Jinnarin, this is a tale I've got to hear. In fact, tell me everything, everything that happened since last I saw you."

"All right, Farrix. My story first, but then yours. I mean, you've given us quite a chase you know, and we've been over half the world trying to find you. I'd like to know just how you managed to get into the mess where we discovered you at last, and how Durlok figures into all of it, and what he's up to, and—"

Smiling, Farrix touched a finger to her lips to stop her rush of words. "You haven't changed a bit, my sweet, and I love you for it. As to Durlok"—his face fell flat and his eyes grew grim—"we will speak of that later, after you've told me your tale."

Jinnarin nodded and took a deep breath: "Where shall I start? Wait, I know—as I've been told, begin at the beginning." She paused a moment, gathering her thoughts, and then her words came softly: "Well, after I got your note, the one you sent by Rhu, I didn't start to worry until I began having these dreams. And then I went to see Alamar ... Alamar the Mage...."

And as the line of dinghies struggled westward through grasping weed and past ships ancient and water-logged and trapped in the Great Swirl, in the bottom of a boat the two Pysks leaned back against a sleeping fox ... and Jinnarin told Farrix her tale.

Dawn found the dinghies sailing west, tacking against the wind, the shallow-draft, flat-bottomed boats skimming barely above the weed. Occasionally the tiny flotilla would encounter stretches where the Dwarves needed to row, but for the most part they evaded the clutch of the Great Swirl, though now and again the person at the helm would lift the steering oar clear and rid it of green sea moss. Dawn also found Farrix and Jinnarin asleep in each other's arms in the bottom of one of the crafts, though when Jamie stepped across Rux and the fox shifted about, it brought both Pysks awake.

Jamie relieved Lork at the helm, and sighted on the other craft. Aravan's boat was in the lead, all others following in file—Bokar's boat was second in line, then Aylis's, Alamar's coming after, with Jinnarin and Farrix's boat following, then Kelek's, and last of all, Jatu's.

As Relk broke out rations for the morning meal, Farrix glanced at the rising sun. "Are we sailing by dead reckoning?" he asked Jamie.

The Man laughed. "Nay, Master Farrix. Cap'n Aravan, although he doesn't use an astrolabe, he doesn't need one. He's an Elf, you see, and the best pilot of all. Dead reckoning? Not as long as he can see the Sun or the stars."

"Oh look!" cried Jinnarin, gripping Farrix's hand. "Alamar: he's sitting up!"

In the boat ahead, the eld Mage sat in the bow, facing backwards. Wind blew through the wisps of his white hair, and his frail hands desperately gripped the wales.

He was pale, drawn.

He was ancient.

Jinnarin turned to Farrix, tears welling in her eyes.

* * *

Jamie looked into the boat ahead. "Cor, what a change! Why, when I first clapped eyes on Mage Alamar, I'd have said he was an old Man of seventy or thereabouts. But now he looks to be in his doddering nineties."

Jinnarin peered up at Jamie. "Oh, Jamie, he is not a Man, but a Mage instead, and as such he is much older than ninety. In fact, from what I've gleaned, he is thousands of years old. But Mages can spend their youth and then gain it back again."

"How so, Lady Jinnarin?"

"If they cast no spells, Jamie, they do not age, ever. But when they do a casting, it drains youth and energy— the greater the spell, the greater the drain. And Alamar cast a very great spell to fool Durlok, and it nearly cost Alamar his life."

"Durlok casts spells and he does not age," muttered Farrix.

"That is because he is a Black Mage and steals the youth of others. Alamar told me that the astral fire can be leeched from those in great emotional distress. Like bloodsucking lamias, Black Mages do this, living off the youth of others, hence spending none of their own."

Farrix slowly nodded. "I knew that Durlok used the agony of others to power his spells, but I did not know that by doing so he preserved his own youth."

"Hm," mused Jamie, then asked, "but then how do Mages regain their youth?"

"Alamar says they must rest a long while. Cast no spells. He also says that on Mithgar, this takes ages, but on the Mage world of Vadaria, it goes much more swiftly." Jinnarin's gaze sought out frail Alamar in the boat ahead. "Oh don't you see, Farrix, *that* is why we must return to Rwn—for on that isle is the only known crossing to Vadaria, and Alamar needs desperately to go home."

Throughout the morning the boats sailed west among trapped drowned hulks, the chill wind shifting about, growing warmer as it swung from the southwest to the west and then on around until at last it blew straight from the north, straight from the high northern Sun.

"Ha!" crowed Jamie. "That's the last of the tacking if the wind'll just hold abeam."

"But not the last of the rowing," growled Tolar, the warrior shipping out his oar and nodding ahead where Dwarves in Aravan's boat now rowed across weed.

As the Dwarven rowers pulled oars, Farrix shaded his eyes and looked at one of the derelicts a mile or so to the north. "I say, Jinnarin, what d'you think might be on these ships? What cargoes? What curiously wrought artifacts? What things of mystery and wonder?"

Jinnarin shuddered, her mind returning to the night when they had seen a hulk glowing with green witchfire. "I don't know, love, and I don't believe that I want to know. I do know, though, that some of these drowned relics cause Aravan's amulet to grow freezing cold."

"Meaning . . . ?"

"Meaning that something perilous lurks thereon."

"Perilous?" Farrix glanced at her, then swung his gaze back to the distant hulk. "Witches, liches, lamia and the like?"

Jinnarin shook her head. "I don't know, love. Just perilous."

Farrix sighed. "Well, still I would like to know what these ships bear. One of these days, perhaps I'll—"

"Oh, Farrix, it's your curiosity that got us in this fix to begin with. Besides, from the looks of Durlok's treasury, it seems as if he might have already plundered the victims of the Great Swirl."

A grim aspect swept over Farrix's face. "Yes, love. He indeed used the Swirl to ensnare victims, though it was the people he wanted and not the cargo."

Jinnarin cocked her head to one side and looked at her mate. After a moment she said, "Well, Farrix, it seems as if all this is leading to your tale. I know you don't want to relive the bad memories, but I think you must. We need to know what Durlok is up to so that the Mages of Rwn can block him, stop him cold before he does something vile."

Farrix clenched his hands in frustration. "But that's just it, Jinnarin—I don't *know* what Durlok is up to! Ah, but that it is something vile . . . well, it goes without saying. But just *what* it is, I don't bloody know! Burn me, I haven't a clue!"

"Well, love," said Jinnarin, "I don't know whether or not I can help, but why don't you tell me your tale and then we shall see. As Alamar says, begin at the beginning, which in this case I believe is when you and Rhu left our home in Darda Glain."

Farrix nodded and took up a portion of a crue biscuit and bit off a mouthful, feeding the rest to Rux. He sat and reflectively chewed, gathering his scattered thoughts. At last he took a drink of water, washing all down.

Turning to Jinnarin, he said, "It was still winter when Rhu and I set out to track down the plumes...."

"Love, I'm off to follow the flumes, to see just where they are going."

Farrix looked at Jinnarin, noting the touch of sadness that came into her eye. Even so she did not argue with his decision to chase this will-o'-the-wisp of spectral light, but instead she stepped forward and hugged and kissed him. His heart felt somewhat heavy, though not extraordinarily so . . . for he and Jinnarin had been mates for several millennia, and she seemed resigned to his "whims."

With a whistle, Farrix mounted up on Rhu, and off through the forest of Darda Glain they headed north-easterly, the black-footed red fox padding across the snow. And Farrix looked back to see his loved one standing before the hollow tree where they lived, and he waved good-bye then turned and urged Rhu into that ground-eating trot which would carry them miles before nightfall.

North and east they fared among the winter-barren trees of Darda Glain, Farrix heading inland to skirt around an arm of ocean barring the way directly east. Surrounded on three sides by water, Darda Glain was a hoary old forest, forty or so miles across from east to west, and fifty from north to south. It occupied the whole of an outjut of land protruding into the sea, there along the southern bound of Rwn, where it was sustained by misty rains of summer and swirling snows of winter which blew in from the Weston Ocean to fall upon the rich loamy soil. Closed to all but the Hidden Ones, Farrix and Jinnarin dwelled near the center, though now and again they moved to the margins to stand their turn at ward. But now Farrix rode away from the heart of the woods, driven on a mission of his own, and once again 'twas not Duty who summoned but Curiosity instead, her silent call luring him across the ancient island of Rwn.

Rwn itself was roughly circular, spanning nearly a hundred and fifty miles in any direction—give or take an arm of the ocean or peninsula thrust out into the sea. Some fifty miles inland all way 'round, the island rose up into a central region rough with craggy tors and steep hills and stony mounts. In the north lay coastal plains, scrubbed raw by northern winds, the grassy expanse sparsely dotted here and there with wind-twisted trees and small coppices of pine, and only a handful of people dwelled upon the plains. To the east and south and west, the margins of the isle were more hospitable, though just as sparsely populated—with the exception of Darda Glain in the south, where dwelt the Hidden Ones, and the Kairn peninsula to the west, where lay the City of Bells on the far western edge of rolling farmlands running to the east, running all the way to the old defensive rampart of the Kairn Wall some twenty-five miles from the town.

And it was on this isle in the woods of Darda Glain on the southern marge of Rwn that a Pysk rode a fox, heading north and east, drawn onward by a falling sky.

Over the next two days they fared, heading ever northeastward, but at last they emerged from Darda Glain along the shores of Lac Rwn. Ice extended out from the shoreline, though the center was clear. Clear as well was the river flowing out from the southern end of the lake and down toward the sea. Disappointed that they couldn't cross the wide race, Farrix turned northerly, intending to 'round the top of the lake where they could then head east. And so for the next two days they skirted along the western shores of Lac Rwn, the body of water some fifteen miles long, though much longer by the route Rhu scurried. As they came to the tributaries running down from the tors of Rwn, they went upstream to find crossings, sometimes skittering over ice, at other times faring upon logs fallen across the tumbling waters, and once or twice swimming in the frigid rush—Farrix building a fire to warm and dry them when they reached the opposite side.

On the fifth day in the middle of a snowstorm they finally turned eastward, having come to the northern extent of Lac Rwn, and they wove through foothills, angling somewhat south whenever they could, for Farrix was aiming for a headland that lay one hundred miles or so due east of Darda Glain. And five days later, nine days after setting out, at last they came to that distant peninsula overlooking the Weston Ocean along the southeastern margin of the isle.

Rhu found a small cave where they denned, and Farrix set him free to hunt. And that very same night the aurora flared and a plume plunged down to fall into the sea . . . just beyond the horizon! *Damn!*

Frustrated at having come all this way and still not knowing a whit more than he had known when he had begun, Farrix began skinning the small animals that Rhu caught to eat—mice, hares, stoats, and the like—the fox looking on with approval, for he didn't relish hair. And Farrix found a willow tree and cut branches to fashion a coracle frame, though more pointed than round, lashing it together with thongs. He covered the structure with stitched-together hides, including a flexible one to cover the top, with a hole in the center through which he could slip his legs and tie tightly about his waist, making the interior of the craft waterproof. He treated all seams with a pitchy tar he made from pine cones covered with earth and baked. This took sixteen days to accomplish . . . yet two days before it was finished, another plume plunged beyond the horizon and down to the sea.

"Pox and plague! But I am not ready!" Farrix cried, shaking his fist at the distant flare.

Two days later, Farrix dropped two carven double-ended paddles down beside the hide boat and looked at the sky and declared, "Now! Now I am ready!"

Farrix studied his journal, notes he had been keeping ever since he had first seen the plumes, muttering to himself and Rhu: "Sometimes the skies are cast over. Other times the aurora does not glow. But every two weeks when the skies *are* clear and the aurora *does* flare, then a plume falls to the east, as if it is on a schedule.

Ah, Rhu m'lad, come twelve days, er, nights from now, if it is clear, if the sea permits, I'm off in my wee boat."

The days passed slowly, though Rhu and Farrix found things to occupy their time—the fox hunting or sleeping or watching Farrix with some concern as the Pysk tested his craft in the waters of the ocean, learning how to paddle it, learning as well how to tip it over and turn it upright again, each time emerging spluttering and laughing while Rhu barked and ran back and forth along the beach and seemed on the verge of leaping in to rescue his foolish master.

The dawn came crisp and clear fourteen days after the last plume had fallen. Farrix drew out his journal and pen and ink and wrote a short note to Jinnarin.

> *My love,*
>   *Here I am at the edge of the isle, and the plumes continue to flow easterly. It appears, though, that they arc down to strike in the ocean nearby. I have made myself a coracle, and I plan on paddling a bit out to sea, out to where it seems they might splash, just beyond the horizon, I think.*
>   *I have told Rhu to wait awhile, a day or so. If he returns without me, you will know that I am off on another of my ventures.*
>
> *I love you,*
Farrix

When he finished the note, he packed the hide boat with his bow and arrows, and with a bit of food and two skins of water.

At mid of day he placed the note in the special pocket in Rhu's collar and instructed the fox to wait two Suns as trained and then to go home. Farrix knew that he could always countermand the order if he got back to Rhu before then.

Farrix then launched his coracle, climbing in and lacing the cover tight about his waist. He tied one oar by slipknotted thong to his wrist, the second oar was stowed inside in case he lost the first. And with one last look at the clear skies and a call of good-bye to Rhu, he began paddling out across the rolling sea.

*   *   *

Some twelve hours later beneath a spangle of stars as night drew near the nadir and still no aurora writhed in the crystal skies above, Farrix stopped paddling well out to sea. He had no idea how far he had rowed, but he could no longer see any part of the headland, had not been able to see it for more than an hour. And so he knew that he was well beyond the horizon, and might in fact be near the place where the plumes mysteriously fell. He did know one thing, though—he was weary beyond measure. He had not anticipated how difficult it would be for someone of his stature to row across the horizon, and every time he had looked back, the headland was yet in view, diminished somewhat, but still visible. And so he had rowed onward, hour after hour, the Sun had set and still he rowed, the night growing deeper. And still by the light of the stars, the headland could yet be seen, and so on he pressed ... until at last after long toilsome hours, the headland finally disappeared.

A thin crescent Moon rode low in the west, and the crisp night air remained clear. And still no spectral lights blossomed above. Spent, Farrix laid his head upon the taut boat cover, his eyes fixed on the northern skies. *I will rest but a moment, gather my strength, for who knows when and where the plume will fall should the borealis appear, eh? I might have to row some more. Ha! I know I will have to row to get back to shore, once this is over.*

And so the weary Pysk lay against the yielding cover, his head cradled in his arms, as Mother Sea softly swashed and murmured in his ear, all the while gently rocking the Pysk upon her bosom.

"Yarrah!" something bellowed, jolting Farrix awake at the very same moment a monstrous grasp seized the boat and smashed him against the hide cover, pinning his arms, trapping him. Reflexively he clutched shadow about him, and Pysk and boat became a dark blot ensnared in a mashing grip. He was hoisted upward out of the water and alongside a looming black wall, and he desperately struggled, trying to get free, trying to reach the thongs about his waist to loose them and snatch up his bow and arrows from inside the craft—but he could not. A netting of some sort enwrapped him, and he

could not move—it was all he could do to breathe, clutched as tightly as he was. And as he was swung through the air, he could hear voices yammering words of a sort, though what they cried out, he could not say. Of a sudden he was slammed down, and a voice snarled—*"Balaka!"*—but it was in a tongue he knew not. Silence fell. Unable to turn his head, he could not see anyone, though he could hear footsteps nearing.

Adon, I am captured by Humans!

But then, in the direction he faced, a hulking form moved into view, monstrous, towering, leering—*Oh, Adon! Not Humans but a Troll instead! I've been captured by a Troll!* Farrix's heart hammered wildly in his chest, and he could not seem to get enough to breathe.

Above him and behind, the footsteps stopped. Moments passed, and in the silence, just into the edge of his vision stepped a Lok and then a Ruch. *Foul Folk! Captured by Foul Folk!* His mind screamed for him to flee, but he could not even move, much less escape his bonds.

Behind him, a voice hissed, *"Opsi emoì dós!"*

Then came cold laughter, followed by a whisper, *"Eórphne analótheti!"* and suddenly the shadow Farrix clutched to himself was gone.

"Aragh!" grunted the Troll in surprise, his bat-wing ears twitching outward. The bandy-legged Ruch's serpentine eyes bulged wide and he started to step forward, only to be slapped back by the Man-sized Lok.

A stream of guttural words snarled out, and Farrix was clutched in rough hands and extracted from the net and jerked free of the boat, the Lok doing so not bothering to untie the waist thong.

As he was swung up and about, Farrix could see that he was on the afterdeck of a boat of some sort, a ship large and black, lateen sails amidships and fore. Down each side were banks of oars powered by enormous Trolls. Rucha scuttled here and there, Loka among them. He had no time to see more, for the Lok tightly grasping him drew a kris and cut loose the paddle yet tied to his wrist, then held him out toward a Man. —Nay! Not a Man, but a Mage instead!

His long, angular features were pasty white, his nose long and narrow and hooked; his thin bloodless lips sneered in triumph and his piercing black eyes danced in gloat; he had not a hair on his head, not even eyelashes or brows. Dark robes cloaked him, and he was tall, and his fingers were long and grasping, with sharp nails painted black. He held a tall, straight, dark staff in one hand.

"Well, well," he whispered, "what have we here? Do my eyes deceive me, or is it truly a Pysk we have captured?"

"Let me go, Mage!" spat Farrix.

"*Akahl!* So you know that I am a Mage."

"Of course I know," shot back Farrix. "I have friends who are of Magekind."

"Pah! Name one."

"Alamar! He is my friend."

Farrix was shocked by the reaction to his words, for the Mage's eyes bulged with hatred and his mouth twisted into a snarl, and he stepped forward, his free right hand raised and clawlike, black nails gleaming wickedly, ready to slash, to pierce. The Lok holding Farrix cried out in terror and flinched back, thrusting the Pysk forward, as if he were a tiny shield, and Farrix braced himself for death. Yet in the last instant, the Mage stayed his hand. "Alamar," he hissed through clenched teeth, his nails poised a hairsbreadth from Farrix. "What does he know?"

Farrix's eyes widened. "Wha—?"

"What does he know?" shrieked the Mage, striking the butt of his staff to the deck.

"How should I know?" replied Farrix.

"Because I am the one you seek, spy. I am Alamar's nemesis. I am Durlok!"

"Spy? I am no spy. And I never heard of anyone named Durlok."

"You lie!" snarled Durlok.

The Mage turned to a nearby Ruch and gestured toward Farrix's boat, guttural words snapping commands.

The Ruch turned up the tiny boat, shaking the contents out: a two-ended paddle; a ration of food; two diminutive water skins; a wee bow and a tiny quiver filled with minuscule arrows. As the Ruch peered inside the boat to see if that was all, a second Ruch pulled one of the arrows from the quiver and examined it, sneering in laughter at the tiny barb and touching the tip with a finger in spite of Farrix's warning cry. "Ooo," leered the Ruch, his mouth gaping in a mocking grin, japing, acting as if he were afraid. "Ooo." And once more he pricked at his finger, but this time he flinched back as the sharp point penetrated. Then his eyes flew wide in alarm and his mouth rounded in a silent *O* of horror. He just had time to look up at Farrix before he fell dead.

Durlok stepped forward and looked down at the dead Ruch. Carefully the Mage plucked the tiny shaft from the slain creature's fingers and examined it. Then he whirled upon Farrix. "An assassin!" he cried, his eyes glaring in hatred, his black staff raised as if to strike. But then the look on his face altered, shifted, transformed into a sneer and he held up the arrow. "Ha! Do you actually think this would work against me? Pah! You are a fool! And Alamar is a fool for sending you on a fool's errand!"

"Skalga!" came a cry from the lookout atop the mid ship mast. *"Skalga!"*

Durlok whirled and looked at the sky. High above and to the north, the aurora began to glimmer. He glared back at Farrix and hissed, "We will finish this later, Pysk." Durlok snarled several commands, and Rucha and Loka scrambled to obey. While two Rucha hurled their dead brother over the rail, another gingerly took the arrow from Durlok and carefully slipped it into the quiver. All his goods were then put back in the boat, and the whole of it carried off. A Ruch appeared, bearing what seemed to be a bird cage, and Farrix was thrust inside and the door latched behind, a tiny hasp lock barring escape. The cage was then hung from the forward railing of the afterdeck and the Pysk was then ignored.

Farrix could see that overhead, the aurora strengthened, the glowing drapery rippling bright. And down on the decks Foul Folk scuttled, as if something imminent were to occur. And as Farrix watched, a Man was hauled up from below decks, gibbering, howling, weeping, his arm clutched in a Troll's unbreakable grasp. He was taken forward to the prow of the craft, where Durlok awaited. At sight of the Mage the Man shrieked in terror, and wrenched and jerked, trying to escape, all to no avail. His clothes were cut from him and cast overboard, and screaming, he was shackled to a large wooden block. And from a brazier filled with burning coals, Durlok drew forth glowing tongs, while a Lok stood at hand holding a dark metal cask and another held a rough flint knife. And Durlok took the burning tongs and reached out toward the Man and—

Farrix jerked his head aside and squeezed his eyes shut, for he could not watch such a hideous thing, and he jammed his hands against his ears, though he could still hear the Man's harrowing shrieks. The agonized howling went on and on as abomination after abomination took place there in the bow, screams of agony piercing the winter air as the spectral lights above grew bright. And in his cage, Farrix shrilled in fear and rage and loathing, shrieking at Durlok to stop, though the hideous mutilations went on and on. And of a sudden Durlok snatched up the stone knife and plunged it deep into the Man's abdomen and wrenched it through his flesh, eviscerating him. With a final shriek of agony, the howling stopped as life was hideously torn from the Man ... and then stark silence fell, soundless but for the swash of the ocean and the quiet weeping of a Pysk.

In the stillness, Durlok opened the metal cask and withdrew a dark crystal, long and sharp. And he held it up to the sky, up to the aurora, and muttered a word of <power>, invoking a strange name.

Farrix's hair stood on end, his arms atingle, and of a sudden from the aurora a great plume streaked down toward the ocean, toward the ship, toward the crystal, to slam into that mystic stone, staggering Durlok backwards. Yet the Mage managed to withstand the onslaught, and he held the crystal as coruscating light roared and flared, burned, blinded the eye, the crystal blazing with absorbed light. But just as suddenly as it had appeared, the raging dazzle vanished, and now by contrast the ship seemed plunged in utter darkness and silence, though stars yet shined above and the sea rolled below.

And locked in a bird cage on the aft of the ship, in the quiet a light-blinded Pysk moaned and wept, "Oh god, oh god, oh god. I have found where the plumes are going and I wish to Adon that I did not know."

* * *

Over the next six weeks, powered by the wind and by Trolls, Durlok's black galley plied the seas north-northeast to the coast of Thol, and then south-southwest to Rwn. Every night that the aurora flared, he would perform his abominations and sacrifice another screaming victim and draw down a plume into the crystal.

And in those same weeks he threatened Farrix, vowing to torture him, to kill him, to use him to draw down a plume. Yet always the Mage stopped short of his promises, stating that because Farrix was an assassin spy for the Mages of Rwn, in particular for Alamar, that he, Durlok, would do nothing that might provide a seer's link to him, and the torture or death of Farrix perhaps would do just that—in fact, Alamar probably planned it that way, planned for Durlok to slay the Pysk and provide a seer's link to him from Alamar's very own spawn, a daughter, he believed—and *that* he would avoid. Instead, he would keep the spying Pysk captive until he found a suitable use for him, perhaps to entrap the very ones who sent him in the first place. That way, not only would Durlok wreak his vengeance upon all of those of Magekind who had banished him, he would also avenge a terrible wrong done to him by Alamar in particular. Yes, yes, the Pysk was of more use alive than dead, of that, Durlok was certain. Hence, locked in his cage and cared for by Rucha, Farrix stopped denying Durlok's accusations, for should he convince the Mage that he was not a spy, then Durlok would be free to perform his hideous abominations on the tiny Pysk.

Twice, Durlok sent his Foul Folk on coastal raids and each time they returned with prisoners, victims for his terrible rites, Humans all, for they were of Mithgar and most fit to his purpose.

Farrix discovered that Durlok used their agony to power his castings—that Durlok was by his own admission a Black Mage, outlawed by the bulk of Magekind. Too, he worshipped Gyphon, and somehow his rites were serving that end. But this meager knowledge that Farrix gleaned paled into insignificance when compared to the terrible knowledge of the things the Black Mage did to the Men and Women he trapped.

And so sacrifice was heaped upon sacrifice, the mutilated, burnt, gouge-blinded, eviscerated corpses thrown overboard as plume after plume was drawn down. But then spring came and the aurora became sporadic, then faded altogether. Finally Durlok turned his galley southward, heading for his lair, a place he had stumbled upon, hidden from the Mages of Rwn.

It was during this journey that Farrix discovered the Trolls' utter fear of the ocean, though he did not discover why. That they were on the ship at all seemed a paradox to him; yet it was because of their dread of Durlok that they served aboard the galley. Except for their fear of the ocean, they were ideal for this task, the hulking brutes easily powering the ship a hundred and fifty miles a day. Ordinarily they worked in two shifts of fourteen, seven to a bank of oars, seven to a side; however, when pressed, six more oars were mounted, three to a side, and then twenty Trolls rowed.

The lateen sails, too, propelled the ship, adding considerably to its forward motion. But with the Trolls rowing no tacking was ever needed, hence the galley could run the very shortest course to a given goal, no matter the quarter of the wind. If the wind aided, well and good; if it did not, it was of little consequence.

Some weeks later they came to the Great Swirl, and Durlok sacrificed another victim. The weed was no hindrance at all.

Hidden away in a crystal cavern in a high stone island where no one would think to look, Durlok continued his hideous practices, torturing, mutilating, sacrificing a captive now and then. "Pah! I can always capture more at need," he sneered . . . then gloated and gestured outward toward the Great Swirl beyond the stone of the cavern, "There are times, of course, they even come to me, their ships snared in my great green web." Trapped in his cage, Farrix shuddered at the thought, envisioning a monstrous spider sitting in the center of its lair.

When his captors were asleep, Farrix tested the bars and the lock of his prison, seeking escape, to no avail. And under Durlok's vigilant eye, nothing that could be used to pick the lock was ever left at hand. But Farrix waited patiently, for one day, one day, they would make a mistake. . . .

And in the darkness when all was still, he sat in his cage and thought of Jinnarin. Oh, if only somehow he could get word to her and tell her of the crystal cavern in the high stone island in the center of the Great Swirl and of Durlok and his black galley of death, then perhaps she could gather together those who could stop this monster once and for all. But that was not to be, for how could anyone locked in a cage get word to someone half a world away?

Three months after the galley had come to the island, Durlok took his prisoners and his ship southward, down to the southern aurora, where he resumed his terrible practices, drawing down plumes.

Finally he returned to his understone hideaway, to his temple to Gyphon. And there he conceived a cunning plan should Alamar establish a link and come looking for his pawn. And in unholy glee he sacrificed victim after victim, gathering hideous energy to power a terrible spell, to summon a demon, to lay a trap, to cast Farrix into a coma, into an enchanted sleep.

CHAPTER 35

Questions

Spring, 1E9575
[The Present]

A nd then you came and freed me from Durlok's enchanted sleep," concluded Farrix, his eyes sweeping
across all those in the dinghy, Dwarves, Man, Lady Pysk,
and fox, "for which I will be ever grateful."

Jinnarin leaned over and gave him a kiss but then sat
back, a pensive look upon her face. Yet it was Jamie
who expressed the thought that each of them were thinking. "Lor, Master Farrix, what a horrible time you've
lived through, what with the torture and sacrifices and
all. Brrr, gives me the blue willies it does, and I mean
the deep blue willies, I do."

Koban slammed a fist into palm. "Damn Durlok!
Would that I could caress his neck with my axe." A
rumble of agreement muttered throughout the warriors
aboard.

After a moment of silence, Relk looked at the others.
"Why does Durlok invest the plumes in the crystal?
What is his purpose?"

All eyes swung to Farrix, but he turned up his hands.
"If I knew, then I would say. Yet it is as much a mystery
to me today as when I first saw him do it."

Throughout the day the craft fared westward across
the pale green sea, the boats impelled by a wind abeam
blowing from due north, rare in these latitudes no matter
the season south of the Calms of the Goat. Past half

sunken hulks they sailed, derelicts covered with moss and fungus and rot, steering well clear of many, Aravan's stone running chill in their presence.

In mid afternoon the wind began shifting about until it blew directly from the west, and into the teeth of the blow they tacked to and fro, the flat-bottom boats slipping sideways as well, now running twice as far to cover half the distance. "If we only had a keel, we could make better of it," grumbled Jamie, clearing sea moss from his steering oar. "Of course, had we a keel, the weed'd snag us right up, 'twould , then we wouldn't go anywhere. Drat! Can't win for losing."

The rest of that day and the next as well, the wind blew in their faces. And throughout it all, Jinnarin sat in abstracted silence, speaking only when spoken to, her mind worrying over Farrix's tale as a fox would worry a bone, the Pysk seeking some clue as to the Black Mage's intentions, her thoughts running in circles of surmise and conjecture and speculation. Finally, late in the night she said, "Farrix. Tell your tale to Alamar. He's a Mage. Perhaps he'll discern what Durlok intends."

"Ha! I was right then about the lightning," quavered Alamar in a reedy voice, the eld Mage nodding unto himself.

"Lightning?"

"Your dream. The sending. The lightning, Pysk. It was the plumes."

Farrix now sat in Alamar's boat, having transferred there mid morn. It was the third full day of sailing westward, and above, the skies were overcast, roiling with dark clouds. And still the wind blew from the west. "What else, Alamar? What else did you glean from my tale?"

"Nothing you don't already know, Pysk. The sacrifices, well, they give Durlok the unholy <power> he needs for his blasphemous rites. But why he draws the aurora into the crystal . . . eh, I don't know. —Say, did you overhear the <word> he used when he drew down the <fire>? That might help."

Farrix shook his head. "Kry—krsp—loper— Oh, if I heard it, I would probably recognize it. But it was in a tongue strange to me. Not Slûk. I heard enough of that foul speech to know how it sounds. Instead it was—it was—"

"Probably the Black Mage tongue," interjected Alamar, running a palsied hand through the thin white wisps of his remaining hair.

In that moment it began to rain, the chill downpour drenching all. After they had pulled the silks of the spare sail over them, Alamar said above the drumming of the drops, "Tell this tale to Aylis. She's a seer, and seers are used to ferreting out things hidden, things mysterious. Go tell Aylis."

Alamar began coughing.

The remainder of that day and part of the next the rain poured down unremittingly. But at last it turned to a drizzle and finally stopped altogether, though a chill westerly yet blew. Throughout that night Alamar's coughing worsened, and by the next day he was racked with fever. After brewing a hot herbal tea over the flame of a small oil lamp, Burak directed Alamar to inhale the pungent fumes as he drank it. Alamar took one smell— "Gack!"—and tried to push the cup away. But Burak snarled, "If you would live to see Fager aboard the *Eroean* and receive proper treatment, then by Elwydd, Mage Alamar, you *will* drink this tea!" And he forced the drink upon Alamar, the elder too feeble to resist, though not too feeble to execrate the Dwarf and all of his Kind.

When came the fifth dawn of travel, the wind died altogether, and Farrix transferred to Aylis's boat and told the seeress his tale as the Dwarven warriors rowed. Yet during the telling she seemed to be but half listening, her mind instead on the sick oldster cursing in the boat behind. Even so, at the end of his tale, Aylis murmured, "It is probably when you were caged and thinking of Jinnarin that the seeds of the sending were formed. And when Durlok cast you into a deep sleep within a sleep—a trap, we know—it was a casting with an unintended side effect, for your dream reached across the world."

Farrix protested. "But my dream was of a crystal castle, a lightning-stroked ship, a pale green sea, a spider and a web. All in all, not very accurate, if you ask me."

Aylis smiled, her eyes lost in thought. "My father often told us that dream images are not what they seem. Yet, your images served well enough, for did we not find you?"

Farrix laughed. "Yes indeed, *that* you did. But it was through your cleverness and skills, and not any effort on my part."

Aylis sat without speaking for a moment as the oars plashed in the water. But then she asked, "Did you overhear the <word> Durlok used to summon the <fire> to the crystal?"

"Your father asked me the same thing, Aylis, and I couldn't tell him either. Strange it was, and at times it seemed harsh and at other times sibilant, and if I heard it again, I could say yea or nay."

Aylis took Durlok's lexicon from her pocket. "Farrix, I have here a listing of Black Mage words, and when we reach the *Eroean* and start for Rwn, I will read to you from it, and when you hear the word, then we will perhaps have a clue to Durlok's aims."

The following day, it rained again and a gusty wind blew strongly and shifted about without warning, and Farrix and Jinnarin sat in their craft and watched and listened as Jamie cursed and fought for control of the flat-bottomed boat skittering across the choppy waves, and the Pysks learned several new words of interest.

When came the seventh dawning the skies cleared and wind again blew from the west, and Farrix transferred to Aravan's boat and told the Elven captain his tale as the dinghies tacked across the pale green sea. At the end of Farrix's story, Aravan was just as puzzled as all the rest, though he did clarify a point:

"Even though Trolls rowed Durlok's ship, it is not strange for them to fear the ocean. The bones of Trolls are as hard and as dense as iron, some say even denser. They cannot swim a stroke, plummeting to the bottom like rocks cast into a pool. And *that,* Farrix, is why they fear the sea, for should the black galley founder, then they would be lost, drowned.

"Yet heed, although they might fear the sea, they are even more afraid of the Black Mage, and with good reason, as thou thyself hast seen. He is more powerful than they, and that is a great power indeed, for it is as Bokar says, Trolls are a fearsome foe, and twenty-eight Trolls have power beyond measure.

"But as to the rest of thy tale, Farrix, I have no mark of what Durlok has in mind. Yet of this we can be certain: it is evil beyond measure."

Farrix sighed and nodded. "Perhaps the Mages of Rwn will know."

In that moment a voice called out, "Ship ho! Ship ho on the starboard bow!"

Farrix looked, and a magnificent tall ship bore down toward them, silken cerulean sails flying in the breeze, dark blue hull heeling over, silver bottom glimmering through the waves.

It was the *Eroean*.

They had come to the Elvenship at last.

CHAPTER 36

Pursuit

Late Spring, 1E9575
[The Present]

I tell you, Father, we must get to Rwn!"

"And I tell you, Daughter, we've got to stop Durlok. He blatantly spoke of a wedding gift, taunting us all, believing that we are powerless to stop him."

"Wedding gift?" Jatu raised his eyebrows and he leaned forward on his fists. "What is this wedding gift?"

Alamar glanced across the map table at the big black Man. "I think he hints at an alignment . . . and one is coming soon, and whatever he's got planned is certain to be deadly."

Aravan nodded his agreement, but Jatu asked, "Alignment?"

Alamar groaned with exasperated impatience. Aravan looked briefly at the elder then said to Jatu, "It's when the wandering stars are all in the sky at once. The closer they are to one another, the stronger the alignment. Once in a great while, they all seem to gather at virtually the same place, and this is called a grand alignment. If the Moon is in the heavens and clustered with them, it is even more portentous. Periodically one or more of the wanderers march across the daytime skies, when they cannot be seen, and many people know not they are there, but—"

"Eh!" snorted Alamar. "Any stargazer worth his salt knows exactly where they are, whether or not they are visible."

Aravan inclined his head in agreement, then said, "There are times, Jatu, when the Sun, the Moon, and the five wanderers are all present in the day, though the eye sees only the Sun."

"Kruk!" spat Bokar, glancing at the others in the captain's lounge. "What does this have to do with a wedding, Captain?"

"A so-called wedding alignment is when the Moon and Sun kiss one another while all five wanderers watch—that means all are in the day sky at the same time, though not necessarily clustered tightly together, not a grand alignment."

"Kissing one another?" blurted Jinnarin, sitting next to Farrix on the tabletop. "What does that mean?"

"Just what he said, Pysk!" snapped Alamar. "The Sun and Moon are touching."

"Oh," said Jinnarin, "like the occultation we saw at Rwn on the day of Year's Long Night."

Farrix looked at Jinnarin in startlement, silently mouthing the word, *Occultation?*

"When the Moon eats the Sun," she whispered to him.

"It doesn't have to be a full occultation, Pysk," muttered Alamar, running an age-spotted hand through his wisps of hair. "The only thing that matters is that they touch."

"When will this so-called wedding occur?" asked Frizian.

Alamar slapped a hand down on the table. "That's just the problem! There's a wedding due each month for the next several. The first one comes . . ." Alamar pursed his lips in thought—

"June fourteenth," said Aravan quietly.

"Yes," agreed Alamar, an eyebrow cocked at the Elf, adding, "and then they occur about once a month until . . ."

"The last wedding this year," interjected Aravan, "occurs November ninth, and that one just barely, for even as the Moon kisses the Sun, one wanderer is just setting as another is rising. The following month there is no—"

"Do you always have to interrupt, Elf?" snapped Alamar.

Farrix looked at Alamar. "I seem to recall that Durlok said it was a grand wedding gift. It occurs to me that the words 'grand wedding' might make a difference, neh?"

Alamar's face lighted up. "Heh! Out of the mouths of babes— Of course they make a difference, Pysk. A grand wedding is when the kiss comes near midday, preferably at noon, though a bit to either side is perfectly good. And that will occur in"—Alamar threw up a hand to stop Aravan from saying anything—"in ... hmm ... in ..."—he glared at Aravan and snapped, "Well aren't you going to help?"

"The next four will be grand weddings," said Aravan, "September the eleventh, the last."

Alamar turned to Aylis. "And *that,* Daughter, is why we must go after Durlok. To stop him from delivering his grand wedding gift to—how did he put it? ah yes— his gift to all of my ilk."

"What do you suppose he meant by that?" asked Frizian. "Just who are those of 'your ilk'?"

Before Alamar could answer, Bokar growled, "If we go after Durlok, what do we do about the Trolls? After all, they yet ward him."

"I know!" piped up Farrix, glancing at Aravan. "If we can sink the galley, they'll most certainly drown, heavy bones and all."

"But wait," muttered Frizian, "we don't even know where Durlok and his black galley are."

A grin creased Alamar's aged face. "Aylis can find him. She has his lexicon."

"Even should we discover his whereabouts, Father, still he is a Mage, a powerful Mage and a Black one. We have no way to counter his castings, and even if we did, it is questionable whether we could capture him."

"Capture him Hèl, Daughter, I mean to kill him!"

Bokar stroked his beard. "If we could take him by surprise, sink his ship ..."

"If I remember correctly, Armsmaster," said Aylis, "we talked about this before. To surprise him is unlikely, and to sink his ship, well, he would simply walk away."

"Mayhap, Lady Aylis, but as Master Farrix says, his Trolls would not."

Aylis shook her head. "I think we here do not have the wherewithal to destroy the Black Mage, and instead of pursuing him we should go to Rwn and tell our tale to the Master Mages and let them deal with him. Besides, my father must cross over to Vadaria."

"What of the grand wedding, Daughter. The next four are critical. Whatever Durlok has up his sleeve, he has but four separate days in which to perform it. We don't even need to confront him directly, but merely distract him, turn his energies aside. Can we just divert his attention at mid of day on each of those days, a total of four or so hours altogether ... well, we will have thwarted him. *Then* we can go to Rwn."

"What do you propose, Father? How will we distract him? And should we succeed, how will we keep him from destroying the *Eroean* and all who sail upon her?"

"Look, Daughter, I don't claim to have all the answers. All I know is that Durlok has said that he needs to conserve his energies for whatever it is he plans. That should protect us somewhat from his <power>; he will save it for his vile scheme, hence will not loose it upon us. As to how to distract him"—Alamar shrugged—"we'll think of something."

Silence fell, and all eyes swung to Aravan, for he was their captain. He looked at Aylis. "Canst thou find the whereabouts of Durlok?"

Sighing, she nodded.

"Then do so, *chieran*. Tell us where he fares. Mayhap it will affect our decision."

Aylis looked about the salon. "A darkened cabin would help. Less distraction."

As the seeress sat down, Jinnarin stood and quietly pulled Farrix to his feet and led him to a far corner of the table, whispering, "I think we need to get out of her range, for at times she faints and falls forward."

They drew the curtains over the portholes and lit a single candle. Aylis took the lexicon from a pocket and held the small book in both hands. When all motion and shuffling of feet stopped and silence descended, she took several deep breaths as if to calm herself, then closed her eyes and murmured, *"Cursus."* She sat without moving for a while, then raised one hand and pointed. "There. There is where fares Durlok."

"Sou'sou'east," muttered Frizian, "toward the polar lats."

"How far, Daughter?"

"More than a thousand miles, but less than two," replied Aylis, her eyes yet closed.

"Where bound?" asked Aravan.

Aylis frowned, as if seeking, and finally said, "Where bound? I cannot say. Only where is." Then Aylis's shoulders slumped, and slowly she opened her eyes, her casting done.

As the drapes were pulled aside to let daylight in, Aravan selected a map and spread it upon the table. "Here we are in the Sindhu Sea on the west marge of the Great Swirl. Durlok's ship is somewhere between"—his finger stabbed down to the map twice—"here and here. He could be bound for"—Aravan touched several points on the map—"the Great Island continent in the south of the Bright Sea, the polar land, or east to the southern continent and beyond."

"A thousand miles is quite a lead," said Farrix. "We may never catch him, wherever he is bound."

"You forget, tiny one," rumbled Jatu, "the *Eroean* is the fastest ship in the world. A thousand miles or a thousand leagues, it matters not. Given that he runs long enough, we will surely catch him."

As Farrix nodded, Frizian looked at Aravan. "Well, Captain, if the black galley is somewhere sou'sou'east, where do we run?"

Aravan glanced at each and every one and finally said, "Set our course south-southeast, Frizian. We'll follow Durlok, and if we can sink him we will."

A pent-up exhalation sounded throughout the room, as if all had been holding their breath until a decision was made.

"But what of our journey to Rwn?" asked Aylis, glancing at Alamar then looking at Aravan, her voice filled with distress.

"*Chieran,* I know thou art concerned for thy sire, and so, too, am I. Yet Alamar is right: can we thwart Durlok, then we set his plans in disarray. But this I *do* promise— can we not think of a way to hinder the Black Mage, then will we sail on to Rwn by 'rounding the Silver Cape."

Jatu started, and dread sprang up behind his eyes. "But, Captain, the Silver Cape—we'll be crossing in the dead of summer!"

Aravan's look was grim. "Aye, Jatu, yet heed: if any ship can 'round that horn in summer, 'tis the *Eroean*."

Jinnarin's own heart was hammering with fear, and she squeezed Farrix's hand. He looked at her with surprise and whispered, "What is it, love? What is so dreadful about the Silver Cape?"

"The seasons," she whispered back, "they are reversed down here south of the midline. Though it is called summer, it will really be the dire dead of winter if or when we try to go through the straits—howling blizzards, crushing ice, thundering winds, no day, no Sun—and I've been told by crewmen that it cannot be done."

Captain Aravan called a shipboard meeting and stood Farrix on the wheelhouse so that all could see him, the Elf declaring that that part of the mission had been accomplished—Lady Jinnarin's mate had been found. After the cheers subsided, Aravan then spoke of Durlok and the black galley, and of the unknown threat the Black Mage represented. As was his wont, Aravan then admitted the crew into his confidence and spoke of the plan to pursue and if possible to destroy the Black Mage. The crew took this all in stride—until he came to the part concerning the possibility that they might need to sail 'round the Silver Cape in the dead of summer. A stunned silence greeted this news, sailors and warriors alike looking fearfully about, for it was common knowledge that this had never been done. Finally someone, Lobbie it was, called out, "Cap'n, I mean, it's hard enough in the dead o' winter, when the air is shriekin' mild and gentle compared to the rest o' the seasons—but in the summertime? Might as well try to sail in and out o' the depths o' Great Maelstrom in the Boreal, wot?" But someone else, Artus, spoke up. "Ar, Lobbie, has the Captain ever asked us to do what couldn't be done?" And then Jatu's voice called out, "There's always a first time for everything—after we've done the cape, Lobbie, then we'll think on doing as you say and sail the Maelstrom next," and then the big black Man bellowed with laughter and soon all the crew was howling along in glee.

In mid afternoon the silks were haled about and the *Eroean* was set on a course due south, for she was yet in the marge of the Great Swirl and must needs run out of the weed before turning to pursue the black galley.

Jinnarin took Farrix about the ship, introducing him to the crew. And when she came to Rolly and Carly and Finch and Arlo, these four seemed to look down at Farrix with suspicion in their eyes, as if wondering if he was good enough for *their* Pysk—Lady Jinnarin. In the end, it seems, Farrix passed their muster, for Arlo set about making a larger pallet for Jinnarin's under-bunk quarters for both of the Pysks to sleep upon, and Rolly, Carly, and Finch began fashioning a tiny sea chest in which Farrix could store his things.

That evening, Jinnarin arranged with Ship's Cook Trench for hot water for baths for Farrix and her. Tink and Tiver delivered a washbasin full of hot water to the under-bunk quarters, the cabin boys supplying as well chips of soap and scant cloths and towels. Jinnarin sent Rux to hunt for rats, the fox happily complying, for he had been cooped up in a tiny rowboat for the last seven days running. And the Pysks stripped off their leathers and climbed into the bath, luxuriating in the warmth and water. Soon Farrix was washing her and she him, and alone together at last, Farrix took Jinnarin in his arms and kissed her tenderly, and they clambered out of the basin and hurriedly dried off and then lay down together and made love. . . .

. . . And then again, for it had been two and a half years since Farrix had set off to find the plumes, two and a half years of loneliness, of reaching out to someone who was not there. . . .

. . . And once more . . . this last interrupted by Alamar stomping across the room and banging on the wall of their under-bunk quarters and querulously demanding quiet—"I'm trying to sleep, you know!"

Aylis sat up in the bed, her fine brown hair tousled, a knowing smile on her face. Aravan was gone somewhere, though the stateroom yet breathed of his elusive scent. Yawning, she stretched, full and long, then leapt out of bed and dashed water on her face then swiftly dressed, and ran a quick comb through her hair. When she entered the salon, Alamar was sitting at the table and cursing. "What is it, Father?"

The elder looked up at her. "Eh, it's not enough that there was all that ruckus under that bunk last night, but this morning when I woke up, there was a dead rat in my shoe."

Aylis heard the hint of a giggle, and when she looked, a dark cluster of shadow ducked back into the corridor. Alamar, too, heard it, and the eld Mage swung about and pointed a quavering finger at the hallway. "All right, you miscreant. Show yourself."

Nonchalantly, Farrix strode into view, innocence written all over his face, though his ice-blue eyes danced in glee.

"Don't play the innocent," snapped Alamar, "you're not fooling me."

"What?" Farrix clapped a hand to his heart, his eyes wide. "Is something wrong?"

"There's a dead rat in my quarters, Pysk, and you know it."

"Oh?" Farrix's eyebrows shot up, then back down in frowning concentration. "It must be Rux, that scoundrel."

"Rux, my foot!"

Uncontrollable titters bubbled from Farrix's mouth. "I think, Alamar, you meant to say, Rux, my shoe!" Farrix doubled over laughing.

"You dratted Pysk," gruffed Alamar, now grinning in spite of himself, "you haven't changed a bit!" Alamar looked up at Aylis. "This Pysk, Daughter, even when I was lying there pig-wounded, my leg about to fall off, would use stink bugs to wake me up! And that's not all. Why, once he 'accidentally' dropped a diuren leaf into my tea—"

"That *was* an accident, Alamar!" protested Farrix.

"Ha! I about piddled myself to death."

Farrix laughed. "But I was the one who had to lug all that water up the hill for you to piddle away! I think you did it just to watch me work."

Alamar cackled. "But if you remember, Pysk, I got even for that diuren leaf—"

Gladdened to see her father in good spirits for a change, Aylis interjected, "I'll let you two renew acquaintances and dredge up memories of suitable revenges for foul deeds done." Smiling, she left them behind, her heart lighter.

On deck she found Aravan at the wheel, the ship now running south-southeast on Durlok's track. Aravan, though, had a frown on his face. "The air is light, *chieran*," he explained. "We are barely making six knots."

"Perhaps it is light for Durlok, too."

Aravan shook his head. "Wind or no, for him it matters little—he has the Trolls to row." Aravan looked up at the silks. "The *Eroean* is the fastest ship in the world, but only when she has the wind."

Over the next week the wind was light and shifty, and at times it died altogether. The following week it blew straight at them, and the *Eroean* tacked a zigzag course, Aravan fretting, for the black galley could run a straight line no matter the wind, while the Elvenship could not.

During this time, Aylis read from the Black Mage lexicon, the seeress casting a spell to do so, noting phrases and words in her own journal, noting how they were spelled, their meanings, and their pronunciations. Often she would sit with Farrix, saying words to him, seeing if any sounded familiar to the Pysk. Farrix would listen and shake his head, *No,* the words striking no chord of memory . . . until one day—

Aylis sat in the lounge reading the book aloud, Jinnarin and Farrix listening.

"Hmm," she murmured, turning a page, "these are names of gemstones: *adamus* is diamond; *erythros* is ruby; *smaragdos* is emerald; oh, here is one that at least *sounds* familiar, *sappheiros* is sapphire." Aylis glanced up at Farrix, but he sighed and shook his head. Her gaze returned to the page. "Crystal, too, is a sound-alike: *krystall.*"

"I say," piped up Farrix, "something about that last rings a note."

"Krystall?"

Farrix frowned, seeking an elusive memory. He cocked his head, his gaze lost, and finally muttered, "Perhaps."

Jinnarin smiled at Farrix as Aylis jotted a note in her journal.

Then the seeress continued her reading, pronouncing many a strange-sounding word, all to no immediate avail for he recognized none.

Jinnarin and Aylis stood together on the foredeck, the Pysk on the stemblock peering forward, the seeress at the rail looking down. Below, the clear waters slid past.

"Do you have any brothers or sisters, Aylis?"

Aylis looked up at Jinnarin and shook her head. "None. Why?"

"Oh, I was just talking with Boder. He has four sisters and three brothers. Can you imagine being raised in a family of eight? —No wait, ten, counting the father and mother. They had *eight* children in nine years. . . . Whereas among my Kind, we have perhaps but one child in nine thousand years . . . and then only if someone has died—by accident, disease, or foe. But eight children in nine years I find it quite unimaginable."

Again Aylis shook her head. "Humans—that's the way of Humans. They seem to believe that they can multiply without number. My father was right when he said that the gift of Humanity was fecundity."

Jinnarin nodded and fell into silence. After a while she said, "Even so, it must be special to have a brother or sister. I've often wondered what it would be like to have one."

Aylis pursed her lips. "I was raised in a family of two. There was just my sire and me."

"What about your mother?"

Aylis sighed. "I don't remember her. She died when I was but a few months old."

"Oh, I am so sorry, Aylis. Everyone should have a mother . . . a loving mother that is . . . like mine."

"Does she live in Darda Glain?"

Jinnarin shook her head. "No, she and my sire now live in Blackwood. I haven't seen them for millennia— ever since the wedding. They went from Darda Glain to the Blackwood, seeking a larger forest, more space."

They stood in silence for a while, then Aylis said, "Your mother, she was nice, neh?"

"Oh yes. I always felt loved."

Aylis nodded, then sighed. "I wished that I'd known my mother. Father seldom speaks of her. I think it hurts him to do so. He says I look like her, like Lyssa ... all but the eyes. I have my father's green eyes. He tells me hers were blue."

"How did she ... ?"

Aylis's gaze turned grim. "Ravers slew her. Foul Folk. During the War of Rwn."

Jinnarin glanced up at Aylis. "Many were lost in those battles. But the Foul Folk, we took their measure in Darda Glain and they were afraid to enter thereafter."

"So I heard."

Again a silence descended between them, each lost in her own thoughts as the *Eroean* cut through the waters. At last, however, Jinnarin softly asked, "Will you be my sister, Aylis?"

Aylis turned and looked at the tiny Pysk, and tears welled in her eyes.

Adverse winds continued to plague the *Eroean*, and every day the black galley drew farther away. Out of the Sindhu they sailed and across a short stretch of the Bright Sea, and then they fared south of the Great Island and into the waters of the Polar Ocean. And each day the Sun rose later and set earlier as they came into the frigid mar, for summer drew nigh and in these south polar seas that meant the coming of the days of no Sun whatsoever, the coming of the long night. And toward the dark they sailed, into stormy waters.

As the ship plunged through the hammering waves, Aylis sat at the map table, dealing cards from her seer's deck. "Oh my," she murmured, her lips drawn thin, "the Drowning Man."

Quill in hand, Aravan looked up from the ship's log. "What is it, *chieran*?"

Aylis turned to him, a stricken look on her face. "The Drowning Man"—she gestured at the spread of cards— "a harbinger of disaster. Although I cannot break through Durlok's shielding, it may mean the *Eroean* and all on her are heading toward ruin."

"But thou art not certain?"

Aylis shook her head. "No. I am not certain. It could mean disaster for but a few on this ship ... or for someone else altogether."

Aravan came and stared down at the card, his hands

kneading the knots loose from her taut shoulders and neck. At last he said, "I shall warn the crew to make certain to clip to the safety lines."

"Hmm, this is strange."

"What is it, Daughter?" Alamar looked up from the tokko game. Jinnarin, too.

"Father, Durlok has circled a word, see?"

Aylis passed the lexicon across the table to Alamar. The eld Mage took it up in palsied hands, and then laid it back to the surface of the table. Both Jinnarin and Farrix stepped to the side of the book and peered down at it.

Κρψσταλλοπψρ was the encircled word.

"How do you say it, Daughter, and what does it mean?"

"Well, it could take on either of two pronunciations: Krystallopŷr, or *Krystallopýr*."

"That's it!" exclaimed Farrix. "That's the word Durlok used to draw down the plumes!"

"Which?" demanded Alamar.

"The last one: *Kry-kr*—"

"Krystallopýr?" asked Aravan. Something about the word rang a faint echo in Aravan's mind, but he could not dredge up the elusive memory.

"Yes. What you said. *Kry-krys-rystallo*— Oh, I give up!"

"Ha!" barked Alamar. "One is what it is; the other is its Truename!"

"What *what* is, Alamar?" asked Jinnarin.

"The crystal that Pysk told us about, Pysk."

"Oh," said Jinnarin, enlightened.

Farrix looked at Alamar. "You mean the crystal itself is called, uh—"

"Krystallopŷr," supplied Jinnarin.

Farrix nodded. "Yes, what she said. But about this Truename . . ."

"Krystallopýr," said Alamar, "that's the way it is invoked, the word used to call the <fire>. Ha! I *knew* that it wasn't a casting!"

"Hoy now, just a moment," said Farrix. "If it wasn't a casting, then why did Durlok need to—to horribly sacrifice someone? When I was captive on the black galley,

I learned that by torture and maiming and mutilation he could somehow use a victim's agony to power his castings."

Alamar stroked his thin beard. "Hmm, good question, Pysk. As to why, I can't say for certain ... but knowing Durlok, he probably did it just for the sheer pleasure it gives him."

Aylis shook her head. "More likely, Father, he did it to protect himself from the crystal. Invoking its Truename may have made it dangerous to hold."

Alamar shrugged. "I wouldn't know about that, Daughter, but this I do believe: Durlok found the crystal and somehow teased its Truename from it."

Aylis shook her head. "No, Father. Truenames are embedded into things during the forging, and unless Durlok is a seer, he cannot discover such. He must have created the crystal and given it its Truename."

"Well he didn't *forge* it, Daughter!" snapped Alamar. "He does not have the training."

"Then, Father, he must have read it in a scroll, or else someone told him the crystal's Truename, or someone of knowledge and <power> forged it for him."

"Bah! He has no friends. Who would do such a thing?"

Silence fell upon them, Alamar's last question ringing on the air. Moments later, "How about Gyphon?" suggested Jinnarin.

On the eighteenth of June the *Eroean* at last came full into the South Polar Sea, and a shrieking wind howled easterly, hurling snow and ice and the Elvenship before its brutal blast. Great greybeards loomed over the ocean, dwarfing the tall *Eroean,* and though her sharp bow cut through the peaks of the towering crests, her hull jarringly boomed down into the troughs beyond. The Sun no longer rose, day now as dark as night, and the screaming air was frigid beyond endurance. By Aylis's casting and Aravan's charting they knew that their quarry sailed eastward far ahead, some twenty-eight hundred miles in all, the black galley seemingly on a direct course for the Silver Cape, Durlok yet some twelve hundred miles from the straits, the Elvenship nearly three thousand.

"Kruk!" cursed Bokar, slamming his fist to the table. "I had hoped to catch him before the pinch of those dire narrows."

At Bokar's words, Aravan's eyes lighted up and he glanced down at the map. The ship whelmed down into the brine and slid into the trough below, then began a climb up to the crest ahead. None said aught as the lantern cast swaying shadows in the rocking salon, and by its yellow light Aravan gauged the distances. At last he looked to Frizian. "What silks are we running?"

"Nought but the mains, Captain, and those goose-winged."

"Then, Frizian, set the mains at full, all topsails, too. Fly the jibs and stays as well, yet mount not the gallants and above."

"But, Captain," protested Jatu. "This air. It blows. Oh how it does blow. And that much silk endangers the masts."

Aravan turned up a hand. "Mayhap, Jatu, yet I deem she can withstand the press." The Elven captain then glanced at the others. "Heed me, all of ye. We're going to try to ride the Hèlbent wind and catch the Black Mage in the straits."

"*In* the straits!" exclaimed Bokar. "Are my ears deceiving me? Did I hear you say *in* the straits?"

"Aye, Bokar. What better place to take him by surprise?"

And the hull of the *Eroean* boomed down.

In the dark thundering wind, sailors in polar gear clambered up the ratlines to unfurl the silks. Even though dressed to withstand the blast, still the Men spent as little time aloft in the savage blow as completing the task allowed; no sooner would one crew finish and come running back into shelter, than another crew would charge across the deck and up to a given yardarm to loosen ties and lashings, then scurry back down as mates on the deck haled the halyards about and set the silk to the wind. In short order the mains and tops were deployed, the jibs and stays swiftly after. And the masts groaned and ropes thrummed under the shrieking burden as great greybeards hurtled through the night across the frigid polar sea.

And in the wheelhouse, Aravan called out to be heard above the roar, "Set her course for east-southeast, Jatu."

"But, Captain, that will take us to the polar cap, and should we get caught in the ice . . . we'll be crushed."

"Nevertheless, Jatu, it is the shortest route to the straits. 'Tis a great circle we run on this globe and not some flat-world path, so point her stem to east-southeast."

"Aye, Captain," replied Jatu, relaying the order to Boder, with Rico piping the sails to trim her up in the hurling wind.

"Twenty-nine knots, Captain," bellowed Jatu over his shoulder, awe in his voice as he and Artus entered the dimly lit wheelhouse and struggled to shut the door against the brumal blow. "By Adon, but I can barely believe it—do you realize that in the last three days we've not been below twenty knots? Adon and Elwydd, in but three days we have run nearly two thousand miles! No other ship has ever before done so."

"No other ship has e'er before been driven by such a thundering wind," replied Aravan.

"Jatu," called out Jinnarin, she and Farrix standing on the sill of the forward window, "don't you remember you once told me that had we a polar blow abaft we could sail entire oceans in but a week or so."

"Yes, tiny one. But never did I think to see the day."

"At least it's stopped snowing," said Farrix as he squinted out into the polar night. Of a sudden he pressed his face to the window and cupped his hands about his eyes to shield out the light from the hooded lantern behind. "I say, Aravan, is that a white mountain ahead?"

Aravan whirled about and peered through the glass. "Lantern out!" he barked, and Geff leaped to comply and slammed the shutter to. As the wheelhouse was plunged into near darkness—pinpricks of light leaking through the closed shield—"Yes," cried Farrix, "either a white mountain or a wall of ice, and I know which I'd wager it is!"

"Where away?" snapped Aravan, peering into the long polar night, moonless and starless beneath the racing black overcast above.

"In the distance ahead. To the right, the starboard."

Farrix pointed. "We are going to come very close, maybe even graze it. Don't you see it?"

"Nay, I do not! Hegen, larboard two points! Put the wind on our aft quarter! Reydeau, pipe the sails! Take care, ye both, for she'll founder if we put her broadside to these waves!"

Driven before the shrieking blow, the *Eroean* plunged ahead, curving in a long, long arc as she answered the helm—swiftly for a ship of her size, slowly given the hazard. Hurriedly the standby crew scrambled onto the deck, swinging the halyards about, as well as trimming the jibs and stays. And the Elvenship curved through the towering rage to swing alongside and then away from a vertical wall of ice looming some eight hundred yards to the starboard.

Above the squall and boom, Jinnarin called out to Aravan, "I told you Farrix's eyes were keen."

Aravan nodded. "Keen indeed is thine eyesight, Farrix, Pysk of Darda Glain, for thou didst see the floe by dark of night some two or so miles away. In this polar darkness without stars or Moon, mine own eyes see a mile or less."

"At the speed we are travelling, Captain," rumbled Jatu, "nearly thirty knots, should we encounter something directly in our line less than a mile away, we will collide with it in under a hundred heartbeats."

Hegen cleared his throat in the dark of the wheelhouse. "With your permission, Captain, I think we need such a lookout as Master Farrix here to steer us through this cursed everlasting night. I hear tell that the Silver Cape, well, she be named 'silver' because of the ice which lies in the straits summer and winter all 'round, though worse at this time of year. And, well, the throat of the pinch can not be more than two days ahead, given the rate we run."

"I'd be glad to stand watch, Aravan," declared Farrix. "Burn me, but there's little else to do. And though she doesn't think so, Jinnarin's eyes are as keen as mine."

Jatu rumbled, "Even given a Pysk warning of two miles or three, still I doubt that we could miss something large in our path if we continue running at this speed. Our chances of doing so would be slim at best."

"Nevertheless, Jatu," replied Aravan, "a slim chance

is better than none. I deem Hegen has the right of it—
we should have Pysk eyes at watch."

"What about Alamar and Aylis?" asked Jinnarin. "I
mean, they have magesight. Perhaps they can stand
watch as well."

"With your permission again, Captain," said Hegen,
"Lady Jinnarin is right. We can use all the eyes we can
get . . . though Mage Alamar, well, I'm wondering if he
has the strength in him, what with him now being so old
and all. I mean, he was old before he went into the
Great Swirl, but now he looks to be on his very last
legs."

Farrix turned and looked at Aravan. "Captain, let him
stand watch with me. He desperately needs something
to do."

Pondering, Aravan stroked his jaw. At last he said,
"If Lady Aylis says that he can afford to cast the spell,
can withstand the drain of astral fire, then, aye, he can
stand watch with thee."

The next day the skies cleared and austral stars shone
down and on this day a waxing half Moon would rise in
the southeast and circle low to the horizon up 'round
the north and down again to set in the southwest. And
though it was clear, still the thundering wind continued
its savage blast, and great greybeards towered over the
seas. And still the *Eroean* raced across the icy brine,
cutting up through mountainous crests to slam hard into
the water and ride down through abyssal troughs, the
ship now running east-northeast on a great circle leading
to the straits of the Silver Cape.

As she had done every day, Aylis cast a spell to locate
Durlok, the lexicon a seer's lodestar to the Black Mage.
"There," she murmured, pointing, "three hundred fifty
miles or so."

Aravan noted the direction, and plotted a point on
the map. "He yet fares toward the straits, some seventy
leagues before him, some two hundred leagues from us."

"Captain," rumbled Jatu after a swift calculation, "can
we continue to run at this pace, tomorrow we will be in
the straits nigh mid of night."

Bokar looked at the darkness showing through the

portholes. "Ha! In an everlasting night, when does mid of night come?"

In the swaying lantern light, Aravan glanced up from the map. "Tomorrow comes the summer solstice—Year's Long Day in the north, Year's Long Night down here."

As the wind howled and the ship rode up to crests and plunged down into troughs and the sea boomed against the hull, Jinnarin braced herself against the roll and looked down at the map. "Will we catch Durlok at the straits?"

Spanning between the marks which registered Durlok's daily positions, Aravan used thumb and forefinger to gauge when the Black Mage would enter the straits. Then he looked at Jinnarin and said, "Aye, if the wind holds, 'tis likely that we will catch him up somewhere nigh."

Jinnarin suddenly shivered. "Ooo, I just remembered: the last time we met Durlok on a Year's Long Night, he nearly sank us."

Braced by Aravan, Aylis stood in the wheelhouse, her eyes closed, the lexicon in one hand, her other outstretched to the fore. "Twenty miles, *there*."

"A point larboard, Boder," hissed Aravan. "Rico, trim her up. At his rate and ours, we will be on him in less than an hour."

Bokar gritted, "The ballistas are ready, Captain. Warriors stand by below the hatches waiting my signal."

Farrix peered out into the starlight, Jinnarin at his side. In a tall chair fastened to the deck sat Alamar, the elder peering out as well. The *Eroean* raced toward the throat of the strait, massive bergs and floes to left and right and fore, monstrous waves smashing against mountains of ice. And should the starlight fail, Aravan would depend on the Mage and Pysks to guide the ship safely through. But now the starlight shown down, and Aravan needed nothing other than his own keen Elven sight.

Whoom! Again the hull crashed down into the brine, and Alamar groaned, "If I have a brain or guts or a kidney left when all this is done, I'll light a candle to Elwydd! Lor! No wonder sailors are half-daft!"

In that moment the door opened and wind and howl

and spray raged inward. Battling the blow and wash, Jatu stepped into the wheelhouse and slammed the door to, shutting out the yowl and drench. "Captain, a storm comes abaft."

"Nigh?"

"Aye, Captain. It flies on the wind."

Again howl and spray raved through the wheelhouse as Aravan stepped out the door and peered aft. Moments later he stepped back in. *"Vash!"* he spat, "it will be on us in less than an hour."

"Damnation!" quavered Alamar, "if the storm is anything like the one before, Durlok will lose us in a blizzard."

"Father, I have his lexicon. He cannot lose us forever."

Jinnarin turned, her face grim. "But he can ram us in the storm, when we are blind to him, as he did in the Northern Sea. But should he ram us here, in these seas we will not survive."

"Damn and blast!" gnarled Alamar.

Once more Aravan stepped out and peered aft through the blow, and the hull of the *Eroean* slammed down. Moments later Aravan reentered. "Rico, pipe the full crew and rig the gallants and up."

"But Kapitan," protested the bo's'n, "this wind! By damn, all sail will break mast!"

"Rico," snapped Jatu, "you heard the Captain. Full crew. Rig all sails but the studs. And caution the Men to clip up."

Like a monstrous harp the rigging howled in the brutal wind, the masts groaning in mortal agony, and racing across the South Polar Sea plunged the *Eroean,* riding up curling crest after curling crest to slam down and plummet into the churning depths beyond.

"Adon!" cried Farrix. "The black galley! There it is!"

As the *Eroean* rode up the next crest and over, all eyes peered where the Pysk pointed. Through the snow flurries forerunning the storm, the top of lateen sails could just be seen ere they disappeared down, the black galley plunging into a trough. The Elvenship, too, slid down the roiling face of a wave and into a deep hollow beyond.

"A mile I would say," muttered Alamar, Aravan agreeing.

"Armsmaster, signal thy warriors. We will be on him within two hundred heartbeats."

"Aye, Captain!" cried Bokar. And he threw open the trapdoor and slid down the ladder to the deck below, and all could hear the sound of his horn as Bokar ran forward. Out on the decks, hatches flew open and Dwarven warriors swarmed up and out. They hooked their safety harnesses to specially rigged lines and made their way across the pounding, plunging ship to the loaded ballistas, where they cast loose the stays.

"Eh, I should be out there to guide their fireballs," Alamar grunted as the ship whelmed down into the icy brine.

"Father, it is all you can do now to take this pounding, much less stand on the deck in this sea."

"Damn, Daughter, don't you think I *know* that?"

"Oh Hèl!" shouted Farrix in frustration as suddenly the ship was enveloped in blinding snow. "The storm! The bloody storm!"

"Can you see the black galley?" cried Jinnarin. "I've completely lost it!"

No! cried Farrix and Alamar simultaneously, rage filling each voice.

"Stay the course, Boder," snapped Aravan. " 'Tis likely we will pass close enough for Bokar's warband to sight it and cast fire."

Onward plunged the *Eroean,* her rigging shrieking, her masts groaning, her timbers moaning, the hull booming down into the polar brine beyond each curling crest. Monstrous waves rose up and smashed down and the storm-strengthened wind thundered past. Of a sudden through the hurtling snow, fire flared at the forward ballista and a streak of flame shot larboard, another flying forth immediately after. A heartbeat later the midship ballista loosed fire, too.

"Did ye see aught?" snapped Aravan.

"A dark shape larboard," replied Farrix. "Yes," concurred Jinnarin. "Nothing!" spat Alamar. Aylis shook her head, *No.*

"But I don't know if Bokar's fireballs struck home," added Farrix.

"By now we have overrun the galley," muttered Aravan, as the hull thundered down, "and we cannot come about in these seas, else we'll founder broadsides."

"We might slow and let him run past," suggested Rico.

"Oh no, Rico," protested Jinnarin, "I think he would ram us instead."

"If he can find us," muttered Alamar, peering out into the wall of white shrieking past as the ship pitched up to a crest and cut through to smash down beyond.

Cursing, Bokar came climbing up through the hatch. "We may have set a sail on fire, but if we did it was by sheer fortune."

"See," querulously snapped Alamar. "I told you I should have been there to guide Bokar's fireballs."

"Alamar," cried Jinnarin, "that's old ground already gone over. Besides, you did not even see the galley."

"Well, had I been on deck, I might have! —Hèl, if a Dwarf saw it, I *would* have!"

"Regardless, Father," said Aylis, "we can always come at him again. After all, we have this." She held up Durlok's lexicon, and in that very moment, it burst into furious flame.

Suddenly, Alamar howled, fire flaring forth from his robes. And a pocket in Bokar's parka blazed up.

Jinnarin screamed as Aylis dropped the lexicon to the deck, and Aravan stamped on it to put out the fire. Bokar ripped off his jacket and threw it down. Alamar shouted, *"Abi!"* and forth from his robes flew a burning page, even then turning to ash. *"Exstinguete ex omni parte!"* he called, and all fire was quenched.

And as the *Eroean* thundered into the waves, "What is it?" cried Jinnarin.

"Durlok!" spat Alamar. "The fireballs alerted him that we are on his trail, and he seeks to destroy that which we use to trace him."

Aylis looked at the scatter of ashes on the deck where the lexicon had fallen. "I deem he has succeeded, Father, for I fear all is burned."

"Oh, Adon!" cried Jinnarin. "Our pages are in our under-bunk cabin with Rux!"

As Jinnarin and Farrix leapt down from the shelf to head for the door, following after Jatu—for his page had been in his cabin as well—above the roar of the wind, from the deck there came a great creaking groan, and suddenly the mizzenmast shattered, silks and halyards and yardarms thundering down, crashing into the main-mast, and that great timber, too, burst and hurled forward to the deck slain; and along with her silks the mizzen took with it the spanker and gaff and two stay-sails, while the main shattered down carrying her own sails and hurtled into the foremast and ripped through the fore lower topsail and the foremain as well.

And then in the blinding storm, as monstrous waves roared across the deck, the hull crashed against a mountain of ice.

CHAPTER 37

Deliverance

Summer, 1E9575
[The Present]

A don!" cried Farrix, pulling Jinnarin behind him as the masts and silks and yardarms and halyards thundered down. And then a great judder jolted the ship, hurling Jatu and Artus and Rico to their knees and slamming Aravan and Aylis and Bokar to the wall. Both Jinnarin and Farrix kept their feet as they managed to grasp one of Alamar's anchored chair legs. Boder, too, remained standing, for he held onto the wheel.

"Oh bloody Hèl!" cursed Alamar as he sighted a monstrous white wall looming to starboard, the ship scraping and grinding alongside.

"Ice!" shouted Jatu, gaining his footing, but of a sudden the *Eroean* was past, the wall gone, the grinding no more.

"We are free of it," gritted Aravan, as the hull rose up then slammed down into the brine.

Jinnarin stepped past Farrix, her words coming in a rush: "Love, I will make certain that Rux is all right. And if our quarters are aflame, I'll get help. You remain here, for your eyes will be needed if the wretched snow ever abates." Without waiting for a reply, Jinnarin darted from the wheelhouse.

As she vanished into the corridor leading to the aft quarters, Jatu barked, "Artus, see after her. Too, in a metal box in my sea chest is one of the pages. Make certain that no fire burns."

As Artus turned to go, Aravan snapped, "Artus, in the log on my desk is another lexicon page. See to it as well."

"Aye, Captain," replied the young Man, and he ran after Jinnarin.

"I'll go, too," said Aylis, and she followed Artus into the passage.

Again the *Eroean* thundered down into the waves.

By this time, Farrix had regained the window ledge and he braced himself and peered outward. The blizzard yet raged and the Pysk could but barely see past the wreckage of masts, his vision not quite reaching to the bow of the ship. As Aravan stepped to his side, Farrix said, "Blast, Aravan, I cannot tell what lies before us, but this I do know—we are dismasted."

Boom! down hammered the hull, water thundering across the decks, bearing downed spars and silks and halyard to slam into rails and ladders and cabin walls.

Bokar took up his jacket and briefly inspected it; the pocket where the page had been was no longer burning. As he shrugged into it, he said, "Captain, I'm going to see if any of the Châkka were injured then do something about the ruin."

The armsmaster opened the trapdoor, and in that moment up popped Tivir, the lad dressed in his arctic gear. "Cap'n, Oi'm t' tell y' wot Frizian said: 'e's got a party t'gether, 'n' they're goin' up 'n' out t' gauge th' damage 'n' secure th' wreckage."

"Well and good, Tivir. Tell him I need a report and swift, for the Black Mage is yet somewhere nigh."

As the ship whelmed down in the water, "Aye, Cap'n," replied Tivir and slid down the ladder. Bokar followed, the Dwarf slamming the trap to.

"Bah!" snarled Alamar. "Durlok can no more see in this blizzard than can we."

Without turning around, Farrix asked, "Don't you have some kind of magery that will allow you to look through the storm?"

"Magesight is all I have, Pysk. In some things it serves me well; in others it is no better than your own."

"And in the blizzard . . . ?"

"In the blizzard, Pysk, your eyes see better than mine."

Again the Elvenship thundered down in the waves.

Jatu stepped from the wheelhouse and into the howl, and after a while he returned, snow and wind whirling in after.

"Captain," said the black Man, "we are now but barely faster than the following seas. Should the wind fall the slightest, these greybeards will get behind us and swing us about until we are rolled and founder."

"I know, Jatu," replied the Elf, his features grim, and again the hull slammed down.

"If we don't get some sight, we're likely to run into more ice," snapped Alamar. "Only Dame Fortune guides us now."

"Well why don't you use your magic?" called out Jinnarin, entering the wheelhouse once more, Artus at her side.

"Argh!" growled the elder, but saying no more.

Artus said to Jatu, "Your metal box was filled with ashes; nought else in your sea chest was harmed."

Jinnarin clambered up beside Farrix. He looked at her and raised an eyebrow. She answered his unspoken question: "The pages burned, but nothing else, although some of the wall was scorched. Rux is all right, though he was upset by the fire and whatever hit the ship. I found him outside in the passageway, coming after me."

Jinnarin turned. "Aylis is in your cabin, Aravan. The ship's log was smoldering when she and Artus got there. Durlok's page was destroyed, and a number of pages in the log were charred beyond recognition. Aylis cast a spell, and she is now copying all that was lost while it's still fresh, she says, though I don't know how she can tell what used to be there."

"Magic," muttered Farrix.

"Pah!" snorted Alamar.

Jinnarin turned to the eld Mage. "Speaking of magic, Alamar, why not cast a spell that allows you to see through the snow?"

"I already asked him that," hissed Farrix. "He says he doesn't know how."

"What I said, Pysk," growled Alamar, "was that magesight made my eyes no better than yours."

"Oh," said Jinnarin. "But wait, if you could—"

Again the *Eroean* slammed down into the sea, and at

the very same moment the trap popped open and Tivir stuck his head through. "Cap'n, Frizian says th' mizzen 'n' main 'r' gone. Th' fore yet stands, though th' fore-main 'n' fore lower top 'r' ripped down. Th' jibs 'n' forestay 'r' worthy, as is th' fore upper 'n' all above, 'n' those 'r' th' sails wot yet carry us. Th' mizzen is shattered f'r more'n half her length; th' main f'r a quarter. 'E says it looks loike th' mizzen failed 'n' carried th' main adown wi' it. 'N' Finch says that 'e's got below a timber wot'll fix th' main, but nothin' f'r fixin' th' mizzen. But 'e says there's nary no way t' fix 'er in these seas, 'n' that y've got t' find shelter or flat water afore repairs c'n begin."

"Damn!" spat Jatu. "Where in Hèl are we to find flat water in the middle of the South Polar Ocean?"

" 'N', Cap'n," added the cabin boy, "there's smash everywhere 'n' Frizian 'n' Bokar has all hands trying t' lash it adown so as t' keep it from crashing th' ship apart."

"By your leave, Captain," rumbled Jatu, "I'll go and help."

Aravan nodded, then said, "Jatu, I'll run a course straight with the waves until all is lashed securely, turning only as needs to avoid ice, can we see it in time. But hurry, for we must find relief 'round the horn and up the coast in the shelter of the cape ere the foremast, too, gives way."

"Aye, Captain." The black Man then disappeared down the ladder to make his way forward below deck and then up and out, Tivir going with him.

Aravan turned to Rico. "Bo's'n, we need more head-way; choose some of the Men and see if you can replace the top and main on the foremast. Artus, thou goest as well."

As Rico and Artus slid down the trap ladder, Alamar growled, "Look here, Elf, we're blind! More sail will just make us run faster into the danger ahead. Are you trying to drive us into the storm-hidden ice all that much quicker? Or instead do you merely seek to break our last mast?"

"Nay, Mage Alamar, I seek to do neither. Yet heed, wouldst thou rather we miscarry on a wave and founder?"

Alamar growled under his breath but said no more.

Farrix turned to Jinnarin. "Love, you were about to say something when Tivir interrupted."

The ship juddered down as Jinnarin searched her mind for the elusive idea but could not find it. Yet even as she turned to peer out at the storm, of a sudden it popped back into her thoughts. "I know what it was. Alamar, why don't you give Farrix your magesight? I mean, he can't give you his Pysk eyes, but surely you can cast a spell to let him see astral fire, neh? Perhaps together—Pysk sight and magesight, I mean—they will penetrate the storm."

Alamar was taken aback, his eyes widening.

Grinning a great grin, Farrix squeezed Jinnarin's hand. "Burn me, but that's clever!" Then he turned to Alamar. "Whether or not it succeeds or fails, it is worth a try. Anything is better than running through these waters blind. Can you do it?"

"I can try, Pysk. I can try."

Alamar held out his palsied hands and tried to control the trembling, the elder muttering "Damn!" under his breath. Gently he cupped his fingers 'round Farrix and placed his quavering thumbs feather-lightly against the Pysk's eyes. "I think I will have to change it slightly, the casting, that is. Let's hope it doesn't instill blindness instead."

Jinnarin gasped and called out, "Blindness? Wait!"

But at the very same moment, Alamar muttered, *"Transfer visum."*

Alamar took his hands from the Pysk.

Whoom! the ship whelmed down.

Farrix opened his eyes.

The irises were no longer ice-blue, but utter black instead.

Farrix's mouth dropped open, and slowly he shifted his gaze about the wheelhouse, pausing at each person there, finally stopping on Jinnarin. "Adon," he breathed, "everything glows."

"Ha!" wheezed Alamar. "It worked!"

"Everything glows," repeated Farrix.

"Of course it does Pysk," quavered the elder, the

snap gone from his voice, "but can you see through the storm?"

Farrix whirled about and peered through the glass. "Lor, everything's strange; different colors. But wait, yes, I can see! Ha! Rico is up the foremast with a crew. They are trying to get the fore lower topsail rigged. Some are working on the foremain. —And wait! There's a tall thing—a mountain—to the right; probably ice, though it's not white but instead it is . . . it is a color I have no word for. We'll miss it."

Farrix turned his black gaze to Alamar. "How long will this vision last?"

"Eh? Why, till you will it gone, Psyk," hissed the elder. "But the important thing is, what do you see ahead? You've got to guide the ship, you know."

As the *Eroean* rode up to a crest, Farrix moved to a place where he could see past part of the downed wreckage. "It seems to be clear for the moment," he said at last.

"Canst thou see the black galley?"

The *Eroean* hammered down in the waves.

Farrix ran to the larboard window and then to the starboard, staring out each side as the waves lifted the *Eroean* up. "Not from here, Aravan. If Durlok is about, he's not where I can see him."

"Directly aft, Cap'n?" suggested Boder.

"Mayhap," acknowledged Aravan.

"Lor, the strange colors," breathed Farrix. "Even the waves."

Whoom! down thundered the *Eroean*.

Time passed, with Boder occasionally adjusting the wheel at Farrix's beck, the Pysk guiding the ship to avoid mountainous ice in their line. Each time, though, the ship rolled dangerously as the following seas tried to overturn this intruder in its violent domain. At last the trapdoor popped open and Rico climbed up and out. He cast back his parka hood, his face burning red with cold. "Kapitan, she now bear all silk but stud. But she groan somet'ing fierce. I be afraid she break, too.

"And, Kapitan," added the bo's'n, "Frizian, he say most wreck be lashed down."

"Well and good, Rico." Aravan stepped to the door-

way and out into the brawling storm. Clutching a safety
line, he made his way to the rail and peered through the
blizzard and over the side and held on tightly as the ship
rode up to curling crests and whelmed down into the
frigid sea, the Elf gauging the speed of the ship with
respect to the towering waves. When he returned he
said, "Boder, steer a point larboard. Rico, trim the foremast. We will run for the shelter of the cape. Farrix,
keep an eye out for ice and the black galley."

Two hours they hurtled among looming waves, driven
by a thundering wind, the ship rolling and the foremast
groaning under the strain as they ran northeast in the
blinding blizzard through the long, dark polar night.
Channeled by the stricture of the Silver Straits, wind and
water and hurling snow rounded northerly. And into the
ice-laden maw they plunged, Farrix guiding them past
the monstrous floes. And just as they came to the crux
of the throat—

"Bloody Hèl!" cried Farrix, his eyes wide and staring.
"What is that?"

Whoom! crashed the *Eroean* into the howling sea, the
ship slowly uprighting as it slid down the face of the
wave and into the deep churning trough.

Jinnarin looked starboard to where he pointed, but all
she saw was a hurtling wall of snow. "What? What did
you see?"

Farrix turned his utter black gaze upon her and she
shivered in apprehension, his eyes so alien, so strange.
"I thought I saw . . ." His words ceased altogether.

"Saw what?"

Farrix shook his head. "Another ship."

Aravan stepped forward. "Durlok?"

"No, it was a galleon, I think. Her sails were tattered
and blowing in the wind, her rigging burning with
witchfire."

At the wheel, Boder gasped. "The *Grey Lady*."

"What?" asked Farrix.

Boder looked at Jinnarin. "Didn't you tell him, Lady
Jinnarin?"

"No," answered Jinnarin, shaking her head. "I hadn't
got around to it."

"Got around to what?" asked Farrix, his eyes now

fixed to starboard as the *Eroean* climbed up the face of the next towering wave.

"A sailor's legend," replied Jinnarin, "the *Grey Lady*—a ghost ship."

"Aye," added Boder. "A cursed ship sailing endlessly through the night 'round the Silver Cape, her masts and rigging glowing with green witchfire, her ghostly crew forever trapped aboard, searching for the lost lad of a sorceress dire."

Farrix glanced at Jinnarin. "A sorceress?"

"A kind of a Black Mage," answered Jinnarin.

"Bah!" snorted Alamar. "Most are not Black Mages at all."

"Well this one was one, Mage Alamar," protested Boder. "From Alkabar in Hyree, she was, and as Black a Mage as they come. Cursed the *Grey Lady* to sail the seas till they found her son who washed overboard in the Silver Straits.

"But that's not the total of it. They say that as the *Grey Lady* sails about, trying to find the lost passenger, the ghost captain calls the lost one's name out over the waters. They also say that if you hear what that name be, then you will suddenly find yourself trapped aboard the *Grey Lady* herself, sailing the seas forever ... or till the lost one's found."

"Humbug!" muttered Alamar.

But Farrix said, "I doubt if we'd hear anything above the shriek of this storm."

"Well if she comes near, stuff up your ears," advised Boder, "just in case. Better safe than sorry."

With the wind screaming in fury and the rigging of the foremast howling in kind, the canted *Eroean* topped the crest of the wave and Farrix peered intently starboard.

Boom! the Elvenship hull slammed down to the face of the slope beyond.

"Well?" asked Jinnarin, her heart hammering.

Farrix shook his head. "Nothing. If it was ever there, it's gone now. Though I could have sworn—"

"Poppycock!" muttered Alamar.

Farrix glanced toward Boder, then looked at Jinnarin. "Perhaps instead it was an oddly shaped greybeard."

"What about the witchfire and tattered sails and all?" asked Boder.

"With magesight, Boder, everything glows," answered Farrix. "And the tattered sails ... perhaps it was merely spray...."

Slowly Boder shook his head, unconvinced, yet remaining silent.

Troubled, Farrix turned and peered again forward, and as the *Eroean* rode up to the towering crest of the next hurtling wave, the ship rolling to starboard as all sails rose up into the quartering larboard wind aft, "Floe ahead," he called and pointed. "Starboard."

At Aravan's command, Boder turned the wheel a bit.

Ten hours later due north they ran, dodging among gigantic floes, the wind now gradually diminishing though air and wave yet raged. Borne on the sails of the foremast alone—squares and jibs and a stay—they had finally passed beyond the shoulder of the cape, where the shelter of the stark mountains thereon began abating the blow. Farrix, Aravan, Hegen, and Reydeau now stood in the wheelhouse, the others having gone to their quarters to collapse in bed. A crew remained at standby forward below decks, ready to hale the silks about should steering be called for in the blow.

Five more hours they sailed, the snow diminishing as well, until at last it stopped altogether. Rico and Boder came back to the wheelhouse, and Reydeau and Hegen retired. Jatu and Artus entered the cabin, and the black Man reported their speed as nine knots—"A long way from thirty," he added.

Another hour passed, and the overcast began to break as they ran out from under, and a star glimmered here and there, and now Aravan could see the waters far ahead.

"To bed, Farrix," the Elf told the weary Pysk.

"But Aravan," Farrix protested, "you have not rested either."

"Nevertheless, Farrix, thou take to thy bed. I will remain here. Eyes are needed to pilot the ship, eyes that can see by starlight."

In that moment Aylis stepped into the wheelhouse. "I

can see by starlight. I will stand watch while you *both* take to your beds."

As Aravan looked at her, Jatu rumbled, "Lady Aylis is right, Captain. She and I will command the *Eroean* while both of you get some sleep."

Aravan kissed his lady's hand then turned to Jatu. "Sail due north. We make for Inigo Bay. There we will lay up and harvest the tall timbers for repairs."

When Farrix came to the door of the under-bunk quarters, Jinnarin called to Tivir, who bore to the Pysks a tin lid on which was bread and honey and tiny pot of hot tea. "They say as y' saved th' ship from th' ice," declared the cabin boy, bobbing his head to Farrix, " 'n' saved us all from th' *Griay Laidy,* too. For both y' 'ave me 'n' me mates' sincerest thanks."

"Oh, Tivir, it was Jinnarin's idea and Alamar's magic that let me see the ice. And as to the *Grey Lady,* well, it is not certain that she was out there at all. —But if she was, well, they were sailing dead against the wind while we ran the other way. And so, if any ought to receive your thanks, then 'tis Jinnarin and Alamar and the crew entire, for all worked to keep the ship afloat, when surely any other ship in like circumstance would have gone down."

A great smile flashed over Tivir's face and again he bobbed his head then turned and sped away.

Carrying the largess, Jinnarin stepped into their quarters, Farrix behind. As she set down the tray, she said, "Oh, Farrix, if it *was* the *Grey Lady* then I'm glad you didn't hear the captain call out the lost passenger's name. I do *not* wish to chase after you again, this time with you sailing through endless nights aboard a ghost ship. I especially wouldn't wish to hunt for you in these deadly seas."

Farrix smiled at her. "But you would come seeking . . . wouldn't you?"

She smiled back at him, then inspected her fingernails and nonchalantly said, "Perhaps."

"Oh, you," growled Farrix, taking her up and swinging her about.

As he set her down she kissed him then said, "Can't you get back your own eyes? I miss them."

Farrix closed his eyes and concentrated as Alamar had

told him to do. When he opened them again, the utter black was gone, replaced by ice-blue. Gone, too, for Farrix was a wondrous world of light and fire, replaced by one dull and drab.

Eight days later on the thirtieth of June, they limped into Inigo Bay. And deep in the bight they came to a narrow cove, shadowed by tall evergreens high on the snowy slopes above. It was mid of day when they anchored, the low-hanging Sun hidden behind the northern hills—they had run out from the polar night some seven days past, the Sun rising in the north-northeast to cut a shallow arc low across the northern skies and set in the north-northwest, each day but a few hours long. And in this twilight 'scape, Aravan sailed the Elvenship into the firth and dropped anchor.

As Jatu and Finch and a crew of Men and Dwarves haled a great timber out from the main hold, Aravan and another crew gathered cutting tools and debarked for the hillsides. Farrix and Jinnarin and Rux accompanied the landing party, as well as Aylis and Alamar, the eld Mage insisting over the objections of his daughter that he needed to "get off this wet pitching rollabout and onto dry, stable land."

They landed along the eastern rocky shore of the tree-laden narrows.

Jinnarin set Rux free to hunt, the fox barking and bounding with joy to be on land as up through the trees he ran, lunging across the deep snow. Alamar watched as Rux disappeared among the Inigo pines. "Ha! At least someone else shares my need to be aland," he muttered, then turned and hobbled to a large boulder by the water's edge, where he sat overlooking the sea.

While a contingent of men set up camp along the shore, Farrix and Jinnarin and Aylis trekked in the trail of the cutting crew wending into the forest above, the Pysks and Lady Mage walking the deep slot through the snow that the Dwarves and Men had left behind.

After taking the measure of several trees, Aravan selected two tall, straight pines, each towering upward some hundred feet. "From these will come a new mizzen," he said, eyeing the lay of the land. "We will fell them downslope."

As the sound of axes echoed through the woods, Jinnarin and Farrix followed Aylis through the snow to come to an outjutting stone on the face of a precipice overlooking the bay. In the distance below they could see the *Eroean*, Men and Dwarves swarming about, readying the huge timber they had brought up from below to repair the mainmast.

"Burn me," exclaimed Farrix, "but like ants they look."

"Hmm?" distractedly murmured Jinnarin. "Oh yes. Ants." She sighed.

Farrix took her hand. "What is it, Jinnarin? Why the long face?"

"Oh, I was just looking at Alamar. He seems so alone, so despondent. . . . So used up."

Down through the trees alongside the shore near the campsite they could just glimpse the eld Mage through the branches. Water lapped against the boulder he perched on.

Aylis looked long, then said, "Used up, yes. The last spell he cast—the one that gave Farrix magesight—well, it took a lot out of him. Giving magesight to another, it was a remarkable casting, but costly."

"Costly?" exclaimed Jinnarin. "I thought it was easily done. A natural talent of Magekind."

Aylis glanced at the Pysks. "Aye, to <see> is indeed a natural gift of Mages, but to cast it onto another, well, I am not at all certain that I could cast it upon someone else, as did my father."

"Oh?" said Farrix. "Why so?"

"My discipline is that of a seer; his of an elementalist. They are greatly different. I believe I would need long training to be able to do what he did."

"Well then," said Jinnarin, "I am certainly glad that an elementalist was along, for surely we would have perished in the Silver Straits had Farrix not been given magesight to guide us."

Aylis sighed. "Yes. No doubt. Yet it took much <fire> from my father. <Power> he did not have to spend."

Now the burr of a crosscut saw echoed among the pines.

The Pysks and seeress stood and watched the crew aboard the ship working on the stub of mainmast jutting up like a broken finger. In the still air, Farrix and Jinnarin and Aylis could hear them calling to one another above the sound of the saw ringing through the trees. As they gazed down at the *Eroean*, Jinnarin said, "You can no longer sense the whereabouts of Durlok, eh?"

"No," responded Aylis. "With the destruction of the lexicon, he is lost to me. Where he is, I cannot say."

"Couldn't we go back to his lair in the Great Swirl and get something else of his?" suggested Jinnarin. "Track him that way?"

"Yes, we could," answered Aylis. "Yet heed: when we were there and my father and I saw Durlok's <power>, it was nearly beyond comprehension. If we are to face him again, we will need powerful allies of our own . . . hence we need go to Rwn and gather aid from among the Master Mages."

Once again they fell silent, and far below, Dwarves came up from one of the holds, bringing a forge and bellows, which they proceeded to set up on the deck. They kindled a fire and added charcoal to the blaze. But Aylis's gaze strayed down to her father sitting at the shore. Blinking back tears, she said, "I think I'll go back and watch them fell the trees. Will you be all right?"

Farrix and Jinnarin nodded, and without another word, Aylis left. After a long while, Jinnarin reached out and took Farrix's hand. "Aylis says that Alamar's fire burns low."

Now Farrix sighed. "She is right. Alamar's fire *is* low, at least compared to the fires of everyone else who came to the wheelhouse."

"You could see the astral fire in people?"

"Yes. And your fire was brightest of all, Aravan's next, each brighter than that of any Dwarf, Man, Mage, or Lady Mage. Alamar's was dimmest."

"Oh my, then he does indeed need to go back to Vadaria."

Farrix looked down at the distant Mage. "Yes. And soon. Else, as Aylis says, he will die forever."

Timber! came the cry from behind, followed by the sound of shattering branches as the forest giant came crashing down among the Inigo pines.

Axes rang through the woods as the log was shorn of branches, then adzes stripped the bark from the length of the pine. The crosscut saw topped the tree, and the base shaft of the mizzenmast was cut to length. And during the stripping, the second tree was felled, and the shearing of branches begun. Then all turned to stripping the bark from the second tree, after which the middle shaft of the mizzenmast was cut to length. Finally they began sliding the logs down the slope through the snow toward the water below. And in the campsite they took a meal and a hot bracing drink.

During the work the Sun set and a full Moon rose, the silver orb rising in the east-southeast and circling low to the north before setting in the west-southwest.

And as the Sun rose on the following day, crews were rubbing the wood with the special oils prepared by Aravan. When this was done, they floated the sections of logs out to the *Eroean* and made ready to winch them aboard.

Alamar insisted on remaining ashore.

In the following days, working nonstop, the masts were reset: massive iron bands were forged to hold the sections of masts together, and heated by Dwarves till they were glowing yellow-white, they were slipped over the ends of the shafts and hammered up onto the shank, the wood charring and sizzling and lighting afire as the rings were pounded into place. And as the iron cooled and shrank, the sections of mast were tightly bound together as surely as if they had been forged as one. This was repeated, and then once again, as the two broken masts were made anew, each mast consisting of three sections—lower and middle and top—the solid iron bands clutching tightly, holding all together.

They winched the mainmast into its footing, a length of the shaft going all the way through each of the decks and down to the mainmast base collar at the keelson. And when it was fixed in place, the mast raked back at an angle, the mizzenmast was likewise set. Then the crews swarmed up the main and mizzen and began refitting each mast with yards and crosstrees and other such. Up went the ratlines and nests, up went the blocks and halyards and other rigging.

And during it all, hidden by the hills, the Sun rose and set and rose and set again—several times altogether—each day a fraction longer than the one before as icy summer gradually edged toward the distant renewal of life that would come with autumn. Nightly, the fulgent Moon looked silently down as it circled 'round east to north to west, rising later and later in the passing eventides, the silvery disk waning with growing age.

And as the work progressed, Alamar and Rux tarried ashore, along with a single crewman to aid the eld Mage, should such aid be needed.

Finally the work of refitting was done, and two crews set out in boats to break camp and to retrieve Alamar. Jinnarin came along as well to fetch Rux. As the crews disassembled the camp, Jinnarin walked up into the woods and whistled a silent whistle, a call beyond earshot of Man and Mage alike. Soon Rux came trotting among the pines, and Jinnarin rode him back down to the boats.

On the sixth of July, with all silks flying, the *Eroean* sailed away from Inigo Bay and out into the wide waters of Weston Ocean beyond.

"Where away, Captain?" asked Jatu, the offshore wind belling the sails.

Aravan looked up at the early morning stars, the Sun not yet risen. "Take her east till we clear the coast, then north-northwest, Jatu. Set a course for Rwn."

At these words, Aylis heaved a great sigh of relief and peered forward to where her father stood clutching the starboard railing.

As if sensing that a course had been chosen, Alamar turned and slowly made his way aft. Finally he stood at the foot of the steps leading up to the aft deck. And with his wisps of remaining hair blowing in the wind, and his rheumy eyes looking up at Aylis and Aravan, Alamar bitterly asked, "Are we headed for Rwn?"

At Aravan's nod, Alamar groaned.

Aravan added, "Without the lexicon, Durlok is lost to us."

"Don't you think I know that, Elf?" querulously wheezed Alamar. "Of course he has escaped for now! And he's up to evil, I can smell it! The grand weddings, you know. And speaking of them—nothing we sensed happened on the one in June. Perhaps somewhere, a terrible thing occurred; what it might be, I cannot say. But remember, we were hot on his track at the time and perceived nothing in his wake, and so *nothing* may have happened. If so, there are three grand weddings left this year—in July, August, and September. We've got to find him before he does something dreadful. Yes, he is lost to us, but perhaps not for long—the Children of the Sea are searching for the black galley."

Aylis's eyes flew wide. "You called the Children of the Sea?"

"Of course, Daughter," puffed Alamar. "What did you think I was doing back there on shore, sucking my thumb?"

"No, Father, I just—"

"Never mind, Daughter. It doesn't matter what you think of me. The fact is, I called them and asked for their help. They came in the moonlight the day before yesterday, and even now are sending word to the *Ut!¡-teri*—the whales—and to the *A!mii*—the dolphin. Soon they will be searching the seas for the black galley, and when it is found, they will locate the *Silver Bottom* and inform me or you, Elf—after all, you *are* known to them as a Friend—as to the whereabouts of Durlok's ship."

"Father," said Aylis softly, "I did not think you were sucking your thumb. Pouting, perhaps, but not sucking your thumb."

"Heh!" cracked Alamar. "Pouting. Hch! Well, to tell the truth, Daughter, perhaps I was pouting a bit."

"Regardless, Mage Alamar," said Aravan, "mayhap thou hast given us the means to find Durlok, perhaps to stop his scheme, whate'er it may be. Till then we sail for Rwn."

Day after day, northerly they fared, running on the larboard wind for Rwn. Across the Lat of the Goat they sailed, the air light and shifty but they did not need to row. Another grand wedding came and went, and they knew not if aught had occurred. And on northward they voyaged, the wind generally to starboard aft as they sailed into summer.

They crossed the midline on the twenty-second of July, and once again Fortune smiled down upon them and the winds did not die, though they did shift to the starboard fore. It was in the middle of the following night that a great shower of falling stars scored the vault above, a shower so bright as to light the entire sky with the luminance of day. Jinnarin and Farrix *ooh*ed and *ahh*ed, but all the Dwarves on deck at the time moaned in terror and threw their hoods over their heads—a sign of mourning—and refused to look at the blazing sky. In solemn silence they tramped down to their quarters below deck and none else came above to see.

"What's the matter?" asked Jinnarin, concern filling her hushed voice.

At the wheel, Aravan answered, " 'Tis a belief of the Drimma that when a star falls it means someone will die, usually a comrade, though not always."

"Oh, how dreadful," said Jinnarin, as stars without number flared across the heavens above. "That something so beautiful could be a symbol of doom ... how unfortunate."

Aylis nodded in agreement. "Yes indeed, Jinnarin, and I wonder how such a belief came about? That such a dazzling display as this could cause fear ... why, it is as if rainbows or butterflies had been made into symbols of death."

"Perhaps," mused Farrix, "it is because the star dies in a blaze of glory, whereas the rainbow merely fades and a butterfly flutters away."

"Regardless," said Aravan, "it is the belief of the Drimma."

"Let's go get Alamar," said Jinnarin. "He will want to see such splendor."

As the Pysks ran below, Aylis leaned her head against Aravan's shoulder and looked at the sky and murmured, "What wonders the heavens are, my love."

Aravan embraced her with one arm and whispered, "I have seen myriad wonders since I came to this world—temples of gold, rivers of fire, jewels of a thousand rainbows, great luminous wheels of light turning in the midnight sea ... and more. But of all these marvelous things, *chieran*, none can compare with thee, for thou art the most wondrous of all."

Onward they sailed, their course set for Rwn, now in the fullness of summer, but when they came to the Lat

of the Crab the wind died and towing gigs were called
for. Across the calms they rowed, finally breaking into
the wind once more, blowing on the larboard beam.
Again the *Eroean* put her shoulder to the sea and raced
toward the northerly isle.

On the sixth day of August, in early morn a judder ran
throughout the ship, as if the hull had struck a shoal, but
no shoals lay in these waters near Rwn. And although it
seemed as if the *Eroean* had collided with something,
the ship slowed not, as if whatever the hull encountered
was ephemeral. Members of the crew ran to the railings,
but nothing beneath did they spy. "Possibly we struck a
great creature of the sea," suggested Jatu, "one of those
giant turtles, or the like." Yet Aylis did a casting but
sensed no <sentient> life below, while Alamar's casting
could detect no spells being hurled against the ship.

Onward they sailed, and as the Sun crawled up the
sky, again the ship juddered, but once more nothing was
sensed or seen to account for the vibration. Lookouts
were stationed along the railings, yet none saw aught
as once again and then once more the Elvenship was
mysteriously shaken.

In mid morn, they came within sight of Rwn. Standing
on the stemblock, Farrix turned to Jinnarin. "Do you
hear that?"

"What?"

"Bells. I hear bells."

"Kairn is known as the City of Bells."

"Do they normally ring in mid morn?"

Jinnarin shrugged. "I don't know, but here comes Alamar. Let's ask him."

"Bells?" quavered the elder, glancing at the Sun in
the sky. "Are you certain?"

"Yes," replied Jinnarin. "Farrix heard them first, but
I hear them now."

"Go tell Aravan," hissed the Mage. "At this time of
day they can only be ringing in alarm."

Under full sail the Elvenship raced toward the docks
at Rwn, furling her silks at the last moment and gliding
into the quays. High on the rim of the isle there seemed
to be a great commotion, with people rushing to and

fro, and above the thunder of the River Kairn plunging in cascade to the ocean, all aboard could hear the bells of the city wildly ringing in alarm.

Swiftly they debarked, Jinnarin riding and hiding in the hood of Jatu's cloak, Farrix in Aravan's. And as they made their way toward the long staircase leading upward from the docks, a prolonged judder shook the stone of the quay as a tremor ran through the isle.

CHAPTER 38

Conjoinment

Summer, 1E9575
[The Present]

The city was in chaos, people rushing to and fro as buildings shook and swayed, some having collapsed into piles of rubble. Fires burned here and there, and bucket brigades of Men and Women struggled valiantly to extinguish the blazes. Galloping horses careered through the cobblestone streets, their riders bent low over their necks as if expecting arrow fire. Teams hammered past, drawing jouncing wagons after. Like flocks of gabbling geese, calling mothers herded crying children away from juddering homes. And throughout all, the bells of Kairn rang out their alarm.

Amid the confusion, Aravan, Aylis, Alamar, Bokar, and Jatu made their way along the chaotic streets toward the ferry leading to the Academy of Mages, aged Alamar setting the pace. From her hiding place in Jatu's cast-back cloak hood, Jinnarin peered at the tumult and gathered shadow unto herself. In Aravan's hood, Farrix did the same.

At last they came to the ferry, but no ferrymen manned the craft. As another tremor rattled Kairn, Jatu and Bokar took up the pull ropes, and across the waters of the River Kairn they haled the barge, landing at the north pier of the Island of Mages.

"Daughter, it's Drienne we need to find. Know you her <aura>?"

Aylis nodded, and murmured, *"Ubi est Drienna?"*

Following the seeress, up toward the academy they went, and all about them Mages strode purposefully this way and that, as if on specific missions. Entering the central tower, Aylis found Drienne at a table in the middle of the library, paging through a tome. She looked up and brushed back a stray lock of raven-black hair as the comrades approached. Her hazel eyes widened at the sight of aged Alamar. But without preamble, she said, "Something is happening. The entire island of Rwn is endangered."

"It's Durlok's doing," quavered Alamar.

"Durlok?"

"The Black Mage," called Jinnarin, the shadow-wrapped Pysk peering over Jatu's shoulder.

Again Drienne's eyes widened, emerald flecks stirring, but she looked back to Alamar. "Durlok? I thought him dead."

"Not bloody likely, Dree," wheezed Alamar. "We found him in the Great Swirl."

"Great Swirl?"

"It's a long story, and one that will wait."

Drienne nodded sharply, then asked, "Regardless as to where you found him, what does Durlok have to do with these tremors?"

Alamar sat down opposite her. "He promised a grand wedding gift for me and all of my ilk."

"Grand wedding?" muttered Drienne, then she cocked a dark eyebrow. "August twelfth? Six days away? That grand wedding?"

Alamar nodded. "That, or the one in September."

"We've got to stop him, then. Where is he?"

Alamar clutched a frail fist and feebly struck the table, and he quavered, "Damn! That's just it! We don't know! He got away."

"And without something of his, imbued with his <aura>, he is warded against seers," added Aylis. "Just how, I don't know. There is this, too: while in the Swirl we saw his <fire>; his <power> is nearly beyond comprehension."

Drienne looked to Alamar, and the elder sighed and nodded in confirmation.

Drienne leaned back in her chair and steepled her fingers. After a moment she said, "I will call all Mages

together and propose that we form a Great Conjoinment
and try to locate him, try to determine what is happening, try to stop it."

"Conjoinment?" blurted Aylis, glancing at her father
then back to Drienne. "But that will drain—"

"I know, child," responded Drienne. And she fixed a
steely gaze on Alamar. "All Mages must join ... but not
you, Alamar, your fire is nearly gone. You must go back
to Vadaria. If we do not survive, avenge us."

Alamar puffed up to make a reply, but Drienne cut
him off. "As Regent of the Academy it shall be as I say,
and I will brook no disobedience."

Alamar muttered, "See what happens when you give
a sorceress a little authority?"

"Sorceress!" gasped Jinnarin. "Oh my!"

With an eyebrow raised, Drienne looked up at the
shadow lurking behind Jatu's shoulder. "She heard the
tale of the *Grey Lady*," rumbled the black Man. Drienne
grimaced, then nodded.

By mid afternoon, all Mages as well as the comrades
had made their way to a walled garden on the western
end of the river island. As they had come down toward
the white stone wall, Jinnarin could see the River Kairn
flowing on to the west, where it passed under a pontoon
bridge and coursed onward to plunge beyond sight over
the linn and down the sheer drop of the Kairn Falls to
thunder into the Weston Ocean. The garden itself was
guarded by two Mages standing at the one gate, for here
was the only known crossing to Vadaria, and they
warded it well.

Jinnarin's heart thudded in her breast as she looked
to the northwest, where a crescent Moon was just then
setting, a Moon that would wane day by day as it edged
toward the Sun, preparing to kiss the golden orb in but
five days and some. Jinnarin tore her gaze from the pale
arc as Jatu stepped through the garden gate, the warders
nodding to Drienne as she passed the comrades through.

Within the white stone walls stood a grove of silver
birch, the trees but arm's lengths apart from one another
and filling the whole of a natural amphitheater whose
nadir stood in grove center. A green sward covered the
ground, except for moss-banked rivulets which sprang

from the earth and ran down to the heart of the tiny vale, where lay a crystalline mere, white hyacinths floating within. There seemed to be no outlet, yet the waters did not rise, and Jinnarin assumed that they seeped away underground.

And into this garden, into this grove, into this amphitheater streamed the Mages, while now and again the land did quake, the leaves on the birches shivering and rustling in the tremors. They all took seats where they could see among the boles of the trees and down to the mere where now stood Drienne. Seated among the trees as well were the comrades, Jinnarin and Farrix yet shadow-wrapped. At last the gates were closed and a hush fell upon the throng. When all was silent, Drienne called upon Alamar to speak.

The eld Mage shuffled down through the grove and to her side, while all other Mages looked on and whispered among themselves, some shaking their heads at his age-worn state: *Can this be Alamar? Surely not. He is so— so old! What happened to him? . . .*

As a tremor ran through the island, Alamar gestured about at the shaking grove and in a thready voice said, "This is the doings of Durlok, the Black Mage." A mutter of disbelief whispered throughout, but Alamar raised his voice above it. "He seeks to destroy us all, or so I deem.

"We came across him on an island in the middle of the Great Swirl, a place where none would think to look. And in a crystal cavern on that island he worships Gyphon, and there I discovered that Durlok has the means to bridge the In-Between and converse with Him."

A collective gasp greeted this news, and one Mage, a healer named Rithia, called out, "But Adon forbids—"

Alamar quavered, "Do you think that would stop either Gyphon or a Black Mage?"

"What were you doing on this island in the Great Swirl?" called out a voice.

"None of your business," snapped back the elder.

"Then how do we know this is true?" called someone else.

"Because I say so, you idiot!" shouted Alamar, his face turning red.

"Well, if you don't tell us what you were doing, well then, why *should* we believe you?"

Alamar could do nought but wheeze.

"He was rescuing me!" piped up a voice, and a tiny cluster of shadow struggled out of Aravan's hood and dropped to the ground and ran down to stand at Alamar's side. Of a sudden the shadow vanished, and Farrix stood revealed.

A murmur of wonder rippled through the gathering: *Aha! A Fox Rider! One of the Hidden Ones!* . . .

"What Alamar says is true," called Farrix. "I know, for I was Durlok's captive until Alamar and other comrades came to save me." Farrix held out his hand, and down among the silver birches came Jinnarin, her shadow-wrap gone. And stepping in her wake came Aylis and Aravan and Bokar and Jatu.

The debate in the Mage Grove lasted for most of the afternoon, but in the end the Mages decided to band together to stop Durlok, Regent Drienne to be the focus and the wielder of the Great Conjoinment.

"What is this—this conjoinmen*t?*" Jinnarin whispered to Aylis.

"It is when one or more Mages yield their <power> to another Mage, thereby combining their <strength>, their <fire>. The one who wields the conjoinment, usually a sorcerer, for they have the training—in this case Drienne—her powers will be magnified beyond what she alone could brandish."

Aravan looked into Aylis's eyes. "It is . . . dangerous, *chieran?*"

"At times, for <power> flows from all to the wielder."

"Hold on, now," muttered Farrix. "Isn't that the same as Durlok stealing the astral fire from his victims? What did Alamar call it? Oh wait, I remember—he said it was like a bloodsucking lamia draining life."

As if to stave off an accusation, Aylis held out a hand, palm facing the Pysk. "In some ways, Farrix, it *is* like a lamia. But heed: in a Great Conjoinment, all freely volunteer to yield their <fire> to the wielder, whereas a Black Mage simply takes it, permission or not."

"But, Aylis, won't you age?" asked Jinnarin. "I mean, spending your astral fire means losing your youth, and whether it is in a casting of your own or lending it to another, well it seems to me that the effect on you will be the same."

Aylis nodded. "Yes, I will age. But remember, I can regain my youth."

Aravan took Aylis's hand. "*Chieran,* thou hast not said how a conjoinment can be a danger to thee."

Aylis sighed. "During my schooling there came a time when we practiced a conjoinment. It was then we were warned that a wielder can draw too much <fire>, in which case, those conjoined will die."

Dusk descended across Rwn, and the Great Conjoinment began, Mages sitting on the sward running down to the crystal mere. Jinnarin, Farrix, Aravan, Jatu, and Bokar sat among the silver birches of the Mage Grove and watched as Mage after Mage in sequence murmured a word—"*Coniunge*"—and then sat in silence thereafter. Down in grove center by the flower-laden waters sat Drienne in a high-backed crimson chair, one which had been brought in for the occasion. Drienne's eyes were closed, and Jinnarin beheld a pale jade nimbus glowing about the raven-haired sorceress. Farrix, too, noted the astral glow, though none of the other comrades could see it.

As the twilight disappeared, night fell and a panoply of brilliant stars wheeled into view above. And still the island of Rwn juddered and jolted as tremors racked the land.

It was just before mid of night when Aylis came to Aravan. Her light brown hair was now lightly threaded with silver, and a tracery of fine lines clustered 'round her eyes. She was weary, drawn, dejected . . . she was older. She took Aravan's hand in hers and gently stroked it then held it to her cheek, and her pale green eyes gazed into his of dark sapphire. "There is great <power> flaring somewhere in the world, my love, though we cannot seem to isolate it. Drienne is drawing all the <fire> she dares, yet the conjoinment is unable to do more than somewhat stem the flood. Whatever his scheme, we cannot stop Durlok but can only delay him. And so I have come to you for a boon."

Aravan kissed her fingers. "Thou hast only to name it, *chieran*."

"You must sail the *Eroean* to Darda Glain and evacuate the Hidden Ones."

Aravan's eyes widened. "But I would not leave thee," he protested.

"Love, you must go. No other ship is swift enough to get there in the little time we have left."

"Dost thou know how much time remains?"

Tiredly, Aylis ran a hand through her silver-shot tresses. "If Durlok keeps his vow, perhaps we have five days and a bit—not quite six."

"Then come with me, *chieran*."

"I cannot. I am needed here."

Aravan looked long into her eyes. Above, the silent stars shown down upon the heartrent lovers. At last Aravan took her in his arms and gently kissed her. And he whispered, "I will come back for thee."

Tears slid down Aylis's cheeks as Aravan turned and strode to where the others waited. After a few words, Jinnarin came running to Aylis. "We will return, sister of mine." Then the Pysk ran to Jatu, and the big black Man lifted her into his cast-back cloak hood. All waved to Aylis, and she to them, then they turned on their heels and strode toward the garden gate.

And the world trembled once more.

As the comrades came down to the docks, they noted a small number of frightened Men and Women sitting on the quay, waiting to set sail. These passengers knew not what danger threatened; they only sensed that something dire was afoot. And the trembling isle to them seemed disastrously unsafe, whereas a ship could weather any storm—or so they thought. And so they sat quietly and waited to board the given ships upon which they had purchased passage.

And as Aravan and company strode across the quay, another tremor juddered the land. Sensing their parents' alarm, children clutched fathers and mothers and wept in fear.

Aravan with Farrix, Jatu with Jinnarin, and Bokar finally came to where the *Eroean* was docked. They found the gangway hauled aboard and the warband standing guard along the railing. As they approached, Kelek called out and the ladder was lowered. A Man bearing a sleeping child stepped before Aravan. "Are you setting sail now? If so, I would book passage, though I have no money. I am a good worker."

Aravan looked into his pleading eyes. "Nay, we but go to another part of Rwn. If thou and thy daughter would set sail away from this isle, here is enough to pay thy way." Aravan took a small pouch from his cloak, coins clinking within, and pressed it into the Man's hand. Aravan turned and pointed. "That ship yon is even now loading."

"Oh sir, I don't know—"

Aravan held out a hand to stop the Man's words. "Repay me by doing well unto others." He glanced at the far-docked schooner. "Go now; thou must hurry."

As the Man hastened away, the child awakened. "Oh, Father, a little person," she called out, but he did not turn to see.

Aravan looked at his comrades. "If we take strangers to Darda Glain, we will never get the Hidden Ones aboard. Yet how can I refuse them?"

"Captain," rumbled Jatu. "Our first loyalty is to the Hidden Ones. If we have room after they board, then perhaps we will discover a way to take on others as well."

Aravan gave a sharp nod, agreeing, then said, "Let us away."

As the comrades boarded the *Eroean,* again the island quaked.

Running against the morning tide, the Elvenship sailed away from Kairn, with her silks unfurled full. Due south she ran, bells ringing in her wake, the wind on the starboard beam, and now and again the ship would shake in the juddering of the sea. As dawn began to pale the skies, Aravan stood on deck with Jinnarin and Farrix. He pointed to the heavens where rode a quarter Moon above. "Ye can see four of the five wanderers: the red one nigh the zenith, 'tis named *Reier* by the Lian, Red Warrior in Common; next to the Moon is *Veorht Íian,* Bright Voyager; 'tween the Moon and the eastern horizon lies *Cianin Andelé,* Shining Nomad; and below, down on the rim of the world is *Wifan Aun,* Swift One. The fifth wanderer, *Rul Pex,* Slow Foot, will not rise until shortly after the Sun, hence cannot be seen until the coming of the eventide when the Sun has set, and then for but a brief while."

Farrix pointed a finger at the sky and counted off, "In the order you named each wanderer, we instead call them Red Vixen, Snow Bear, Bright Lady, Sun Rider, and Traveller."

Jinnarin looked at them all, running from high above in what seemed to be a line down to the eastern horizon. Then her eye swept back to the crescent quarter Moon, and a cold shiver ran over her frame. His arm about her, Farrix looked at Jinnarin and asked, "What is it, love?"

Jinnarin sighed. "That such splendor could be twisted for evil ... it speaks of a vile mind."

"I know," replied Farrix softly, and together they stood on deck and watched the dawn brighten until at last the Sun rose. And when it was full above the horizon and day was on the deeps, no longer could the wanderers be seen, though the waning Moon yet rode the sky above, the silver crescent steadily edging toward the Sun.

Due south they ran until early morn, the wind on the starboard, Rwn on the larboard, until at last they rounded a broad peninsula outthrust well into the sea, where they swung east-southeast. And with a following wind blowing on the starboard aft, they headed for the great outjut of land on which lay Darda Glain. Aravan was heading for a long bight of sea that reached deep into the ancient forest, falling short of the center by only ten miles. Both Farrix and Jinnarin had assured him that ships could sail into the firth without fear of attack, just as long as they did not put ashore. They would, however, be well watched, for eyes of the Hidden Ones would be upon them from the moment they entered the bay.

It was high noon when they sailed past the mouth of the long inlet, and the ship swung to the east-northeast to follow the bight inward. Aravan had all hands piped on deck. "I would have the Hidden Ones see ye so that they will know who comes calling. Leave thy armor and weapons below so they will know we come not in War."

Bokar arranged the Châkka so that half stood along the starboard rail and half on the one to the larboard. Somehow without their crossbows and axes and warhammers and shields and without their armor and flaring steel helms, they looked like nothing more than crafters and merchants ... or so Jinnarin surmised. And on the part of the Men, Jatu placed his unarmed sailors up the ratlines and along the yards in the crow's nests as well, so that they bedecked the ship as if it were on parade. And down the center of the fifteen mile long firth they sailed, the *Eroean* running at eight knots, her cerulean silks belling in the aft quartering wind, while the silent forest watched to left and right no more than a mile either way.

The Sun had progressed one third part down from the zenith when the *Eroean* at last came to the wide root of the firth, where she dropped anchor.

"Stand by to lower a single gig," called Aravan.

The Elf looked down at the Pysks and fox. "Ready?" They nodded, Jinnarin adding, "And eager, too!"

Bokar turned to Aravan and gritted, "Captain, I mislike this idea of you going ashore alone. Darda Glain is closed to outsiders. What if you are attacked by the Hidden Ones? Little good will my warriors be with you there and we here."

"He's not going alone, Bokar," said Farrix, waving a hand toward Jinnarin and Rux. "We will be with him."

"And as to attacks," put in Jinnarin, somewhat miffed, "he wears his stone and all will know him as a Friend. We're not bloodthirsty savages, you know. Besides, I thought we discussed this and you were in agreement."

Bokar growled, but said no more.

"Ready with the gig, Cap'n!" called Slane.

Elf, Pysks, and fox stepped across the deck, where Jinnarin was lifted into the boat by Jatu, Farrix after, and Rux leapt in at Jinnarin's command. Aravan stepped aboard, and the gig was swung out on the davits. "Lower away," rumbled Jatu.

Even as the keel of the gig scraped sand, the island shook with a tremor, the leaves of nearby forest trees rustling as if in protest. Jinnarin said, "We will be back as soon as we can, Aravan. There's much ground to cover, and many to warn. I am just hoping that most will respond, for I think something ... dreadful ... lies but five days away."

Aravan glanced at the Sun. " 'Tis early afternoon of the seventh. Try to be back by sundown of the tenth, bringing all with you who will come. I would be at sea early morn of the eleventh to make a run back to Kairn."

Jinnarin and Farrix canted their heads in agreement. Then they both mounted Rux, Farrix behind his mate, and at a command from Jinnarin the fox leapt over the side and darted across the shingle of sand and into the dark forest beyond.

"Fare ye well," called Aravan after, but he doubted the Pysks had heard.

And the island shivered again.

Gradually the time eked toward the tenth, when the Hidden Ones were due on board, for Aravan hoped to set sail the day after—on August eleventh. And as time crawled by, the waning crescent Moon, now fingernail thin, crept closer to the Sun, while at the same time the tremors worsened. Aravan and the crew entire paced the deck of the *Eroean* and fretted, for they'd had no word from the Hidden Ones and neither Jinnarin nor Farrix had returned. And gradually the breeze blowing up the firth dwindled, dwindled, diminished, until on the tenth of August at mid of day the wind died altogether and nought but a hot summer stillness lay over the forest and across the bight. And the Moon would kiss the Sun in but a two-day.

Night fell and still no word arrived. Yet as the midnight hour drew down upon the *Eroean,* a knock sounded on Aravan's door, and when the Elf opened it, Geff stood there. "Cap'n, they's a small signal fire blazin' on the shingle ashore."

Swiftly a gig was lowered, and Aravan rowed toward the tiny flame. As the keel of his boat scraped sand, Aravan turned about to see Jinnarin and Farrix standing by the fire, along with Rux and another fox he took to be Rhu. There, too, were clusters of shadows—other Pysks, he presumed. And back in the fringe of the forest, something . . . huge . . . loomed in the darkness among the trees.

"May I come ashore?" he asked, standing in the boat.

"Oh yes, Aravan," said Jinnarin, distress in her voice, "please do. Perhaps you can talk some sense into these—these log-headed, stubborn fools!"

Aravan stepped into the shallow wavelets lapping the shore and dragged the gig a bit higher onto the sand. Then he walked to the fire and knelt. The clusters of shadow moved back.

"What yields?" asked the Elf.

Farrix drew in his breath and blew it out slowly. "They will not come."

"Oh? None? Neither the tree nor hummock nor hole dwellers? The fen swimmers? The forest runners? Others?"

Jinnarin plopped down in the sand. "Some are afraid. Others refuse to be seen by Humans, Dwarves, or Elves. Still others do not believe that a fight between Durlok and Alamar or any other Mage is of concern to them."

"Meddle not with Mages!" muttered Farrix. "It is an old saying, and many will not go against the adage."

"Did ye tell them of the Black Mage, of Durlok's evil?"

Farrix nodded. "Even so, most claim it is the business of Magekind."

"If he comes to Darda Glain" came a whisper from a cluster of shadow, "then will we deal with Durlok. Else we let the Mages police their own."

A low, heavy wordless rumble came from the massive, looming darkness in the fringe of the woods.

As a tremor shook the land, Aravan turned and addressed the gathering. "Do ye not see that Durlok has already come unto thy domain? This shaking of the land is his doing. It presages something dire, of that ye can be certain."

"Perhaps," replied a voice from yet another cluster, "but whatever it is, it is aimed at the Mages and not at Darda Glain."

Jinnarin pounded a fist into the sand. "It's no use, Aravan. We've argued until we are blue in the face. The LivVolls, Vred Tres, Sukke Steins—none of these would come, saying that it would take too long. The Sprygt will not leave their Tres, the Tomté stay with the Volls, and the Ande say they are linked to the glades. As to the others, they would not listen at all."

"What of thy Kind, the Pyska?"

Jinnarin waved a hand about. "A few came to see the ship and the Friend who saved Tarquin, that's all."

"They will not come?"

"Right, Aravan, it's simply no go," added Farrix.

"We will not abandon Darda Glain," whispered a voice from one of the clusters.

A tremor jolted the land.

Aravan knelt in silence for a while. At last he stood and brushed off the knees of his breeks. Then he addressed the clusters. "We go now to return to the *Eroean*. Come the dawn, if there be a wind, we set sail for Kairn. Should a change of mind come upon any of ye, light a fire along the shore ere we reach the open sea and we will come for ye. And that goes for thy immense friend standing at yon forest edge, or any other Hidden One."

Leaving Jinnarin and Farrix behind to say farewell, Aravan walked to the prow of the boat and waited. Moments later, both Pysks turned and came to the gig. Rux and Rhu leapt into the boat, and Aravan lifted Jinnarin and Farrix to the craft and settled them in the bow, and Jinnarin leaned her head against Farrix's shoulder and wept.

Just as the Elf prepared to shove off, there sounded a call from the woods, and riding into view came a band of Pysks, ten altogether, males and females alike. Jinnarin and Farrix leapt to their feet and watched as the Pysks approached, Jinnarin wiping the tears from her eyes. Dressed in leathers and armed with bows and arrows, the band of riders rode their red foxes down across the shingle of sand to come before the gig, where they stopped.

In the lead was a russet-haired female, and she sat before Aravan and looked up at the Elf momentarily. Apparently he passed her muster, and she turned her brown-eyed gaze upon Jinnarin. "We have come to join you."

Jinnarin's tear-streaked face lit up. "Oh, Anthera, we are so glad you changed your mind . . . all of you!"

Again Anthera looked up at the Elf then back to Jinnarin. "Long we debated ere we decided. Had it been any other than you and Farrix and a Friend, we would not have come."

The land shivered again.

"Thou didst well to come, my Lady," said Aravan, "for Rwn itself may be in danger."

Anthera shook her head. "Oh, we do not believe that the island—or even Darda Glain—is in any danger. Oh no. Instead, you see before you a warband. We came to oppose the Mage who took one of our own as a prisoner. Never again will we allow the return of the old days unto our world, when the capture or killing of Hidden Ones was a common practice. Never again!"

Behind her, Pysks raised their bows and shouted out, *Never again!*

When Aravan returned to the *Eroean,* he came in a gig filled with foxes.

Dawn came and still no breath of air stirred, and the silks were unfurled to hang lank in the summer morn. Too, no fire was lighted on the narrow beach. And the slenderest of Moons rode near the burning Sun. It was the eleventh of August and the morrow would bring the grand wedding.

Like a caged beast, Aravan paced the deck. And just ere midday he called to Jatu to break out the rowing gigs. "We will pull the ship down to the sea where we may find a breeze."

The gigs were unshipped and towing ropes affixed, and Dwarven warriors began to row, canting their warlike chants. Slowly down the still bight they fared, heading for the distant sea, crews straining at the oars, the forest gliding steadily by, the Sun creeping down the sky. Now and again the lookouts reported movement among the distant trees. Yet when they stared at the forest marge, nothing afoot did they see.

And still the Dwarves rowed.

"Two knots at most I gauge it, Captain," replied Jatu to Aravan's query.

The Elf sighed. "I agree. At this rate we'll come to the ocean at dusk."

"By damn, if there be wind, Kapitan," said Rico, "she make it to Kairn in time, will *Lady Eroean*."

"I can only hope thou art right, Rico."

And onward rowed the Dwarves.

It was nigh sunset when the first faint trace of air belled the sails backwards. "Rico, pipe the yards keelways to the ship. We've another long hour ere we come to the waters where we have sailing room. If need be, furl the silks altogether."

"Aye, Kapitan."

Slowly the hour passed, and the Elvenship came down toward the sea, the Dwarves haling on the oars, towing the craft behind. A gentle breeze, light and shifty, stirred the silks, and Rico furled them full so that they would not oppose the rowers. At last at dusk they debouched into the Weston Ocean, and Aravan ordered the gigs back aboard.

"Rico, prepare to sail. Boder, we'll set the course tacking westerly, for the wind will be in our face."

Yet as the purple twilight settled over the sea, a lookout called, "Dolphin, Cap'n! Dolphin off th' larboard beam!"

Aravan stood at the rail and peered outward with his Elven eyes, and then he said to Rico, "Belay those orders, Bo's'n, at least for a while," for Aravan could see that among the dolphin racing for the *Eroean* came swimming a Child of the Sea.

Jinnarin and Farrix came running and climbed to a belaying-pin rack and peered down over the side. And as the pod of dolphin reached the Elvenship, Aravan leaned over the larboard railing and called down to the circling Child, "Speaketh thou the Common Tongue?"

The reply came, strangely accented and full of pops and clicks and chirps, and Jinnarin only understood two words in all: *Ut!¡teri*—whales; and *¡g!alley*—the Merfolk attempt to say galley.

But Aravan seemed to understand the sense of what the Child was saying—perhaps it was because he was a Friend; perhaps it was because of his amulet; perhaps it was something else altogether; who can know? Regardless, he turned to the others, his voice grim as he said, "The whales have found the black galley."

CHAPTER 39

Grand Wedding

Summer, 1E9575
[The Present]

Jinnarin's heart hammered in her breast. "Where?" she called down to the Child of the Sea. "Where *is* the black galley?"

The Child cocked her head to the side and rattled a string of clicking, chirping, whistling words at Aravan. "She does not understand thee, Jinnarin," he said. Then Aravan called down, "Where away the black galley? How far?"

The Child turned and gestured southwesterly, chattering her clatterous speech.

"Only halfway to Atala," relayed the Elf, "surely *Silver Bottom* can sail that far. It is not even a half a day as the *¡Nat!io* run. —Ah, yes, my Child of the Sea, less than a half a day for thee and thy Kind, but longer for me in this light breeze."

Again the Child clattered back at Aravan.

"Neither *¡Nat!io* nor *Ut!¡teri* nor *A!miî* can get near the black galley, for terrible power is pouring from it and doing something to the bottom of the sea." Aravan's eyes widened. "Durlok does something to the sea bottom! What?"

Aravan listened then repeated the sense of her reply. "Thou knowest not, for the terrible power goes down and the Sea Folk cannot go nigh."

"Kruk!" cursed Bokar standing next to Aravan.

Jatu held a hand up in the breeze. "The wind freshens

a bit, Captain. There is a chance we could get halfway to Atala ere the Moon kisses the Sun on the morrow."

Bokar growled, "Mayhap the Children and whales and dolphin cannot get near the galley, Captain, but by El-wydd! my ballistas can reach far over the waters."

"But what about Kairn?" asked Jinnarin, anxiety in her voice. "Aylis is there."

"Ah yes, love," said Farrix, "Aylis is indeed there, and perhaps Alamar, if he's not yet crossed over to Va-daria, that is. But listen, Alamar did have a good plan back when first we began to pursue Durlok, before the Black Mage destroyed the lexicon: if we can distract Durlok for but an hour 'round noon tomorrow, well burn me, I think we can upset *whatever* his scheme is."

Indecision filled Jinnarin's eyes. "But if we fail—"

"If we don't try, we've already failed," interjected Farrix.

The Child below chattered and clicked and chirped. "She says she will lead us to the black galley," relayed the Elf.

Jatu looked at Aravan. "Time is passing, Captain. What'll it be: Kairn . . . or Durlok?"

Aravan glanced up at the windage pennons fluttering in the strengthening northwesterly breeze. And his gaze strayed to the west-southwest, where Atala lay one hundred forty-four leagues away, some four hundred and thirty-two miles, toward the west-southwest where also lay the black galley, perhaps half as far. Then he looked to the northwest where lay the City of Bells, which held the grove where was his true love, a mere ninety miles beyond the horizon as the albatross flies, though a longer route by the sea.

"Captain?" said Jatu.

Aravan looked at the big black Man and finally said, "West-southwest, Jatu. We follow the Child of the Sea."

In a grove of silver birch, Aylis glanced up at the stars. Her fine silvery hair fell down 'round her shoulders, nearly all the brown now vanished. And she wondered if the evacuation of Darda Glain had gone well, for in but fifteen hours the unseen Moon would kiss the Sun. At the moment none of the wanderers were in the sky, would not be there until an hour before mid of night

when the Red Warrior would come over the horizon
first.

She wondered as well when Aravan would return, for
he had promised he would come for her.

Aylis lowered her eyes and glanced down at Drienne,
the sorceress sitting beside the crystal mere, her skin
translucent with age. Nearly all of her raven-black hair
had turned pearlescent. White, too, were her knuckles
as she tightly gripped the arms of the crimson chair and
channeled the <power> of the conjoinment into the aethyr in an attempt to quench the burn of Durlok's <fire>.
They had not been able to locate the whereabouts of
the Black Mage, and even had they, still it is questionable whether it would have improved their chances.

Yet could they delay Durlok's scheme until the wedding was past, then all would be worth it ... or so
they hoped.

Swiftly the *Eroean* cut through the waves, the ship running wet, her stem aimed west-southwesterly, a braw
wind on her starboard beam, quartering toward the bow.
But out ahead of the Elvenship coursed a pod of dolphin, effortlessly pacing the ship, and in their midst
raced a Child of the Sea. High in the aft skies the Red
Warrior shown, and lower easterly stood the Bright Voyager, followed by the Shining Nomad. And Jinnarin had
watched as each of the wanderers had risen, her hammering heart pounding rapidly as each climbed into
view.

Bokar and his Châkka warriors had donned their
armor and cleaned their weapons and had thoroughly
checked the ballistas, and crates of fireballs and javelins
sat ready at hand. And as Bokar had told his warriors
what was afoot, Engar had called out, "Well and good,
Armsmaster. When we sink the black galley, we will
send twenty-eight Trolls down to the bottom with her!"
An uproar of approval had greeted Engar's remark.

As to the band of Pysks, they had taken quarters in
Alamar's former cabin, and they, too, prepared, though
not in the open, for they were not yet comfortable
around Humans and Dwarves ... nor even an Elf, in
spite of the fact that he was a Friend.

Onward sped the Elvenship in the sometimes juddering sea, false dawn coming at last, and with it rose the wanderer known as the Swift One; and Jinnarin thought her heart would burst with the tension, for they still had leagues upon leagues to go, but the inexorable turning of the unstoppable heavens heeded not their plight.

The Sun rose.

"Lord god, Aravan," gritted Farrix, "where is the Moon?"

Aravan pointed slightly above and east of the Sun. "There, though it cannot be seen."

Farrix looked, but the Sun was too bright for him to find the other orb.

The wanderers, too, had disappeared with the coming of day.

"Slow Foot will rise shortly," added Aravan, "though it, too, will be hidden from sight."

"Captain, we now run at fifteen knots," said Jatu. "Will we arrive in time?"

Aravan glanced at the Sun, then away. "I don't know, Jatu. It depends upon exactly where Durlok's galley lies. This I do know: given our current speed, we will arrive at a point precisely halfway between Rwn and Atala exactly at high noon. If he is closer ... well and good. But if farther ..." Aravan did not finish the sentence, but all knew what he meant.

Farrix jittered about on the deck, unable to sit for any length of time. Jinnarin snapped at him to "give it a rest," but no sooner had he plopped down than she took his place, muttering, "Come on, wind, can't you blow harder?"

And across the sea ran the *Eroean* as the hours counted down.

The Sun stood nigh the zenith when the mainmast lookout bellowed, "Cap'n, the dolphin break away!" and at the same time the foremast lookout cried, "Cap'n, ship ho, dead ahead!"

As the *Eroean* thundered past the circling dolphin ringing 'round the now halted Child of the Sea, Bokar shouted a command and Dwarves scrambled toward the ballistas. Dodging among the rushing warriors, Jinnarin and Farrix raced to the foredeck and scrambled up onto the stemblock and peered into the distance ahead. And just as Aravan joined them, low on the horizon and barely in their view they could see the black galley in the water.

"Good lord!" breathed Farrix.

"Adon!" gritted Jinnarin.

Hearing fear tingeing their breath, "What is it ye see?" asked Aravan.

"Don't you see it, Aravan?" cried Farrix, his eyes wide in dread.

"The galley, aye, but nothing more."

"Oh, Aravan," breathed Jinnarin. "The galley, it is covered over with a boiling nimbus of horribly writhing black fire."

Aylis, her hair now completely silver, the brown gone with her vanished youth, glanced at the sun overhead. It was near high noon and the unseen Moon would any moment kiss the Sun. She sighed and slowly peered 'round the slopes of the amphitheater, eyeing each and every Mage, all now burdened with age. Her eye stopped on a bent, wrinkled, hairless, stooped elder, partially hidden behind a tree, his arthritic hands knotted and trembling. Slowly, Aylis made her way down and across the Mage Grove and up the opposite slope. At last she reached the ancient one's side, and weeping, said, "Father."

Alamar looked at her with his rheumy eyes, his mouth gaping in a toothless grin. "Do him in the eye, Daughter," he whispered. "We'll do him in the eye."

Yet even as Aylis looked on in distress, tears running down her aged face, she knew that neither he nor she could leave the Great Conjoinment until Drienne broke it. And weeping, she gazed upon her father, and his brown-mottled skin drew taut across his skeletal face as the last dregs of youth poured from him.

And in that moment the island lurched violently sideways, as if a vast hammer had struck an immense blow. The ancient Mage collapsed, and Aylis was knocked from her feet.

And the sea began rushing away from Rwn.

"Trim her up, Boder. We'll pass with her on our larboard. Rico, get all the speed from the silks thou canst."

"Aye, Cap'n," muttered Boder, sighting down the

length of the *Eroean* at the black galley five or so miles distant. "How close do you want me to come. I'll graze her, if you like."

Aravan grinned. "A hundred feet will do." The Elf turned and called out, "Bokar, we'll make the first pass with her a hundred feet on our larboard."

The Dwarven warriors on the starboard ballistas groaned and growled and shook their fists at the larboard crews and shouted out curses in Châkur.

And in the bow as brine and spray washed across the decks, Jinnarin and Farrix ensconced themselves among the jib sheets wrapped 'round the belaying pins in the forward rack, where neither wind nor wave could wash them free.

And Aravan glanced at the Sun where he knew even now that the unseen Moon was within mere moments of kissing the golden orb.

But Rico and crew had trimmed the silks to take the very last part of the final knot from the air, and the Elvenship thundered across the sea.

The ballistas were ready.

The Dwarves were ready.

And Boder had his line. . . .

. . . And in that moment the Moon kissed the Sun—
—The world lurched—
—And the bottom seemed to drop out of the sea—
—The entire surface fell away beneath the *Eroean*—
—The ship falling with it—
—And spinning beyond control, with Men and Dwarves hurled about the deck like ten pins scattered, the Elvenship slid down a long slope of water, the whirling *Eroean* rushing headlong *downhill* toward the motionless black galley—
—And as they plunged wildly down the steep slant and toward the far dark ship, and down and down and down, a great wall of water seemed to rise up before them in the distance between, and thundering toward them came hurtling a monstrous wave.

In the grove of silver birch, of a sudden the Great Conjoinment vanished, and Drienne, her hair now utterly white, painfully stood and called out, "We have lost the battle and are now in great peril. Vadaria is our only hope, can we cross over in time.''

And with this pronouncement, among the birches, all the Mages, their backs stooped with age, began the intricate steps and the arcane chant that would take them to Vadaria.

Aylis, now free of the conjoinment, knelt by her father's corpselike form. She could not tell whether he was alive or dead, but nevertheless she took up his frail frame in her arms. Struggling, for now she was terribly weak, Aylis managed to stand at last. And bearing his unmoving body in the desperate hope of saving him, she began chanting and stepping the pattern as well.

And all about Rwn the bare ocean floor was exposed for mile upon mile—sand and mud and rock and weed lay in the sunlight, and fish gasped and flopped about, and eels slithered, and things unnamed wriggled and squirmed and oozed, and the River Kairn plunged over the falls to roar down upon the bared expanse—the sea having fled southward to fill the colossal emptiness left behind by the sudden vast collapse of the abyssal depths below. And far to the north of Rwn, the waters of the Northern Sea were just now beginning to react, a frigid flow running down to fill the hollow abandoned by the fled-away sea.

A howling wind preceded the monstrous crest, blasting against the *Eroean* like a giant, angry hand, slamming her hard, heeling her over, the monstrous slap stopping her spin, for her sails were set for a reach. Her stern was to the oncoming wave, and Aravan called out above the howl, ''Rico, square the yards! Boder, run a straight course! Frizian, batten all hatches! Jatu, ready a sea anchor—no, two! By Adon, we cannot outrun this wave but mayhap we can ride it!''

As Men and Dwarves scrambled to comply, Aravan shouted for all to get below decks as soon as they could—''We may be swamped, and I would not have any washed o'erboard.'' And he took control of the stern helm and ordered Boder to the one in the wheelhouse.

And behind, the monstrous wave thundered toward them as they fled before it in a howling gale, yet even now the Elvenship began riding up the forerunning slope.

Higher and higher rode up the ship, the slope steeper and steeper, a titanic curl of roaring water plunging down from the crest. Rico and crew belayed the last halyard, and scrambled below deck even as the curl began hurling spray upon them. Last of all to relinquish his post was Aravan, when he knew that Boder had taken the wheelhouse helm.

And as the captain scrambled down the sloping deck and into the wheelhouse, the Elvenship thundered down into the brine as if she would founder, but in the last instant she pulled herself up and rode the face of the wave.

Bracing himself against the canting deck, "Headcount!" snapped Aravan.

In moments the reports came to him. "Sailors all present and accounted for, Captain," called out Frizian, the second officer hanging onto the ladder below the trap to keep from sliding away.

"The Châkka all are here, Captain," barked Kelek, the Dwarf hauling himself up the slant to hang on beside Frizian.

And as the *Eroean* was borne on the thundering face of the hurtling wave, "What about the Pyska?" snapped Aravan.

"Foxes are below, Captain," shouted Frizian, "but me thinks all the riders above."

"Boder, I'll take the wheel! Thou search the aft quarters for them."

As Boder clambered through the doorway and up the high-pitched corridor to the stern quarters, in the howling wind the Elvenship forever plunged down the face of the wave, the thundering waters of the vast curl whelming down just aft.

Moments later Boder returned. "All the riders are in their cabin, except Lady Jinnarin and Master Farrix. Those two are not in any of the aft quarters, Cap'n. Neither theirs, yours, nor any of the others. Cap'n, you don't think they've gone and drowned, do you?"

A bleak look swept over Aravan's face, but he did not reply. Instead he called down to Frizian, "Jinnarin and Farrix are missing. Search below decks, call out for them. If they are in quarters or holds, have them sing out."

And below decks, Men and Dwarves clambered throughout the slanted ship, calling out the Pysks' names, but no one answered their cries.

And out on the deck, on the forward pin rack and anchored among jib sheets, Jinnarin and Farrix gasped for air time after time as the *Eroean* plunged into the seas, the brine seeking to drown them.

And in a silver birch grove the ground began to shudder, as tons unnumbered of hurtling water thundered across the exposed ocean floor and hurled toward the island of Rwn. Aylis carried her father and chanted, as did the other Mages, and none had yet crossed over, for this singular passage to Vadaria was especially difficult.

Onward roared the titanic wave, towering higher and higher as up the slope of the ocean floor it raced, bearing the *Eroean* on its monstrous flank as if the ship were no more than a tiny chip of wood.

"Oh Adon, Adon, Adon," gasped Boder, " 'tis like being on a mountainside."

Alarm filled Aravan's face, and he managed to cross to a window and glance up and back at the Sun. And a desolate howl of unbearable anguish ripped rawly from his throat. And he nearly collapsed to the deck in despair. But Boder's shout of fear for his captain brought Aravan back to his feet. And he took a deep breath and his face went flat, as all emotion was forcibly extinguished.

"Cap'n, what is it? What's happened?"

"Boder, our position," rasped Aravan, devastation in his eyes, "the *Eroean* is passing over Rwn."

CHAPTER 40

Devastation

Summer, 1E9575
[The Present]

The great wave rushed across the ocean, towering high in shallow waters, diminishing in the deep. And wherever it encountered bodies of land standing athwart its track, especially lands with steep shoals, the sea at first fled from the coasts, the waters sucking and hissing as they ran away. And in this vast outrush, boats and ships were dragged from their moorings, snapping their ropes, dragging their anchors as if they were nought. People ran down to the shore to gape at the incredible sight of the fled-away sea, and many scurried out onto the newly bared bottom to gather up the fish flopping about and gasping. But then preceded by a howling gale the waters came roaring back, rising up in a vast wall to smash against the shore and sweep far inland, leaving widespread death and destruction in their wake. And following the first wave came another, and another after, and another—more than twenty in all, for an immense area of the plate of the sea had utterly collapsed the monstrous waves like titanic ripples in a vast pond. Even thousands of miles away, whole villages and cities and dwellings were wrenched from the face of the world, forests and fields were engulfed, and lives unnumbered were drowned. Thus did Atala and Gelen and Thol and Jute and Goth suffer, and even faraway Hyree, as well as the low-lying lands on the distant coasts of the western continent and its sister land to the south. Worst hit of all these distant Lands was the Realm of Thol, for the mightiest crests seemed somehow directed north and east, as if Rwn were the primary target and all else secondary—and for the unfortunate Tholanders, their Realm lay beyond Rwn on this northeasterly track. Here the waves rolled for miles inland and swept all away; nothing was left standing, not even the tower of Gudwyn the Fair which had stood well above the sea on a high headland, the tower vanished along with the town of Havnstad which had lain below. And the juddering of the seafloor had other dire effects, for Karak on Atala begin to erupt, filling the air with ash and smoke, while great rocks blasted up into the sky and red-burning lava ran down its flanks to set the high land afire.

Driven before the thundering gale and riding the monstrous bore, the *Eroean* was hurled across the medial sea lying between Atala and Rwn. But once the Elvenship passed over the isle and into the deep waters beyond, the titanic wave diminished with distance, diminished with the greater depth of the sea, until far to the northeast, some six hundred miles past Rwn, Aravan at last could bring the ship about without fear of being swamped. And as she turned, a number more of the diminished waves—some larger, some smaller than each preceding one—passed beneath the *Eroean* and sped onward into the far reaches of the chill Northern Sea, where they would rise up again into towering monsters as they came to the shores beyond.

"Captain," rumbled Jatu, "our course . . . ?"

"We sail for Rwn, Jatu, to gather up whatever survivors there may be."

"And the Hidden Ones . . . ?"

"I will speak with them. They have yet to be told that the wave passed over Rwn."

In the bow, as Men came to set the sails, both Jinnarin and Farrix extracted themselves from the rigging, the Pysks drenched to the bone and half drowned. "Oh, lor!" exclaimed Lobbie. "Y're safe! Burdun, run quick and tell the Cap'n that Lady Jinnarin and Master Farrix is found safe and sound!"

"How can you be certain, Captain Aravan?" asked Anthera.

"I saw the position of the Sun, Lady Anthera."

"Oh, Anthera," said Jinnarin, bursting into tears, "it's all too true. Farrix and I saw the whole of it. We ran right over the center, right over the mountaintops."

Anthera's eyes shifted to Farrix, and bleakly he nodded, confirming Jinnarin's words.

"And Darda Glain . . . ?"

"Swept under, Anthera," choked out Farrix.

"What about survivors?"

All eyes turned to Aravan. Desolation filled his features. "There is little prospect that any escaped, yet even now we sail in the hope that Fortune smiled on some."

Anthera stood a long while without speaking, her head down. At last she gritted, "Durlok!"

As in a calm after a great storm, for the next three days the winds blew lightly and often shifted about. Even so, steadily the *Eroean* sailed toward the waters of Rwn. And all along the path was evidence of the destruction, a crate or two and barrels, and shattered boards and broken wheels and splintered doors, and shingles and roofs and sodden thatch and parts of walls, that and more—flotsam bobbing in the brine. Great trees they saw, limbs and branches shattered, trunks split, roots broken, as if these forest giants had been ripped bodily from the soil. Saplings there were and underbrush, and now and again stretches of sod as well as great masses of seaweed heaved up from the bottom, all riding the now calm waves. Too, there was straw and sheaves of grain—oats and barley and the like—and fruit trees and cabbages and other such. Small animals were seen floating dead, as well as a deer or two. And once they passed something that looked like part of a Man, but it sank from sight ere they could say.

And Men and Dwarves and Pysks wept to see such destruction as on toward Rwn they sailed.

But the most horrid thing of all was yet to be seen, for when they came to where Rwn was located, nought but empty sea greeted them—the island was completely gone.

"Are you certain, Captain?" asked Anthera, her voice hollow with despair.

With utter desolation in his eyes, Aravan looked at

the auburn-haired Pysk, but it was Jatu who answered her question. "Aye, Lady Anthera, he is certain. We sail where Rwn once stood."

Stunned and unable to see for the tears in her eyes, Anthera stumbled out onto the deck to bear the devastating news unto all.

That day they coursed in an ever-increasing spiral, and the next day and the next as well, looking for survivors, finding none. And out on deck, as the gazes of Men and Dwarves and Pysks frantically searched the water, they spoke to one another in hushed tones:

Do you think that any of the Mages escaped the deluge by crossing to Vadaria? Who can say? Not I. Nor I. Wot o' th' ships, Oi wonder—did any set sail in toime? Lor, if they didn't, surely they sank, for only the Eroean *could weather such. A entire isle agone, 'n' it weren't no tiny spit o' land, neither. Kruk! Can the armsmaster figure a way, we will slay this Black Mage. Hoy, Oi wonder why th' Maiges o' Rwn j'st didn't waive their hands 'n' quell the waives, wot? Them little Fox Roiders, d'y' see the angry set o' their jaws? Durlok is evil, without honor, and for that he will answer to the Châkka! . . .*

Anthera peered out over the empty waters. "For this Durlok *will* pay!"

Jinnarin burst into tears. Farrix put his arm about her and drew her to him. After a while Jinnarin said, "Alamar once set me a problem, and it was to define the nature of evil."

Farrix gestured at the expanse where an island should be. "*This* is an act of utter evil."

"Yes, but Alamar would not have been satisfied with that answer. Instead he would have jumped down your throat and made you explain why. I mean, if nature alone had done this, it would not have been an act of evil. And if something hideously malevolent and destructive had lived alone on Rwn and needed to be destroyed, and if the only way to destroy it was to destroy the island, but to do it in such a way as to bring no harm to anything or anyone else, again it would not have been an act of evil."

"But such was not the case, Jinnarin. Durlok destroyed the innocent."

"As sometimes does nature, Farrix. So Alamar would

say—as do I—that the destruction of the innocent alone lies not at the heart of evil. Instead it is more: heed, Durlok has no concept of free will in others, of the rights of others to guide their own destinies. He looks upon others merely as creatures put here to serve his desires. Hence, Durlok is evil for he destroys others, dominates others, deceives others merely for his own gratification. And *that*, my love, is the true nature of evil."

Farrix slowly nodded, but Anthera turned and looked at Jinnarin. "You say that if something hideously malevolent and destructive needs to be destroyed, *is* destroyed, it is not an act of evil, and on that I certainly agree. Heed me, Jinnarin, Durlok is such a thing."

For three days they searched, all to no avail, and often would grief overwhelm sailor, warrior, and Pysk alike—all but Captain Aravan, who held his grief in check.

But in the dark hours of the third night, alone in his cabin, Aravan wept inconsolably, silently whispering, *"Chieran, avó, chieran."*

"Captain, when first we came to you, we only asked that you return us to Darda Glain once Durlok had been dealt with. Now there is no Darda Glain and so our request changes; instead we now ask that you help us to exact our just vengeance against the Black Mage."

Aravan looked down at Anthera, the Pysk standing on the map table with Jinnarin and Farrix at her side. "Thou art not alone in thy thirst for revenge, Lady Anthera, for every Man and Drimm aboard has asked that we search out Durlok and slay him, and I have said yea.

"Yet heed me, it is a task beyond peril to slay a Mage. And we cannot succeed with nought but simple measures, for Durlok wields power beyond our comprehension."

"But Aravan," protested Jinnarin, "do you not think that his destroying Rwn has taken much from him? I mean, look what the expenditure of astral fire did to Alamar, to Aylis, to all the Mages in the grove. And Durlok is but one, whereas they were many, and so he had to overcome their formidable opposition as well as do whatever he did to destroy Rwn. So I ask, do you not think that he has but little power left? Dregs of what once was?"

"I know not, Lady Jinnarin. Mayhap thou hast the right of it, and Durlok is indeed weakened. But this I do know, and that is—it is perilous to stand in opposition to a Mage."

Farrix grimaced. "There is this, too, Aravan: as long as Durlok has victims, he has power."

"Kruk!" spat Bokar. "Give me one good swing of my axe, and I will deal with Durlok. It is not the Black Mage that concerns me, but his twenty-eight Trolls instead."

Silence fell among the comrades as each pondered their plight, and only the *shssh* of wind and *plsh* of wave and *rrurrk* of rigging sounded in the salon. Farrix looked over at armed Anthera and then to Jinnarin and then to Bokar. And he said, "Let's go see Tarquin, for I have an idea."

CHAPTER 41

Pŷr

Autumn, 1E9575
[The Present]

Like silent ghosts, the shadow-wrapped foxes slipped across the island in the night. In groups of three they ran, flitting among the stony crags, the riders upon their backs armed with tiny bows and deadly arrows and armored in darkness cloaked 'round. Southward they hastened, away from the temporary encampment hidden on the northern bluffs and toward the steeps above Durlok's lair. In the lead of one group ran Jinnarin on Rux. Behind and to her right sped Farrix on Rhu, Anthera on Tal to her left.

A distance hindward came Aravan, and with him both Tivir and Tink, for these three were the slenderest of all the *Eroean's* complement. And they were accompanied by three more of the tiny riders faring to fore and flank. Aravan carried rope and cord and a crossbow with a quiver of bolts fastened to its stock, and on his thigh was strapped a long-knife. And each of the cabin boys bore a crossbow and quiver and a cutlass girted to the waist, and each bore as well one of the small brass and crystal Dwarven lanterns, its phosphorescent glow well shielded. Too, both Tivir and Tink carried long, forked sticks carven from straight alder saplings. And across the center of the isle they fared.

Westward a half mile or so, another trio of the shadow-wrapped scouts sped toward the island rim, and striding after those three went Jamie and Slane, armed and bearing lanterns, the two sailors warded 'round by the last three of the Pysks.

Thus did twelve Fox Riders, two Men, two slender lads, and one Elf cross the island above, while sixteen Men and forty Dwarves sailed westward in the dark 'round the isle below.

To the east-northeast a waxing half Moon rode just above the horizon, and high in the northeastern sky among the turning stars silently fared the Bright Voyager, the Red Warrior on its heels.

It was the last night of October—eighty days after the destruction of Rwn.

Jinnarin flung up a hand, while at the same time bringing Rux to a halt. Farrix stopped on her right; Anthera on her left. They had come to the edge of the isle.

"Somewhere below," hissed Jinnarin, and all three dismounted. The Pysks spread out and waited, now and again peering over the edge of the cliff and down at the foot of the bluff, where the Sindhu Sea washed against adamant stone.

Rux turned his head and peered inland, as did Rhu and Tal, and out from the darkness came Aravan and Tink and Tivir, escorted by Bivin, Reena, and Galex on their foxes.

Aravan held his amulet and paced back and forth along the rim of the bluff. At last he stopped at a point and whispered, "Here the stone seems coldest. I ween the window is warded and virtually below." He stepped five paces easterly. "This should put us slightly to the side."

Aravan uncoiled the slender cord and tied one end to a boulder. Then he nodded to Farrix who whispered a command to Rhu, and the fox slipped beyond seeing back among the crags. Farrix shot a smile toward Jinnarin and then slid a hand through one of the many loops tied along the length of the free end of the heavy twine.

Down Aravan lowered the Pysk, while all the others peered over the edge and watched as Farrix descended to the ledge below. When he reached the shelf, he stepped away from the line and crept along the stone, listening. After a while, he signalled up to the watchers, and then he backed away and sat down.

"Good," breathed Anthera. "He hears the warders. Now we know where the window lies."

"Jinnarin, keep watch o'er Farrix. Tivir, to me. All else, take ease," murmured Aravan.

As Aravan and Tivir began pacing easterly, Jinnarin lay on her stomach and peered down at Farrix. Anthera and the remaining Pysks spoke commands to their mounts, and the foxes fanned out to watch the approaches. Some two hundred fifty feet easterly, Aravan and Tivir marked a place on the rim with a circle of stones, then they came back to the group. And while the Pysks knelt and inspected their weaponry for perhaps the thousandth time, and Aravan looked over the rim at Farrix below, Tink and Tivir warily peered into the moonlit darkness, their eyes searching—for what, they did not know.

And they waited.

The Moon had crawled the width of its disk up the eastern sky, when the foxes on the western approach signalled an alert, and the Pysks took up a defensive stance—bows strung with deadly arrows—even though they knew who probably came. The cabin boys, too, stood with their crossbows in hand, their breathing coming in suppressed gasps.

Finally six clusters of shadows slipped through the moonlight and to their side: it was Kylena, Rimi, Fia, Dwnic, Lurali, and Temen. And Fia whispered, "They are ready."

Aravan nodded and pulled up the cord, while the Pysks sent their foxes away to hide among the crags. Aravan then gestured to Jinnarin, and she slipped her hand through the very end loop on the line. Aravan lowered her two feet or so then gestured to Anthera, and she slid her hand through the second of the loops. One after another, the Pysks slipped their wrists through loops in the line, and like pearls on a string they were lowered down to join Farrix.

Carefully a rope was lowered, then, silently, Aravan came sliding down, Tink quietly after, the lad bearing a lantern and one of the forked sticks. Tivir remained above. Tink took two lengths of yellow yarn from his pocket and gave one to Jinnarin and the other to Farrix, along with a small bit of spirit gum for each, the adhesive wrapped in paper.

"Listen," breathed Farrix, tying the yarn about his waist, and all could hear a rattling and a muttering mixed now and again with guttural curses. Yet what was said, none knew. "They speak, in Slûk," murmured Farrix. "I think there are two, and they play at casting knucklebones."

Aravan nodded, then lay on his stomach, and with Tink anchoring his legs, Aravan leaned out and looked under the overhang. Slowly he moved along the ledge, looking, listening, turning his head this way and that, trying to see where stone ended and illusion began, yet the glamour was such that the stone appeared natural, the cracks and crevices unbroken as they passed across the face of the bluff. Even so, he used the sound of the muttered curses to site the window slit. Quietly he drew back and pointed straight down and moved five feet to one side. Cord in hand, again he lay on his stomach, and as Farrix slid his hand through a loop, Aravan took the stick from Tink. Then leaning over the ledge once more, Aravan lowered Farrix a ways, and with the fork of the carven branch he maneuvered the Pysk to a slender ledge—no more than two or three inches wide—running along the rough face of the bluff. When Farrix gained his footing, he turned with his back to the wall and slipped his hand loose from the loop. And while Aravan drew up the cord, Farrix strung an arrow to his bow.

Moving westerly three strides or so, Aravan repeated the feat, only this time it was Jinnarin who was maneuvered to the tiny ledge, her position slightly higher than that of Farrix, for the ledge ran at a shallow angle from him up to her.

When she was ready, Jinnarin nodded to Farrix and then gathered shadow unto herself, and with her heart pounding, slowly she began moving toward him—and he to her—Jinnarin cautiously feeling the wall as she went.... At last her fingers passed through seemingly solid stone.

She had reached the window slit.

She stepped back and flattened herself against the wall, and dropping her shadow she signalled Farrix. Trying to quell her racing heart, she waited while his shadow sidled toward her, Farrix moving more quickly now that he knew the approximate location of his side of the slot. And all the while the muttering and cursing rose and fell within the lookout post.

At last Farrix's fingers dipped into the illusory stone. He backed away and his shadow disappeared and he nodded at her. Cautiously, silently, together they explored the dimensions of the window, trying to find the sill, for it was critical that they know where it lay. Sliding her hand down the side, she could not find the threshold; it was somewhere below where she stood.

Jinnarin looked down the rough face of the cliff, seeking a shelf beneath, one she could climb down to . . . but the only ledge below was clearly too far down.

Jinnarin signalled *[Wait],* and she lay upon the narrow ledge, and using her bow as an extension of her arm, she quietly slid the tip along the edge of the window slot and reached down as far as she could, trying to find the sill . . . to no avail. But Farrix, somewhat lower and using the same method, found the brink at the full extent of the reach of his bow. Now they knew exactly where the threshold was.

Standing again, she strung an arrow to her bow and moved to the window end of the ledge, readying for her leap. With her heart wildly thudding, she glanced over at Farrix. He, too, was in position, his own bow ready, and he nodded to her and then gathered shadow, as did she.

Silently, the gloom of Farrix sprang from the ledge and disappeared through the stone. *One, two,* Jinnarin counted, and then followed, springing through the illusion to the opposite side. She landed on the sill, the dark cluster of Farrix front and to her left. Before her in the torchlit lookout chamber, a kneeling Ruch clutched at his throat, while a second kneeling Ruch was just beginning to turn toward the slot. Jinnarin aimed and loosed, her wee arrow hissing across to strike the turning Ruch in the side of the neck. He spun on about and his gaze widened and he opened his mouth to shout, while at the same time he clutched desperately for the bugle draped by a thong 'round his shoulder—but his eyes glazed over and he toppled sideways to the stone floor, his comrade collapsing as well.

Silently, the Pysks slipped the yarn from 'round their own waists, and while Farrix stood ward, Jinnarin, with a dab of spirit gum, fixed one end of her yellow floss to the corner of the sill and cast the free end out the window. She moved to the opposite corner and did the same with Farrix's yarn. Now the window ledge was marked to outside eyes. And in but moments, Anthera came through the illusion and slipped her hand from the cord loop. Quickly she was followed by Bivin, and together they leapt down from the sill and sped into the narrow passage leading into the holt.

Reena followed and then Galex, and they, too, moved swiftly down the corridor.

Kylena, Rimi, Fia, Dwnic, Lurali, and Temen came after, but stayed within the lookout post, fanning out to take up positions to either side of the passageway entry.

When all were in, Jinnarin and Farrix leapt down from the sill, and Aravan wriggled through the narrow slot, then pulled in his crossbow and quarrels tied to the end of the rope, then he gave the line a tug.

Outside, Tink pointed his lantern up toward Tivir above and momentarily cracked the hood, signalling him that the Pysks and Aravan were safely within the lookout chamber.

With a brief flash of return light, Tivir acknowledged the signal, then turned and sent a signal westward. A half mile away, Jamie flashed Tivir a recognition, then turned and signalled the boats below.

And the warband set sail for the illusion-covered entrance to the understone lagoon.

Jamie and Slane then sent a flash of light to Tiver, and he in turn to Tink, and moments later Tink slithered into the chamber and nodded to Aravan. And the Elf and the lad dragged the dead Rucha to the side of the chamber.

And they waited.

Time passed.

Finally Tivir came wriggling in through the window, for Jamie and Slane now stood watch above.

And again they waited as time limped past.

Finally Aravan sissed and pointed; by moonlight the warband sailed the waters below, eight dinghies in all—forty Dwarves and sixteen Men.

Turning from the slot, Aravan silently gestured to the others, and into the narrow passage they went.

Standing on the rim at the circle of stones, Jamie flashed a signal down to the boats, then slightly cracked the hood, dim illumination leaking out.

In the lead, "Down sail and unship oars," whispered Bokar, and Châkka warriors moved quietly to obey, the boats behind following in kind.

Guiding on Jamie's light, toward the cliffs they rowed, for somewhere in the shadows beneath his dim beacon stood an illusion.

Quietly they rowed, listening for the hollow echo of the surf which marked where they would find the understone lagoon, seeking to see where the waves rolled through seemingly solid rock. At last they found it, and through the glamour and into the channel they slipped, one after the other.

Once past the illusion they could see the dim glimmer of torchlight afar. And as waves swashed against the distant walls, down the strait and into the cove they fared, dipping their oars carefully even though the murmur of waves and boom of surge filled the vast hollow with a tumult of sound.

Now by the torches burning in their cressets at the far side of the stone dock, they could see the whole of the lagoon . . . and moored at the quay rode the black galley, a hundred dark feet in length, her oars shipped in, her mainmast stepped down, her shorter foremast yet mounted, the lateen sail unfurled.

Nodding in silence, Bokar gestured toward the steps at the end of the landing, and toward these they rowed. Quietly, they came to the stairs, and Bokar along with six others crept up and to the black galley, and they slipped over the side.

Moving in stillness, they searched the ship, and below deck they found a single sleeping Ukh and silently they slew him. They then returned to the deck, where Bokar signalled to the remaining boats. While the armsmaster and his squad brought galley oars topside and laid them on deck alongside the larboard rail, swiftly the remaining boats landed, one after another, and Châkka debarked and came up to the black ship, carrying the ballistas and crates of lances, lading all aboard. As they did this, the sailors behind rowed the emptied dinghies away from the quay and into concealment on the lagoon side of the galley, where they cast lines upward to be tied to the craft, and the sailors then clambered aboard, Jatu the first one over the rail.

But as the last ballista was laded, there sounded the loud, raucous blatting of a *Squam* horn, filling the cavern with its harsh blare. Bokar whirled about, trying to spot the Grg blowing it, sounding the alarm. Again it blatted, again and again. Of a sudden, Arka raised his crossbow and—*Thnn!*—let fly with a quarrel, and with a skrawk, the bugle ceased, the Ûkh plummeting from the foremast crow's nest to smash down on the deck.

And from the corridor leading into the caverns beyond the quay, there came the blattish answerings of an Ûkkish horn within.

As the boats of the warband sailed past in the waters below the window slot, Aravan, Tink, Tivir, and eight Pysks slipped down the narrow passageway toward the main corridor of the understone holt. Some hundred feet from this central passage they came upon Reena and Galex, two clusters of shadows hiding in folds of stone along the passage. They had been stationed here to bring down any Rucha or Loka who might have gone toward the lookout post, and who might have managed to escape Aravan's party waiting there and come fleeing back down the way. And somewhere ahead were Anthera and Bivin to stop any who might get past these two.

As Aravan and party came to Reena and Galex, these two made themselves known, and here Aravan stopped.

And they waited for Bokar's signal that all was ready.

Time eked by.

How long they stood in the dark cleft, Jinnarin did not know, but of a sudden she heard the distant raucous sound of a *Rûptish* horn.

"Vash!" hissed Aravan. "We are discovered! Quick,

Tivir, Tink, now may be the time of our contingency. Remember, if it comes to it, ye must run fleetly!"

Toward the main corridor they moved, coming to the place where Anthera and Bivin waited. And as they reached them, with a squawk the horn was silenced.

Moments passed, and then they heard the sound of another *Spaunen* horn, this one from the interior caverns. Peering up the hall, they could see torchlight emerging from the Trolls' quarters, and then they heard a ponderous treading. Trolls emerged, monstrous creatures, twelve feet tall, broad and brutish. And they filled the wide corridor and looked up the passage away from the quay, up to where the trump blared.

"Well, Cap'n," said Tivir, "looks loike we're on. Tink, y' ready naow?"

Tink swallowed and nodded and leaned his crossbow against the wall next to Tivir's. Then he glanced down at Jinnarin and she smiled at him, but her eyes were filled with fright. Tink flashed her a fleeting grin, then looked up at Tivir. "Let's get to it, boyo."

With a nod to the captain, the cabin boys stepped from the narrow cleft and into the main corridor. They silently ran a few steps down the passageway. Then, throwing the shutters of their Dwarven lanterns wide, "Hoy!" Tivir shouted. "Y' big lummoxes! Here we be, y' stupid gobs!"

"Yah, y' bloody arses!" shouted Tink. "Catch me if y' can!"

Trolls turned, their eyes flying wide at the sight of the lads.

RRRRAAAWWWW! bellowed a Troll, roars of the others thundering after, rage echoing down the stone corridor. And then the monstrous Spawn lunged toward the two. Tivir and Tink turned on their heels and raced toward the quay, Trolls plunging after, gaining with every stride.

"Brekka! Dett! Cut the lines!" barked Bokar. "All others, grab oars! Shove off! We may save this mission yet!"

With axes, the lines were severed. And using the

ship's oars, sailors and warriors shoved against the stone quay. But the ship was massive and moving thwartwise in the water. Sluggishly it responded as straining Châkka and Men pressed mightily to push the galley sideways away from the dock.

And all the while deep within the caverns there sounded the blatting alarm of a horn.

Slowly the ship drifted free, moving out from the landing.

And now they could hear the ringing of shouts, and a vast roar, followed by more shouting and the hammer of running footsteps, and the massive thud of lumbering feet.

Of a sudden, Tink came running, Tivir at his side, huge Trolls roaring and thundering in pursuit, more Trolls plunging after. And Tink ran straight while Tivir veered to the left, a Troll chasing each, the monsters reaching out to grasp the lads. But both boys made running dives, knifing into the black waters of the lagoon. The Troll chasing Tivir bawled in fright and tried to stop, but could not, and he skidded off the stone quay to fall into the brine and plummet from sight in the dark sea. But the Troll chasing Tink made a prodigious leap over the open water between the quay and the black galley and crashed into the side, and with a desperate grab he managed to clutch the top wale of the ship, the craft listing with his weight. And leering at the Dwarves, the monster clambered aboard as Dwarven axes and Jatu's warbar bounced off his stonelike, green-scaled hide.

Wrapped in shadow, Jinnarin watched as Trolls thundered by, her breath coming in gasps, for these were terrible monsters. And she prayed to Adon that Tivir and Tink had escaped, and that Bokar and the warband had managed to free the galley before the alarm sounded.

"Ready!" hissed Aravan. "The Trolls are past. The *Yrm* come after. We cannot let them get by to take command."

Jinnarin peered out into the corridor. In the distance oncoming torchlight shone 'round the bend. "Let's go!" she hissed, and into the passageway scurried dark clusters to run alongside each wall, Aravan following, his crossbow cocked and loaded.

As they came to the side passage lending to the Trolls' den and Aravan stepped within, 'round the main passage came the torchbearing *Rûpt,* the Spawn armed and armored and heading for the quay. And into the innocent shadows they stepped, but of a sudden they clutched at necks and cheeks, as if stung by bees. And as those in the fore were felled, those bringing up the rear shrieked in alarm and turned to flee even as the Pysks set arrows to string.

Aravan sighted his crossbow, but from behind there came a grunt, and he whirled about just as a monstrous grasp caught him up and slammed him against the stone wall, stunning him, his crossbow clattering away in the dark.

Into the hallway lunged the Troll, roaring in monstrous glee, dazed Aravan trapped in his crushing grip.

Shouting for help, Jinnarin loosed her tiny arrow at the brute, but it merely bounced off the scaled hide.

In the water below the galley, Tink and Tivir clambered into a dingy and then up the line to the deck of the galley, where they found Dwarves and Men desperately hewing at a Troll, gallantly trying to bring it down. But their axes and cutlasses and Jatu's warbar merely clanged against scales like stone, while the Troll smashed the warriors and sailors aside as if they were nought but pests, and bones were broken with each of his blows. And Trolls ashore jeered as the defenders were whelmed away.

Tink grabbed Tivir by the arm. "C'mon! Let's kill'm!"

Together they ran to one of the ballistas and set it up on its footing. As Tivir wound the crank, Tink opened one of the boxes of javelins, taking care not to touch the dark smut smeared along the length of the steel point.

Tink placed the shaft in the ballista groove.

Then, while Tivir braced the pedestal, Tink stepped to the stock and aimed. "Dona hit no Dwarf nor Man!" barked Tivir.

" 'Don, guide me," Tink prayed, and then loosed.

Thnn! the shaft hurtled through the air, the recoil knocking Tink and Tivir flat to the deck, the ballista landing atop them.

Thok! the spear slammed into the Troll, striking him in the full of his back, running him through, the dark-smeared point emerging from his chest. His eyes wide, the Troll looked down at this thing piercing his body and opened his mouth to roar, but staggered hindwards instead, toppling over the rail and into the water with a great splash, to plummet from sight.

From the deck where he'd been knocked, a ballista in his lap, Tink looked at Tivir and said, "I'll be damned, Tiv, we got him!"

Laughing insanely, and ignoring the shadows, the Troll raised up Aravan, preparing to dash his skull against glittering stone, while all about him Pysks loosed their tiny arrows, to no avail, for they merely bounced from the monster's scaled hide.

But before he slammed the Elf into the wall, a look of cunning swept over the Troll's face, and instead he clutched Aravan's chest in both hands, the thick fingers wrapping completely 'round, the creature preparing to crush the life from the Elf, to slowly squeeze the air from him, to shatter ribs, to hear him bubble on his own blood, the brute now leering at this most clever plan. And deliberately he tightened his grip.

The pain brought Aravan awake, and with his ribs creaking under the strain, gasping, he heard Jinnarin shouting, "Do him in the eye, Aravan! Do him in the eye!"

Desperately, Aravan scrabbled at the long-knife strapped to his thigh, while the monstrous Troll laughed in cruel glee and slowly squeezed. In an agonized groan, air hissed out from Aravan's lungs, and there came the crack of breaking ribs. The Troll's eyes flew wide in delight at this sound of damage and torment from his helpless victim, and he held the Elf up to his ear to hear better, and squeezed again. But as another rib snapped, Aravan jerked his long-knife free and before the Troll could react, he slammed the dark blade straight into the monster's ear, the grumesmeared tip punching through, delivering Fox Rider poison directly to the creature's brain.

In agony, the Troll sucked in a great breath of air as if to shout, but instead collapsed sideways, slamming Aravan to stone, while shadowy clusters scattered away to escape the falling monster.

And the passage filled with a sickening stench as death loosed the Troll's bowels and bladder.

Struggling, Aravan managed to free himself from the creature's grip. He painfully stood and tried to take a deep breath but could not, for five of his ribs were cracked.

"Quickly," commanded Bokar, "set the ballistas in place. Burak, Fager, Jatu, you others, tend the wounded. Tink, Tivir, jeer at the Trolls. We must keep them here until Captain Aravan deals with the Black Mage."

"Ar," shouted Tivir, grasping the foremast rigging and leaping to the rail and waving at the Trolls, "y' stupid gobs of snot! We kilt y'r mate, we did. Me 'n' Tink done it, roight enough."

"Right you are, Tivir me lad!" shrieked Tink, climbing up to stand beside Tivir. "And if any of you ugly toad suckers want a taste of th' same, come and get it. We're waiting, or are you too frightened to face us mighty Troll killers, eh?"

" 'N' besides bein' toad suckers," added Tivir, "y'r so oogly y'd spoil milk. O' course, that's th' way y' loike it, Oi shouldn't wonder, good 'n' blinky!"

" 'N' lemme tell y' about y'r oogly mothers . . ."

It is uncertain whether any of the Trolls understood a single word shouted at them by the two lads, but that they were being jeered at, the creatures had no doubt at all. And while some Dwarves hammered spikes to mount the ballistas to the deck of the drifting ship, and others uncrated the javelins—javelins whose blades were coated with Fox Rider poison brewed in secret by the Pysks in Tarquin's woods—and while Fager and Burak and Jatu and sailors tended the wounded, the Trolls roared out Slûkish curses and raved back and forth along the dock, and two or three, frothing at the mouth in anger, disappeared into the passageway behind.

Groaning and holding his rib cage, Aravan stepped to the dead Troll and retrieved his long-knife. Then in the shadows of the side passage he found his flung-away crossbow, the weapon spent, the quarrel gone, the bow having fired when it had hurtled against the wall, though the bow itself was unbroken. Sissing in pain, he managed to cock it and lay another poison quarrel into the groove. And through clenched teeth he said, "Let us go on."

Down the passage they scurried, did the shadows, 'round limping Aravan, while behind from the direction of the quay there sounded the roaring of Trolls. Moments later the Pysks and Elf came to the side passage leading to the Ruch and Lok quarters, and they could hear scrabbling down that way. Squatting, wincing, Aravan whispered, "Anthera." When a shadow approached, he jerked his head toward the passage and said, "I would have no *Rûpt* at our backs; take half and deal with them while the rest of us go on. Follow as soon as ye are done. —Jinnarin, Farrix, stay with me."

Six clusters of darkness broke away and headed down the rough-hewn side corridor, while Aravan and the others pressed forward along the main way.

'Round a long curve limped Aravan, shadows running fore and aft, and at last they came to the split where to their right lay the gathering hall and the three chambers on past, and to their left lay the crystal chamber, Durlok's quarters beyond. Again Aravan squatted, his breathing shallow, labored. "Who is left?" he whispered.

Jinnarin dropped her shadow as did the others. Aravan scanned them all. "Fia, Dwnic, Lurali, Temen, again I want no *Rûpt* at our back; if any hide in the gathering hall, galley, privy, or prison, deal with them. If there are prisoners, I would know that as well." Aravan gestured at the passage leading toward the crystal chamber. "Seek us yon when ye are done."

Once again all the Pysks gathered shadow unto

themselves, and four slipped down the right-hand way, while Aravan and two went left.

Shouting oaths, Trolls brandished their clubs and warbars at the japers, some even hurling their ungainly weapons at these invaders aboard their ship. The lads dodged this way and that as the inept missiles came whistling past. The three Trolls who had gone down the passage returned, each bearing a large stone or two. And they threw the rocks at those aboard the black galley, hurling them with such force that they *hummed* as they flew through the air, and one badly aimed stone broke through the hull of the craft just above the water line. "Oh, lor!" exclaimed Tivir. "Oi j'st hope they dona get th' idea t' sink th' ship."

But those words were said in vain, for the Troll whose rock had smashed through the ship's side shouted and threw again, this time deliberately taking aim to send the galley down.

Yet at that moment, Bokar shouted, "Ready! Loose at will!"

And ballistas were cranked and javelins hurled, piercing Trolls on the quay, the poison tips deadly. Trolls fell where they were pierced, some toppling from the landing, dead before striking the water. Others were shoved from the dock as their comrades panicked and sought to flee, and bellowing in terror, they drowned, plummeting from sight as if made of stone. Some Trolls stumbled and fell over their dead brethren, and they scrambled up only to be slain by another deadly round of ballista bolts. Still others escaped, running back into the passageway behind.

"Kruk!" spat Bokar, as the dock emptied.

"Damn!" gritted Jatu. "Just what we didn't want!"

And at the fore of the ship, "Cor," breathed Tivir. "Oi do 'ope th' cap'n 'n' Pysks 'r' safe."

"Let's hope," agreed Tink. "If not in the skinny passage to the lookout post—"

"Then safe past th' narrow doorway into th' Black Maige's alchem'stry plaice," interjected Tivir, "where th' Trolls can't squeeze in t' get'm."

"How many Trolls are left, I wonder?"

"Har, there's th' one what we killed, 'n' Oi count

nine more alayin' on th' dock, 'n' one fell in chasin' you, 'n' three more was accidental' shoved off by their mates 'n' drowned. That makes"—Tivir counted on his fingers—"ten and four deaders, and that still leaves, um"—again Tivir counted on his fingers.

"Fourteen," supplied Tink.

"Yar. Fouteen more. But those 'r' runnin' toward where th' cap'n 'n' th' others are."

"The Trolls aren't what worries me most, Tiv," replied Tink, "but the Black Mage instead. The cap'n, now, he said himself that the Fox Rider poison on the ballista javelins would take out the Trolls, just as Master Farrix figured. But the Black Mage, well, the cap'n still didn't know what'd do him in, though Armsmaster Bokar says that if the cap'n or the Pysks get a clean shot, Durlok is dead. Let's just hope he's right."

Tivir nodded slowly, but added, "Yar. But let's also 'ope th' Trolls can't get at th' cap'n neither."

While Tivir and Tink were toting up the dead foe, at the other end of the galley, Jatu and Bokar and Kelek stood at the rail and did the same. Jatu turned to the Dwarf and said, "There's fourteen of them slain, Armsmaster, and six of our own are dead—two of my sailors and four of your warriors. Too, we've another nine with broken bones—three Men and five Dwarves. More will die when we go after the remaining Trolls, perhaps none will survive. But if we don't go after them, then likely they'll kill the captain."

Bokar glanced at the black Man and nodded, then turned to Kelek. "Ready the new-forged crossbows—"

In that moment from the corridor leading inward there came a great clanging of picks against stone.

Limping and hissing quietly in pain, Aravan made his way down the passage toward the crystal chamber. Before him trotted Farrix, Jinnarin coming after, both Pysks cloaked in darkness and nearly invisible in the shadowy corridor. In the distance behind them they could hear the far-off bellowing of Trolls, punctuated now and again by a closer shrill cry . . . the shriek of a Ruch or Lok or somesuch.

As thcy came to the first cavity on their left, they

heard hoarse breathing back among the wares, and while Aravan waited, Jinnarin and Farrix slipped into the dark area. Moments later there sounded a sodden thud, and the shadowy Pysks emerged, and Jinnarin whispered to Aravan, "It was one of the Rucha."

Onward they went, and ahead they could see the glimmering of magelight seeping down the corridor, but ere they reached its source, the second storage area gaped to their left. Once again Jinnarin and Farrix slipped in among crates and bales and kegs and the like, but this time they found no one hiding among the goods.

Onward they pressed toward the crystal chamber, the light growing brighter as they neared. And Jinnarin could not seem to get enough to breathe, and her heart leapt about in her breast as would a caged wild bird.

And then they came to the entrance, the crystal chamber glittering in the phosphorescent blue light.

With shadows clustered about her, Jinnarin peered into the temple. It was empty. —No wait! Down on the crystal altar lay a mutilated corpse, blood runnelling adrip.

"Take care," hissed Farrix, "he has slain a fresh victim."

"One at a time we will enter," whispered Aravan. "Remain spread out; give him less target. I deem we must search the quarters beyond."

Into the crystal chamber they slipped, one after another, the trio spaced wide—Farrix first, Aravan next, Jinnarin coming last, her heart trapped in her throat. Along the curving wall they crept, bows and crossbow ready, Farrix in the lead heading for the distant doorway. His shadowy cluster had nearly reached the opening when—

"Fools!" sneered a voice, echoing in the chamber.

Jinnarin whirled, seeking the source, and down at the altar as if appearing out of thin air, stood a tall hairless person in dark robes, a long black staff in his left hand.

Durlok the Black Mage had come.

"Stand by the ballistas!" cried Bokar. "I think they mine rock to sink the ship."

The *chnk!* of pick on stone was followed by the *dnnk!* of sledge on drillbar, and Bokar paced back and forth along the line of ballistas. "When the Trolls come, Relk, you and your crew shoot first. Varak, your ballista is next. Alak, you are third. Bral, next. . . ."

Jatu called the remaining unscathed sailors to him, eight in all—Tink and Tivir included—and said, "Man the dinghies. We need to square the ship to the quay. And should the Trolls succeed in holing the galley, we will need to evacuate. If they fail, still we will need to draw the ship deeper into the lagoon a bit beyond their range, but not beyond ours."

As Men and lads scrambled over the side and into the boats, shadowy movement was seen at the entrance to the corridor, and a Troll stepped forth, a great jagged rock in his hand. But even as he drew back to hurl it, *Thnn!* Relk's javelin hurtled forth and slammed into the monster's gut, running him through. The Troll staggered sideways and fell, the rock thudding to the quay, but another of the creatures leapt forth and scooped up the stone as a javelin splintered against the wall beside him. Another javelin missed as the monster straightened and turned, but even as he hurled the stone, the next javelin pierced his groin, and down he crashed, howling as black blood gushed from him and where it fell smoke curled up from the quay, even as the monster's yowls chopped into silence.

The great rock smashed down onto the stern of the galley, shattering planks as it holed the afterdeck and fell through to crash into the quarters below. Slowly the ship turned in the water, the impact of the stone swinging it 'round. But Jatu called down to the sailors in the dinghies; and some rowed away and hauled on lines while others rowed to push against the galley with the bows of their boats. They stopped the swing and began to square the ship to the quay even as the Dwarves cranked the ballistas, recocking and reloading them.

Within moments, two more Trolls were felled, their hurled rocks thundering harmlessly into the waters between.

And all sound of pick on stone and hammer on drill-bar ceased.

"They have given up trying to sink us, I think," said Jatu.

"Aye," Bokar grunted in agreement. "But heed me:

if we would save Captain Aravan"—Bokar motioned to Kelek—"it is time for us to enter the tunnels."

Swiftly, Bokar and Jatu rattled off orders, Men and Dwarves springing to respond. Down into the boats they clambered, leaving the dead and wounded aboard, Chirurgeon Fager in attendance. Led by Bokar, all remaining warriors ferried in the dinghies to the landing. Along with the armsmaster and five other Dwarves, Jatu stepped from the lead boat and onto the quay, and behind him Tivir whispered, "Fortune be wi' you, Mister Jatu." Then the lad began rowing back to the galley, where he and the rest of the Men were to tow the ship beyond range of the Trolls' rocks.

Armed with massive crossbows, each requiring two Dwarves to cock and load it, up the steps and toward the silent, dark entrance went the warband, threading among slain Trolls.

"Remember," hissed Bokar, "aim for the throat."

Ignoring pain, Aravan whipped the crossbow to his shoulder and loosed the poison quarrel, the bolt streaking down at the Mage. But Durlok threw up a hand, and spat, *"Peritrapoû!"* and the quarrel flew straight back at Aravan, the Elf jerking aside as the bolt hurtled past to shatter against the crystal wall.

"Once more I name you fools," sissed Durlok.

Widely separated, two shadowy clusters darted down toward the Black Mage, but again he threw up a hand, pointing first at Farrix and then at Jinnarin, hissing at each, *"Anoémon genoû!"* and both Pysks fell stunned, their gathering of darkness gone.

Aravan gritted his teeth and casually moved toward the doorway leading to Durlok's quarters.

Durlok laughed wickedly. "Do you seek to draw my attention away from your allies?" He pointed a finger at the door leading to the quay—*"Emphragma!"*—and the portal filled with darkness. "Again I name you fool, for just as you, they are no threat to me."

Once more Durlok raised his hand, this time pointing at Aravan—*"Parálusis!"*—and the Elf staggered and fell to the floor, sensing all but unable to move. And he watched as Durlok cast the mutilated corpse from the altar and then turned and strode up to where he lay.

Durlok grasped Aravan by the collar of his jerkin and then began dragging him down toward the altar. "You think to defeat me? Pah! *I* am the one who conquers. Don't you yet realize, fool, *I* am the one who caused the Pysk to dream the dreams that would draw you and your allies into my trap. And although that imbecile Alamar slew my Negus of Terror, he paid for that deed and now lies dead below the waters of Rwn. And thinking of revenge, you were drawn again, and now I have you!"

Durlok laid his staff aside and, grunting, lifted Aravan to the crystal block. As he did so, through the dark barrier at the entrance Aravan could see shadowy figures moving beyond, and he could dimly hear a muffled shouting. Durlok looked up and laughed. "Do you think they will rescue you? Pah! Again you are a fool. They cannot get in, and I will deal with them after I have dealt with you. In fact"—Durlok squatted at the altar side, then stood, and in his hands he held a long, sharp, dark crystal—"I will draw out your <pyr> and use it to defeat those who seek to save you, just as I used the <pyr> of the aurora to collapse the bottom of the sea. Does that please you, Elf?"

A groan escaped Aravan.

"Oh. What's that? You would speak? Well then, fool, speak." And Durlok muttered, *"Elattótheti!"*

A degree of the paralysis lifted from Aravan, and he managed to turn his head toward Durlok and whisper, "Why?"

Durlok's eyes widened in amazement. "You are even a bigger fool than I thought, for when I grant you speech, instead of begging for your life, you stupidly ask a question instead. —Why what?"

"Why dost thou do these evil things? Why didst thou destroy Rwn?"

Again Durlok's eyes widened. "Evil? Evil! The destruction of Rwn was not an act of *evil*. Nay, not at all! Instead it serves the purposes of my Lord Gyphon. He has plans. Yes, He has plans. —Damn Adon for opposing Him!"

Beyond Durlok, Aravan saw shadow fluctuate about Jinnarin.

"And thou, hast thou no plans?" whispered Aravan.

"Oh my yes, fool. My plans are many. I will rule upon Mithgar."

More shadow gathered about Jinnarin, her form obscure yet unmoving.

Aravan opened his mouth to speak, but Durlok hissed, "Enough, fool!" He took up his long, black staff in his left hand and raised up the crystal in his right and paused as if admiring the smoky gemstone. Muffled shouting came through the dark barrier at the entrance, and there sounded picks on stone. Durlok laughed and looked down at Aravan, then held the crystal before his eyes. "This crystal is now without power," whispered Durlok, "but I will Truename it and draw out your astral fire."

In that moment, Aravan remembered Aylis's prophecy, and her instructions in magewords, and the circled word in the lexicon of the Black Mage. And he struggled to move, to grasp the stone all in vain for he was yet held by Durlok's spell. And Durlok laughed at Aravan's feeble efforts and raised the crystal on high and opened his mouth to speak—

—And shrieked and clutched the back of his neck, his staff clattering away on the chamber floor and the crystal falling to the altar.

And his face turned grey and he staggered, and he turned to see Jinnarin standing behind, the Pysk stringing another minuscule arrow to her tiny bow.

"Iè húdor genoú!" he managed to gasp, and the grey fled from his features.

And he raised his hand to blast Jinnarin from existence, shrieking, "You are dead!" but the paralysis had lifted from Aravan the moment Durlok had turned away. And the Elf took up the dark gemstone, and with all his might he stabbed it into Durlok's back, while at the same time crying out, *"Krystallopýr!"*

Aravan had *Truenamed* the stone.

And it flared hotly and drew astral fire unto itself.

And Durlok's eyes flew wide in horror, and shrieking he clawed at his back, trying to reach the stone but failing. And shrilling, he turned and lurched toward his staff, but the burning dark gem piercing him sucked away his <fire>, wrenched out his <power>, the screaming Black Mage ageing even as he stumbled toward his goal. His flesh sagged then seemed to draw in, his back bent, his skin turned mottled brown and withered, his eyes grew dim and his hands shook with palsied tremors, his throat and jaw and brow and cheeks shrivelled and sank until his face seemed to be nought but a parchment-covered skull. His horrified screams turned to croakings, to hollow whispers, and still he tottered toward the black staff. Ancient, feeble, he fell to his knees, no longer able to walk, and moaning and sissing crawled weakly forward, stretching out a skeletal hand. And as he reached the staff—

—Aravan squatted down and stayed the Black Mage's hand, the Elf whispering, "For Aylis and Alamar and all the others."

—And Durlok's mouth hinged wide in terror, in the gaping silent scream of the dead, and then he collapsed, his brittle bones shattering, his flesh turning to dust.

—And amid the stirring ashes, a gleaming dark gemstone lay.

CHAPTER 42

Scatterings

Autumn, 1E9575–Spring, 2E1
[The Present]

Suddenly the crystal chamber plunged into darkness, the faint glow of Krystallopŷr providing but feeble light. But moments later, from the doorway came the glow of a Dwarven lantern piercing the dark. Dwarves and Pysks came boiling into the crystalline room, Jatu as well, for with Durlok's death the barrier had vanished, just as had the magelight within. And Bokar shouted, "Captain Aravan, are you all right?"

Aravan stood holding onto his ribs. " 'Ware, Bokar, *Yrm* may lie in Durlok's rooms. Too, be there a healer with thee? Farrix lies yon—stunned or slain, I know not."

Bokar barked out orders to the Châkka, and as Burak moved forward to tend Farrix, a contingent of warriors hefted their axes and stepped across the chamber to cautiously enter the doorway to Durlok's quarters, several enshadowed Pysks going before them. Some Châkka and Pysks stayed behind and stood guard.

Jinnarin knelt at Farrix's side, along with Burak. Moments later she called out, "He is coming 'round now."

Jatu trod down into the temple and squatted by Durlok's remains, now nought but a pile of char. And Aravan hissed, "Touch not the crystal, Jatu. It is deadly."

Jatu glanced over at the black staff then up at Aravan. "We could see, Captain, though darkly. Durlok seemed desperate to reach this length of wood. I wonder why?"

The Elf shrugged, then turned and glanced up at Burak and Jinnarin and Farrix. Farrix was now sitting up.

Gingerly, Jatu touched the staff with a finger, quickly jerking it away. Then he touched it again, and once more, finally taking the staff in hand. He stood and measured its length: it was as long as the big black Man was tall. "Strange wood," murmured Jatu. "Like ebony, but not."

Accompanied by Anthera and Fia, Bokar came down to the altar, and Aravan asked, "The Trolls, Armsmaster, be they slain?"

Bokar nodded, but his eyes harbored pain. "Aye, Captain, they are all dead. But thirteen Châkka are slain, and two Men. Too, we have fourteen wounded—eleven Châkka and three Men—most with broken bones."

"My ribs among them," said Aravan, "cracked by the Troll I slew."

"Aha!" barked Bokar, as he turned and summoned Burak. "So that was you, Captain. How done?"

"Poniard in the ear," answered Aravan.

"We wondered how it was done and by whom."

Burak aided Aravan to remove his jerkin, then the healer began binding the Elf's rib cage.

"What of the *Yrm?*" asked Aravan.

Anthera raised her bow and said, "Lest there be any Rucha or Loka hiding under Durlok's bed, we deem all are slain."

Aravan glanced at the mutilated corpse lying on the far side of the altar. "Had Durlok any captives?"

Fia shook her head. "There was a Man in chains in the prison, but someone had just cut his throat, we think to keep him from calling out for aid. Most likely he was slain by the Ruch we slew in turn."

Farrix now stood and with Jinnarin came down to Aravan. Pointing at the ashes, he muttered, "That's Durlok?"

Aravan nodded.

"Well, there lies the crystal he used to draw down the plumes."

"Touch it not, Farrix, for I spoke its Truename and it is hazardous."

Jinnarin glanced up at Aravan. "We can't just leave it here."

"I know, Jinnarin." Favoring his freshly bound ribs, Aravan squatted. Reaching out, he held his hand above the bladelike gemstone and whispered, *"Krystallopýr,"* and the hot gleam vanished from the smoky crystal. Aravan then cautiously touched the stone, ready to draw back at the first sign of danger; sensing none, he took it up. He considered for long moments, then handed it to Jatu, saying, "Keep this safe until we find a way either to use it or to destroy it."

Pysks and Dwarves came back from Durlok's quarters and into the chamber. "All clear, Armsmaster," called down Lork, second in command to Bokar now that Kelek was dead, "no Grg within."

After retrieving the ballistas, they sank the black galley in the deep waters of the understone lagoon, the sinister ship hissing in protest as it went under, great bubbles rising long after it had vanished down into the dark, unplumbed depths.

At Aravan's command, splinted and bandaged, the wounded were sailed 'round to the temporary camp on the northern bluffs. Then they laded the dinghies with their slain comrades, and sailed them 'round as well. The remains of the Men were buried at sea, Aravan entrusting their souls to Adon, but the bodies of the Dwarves were carried up to a great pyre atop the bluffs and gently placed thereon, along with Troll warbars and clubs and war mattocks—the weapons of their slain foe.

As twilight fell, all gathered 'round—Men and Dwarves and Pysks on foxes—while Bokar spoke the service for the Châkka, calling upon Elwydd to watch over the spirits of these slain heroes as they roamed among the stars awaiting the time of their rebirth. And as the great pyre was ignited, the scrub and brush flaring up, Bokar stepped back to Aravan's side. They solemnly watched the smoke rise into the darkening sky, and Bokar said, "They died in honor, Captain, which is the best death a Châkka warrior can hope for. Ah me, but were we not sworn to secrecy concerning this mission, the battle to bring down Durlok would be a feat of which the bards would ever sing. Twenty-eight Trolls did we altogether slay in this battle. One by you, Captain Aravan—by poniard in his ear. Two by Tink and Tivir: one by drowning; one by ballista bolt. The rest by Châkka hand, or as good as. Never before has such been done by so few. And as for our own dead, no warrior could ask for a better fate, even though it will go unsung." Bokar turned and glanced out to the sea, as if seeking solace on the distant horizon, the sky now pink and violet and indigo in the dying light.

Aravan stood silent for long moments, and only the murmur of the wind and the crackling of the fire and the rolling boom of surf below disturbed the quiet. But at last he said, "Forget not the Pyska, Bokar, for without them, it could not have been done. And as for these deeds going unnoted, 'tis not so. I will record the measure of this battle in the logbooks of the *Eroean*. Too, I deem there will come a time in the far future when the veil of secrecy can be lifted—when, I cannot say, but surely the day will come, and then shall the songs be sung. This I swear, my friend ... my valiant warrior friend."

Bokar did not turn his face from the sea, but he nodded sharply, once, unable to speak for his tears.

The next day, Aravan called Jatu to him and said, "There is much wereguild to pay for the slain, Jatu, for the care of the families they left behind. Too, the Men and Dwarves and Pyska deserve reward for a task well-done. Take Bokar and a Pysk or two and select a crew and go to Durlok's treasury. Choose among the things of value for us to take back."

Jatu nodded. "Aye, Captain. How much?"

Aravan considered. "We could safely lade three dinghies, neh?"

Jatu smiled grimly. "If we run into weather on the way back, we can always cut them free and come again another day."

A bleak look swept over Aravan's face, and he shook his head. "I doubt that we will ever come here again."

In a trice Jatu had selected those who would go with him, Anthera and Jinnarin among these, though the Pysks had merely shrugged at the thought of taking any of the treasure for themselves.

* * *

The next day, the second of November, they set sail from the isle, this time running down the prevailing wind, heading easterly to find the *Eroean*—eight dinghies with people and foxes in them, and three more dinghies laded with treasure and being towed. They moved slowly through the grasping weed, for there were but thirty-one healthy rowers spread among the eight crewed boats, the eleven wounded dwarves and three wounded Men and the rib-cracked Elf distributed among the craft. Yet the wind helped, for it blew directly astern as among the weed-clutched hulks they fared. And still Aravan swung wide of these when the stone at his neck grew chill.

Easterly they ran, coursing with the wind, at times running swiftly, at other times sluggishly, as day became night and vice versa. They were heading for the waters along the eastern rim of the Great Swirl, for patrolling up and down along that marge ran the *Eroean*.

Two days after setting sail, chill rain fell upon them in torrents, and great swells ran under the weed. The storm lasted for two more days, yet in the end the skies cleared, and the Sun shone brightly down. And still they towed the treasure after, for the blow had not been fierce.

The next day the wind died entirely, and slowly across the pale green sea they fared, rowers alternating, conserving their strength.

But the following day the air returned, blowing slightly south of east. And onward sailed the crews, though both Tink and Tivir came down with a case of the chills.

Easterly they fared in the flat-bottomed dinghies, cruising just above the weed, until on the ninth of November just after dawn Aravan glanced at the Sun then brought them all to a halt. They lowered sails and drifted, there among the slow-turning weed. At last, late in the day, they sighted the *Eroean* running north. Within the hour they were taken aboard.

The *Eroean* headed for the Silver Straits, for it would be the dead of winter when she reached there, the mildest time of the year in the South Polar Sea. And as the days grew longer and the nights shorter, southeasterly fared the Elvenship, down through the Sindhu Sea. During these same days and nights, Captain Aravan could often be seen standing alone at the railing, staring out at the horizon, mourning for his lost Lady, or so said the crew. There came a night in the salon when the captain and Jinnarin sat talking. . . .

Jinnarin sipped from her acorn cup. "What do you suppose Durlok meant when he said that his Lord Gyphon has plans?"

"Thou heard him say that?"

Jinnarin nodded. "I heard nearly all of what he said, Aravan. I was conscious for the most part."

Aravan looked intently at Jinnarin, his gaze piercing, as if to penetrate a secret. "How is it that thou didst not succumb wholly unto Durlok's spell as did Farrix?"

Jinnarin shrugged. "I don't know, Aravan. But there is this: between the time he cast his spell on Farrix and then turned to me, I remembered a word that Aylis had said during Alamar's battle with Durlok—when the Black Mage hurled a lightning bolt at us—and so I said it just as he pointed his hand at me. '*Averte!*' That was the word I said. '*Averte!*' And I tried to envision his spell going astray. —Why this might have worked for me, I do not know, for I am certainly no Mage."

Aravan looked at her speculatively, then stood and refilled his cup from the teapot on the stove. "And then . . . ?"

"And then, well, it seemed as if I'd been hit a glancing blow by something invisible, something that stunned me a bit, though what it was . . ." Jinnarin shrugged. She looked up at Aravan. "I could hear him talking to you, crowing like, bragging. That's when he spoke of Gyphon and His plans, though he did not say what they were. Then, of course, that's when I managed to get to my feet and shoot him."

" 'Twas well-done, too, Jinnarin, for hadst thou not shot him, we would not be here speaking now."

"But the poison didn't work, Aravan. He somehow threw it off."

"What he did, Jinnarin, was cast a spell, for he said in the Black Mage tongue, 'Poison, become thou water.' "

"Oh," murmured Jinnarin. "Magic. I knew it had to

be somesuch. —He was getting ready to do me in, too, regardless as to whether or no I called out *'Averte!'* But of course that's when you stabbed him with the crystal, Truenaming it. —Tell me, how did you know that it would work?"

Aravan swirled his tea and then drank it all. Setting the cup down, he said, "Dost thou not remember, Jinnarin? It was here at this very table that Aylis spoke her prophecy to me about the cards: *'Introrsum trahe supernum ignem—pyrà—in obscuram gemmam!'*: 'Draw the heavenly fire—*pyrà*—into the dark gem.' "

"Oh!" exclaimed Jinnarin. "Of course!"

Aravan sighed. "As we studied the lexicon of the Black Mage, I learned many words, *Krystallopýr* among them, Alamar saying that it was a Truename."

"The circled word," breathed Jinnarin.

Aravan nodded but remained silent.

"Oh my, but what a long string of happenstance to come to that end," added Jinnarin.

Aravan made a negating gesture, saying, "Nay, I think it was no happenstance that brought us there. Thou must remember, my beloved Aylis *saw*."

"But I thought she was blocked by Durlok."

Aravan sat back down. "Aye, she was. Even so, still she managed to gain truth in some matters from the cards, even when they seemed but randomly scattered and without purpose. She saw danger. She saw the Dark Mage blocking. Too, she used her seer's powers in other ways: she touched Durlok's victim and saw his death. She touched wood and saw the ram of the black galley. She followed the Black Mage across half the world." Aravan paused, then with grief in his voice said, "And once when dealing the cards, she turned up the image of the Drowning Man, a harbinger of disaster. She knew not what it meant at the time, thinking that perhaps it signalled peril for the crew of the *Eroean*. Too, she said that it could perhaps signal catastrophe for others. I knew not what it might have portended, but, oh, I do now know, much to my sorrow, for it signalled the drowning of Rwn and the loss of all thereon."

"But we don't *know* that, Aravan," protested Jinnarin. "Some may have survived."

"Jinnarin, dost thou not recall Durlok's boast that Alamar had been slain?"

"Yes, I heard him say that. But listen, he also said that Alamar had slain his 'Negus of Terror,' meaning the Gargon; well, in that, he was wrong. And if he was wrong about who killed the Gargon, well then, he could just as likely be wrong about the death of Alamar. — Surely Alamar escaped to Vadaria. Surely."

"Mayhap, Jinnarin. Yet Aylis was bound to the conjoinment. Had I stayed in Kairn, mayhap I could have saved her."

"Had you stayed in Kairn, Aravan, then likely none of us would have survived. We'd all of us have drowned—Dwarves, Men, you, Farrix, me—as well as Anthera and Bivin and those who came with us out of Darda Glain . . . we all would have been lost. And worst of all, Durlok would still be alive."

Tears ran down Aravan's face. "Ah, Jinnarin, thou art right, and had I to do it all over again, I would choose the same. Yet it is a choice that leaves my heart sundered in twain, for my true love is gone from me just as surely as Rwn is gone."

"Look here," interrupted Jinnarin. "You must stop all this talk about Aylis being drowned. Just as did Alamar, she too must have crossed over. After all, she is my sister. We dreamwalked together. And if something went wrong, I would know . . . I would simply know."

But the look deep within Jinnarin's eyes belied her words.

The farther south they went, the longer became the days as winter deepened in the South Polar Sea. In late November they had come enough south that the Sun no longer set, but merely circled round the full of the sky. And on December the thirteenth they sailed into the watery margins of the Silver Straits, and on that same day Boder came to Farrix, the helmsman acting on behalf of the crew.

"Master Farrix, we'd rest more easy if you'd stand watch up in the main crow's nest, we would."

"But why, Boder?"

"Because, Master Farrix, you've the eyes to see the ghostly galleon."

"Ghostly galleon?"

"Aye, Master Farrix, the *Grey Lady*. What we mean to say, sir, is even though it's bright daylight and all, still she might be roving these waters and looking for the lost lad, and any one else she can catch. And well, you saw her before, and we'd like your eyes atop again so that we can take proper evasive action should it come to it."

"But Boder, what I saw may have been nothing more than wind-driven spray from a greybeard. Besides, I was endowed with magesight at the time, and none here knows how it is done, and so it won't be the same at all."

"That is as may be, Master Farrix, but you have seen her and we have not, so the crew entire would take it as a personal favor would you ride the nest."

And so, with Slane's help, up to the mainmast crow's nest went Farrix to watch for the *Grey Lady* as the *Eroean* fared through the straits.

Shortly after he had reached the nest, Jatu came climbing up bearing Jinnarin. "I came to watch as well," she said. "If there's to be any ghost ship sighted, I want to be here when it happens."

Jatu laughed, and after a word or two to Slane, back down went the black Man.

'Round the horizon they looked, and Farrix said, "How different the view from when last we were in these waters. —Hoy now, was it only six months past? Why, burn me, I believe it was. Regardless, this time there are no great greybeards trying to drown us, no hurtling snow trying to blind us, no screaming wind trying to sunder our masts."

"Right, Master Farrix," replied Slane, "and I'll take this mildness just the same, and I'll thank you to leave it be, if that's all right with you, now, eh?" Both Slane and Farrix broke into guffaws, while Jinnarin giggled.

With the mast slowly swaying back and forth, they sailed in silence for a while, the ship heading northeasterly. Of a sudden Farrix pointed north, "Hoy, what's that glint?"

Low on the horizon something glittered in the bright winter Sun.

Slane looked long, but at last said, "That's the silvery glitter of ice in the sunshine, Master Farrix. It's ice that gives the Silver Straits her name, glinting silver, like. To larboard and starboard lays the ice, and before we're through the straits, we'll see it good and proper."

Onward they sailed in the high, clean air, the three of them saying nought, the sway of the ship mesmerizing as they cut across the sea, silks belling outward in the following wind. After a while Jinnarin looked down from the height of the mast to the deck of the ship, and her heart pounded unexpectedly at the sheer drop below. But then she nudged Farrix and pointed downward. Below, Aravan stood alone at the midship rail staring down into the sea. "Oh, Farrix, I feel so sorry for him. He is so lost without Aylis."

Without shifting his eyes from Aravan, Farrix gently reached out and took Jinnarin by the hand. "Just as I would be lost without you, love."

Jinnarin sighed. "Oh, I *do* hope that she's in Vadaria."

Farrix nodded. "So do I, love. So do I."

Again Jinnarin sighed. "The trouble is, Rwn held the only known crossing between Mithgar and the Mage world. And now it is gone."

"Maybe there's another one, Jinnarin."

Jinnarin shook her head. "I don't think so, Farrix, for the Mages long ago would have found it if there were."

"Perhaps they just haven't searched well enough."

"Perhaps," Jinnarin sighed. "You know, Farrix, I have tried walking a dream to her."

"And . . . ?"

"And nothing. I couldn't form a bridge. You see, she has to be dreaming at the same time as I."

"What if dreamwalking doesn't work between Planes?"

Jinnarin shrugged. "There is that. There are also other things . . . worse."

"Such as . . . ?"

"Such as, if she were dead. Then it would be the same."

"The same?"

"Yes. If she were dead, well, I don't think I would be able to dreamwalk to her."

"Oh."

Slane turned to Jinnarin. "Oh, I don't know about

that, Lady Jinnarin. I mean, I've heard tales of the dead speaking to the living in their dreams, right enough."

A stricken look came over Jinnarin's face. "Oh, Slane—"

"Oh, don't take me wrong, miss. I ain't saying one way or the other whether Lady Aylis is dead. I'm only saying that spirits and ghosts can come to your dreams, they can, and that's a fact."

Jinnarin nodded bleakly, and resumed her vigil of Aravan below.

After a while he turned away from the railing and went toward his quarters. When he was gone from sight, Jinnarin turned to Farrix, tears in her eyes. "You know what the worst thing is, Farrix? We can't even put our arms about him and comfort him, for Pysks and Elves are not of a size."

Through the Silver Straits they sailed without incident, and then on up into the Weston Ocean. The winter solstice found them anchored in Inigo Bay, crews ashore taking on fresh water from the clear streams flowing down to the sea. And that night, the rites of the solstice were held—three altogether: the Pysks and foxes in the courtly dance of rider and mount, the foxes moving in a statcly circle, turning and bowing in unison; the Châkka chanting their paean to Elwydd, the Giver of Life; and Aravan pacing the Elven rite, tears flowing down his face, for when last he had stepped the steps, his *chier* was at his side.

It was the day after the solstice that Aravan and Jinnarin again sat in the lounge and spoke of things that had been and of things that were and of things yet to be. Rux lay on the floor, dozing, for it seemed that all rats had gone missing, what with twelve foxes aboard. Aravan reached down and scratched Rux between the ears, then sat a moment in deep thought. At last he looked into his cup, the tea gone cold, and softly said, "This is the last voyage of the *Eroean*, Jinnarin. I am giving up the sea."

Jinnarin said nothing for a while, the sounds of wind and wave and silk and rope filling the salon. Finally Jinnarin said, "I know that a great melancholy lies over all the crew, for many a good friend was lost there in the crystal caverns. But to give up the sea—it is your life, Aravan.''

Slowly Aravan nodded, and his eyes glittered with unshed tears. "It is too painful for me. Everywhere I look, she is there. At every little sound, I turn, expecting at any moment for her to step from seclusion, her green eyes dancing in humor, she laughing her throaty laugh. I waken at night and it is as if she has just slipped from my bed, and I lie waiting but she does not return.

"The *Eroean* is where I knew her. Where we laughed and loved. Where we strove against evil. Where we celebrated good. And without her at my side, the *Eroean* no longer brims with the bright promise of the morrow, but is filled to choking with dolor instead."

Aravan buried his face in his hands, while tears spilled down Jinnarin's cheeks.

The following day Aravan gathered the crew together and announced that this was the final voyage of the *Eroean,* for a while, at least. There were some cries of protest, but most of the crew understood. "We will sail to the hidden grot in Thell Cove where we will stow the ship," added Aravan. "Then we divide the treasure, and when added to what we've already stashed away in the banks of Arbalin, then I say ye and yours should all have comfortable lives, whatever ye decide to do."

Aravan then asked if there were questions, but none spoke, the crew too desolate to think of any.

As the meeting broke up, Jinnarin asked, "What are your plans, Jatu?"

The black Man sighed, then said, "I think I'll go back to Tchanga. Settle down."

"Take a wife?" asked Farrix, grinning.

"More like several," growled Bokar.

Jatu smiled. "Aye, more like several."

"What about you, Bokar?" Farrix looked up at the Dwarven warrior.

Bokar stroked his beard, then said, "There is a new Châkkaholt in the Grimwalls. Kachar, by name. I think I will go take a look, and if it's to my liking, there will I settle."

"Meself, Oi'm goin' back t' Gelen," said Tivir. "Run me a fishin' boat."

"Not me," said Tink. "I'm going to get me a manor in Rian, down by the Argent Hills, and be the squire of the land. Raise crops and suchlike."

"Ar, wot d'y' know about croftin', eh? Nothin', says Oi. . . ."

There sounded a pipe on deck, and both lads jumped up to answer. . . .

. . . And for the weeks to come, talk of the future occupied those aboard.

On February first, the *Eroean* hove to along the coast of the western continent, and all the Pysks and Aravan debarked. Into the forest they went, journeying to Tarquin, and he welcomed them with open arms. Here would Anthera and the Fox Riders stay, the ones that had come with her on that fateful day, for their home, Darda Glain, was gone. But Farrix and Jinnarin wished instead to go unto far Blackwood—called Darda Erynian by the Elves—there where Jinnarin's sire and dam dwelled . . . for Aravan planned to go to Pellar, and he would take these two with him.

They stayed with Tarquin for a sevenday, and on the eighth when Aravan was to depart, the Hidden Ones approached him and Anthera said, "When you came to Darda Glain, you said that you had come to rescue us. We came, but for a different reason—to make an example of those who would seek to enslave a Hidden One. We stayed for yet another reason—to seek revenge for the destruction of Rwn and our kindred in Darda Glain. Yet heed, Aravan, you were right all along—you *did* come to rescue us, though none knew it at the time. For this, my band and I will never forget. And we have made for you a gift to remember us by; it is a truenamed weapon, a crystal spear: Krystallopŷr."

As Jinnarin and Farrix flanked Anthera on one side, and Tarquin and Falain on the other, nine Fox Riders from Darda Glain—Bivin, Reena, Galex, Kylena, Rimi, Fia, Dwnic, Lurali, and Temen—stepped forward, and they bore a crystal-bladed spear with a long black shaft. "It is the dark crystal that slew Durlok," said Anthera, "starsilver-mounted on the Wizard's staff. As you know, this crystal is devastating in its power. Use it well and rightly, and guard forever its Truename—*Krystallopýr*—for in ill hands great wrongs can come of it."

Aravan took up the weapon, nearly eight feet in length overall. Slowly he turned it in his hands, and peered at the dark silveron mount holding blade to shaft. It was chased 'round with strange runes, tiny in their incising. He looked at Tarquin.

"It was forged by—by ... hmm, you would call him Drix. He is too shy to come forward, but he is watching even now." Tarquin tilted his head to the left.

Aravan turned that direction and bowed to the woods. "I thank thee, Drix," he called. "I will try to bring honor to this weapon." Aravan turned to Anthera and the Fox Riders, and there were tears in his eyes. "I will try to bring honor."

In the dark of night of the vernal equinox, the *Eroean* sailed into Thell Cove along the coast of Pellar. There the Elvenship was secreted in a hidden grotto, the very place where she had been born. And the Men and Dwarves set about laying her away, putting her down for a while.

Two days later they divided the treasure, shares being given to the dead as well as to the living, Jatu and Bokar taking on the task of seeing that the families of those who had been slain received their proper due. The only thing that Jinnarin took was a simple silver ring, a ring she slipped over her hand to wear as a bracelet. Farrix took a small red jewel on a golden chain, which he clasped about his waist.

Before any departed, Aravan called one last shipboard meeting, and he and Jinnarin and Farrix and Rux and Rhu stood atop the wheelhouse as the crew gathered on the decks before them. And when all were assembled, Aravan said, "I mind ye each that ye are pledged to me to keep the secrets of the *Eroean* tight—how she is built, how she runs, and where she is stored.

"And there is this, too: Ye hath completed a quest of the kind which bards extol. Yet none but we shall know of it, for I would remind ye all that drunk or sober, healthy or sick, in torture or pleasure, sadness or joy, we all of us are pledged to secrecy concerning this mission. Ye may not speak of such except to one another, and then and only then if ye cannot be overheard. The truth of the Hidden Ones shall remain but fables in the minds of all but the crew of the *Eroean,* and we shall keep such truth locked tight.''

Aravan looked from Man to Man and from Dwarf to Dwarf, and when his eye fell upon Bokar, the warrior dropped to one knee and, with a fist clenched to his heart, shouted, ''For the Lady Jinnarin!''

And so did all the crew go down to one knee with hands clasped to hearts and shout, *For the Lady Jinnarin!*

And tears welled in Jinnarin's eyes, for the last time she had heard such a pledge, the quest was just beginning, and an old Mage had stood nearby.

Farrix reached out and took her hand, and she looked at him and smiled, and he whispered unheard, ''For the Lady Jinnarin.''

At last Jinnarin held up her free hand and quiet fell. Her gaze swept across the full of the crew, friends all, and they waited in silence for her to speak. At last she said, ''We ridded the world of a great evil, did you and I and others, and some of us gave up our very lives to do so. Yet heed: evil never sleeps. The challenge we face is to be ever vigilant against such happening again, and I know we all will maintain our guard. This, too, do I know: you are all my comrades. Should any of you ever need help, come to the Blackwood. Farrix and I will be there.''

Jinnarin fell silent, and once again a lusty cheering rang out, and Farrix raised Jinnarin's hand into the air.

The crew disbanded and scattered to the four winds. Many of the Men sailed away in dinghies, heading to Arbalin to gather their fortunes, Jatu in the lead boat. Others struck out cross-country, mostly Dwarves, heading for the Red Hills, or Kraggen-cor, or Mineholt North, or elsewhere, Bokar among these.

Aravan and Jinnarin and Farrix set out northeasterly across land, Aravan stopping long enough in the Pellarian village of Whitehill to purchase a buckskin horse and a roan pack mule and supplies. And when he was gone, the villagers whispered among themselves concerning the taciturn Elf with the crystal spear.

Slowly they made their way up through Pellar, camping by day, riding through the night, the Elf ahorse, the Pysks mounted on foxes. They avoided villages and farms, keeping to out-of-the-way trails, for the Hidden Ones would remain just that—hidden from the eyes of Men and Dwarves and even Elves, except for those accounted as Friends. Spring stirred in the land, and water seemed to run everywhere, with green shoots bursting through the soil and early flowers blossoming.

Near the end of April they passed among the Fian Dunes and crossed over the Pendwyr Road. And still they fared northeasterly, for in that direction lay the Greatwood, where they would swing northwesterly and ride among those hoary trees until they came to the Rissanin to cross over Eryn Ford to come into Blackwood.

It was early June when they passed through the Glave Hills and entered the Greatwood, a mighty forest stretching northwesterly some eight hundred miles, the forest nearly two hundred miles wide.

Up through these woods they went, now riding by day and camping at night, for herein the Pysks felt sheltered from prying eyes. June passed and then July, and at last they crossed Eryn Ford.

They had come to Blackwood.

That night, Aravan and Jinnarin and Farrix sat by the fire and spoke of many things.

"What will you do, Aravan?" asked Jinnarin at last.

Aravan sighed, then looked to the west. "I deem I will live in seclusion for a while by the Great River, by the Argon, where I can rest in solitude a century or so."

Farrix cast a twig on the fire. "Broken hearts do mend, or so says Jatu."

Aravan sighed. "Mayhap for mortals it is so. But for Elvenkind . . . I know not. When we love, it is profound. I deem my heart will never mend, but perhaps one day I may come to know peace."

"Peace?"

Aravan nodded. "Aye, peace. Last night I felt her fine silken hair brushing my face, and I startled awake to discover it was nought but a gentle breeze. Every day and night it is so—something reminds me of Aylis, and it wrenches at my heart."

They sat in silence for a while, then Farrix said, "Cherish those memories, Aravan, for they speak of times of joy."

The next morning as Aravan saddled his horse and placed the frame pack on the disgruntled mule, Farrix and Jinnarin filled their own packs and draped them across Rux and Rhu. On this day Aravan would set out west, while Jinnarin and Farrix fared north.

At last came time for them to part company, and Aravan knelt down and held out a hand, and the Pysks came and touched his palm. As she did so, Jinnarin looked up into Aravan's eyes. "Thank you," she whispered.

Aravan mounted his horse, and Jinnarin and Farrix leapt astride the foxes.

"I say!" called Farrix.

Aravan looked down at the Pysk and waited.

"If you should ever take to the sea again," continued Farrix, "be it adventure, War, a quest, whatever, come first to the Blackwood to find your crew, for Jinnarin and I will be waiting."

"And if not us," added Jinnarin, "then our son or daughter—especially our daughter—should we have one." Jinnarin raised her bow. "We are mighty fighters, you know!"

Aravan laughed, the first he had done so since the destruction of Rwn. Then he wheeled his horse and galloped off through the woods, the ill-tempered mule on its long lead line protesting but following after.

Behind, Jinnarin and Farrix watched him go. And when he was gone from sight they turned their faces to the north. And with cries of *"Hai, Rux!"* and *"Hai, Rhu!"* away into Blackwood they rode.

Epilogue

Times Following
[... Immediately and After]

The cataclysmic destruction of Rwn marked the end of the First Era on Mithgar, for not only had it been a world-shaking catastrophe, but the Mages of Vadaria could no longer freely come and go, and this exclusion was to have profound effects upon the affairs of all.

As to Rwn itself, there were few survivors of its ruin: in the days immediately after, among the flotsam, the barque *Beau Temps* out of Gothon recovered but a single pair of survivors clinging to a gigantic tree. Lovers they were: one a golden-haired Elfess in grey leathers, a jade-handled sword in a back-slung scabbard marking her as a Lian Guardian; the other a dark-haired young Man, a bard, a silver harp slung across his back. Rein and Evian were their names, and they knew not if any of the Mages on the island had escaped back to Vadaria. The rescue of these two is mentioned here in passing, for two thousand years later Rein's truenamed sword would be given over to her daughter Riatha, where it would be used in the bitter strife between Gyphon and Adon.

As to the first of these struggles, it finally erupted into what is now known as the Great War of the Ban. During this War, the battles were mighty, and the Alliance of the Free Folk was sorely pressed, for most of Magekind was prevented from entering the conflict, trapped on Vadaria as they were, with no known way to cross over to

Mithgar. Many believe that Gyphon had precipitated the destruction of Rwn with that very purpose in mind—specifically, to preclude Magekind from joining the Free Folk should War come, as it did. Even so, there were Mages who had been elsewhere on Mithgar at the time of the destruction of Rwn, and virtually all of these joined the Alliance. In the end the War was won by the Free Folk, though at a great cost. Afterwards, in the main the Mages on Mithgar retreated to Black Mountain in Xian, where they shut themselves away and began the long slumber to recover their <fire>. They knew that their <powers> would be needed again, that Gyphon was not quit of His ambition to rule all—for as He was cast into the Abyss did He not say to Adon, "Even now I have set into motion events You cannot stop. I shall return! I shall conquer! I shall rule!"?

Haunted by the loss of Aylis, Aravan fared to Darda Erynian, where he dwelled in seclusion for a century or so along the banks of the Argon. And then he came to the Elvenholt of Caer Lindor to live once again among Elvenkind, there on the isle in the Rissanin River along the marge between Blackwood and the Greatwood. But his ready smile was yet subdued, and a tormented look dwelled deep within his eyes.

And he bore with him a black-hafted crystal-bladed spear.

Millennia passed, and War came, and Aravan fought valiantly in the Great War of the Ban, and he was present when the Dawn Sword was lost. For many millennia he sought that talisman . . . and the yellow-eyed "Man" who caused its loss.

Aravan did not sail the *Eroean* again until the Winter War, and then it was to savage the ships of the Rovers of Kistan, after which it was hidden away once more in the grotto in Thell Cove. It is told that during this foray against the foe, he was accompanied by three of the Pyska: Jinnarin, Farrix, and one named Aylissa; just who she was, this Aylissa, is not clearly known, yet some say she was the daughter of Jinnarin and Farrix.

As to the gift given him by the Hidden Ones, Krystallopŷr remained in Aravan's possession, its Truenamed burning crystal blade devastating in its power. Yet the givers of the spear had no inkling of what they had done when they had used a Wizard's staff as the haft of the weapon, nor did they know of the terrible consequences that would be wreaked were the staff's Truename ever to be invoked.

Lastly, you may wonder, did any of the Mages of Rwn survive? Did Aylis? Did Alamar? Is there another way between Vadaria and Mithgar? The Impossible Child found the answers to all four of these questions . . .

. . . But that is another tale.

It is said that when the air is calm and
the water nought but a glassy mirror,
there is a place in the sea where at times
if you are very still . . .
. . . you can hear bells ringing far below.

About the Author

Dennis L. McKiernan was born April 4, 1932, in Moberly, Missouri, where he lived until age eighteen, when he joined the U.S. Air Force, serving four years spanning the Korean War. He received a B.S. in Electrical Engineering from the University of Missouri in 1958 and an M.S. in the same field from Duke University in 1964. Dennis spent thirty-one years as one of the AT&T Bell Laboratories whiz kids in research and development—in anti-ballistic missile defense systems, in software for telephone systems, and in various management think-tank activities—before changing careers to be a full-time writer.

Currently living in Westerville, Ohio, Dennis began writing novels in 1977 while recuperating from a close encounter of the crunch kind with a 1967 red and black Plymouth Fury (Dennis lost: it ran over him: Plymouth 1, Dennis 0).

Among other hobbies, Dennis enjoys SCUBA diving, dirt-bike riding, and motorcycle touring—all enthusiasms shared by his wife.

An internationally bestselling author, his critically acclaimed fantasy novels include *The Eye of the Hunter, Dragondoom, The Silver Call* duology, *The Iron Tower* trilogy, and now *Voyage of the Fox Rider,* to be followed by the story collection *Tales from the One-Eyed Crow.*

Never one to sit idle too long, Dennis has also written *The Vulgmaster* (a graphic novel) and several short stories and novelettes which have appeared in various anthologies.

He is presently working on his next opus.

CASH BACK

Get $2.00 off
TALES OF MITHGAR!

Now that you've bought bestselling fantasy author
Dennis L. McKiernan's VOYAGE OF THE FOX
RIDER, you can get $2.00 back when you buy his
special trade paperback, TALES OF MITHGAR.

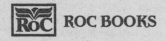 **ROC BOOKS**

To receive your $2.00 rebate, you must purchase both
VOYAGE OF THE FOX RIDER and TALES OF MITHGAR
(keep the receipts, please).

Then to get the $2.00 rebate, send in:
1. Sales register receipts for *Voyage of the Fox Rider*
   and *Tales of Mithgar* with prices circled
2. This rebate certificate completely filled out with
   your name, address, and UPC numbers from
   appropriate books

NAME_____

ADDRESS_____

CITY_____STATE_____ZIP_____

upc#_____ upc#_____

   3. Mail to:
VOYAGE OF THE FOX RIDER/TALES OF MITHGAR rebate
P.O. 1230
Grand Rapids, MN 55745-1230.

PENGUIN USA
Offer expires 11/30/94. Mail will be received until 12/16/94.
This certificate must accompany your request. No duplicates accepted. Void where
prohibited, taxed or restricted. Allow 4-6 weeks for receipt of rebate. Offer good only in
U.S., its territories and Canada.
Printed in the USA